To
Mary
Margaret —

The Qaraq and the Subversive Manuscript

Congratulations!
Welcome to the Qaraq
family —

Enjoy!

Steve

PRAISE FOR *1001, THE REINCARNATION CHRONICLES*

Amazon reviews:

"The kind of book that keeps you up later than you intended at night!"

"Whether you believe in reincarnation or not, this is a book which will expand your universe."

"It's amazing to have so many different tales within one book - and so much juicy variety."

"There is nothing in contemporary as well as historical myth or legend or literature to compare with *The Qaraq*. Weinstock has created an entirely new genre for himself!"

"Mr. Weinstock delivers passages of exquisite lyric prose that I will go back to read numerous times."

OTHER BOOKS by STEPHEN WEINSTOCK

1001, The Reincarnation Chronicles:
   Book 1   *The Qaraq*
   Book 2   *The Qaraq and the Maya Factor*

BLOG/WEBSITE

1001/Qaraqbooks News   http://www.qaraqbooks.com/subscribe

1001

The Qaraq and the Subversive Manuscript

Book Three

of

The Reincarnation Chronicles

by

Stephen Weinstock

Qaraq Books

A Qaraq Book.

Copyright © 2017 by Stephen Weinstock

Excerpts from ARABIAN NIGHTS, translated by Zack Zipes, translation copyright © 1991 by Jack Zipes. Used by permission of New American Library, an imprint of Penguin Publishing Group, a division of Penguin Random House LLC.

ISBN-13: 9780692924297 (Qaraq Books)
ISBN-10: 0692924299
Library of Congress Control Number: 2017949732
Qaraq Books, Glen Ridge, NJ

Author Photograph: Scott Allen

Qaraq Books
17 Sommer Ave.
Glen Ridge, NJ 07028

Subscribe to 1001/Qaraqbooks News: www.qaraqbooks.com

DEDICATION

To all those seeking a resolution to the conflict of
Otherness,

through stories, humor, and love.

"Scheherazade stubbornly insisted until her father, the Vizier, approached King Shahryar. The King, who had held Scheherazade exempt from his bloody practice, warned that the minister would have to kill his daughter the next day.

That night, as Shahryar prepared to penetrate her, Scheherazade begged to see her sister for the last time. Dunyazade was allowed to sit at the foot of the couch and later asked Scheherazade to tell a marvelous story.

When dawn arrived, Scheherazade broke off in the middle of her tale, and King Shahryar granted her another night to continue her storytelling. In this way Scheherazade prolonged her life for a thousand and one nights."

From the FRAME TALE of *The Thousand and One Nights*

TABLE OF CONTENTS

APPENDICES

A NOTE FROM THE AUTHOR TO HIS DEAR READERS

1001, The Reincarnation Chronicles is an 11 book series containing 1001 chapters, and in the tradition of *The Thousand and One Nights*, each chapter contains a story. That's 1001 past life stories! Holy Scheherazade!

The 11 central characters in the present day narrative belong to a *qaraq*, a group of souls who have reincarnated together lifetime after lifetime, accruing an interlocking karmic history. The interaction between this history, the qaraq's present day drama of discovery of it, and the characters' choices to perpetuate or repair their karma, form an intricate and challenging narrative. In addition, there are 11 hidden numerological and literary structures lying beneath the complex history, supporting the arcane operation of the laws of karma.

Why so complex, the Dear Reader begs to ask? Because your wondrous soul is immortal, the sympathetic Author replies, and deserves a worthy reflection of all it has been through.

Despair not, Dear Reader, there is hope! Yes, each of the central characters has dozens of incarnations appearing in the series. And yes, there is a tangle of names, many unpronounceable, since they derive from fantastical worlds. However, the kind Author has given each incarnation the same initial as its central character. Thus Naji is incarnated as Nyw, $NO(z)^{14}$, and Noam.

As the *1001* series unfolds in its eleven books, the astute Reader will become aware of the interplay of the hidden structures. In anticipation of that glorious day, the helpful Author has supplied each chapter's place in the past life Chronological Order and present day Narrative Order, alongside the chapter number at the beginning of each chapter. (See A NOTE ABOUT CHAPTER NUMBERS below.)

Next, if the Careful Reader loses track of an incarnation, a past life incident, or an historical event, the compassionate Author offers comprehensive lists in the Appendix section. In the back of each book, here can also be found the story of Scheherazade, so important to the nature and interaction of the souls in the qaraq.

Finally, the biggest boon that the sweet Author will ever give the anxious Reader. If at any moment things seem complicated, especially at the beginning of any book, put fears aside and simply READ ON! One of the central actions of *1001, The Reincarnation Chronicles* is the qaraq's tireless effort to understand the karmic history and mysterious structures controlling past and future. In any chapter the characters examine events in this glorious puzzle. If the Reader is ever daunted, trust that the qaraq will provide whatever needs to be understood at that moment. All that is required is patience, a bit more than needed for a genre bestseller.

Good luck, brave Reader!

A NOTE ABOUT CHAPTER NUMBERS

Three numbers appear before each chapter:

155   **806**

1

Narrative Order   **Chronological Order**

Chapter Number

The center number is the Chapter for this particular book.

The left-hand number is the cumulative chapter number for the series, that is, out of the 1001 chapters that make up *1001, The Reincarnation Chronicles.* So Book 3 starts with #155 out of the 1001 chapters in the series' **Narrative Order**.

The right-hand number represents where the chapter's past life tale falls in the **Chronological Order** of the qaraq's history, the 1001 lifetime stories that comprise that history. So Ooma's tale of The Seven Rooms is

#806 out of the 1001 lifetime tales in the **Chronological Order**; falling during present day of qaraq history.

See the Appendices for the Narrative Order, Chronological Order, and lists of Incarnations, all helpful to keep track of the multiple characters and narratives.

WORLDS MOST FULLY REVEALED IN BOOK THREE

THE ARABIAN INCARNATIONS

THE EARLY ISLAMIC INCARNATIONS

Udir, Indian garbage collector	Ooma
Humai, originator of *The 1000 Tales*	Ooma
Sheikh Ba'Tr ibn Halali, incarnation aficianado	Bax
Hazar, muhaddith in early Islam years	Porcy
Hammad, Bedouin poet, end of Umayyad era	Porcy
Zabbah ibn Sayyar al-Sakkak, Basran scribe	Zack
Wahid, papermaker and book collector	Verle
Sahra, ally of Zabbah and Wahid	Sahara
Narob, mahout	Naji
Scholar in House of Wisdom	Diana
Hu Ma, Chinese captive of Sheikh Ba'Tr	Ooma
Khadija, daughter of Hu Ma and Ba'Tr	Ooma
Logic Puzzle Suicide	Ooma
Umnia, Cairene Nights enthusiast	Ooma
Hanbal, Umnia's husband	Porcy

THE SASSANID INCARNATIONS

Uzmeth, 140-year-old Sassanid Queen	Ooma
Dinzadeh, slave of Uzmeth	Diana
Ba'ash, slave and favorite of Uzmeth	Bax
Shah Zabar, Sassanid Prince	Zack
Ardryashir, slave to Uzmeth	Amar
Sharzad, daughter of Sassanid vizier	Sahara
Purzai, Uzmeth's final victim	Porcy
Sharzad's First Child	Zack
Sharzad's Second Child	Cachay
Bahram V (Narses/Gur)	Naji
Humai, Sharzad's granddaughter	Ooma

THE 379 GROUP INCARNATIONS (V2)

Sanaa, 10th C. Baghdadi/Cordovan story collector	Sahara
Oamra, Sanaa's partner	Ooma
Oamra's stillborn child	Amar
'Umar ibn Anbari al-Raqa'maq, Frankish scholar	Amar
Masiama ibn Ishaq ibn al-Di'nam, bookstore owner	Diana
Abu ibn Ahmad al-Turtushi, Tortosan pornographer	Bax
al-Izjis, Cairene scholar	Zack
Ali ibn Abd Allah ibn Wasif al-Wa'wa, scholar	Verle
Muhammad ibn Darraq abd al-Qastali al-Khwarazmi, Cordovan scholar-courtier	Cachay
Paulina, Cordovan orphan	Porcy
Homma, an Indian elephant in Baghdad	Ooma
$NO(z)^{14}$, microbiome phage	Naji
Nasal microbiome microbe	Cachay
Madame Hunj, 11th C. Baghdadi brothel owner	Porcy
Nazir, 11th C. Baghdadi criminal	Naji
Balthasar, Italian boy with Ba'Tr's karma	Bax
Ursalina, Italian girl with Hu Ma's karma	Ooma

SHY TEACHER/FRANKOVIC INCARNATIONS

Unfanta Rishi, illustrious alumna	Naji
Hra Zamen, shy teacher	Zack
Uor Qxalm Taki, prima political ballerina	Ooma
Hra Eldon Kor, MAMESS teacher	Cachay
Taki's dance student	Sahara
Povi, dance student's best friend	Porcy

THE EXPLORATION INCARNATIONS

Vas ibn Bad'r Ens, Anatolian merchant	Verle
Si, Malaccan lover of Vas	Sahara

CONTINUING WORLDS FROM PREVIOUS BOOKS

THE BORZI INCARNATIONS

Borzu, legendary hunter, clan leader	Amar
Haughty Fern	Cachay
Strangler Fig	Diana
Tau Lepton	Cachay
Early Vawr tribesman	Zack
Ice Age Weather system	Cachay
11 Generations of the Vawr	Verle
Baby Mammoth	Cachay
K'Chung, Warlord of the Eastern Borzi	Cachay
Later Vawr tribesman	Naji
Ourm, Borzi female	Ooma
Short-lived Glacier	Bax
Brawr, Vawr male	Bax
Borzi female victim of Brawr	Sahara
Half-breed, child of Brawr and Ourmi	Porcy
Hotly pursued Vawr cavewoman	Diana

THE STONE CLIFFS INCARNATIONS

The Old Man in the Mountain, origin	Sahara
Xani, Tuvan exile	Sahara
Naxi, her tormented child	Naji
Principice Nongsch of the Three Valleys	Naji
Mountain looking within	Amar
Cliff Face in staredown	Zack
Vlaler-rawk, Principice assistant	Verle
Takharghock, warrior	Bax
Cliff Eyes	Diana
Cliff tears	Porcy

THE EGYPTIAN INCARNATIONS

Vraawr, neopheline tombleur	Verle
Saqqarah, messenger to Imhotep	Sahara
Nyw, Imhotep's cat	Naji
Animal mummifier	Amar
Atu, Sumerian priest	Amar
Ur-zamma, Sumerian princess	Ooma
Ka Lal, Old Kingdom priest	Verle
Zenkket, Ka Lal's apprentice	Zack
Laundromat Manager, parallel universe to Egypt	Cachay
Kha-nan-set, tomb aalesman	Cachay
Aapep/Pyramid thief	Naji

THE DRAILL U INCARNATIONS

Do'en Kvevely, Dean of Draill U	Verle
Ctatlo, performing arts theorist	Cachay
Pr Daywa, neuromistressa	Diana
I-Zaea, indaki	Zack
Inspiration for *Asd and Ajd* score	Bax
Poito, spacewright of *Asd and Ajd* multiperf	Porcy
Siyam, neurodancer	Sahara

Amat, telepactor	Amar
Naqoeo, telepacting student	Naji
Om-na, xalantangist	Ooma

THE THIRTY YEARS WAR INCARNATIONS

Dike, The Zyp, Low Countries	Zack
Anno, Dutch child, coven adoptee	Amar
Army camp follower, 30 Years War	Diana
Swedish Soldier with pox	Bax
Old Umh, Egyptian spirit, from Ramses III era	Ooma
Atu, Sumerian priest	Amar
Ur-zamma, Sumerian princess	Ooma
Old/New Umh's incarnations	Ooma
Lady-in-waiting	
Ormgarde, maid to Kristina	
The Lady in Red, provocateur	
The witch in red	
Picture with mirror, Donne's room	
Key-shaped Cudgel, Donne's room	Zack
Casket, Donne's room	Porcy
Kristina, Ophelia's cousin, Denmark	Cachay
Colonel Walker, British spy	Verle
Deserting soldier	Amar
Sondre, refugee	Sahara
Nils, six-year-old boy in 30 Years War	Naji
The Idea, Donne's room-as-the-universe	Naji
11-year-old Witch, Scottish coven	Cachay

THE EUROPEAN NIGHTS INCARNATIONS (V3)

Veronique d'O, follower of Galland's Nights	Verle
Rebbe Yisroel	Porcy
Alter, eldest Okopy brother, ghost	Amar

Shemuel, middle Okopy brother, hermit — Sahara
Noam, youngest Okopy brother, twister spirit — Naji
Zadek, Veronique's servant and disciple — Zack
Dom Denis Chavis, continuer of Galland's edition — Bax

OTHER WORLDS IN BOOK THREE

Ga-Men, proboscidian planet	Diana, Zack, Porcy, Verle
The Magickwald	Sahara, Verle, Naji
Maya civilization	Naji
19th C Eastern Europe	Ooma, Bax, Sahr, Amar
The Interlife	Naji, Cachay
Future lives, 22nd C	Zack, Diana, Amar, Sahara
Deep future lives	Verle, Diana, Amar, Sahara, Cachay

OTHER WORLDS IN BOOK TWO

The Xoo	Verle, Bax, Diana
First Cavedogs	Sahara, Amar
New Orleans	Ooma, Verle
Present Day lives-within-lives	Cachay and qaraq

ALL WORLDS REVEALED
IN BOOK ONE

10 - Dragonfly

9 - The Red Isle

8 - Gondwanaland/pre-Stone Age

7 - Persia/Mideast

6 - 30 Years War/Donne Idea

5 - Borzu + North-South Winds

4 - Story collection or Interlife tales

3 - China, The Seven Palaces

2 - 1500s France or Suburb

1* - Tree or Atom tale   Plus: 15 - 'lives within present lifetime' stories

* 1-10, 15 = number of lifetime stories appearing in Book One

ق

PART ONE

1

—◦◦◦—

September 11, 2001. 8:46 A.M. Impact.

When the first plane hit the North Tower, Ooma Qadir was already in trouble.

Two and a half hours earlier, on the 6:11 to Hoboken, her attention had wandered from the article she was reading for her Global Markets class. Ooma thought about her boyfriend, Bax. Boyfriend. Bax had certainly acted like one that summer. It was adorable to see this giant of a boy stare at her with watery eyes to check if he had done or said the right thing. Now her senior year at Glenclaire State had started, which included an internship at Bruckner Associates and a daily commute from New Jersey to Wall Street. Ooma would see what the added pressure would do to Bax's devotion. He'd probably be more forlorn than ever.

Ooma transferred from New Jersey Transit to the PATH train at Hoboken. She would get to the World Trade Center around 7:00, an hour before her boss, Amar Rash. He was a good boss, and had taught her more than she had bargained for as an intern. His over-reactive personality sometimes manifested as a tyrannical side, but he could also be warm and intimate. Ooma enjoyed flirting with him: he was a light-skinned Indian man, similar in tone to Ooma's caramel coloring. She had considered going beyond flirting, but Ooma was interning to improve her skills, not indulge in an office romance. And Amar was married to that intense woman, Sahara Fleming.

Ooma came from a strict Islamic background. She still lived with her parents and honored their beliefs. Ever since she was a girl she had taken comfort in Islam, loved reciting verses to the Muslim guests at her parent's parties, and even kept a special book in a Middle Eastern language she did not recognize, hidden away in her closet, a spiritual talisman in her own secret world.

Ooma's fantasies made her oblivious to the arrival of the PATH train. She jumped up at the World Trade Center station just as the doors were closing, and scurried up to the lobby level of the South Tower, through the maze of hallways and people. Flashing her ID to the sleepy security guard, she waited by the bank of elevators. She felt privileged to be a twenty-year-old student working at 2 World Trade Center.

Ooma loved working at the Twin Towers, in part for the welcome to the Islamic population. In her first month there, a construction worker, recognizing the significance of her headscarf, greeted her with "Salaam aleikum." Before she could respond, two men in suits replied "Aleikum salaam." One of Amar's colleagues, a Jewish trader, had told her about the Muslim prayer room on the 17th Floor, an oasis of spiritual calm in the frenzied world of capitalism. She enjoyed her visits to the prayer room: she might find anyone there, from financial analysts to secretaries, American natives to foreign visitors. Ooma felt at home in the South Tower.

Settling down at her makeshift workstation on the 77th Floor, Ooma prepared for her boss' arrival at 8:00 AM. At 8:30, she became worried about Amar's lateness and reached his cell phone. He had slept in after a late night, he said, but was at the PATH station and would be at the office in fifteen minutes. Ooma hung up with relief, but wondered what had kept him up. He had healed his rocky marriage with his wife Sahara, at the same time that Ooma and Bax had tightened their relationship. But Ooma ached with the thought that Sahara had kept her boss up late.

Ooma imagined Sahara spinning one of her fantastic stories, spellbinding her husband. Ooma had tried to penetrate what was behind Sahara's mystique for over two years, but Sahara had kept her at bay, often with inexplicable spite. Sahara was part of a clandestine group, a *qaraq*, joined by other members of her hometown of Glenclaire, New Jersey. Including Bax! When it became clear that Ooma and Amar had every right to join the group, but were locked out, it had bonded her to Amar even more. So the suspicion that Sahara let Amar in on secrets of the group hurt Ooma.

Obsessing about Sahara and the mysterious stories, Ooma felt herself slip into a suspension of reality. It was a familiar sensation, a powerful hypnotic state she had experienced at Bax's touch. More recently, she had shifted into the trance state all on her own. In this mindset, Ooma heard the archaic tales Bax shared with her, the enigmatic visions the qaraq discussed. She had even received some herself. But the hypnotic episodes were unpredictable and often unsettling.

Ooma had to get back to work. She was a capable worker, and Amar valued her competence. Shaking off the mild buzz, she organized his desk, sorting the current files in order of importance. She renewed her pride in her situation at the trading firm.

Where was Amar? Her mind drifted away again, anxiously awaiting her boss. Ooma fought the seductive sensation, but she was losing the battle. She hovered in thrall for several minutes, staring across the office space, out the windows, and over at the North Tower, the twin monolith. In a split second a bizarre vision appeared to Ooma: the North Tower appeared to flash, crumple at one layer above Ooma's sight line, and burst into flame and smoke. Ooma's mouth opened involuntarily: the horrible spectacle was not her fantasy.

The entire office went into high alert about the billowing smoke. Her office mates were arguing about whether a fire had erupted across the way, or whether something had struck the building. Others questioned whether their own building was safe. One hysterical receptionist pointed out the windows at the falling glass and debris, and the shower of paper raining down onto the streets below.

Ooma brought her mind into focus to realize that Amar was probably down there, emerging from the PATH train. He might be safe inside the bowels of the South Tower, but her stomach tightened. She speed dialed his cell phone. It went to voicemail. She stood up with an instinct to rush down in the elevator and look for her boss. A scream stopped her cold.

The receptionist got everyone's attention, with wild gestures toward a harrowing sight: bodies flinging themselves out the burning windows of the Tower, jumping to their death rather than face the torturous heat. *These are our twins*, Ooma thought. *We could be in that situation.* A young analyst with a radio held to his ear called out. A news report claimed a plane had flown into the building. Accident? A frantic manager shouted for everyone to be quiet and listen to the PA system.

Still standing, Ooma's eyes fixed on the smoke, debris, and falling bodies across the chasm between the buildings. She could not get a grip on the horror in front of her, her anxiety about Amar, or her previous reverie. The explosion in the North Tower had occurred when she slipped into that hypnotic moment. As her brain swirled in confusion, she had the dreadful thought that her mysterious mindset had brought on the catastrophe. The thought possessed her: if she could only understand the power of that state of stillness. It could bring her peace.

Ooma made one final effort to come back to reality. It was vital to maintain a calm, capable demeanor. Something horrible and unprecedented was happening, and she needed to be alert. But the pull of her disassociated state was too alluring.

She remembered a similar struggle, a similar need to understand something unprecedented. It was at Amar's New Year's Eve party of 1999, which she had helped cater. That was when it had all started. Her fascination with Sahara, Sahara's cold eyes on her, her first encounter with qaraq members, some casual, some intense. Ooma had fought a losing battle then too, to maintain composure as the party's events overtook her. She had lost herself to a sweet oblivion.

Ooma barely took in the flurry of activity in the office. It was too much. She re-entered that sweet oblivion instead, as a shield to the surrounding chaos. She let the hypnotic state envelop her mind. Reverie returned her to the 1999 party. She saw a moment with Bax, an intense kiss.

Ooma's eyes glazed over, now oblivious to the devastation. Safe inside a memory, Ooma re-experienced the New Year's party. She had worked on Amar for weeks to invite her. The party was mostly for business associates, so she had lobbied heavily to assist. Finally he had consented.

She remembered the preparations, the start of her work that night.

The Memory of the Seven Booms

1

In the kitchen, I manage the curries, kabobs, and other Middle Eastern delights for Amar and Sahara's menu. I like preparing this food more than eating it; I keep a trim figure by not eating much. I'm not in the market for a boyfriend – college and work first – but I like feeling attractive.

Just before the guests arrive, Sahara brushes through the kitchen, eyeing my work with a slight scowl. She wears a stunning turquoise sari, no doubt a gift from Amar. With her brilliant golden and tangerine hair, Sahara looks less like an Indian wife than a hippie poser. Is she really an Arabian Nights expert, someone in touch with great mysteries? Maybe I'll find out something tonight, for I'm very curious about her secret history, more curious than I understood why.

Sahara comes through a few other times as the party progresses, approving platters, tweaking spices, reporting shortages. I chop, roll, and skewer for an hour before I allow myself a glass of wine. I look up at the clock a hundred times, staring at the sword-shaped hands pointing to numbers that lose their meaning for me. The fountain motif on the kitchen backsplash tile gives me a curious chill. How long have I been working? Maybe a second glass of wine. Don't tell mother.

Proud my tasks are almost complete, I need to get out of the kitchen. One more batch of hors d'oeuvres into the microwave. I've been in here seven hours straight! Everything's in good shape. I'll go check on the servers.

Before I can plan my escape, in walks Porcelain 'Porcy' Honeywell. She's coming over, okay, focus, this woman'll talk your head off. Just fold these babies over, nuke 'em, and you're done. Stay focused.

"Ooma, sweetums, look at you slaving away!" Porcy says. You should join the party, pretty little thing like you. Meet one of these execs and you can end up in a house like this, eh? I'm proud of this palace, one of my best sells. Couldn't have done it without my little spy."

Porcy had asked for my help tormenting Amar into using her as a real estate agent. She keeps talking, so I keep folding, and keep looking at the fountain backsplash tiles. Almost there.

Porcy calls out the kitchen door. "Hey, Bax, come over here. This is Ooma. Cute, eh? I'm helping Bax out for a while, Ooma dear. Saved my life on the subway. Putting him up till he gets some work. Maybe you'll help him mingle, doll. I'll leave you two. Got to network."

2

Okay, don't get into this guy. You've got work to finish. Hide in the pantry. Look at the recipe for the microwave timing. Study it closely like a precious map. Didn't work: he's followed me in here. How come he looks familiar? Hollywood good looking. Big chest.

"You're the Rock-It girl," Bax says.

"Excuse me?"

"I saw you in Rock-It. The CD place."

"That's who you are!" Maybe I'll get into him later. "Listen, I've just got to pack these babies in the microwave." I do so, set the timer, return to the pantry. "When they're done, I'll introduce you to people from Glenclaire here. What do you want to do, odd jobs, yard work?"

"Whatever." Uncomfortable with that question. He's playing with a pile of cloth napkins. Cute. He folds one like a bandit's kerchief. Puts

8

it on, fake tough guy. Folds it again. Looking at my face. Map of the world. Places the napkin up to my face. Soft touch for a big guy. Covers me up to my eyes, wraps it over my eyes. A veil.

"You've got amazing eyes," he says. "Deep."

I stare back, a big, mysterious look. The microwave dings. I flinch, the napkin falls. I retrieve the plate of hors d'oeuvres, and Bax and I walk into the living room.

3

The place is brimming. I hand off my plate to one of the servers, ask about what's needed, but they tell me everything's under control, have some fun. I grab a mini samosa, scarf it, suck on the toothpick. Bax is served a glass of wine, gets one for me. The third. Forgive me, Allah.

I bring Bax over to a group of Glenclairians, introduce him. I get cornered by a few office types, leave poor shy Bax stranded. They offer more wine. Third topped off? Fourth?

"So where's Amar?" I ask one balding man with a mustache full of hummus.

"Outside, maybe. The secretary yearns for the boss as the stick yearns for the dog?"

Some ancient saying? "You know what Alexander the Great said," I answer. "My secretary is the controller of my wit. Can't have the boss talking trash." I hang out a bit, spouting off lines from the Qu'ran, Rumi, Nirvana songs. Head spinning, I feel like the little girl at my parents' parties, performing Farsi poems for the guests. I love it.

I make a dramatic gesture and knock a guests' plate of curry onto the floor.

"Whoa, slow down," the sweet-faced guest says. "It's okay," he whispers, "I hate shrimp."

We both bend to the floor, cleaning up the mess. "I'm Zack, next door neighbor. Crashing the party. I should stay hidden down here."

I like this guy. "Me too, I guess." As I stand up, I feel woozy and Zack steadies me. "Thanks. Got up too fast. Let me go dump this."

I dispose of the plate, start to bring Zack more food, but I think I see Amar from the back. I move over to him, but it's another Bruckner trader, giving me another drink. Losing count. Losing myself. I see Bax looking around the room as Sahara enters. He sees me, heads over.

My beeper goes off like an alarm. I flinch, then extract myself from Bax's oncoming need. My beeper flashes Amar's home number, familiar from the office Rolodex. Who's calling? I look around the room. There, on the other side, stands Sahara with the phone receiver in her hand. She holds it up, beckons me with a finger, like some coded sign, and disappears down a hall.

4

I stagger across the room, holding onto furniture like a one-year old. By the time I manage the cross, I am in between two hallways. Did she go down this one? Peek down, see the ornately curved arched doorway into the patio. Can't be right. But is Amar outside? Inch my way up to the glass, stare out at the guests.

Where is Amar? I'm here for him dammit where is he? Typical: do this, have that ready, and I do, capable Ooma. But he's not ready, doesn't need it anymore, has gone home. To the wife. To find his father. Grandfather. Come over to the house. Yeah right. Oops not this weekend we got a thing. Yeah right. Other side of the tracks. Mansion, Amar. Parents' house, Ooma.

What am I doing? Interning for a Wall Street hotshot. Is it money? Power? A mansion of one's own. Become more of an American. Bullshit? What else do I want?

Cool glass from door on forehead. Breath fogs it up. Foggy night. Strange. Shadow patterns from the hall light fixture, looks like an Arabian oil lamp, Persian ewer. Sahara probably picked it up at Pier One. Where all the Near Eastern scholars shop. Light on foggy glass makes people out on patio look frozen, like chess people. Courtiers. Familiar. Deja. Deja fogged.

I scream! Who's got me? "Oh, Bax, you scared me." His grip sobers me up momentarily. "Thanks, made a wrong turn. No Amar. No Sahara."

10

"She beep?"

"You saw? Let's try the other hallway."

5

Down the other hall I walk through an open door into a den lined in dark wood. Arabesque wallpaper border, jewel trim on boxes, an old ud missing its strings hanging on the wall. Sahara, in her turquoise sari, waits for me. Bax waits in the hall.

"The boss' favorite color," I say to Sahara.

"Did you get lost on the way?" she asks, ignoring my comment.

"Kind of," I say. "Big house."

She ignores this, too. "I just wanted to thank you for all your hard work."

"Oh, please, it's my job."

"But it's not your job, Ooma." Is there a criticism here? "You've really gone out of your way. Especially mingling with our guests. You're quite the entertainer."

I get it: that's *her* job.

"But sweetie, are you okay? You're all clammy. Why don't you just rest here for a half hour. Should I call your parents?"

Is she trying to make me sick? She indicates a built-in divan, wrapped around the far corner of the room and stuffed with pillows. I walk across the room. Drunken driver on a police line. Plunk myself down. "Thanks, this feels good."

Sahara walks over to the stereo. "You just leave the entertaining to me. I'll put on something so you can sleep." An Indian raga. "Nightie night," she says, having put me in my place.

6

Music is soothing. Slow. Wafty. Watery. Brain refocuses out of edgy alert, back into stupor. But now it's nice: warm, buttery ribbons of pleasure throbbing behind my eyes.

11

Bax walks in. He looks around the room, goes to the stereo, looks at CD cover. Turns to me, dark god of desire; over to the divan, muscular body dropping next to me. He pulls out a joint and picks up from one of the pillows a matchbook from Taj Indian restaurant with silver elephant on cover. He lights up, helps himself, passes the smoking gun. I take a puff, having only one brain cell remaining to tell myself to stop. I put the joint down and lean back on the pillows.

What happens next is a blur, but there is kissing and fondling. With each kiss comes a stillness and a vision. A strange sensation, like I had at the patio glass. Ooma through the looking glass. Something about the house the rooms this room? Den of iniquity. I am so close to Bax he must be having these same visions. Or different ones?

What are these visions? Flashbacks? To what? When? They are so vivid and detailed, like short films. And they feel so familiar. Like I know people in them, like Amar, Sahara, and even their neighbor Zack. Why does this happen when I kiss Bax? Even if Bax is somewhere else, some other vision, we are connected, entangled, like two atoms. Scary. Who is this guy?

The next thing I know there is a quiet cough. Amar stands over us. Allah! How long has he been there? Is he grinning, angry, leering? Get out of here, Bax. Get off, get up. Bax dislodges himself, stands, unsure where to go.

Amar reaches down to help me up, then thinks better of it, goes to turn off the stereo. I slowly rise, test my balance. As my strong, silent boss moves to the door, Bax darts out of the room. Amar looks at me. Our eyes lock. A long moment. Deep. I signal I'm fine. He gestures for me to follow him. Non-verbal communication. Strange moment: never like this at the office.

7

I stagger through the hallways, out the looking glass doorway, onto the patio. Winter air hits me, but there are heaters set up, so it's hot and cold flashes. The whole party is out here now, a sea of people. The

12

sea parts and there's the fountain, on the far side of the patio, an ornate Moorish water display that splashes onto three tiers, with tiny Christmas lights blinking all through its crystalline reflections. It is a bright container of magic.

I have never seen it, and yet it is so familiar. "Amar, it's beautiful!"

Before Amar can brag, Porcy pops up. "It's what sold Sahara on the house."

Then Sahara bursts through the crowd. "What are you doing up, Ooma? Amar, did you rip this girl out of her sick bed? We should take her home."

Amar volunteers to drive me, Sahara rebukes his abdication as host. Bax reappears to offer, Amar denies him any more access. Glad the boss is not mad at me. Maybe he is. Porcy is too busy with clients to drive me, so in the end, good neighbor Zack materializes, becomes my chauffeur. He rounds out the quintet of admirers who ushered me through this night. Do I sense a sixth presence, near Sahara? Inside Sahara? Better go home.

I retrieve my stuff from the kitchen. Amar and Sahara see me to the door, Bax puppies behind. I slosh across the lawn to Zack's driveway, flop myself into the Good Will box of his front seat. Bax stands on the lawn, waving, his face dark in the winter moon.

Somehow Zack delivers me to my parents, praising them for such a hard worker. "Ooma means capable," my father beams. It's just enough of a distraction for me to get upstairs without anyone noticing I'm shitfaced.

I sleep deeply that night, but not peacefully. Something ominous emerged during the party, during my stupor, during those kisses. Something that will remain ominous as long as I struggle to remember it, and when I do remember it, I fear it will be worse than ominous.

ق

For two and a half years Ooma Qadir had been trying to remember the visions she had experienced during the party. At the Twin Tower

13

office, as the events of the night passed through her mind for the thousandth time, Ooma learned something new. In that first kiss, and the first stillness inside it, there had been a gateway to another world. Ooma yearned to stay in the memory, for she had a glimpse of the truth. Seeing more would deepen her understanding and connection to the visions, to Sahara, and to the qaraq.

Despite the promise of this memory, something nagged Ooma to stop telling her tale inside her head. There was imminent danger around her: was it something in the visions? What could be more pressing than recalling what she had seen that night? Some matter of life and death hid within those visions, some guarantee of her existence in the qaraq. Now that she was ready to re-experience every detail, what was pulling her back into the real world? What was the real world anyway? Even if it was falling apart around her, she had to get back to her memory of the visions, for she had realized something vitally important about this gateway to another world.

The visions were not phantasms, but memories. Of past lifetimes.

2

September 11. 9:40 A.M. An hour after Impact.

When Baxter Tenderheel got to Penn Station, he knew things were bad. No buses or subways were running, and Bax had to walk downtown, toward the Twin Towers, toward Ooma.

Less than an hour earlier he had been at home in Glenclaire, watching the morning news with Porcy. The middle-aged, light-brown skinned woman and the tall Coloradan had an odd living arrangement. They were neither lovers nor guardian and child, and Bax had been slow to be a friend given his shyness. But there was an important bond between them, not just in this lifetime.

When they saw the first report of a plane hitting the World Trade Center, Bax jumped up to catch a train into the city.

"Where are you going?" Porcy said, without taking her eyes off the television.

No words had formulated Bax's impulses yet. Finally he said: "Ooma's in danger."

"And you're off to rescue her? It's not even her building, Bax. It's crazy to go."

"Like jumping on the subway tracks that time? To rescue you?"

Bax's reminder of his rescue, a vital source of their bond, tightened Porcy's throat. In the qaraq's support group meetings, the young man had discovered an outsized fear of death that ran from many past lives into the present. Yet he had risked an oncoming subway train to pull her off the tracks. In return she had taken him in, in compassion for Bax's homelessness at the time.

She looked up from the TV. "Pack a lunch, dear. And be careful."

Bax grasped the front doorknob, lurched back to give Porcy a kiss on the head, and bolted out of the house. Bax ran for the nearby station; he could just make the 9:00 train. He barely had a thought for Porcy, but was relieved she had let him go. He valued and respected Porcy, but had little patience with her meddling.

On the train, thoughts raced through his mind. If Ooma did not live with her parents, Bax could move out of Porcy's house and into a place with Ooma. He felt a new commitment to her, but how would Porcy feel about it? Porcy liked Ooma, and had often advised Bax to do the right thing toward her. Ooma's parents tolerated him; they were used to Ooma's freewheeling choices. But would they ever accept her living with a white, Christian cowboy from Colorado?

Bax made the connection at Newark, and heard that they were canceling PATH trains into the World Trade Center. He could still get into Penn Station. Rumors of a terrorist attack on the city made everyone on the train anxiously conscious of traveling through the tunnel under the Hudson River. Imagining an underwater explosion, Bax felt his stomach contract. The idea of Ooma inside a burning skyscraper crowded against his fear like the passengers on the packed train.

Bax's first sight of Ooma had been at the punk rock CD store in Glenclaire. What was a quiet-looking girl in a headscarf doing at a grunge shop? He was too shy to brave even a few words to her, but at one point he met her eyes, and in them he saw a wilder soul. Later Bax heard of Ooma's club-going, her Goth friends, and many adolescent sins against her beloved Islam. Although she had chosen assimilation and wildness as a teenager, and was now on the path of the corporate

16

American woman, anathema in many Islamic households, she never rejected her religion.

Given Bax's roots, a Westerner from out West, he knew that Ooma did not understand the intense, electric connection with the twenty-three-year-old man. Sexual magnetism had been there from the start, but soon after, they had experienced magical moments where, with a mere touch on the arm, they had brought visions of other worlds into each other's minds. Their first such encounter had been at the New Year's party Porcy dragged him to. On the pillows of Ooma's boss' den, their kisses and touches summoned visions of far-off times.

It had taken Bax a year to accept that these fantasies in his brain, with or without Ooma's stimulus, were memories of past lives, clear enough to recount as stories. Porcy discovered that her bond to Bax stretched back in time. She dragged him to meetings held at the Glenclaire Universalist Unitarian Church, a support group for locals having memories of their past lifetimes. As the group recounted their stories, it became clear that their lives were intertwined, that they shared the same karmic history. Elvira Young, their facilitator, called this kind of soul group a qaraq. The qaraq's past life tales elucidated their inter-relationships, revealed secrets, and healed Bax's deepset fears.

Though Ooma received her own stories related to the qaraq, she was barred from the group. Sympathetic to her unfair treatment, Bax took on the task of bringing her news of the group and sharing her tales with the qaraq. Ooma pressured him to lobby for her acceptance into the group. It felt like a secret pact, an illicit alliance, which added to their preternatural bond.

Penn Station was a madhouse: the entire transportation system shutting down, thousands jamming the halls. Everyone was nervous that Penn Station could also be a terrorist target. The atmosphere dwarfed Bax's natural predilection to fear death. What am I doing, he thought? How can I who feared every little thing chase down a catastrophe? When Bax shoved his way outside onto Seventh Avenue, all he wanted was to return to his reverie of Ooma.

Out of nowhere he felt an inexorable pull to recall the visions spurred by Ooma's kisses at the 1999 party, lost in his memory. He matched this force with his intense drive to get past the crowds, to get to Ooma. Incredibly, Bax felt Ooma reaching out to him to recover their time together during that first kiss, clutching in that niche decorated like a palace from the Arabian Nights. It was as if the bizarre nightmare of this day had a hypnogogic power over him, allowing him to be at once awake, darting in and out of people on the sidewalk, and asleep, drifting into a subconscious recollection of the visions with Ooma. In this state, Bax recalled his encounter with Ooma at the party, projecting the memory back out to her mind.

The Recollection of the Seven Kisses

It all led to this moment. Was there seven of everything? Did we pass through seven rooms together? Kitchen. Pantry. Living room. Few more till we arrived here. Bright things along the way. Halo of light around them. Little fountains on kitchen tiles. Napkin veil on Ooma's pretty face. Funny guitar on wall over there. Something in every room? Seven objects?

What else? Seven glasses of wine? Maybe between us! Wine helped me brave the Wall Street types. Ask for work. At least one gig. Wish it were seven.

Did I see Sahara Fleming seven times tonight? Saw her three times coming across country from Colorado. Strange that. Mystical appearances. Golden hair. Flaming. Fleming. Now I'm in her house. Wine helped me look her in the eyes. Only once.

But Ooma. Seven kisses. The other sevens led right to her mouth. Inside. Hoping for it. Wine dared me follow her into the den. After Sahara left. Lucky break. Moved over to Ooma on pillows. Elephant design on matchbook and pillows. Pulled joint out of pocket. Ooma had no problem with it. Not strict Muslim? Open to everything? Why headscarf?

A signal from Ooma. Come to me. Plump up to her. Put her legs on my lap. Lean down next to her. Our heads pull in. Slow insinuating music. We sink into elephant pillows.

A brief, soft kiss. Acknowledgement.

A second small kiss. Gauge appetites.

A third, long kiss. Testing pleasures. Delicious small mouth. Short pause.

A fourth, longer kiss. Diving connection, tongues, whole mouths. A respite for eye contact. Knowing agreement of delight. And wonder. Is this happening to you, too?

Another, fifth, long kiss, mashfest overflowing lips over lips, hands over bodies.

A break. Chuckles.

A fast, hard, hot, sixth kiss, exploiting reinforcing mouths.

A seventh, longest kiss, back into the fray, more tongues, hands, hand under her, under clothes, a finger, probing, searching, finding.

Seven kisses. Not just pleasure. Something more powerful. A silent moment. Deep inside each kiss. When the world goes still. A microsecond that feels like a year. An eternity.

Like times when sleepy. Nodding off for a brief moment. Then waking with a start. Totally refreshed. Like having passed through a new world. Unsure where you've been. Surprised by lost awareness. Split second of unreal time containing another reality.

Still moment during kiss is deeper magnification of Nodding Off sensation. Dark mystery unfolding in stillness. An entire history in half a second. Formal but familiar. Each kiss a wormhole to an infinite narrative. Summons another time period. Entangles me at arm's length.

Ooma: do you have the same feeling? In control? Receiving same race of images? Kissing of the earth seven times. Lady's exhortations. King listens on the divan. More pillows. A sister asking for a tale.

Whose sister? Sahara? Talking about Scheherazade at party. Story collections. Middle Ages. Arabian. Nights.

Each kiss contains a story. Each story a world. The gate leads into a garden of tales. In which we are all entangled. For an eternity.

ق

3

September 11. 7:10 P.M. The night after Impact.

As the beautiful summer sun set on the evening of September 11, neither Amar, Ooma, nor Bax had returned from the city. After Bax had dashed for the train, a worried Porcy was unable to remain alone, so she drove to Sahara's house and the two friends remained glued to the television. Like so many family members in the outlying areas of New York City, by evening both women were ragged with concern. Those lost in the buildings were unaccounted for and unnamed, many survivors had not been able to contact or return home, and the media was a relentless source of dreadful information. Hours of watching the gruesome coverage had drained Sahara and Porcy.

Was it just yesterday that Sahara had moved back into the house after a year and a half separation from Amar? Sahara confided to Porcy that only last night had she felt it was the right choice, that her love for Amar could overcome the innate storminess of their relationship. Having borne Amar's temper more than once herself, Porcy was skeptical. But despite her concern for Sahara, it was not the day to add tension by confronting that situation.

They endlessly second-guessed where Amar and Bax might be. How long before they knew? Would the first responders rescue any survivors that night from beneath the dark rubble? If Amar died, how could Sahara forgive herself for wasting the year when she shut him out?

But he had threatened her violently while she was pregnant with their child Naji. He had erupted in anger in front of her past life support group, and the qaraq had banned him from meetings. He had scandalized her in front of his colleagues and clients at their 2000 New Year's party. There had been no choice but to keep their child away from him.

Yet he had worked so hard to show his repentance, his generosity, and his magnanimous spirit. In order to repair the marriage, he had even given up his jealousy of the qaraq's attentions and accepted the members. Given that Amar was entangled in the past life stories, he was one of the *qaraqis*. He had proven a good husband and father. And the make-up sex had been incredible.

An hour past her son's bedtime, Sahara knew she had to attempt to put down Naji to sleep. Cradling his little body in her arms, she could hardly believe he would turn two in a few weeks. Sahara laid her baby gently in his crib. Curling a lock of her hair around a finger, she stared at her perfectly still, perfectly awake child. She picked through the pile of books nearby. She debated between the tale of Ali Baba or one of the animal fables from *The Thousand and One Nights*. She laughed to herself for hesitating to choose Ali Baba because she knew it was a later European addition to the famous story collection. Researching her doctoral thesis on the origin of the Nights over-prepared her for bedtime stories. Just read the damn story!

It did not matter what she read, anyway. Naji lay on his back, oblivious to her voice. At times he would stare at her with his eyes, as dark and piercing as his thirty-three-year-old father. Sahara held up an elaborate illustration of the forty thieves climbing inside the jars. She had no idea whether Naji was responding to the image or off in some other world. And it was not some candy-coated infant's world either. This was the child that had spoken to her mind from the womb, and told her tales of his past lives! Marvelous, scary child, who, now that he had lost his telepathic ability and was developing normal baby speech, often sank into a silent void. She read another paragraph, but Naji shifted his gaze to a corner of the ceiling.

More than ever she had been convinced of her connection with the Scheherazade archetype, a truth suggested by Sahara's past life memories. Now pregnant with twins, she would soon have three children, the size of Scheherazade's family at the end of some versions of the story. But given that Naji had distanced himself from their mother-child bond, this idea of the 'right' family seemed deluded. Even if she had Scheherazade's storytelling powers, they were wasted on her child.

When carried around the house, Naji would point at an object and try out its name. He understood simple commands and made more sounds than ever, but it was a shock that a being who had articulated entire histories telepathically had been reduced to this primitive state. To other mothers, the utterance of "Mama" would be a joyous miracle; to Sahara it was a baffling curse.

Sahara had considered bringing Naji to a speech therapist, but there was nothing wrong with him normatively. How could she explain the loss of Naji's magical abilities, his power to recall and describe past life stories? Sahara wondered if she should seek advice from Elvira Young, the mystreious woman who led the past life group. Elvi seemed to understand arcane truths. Since the problem haunted Sahara, what would she do when the twins were born? They were due on October 1st, Naji's birthday and a symbolic date for her work and lifetimes: 10/01. Would it be too much for her to handle?

But what could be more overwhelming than this very day? Sahara put the book down and returned to twirling her orange-blond hair around a finger. Perhaps Naji was more sensitive than she realized; perhaps he absorbed her anxiety and that was why he could not sleep. But how could she know that? How could she know anything he was feeling? None of this speculation mattered if her children's father did not return home.

Unbeknownst to Sahara, Naji could barely keep track of his feelings. His normal brain development might be blocking his telepathic powers, but he still retained glimpses of past lives. And of the interlife, the place between lives where he had come from only two years ago. He tried to stay aware of the physical world around him, but strange images pulled him away constantly. Whenever his mother read him a story, the archaic words and fantastical pictures led him into a fantasy universe. Sometimes it was too much for him and he looked away into emptiness.

Confused by the battle between normal behavior and extra-normal impressions, Naji longed to be a 'real boy,' like the puppet with the long nose in one of his mother's tales. Naji had stopped talking in people's minds when he began to speak aloud; now his speech was hampered by his concerns for the twin babies inside his mother. Given his proximity to the interlife, he should be aware of their presence as souls entering the world. But he was unable to sense their thoughts or contact them. Where were they? Was it his limitations? Was something wrong with them?

Now, on top of all these confusions, something was dreadfully wrong with his mother. She and Porcy had been worried all day; he knew his mother worried about him, but today was much worse. He had heard them say something about twins, or Twin Somethings, but it was something outside, not inside his mother. She was so fraught with fear that Naji worried for the health of the babies inside her. What had gone wrong? He could not help his mother, so Naji determined to contact the twins at last, and make sure they were safe. Willing his mind to search for their souls, Naji became even more detached from the normal world. Shutting himself away from the tensions in the household, he retreated into another realm.

The Tale of the Locked Corpseroom

There are as many versions of the interlife as there are individual souls. There are endless variations on Heaven and countless kinds of

Hell, and there are Ethers and Purgatories and Paradises of all sizes and shapes. When Naji decided to go look for the twins, two beings who may or may not have already made it through the interlife to be ensouled in their mother's womb, he did not know where to begin. The Infinite Intelligence, the powers that be, made an exception for this magical child and allowed him to pass from the living world back into the interlife, but they did not make it easy for him. Naji was on his own wandering through Limbo and Underworld.

The first thing Naji knew was that he was sucked back through a liquid canal at great speed. Surely he would see the twins, almost fully formed, ready to emerge in a few weeks. But he was moving too fast. If there were two souls smiling at him he missed them; if there were two natal bodies there, they were gone in a flash. Naji slid and corkscrewed through the tunnel, wondering where his journey would take him.

Finally, he flew out of the tunnel with explosive force, shooting forth into open air. Suspended in a vast sky-blue space, Naji delighted in the iridescent color. He forgot all about the twins. As he floated in the heavenly ether, luminescent souls drifted past. Naji remembered the way decrepit flesh resuscitates into youthful radiance in the interlife.

As Naji tired of his airborne excursion, he sighted a garden-filled landform below him. He descended gracefully into a grove of white and green dappled trees. He drifted past banks of bright pink and red flowers with enormous curving bells. He walked bare-footed on a path of soft moss. The path led to a clearing surrounded by lush red and green ferns, where a dozen damsels in flowing pastel robes sat on a semi-circular white bench. As Naji quietly took a seat on the bench, one of the damsels stood up and walked toward a small, twisted Japanese maple tree that spiraled out of the earth in front of the semi-circle. When she stood behind the tree, which rose no higher than her shoulders, Naji realized that it served as a lectern.

The damsel recited a devotional poem about a bear surviving the winter by hibernating. When she finished and sat down, a second damsel walked to the lectern and recited a quotation praising the art of empty-ing the mind. A third damsel told an anecdote about Saint Hrosvita, who protected her disciples from harm by enveloping them in soothing music. As Naji listened, he understood these were not random passages, but pertained to each individual.

Naji remembered this realm of the interlife he had entered. These were souls that had looked back on their lifetimes, examined them deeply, and purified their observations into important lessons. Souls must pass through here before rebirth, a thought that reminded Naji of his search for the twins. If they had been here recently, he could get to the bottom of what happened. None of the damsels knew of any twin souls, but graciously sent him where he could find help.

In Celtic mythology this interlife is known as The Dreaming Back, the place between existences where souls must revisit their former history and learn from their mistakes or best actions. This practice unfolds in the **corpyrooms***, the viewing stations where a soul can re-live or* **re-do** *its life, as if watching a film and acting the lead role at the same time. While re-doing a lifetime, a soul processes the information with a spirit guide. At the end of the first viewing, the soul starts re-doing the lifetime for a second time, only experiencing those moments still to be processed. This process continuea a third time, and a fourth and so on, until the spirit guide feels the soul has accomplished enough work for that inter-life. What Naji witnessed in the semi-circle of damsels was a kind of final examination after the corpyroom process.*

For hours Naji waited for souls to exit the corpyrooms, stopped guides on the paths of The Dreaming Back, and inquired after the twins. Many wondered why he was asking such questions about other souls, and entreated him to remain focused on his own soul. Some patronized Naji by explaining the corpyrooms. Others were so intent on what they were in the midst of that they could not hear his question. Naji became impatient with the useless answers. Was this not Heaven, where souls are caring and responsive? Naji brooded, frustrated with his lack of progress, and talked back to the fools with childish name-calling and impish taunts.

Finally, a more authoritative spirit guide took him by the hand (not very gently at that!) and thrust him into a corpyroom. Locked in, Naji sank to the floor and cried.

Sahara lost patience waiting for Naji to fall asleep that evening. She ceased fingering her hair and thought of a line from Scheherazade: "This is nothing compared to what I could tell you tomorrow night." Then she spoke aloud to Naji, "But there'll be no story if you do not go to bed right away." With that, she left the child in his crib and returned to the living room. She felt terrible, and expected him to burst into tears. Naji was silent.

Downstairs, Sahara found Porcy talking with Dr. Diana Machiyoko, another member of the qaraq. Diana had been Sahara and Amar's therapist, but Sahara had stopped seeing her when she separated from Amar, and had in fact moved into Diana's house for a year and a half. Their living relationship had been tense and full of squabbles, for the Asian-American therapist was a very private person, with low tolerance for a working mother with a one-year-old. Nonetheless, Diana had baby-sat Naji enough to develop a warm rapport with the child. As soon as Sahara decided to move back with her husband, Diana became her closest friend and ally.

Diana explained to Sahara that she had been swamped with patients all day, unscheduled drop-ins full of angst over the disaster. She knew the next weeks would be jam-packed, so she did not delay checking in with Sahara about Amar. Sahara was grateful for her friend's arrival, at least to buffer Porcy's obsessive TV viewing. She unloaded her grave concern that Amar was missing, and fretted about Naji's aloofness. Diana advised her to let Naji be for now: he was a special child on his own path, and in her anxious state Sahara was little able to help him.

In fact, the twins were due in three weeks, and everything was fine, but during her pregnancy with Naji, Sahara had suffered a medical scare and a psychological meltdown after delivery. Dr. Lake had simply advised her to take it easy, but another doctor she had consulted, Dr. Hajjaj, had insisted on bed rest. Sahara had chosen to ignore this advice. Diana insisted Sahara relax if only for the sake of her health. And the twins.

Getting signals from Sahara, Diana promised that she would stay and wait for Amar, and invited Porcy to return home if she wished. But Porcy could not face being alone without knowing Bax's whereabouts. Finally Bax called. The Hudson River cruise lines were voluntarily shuttling passengers to New Jersey and the Hoboken trains were running again. Porcy grilled him about what had happened, but he assured her he was safe at home. He thought he had seen Ooma in the aftermath, but things had been too chaotic for him to be sure. After more hysterical questioning from Porcy, Diana calmed her down and strongly suggested she go home to be with Bax. He needed her as much as she needed him. Porcy accepted the advice gratefully and hugged her two friends goodbye.

Sahara thanked Diana profusely for her intervention. Porcy could be a handful, even without the world falling apart. Sahara went into the kitchen to open a bottle of wine. Diana went upstairs and observed Naji staring at the ceiling. Rejoining Sahara for a glass of Cabernet, she reassured the mother of her baby's peace of mind.

The Tale of the Locked Corpyroom, conclusion

In his crib, Naji went in and out of seeing his bedroom, nodding off, and returning to the interlife, locked inside the corpyroom. Once he ceased crying there, Naji knew he had to find a way out of his prison. How could they do this in the interlife? He recalled no other times between lives when he had been treated so badly. Would someone come for him eventually? Would they banish him as an outcast, having breached the world of the living to return to the land of the dead? He could not let that happen before he had discovered what had become of the twins.

Investigating the corpyroom, a darkened screening chamber without windows, Naji had difficulty locating an alternate way out. There was no external projection booth or separate chamber for projecting a soul's life. But he needed to escape! Naji felt along the walls in the dark, and in one corner found the metal slats of an air vent. He could not budge the vent's frame, but thought the spaces between the slats might be large enough for him. Squeezing tightly through them, Naji succeeded in forcing his body into the airshaft on the other side of the wall. He crawled along the vent for a time until he was able to squeeze through another vent and into a hallway. Under dim light, Naji walked cautiously along a warren of corridors. Soon he felt as imprisoned in this maze as he had in the enclosed corpyroom.

Just as he was about to give up hope, Naji saw a shadowy figure in a robe down the hall. His first instinct was to run in the opposite direction, but then the figure gestured toward him. The ghostlike presence wore a hood over its head and held something in its gesturing hand. Naji walked toward the hooded form, who began leading him through the network of halls. At every corner the apparition beckoned Naji with the object. Naji hurried faster: what was the object? Moving down brighter corridors, up and down stairwells, and through many doorways, the figure finally halted at a locked door. It reached out its hand and unlocked the door: the object was a key!

The figure threw open the door and stepped out into blinding light. It sped across an open yard. Naji walked outside, grew accustomed to the light, and saw that the figure had joined a second hooded form on the other side of the yard. The first figure signaled Naji once more with the key, and then, as the child approached, the two robed beings lifted the hoods off of their heads.

Naji had found the twins.

ق

4

———〰———

September 11. 8:50 A.M. Hour 1 (first hour after Impact).

After only two hours of sleep, Amar Rash was an hour late to work. Impatient for the train to move faster, he calmed himself by thinking about the day before, the first day his beautiful wife had moved back in with him. Laughing to himself, Amar thought of how mundane the day had begun, with the two of them trying to fit a new couch into their den. Amar had done all the moving, while his eight-month pregnant wife directed from the pillows of their Arabian niche. He did not want her to lift a finger, especially her blood pressure scare during pregnancy with Naji.

Sahara had stayed up all night telling him an intricate past life tale. His own Scheherazade. The story was about Antoine Galland, the first European translator of *The Thousand and One Nights*. Her tale had ended with a visionary tirade by Veronique d'O, the daughter of Galland's patroness. She saw the collection of a thousand and one story parts as a container for the endless events of the universe. It was an expansive vision they had never considered. Nor had the qaraq.

Amar had loved the Nights, and ancient Indian story collections, ever since his mother had read to him as a boy in New Delhi. These story collections had brought Amar and Sahara together, on a romantic level, on a physical level (in the South Asian library stacks at the University of Chicago), and on a spiritual level. In several of the qaraq's fantastical past life memories, he and Sahara were incarnations of the historical models for Scheherazade and her captor, King Shahryar.

It was sweet Sahara had kept him up with a story, but not so sweet that he was late. Amar had made many mistakes in the past two years, with his wife, with her new friends in New Jersey, and with his colleagues at work. For a year he had been a pariah at his Bruckner Associates workplace. The dotcom boom had saved him, but now that it seemed to be ending, he had to be extra careful not to do anything conspicuously wrong.

But Ooma would cover for him. He could always count on Ooma. And he supported Ooma, despite office prejudice against her youth and religion. He took care of her and she him.

Amar rushed from the station underneath the Trade Center, but slowed when he reached the public spaces leading to the South Tower's lobby. People were running or standing still, pockets of smoke and dust appeared everywhere, and there were too many police officers. Forgetting his rush, he headed toward the street to see what was happening. Glass and paper littered the cement outside. What had fallen to the ground? People were shouting about a plane crash into the North Tower. Bodies falling from above! A crowd formed, but the police urged everyone to disperse.

"If you work in the South Tower, the safest thing would be to go there immediately. The street's too dangerous, and there's nothing wrong with that building." Amar knew they did not want injuries, but sensed no one really understood the situation. He entered, hurried to the 77th Floor.

The office was a confused mess. Some tried to keep order, pushing everyone to stay at their desks. Others shouted they should get out of the building. Or go help. Amar broke up arguments, saying the police wanted them to stay in the Tower. He received a few insults for his trouble.

Finally, his eyes came upon Ooma, standing frozen in front of the windows facing the North Tower, toward the billowing smoke and falling objects across the way. He raced over to her. Was she in shock? She looked as though in trance, like when the qaraq's members went into *regression*, recalling past lives. A real life sensation could trigger a regression, so Ooma might glimpse a lifetime of disaster, entrapment, or escape. Amar wanted to shake Ooma out of her detachment from reality, but he feared what it might do to her psyche.

In her protective bubble, Ooma recalled the first kiss from the 1999 New Year's party. After several years of searching for it, the first vision from that night appeared in her mind.

The Tale of the South Chinese Harem Girl

How horrid to sail on these unfortunate seas for months. My father had warned the Chinese lords: the great empire of *Chung Kuo* could no longer exist in a protective bubble of isolation. But I, Hu Ma, daughter of a sought-after mystical scientist, never imagined I would risk penetration by the barbarian conquerors from the desert lands, spreading a new religion just as their greasy sailors wished I would spread my legs. Father was little protection; he was enthralled that the Arab navigators Wahab and Abu Sa'id rendered the oceans between the desert peninsula and South China into a mere stream to cross, and they were equally dazzled by his science and philosophy. Our lords granted Father leave to voyage to Basra with the Arab fleet, secretly grateful to save their domains from destruction by sacrificing our family sacrificing me to lonely sailors and hormonal cabin boys. I was nearly ravished a dozen times protected only by the intervention of Sa'id who had promised me as a gift for an Emir; the captains would not tolerate the crew relieving themsleves in the hold of rare tea so why despoil the even bigger prize of my virginal state?

When we arrived at the swarming port of Basra, instead of continuing up legendary rivers to the Empire's capital of Baghdad we disembarked and were ushered into the custody of a local Sheikh who we learned was frustrated by his distance from the central nexus of the Islamic Empire. The Sheikh longed for the victorious cosmopolitanism of the City of Light the Caliph the wonders of art and literature such as the marvelous *One Thousand Tales*, that compendium that could have hailed from Sind or China or Persia but now was called Baghdadi material. The Sheikh took every advantage of the port of Basra as the Empire's reach into the oceanic world bribing his way to being first receiver of all news and materials from abroad for in this trickery he felt superior to the Caliph.

Thus we became captives of the Sheikh who gloried in the acquisition of the first visitors from South China and as we disembarked Father and the males of our contingent were taken into the Sheikh's court rooms while I and the females were pulled into the darkened chambers of the Sheikh's harem but I shrieked that I was the noble Hu Ma daughter of a great magician. My insult deepened when I came into contact with my handler an overpainted woman twice my age who instructed me on methods of the singing slave girls the flirtatious wiles the sexual signals the entrapments that could gain me favor and influence over men. There was no misunderstanding this advice despite the difference of our languages and there was no misunderstanding when I rejected such debasement and my grotesque handler applied several slaps with the back of her hand

She handed me off to two harem girls who had the greatest sympathy for my plight and fed me strange pastes and tiny black salty spheres to restore my health and attitude. I implored them to send to Father a plea but since they had no power to command they assured me with the most expressive gestures that if Father was a great sorcerer it could only benefit my family.

I learned that the Sheikh's great interest was in the longevity of his life and he had studied a great many texts and theories to gain the secret of endless life, his belief being the connection between youthfulness and the sexual life force. With the girls' whirling gestures I understood on the most primal level that this Sheikh saw sexuality as a magical thing and I saw in my mind's eye a Sexual Force as powerful as any planetary energy interwoven into the ether around our planet harmonized with our mysterious Chinese concept of Qi energy. It would be my escape – Hu Ma's salvation -- to seduce this Sheikh not with flirty signals but with the power of Thought and Qi and Endless Life. When my cruel handler next grabbed my arm I said I welcomed her Commander so she dragged me through the luxurious halls of the palace and I was brought to his bath where he was hidden under the folds of a soft towel and when he was told of my arrival he slowly turned to look at me and at once I regretted my decision to embrace interaction with this man because I was face to face with the oldest most wrinkled and decrepit human I had ever seen!

ق

Like waking with a start from a dream that ends in sudden disaster, Ooma gasped as Amar took hold of her shoulders. "I don't know what the hell's happening with you, but we've got to get out of here." Over-reaction had been Amar's way for many lifetimes, no less this one. Often his impulses had cost him relationships and reputation, but now it might save his life. He grabbed Ooma's hand and took off for the elevators.

Just as her incarnation had carried her soul from the safe Chinese world to the dangers of Arabia, so Ooma was torn from her protective memory back into the horrific world of flying machines crashing into gigantic towers. As Amar tugged her out of the office, her mind fought to connect the world she had just encountered with what she knew as the real world.

One thing was certain. For the first time, Ooma had envisioned a life unfolding in the time of *The Thousand and One Nights*, tremendously valuable information to the qaraqis who had been less than welcoming to her. Crucial to her acceptance, she felt a need to relay her visions to the qaraq.

34

Amar Rash saw Ooma come back to reality and was glad of it. At the elevator, he punched the down button several times. "The skylobby's one floor above on 78. There may be a lot of people there with the same idea. To escape this madness."

"And let me live," Ooma replied, thinking both to escape disaster and the harem of the decrepit Sheikh. And stay in touch with her new memories. She would need Amar's help. "I have to tell the qaraq my new recall. It's important to them, especially Sahara."

"You're nuts," Amar said, stabbing the button a few more times. "Please stay with me and don't go into Reincarnation Land in your head."

The elevator doors opened. There were only three persons inside. They entered and Amar pushed the unlit ground floor button. These people aren't even trying to leave, Amar thought.

"It's a way for us to be included in the meetings," Ooma said. "Of belonging. But you're right. First we must escape."

Before Amar could agree, the second plane hit the South Tower, smashing through eight floors above them.

5

———◈◈◈———

September 11. 9:55 A.M. Hour 2 (1 hour after Impact).

Bax bumped shoulders with someone on Seventh Avenue and 21st Street and realized he had been walking in a fog. There were plenty of dazed persons walking uptown toward him, workers escaping the World Trade Center. Bax heard that a second plane had flown into the South Tower. There was little doubt about an attack on the city now. Instinctually, Bax looked downtown in the direction of the Twin Towers, and gaped at a surreal vision. Instead of the familiar, iconic shapes of New York City, above the Wall Street skyline rose the unmistakable, ominous form of a mushroom-shaped cloud, formed from the smoke and dust of the plane crashes. Having fled his native Colorado because of his fears of the missile silos and nuclear industry there, Bax was racing toward the very spector of his phobia.

But he had to find Ooma. It did not matter whom he bumped or what else he heard or saw, he had to focus on getting to Wall Street. The more he intensified his drive to reach Ooma, the more Bax felt her presence near him, inside his thoughts and feelings. During their seven kisses he had been aware of times his story was interrupted or continued by another voice. Only now did he understand that he and Ooma had been receiving each other's past life visions.

He felt the same sensation now, the same connection to Ooma. Was Ooma sending him the visions from *that night* during this hellish morning? How was that possible? Was it some frightening consequence of the traumatized mental state of the city? Were their minds so open and vulnerable that they had access to each other?

Bax remembered a story Ooma had told him, of her life as an Indian elephant named Homma, who had traveled to Baghdad. In Homma's tale, the baby elephant had many fragmented visions, including one of seven kisses! Elephants have incredible memories, but how else could Homma 'remember' something from a thousand years later? Just as Ooma's visions during the seven kisses had bled into his mind, they now projected out into the world, across time and space.

These baffling thoughts pushed Bax to a memory of the Arabian niche. His vision during the first kiss came into view as he walked downtown toward the mushroom cloud. Could he face his fears of what was down there, fears inherited from his incarnations, from one past life that ended in violent death, or another cut short too soon? Or from the man in the vision forming now, an old man obsessed with Death and immortality. Recognizing the voice of his soul, the fragmented, sparse phrases, as clouded as the smoky sights on the street, Bax drifted into a memory of his life as the Sheikh from Ooma's first kiss vision, Hu Ma's tale.

The Tale of the 111-Year-Old Sheikh

I, Sheikh Ba'Tr ibn Halali, have never been so close to Death. One hundred and eleven years of the Moon have I lived. Yet I will conquer

Death! All my life I have studied. Questioned. Welcomed foreigners. All to understand Death. How every culture believes in Life beyond. Most of them believe in Return. As a new Life.

I work closely with the Zanj. From East African coast. Below Egypt, Land of the Afterworld. My Zanj work as navvies outside Basra. Dig canals through swampland. We sweat side by side. I ask them: what is after Death? They say: we become the rocks. The mountains looking down on our families. I do not like this belief. I do not wish to be a rock. I lower their rations.

I blame it on Basra. Central seat of mystical Sufi. They moved here when the Umayyad dynasty was driven from Damascus. Mysticism alive for a century here. I grew up hearing Seventh Heaven chatter. Gardens of the Afterlife. Made me thirst for life after. Gained wealth through business to entertain great Sufis. Egyptian Pyramid moguls. Reincarnation theorists.

I collected manuscripts. Ritual objects. Tiny shabtis from Pyramid tombs. Avatars for dead souls. Plunder from Arab raids. Parthian star lamp from ruins of Ctesiphon. With secret latch. Hidden code phrase. Said to add one hundred fifty years to a life. If used during sexual act. Worked for demented Queen Uzmeth. Worked for me. But do I want only longevity? Too old. Dying. Need immortality. Need more than star lamp? More to sex? Greater power?

Caliph keeps me here in backwater. But I bring new ideas from Cordoba. The other Empire. Umayyad survivors. In defiance to Baghdad. Open relations with Europe. Acquisition of Greek and Roman texts. Translate wise tomes into language of the Prophet. Elderly ideas become youthful. Pneuma: soul to Aristotle. Literally: breath. Carries the soul. Pneuma infuses the soul during the procreative act. The star lamp phrase uttered during the act. Create immortality?

Ask the Chinese sorcerer. He insists on potions and spells to do the work. But nothing works. Lock him up with his vials. Mix his powders with the desert sands. The daughter implores me. Hu Ma. Will do anything to save father's life. Delightful. I consider her pleas. Could use star lamp once more. With this beauty. But Father deserves no mercy. He must die. As I am.

Hu Ma shifts tactic. Demands private audience. Demands! Alone, she flirts shamelessly. Harem mistress taught her well. Offers herself. For my experiment. Gentle blushes. I show magnanimity. Praise Hu Ma's compassion. (Will execute father later.)

Conjugal night prepared carefully. Immortal life or death matter. No expense spared for Hu Ma's habiliment. Rings braids perfumes flowing silks from her native land. She is ravishing. Hu Ma shows no sign of resistance. Despite my age. Decrepitude.

Finally together in the bed chamber. Her ritual display before me unprecedented. Revelation of flesh like rising of the Moon. Her touch is unexpected. As if lovers forever. Knows my body. My soul. By Allah, I will not slay her afterward.

Star lamp is lit. I utter the phrase. Ancient command. Hu Ma shudders. She insists: what are these words? Insists! She recognizes something. Fear creeps into her serene face. Then gone. She mounts me. *She* mounts *me*! Her movements take my breath. Pneuma. Unchecked passion. Loss of control. She truly has power over immortality. Or she'll be death of me. Sweet death.

Height of love. Seed penetrates. Breath of life. Feel pneuma whirling inside. Both of us. Hu Ma shudders again. Collapses on me. Her lips crush mine. First kiss! My mouth presses to hers. No response. More effrontery? Press harder. Nothing. Her weight is dead against me. Unconscious. As I realize her inertness my own breath fails. The world spins. Soul into nowhere.

I travel. Transform. Am I dead? Whirled about. Pneuma? Hu Ma? Coma? Ooma? What is this name? I hear it called. A young woman appears to me. Answers the call. I am called. By this Ooma. Hu Ma? Enter a chamber. Kitchen. Recognize olives. Ooma beckons me to another room. Guests. Celebration. Wine.

I am alive! In a youthful body! But where? Strange time and place. A reincarnation? Follow Ooma to back room. Beautiful woman exits.

Golden red tresses. I enter room. Ooma lays on pillows. She is ready for me. First kiss. Vision of a vision of a vision.

Time stops again. Ooma? Pneuma blows me back. Hu Ma? She is gone. Where is she? Jump out of bed. New strength. New body. Molded out of young body from strange world. Alive!

Rejoice too soon. I have been gone months. Sheikhdom in chaos. The Zanj revolt in Basra. But I am not beaten down. For I have beaten Death! My people marvel. The Zanj cower in fear of me. Restore Zanj as work force. Restore my fortune.

Hu Ma did not share my fortune. I send for her body. There is breath still. Pneuma lives. She is alive but lost to us. I will spare her father. He is dead from grief. Send him back to China. Insists on bringing Hu Ma. But Hu Ma stays here. She gave me immortal life, so I must honor her. Her life is forfeit. But new life grows inside her. She lives to give birth to my heir.

ق

Bax came out of his trance. He was below 14th Street now. He had seen a vision of himself, as Sheikh Ba'Tr, traveling forward in time from before the first millennium AD to the 1999 New Year's party. Bax was too unsettled with the shock of the plane crashes and his eerie connection to Ooma's visions to understand what that could mean.

In the Sheikh's tale something dreadful happened to Ooma's incarnation. Just as the Sheikh felt responsible for protecting Hu Ma and the child inside her, Bax continued to feel driven to rescue Ooma. His mind might be lost in memory and trauma and confusion, but his body moved forward inexorably toward the Twin Towers. As if released from his own ego-soul, he felt no fear.

40

6

—⟋⟋⟋—

September 12. 10:30 P.M. Day 2 (1 day after Impact).

Verlin Walker looked up from his pepperoni slice, and stared at the stacks of computer print-outs that cluttered his living quarters. The attic space, given to him as compensation for his job as handyman at the Glenclaire Unitarian Church, used to be sparse and immaculate. The serene A-frame loft contained a shrine nestled into a gable and a Persian rug warming up the large central space. It was not only Verle's personal sanctuary, but also a special place for the past life support group meetings. One vision had pointed to the attic as hallowed ground for the qaraq.

Now the attic loft was too cluttered to traverse, let alone hold a circle of chairs for a meeting. Verle's eyes strained over the piles of books and files. He patted his gray dreadlocks in thought. He did not know if he had the strength to tackle the mess. Yesterday's events had prompted a flurry of activity at the church, special services, prayer meetings, and community outreach gatherings. Verle had not had a moment to rest since yesterday morning, and dozens of volunteers were still needed for the upcoming memorials. He might be spry for a man almost a hundred years old, but this was too much!

The thing Verle loved most throughout his lifetimes was a well-organized system, so he was especially vulnerable to the mess in his attic and the world. He and Zack Goodkin, another qaraqi, had set out to accomplish a beautifully structured archive for the qaraq's past life stories, including commentary and cross-references from the meetings. The goal was a long way off: they had transcribed only half the tales remembered so far.

He needed order! Laying out a set of stories on the floor, Verle glanced back and forth at their contents. If he could find a pattern somewhere, he could re-organize the chaos into some semblance of order. He shuffled the pages, brought out new files, and re-positioned piles. In frustrated annoyance, Verle picked up two fistfuls of pages and threw them randomly on the floor, then sat cross-legged amid the chaos, head in hands, on the verge of tears.

When he lifted his gray-brown-skinned head, Verle detected a meaningful arrangement of the papers. He felt idiotic not to have seen what now was so obvious before him. Along with seeing the structure, Verle felt accompanying sensations, as if he had performed this random selection process many times in the past. But then he envisioned future scholars debating the organizing principle's worth. This vision opened up in his mind, a precognition of his life deep in the future as an academician of past life texts.

A Grant Proposal in Favor of the World Types Structure

I make this plea to the Board of Raegents of the Univertatum d'Ausbourg to dispel the chaos afflicting our society at this time. Given the divide within our population, the encroaching threat of autocracy, and this new meglomaniacal leader, we are in great need of higher awareness. To provide a new truth that might counteract the greed and prejudice rampant in the halls of power, I believe my department is on the brink of a major breakthrough.

For so many semesters I felt like one of those ancient geomancers, who cast sticks or turn knobs on a slab of metal or even throw papers down a stairwell, and then with the faith of the hopeless, attempt to perceive order in the random. I feel a dark connection to those blind prophets. But now that the darkness lies outside in our land, and enlightenment is close at hand inside our halls, I beg you for assistance, financial, personnel, and moral. We need order!

Behold our progress. A recently authenticated story collection from ancient Egypt that surpasses the Westcar Papyrus, a new edition of the *Hazr Afanseh* that clearly tracks the Indian and Persian roots of the *Arabyan Nichts*, and a new Version of our most fascinating collection, where the tales originate less in cultural mythflow and more in past life recollections. That is our work: The Recollection Project intends to continue gathering these memoirs, and there are hundreds of them, but for the first time attempt the geomancer's feat of placing an order on top of the chaos.

No doubt there exists a bonafide sequence to the stories of The Recollection Project. Initial studies organize tales according to the idea of a common group of souls behind the incarnations. The scant evidence for this categorization consists of Character Identifying Traits: recurring name-phonemes, physical attributes or gestures, and archetypical relations to characters from the Nichts. My own soul has been parodied as Ardmin the Rash, who waves his hands wildly like a bloodthirsty King of yore. So much for fighting our meglomaniacal autocrat!

Here is our most recent breakthrough: a categorization scheme so obvious it makes my geomancer's circles in the sand seem ultra-sophisticated. My intrepid (if small) faculty has re-discovered Vlmeer Rwelka's work on *World Types*, lost in the academic mists for centuries. Rwelka, or Papa Vlmeer as my colleagues fondly call him, starts with the notion of a qaraq, the common group of souls inhabiting the same Worlds through-out its past life trajectory.

If a qaraq has ten souls in it, for example, the Rwelkian scholar can detect a set of ten stories with similar characteristics, with one soul featured in each tale, but with interaction between the ten personae over the course of all the tales. This unifier defines a World: not necessarily a location, though the ten tales might all occur on one planet like Aklanon, not necessarily a time, though the stories might all follow the Trojan War, and not necessarily a theme, though I dare say a set of ten might focus on future Scholars who analyze past life story collections. Whatever the glue between stories, a complete set of lifetimes for a qaraq defines a World.

Verle paused in his recollection to experiment with the papers before him. Sure enough, the idea of Worlds bore fruit as an organizational scheme. What an amazing recall! Here was the key to organizing the archives, and an initiation into a World of similar minded analysts. Kindred spirits! Verle even recognized an organizational device from a 'memory' of a future lifetime of his, CHITS, or Character Identifying Traits.

Thinking about the CHITS in this story, Verle knew he was not recalling his own lifetime. More likely he was Vlmeer Rwelka: the name shared letters of his name, Verlin Walker. And Rwelka was as obsessed with structures as he was. The author of the grant proposal, nicknamed Ardmin the Rash, had to be Amar Rash, whose impulsive passion matched that of Sahara's husband.

Why did Amar's voice appear in Verle's mind? It was as if the mind-boggling events of the last twenty-four hours had opened a wound in the psychic universe. The barriers between the qaraq's souls had loosened, giving each soul access to the others' memories. As far as Verle knew, Sahara had not heard from Amar since the attacks. If Amar was lost, was he calling to Verle from beyond the grave? The thought chilled the old man. Shaking off the notion, Verle felt obliged to finish the recall. At least to share Amar's memory with Sahara if something had happened. He took a deep breath and let the text of the Ardmin's proposal return to his mind.

A Grant Proposal in Favor of the World Types Structure, continued

A World can feature more than one lifetime for a qaraqi, or soul in the group. Vlmeer sketches Worlds with thirty, seventy, or one hundred and ten lifetime tales, such as a saga outlining the development of The Arabyan Nichts itself. In these cases, the qaraqis have the same number of (multiple) lifetimes, give or take. Recently, we have hypothesized other number games, even in a set of ten lives. There are Worlds where only nine of the ten qaraqis appear, the missing member reborn for karmic reasons into an exile World. There are other kinds of 'solo' Worlds, where a qaraqi joins a spirit guide for introspection. And there are warring conflict Worlds, where five members belong to one World and the other five to a rival World, such as five Stone Cliffs, overlooking a Valley inhabited by a tribe ruled by five Principices.

It is evident that Vlmeer had found or assembled a complete story collection of past lives. Vlmeer's Worlds represent a great many cultures, known and fantastical. It is of great interest that many of these cultures had their own beliefs and mythology about reincarnation.

Vlmeer used two schemes for his own classification of Worlds: World Types and Character/World Types. World Types were either Earth worlds, Alternate Earth Worlds, Science Fiction Worlds, or Parallel Worlds. Some of these seem arbitrary, such a Shy Teacher World in the Sci-fi realm. The criteria for this categorization seem purely Earth-centric, suggesting an origin to this system predating Vlmeer's time, millennia after the First Galactic Affiliation.

The Character/World Types are less about genre of story and more at the characters' situation in the stories. Conflict tales include the warring 5-character sub-groups; Exile tales include the 9-character Worlds missing an exiled qaraqi; Infinity tales include solo Worlds about introspection with a spirit guide; and Multiple Worlds, which use many lifetimes for each qaraqi, include greater connectivity between characters and events.

With each new idea about the World Types, Verle gleefully shifted piles and re-classified story print-outs. How helpful in prioritizing what to transcribe for the archives! For Verle, the archive was a symbol of his desire to understand the bigger picture of the qaraq's history. Verle hypothesized that the qaraq tended to be around for major historical junctures. It had engaged in a clan war during prehistoric times, and worked on a version of *The Thousand and One Nights* in medieval Baghdad. But none of these events gave Verle a clear picture of its overall history. Grateful for Amar's incarnation text, no matter how he was receiving it, Verle continued.

A Grant Proposal in Favor of the World Types Structure, conclusion

Although we do not have a record of all the Worlds on Vlmeer's lists, we know he had a strict system of accounting, which lessens the sense of arbitrariness:

World/Types	Number of Worlds	Number of Lifetimes
Earth worlds	10	400
Alt earth	40	300
Sci-fi	30	200
Parallel	20	101

Character/World Types

Conflict	40	300
Exile	30	200
Infinity	20	101
Multiple	10	400

I cannot stress my passion for the re-discovery of Vlmeer Rwelka's work. It is an evolutionary step! Just as our souls tired of lives as nuclear material and yearned for organic, physical life, just as unicellular animals divided and started new species, and just as the algae spread onto land, so I yearn for Papa Vlmeer's system that orders our collective stories.

I look at the World Types as a start and finish to the form of all story collections. My staff has the patience of Vlmeer Rwelka, to read, sort through, and analyze, until every last story has found its proper place. They are the ones that need your financing, your encouragement, and your blessing. I humbly lower myself to my knees. I am a man blessed, a scholar enlightened. I submit this report of our progress as my ultimate appeal to counteract the dread direction of our world.

ق

Too tired and overwhelmed to absorb everything, Verle hoped he could call up the particulars later. He was elated by the new vision, which would clarify the archives and the qaraq's history. And clean up his mess.

Verle felt a wave of guilt over his excitement, and an overwhelming grief for his friends in the qaraq. Amar and Ooma could be lost in the rubble, projecting past life tales from beyond the grave! Each qaraqi could be gravely affected by the aftermath of the Twin Towers catastrophe. He was by no means immune to the grief-stricken families who had come by the church. He had to help others. What was he doing, lost in some fantastical puzzle, divorced from reality?

47

Or was it? Suddenly Verle had a joyous inspiration. He could provide a balm for the qaraq's distress, a distraction, and explore the new discovery with his friends. He could not wait to share his findings, hear more tales, and begin the journey.

7

———ครครคร———

September 11. 9:00 A.M. Hour 1 (first hour after Impact).

Amar pushed Ooma in front of him, and leaped out of the elevator. As Ooma landed on the ground, she hit her jaw. The shocking sensation sent her memory back to a kiss with Bax at the New Year's party, an aged Sheikh forcing his mouth down on hers. Amar implored Ooma to rush, but sensed her fall and the shock of the second plane crash had set her mind askew again.

Shoving her through a stairwell door, he grabbed her hand and started down the stairs. She resisted his pull. Ooma had re-entered the mind of Hu Ma, the Chinese captive in Sheikh Ba'Tr's harem, who had fallen into a coma, her mind not lost but more active than ever.

"You must let me help you!" Amar shouted.

Unconsciously, Ooma clutched Amar's hand tightly, and launched down the stairwell. Two floors down a wall of sheetrock collapsed into the stairwell. Amar pulled Ooma back inside a trading floor full of rushing, shouting, and crying victims. They reached the other corner of the floor, then entered another stairwell full of people and smoke.

Amar saw every potential danger around them. Glass and blood covered the stairs. Bodies hurling forward brushed and bumped against them. The building groaned and vibrated and shook as more walls collapsed. Ooma froze, her arms held together against her torso, hands clasped under her chin. Her eyes were closed, shutting out the smoke. Amar could not face the possibility of losing Ooma in the midst of it all.

"Ooma! Save yourself!" In an effort of sheer will, Ooma's body descended flights of stairs with Amar. Strange men with axes and huge dark coats and helmets rushed past them going up the stairs. The crushing debris, poisoned air, the noisome dark – everything pushed Ooma back inside her mind, back into Hu Ma's comatose state, the ultimate retreat from the world, a fractious peace.

Once again Hu Ma felt a pressure on her mouth, this time a sweet pressing of lips. It was Bax's second kiss in the Arabian niche, felt twelve hundred years away. She recognized she was traveling between the different Worlds of a soul's incarnations, here the demented Persian Queen Uzmeth, there a futuristic young Muslim at a festivity. So Ooma in the World Trade Center, Ooma at the New Year's Eve party, and Hu Ma in her coma all received visions moving in flashes.

Amar did all he could to ease Ooma's wild descent down the stairwell, but he had to be constantly vigilant about warding off unexpected barriers. He tried to calculate how many more floors they had to go. He listened to the violent groaning of the edifice, feared it would not stand, but scoffed at the preposterous notion.

No sooner had Ooma gone further into trance than she suffered another blow in the dark from a fellow escapee. Bruised, her clothes ruined from rips and debris, her nerves jolted, her mind hurled back to the lands of medieval Islam, which grew more intense. Enwrapped in a protective aura, Ooma emanated the fantastical imagery out into the world.

Over halfway down the chaotic stairwell, Amar encountered collapsed walls where electrical fires erupted. Ooma crouched down, making gathering gestures with her hands, as if she were cleaning up the debris. Amar coaxed her to stand, but she was lost to him, lost in another vision. Sparks threatened the corner where Ooma cowered. Amar had no choice but to carry her.

Exhausted from lack of sleep and constant focus on the hazards around them, Amar forced his weary body to hoist Ooma into his arms. As their bodies touched, he felt more than a physical bond; her mental state radiated out of her skin into Amar's perception. It was like when he touched Sahara and she received a recall from him. He became aware of an even larger circle of psychic connection, between Ooma and a Chinese captive, Hu Ma, and between Bax, Porcy, and the qaraqis.

They saw Uzmeth, haunted by her evil past, reincarnated as Princess Humai, tormented by nightmares, her grandmother Sharzad telling her night tales to help her sleep. The child pleaded with her father, the legendary ruler Bahram Gur, to commission a story collection. The narrative jumped through time again, to early Islamic invasions two hundred years after Humai. Over this time a wonderful story collection evolved: *Hazar Afsanah*, or The Thousand Marvelous Tales.

Amar and Ooma continued to rest in mutual embrace. Seeing the images of Arab lifetimes swirl in his head, Amar wondered why Islamic history and culture struck their minds at this intense moment. Yes, Sahara is a scholar of the Arabian Nights, yes, Ooma is a Muslim, but what did it have to do with the qaraq, whose presence he felt? Were these visions related to the catastrophe at the Twin Towers, a harbinger of some shift in Islamic-American relations?

The visions settled into a specific tale, seen during Bax's second kiss at the party. Amar flinched at the image of Bax kissing the woman he held in his arms. Hu Ma recognized the world of her captors, but earlier, at the beginning of Islam, when they fought to preserve their ways. And Ooma knew she saw one of Porcy's lifetimes, thanks to the barriers between their souls broken open by chaos, trauma, and near-madness.

51

The Tale of the Muhaddith

We have traditions to keep, hard fought values and sacred words to protect. I spend my days looking at every letter of the law, parsing every phrase of speech to determine its veracity. These Night tales undermine everything we believe. They are vulgar and commonplace, like a shadow in a muddy puddle of The Prophet's words. I overhear the Persian wet-nurse in the evening, reciting the nonsense and lies to my son. I resent her seductive, pernicious wiles.

We are *muhaddith*. We are specialists: we know profoundly the *hadith*, the utterances of those who knew The Prophet's words and deeds. We have memorized tens of tens of thousands of such narrations. We understand the holy significances; we know who the original narrators were.

More than this! We hold in our memory every *isnad*, the chain of narrators who have passed down a saying over generations. We know if a Companion of Muhammad heard it directly from him, or if a Follower of a Companion from the next generation conveyed the message, or if the uncle of the Follower who heard it from the Companion, and so on. The muhaddith scrutinizes each transmitter as to their credibility. Was this narrator reliable as a source or a reputed liar? Did that narrator understand the content of the message, or did he misconstrue the meaning?

The extreme care we take preserving the isnad is pathetically absent from the fantastical stories the round-hipped Persian wet-nurse conveys. Their origin is lost, at best shrouded in shadows, being perhaps from Sind, perhaps from the Sasans, perhaps from street criers in modern Ctesiphon, dodging the blows of the Caliph's troops. When I question her, the wet-nurse claims the tales come from the great collection, the *Hazar Afsanah*, but cannot name its author or the source of any individual story. The very opposite of our endeavors! Here is a text that has no single authentic version. Even the title is shifty and changeable, here *The*

Thousand Tales, there *The Thousand Marvelous Stories*, and over there in the market the people nickname it *The Thousand Nights*. Unacceptable.

It has not been easy to pass the pure light of The Prophet down to the next worthy soul. Our first Caliphs did not have united approval within the *umma*, and there has been much bloodshed and treachery in this community. With all this turmoil whom could we trust with the Truth? Who was craftily fabricating a revelation to politically endorse a conflicting ideology? This was no scholar's game, but a battle to the death. The muhaddith had to be as pure as the original vision, incorruptible. We had to preserve our ways.

In the face of this dangerous effort, how can I let my son's ears be filled with these night tales? The Umayyad dynasty in Damascus may have stabilized the Empire, spread its conquering wings from China to Spain, but there is still endless war and perpetual squabbles. We are not safe for fiction. I see the delight in my boy's twinkling eyes as the nurse prattles on, but all I hear are lies. To encourage the untruth of fiction is to unleash a dangerous freedom: anyone can say anything.

I hear my boy gasp at the story that frames the *Hazar Afsanah*, the tale of the King who kills a new bride every night. My wives complain about the excessive violence in the frame tale, but danger lurks everywhere. Still, the framing device itself is a falsehood: unlike the isnad, which frames a saying, this frame tale allows any random story to follow, a fictional untruth, with an obscured origin. A triple deception!

I feel the power of the *Hazar Afansah*. I have compassion for human joy and human suffering. In my child's face I see the open-hearted feelings inspired by each tale, and my own heart breaks from what I must do. I fear my great work as a muhaddith may be helpless in light of this great work: a thousand tales! Would that I could track down each tale, declare its personal isnad, and tell my son, "This one, the tale of the two prisoners in love, comes from a wise man named Ashanti in a little village in northwestern Hind."

Alas, I cannot, nor can I accept the blasphemy that I am weaker than a bunch of night tales. I must discharge my son's beloved nurse.

Moreover, I must banish her from the city. I will hire assassins to meet her on the road outside the city limits. They will ravish her, slit her throat, and leave her for the beasts. We must preserve our ways! The way is clear! Allah is most powerful!

ق

The violent ending of the tale jolted Amar away from images washing over him. The story was a warning. Danger lay ahead. He had to keep moving! The building was ready to implode! He lifted up Ooma's weight, navigated around the ruined walls and fires, and continued his descent down the burning Tower.

54

8

———◦◦◦———

September 11. 5:00 P.M. Hour 9 (8 hours after Impact).

During the afternoon after the attacks, Naji was not sleeping, but was quiet enough during his nap, too quiet as usual. Sahara left him alone, made a cup of tea, and sat at the wooden dining table to write a few sentences for her thesis on the origins of the Nights. After a few minutes and not a second of concentration, she did something she had been meaning to do for a long time.

"Hello?" A faint voice answered her telephone call.

"Is Ardra Rash there?" she asked tentatively, nervously.

"You have the pleasure of speaking to him," Ardra replied. "Who might this be?"

"Hi. I'm glad I reached you. This is Sahara Fleming. Amar's wife."

"Yes, I know my grandson's wife's name. But I hardly know the woman."

"I know. I'm sorry I've never called before. I know Amar hasn't been good about it. I didn't know who else to call. His father did not answer the phone."

"Sol rarely does," Ardra said. "I believe it's called screening. But I rarely call him, my son, as you may know."

"I thought Amar at least got the two of you talking again," Sahara said

"To his credit." Ardra's tone suggested he did not want to pursue this topic. He had a brief coughing fit, then said, "To what do I owe the pleasure, Sahara Fleming?"

"Again, I apologize to call under such circumstances. Amar hasn't checked in with me from the Twin Towers. With everything that's happened…"

"Yes, that is deeply disturbing. I've been watching the news. Terrible. I am so sorry, I have not heard from him either. He does call me from work occasionally. But not today. How frightening. Can you contact anyone else? An agency?"

"It's impossible to get through to anyone in the city. They're saying some people called home before…" Sahara unconsciously curled a lock around her finger.

"I've heard that. But many who called did not survive. I'm sorry, that was insensitive."

"No, I know you must be as worried as I am. I don't know what else I can do now. They're starting to ferry people to New Jersey, but who knows where he is."

There was a silence. Sahara heard Ardra trying to gain his voice. "You and Amar, my dear, you are … doing well?"

Sahara did not know how much Amar had told his grandfather about their marital troubles. Perhaps everything. Or nothing. "That's just it, Ardra. We're great. Really, really great."

"Then he will return to you," Ardra said. "And Naji. How is my peer-less great-grandson?"

Sahara thought of the child, staring blankly at the ceiling. She was on the verge of tears. Ardra's warm kindness softened her; she could barely contain her feelings. She let her guilt kick in, to push away the other feelings. "Naji's fine. We must come visit you. It's unforgiveable."

"I forgive you," Ardra said mockingly. "A visit would be lovely." He coughed again.

"Are you all right?" Sahara had not even asked after the aging man's health!

"It's just a little nuisance, you know, smoker's cough."

"Have you seen a doctor about it?"

Ardra changed the subject. "You just worry about Amar. And I will, too. He'll be back. He's probably rescuing a few secretaries."

"That's what I'm afraid of." Sahara said it as a joke, but neither of them laughed.

"The three of you will come visit. *When* he comes back."

"Thank you, Ardra. I'll let you know when I hear from him."

"I would appreciate that, my dear. Please take care."

After hanging up, Sahara checked on Naji. He was still in his own world, so distant from her. She was distraught about it, but Naji had broken all rules of babyhood. When babies cannot distinguish between their internal hunger cycle and the object outside that feeds them, Naji had been totally aware of his mother, talked in her mind, and even recounted past life stories to members of the qaraq. In the same year that the qaraq grew to understand that details of everyday life repressed awareness of immortal life, Sahara saw her son's normal developmental growth block his magical power. It was all disturbing and strange, but many things about the qaraq and the visions were disturbing and strange. Even today Sahara had received flashes of lifetimes. Porcy had confirmed that she too had glimpses of stories set in Arab lands. With the news that Arab terrorists may have been behind the attacks, they wondered if today's events suggested the images in their minds.

Something else concerned Sahara. Last year when something blocked the qaraq from remembering past lives, she had learned that the *illusion* of the daily world clouded the *reality* of the immortal world behind it. The qaraq named it *The Maya Factor*, after the Hindu word for the illusion of mundane existence. Today's catastrophe destroyed the belief that everyday existence is mundane: how can so many deaths be trivial? How could she in all conscience reduce this chaos to The Maya Factor? The World Trade Center attacks felt as huge and 'cosmic' as the awareness of multitude past lives. The world would never be the same, and today it took on a heightened reality.

10:10 A.M.   7 hours earlier.

Heading downtown that morning, Bax had similar thoughts. At first the day's events seemed surreal. It was the most beautiful day of the summer, the sun warmly golden and the sky radiantly blue. Then, the mushroom cloud of smoke over the downtown skyline, and the zombie-like forms covered in white dust on the street seemed like an illusion, affirming The Maya Factor.

But below Canal Street the white specters changed. They were running, screaming, and fleeing something unimaginably horrific. The roots of the mushroom cloud became apparent to Bax, no longer surreal but massive, like billowing waves of gaseous fumes. New figures ran past him, blood-soaked and shocked.

The qaraq had also learned that the illusion of everyday existence protects living creatures from burning out on the intense visions of the vast universe and the endless lives of the immortal soul. There was comfort in this aspect of The Maya Factor, and the soul-group had regained its equilibrium and strength after its fearful loss of power.

But the idea of the world as illusion was in doubt: today mundane existence was horrible, not comforting. As the terrifying images ripped away Bax's shield of bravery that morning, he saw The Maya Factor in reverse: the physical world dripping with catastrophic reality. The world of past lives was the illusion, a fantasy to cover up the horror of the world. The qaraq had it all wrong!

The thought that the qaraq's belief system was in shambles was too much for Bax. The temptation to escape into the second kiss from Ooma was too great. Bax reached out to Ooma's soul for this solace. Since the barriers between the qaraqis had lifted, Bax saw another of Porcy's lifetimes, the next vision he had received during the party. It was also the qaraq's next lifetime from the early years of Islam. Why so many Arabic stories in these chilling hours?

The Tale of the Bedouin Poet

Hammad could not believe his good fortune. It had been a grueling journey from the Syrian desert, and Hammad had gambled and won! He was to enter the inner sanctum of the mighty Umayyads, the clan who had brought order to the community of The Prophet. Hammad's great-grandfather had talked reverentially of The Year of Unity, when Caliph al-Malik restored stability to the Faithful, after decades of internal warring. The desert tribes had followed the Word for generations, but when the capitol of the Empire moved to Damascus, they felt closer than ever.

For this reason, Hammad had been inspired to seek out the royal court. He clung to this hope as he was led into the vizier's chamber for an audience. Although he had stopped for the night to clean up and change clothes, he felt all eyes on his tribal garb. As the vizier's attendant whispered the nature of Hammad's business, a disdainful courtier spoke:

"O wise one, it is rumored this tribesman brings something of worth. But is he worthy to bring anything to this court?" The vizier acknowledged his attendant's information, and bid the courtier continue. "There are those of us at court who believe the age of poetry is dead. We all know that before The Prophet received the blessed verses of the Qur'an, the desert Arabs were the masters of poetry. Tell us: is your desert verse superior to the best Umayyad poetry?"

Hammad smelled a trap. If he feigned humility, he would be unworthy and thrown out of court. If he agreed, he would have to prove it. "As far back as pagan times, poetry was the currency of desert interaction. We recorded deeds in poems, preserved genealogies in verse, arrived at water holes singing lyrics. If it is superior to make the daily fabric of life into poetry, then it is so."

It was a good response: the court buzzed with astonished approval. But the nasty courtier was not satisfied; if anything, Hammad had incensed him to battle.

"How can an ode to a mud puddle be superior to an epic about our glorious conquests, as far east as India, as far west as the Spanish peninsula, the end of the world?"

Hammad smiled. "In the remotest oases we have heard of these colossal events, and are humbled. But it is more difficult to create beautiful words describing a single palm tree, than a magnificent conquest. Perhaps your poetry does not work as hard and suffers for it."

Again the court bubbled with approval and the courtier's face reddened. He looked to the vizier, but he was silent and gestured for the courtier to finish his challenge.

"Fine. If the poetry of the palace is so decadent, then grace us with one of your superior, *everyday* Bedouin poems. Recite a *qasida*, an ode to your discovery of the worthy object you bring."

The court murmured assent of the courtier's challenge and leaned forward in anticipation. The challenge was no great dare to Hammad: the qasida was a form heard around the campfire, an elaborately sequenced description of a desert journey. Beginning with the image of his tent rustling in the wind, calling him to roam, Hammad described his wanderings over the dunes like a search for his soul's desire. He evoked the pangs of loss of his loved ones whom he had left behind, the discomforts of heat and thirst, and the great loyalty but worrisome leanness of his camel.

Then Hammad arrived at the heart of his poem, the verses outlining a simple narrative. He wandered in and out of caves where sometimes were found sources of water. In one cave with many side chambers, he found a set of large jars; they were so old that some crumbled to his touch, but one of them contained a few fragile objects. Bringing them out into the blinding light, Hammad saw an odd metal oval piece, and an ancient parchment that appeared to be a map with writing on it.

Hammad's ode continued with a poetic description of his reaction to the discovery. He was used to submerging into a darkened cave and then re-emerging into the searing desert sun. But as soon as he gazed upon the two objects, light flashed before his eyes. He looked above him, convinced he would see spirits or angels. Instead he felt a great foreboding and a message came into his mind: do not return home, continue on with these artifacts, and seek the palace in Damascus.

Concluding as he began, with emotional verses about love's longing and the hardships of his camel, Hammad ended the qasida with a glorious paean to the palace and the welcome he found there, justifying all. The chamber roared with approval. The angry rival knelt before the vizier.

"Yes, a brilliant improvisation. But clearly he has cast a spell on our court."

The vizier smiled at Hammad, encouraging him to respond. Hammad knelt down next to his nemesis. "The Prophet, may his Name be praised, said 'Verily, eloquence includes sorcery.' My friend is correct: I have performed the sorcerer's act on your people. Forgive me."

After this, the vizier got up and insisted the two rivals do the same. "I forgive you both, the one for sorcery, the other for inhospitality. This is one of our loyal desert brethren, who has brought us a mysterious gift, and clearly stands in the lineage of the great desert poets who put our new age to shame. We have a custom to put strange guests to the test, and I thank you both for rising to the occasion. Hammad, you have done well. If I hear of your rival plotting against you, I will have him banished to the deserts of northwest Hind."

The courtier reddened once more, but rose, bowed, and retreated to the back of the chamber with his followers. Hammad rose and received the vizier's welcome.

"My advisers have chosen to dismiss the oval object as superfluous. But they are baffled by the papyrus chart, so I will look at it with the royal astrologers. While you await their judgment, you are a guest of the Caliph."

The wine that went to his head that night, and many subsequent nights, inflamed Hammad's feeling of great fortune. He was happy the astrologers deliberated over the document, for it gave Hammad free reign of the banquets, hunts, singing girls, and company of the Umayyad court. Few courtiers were as insolent as his first rival, and most praised him and insisted he accompany them.

As astonished as he was about this sophisticated court's insecurity about poetry, Hammad soon agreed that the old verse practices of the desert remained the purest and most eloquent. He flaunted his role as a magical manipulator of words: he gave his friends Bedouin nicknames; he prevailed in song contests during drinking bouts; he held forth at nighttime gatherings like a sage in the wilderness. Hammad exalted the free and natural spirituality of his tribesmen against the formal and hampered institutions in Damascus. It was a time when the *muhaddith* established a written record of The Prophet's sayings, each preceded by its *isnad*, the long catalog of narrators authenticating the source. Hammad brashly criticized how this aspect of Islam constipated the art of language, weakened poetry, and denigrated storytelling.

After waiting months for the astrologers' verdict about the papyrus, Hammad grew tired of the shallow life at court. He missed the rawness and visceral stimuli of the desert. He considered returning and seeking no further fortune. His friends at court recognized his malaise and promised to show him pleasure outside the palace walls. So Hammad indulged in the taverns and street life of the great city. He heard dramatic rumors of rebellion against the Umayyad and was warned not to stay attached to them. He delighted in the storytellers of the marketplace. Branded by Islam as fictional lies, the tales nonetheless had a noble charm. Hammad loved the fresh imagery of the fantastical tales. Perhaps the demise of poetry during this time would unblock the Islamic interdiction against fiction and allow these stories to take a rightful place in the culture. Perhaps things needed to change politically before that could occur.

With an inner laugh, Hammad observed how the frame tales and narrative devices included a similar inventory of narrators to the isnad, a handing down of storytellers from one part of the tale to the next, which mimicked shamelessly the work of the muhaddith. Although this practice might have been an attempt to make the stories more legitimate to the ears of the Faithful, Hammad viewed the trick of inserting new narrators as license to fabricate variations and addendums to existing narratives. He thought it a healthy change.

A year passed since Hammad's arrival in Damascus. Spies confided to him that his original nemesis at court secretly obstructed a decision about the papyrus. Inspired by the antics of the marketplace stories, Hammad proposed to his comrades a raid on the astrologers' keep to take back his possession. On the night of the break-in, the palace erupted in chaos and destruction. Hammad and his gang risked their lives, not at the hands of the Umayyad, but rather in facing the Abbasid conquerors, who assassinated all but one of the heirs of the current dynasty. The palace revolt made easy work of the break-in, but Hammad had to flee for his life into the desert. He retrieved only the metallic oval, which remained in his family as a talisman.

Assumed dead months before, the tribe celebrated Hammad's return, welcomed as brethren the friends who fled with him, and marveled at their stories of the palace and the revolution. Hammad astonished his people with accounts of his journey and incredible fortunes, but preferred telling marketplace stories, embellishing details wherever he wished. Free from court stricture!

There was one tale in particular that Hammad loved sharing with his people and local tribes. In Damascus he had learned that it might have hailed from India ages ago, but that more recently in Persia it had picked up details from Sassanian history. One version was the frame tale of the Persian *Hezar Afanseh*, an enormous collection of folk stories. Hammad disliked certain qualities of the frame tale, the extreme violence, a demented Queen, and the carnage of women and children. In one variant, a virgin named Purzai sacrificed herself to incite the vizier's daughter Sharazade to fight against the slaughter. Purzai's demise disgusted Hammad more than any other sordid act.

As a solution, sometimes Hammad eliminated the entire background of the tale, starting with the vizier's daughter telling stories to stop the violence. Eliminating the slaughter of innocents, Hammad felt like Sharazade, a champion saving a nation. At other times he eliminated Purzai but retained the virgin murders, always focusing on the suffering of the people, how the mothers mourned their daughters' deaths, and how the populace enjoyed celebrations after Sharazade extirpated the evil in the land. He told many versions of the tale, until it spread from the Syrian Desert across the Arabian peninsula. But the element of the People stuck fast.

ق

Through the conduit of the New Year's party and Hu Ma's comatose visions, the tale spread through the qaraq, from Bax, Ooma, and Amar's conscious minds to Sahara and Porcy's unconscious. They all sensed the significance of the lifetimes: they were witnessing the evolution of the Scheherazade tale. Amar still wondered why this story, so important to the qaraq and his wife, surfaced on this dreadful day. Ooma still remained in the ancient world as Amar carried her down the last flights of stairs.

9

———〰〰〰———

September 12. 10:15 A.M. Day 2 (1 day after Impact).

The day after the attacks, Zack Goodkin sat in his bedroom at home, staring at the man sleeping in his bed. Zack's emotions bounced from delight to guilt to fear. He pieced together yesterday's events to understand how to process such a complex of feelings.

Zack, Sahara's neighbor, Verle's co-archivist, and the man who had befriended Ooma at the New Year's party, noticed on the morning of 9/11 that Amar's car was still in the driveway next door. Given that Sahara had moved back in the day before, Zack easily guessed what that meant. Amar would be late for his usual train, and Zack considered offering his old friend a ride into the city, but decided to leave the couple to their mischief.

Zack arrived in the city well before the first plane hit. Arriving at the gym in Chelsea, Zack wondered when he had stopped going there to meet guys. Probably the same time he had eased up on his abs workout. After his lover François had passed away from illness in Paris, and Zack had moved back to the US, he had dated half-heartedly. Had he given up on finding a relationship?

He had a meeting with an importer in Tribeca, to pick up some Malaysian articles, and then he would look around Chinatown for any goods to add to his fledgling online business. Heading to his car, he heard the rumors on the street and then saw the billowing smoke further downtown. Jesus! As he drove down Varick toward Canal Street, he could not keep his eyes off the spectacle. When he saw the Tower collapse, he halted in the middle of the street, despite the honking of New York horns, and managed to find a parking spot nearby.

Zack remained in shocked awe as he stood next to his car, frozen in terror. He tried to joke his way out of the anxiety. A suburban housewife greeting her smoldering husband: "Bad day at the office?" The lame attempt at humor did nothing except add guilt to the fear.

Like the other qaraqis that day, Zack was ripe to recall lifetimes from early Islamic history. Being fixed in one spot gave him a strange thought: he wished to explore the wide world but was petrified by the prospect. His mind filled with fleeting images, the familiar flood of memories preceding a past life recall: meeting Ooma at Amar's party, scooping up hors d'oeuvre from the floor; the mind of a comatose Chinese girl (Ooma's incarnation?); parchment scrolls stacked up next to a writing desk. Zack wondered if he should resist the memory, if it was dangerous in the circumstances to let his mind go. And why did he feel that the whole qaraq was witnessing the narrative along with him? Unable to resist, the image of the scrolls led him into his life as an 8th Century Arabic scribe.

The Tale of the Basran Scribe

You are lucky to be alive, Zabbah ibn Sayyar al-Sakkak told himself. Much is changing! Barely into your teens and the Umayyad clan toppled in Damascus. Father worked in alliance with the Abbasids, the new rulers. His guild in Basra had the honor of scribing copies of the famous speech that linked the Abbasid's blood line to the family of The Prophet, may He be blessed for all Time!

When you were given a place in Father's workshop, fresh out of your teens, a new Caliph took power, al-Mansur. The Abbasids refused to reside in the lake of blood that is now Damascus. There is talk of the Caliphate moving to Iraq! Some say that Basra will always be a distant outpost, despite its importance to sea trade. But Father hopes to benefit from the shift in power. May you work for royals, my son, he prays!

If things were not changing fast enough, you heard rumors of a new writing material. Paper! Thinner than parchment. From China! Cheaper than papyrus. The Empire built its first paper mill. al-Mansur commissioned many books, Peace be on Him! Philosophy tracts, poetry anthologies, and these new translations. Ancient Greeks. Roman histories. Lots of copy work.

You cannot imagine where it will all lead. Father went off to procure new manuscripts. How exciting it would be to travel to the Empire's new lands. He returned with tales of the Caliphate still struggling for power, for security, for a capitol. A man was killed in the inn Father stays at, just for waxing nostalgic about the Umayyads. You recognized a familiar feeling: wishing to explore the wide world but being petrified by the prospect. You've been comfortable in Basra your whole life, lulled by its ocean breezes, and content as a scribe in Father's workshop. But the mother of all problems is that itch to experience something else. Which do you want, the changing New or the secure Old? Father answered the question for you.

Abd Allah ibn al-Muqaffa was born in 721 AD/99 AH, of Persian stock. Although he converted from Zoroastrianism, his devotion as a Muslim was in question. More important to him was the edification of the new Abbasid ruling class through the translation of Sassanian Persian texts on ethics and politics. He was an early advocate of adab, the courtly practice of etiquette and wit. Although he wrote a number of works on moral behavior, his Kalila-wa-Dimna *is his most famous work, an Arabic translation of ancient Indian animal fables illustrating proper morality.*

"I don't understand," you pleaded with your father. "Stories and legends aren't written down. They're told in the streets and markets and drinking dens."

"Yes they are, Zabbah," Father agreed calmly, exasperated by your resistance. "But in other nations they have been written down, huge collections at that. This text began as the great *Panchatantra* in India, a five-part cycle of animal tales."

"But father, is this task worthy of us?"

"It will be worthy of *you*, my lad! This is a great honor, to have our guild recognized by Abd Allah ibn al-Muqaffa, a royal secretary of the Caliph and a renowned author in his own right. I send you to represent us, the opportunity of a lifetime!"

"But it is forbidden to glorify the false witness, to pass down unsubstantiated words. Is not the telling of fictions no better than lies? Why commit them to the pen?" You shook from passion.

Father sighed. "I see you are fearful of this journey, Zabbah. Every one of the Faithful has had to take such a journey into a new land. Here is another new dawn, under the guise of *translation*. This text will be the first Arabic translation of a fictional epic. The court ushers in a new acceptance of such fictions. By rendering an Indian classic, which was transformed into a Sasan tome, into our holy tongue, al-Muqaffa imitates the isnad, the chain of narrators authenticating a text."

"That is blasphemy, Father," you cried. "This is no authentication."

"Enough!" Father said. "Caliph al-Mansur enjoined al-Muqaffa to create the *Kalila-wa-Dimna* from its Persian source. The translation is complete, the Caliph is pleased, and wishes a hundred copies to be made. Scribes are needed. Go represent us!"

So you went to the scribe and author Abd Allah ibn al-Muqaffa, who still utilized his original workspace in Basra. You did not have to give up familiar surroundings all at once. For this reason, you excelled at your

duties copying *Kalila-wa-Dimna* for local booksellers, and were promoted to higher purposes. At first al-Muqaffa shipped you out to wherever he oversaw an important manuscript meant for an Emir or Prince.
Relieved you would return to Basra, you excelled in these situations as
well. Your father glowed with pride at his son's success.

Now an indispensable journeyman in al-Muqaffa's enterprises,
you became a permanent member of the great man's employ. When
the Caliph announced he was constructing a new capitol in Iraq, you
moved with al-Muqaffa to the future City of Brass, the great circular city,
Baghdad.

Still standing in the middle of Varick Street, Zack was unsure what he
had recalled when a young man touched him on the shoulder. Looking
into the man's face, Zack thought he saw the mirror of his own anguish
and terror. The two men spoke the same words, simultaneously:

"Are you all right?"

Zack could not help laughing, and the young man responded with a
stiff, half-smile.

"I'm fine," Zack said. "Just standing here, frozen."

"You should move." The man offered his arm. Zack took in his
fragile guide: rail thin, bushy brown hair, and delicate, agreeable facial
features. He gratefully allowed him to interlock arms and found he could
move. On the sidewalk, Zack took a deep breath and exhaled.

"You look as panicked as I feel. How are *you*?"

"I was down there." The man took a breath between each phrase,
short shallow gasps. "My apartment is across the street from Building
One. I saw them jumping."

Zack gasped. "From the building? Jesus!" Zack was unsure what to
say. "I think the other building's exploded, too."

"Oh my God," the man said. "I can't go back there. I won't."

"Don't worry about that now," Zack said. "Obviously I'm not capable
of going anywhere. Maybe I need a seeing-eye guide. Do you want to
go sit somewhere?"

The man took in what Zack was asking. "That'll be good."

"Sorry, what's your name?" Zack inquired.

"Jobim."

Zack smiled. "And I'm Astrud Gilberto."

For the first time Jobim's face brightened. "You know Brazilian music?"

"The best in the world, after Hendrix," Zack said. "So who loved samba so much?"

"My mother is Brazilian. My Dad's from Florida. Jobim Jones."

"Even better." Zack extended his hand. "Zack Goodkin. Coffee?"

Zack and Jobim spent hours in a café, listening to news reports, comforting each other, discovering their common likes and dislikes. They joked about having rescued each other. Privately, Zack felt that Jobim had not just physically rescued him from getting run over in the street. Had he recalled a lifetime of an Iraqi man afraid to venture out into the world because Zack had been afraid of venturing into another relationship, which might end in disaster? Why on this morning, when another disaster appeared before his eyes, possibly also with an Arab source? Was Jobim there to rescue him from his fears?

Later in the day the Hudson cruise ships ferried people across the river. Zack would have to retrieve his car some other day, so he invited Jobim back to New Jersey on the ferry. The gorgeous summer sunlight on the river was an eerie contrast to the huge plume of smoke rising from the depths of downtown. As the ship docked at Weehawken, Jobim was horrified to see another building collapse, World Trade Center 7. On the walk along the river from Weehawken to the Hoboken train station, Jobim burst into tears at the terrible new cloud of dust. Waiting forever for a crowded train to Glenclaire aggravated his fragile state.

Arriving in the placid suburb after hours of travel, Zack noticed Jobim take comfort in the beauty of the houses and gardens. Zack wondered who was rescuing whom. He tensed seeing his mother's car in the driveway, then eased up when the house smelled of sweet potatoes and chicken. He displaced the awkwardness of introducing his mother,

Cachay Goodkin, to Jobim by gorging on the food. Though he ate little, Jobim was so effusive about the food that he charmed the frosty Cachay.

After dinner, Jobim insisted on cleaning up, earning him more points with Cachay. After her intense day at Social Services, fending off callers traumatized by the attacks, Cachay was happy to slink off with a glass of wine. Zack and Jobim settled in the living room to watch television reports.

Normally, sex would have been the natural outcome of their meeting, but with his mother in the house and the tangle of raw emotions in his gut, Zack offered Jobim his bedroom and went to sleep on the sofa. It was a mutual decision, with the promise of intimacy in the near future.

The next morning, Zack checked on Jobim, admiring his sleeping friend's delicate face. Basking in the sublime feeling in his heart, Zack thought back to the end of the recall.

The Tale of the Basran Scribe, conclusion

al-Muqaffa added his own prologue and substantial new scenes to the story cycle of Kalila-wa-Dimna. *One such scene is Dimna's trial, where he has to tell stories to save his neck, a parallel to Sharazade's storytelling. al-Muqaffa's additions rendered Kalila a book containing great wisdom. His simple prose style made the work a reading primer for centuries and a perennial favorite in medieval Arabic fiction. In its own day, the work had its dissident elements: the fables questioned the rights of Kings and the nature of religion. al-Muqaffa was killed circa 758/136, in suspicious circumstances, most likely by a political enemy.*

What will you do now that al-Muqaffa is gone? Zabbah, you are one of the leading experts on *Kalila*, at least on his Arabic version of it. You have made more copies than any other scribe, and memorized more fables than anyone in their right mind. The epic is a comforting solution to your fear of being thrust out into the disparate lands of the Empire. You yearn for the foreign cultures Islam has permeated, but fear them; the Persian/Indian story collection has been the perfect way to bring the wide world into the safe, contained milieu of court and guild.

By empowering you with advocacy for a multi-volumed story cycle, al-Muqaffa opened the door for more fictional works to be translated, despite the controversy surrounding this genre. Caliph al-Mansur has requested a new collection to be translated, and with your reputation, you have the opportunity to suggest an appropriate choice. There is only one choice, so obvious that you feel strangely obsessed with it, to the depths of your soul.

The Abbasid court expects another work with an impressive lineage. The *Hezir Afsaneh* has hundreds of stories from both India and Persia, the Persian frame tale of Sharazade, and variants that the desert tribes have been riffing off for decades. The Abbasids, much looser than the Umayyads, welcome additions, omissions, and alterations of narratives.

But to walk the road of fiction is to step off the strict path of Islam. If Sharazade's story is to win the hearts of the court, certain immoral elements must be modified, those from Sassanian history and legend. This Ouzmeth, with her sexual dementia, this Ardryasher, weak-willed Prince hidden as a slave, this Dinzade, with her sly powers but victim's soul, and this Zahbar, cuckolded, murderous, manipulated, obsessive being – all are sordid characters that put moral values to shame.

There is no getting around the murder of virgins; Sharazade would not tell her stories otherwise. But it is too perverse and complex. Get rid of the insane Queen, promote her slave to King, and give him the burden of anger and murderous intent. Make Zahbar his brother, perhaps sharing a similar fate, cuckoldry if need be. Focusing on the two brothers also lessens the knottiness of Dinzade in the tale. Maybe eliminate her.

To test the waters for the acceptance of the *Hezir Afsaneh*, you should spread your version of Sharazade around the court. Creating the King character might be offensive to those close to the Caliph; will a King's crimes undermine the Caliphate? al-Muqaffa certainly did so with *Kalila*, and look what it got him. Tread carefully, Zabbah. But venture forth.

ق

Zack loved the outcome of the past lifetime. Back in the 8th Century, he had influenced the Scheherazade narrative! Sahara will be ecstatic! As long as Amar comes home from the World Trade Center, Zack thought soberly. Once again, he sensed that his memory had somehow projected the story out to the qaraq's minds, including Amar and Ooma, who would have been at work in the Towers. Did that mean they had evacuated in time and were alive? How strange!

Zack could not help smile. Most of the qaraq had discovered that their souls related to one of the archetypes from the story. Zabbah had done away with Uzmeth as the antagonist (Ooma's archetype), and replaced her with the murderous King (Amar's archetype). In their earlier 4th Century Persian lifetimes, the historical precedent for the Scheherazade tale, Amar had snared Zack into a nasty, vengeful killing. By putting blood on the King's hands, and spreading the tale through the Abbasid court, Zack had gotten even with Amar.

It was interesting that Zack had baby-sat Amar in their childhood; he often called him 'Little Brother.' Over a thousand years ago, Zack, as Zabbah, had created his own archetype, the King's brother. Zack chuckled inwardly that he had tried to scratch Dinzade from the picture (Diana's archetype), a reflection of his tension with the therapist. Finally, Zack wondered about the vizier, Scheherazade's father: the King might murder his wives, but did not call upon the vizier to perform the execution. Was this a later development?

Zack startled when Jobim spoke: "Good morning! You look lost. Where have you gone?"

Zack smiled at his new friend: a pleasant vision. How could he possibly answer Jobim's question? Jobim might have rescued Zack from himself, but he had to take some things slowly, like divulging the existence of the qaraq. Did Jobim have something to do with the qaraq? Zack stopped his obsessive thinking and just gave Jobim a little shrug in answer.

Zack realized he had not given up on relationships.

10

—∽✽∽—

September 11. 10:30 A.M.   Hour 2-3 (2 hours after Impact).

When Bax was a number of blocks away from the World Trade Center, he witnessed the North Tower accordion down into a chaos of smoke. The horrendous sight threw him into a protective trance. Slipping back into his vision during the third kiss at the New Year's party, he reconnected to Ooma, so close to him back at that moment, and Hu Ma, lying in a coma, seeing all.

As Bax and Ooma re-experienced the vision, it appeared in Amar's mind, physically holding Ooma, spread to Zack, still adrift on Varick Street, and even reached across the Hudson River to Verle in Glenclaire. The old man sat in his attic room, minutes away from hearing about the attacks. Shaking his gray dreads back and forth, he sensed he had connected to some weird kind of psychic qaraq meeting, but soon realized he was seeing his own past life as Wahid the paper-maker.

Together this half of the qaraq continued the journey in Time, witnessing the introduction of the *Hazir Afsaneh* into Baghdad, and its struggle for acceptance within Islamic culture.

$\mathcal{T}he$ $\mathcal{T}ale$ of the Introduction of
Paper to the West

It had taken Wahid forty years to get to this point, stretching back to when the great Umayyad armies made inroads into China. After the Abbasids took power, Islamic forces captured a few Chinese papermakers in 129 AH (751 AD), employed them to make paper in Samarkand, and opened the first Arabic paper mill the following year. Due to its thinner consistency, readily available raw materials to manufacture it, and faster production time, paper was a vastly cheaper and superior substance than papyrus, parchment, or vellum.

Having spent a bit of his youth as a soldier in the Eastern regions of the Empire, Wahid had heard of the paper mill; when he was discharged he traveled to Samarkand to gain employment in the innovative factory. Though not of the aristocracy or scribe class, he learned to read and developed an uncanny knowledge of the many proclamations, mercantile records, and books requisitioned; Wahid's superiors noticed his ability to keep all the items organized in his head and made Wahid manager of accounts, a high level occupation for his background.

Caliph al-Mansur began building the new Abbasid capitol, a stunning circular city in the center of the Empire; the gleaming metropolis of Baghdad grew, its cultural output caused a proliferation of documents, and the new paper mill's productivity quadrupled. Wahid enjoyed a string of promotions, leading to Associate Advocate for Paper Publications in greater Baghdad. Under this title, he addressed his pet peeve for two decades, under both Umayyad and Abbasid Caliphates: the poor conditions of the storehouses for preservation of the fragile paper. If the Caliph inspired a new era of translation, why rebirth classics into the glorious language of the Qu'ran only to condemn them to an impermanent paper netherworld? Wahid started his own library.

In the glorious year 164 after The Prophet's Flight, the Caliphate once again changed hands and Harun al-Rashid became Commander of the Faithful, adopting the use of paper for matters of state. Wahid worked his way up hierarchical ladders, until he finally gained an audience with Harun's Minister of Literatures, Zabbah ibn Sayyar al-Sakkak, a very nervous looking man. Wahid unfurled a beautifully drafted paper blueprint of his ideal storehouse, reviewed a pamphlet freshly copied onto the finest Basran paper, and outlined his immaculate system for the organization of volumes. Zabbah ordered drinks somewhere between the blueprint and the pamphlet. Then Wahid presented Zabbah with a catalogue of his enormous library, personally copied on his private stash of paper from the original paper mill in Samarkand. Zabbah anticipated the next move as if looking into Wahid's soul: to gift the Caliph with this collection, in exchange for proper safekeeping.

Wahid and Zabbah developed a fast friendship, the Minister gave Wahid a post within the Ministry, and Wahis recommended volumes for the court's pleasure and edification. Still, the two men sustained emotional reservations: Zabbah's fearful attitude toward the intrigues he would face by appointing an outsider; Wahid's mistrust of imperial process and Zabbah's promises. Court officials approved funding for Wahid's storehouse, and construction began, with courtiers offering cartloads of books to add for a fair price.

Among these literate supplicants was Sheikh Ba'Tr ibn Halali, whose emissaries appeared on Wahid's doorstep seeking no courtly favor, which made Wahid immediately suspicious. Ba'Tr was an avid collector, but his specialty was tomes on the attainment of eternal life, for which he requested a list of new volumes. Wahid balked at his first request for a *borrowing* from his library, turned the emissaries away several times until the Sheikh himself appeared. Over tea and date cakes Ba'Tr offered Wahid a treasure worthy of all the jewels in Baghdad: a rare manuscript of mysterious provenance that listed a series of lifetimes, some in the past, some yet to occur, and some which had come to pass at the time of the manuscript.

Wahid was fascinated with the fantastical manuscript, but begged Ba'Tr to understand the time pressures on him; when the Sheikh asked if there was an existing catalogue, Wahid explained he had gifted it to the Caliph. To placate the relentless man, Wahid finally opened his private ledger of recent acquisitions and let Ba'Tr pore over it for an hour; he felt he had extended a generous amount of hospitality. The Sheikh scribbled down an entry on his own paper (third-rate Basran grade, Wahid noted), and left Wahid's premises, barely concealing his anger. The strange manuscript ended up in a pile awaiting the storehouse.

Zabbah brought Wahid a new project, a second great story collection translation. Zabbah had advocated for the translation of the story cycle the *Hezir Afsaneh*, or One Thousand Fantastical Tales, but the traditionalists at court shunned the unbelievable stories of magic and monsters, and prurient character interactions. Zabbah had propagated alternative versions of the Sharzad frame tale throughout the court, in the hopes of softening its indelicacies; while at a paper mill in central Persia, Wahid had heard a few variants of the story himself, but only Zabbah's version with a scorned King out for vengeance stirred Wahid's blood.

Wahid questioned the usefulness of the King's brother as a character, since he duplicated the King's plight, a criticism Zabbah heard with an internal flash of anger; however, how could the King pull off an extermination of his female population without a loyal, unflinching Vizier? Wahid suggested the Vizier talk sense to the King through storytelling, but Zabbah argued that too much heat escapes if the storytelling reformer is not the next female victim, feeling her death crawling up between the sheets. Let the Vizier choose a victim with knowledge of history and stories.

With an ally in his conspiracy, Zabbah introduced Wahid into court for the purpose of spreading this new variant with the Vizier; the court agreed it was a more logical rendition, and praised the Vizier as a paragon of virtue. Here was the first variant to stand the moral test of Islam. Zabbah seethed at Wahid's success at court, but was grateful for the ascendance of the frame tale; Wahid expounded on the wonder of the

Hezir Afsaneh as a protean jumble of cultures, not unlike the glorious triumphs of the Islamic Empire.

Then Sheikh Ba'Tr returned, incensed at Wahid: unable to demand the return of his document and save face, Ba'Tr plotted with a few low-lifes to break into the storehouse. But Imperial guards waylaid his party, and hauled him before the Caliph. Face to face with the Commander of the Faithful, Ba'Tr confessed all, including Wahid's neglectful mistreatment of him. The wise Harun, knowing the Sheikh was a successful trader, issued a small monetary punishment for the attempted theft, and bypassed stricter corporal punishments.

The affair was a scandal for Wahid and his alleged inhospitality, so the court withheld favor toward Zabbah, the translation project, and the *Hezir Afsaneh*. New debates raged concerning Islamic taboos against fiction, which reminded Wahid of an ancient tribal feud between those wishing to preserve the world and those wishing to change it.

It would take the visionary leadership of Caliph Harun al-Rashid, and the cultural influence of his Persian Vizier Ja'far ibn Yahya al-Barmaki, to put *The Thousand Tales* on the table again; but it was early in Harun's reign, and Wahid would wait another decade before achieving his dream.

ق

When Bax revisited the lifetime on 9/11, he thought, "I recognize Wahid and Zabbah as Verle and Zack, but I'm the Sheikh, and he's a bad guy."

When Zack received Zabbah's story that awful day, he thought, "Why are we changing the Scheherazade tale? Why are we all mixed up in that damn story?"

When Verle received the tale in his attic reverie, he thought, "So my incarnation Wahid invented the Vizier, the archetype from the tale connected to my soul. But just as the guilt for the virgin murders is passed from Queen Uzmeth to the King, as an accomplice I inherit a portion of the guilt, too. Every morning the Vizier had to order the execution of the

79

latest virgin, while the King washed his hands of it. Nice to be created, but cruel fate!"

Before Verle could think more about it, the church secretary called to him from the stairs, informing him of the attacks. Church business overtook him until the following morning, when he envisioned the future scholarship into World Types. Feeling an organizational scheme could comfort the qaraq in this hour of need, Verle thrilled that the group was miraculously sharing lifetimes from a Multiple World, a World they had already recalled as the 4th Century Sasan court lifetimes, the Persian historical models for the Scheherazade characters. Now they remembered their role in the Islamicization of the legend, a task defying the Muslim ban on fiction.

It would be uplifting to inform the qaraq that it was accruing dozens of lifetimes from this World, but could they keep it up? More significantly, why were they recalling lifetimes from Islamic history at a time when the President declared war on terrorists, presumably Islamic terrorists? Were current events triggering these memories? Would Verle discover some higher mission for the qaraq in this Multiple World?

11

—⟨ᴠ/ᴠ/ᴠ⟩—

September 24, 2001.   Week 3 (2 weeks after Impact).

Dr. Diana Machiyoko sat with her legs tightly crossed on one side of Verle's attic loft. She stared blankly across the long space. She was trying to remember the A-frame room as she first saw it, pristine and magically inviting, a perfect setting for disclosure of incarnations from distant cultures. All she could see now were the stacks of folders and books, wires for electronic devices, the mounting clutter of the archival project. Her personal preference for spaces was serene, Zenlike sparseness; she had loved the first meetings in the empty openness of Verle's attic. She had offered to tidy up the jumbled disorder, but it had bested her.

On the other side of the space, Verle paused from his transcription work, wrinkling his gray-brown skin. "Tragedy on tragedy. There's a new memorial at the church every few days."

Near Verle, Zack sat back from a computer. It was their first free moment to work on the archives together since the attacks. "Everything's changed. I can't even drive into the city by myself in the morning. You have to have three people in your car. They're checking everyone at the tolls."

"Is this hurting your business?" Verle asked.

"I don't know yet. The big thing will be new customs rules decreasing my overseas trade."

Verle said, "You've been wanting to expand your online business, my friend."

"I know, I know, it would be a good time to shift into it. But everything feels so hard right now. Jobim still can't go back to his apartment, so he's kinda sorta moved in."

"A blessing in disguise?"

"A miracle! But another huge change. I've only got so many pjs to lend. God, I need a therapy session." Zack cleared his throat loudly.

With Zack's words, Diana came out of her tired reverie, unconsciously uncrossed and re-crossed her legs. "I'm sorry, I'm totally wiped. Too much work since the Towers came down. Everyone's daily reality feels way more crucial than past lives, not more trivial."

"My reality isn't trivial," Zack said. "I was down there. You know how I feel about you ending our sessions. That's what patients do to therapists, not the other way round."

"Our relationship is complicated by our past lives," the therapist said. "Right now it's too difficult to sort out."

Zack had heard the argument many times. Her ambivalence incensed him. "Where else am I going to go for therapy? Let's say I sashay over to Dr. Freudenstein in Ho-Ho-Kus, and explain that instead of dreams I get past life fantasies, which I've come to believe are the truth. As he takes notes he's thinking either: 'A) Very interesting, lots of good material here, but obviously zese past lives are metaphors for his twue feelings, not the twuth, or B) I must give my fwiends at the state hospital a little call.' In Version A I rehash the doubts we've slogged through for three years. In Version B you bail me out of the loony bin. Face it, Yoko-san, you're my only hope."

Verle chuckled at Zack's little tirade, but it struck Dr. Machiyoko seriously. It deeply disturbed her, but she could not formulate her distress. Why couldn't Zack find some New Age therapist who bought into past lives? No, something else was bothering her about Zack's dilemma. She was seeing a flood of new trauma patients; perhaps she had absorbed their instability, her usual clear-headedness fogged over like that huge dust cloud at Ground Zero.

Zack carried forth with his complaint. "I have a new relationship brewing; it frightens me."

The last thing Diana wanted was another therapy session. "How can I help you navigate a relationship when ours is so fraught? We were married in some archetypal, psychic version of the Scheherazade tale! It wasn't romantically mutual, so how does that jibe with our present day situations, our different life styles? What am I supposed to do with that *as a therapist?*" The cloud around Diana's brain unleashed a thunderstorm. She erupted out of her fog, yelling and stomping through the piles on the floor. Zack, who had never seen her in such a state, stayed quiet as she continued. "Why do the Scheherazade archetypes haunt our souls? We mind-melded about them during 9/11. Stories from the rise of Islam. And deep into the future! It's crazy! Why is our qaraq connected to the Arabian Nights? How are the Nights even tied to reincarnation?"

Gingerly, Verle answered Diana. "I have asked this question myself, poor dear. The Nights is a cultural icon, yes? Maybe the answer lies in why cultures believe in reincarnation, and how they reflect these beliefs. The concept of past lives is not obvious in the Nights, but it was in the cultures that passed down the stories."

An animated glow lit up Diana's face. "You're right. We should look for evidence of reincarnation belief in the oldest cultures. When did it start?"

"That's a question!" Verle held up an old hardcover from one of the piles. "Here's a goodie, Sir James Frazier's *The Golden Bough*. He leafed through a few bookmarked pages until he found what he was looking for. "Sir James thought the transmigration of the soul was 'anthropologically innate,' that prehistoric people believed in reincarnation before any other concept of immortality, like Heaven. Thought it way more common as a belief than any evidence we have for it."

"Gives me chills," Diana said. She slipped back into her fog, but this time her weary brain searched for a vision of a prehistoric culture. "We've got to find out when humans first believed in past lives. It's the answer we need."

Zack and Verle saw that stress and exhaustion had caught up with the therapist. "Are you all right?" Verle asked. But Diana stared straight ahead. She spoke in a whisper about a vision.

The Regression of the Grave Paintings

-- Do you see that?

"Doc, what are you talking about? What do you see?" Zack questioned.

-- The mountains. Huge. Snow-capped. Like the Himalayas.

"You're in India?" Zack wondered. "Are you alive there? Who are you?"

-- You don't see? Someone is watching. The scene is split in two, between one who is passive, observing, and one watched, who is me. I am a tribal leader, but full of light, like a holy man, a shaman. You're not the other one, hiding, watching me?

"We can't see anything," Verle said. "Tell us what you see." In her light trance, Diana was able to concentrate on her vision and interpret it for the two men at the same time.

-- The shaman is making something, using a primitive stone tool, but it has sophisticated detail on it, made of something besides stone, maybe bone or horn.

"Stone Age man, but fairly advanced," Verle assessed.

"What's he – or you – making?" Zack asked.

-- Can't see much and the images keep shifting. Now it's prehistoric people huddling around fires and tent structures to stay warm.

"An Ice Age," Verle said, "but maybe the latest one, given the tool quality."

-- Now there's a painting inside a cave: a hunter cutting open the belly of an animal. Perhaps this was a chamber for hunters, for butchering the kill. Another room in the cave network, images of dancing figures, performing some ritual: a sacred space? More images, painted on stone slabs, outdoors near little hills.

"Burial mounds," Verle suggested.

-- Yes, these are death images painted on the stones: violent death scenes, decaying carcasses, body flesh vanishing up into the air, the remains of bones. This is an important place for the tribe, and for me, but I feel separate from it. I feel trapped, unable to be involved, but wanting to be. Feels like I'm always in this situation.

"What about our shaman friend," Zack pushed, "your *self* at the time, isn't he involved?"

-- A new image: people dancing in a circle around something at the burial mounds. It's a corpse, a rotting corpse. The dance depicts fighting. Some are dressed like demons, crawling, sniffing, poking, trying to get at the corpse. It's a battle between those protecting the corpse and those trying to destroy it.

"Fascinating," Verle said. "Many cultures believe we fight demons after death, before we can move on. This is an early form, connected to bugs and animals and elements that rot a corpse."

"Physical decay inspired the soul's battle with demons," Zack said.

-- Here is the shaman. It's later, the body has vanished, and all that's left are bones. A new dance shows the successful attempt of the body to overcome the demons and rise up into the air. The shaman communes with the bones at the center of the dance, at peace, transfigured, separate from the vigorous activities of the tribe.

Another scene: in a trance, the shaman paints on a slab meant for the burial mound. It is what he saw from the bones, where the soul went after defeating the demons. It shows the decaying body transform into something new. The stone slabs at the burial mounds are covered with these depictions, some telling elaborate stories. This corpse transforms into another person, this one into an animal, this one – a bad man from the look of his death scene – into a lowly beetle.

Verle patted his dreadlocks. "My goodness. The next lifetimes. Reincarnations."

"Complete with karma for the bad guy," Zack added.

-- The shaman is finished. He raises his paint-stained hands to the sky. He is exhausted, depleted, sad. He looks around for other tribe members, but no one is there. He hears something, looks into the bush, and sees someone. It is the one who has been watching. He gets a fleeting glimpse of a strange figure, in clothes so unlike his skins. For a moment the watcher is visible.

It is also me.

ق

"Holy Twilight Zone!" Zack said. "A future you watching a prehistoric you?"

"Do you recognize the other you?" Verle questioned.

Diana looked up at Verle and Zack and blinked her eyes. "It's gone. Sorry." The image of the exhausted shaman stayed in her mind. She felt great empathy with the healer depleted from giving to everyone except himself. Just like the therapist in this lifetime. Nothing changes.

Verle gesticulated with Sir James Frazier's book. "Don't be sorry! What you saw is the evidence Frazier says we lack, evidence of reincarnation belief among prehistoric peoples. The last Ice Age ended over ten thousand years ago, so this lifetime might have been around 11 or 12,000 BC. By the shamanistic traditions here, I'd bet these beliefs had been around much longer."

"Assuming you *were* in the Himalayas," Zack said, "the vision implies that the seeds of Hinduism and reincarnation values originated long before Vedic culture."

"This is a very profound memory, Dr. Machiyoko," Verle said, with a reverential tone. "It's a starting point for exploring how cultures absorb reincarnation into their belief."

86

Zack mused, "How did these early humans know about reincarnation? Were they told?"

Verle raised his gray eyebrows. "If a very old group believed in it, does that make it a fact? Is it just a global case of cryptoamnesia, one culture believing something because others believed it?"

"Not that old argument again." Diana thought back to when the qaraq bickered for hours about whether their past life recalls came from real experiences or just power of suggestion. "You said my recall was profound, so own it. We're all going back into doubt because the horrors at the Twin Towers make everything else seem meaningless. But if we focus on how 'anthropologically innate' reincarnation is, and search for it in the world's cultures, that can shore up our eroding beliefs. And help get us through this dreadful time."

"I could not agree more, Doctor," Verle said. "I'm pushing you all to explore the World Types vision I had, as another way to stay dedicated to our work. World Types could help sort out different cultures, too."

The same distress Diana felt at Zack's plea for therapy crept into her stomach. Again, she could not formulate her anxiety, but she suddenly felt a great responsibility toward the qaraq. "Pardon me, Verle, but I think we're talking about two different things. You want us to categorize our memories, and I want us to find out what's innately human and soulful underneath them. We need to delve deeper to dig ourselves out from a community-wide trauma."

"Pardon *me*, my daughter," Verle said, alluding to their archetypal Scheherazade relationship, "but we need every way at our disposal." Verle stared at Diana as a challenge, and she held his look. The two had one of the most amicable relationships in the past life group, and the tension between them surprised Zack.

"Pardon *me*, but can we get a little work done? I'm glad you got your passion back, Doc, so could you clean up some of the old man's mess?"

Diana broke her gaze from Verle and looked kindly at Zack. She had never appreciated his humor as much as in that moment. She still felt

87

dread in her stomach, but as she looked about the clutter in the attic she no longer felt daunted. Remembering how the attic had once looked, serene and spare, she understood what the qaraq's work had to be, and she attacked a pile of paper-clipped transcripts.

12

——✺✺✺——

March 14, 2002. Month 7 (6th month after Impact).

On an unseasonable warm evening at the end of a long Winter following the disastrous Fall, Sahara sat on her patio, staring at the Moorish
fountain. Its gurgling waters seemed contemplative tonight, ready for
some important event. Sahara contemplated her best times with Amar. A
past life where they had been married in a place called The Suburb was
perhaps their romantic start as a couple. In the weeks before 9/11 they
had overcome severe problems to reclaim this love. On the eve of 9/11,
Sahara felt her beautiful recall about the famous French translation of the
Nights was a sign that the union of love, past life work, and her Nights
research could revive that idyllic marriage.

But Sahara had spiraled down into depression during the six months
after 9/11, fighting back with manic episodes of work, only to be thrown
into a disconnected sense of time. The six months had been hard on
Naji, too; after 9/11 he had been lost in his own world. She had tried
many ways to connect to him, even reading past life transcripts or Nights
tales to get a rise out of him. Nothing worked. The union between love,
past lives, and the Nights was lost to her.

After her first Persian memory from the 4th Century, Sahara had
thought: if I actually lived as the historical model for Scheherazade, then

I have access to incredible information for my research. The qaraq's recalls of the last six months had been a gold mine for that hope; she had more evidence about the origin of the Nights than she could put into one thesis. Sahara confided everything to her thesis advisor, Prof. Agib, a trusted old friend of her family. He had gently pointed out that past life regression transcripts would be suspect in academic circles. She tried to corroborate even a small bit of the past life evidence with existing documents, but it was a fool's errand. Again, how to unite reincarnation and the Nights? Sahara sighed. The fountain's gurgling quieted. Strange.

The qaraq members were eager collaborators in this work, each with his or her need for distraction from anxiety and depression. Since the day of 9/11, when a number of qaraqis had shared stories about the evolution of the Scheherazade story, all received in a weird telepathic space, the group contributed a great deal to Sahara's research. They also investigated the relation between ancient cultures and reincarnation beliefs. But months later, there were still many missing pieces.

Tonight Sahara enlisted Porcy's aid: the part-time psychic had a few New Age tricks to induce recalls. Cachay came along with her. The newest member of the qaraq was also its most cynical. Bowing out of Porcy's psychic nonsense, Cachay was there to baby-sit Naji while Sahara went off to another world. Cachay felt Sahara was going overboard with this one, so she wanted to be on hand if something serious went wrong.

Sahara needed to re-visit a lifetime that had been borne out of the fourth New Year's kiss, magical information that the qaraq had shared. The party events were disconcerting reminders of her shaky marriage, Amar's interest in Ooma, and Bax's fawning. Popping up again during 9/11, the tale came down to the qaraq incomplete. The lifetime was Sahara's own, a good enough reason for her to want to visualize it. But she was searching for a key to what the qaraq had been grappling with for six months, the link between the Nights research and the past life work. Like many recalls that year, the story tracked the controversy with popular fiction in the Islamic *umma*, or community.

The Tale of the Majlis of Ja'far ibn Yahya al-Barmaki, or, The Sleepless Reader

I was born on the back of a camel. My father was a rich merchant from Khourasan, my mother one of his many purchases from around the world. My true parents were the camel-drivers I traveled with on the caravans my father organized. He rarely went on the expeditions himself, and then only for short legs, but by the time I was seven I was riding a camel between Syria and China.

The use of the camel, easy transport that revolutionized trade, peaked with the Abbasids, and promoted cultural exchange between nations. The best currency for this exchange of ideas was stories of the world, a vast treasury. I learned stories in the saddle, or half asleep under a date tree at the oasis, or in the bazaar selling off my poor beast's heavy load. Searching for a fresh tale, I combed the dark alleys of new towns, taught myself five languages, and bartered at every bookseller's stall. I retold the best of the stories, changing details with the ease I exchanged goods.

The more I desired new stories, the more tired I became of the caravans. I never made friends. Something in my soul mistrusted giving myself to a society. I was alone with my stories.

When my father died and left me with only a modest sum, I decided to choose a home for myself. In those days the place to be was Baghdad, for ten years ambitiously overseen by Caliph Harun al-Rashid, an austere ruler who had twice made the pilgrimage to Mecca. Although Harun imposed burdensome taxes, he governed wisely, encouraging scientific and cultural progress. He appointed advisors from the Barmaki administrative dynasty, the Persian clan that had supported many Abbasid rulers. Under their encouragement, there was talk of an Arabic translation of the Persian *Hezar Afsana*. I could hear stories from *The Thousand Marvelous Tales* if I settled in

91

Baghdad. I took the name Sahra, from the exotic desert of Africa, and rode my camel into the city.

Manuscripts of The Thousand and One Nights *date from after the 14th Century, but there is one existing fragment that comes from the 9th, not only the oldest evidence of the Nights, but also the earliest sample of paper. Clues from the fragment, which contains a few lines from the Scheherazade tale, point to the first Arabic version of the story collection dating from late 8th Century Baghdad, perhaps during the reign of Harun al-Rashid, a frequent character in the Nights.*

Caliph Harun had put a good deal of the treasury into creating Baghdad, the glittering gem of the Empire. Outside the palace, I drank in tales from the market, and paraded out my best anecdotes. My stories stirred my listeners with the truth about life on the road. Lower officials of the court heard my name and I was invited inside the palace walls. Despite his piety, Harun had a weak spot for a raconteur, so the Barmakis brought in credible yarns to soften the Caliph for funding. My tale of the ostrich hunters of Merv gained me daily admission into the palace.

There was so much activity inside those walls, and so much fear of treachery, that the various departments, military, culinary, or literary, were segregated. I was escorted to a wing of the palace for storytellers, scribes, poets, and all who beautify language. I found poets memorizing old desert *qasidas* to honor Arabic verse; I heard young *nadim* composing sweet melodies to toast the Caliph. Most of all I listened to endless debates about *The Thousand Tales*, its title and contents.

While the Barmaki supported their Persian classic, others mistrusted their power and argued for collections from the Greeks or Rajasthani. Harun's companion Al-Asma'i was hard at work on a literal translation of the Tales, but critics conquered the Caliph's ear, aborting al-Asma'i's project. An older paper manufacturer named Wahid, who owned a remarkable collection of books, argued that there were so many delightful tales in the world that the Persian tales should be supplemented. Barmaki stalwarts contended that an Arabic translation of *The Thousand Tales* only contain several hundred, since the storyteller Sharazade told each one over many nights. The literary minister Zabbah, who sided with Wahid's expansive view, advocated for a book of a thousand tales.

No debate was more hotly fought than between poets and storytellers. Promoting Islamic disdain of fiction, insecure versemakers condemned stories as street corner debasement. The storytellers retaliated that new literary forms needed to express courtly achievements and valorous conquests in common language. The Barmaki vizier Ja'far championed the new fiction, but poets had a powerful lobby at court and threatened every fiction project. Influenced by his religious wife, Zubeidah, Harun was conservative in his promotion of fiction translations and warned Ja'far against impiety in the form of bawdy tales.

In my first months at court I gained the attention of Wahid and Zabbah through our mutual fight for fiction. They saw stories as living symbols of human action, replete with hidden messages and universal meanings gathered from different cultures. Steeling myself for their criticism, I dared raise an idea concerning the battle with the poets. "Did not the greatest poetry and stories evolve side by side from wanderers in the desert? Were not *those* nights of wonder full of the back and forth of verse and narrative? Why not create an amazing admixture of the two art forms?"

I explained further. "Every good story has its own natural rise, its quiet resolution, and somewhere in the middle, a rousing climax built on tension and inevitability. Inserted in the proper place, a poem could oil the progress of the action, let the listener down slowly at the end; or help the climax blossom to its fullest and linger in the ear longer than mere prose allows."

Zabbah and Wahid praised my notion with embraces and salutes. Their enthusiasm relieved me, but when it did not abate I grew uncomfortable. I had spent too many years alone with my thoughts to trust any man completely. I expected them to change my idea monstrously, take all the credit, or slander me if it was criticized at court. I avoided the two men.

Sensing my cold distrust, Wahid came to me with a stack of books, both histories and poetry volumes, encouraging me to nourish my idea with examples. He even entrusted me with a rare manuscript given to him by a Basran sheikh, which elucidated a series of past and future lifetimes that supported reincarnation and predicted world events. Though Zabbah and Wahid vied for my allegiance, I was caught between their flattery and the solitude I had enjoyed my whole life. I had made some kind of deal in my soul not to be attached to anyone, perhaps in one of those past lives in Ba'tr's enigmatic manuscript. So I kept to myself, despite accepting Wahid's loads of books.

For Sahara, this past life was most precious, given its mixing of Nights and reincarnation matters. In her determination to flesh out her recall as Sahra, an Arabic male, Sahara had asked Porcy to come to the house and perform a perilous variation of one of her techniques. The qaraq had been targeting specific recalls for months, thanks to Verle's pursuit of World Types, and Sahara was confident she could do the same. Porcy was all for helping Sahara uncover the time when the Nights escaped orthodox strictures to be embraced by the common people.

Interrupting Sahara's peaceful remembrance by the fountain, Porcy came out to the patio to report that Naji was safe with Cachay, and that it was time to begin. Porcy opened a bottle of lavender bath oil from Crystal Charm, a New Age shop on Abbey Street, and emptied the contents into the fountain. She had Sahara immerse herself in the warm bath. The sedating quality of lavender would aid past life remembrance. Porcy recited blessings as Sahara awkwardly stepped into the three-tiered fountain's lowest pool. Sahara's stomach tightened.

As the fountain jets splashed streams into the pool, the oil swirled about in unusual patterns. Focusing on them as Porcy instructed her, Sahara felt an immediate effect. Her body felt heavy and out of control.

As Sahara rushed into trance state, her body slid into the pool until her head was completely underwater.

With great difficulty, Porcy climbed into the fountain's pool, lowered her squat body behind her friend, and gently lifted Sahara under the arms until her head emerged out of the water. Porcy did not wish to rouse Sahara from her deep trance, but that meant holding her until she had completed her vision. Steadying her weight, Porcy held on for dear life. Safely held in place, Sahara let the memory overtake her mind.

The Tale of the Majlis of Ja'far ibn Yahya al-Barmaki, or, The Sleepless Reader, continued

Hoping to mix poetry with fiction, I threw myself into looking for poems that would go well with a particular love story, or dramatic episodes that cried out for verses. Late one quiet night I closed my eyes, meditated on the heart of one poem, and comforted myself by playing with the strands of my beard. Letting an evocative passage take hold, I felt a glimpse of infinity in the intoxicating words. I opened my eyes, picked up a peerless volume of Umayyad poetry, and went farther inside the images to discover an eternal peacefulness. I read for what seemed like hours, then fell into a delightful, bottomless sleep.

The next night I repeated my ritual. I devoured a delightful short collection of fifty tales entitled *The Prisoners of Love*, about two lovers imprisoned for their political views. Then the reincarnation manuscript transfixed me. The thought of an endless series of lifetimes awakened my vision of infinity. I pondered the relation of past lives with *The Thousand Tales*. Many narratives contained moments of humans transforming into animals and magical beings into humans. I wondered if these were allegories of reincarnation, symbolic of actual transmigrations. After many other books, I fell soundly asleep, unaware of the time.

On the third night, I felt a need to rise, stretch, and walk about the streets. I ambled toward the palace through the deserted alleys, until I came across not one, but two or three people in a standstill. When I reached the gates I found the guards similarly immobile, and easily walked past them. Inside the walls, late night parties were in progress, yet no one moved or blinked. Finally I understood: my contemplative ritual had put me in a state of literal timelessness, where I existed in a moment of frozen time. In the last two days, I had awakened refreshed and time continued on its way. Shocked, I returned home and fell into a fast sleep.

I awoke to the hurried sunrise, and spent the day dazed and afraid. That night, when I returned to my prolonged reading, I rejoiced. What harm has this ability done me? What harm has it done the world? I could make my way easily through Wahid's collection. I gratefully returned all the books he had given me, in exchange for more and more volumes. Of course, this was also my downfall, for Wahid and Zabbah became suspicious of the velocity of my reading. They interrogated me about each volume, thinking I was not actually reading them, and I considered feigning ignorance to rid myself of them. But I didn't.

After seventeen nights of stopping time, an incredible realization came upon me. Though I had avoided the company of others for fear of becoming too attached, I was doing just that with my endless nights devouring Wahid's books. I confessed this mind-opening epiphany to Wahid, who had barely taken his eyes off me since I devoured two hundred and thirteen books. Ready to commit myself to their friendship, Wahid cared deeply about my excitement.

Breaking from a lifetime (or more) of withholding myself from society, I confided my time-stopping power to Wahid and Zabbah. They marveled, praising my constructive use of all the time. I had not carried off palace jewels or played tricks on frozen members of the court. With trust, Zabbah disclosed their mission to support a free adaptation of the

Hezar in Harun's court. They had influenced the frame tale, having the Vizier instruct Sharazade how to dupe the King. Having heard many variants on the road, I understood both the audacity and sense of the innovations.

But I confided my own thoughts: if Sharazade was instructed to manipulate the King because of her vast knowledge of stories, then why wouldn't this amazing woman have the idea herself? The old Persian *Sharzad* was a victim hiding out from her fate, drawn out by a slave. Now a Vizier brought her forth, her father no less, ordering her about the palace. I teased Wahid mercilessly about his characterization. What father would order his daughter to sleep with a killer?

No, it's all Sharazade's idea, I contended; she is confident that she can overcome, even re-educate the crazed King. Her father would fight this dangerous notion, and she should fight back, their relationship petulant and equal. To convince her unnerved parent, she would do what is most natural, tell a story to make her point. Imagine: no real plan, just outrage at the slaughter of fellow virgins. In the heat of arguing with a parable, her father interrupts her, and she receives an inspiration: trick the King by interrupting a story. Could she survive a night with the King this way?

Wahid did not take his teasing lightly. If so protective of his daughter, the Vizier would have brokered some deal with the King, so his virgin girl was immune from the King's monstrous acts. What would the clever Vizier have sacrificed in order to gain this immunity? Conversely, once Sharazade convinced him, what embarrassment would he face by offering the King his daughter's body and soul? Could the King even break their agreement; could the Vizier?

Sharazade's plan is a child's cruel independence from a parent. She forces her father to wait sleeplessly for the King's dark summons: prepare the executioner. Instead, the next morning the King avoids his Vizier, who has made things so awkward between them, and conducts his official business without him. After the courtly diwan adjourns, the King returns to his bedchambers, and only then can the Vizier breathe a

97

sigh. Not for long, because once again he must await the fate of his child all night, for a thousand nights! As if I was his cruel, punishing daughter, Wahid scolded me for my heartless idea. But recognizing a great yarn, he surrendered.

At this point in her recall, Sahara's trance lightened, just enough to sense a warm presence behind her. The memories still entered her mind, but now she was able to react to them. She marveled that the Abbasid court had argued about how to translate the story collection. She thrilled that her own incarnation, Sahra, had pushed Scheherazade's character to a new level! Europeans weren't the only ones who messed with the Nights. Spellbound, she re-immersed herself in the past.

The Tale of the Majlis of Ja'far ibn Yahya al-Barmaki, or, The Sleepless Reader, continued

The pious Harun had become tired of reports of Ja'far ibn Yahya al-Barmaki's late night carousing, and insisted his Vizier stop corrupting precious intellectuals and artists. Ja'far complied, for he was a man with higher interests. He organized a series of *majlis*, or salons, where the best minds from all sects and schools debated important topics.

Zabbah and Wahid had spent all their currency at court lobbying for story collections, but I was still in the shadows. So happy with my alliance and brainstorms, Zabbah made plans for me at court. Through his machinations, I received an invitation to speak at one of Ja'far's majlis. The topic for the evening was the immortality of the soul. I was intimidated to find myself in the company of prominent Muslim theologians, philosophers, and free-thinkers, under the critical gaze of courtiers with great influence. Given this great opportunity, I chose to present a complex argument that addressed fiction translation as well as immortality.

I was to be the eleventh speaker. I cowered, hearing one great mind after another parsing texts from Hippocrates or jurisprudence from Shi'a sages. Most intimidating was Sheikh Ba'Tr, the specialist in metempsychosis who had tousled with Wahid over his book collection. Ba'Tr presented a survey of the literature on the subject, all the while casting glances at Wahid and Zabbah.

When it was my turn I shook like a leaf. I introduced myself as a great traveler of the caravan routes, who had encountered many cultures. This provoked a relieved sigh: I was to be a worldly alternative to the heady philosophers. I began my case for combining the great story collections of the world with the wit of poetry, but when the usual fiction/poetry camps heckled me, I steered closer to the theme of the night.

"Having subdued many cultures, Islam embraced many types of stories, as well as many beliefs in the soul's previous existences. Since the soul creates myths and legends, it is embedded in the many stories, and the stories therefore contain myriad reflections on immortality and reincarnation." Citing Wahid's arcane manuscript (a wicked look from Ba'Tr), as well as the *Hezar Afsana*, I pointed out examples of past lives in many tales. Many nodded in agreement, some rolled their eyes, but all were engaged.

"I return to my opening plea to blend fiction and poetry in story collections. Working on an anthology is synonymous with preparing the soul for its immortal journey. Whoever dips his soul there, storyteller or poet, will benefit from great secrets, like imbibing an elixir of immortality. Such work could be the source of a new Arabic literature."

Ba'Tr rose in fury and slandered my views as blasphemy. Easily manipulating the poets, Ba'Tr caused such a stir in the room that Ja'far had to quiet the hubbub. The Vizier could not rebuke this powerful merchant, so he warned me to be careful, since the Caliph did not tolerate any form of blasphemy. Seeing my anger rise, Zabbah stepped in, bowed low, and had me follow suit. We retreated out the door, Wahid following with a hot, backward glance at Ba'Tr.

Sahara felt a shiver up her spine. Here was a connection between reincarnation beliefs and the development of the Nights! Here was evidence that the original Nights might be permeated with such beliefs, even with past life stories. The bubbling water, Porcy's grip, and the chill night air all entered Sahara's excited consciousness. But one more piece of the story came to her mind.

The Tale of the Majlis of Ja'far ibn Yahya al-Barmaki, or, The Sleepless Reader, conclusion

Although silenced at court, inevitably our ideas went forth. With Barmaki support, the *Hezar Afsana* translation began. Different factions worked on it, another inevitability, given the conflicting outlooks. One version kept the number of tales to a minimum, pushing for the title *Alf Leilah, The Thousand Nights*, describing the many nights Sharazade took to complete a story. Other versions bravely included Arab tales alongside the Persian and Indian sources. Zabbah, Wahid, and I joined the scribes working on this version, finding a guild sympathetic to the inclusion of poetry.

As the first Arabic translation of the *Hezar Afsana* neared completion, the court forgot my provocative presentation, but I still felt stung by Ja'far's dismissal of me in the name of the Caliph. It was Zabbah who concocted the delicious idea that gave my wronged soul gritty satisfaction. Harun was already being called the greatest of the Caliphs, though detractors said his cultural tolerance would be Islam's downfall.

100

Nonetheless, scribes contemplated adding new Arabic tales of Harun's exploits; to slip one into a fresh manuscript would be so easy.

Ja'far's partying was out of hand, but though Harun usually reprimanded his Vizier, now the Caliph partook. So what better comeuppance than for us to pen an original tale about Harun and Ja'far: the two sneak out of the palace one night in disguise, carouse with the local singing girls and reprobate poets, and end up sleeping in a ditch. It was a tasty bit of mischief, disguised enough so we would never be suspect. Given how vast the *Alf Leilah* was becoming, no one would notice the satiric bauble about Harun and Ja'far. Content that Sharazade was taken more seriously in the latest telling of the tale, I did not anticipate a cycle of Harun-Ja'far stories evolving from our little prank.

ق

Sahara drew herself out of the fountain, laughing at the joke that ended the recall, since the Nights became full of debauched Harun stories. When she realized Porcy thought she was laughing at her, she hastened to explain. "I've seen a new connection between past lives and the Nights! This can rejuvenate the qaraq's work. And help heal our pain. It's all going to be okay, Porcy."

"Of course it is, sweet," Porcy said, "as soon as we dry off."

Sahara heard the fountain give a chuckling gurgle in response.

101

13

———⟨ᴈᴈᴈ⟩———

October 4, 2001.   Week 4 (3 weeks after Impact).

The din was horrendous: the screams of children, cries of panic and fear.

What in the world had gotten into Porcy, to suggest they celebrate Naji's second birthday at the FunStop in West Orange?   Grateful that nothing had happened to that fool Bax on 9/11, Porcy had thrown herself into helping others, at the church, at the real estate office, and now in Sahara's life.   Anything to mask her anxiety at how the world was changing.   Sahara had been through so much in the last few weeks, Porcy thought a little levity might help.   But this chaos?

It had been hard enough to schedule the qaraq for Naji's birthday on October 1.   When that numerically significant date (10/01) didn't work, Porcy found an opening at FunStop for Saturday.   Angry at Porcy, Bax refused to go: Ooma had been promised she could join qaraq meetings, but she would not be there.   Better he be spared this cacophony; things were already tense between them at home.   Diana thought a party was an indelicate idea after 9/11, and gave Porcy a piece of her mind.   But the therapist wanted to support Sahara and Naji, so she was there, enduring the torture.   Porcy coaxed Cachay to bring her buddy Verle, though neither was eager to come. What was happening to the group's good spirits? Porcy hated the tensions mounting within the qaraq.

What was even harder for Porcy was watching Naji in the toddler party room. Glenclaire was a diverse suburb, and it was heartening to see all the different skin tones of the little friends, especially since she, Verle, Cachay and Zack were all of mixed races. But poor Naji had no friends, and he sat by his mother in a bubble of eerie calm, no doubt shutting out the noisy children. Porcy tried to cheer up the lad, but he was in his own mind. One way to escape the tense new world.

Faking good cheer put Porcy on edge, and she was exhausted from being leader of the expedition. A two-year-old tried to climb on the frail Verle's lap. Diana was hit on the head by a balloon elephant. Just when things could get no worse, Zack walked in, accompanied by his new boyfriend Jobim Jones. Why in God's name did he subject a new beau to this insanity? When Porcy saw everyone's face tighten, at a loss how to include this stranger in the midst of the shouting nest of children, she could take no more.

Porcy grabbed Sahara and Naji's hands, left the toddler party room, and found the prehistoric cave play center. Thank God Naji climbed on the wooly mammoth for a minute, then ducked in and out of the caves. Peeking out from behind a rock, Porcy caught something in her peripheral vision, a twitch of movement between a mother and child. Given her unraveling emotional state, the cave shadows, and piercing noise, Porcy glimpsed a prehistoric world from her past and fell into a memory.

The Tale of the Borzi-Vawr Half-breed

The din was horrendous: the screams of Awrawr's family, cries of mourning in the frosted air. They knew the corpse was inside the cave, but we kept them out. It was cruel, but necessary.

103

I jumped atop the rock and raised my arms, waiting for the screams and weeping to subside. I waited patiently, not wanting to disturb the Vawr clan any more than necessary.

"We must be brave," I communicated, with gestures and grunts. "The Borzi will destroy us otherwise. They have starved us Vawr. Hurt and killed us." I waited for the renewed cries to die. "But we must survive the cold. And the Borzi. To do that, we must protect the body of Awrawr! We must have blood for blood!" Shouts of fury drowned out the mourners. I calmed these voices, too. "This is not about vengeance. This is about making sure there will be a Vawr child and not a Borzi child!" Cheers of triumph allowed me to jump down and enter the cave without obstruction.

It had been hard enough for the Vawr clan to accept my family as their own. The tribe had exiled my father, Brawr, whom I nicknamed Brami, for having a child by a woman from the rival Borzi clan. Infiltrating the debased Borzi ritual, he enjoyed the wild, female leader Ourm, or Yurmi – the name I gave my mother. After Yurmi became heavy with me from trysts with Brami, she confessed her liaison, and the tribes exiled my parents from the Three Valleys. I grew up in the frigid mountain passes, observing the Borzi extermination of the Vawr.

What was even harder was convincing the Vawr what should be done to the corpse.

Back in the toddler room, Diana was sorry not to have gone with Naji, but she was compelled to stay with Zack and meet Jobim. The group understood immediately what Zack saw in the handsome, easy-going man. Jobim scored instant points for charming the raucous children to play on the other side of the room.

"I left Wall Street a few years back and did one of those Department of Education boot camps. Wasn't cut out for second graders, but I picked up some kid skills. Boundaries are us."

Verle smiled. "Bless you for setting up a perimeter, young man."

Diana scrutinized Jobim carefully. "What do you do now, Mr. Jones?"

"Free-lance computer analyst. Making the Internet safe for capitalism."

"Or safe from capitalists," Verle said. "You think the dotcoms are in trouble?"

"No doubt. Bubbles are no thicker than water." Jobim continued the polite banter: he liked these people, especially the old guy, but wondered what was up with the Asian woman, who eyed him when she thought he wasn't looking, and sat with her legs twisted together like a pretzel.

Verle wanted to talk about the latest past life recalls. But he had no idea if Zack had resisted telling Jobim about the qaraq. "Zack, my lad, any new trinkets to add to my collection?"

"You collect Bhutan temple door knockers, too, Mr. Walker?" Jobim asked.

"Please, call me Verle. Or 'old man,' like the rest of them. Zack has been helping me organize my collection of ... rare books from the Near East."

"Like the Arabian Nights?" Everyone looked at Jobim. It was a plausible enough response.

"The *Thousand and One* Nights," Zack corrected, unable to help himself.

"Or just the *Nights*," Verle said. "Anything new since those old ... books you found?"

"Hoping for a follow-up to that work by the Sheikh," Zack said. "No more news there."

"Is this about some version of the Scheherazade story?" Jobim asked.

Again the group stared at him. "Very perceptive, young man," Verle said. "We like to share stories with each other, our little hobby. In fact, I made a discovery the other week. According to times and places the books occur, call them Worlds, we each make a contribution. Tracking who hasn't added a story to a particular World, we know that person has to ... find a tale in that World."

"These are stories from rare books, right?" Jobim clarified. "What if someone can't find one from a World? Do they research the story? Make one up? Remember a past life?"

105

The group was stunned into silence. Having been an observer, Diana couldn't hold still any longer. "That does it! What've you told him, Zack?"

"Nothing! Do you know how hard it's been? It's bad enough I can't confide in a therapist."

Jobim realized he had entered a forbidden chamber, toddlers or not. Then Sahara burst through the door, carrying Naji in one arm, and leading Porcy with the other. Distressed, they came over to the group's corner of the playroom. Sahara found a toy for Naji. Porcy collapsed in a chair.

"Another Borzi recall," Porcy said breathlessly. "We were back there, I was Bax and Ooma's child. Brami and Yurmi I called them." Porcy began recounting the tale, oblivious to the group's discomfort. Then she saw Jobim, and stopped in confusion.

Jobim encouraged Porcy. "You were a caveman? Sounds like an Ice Age. Cool."

"My thoughts exactly, friend." Delighted with Jobim's contribution, Verle took it as an invitation for discussion. "The Borzi were probably Neanderthal, a hundred thousand years ago. Less advanced than the tribe we've been ... reading about, who made grave paintings."

Jobim winked. "In your Big Book of Past Lives, right? Two different cave Worlds, one at the start, one at the end of the last Ice Age."

Porcy whispered to Zack. "This one picks up fast." To the group: "Wanna hear the rest?"

The Tale of the Borzi-Vawr Half-breed, conclusion

I came into this world blazing with anger, so I was ready to fight for any downtrodden people. Growing up, I felt my parents had abandoned their tribes rather than the other way around. I coaxed Brami to launch an attack on the Borzi. I spied on the Vawr to see how we could help.

106

When the ice descended on the land, the Vawr had abandoned the idea of four seasons and talked the tribe out of Winter. The Borzi worshipped the ice, Winter, and Death; the Vawr endured with hope, flower blossoms, and rebirth rituals. Yurmi thought them fools, and argued with my father about his lack of reality. But I was both Borzi and Vawr: I saw a cold-hearted way to survive, and the idealistic means to convince the Vawr to do so. Sneaking down the mountain pass, I entered Vawr territory as a stranger. I kept my parentage a secret.

Choosing a boulder on which to preach, I appointed myself spokesperson for the tribe. Rallying the tribe against the evil Borzi, I went from stranger to clansman overnight. I joined in the rituals, especially for life and death. One in particular gave me the idea to summon their courage.

"We must fight back with something fierce and terrible. We must brave an idea that rivals the Three-Season notion, but promises more success. Whenever a Borzi kills one of us, we must adapt our Passing On ritual to insure the Borzi do not claim that soul."

I convinced the Vawr that we had to capture any Borzi who kills one of our own, isolate the Vawr corpse in a special cave for secret burial, and perform a special task in the Passing On ritual. We drained the captive Borzi of blood, and then, without desecrating the Vawr corpse, transfused enough Vawr blood into the Borzi body. We were insuring that, when reborn, the Vawr soul would re-enter his own clan, and with all hope, the Borzi would be reborn a Vawr.

Through the magic of this new ritual and the hope it gave the tribe, I was welcomed as a permanent resident. My new respect allowed me to introduce my parents. The Vawr welcomed back Brami with open arms, and cautiously accepted Yurmi, insisting that it changed nothing in their hatred of the Borzi. I saw the look of regret on her face from time to time, that her bond with a Vawr mate had not brought harmony to the world, only a child that fomented more war. But the price of survival lies heavy on our souls, the cost being desperate action.

ق

When Porcy finished, tension still held the group, between the raucous children and Jobim's presence. He smoothed things over. "Sorry I crashed your reincarnation toddler party."

Along with the chorus of reassurances, Diana said, "I suspect Zack had a plan, whether conscious or not. How many guys have you invited to a baby birthday party, Zack?"

"I'm learning all kinds of things," Jobim commented, squeezing Zack's arm. "Is there a group discussion now? Does the story fit your World scheme?"

Zack saw Verle's elation at Jobim's question. Jobim totally understood how Verle's mind worked. Was Jobim connected to the qaraq, or was it just his charm and sensitivity?

"I knew the Boreus World was in the Alternate Earth World Type group, one that reveals new perceptions about life on Earth." Verle dodged a paper plane thrown in his direction. "But the Borzi and Vawr are examples of a subset of Worlds, where five qaraqis are in opposition with the other five. We've seen many five-soul Worlds during this time in our history. Great data to use."

Diana interrupted. "Hold the data for a second." The idea of the party had bothered her from the start, and she had a splitting headache from the noise. She could barely tolerate Verle's category nonsense. "What's really extraordinary about Porcy's story is the reincarnation beliefs embedded in Earth culture. Tens of thousands of years before the grave painters, the Vawr ritualized rebirth. This affirms our belief system, which has been shaken."

"If we're so shaky, why won't you have me in therapy?" Zack whined.

Diana wanted to slap Zack – this is not the time! – but she was still disturbed by his insistence. Even if he could find another therapist, a challenging task at best, Diana *wanted* to help the qaraq see connections between their recalls and the current stress. But her role was limited to friend or soul mate, not therapist.

Verle took advantage of Diana's momentary silence. "May I return to my data, Dr. Machiyoko? It concerns you directly." Verle's tone was more abrasive than informative. "In this World, we've met five Vawr: Naji introduced the World as a quiet observer, so I doubt he was Borzi; Zack and I founded the Vawr's Three-Season idea; Bax was Brami, and Porcy his child. But we only know four out of the five rival Borzi: Amar was the legendary Borzu; Sahara and Ooma were Borzi women; Cachay was the ruthless K'Chung."

"That leaves Doc," Zack said, "who must have been a merciless Borzi. You owe us a tale."

Between Zack's attitude, Verle's insistence, and the obnoxious FunStop party, Diana felt hounded. "This is not a qaraq meeting. This is Naji's day, not ours. Jobim shouldn't be privy to this, welcome as he is. "I'll recall my Borzi life when I'm ready. Back off."

Verle lowered his voice humbly. "Forgive me if I overstep my bounds. I know you wish to help us deal with the shock of recent events. But I also hold a valid coping response. The Worlds system affirms the vastness of our history. I won't back off, my dear."

During the argument, Sahara sensed Naji go deeper into one of his still episodes. With the noise, the tensions in the qaraq, and his own sensitive mind, Sahara worried she might lose him. With his father unable to be there, Sahara felt overwhelmed to help.

Recovered from her visionary trance, Porcy saw the concern on Sahara's face. She was glad to have recalled another example of archaic reincarnation beliefs, but it did not make up for roping everyone into this debacle. Interrupting Verle and Diana's tiff, she said, "Could we not start another clan war? How about cake?"

In fact, Naji felt the tension passing through the adults, more palpable to him than the shouting children in the toddler room. His agitated mind sought comfort: the warm physicality of his mother was not enough. His mind drifted off and he found himself back in the interlife, following the twins. He had not caught up to them in those caves; as soon as he got close they rushed ahead. Now they ducked around a new corner of the interlife.

While chasing his brothers, Naji was distracted by the places they led him: intricate mazes with mythical animals, fragrant gardens with streams full of colorful fish, and public squares where spirit guides served cake. As much as he desired to speak with his twin siblings, he appreciated their tour of this Wonderland. How much he preferred what they offered, leaving behind the noise at FunStop and the tense bickering of the qaraq.

14

—◦◦◦—

September 11. 9:47 A.M. Hour 2.

When Amar reached the lower floors of the South Tower, he had to rest. Light as Ooma's body weight was, smoke, fatigue, and fear weighed him down much more. Now that they were nearing safety, he gambled he could take a minute to recuperate. Dozens of World Trade Center workers pushed passed him; he struggled to escape the current of bodies.

After Amar put Ooma down, she asked faintly, "Is Hu Ma out of her coma? Where's Bax?"

Although lifted out of her trance, Ooma made little sense. Amar gave a simple answer. "Hu Ma's still in a coma, and I'm staying right here with you."

Ooma suddenly recognized the man next to her. She listened to the noise of falling debris. "Save yourself! It's too hard for me. Too much in my mind." Ooma wondered if Amar would stay if it meant their death together.

Amar flinched at a crashing sound from the floors above. Picking up Ooma again, he moved as fast as he could down the stairwell. They had a dozen floors left to go, but there was no time left. When they reached the outside plaza, though every molecule of his body told him to get away from the building, he had to put down Ooma again. It hurt to breathe, his lungs clogged with dust and smoke, and he had wrenched his lower back.

Sprawled on the ground, Amar and Ooma gazed at each other. Amar reached out to caress her head and Ooma collapsed on his shoulder.

"I am dead weight. You must continue without me now. Nothing can happen to you. I'd hate to separate you from your wife and child." She clutched his hand. "Children."

"Yes, three children, soon. But I can't leave you here."

"I'm not worthy of it, Amar. I am the bane of your existence. As Uzmeth I was cruel to you, and now I still threaten your life. I am the basest of creatures."

"No, no, dear one!" As Amar held her closer, they both realized they had heard each other's last remarks without speaking. Touching linked their minds. Shocked, Ooma drifted back to Hu Ma helpless in her coma, and the fifth kiss taking control of new images in her brain. Feeling ashamed and unworthy, Ooma saw her lifetime in the lowest caste of an ancient Indian city, long before the creation of the Nights. A new story unfolded in Ooma and Amar's minds together.

The Tale of the Lucky Untouchable

Udir accepted his lot in life more than most from his caste; he believed he had performed evil actions in a previous life, or abused a prominent position. Sweeping the streets and picking up foul debris with his bare hands was his rightful duty; it must be a lesson or punishment. Unlike his fellow workers, who brought their carts to the great piles on the outskirts and dug about in hopes of finding some misplaced treasure or sack of coins, Udir simply emptied his cart, made the long walk to his shack, and enjoyed a quiet night alone after the congestion of the streets.

So on the day that Udir found the book among the filthy detritus, he had no thought of reward. To have such a valuable object cross his path meant that he should return it to a worthy owner. How could an Untouchable approach a Brahmin, even with the humblest of intentions? Udir cleaned off the parchment document and kept it in his shack for weeks. He often looked at it, wondering at the indecipherable letters as he chewed on a cinnamon stick. Holding the soft object in his rough fingers gave him solace, but he chastised himself for this secret pleasure.

Finally, Udir determined a course of action. There was an older Brahmin who always smiled at Udir as he passed him on the street, though such kindness was forbidden. One day he hid the book in his cart and as the Brahmin approached, Udir took it out and placed it on the ground. The Brahmin almost ignored the gesture, but his curiosity got the better of him. He bent down to inspect it, opened a few pages, and gazed in wonder. The Brahmin darted his eyes to see that no one noticed him, picked up the book, and without a glance at Udir, hurried down the street.

Udir was sad to lose the book and the smiles of the older man. After a few weeks the Brahmin acknowledged Udir and discretely offered him a small purse. Udir was uncomfortable accepting the money. The next day Udir repeated the gesture he had made with the book, and the Brahmin was forced to take back his coin purse.

Udir did not see the Brahmin again, but one twilight at the trash heaps a very short man with a long beard waved Udir to follow him. It was extremely difficult to traverse the piles, but the short bearded man moved at an uncommonly rapid speed. Udir chased the man over three piles until he saw him disappear into the nearby woods. Udir ran at top speed, forgetting about his cart or why he was compelled to exhaust himself, and finally collapsed. Lying on the ground, Udir was surprised to see the bearded man sit next to him, and wait patiently. Udir stopped panting, and the man spoke.

"I am called Jbafr and I have been sent by my mentor, the Brahmin, to reward you in a more appropriate way than mere coins, which you so aptly refused."

"I refused them because I deserve nothing," Udir replied.

"You insult the Brahmins by denying it," Jbafr said without malice. "You have earned the right to understand the book's contents, for its disappearance was a wrong you have righted."

Udir accompanied the bearded man through the forest, at a more leisurely pace. "The book you found is no ordinary text, but one full of magic and power. It is full of marvelous stories, but more importantly, it is a manual for imbuing stories with special potency. You would understand if I told you the book's lessons give stories more exciting action or power to make the listener weep. These things are secondary in the use of this manual. To make you understand I must show you."

The two men walked until dark, when Jbafr struck a fallen branch, transforming it magically into a torch. Entering a cave, Jbafr used the torch to show Udir old paintings on the walls.

"Thousands of years ago people employed ritual, dance, painting, and trance to protect a departing soul from the demons of the otherworld, and influence its next incarnation. These practices preceded the karmic lessons of Hinduism by many years, and existed throughout the world. Over time humans lost touch with their awareness of reincarnation; instead, they transferred their knowledge to the Gods, creating endless incarnations for their local pantheons.

"Rather than perform a dance with power to return a dear relative to the family as a child or pet, humans chose the pleasure of envisioning a demi-God as a fierce warrior in one life and a bloodthirsty snake in another. Our tales became entertaining and marvelous, but useless to control the transmigrations of souls.

"Terrified of this consequence for humanity, certain wise ancestors culled together a set of potent tales. Within these caves, they devised ingenious techniques for infusing these stories with truly magical powers.

They loaded the tales with symbols and hidden phrases from incantations. Correctly told, written, copied, or read, these stories could influence a soul's journey."

"How is this possible?" Udir inquired, although he felt it was out of place for him to do so. "How do you know this, and how can a story be given such an ability?"

"I know this because others like me and my master have studied special texts. The wise ones were not the first to imbue tales with power; they possessed texts from far off worlds that contained uncanny prophecies and stories of lifetimes. The collection they passed down was not the first of its kind, even though we consider it the earliest common ancestor of all Indian collections."

Udir felt a chilling recognition when Jbafr mentioned the earliest common ancestor, a pride of place, as if he was the Oldest Original. He blushed at the delusional thought, and knew the chilly feeling was the cave's night air. But he was curious: "Did I find the original set of stories?"

"As I said, it is a manual on how to imbue stories with reincarnative power. We don't know if it contains the actual methods from the ancestors. It contains a set of tales that exemplifies how myths are infused with puissance. And there are baffling lists of incarnations."

It was late and cold, and Udir worried about his cart. "Why do you confide all this to me?"

"You are connected to the book. My master believes it contains prophecies about you."

Udir could not even speak, such was his shock.

The bearded man continued. "There is a prophecy concerning an evil Queen named Uzmeth, which came to pass in recent years. We believe you were the evil Queen in your last life, reincarnated as an Untouchable for punishment, and will do something to preserve the book."

Jbafr's statement affirmed Udir's lifelong feeling about himself. But what will he do? Nervous, Udir rummaged in his shirt for a cinnamon stick.

Jbafr calmed his charge. "For two hundred years or more, the great Indian story collections have been migrating west. The *Panchatantra* is a favorite among Persians. *The Prisoners of Love* is merging with anthologies in Western China. Story collections are the rage among the Sasan royals.

"There is another prophecy that the child Princess Humai of the Sasan household will initiate a collection called *The Thousand Tales*, an admixture of Indian ancestral tales and newer Persian stories. It will purge the shame from the evil Queen. You will be reborn as this child."

Seeing Udir's disbelief, Jbafr said, "By decoding past life information from the stories, we learn such things. As a bridge between your penance in this life and accomplishments in the next, you need a quest that will link you, the book, and the Persians, who will develop the collection of a thousand tales. An invisible mendicant could quietly pass from India to the palace in Persia. You must deliver the book."

Before Udir could protest, Jbafr left the cave and began walking back to town. Udir followed him. Jbafr instructed Udir to continue street cleaning until copies of the book were made. Weeks went by. One day Udir saw the Brahmin approaching. Like the opening of the heavens, the old man smiled at him. Udir left his cart, followed the Brahmin, and never looked back.

ق

When the story ended, Ooma took in the people around her escaping from the Tower. At first all she saw were souls covered in white substance, rushing frantically. Had she died and gone to Purgatory? Was her next karmic punishment awaiting her? Then Amar released his touch on her arm, and Ooma snapped out of her trance, aware of the urgent reality, but still retaining images of herself as an Untouchable. "You see my unworthiness, Amar? I hold you back from survival here. I did so as Queen Uzmeth, forcing you into degrading acts. I was punished for that in this story."

116

"I was just as cruel to you. In the evolution of the Scheherazade tale, I murder you as my Queen, and continue murdering virgins, each one representing you. Why do we torture each other?"

They looked into each other's eyes, in what felt like the first time in ages, and both of them knew the answer to the question. Their passion for each other was so deep and wild that the consequences were unpredictable and violent. In this lifetime, the repression of their feelings for each other was suddenly looming and gigantic. But neither could speak it yet.

Instead, Amar said, "I won't leave you here." Then, with an emotion that frightened him: "I will never leave you."

He touched Ooma's shoulders, and their mental link reasserted itself. Amar felt a surge of gratitude from Ooma that he would bring her to safety. He responded with an expression of joy that she was alive.

Just as they were aware of the seismic forces inside them, the South Tower rippled through its core. They ran, enshrouded by an enormous cloud of white ash.

117

15

—⟩∿∿⟨—

September 11. 2:30 P.M. Hour 6.

Cachay closed the bathroom stall and sat down on the toilet seat fully dressed. She had needed a break hours ago, but the phones had not stopped ringing since the plane crashes. As a public defender in the Social Services Agency, she normally dealt with family, discrimination, or minor criminal cases. Since they were a government agency, everyone was calling for information about survivors at the World Trade Center, who to contact, or who the terrorists were.

The emotional intensity that day brought home how stressful her job already was. The relentless pace of the calls got on her last nerve. Not knowing if her son Zachary was safe worried her to death. What toll was this job taking on her?

She looked down at the stapled document in her hands. Cachay had found it on her desk that morning, of all times, but no one knew its origin. After perusing it she had buried it in a drawer, for fear someone seeing it think her crazy. Now Cachay began reading the text and felt it was her past lifetime. Maybe she was crazy. What in the world was this document?

A Chronology of Dr Winood
Ctatlo, 8101 - 8183

LIFE OF A GENIUS: A TRIBUTE TO THE INVENTOR OF THE MULTIPERF

8101   Born Hamrod, Northern Icarion. Daughter of a local greensmith and children's whakatan teacher. Sits in on mother's song lessons from age two.

8116-21 Attends Glaruda Adolescent Performing Institute (GAPI). Classmates with Waeo Kvevely, future Do'en of Draill U. Graduates top honors.

8121   Freshling year at Draill U. Enters as whakani major, determined to write great Aklanonian playscript. Raped in woods on Isle of Whaka.

8122   Sophmorist year. Switches to telepacting major, then tarakani (nerve dancing). Moves to Isle of Whakatan.

8124   Senieur year. Crosses over to Whakatan Conservatory. Kvevely accompanies her senieur recital, which receives great acclaim. Sensitive blending of dramatic text, telepacting, movement and gesture in Ctatlo's vocal performance.

8125   Politically controversial experimentation in field. Denigrated by critics, audiences.

8143   Kvevely becomes Do'en of Draill U.

8147   Embryonic formation of aesthetics, addressing her critics. "Abuses of Whaka."

In the bathroom stall, Cachay realized the question was not 'What in the world was this document?' but 'Where is it from?' The document came from Draill U, the famous arts conservatory of the planet Aklanon. Cachay recognized this world from a group recall last

119

Halloween, guided by baby Naji! What had she gotten herself into with this qaraq?

A Chronology of Dr Winood Ctatlo, continued

8151   Sympathetic to her failures, Kvevely hires Ctatlo as whakasaja faculty at Draill U.

8156   Chronically airsick from the teleferries, moves onto the Isle of Whakatan; Do'en Kvevely builds apartment complex for her.

8158   Implements cross-training on Isle of Whakatan (composers sing, singers conduct, etc.). *The Whaka of the Whakasagi*. Publishes the classic vocal manual of the modern era.

8162   *An Extended Social History of the Whakasagi*. The story of the great polyvocalists. Also thought of as an anti-imperialistic tract against the Neo-Authouritariunists.

8163   "Heyatt uy Budoyr." Ostensibly a whakasagi teachbook, the essay examines adaptations of the story from the Nichts as political action. Works that stretch social norms (a woman disguised as a Prince must bed a nubile Princess; the two women live happily ever after) necessitate adaptations that stretch art forms. Using the folk novel *Heyatt* and the painting, "Budoyr in Love," Ctatlo's theatrical adaptation involving several arts became famous. Multiperf theory.

Cachay marveled at the skills she had displayed in her lifetime as Ctatlo. Was it the same in this life? She had been a successful career woman when she had decided to go back to law school, and then work for the poor and victimized. She had explained to the qaraq that she had been greedy her whole life and wanted to amend that. They were suspicious of her explanation, since she held many secrets from them.

Cachay looked at the poorly maintained bathroom stall, the peeling paint, the broken toilet paper dispenser. She questioned whether this job was worth the strain, regardless of her good intentions. Was it really her true nature to sacrifice herself for others? She had a protective instinct, but was it enough? What was the alternative? To focus on the qaraq and her past lives? She shook her head at the folly of that thought. Despite her doubts, she kept reading.

A Chronology of Do'r Winood Ctatlo,

continued

8165   *The Whakatica.* Ctatlo's poetics, and the aesthetics of the multiperf.
8170   The Nerve Dancing Workshops. To prove her multiperf theories, Ctatlo conducts experiments with tarakan: if nerve-based, movement should spark audience's sensory reactions. Intimate, vulnerable experiments provoke expulsions and suicides. Kvevely protects Ctatlo's tenure.
8171   Stays indoors most of the school year. Kvevely builds aquatunnels within Draill U.
8172   The Whakatan Lectures. Accused of favoring the musical disciplines despite her multiperf theories, limits sound element to create the setting or environment in a stage narrative.
8173   Do'en Kvevely proposes marriage; Ctatlo neither accepts nor rejects him.

Cachay stared at the document. Who gave her this thing? How did they get into her office? While reading, she saw no flashes of Draill U in her mind. Cachay had not had a recall in months. Elvi, the group's facilitator, had asked for a new tale from her at the qaraq's last meeting; Cachay nearly stormed out. Elvi could have planted the biography, hoping it would bring back Cachay's memories. The qaraq had experienced a similar dry spell; at that time Cachay had been flooded with memories. Perhaps it was a natural cycle, and she was running a year behind the group.

Or had job stress slowed down Cachay's recalls? On top of office gossip and red tape, she was learning new computer programs, helping Zack with his Internet business, acting as unofficial, grumpy webmaster. *No wonder I can't recall a lifetime.* So who recalled Ctatlo's lifetime?

A Chronology of Pr Winood Ctatlo, continued

8174   "The Muse from Beyond," article exploring the compositional process of the whakatang as a model for all creativity. Rebuffed by critics for its postulate that anyone receiving an Idea is experiencing an Inspiration derived from a tangible source in another world.

8176   "The Invention of the Kasatutang." The essay both invents the job of spacewright who unifies everyone's work on a multiperf, and calls on the kasatutangi to weave the story in space.

8177   In a rare interview, reveals pain of rape on Isle of Whaka during freshling year.

8178   In an even rarer solo performance, demonstrates the pointlessness of text as a storytelling device, recounting *The Epic of Frochthyus* using wordless song and abstract gesture.

8179   Tabloid media exposes Kvevely as the rapist in Ctatlo's past. Kvevely denies it and proposes again. After another silent reaction, the press characterizes Ctatlo as so hurt that she seeks safety in control over the world of the multiperf.

Cachay wondered if Kvevely was someone in the qaraq. As soon as she questioned it, she realized it must be Verle. Do'en Kvevely was inextricably bound to Ctatlo. Was Verle's soul capable of rape? She and Verle had a strong connection, possibly something to pursue in this life. Did Verle plant the document? The old man would have struggled to physically place it here. He would have needed help. Again, Cachay pointed her finger at Elvi, often in cahoots with Verle.

Cachay caught herself obsessing about who played this trick on her. She felt like a teenager worried about a love crush. There was dark emotion under the minimal narrative of the chronology, but she refused to get sucked into the melodramatics of the qaraq. She had to finish this thing and get back to work.

A Chronology of Dr Winood Ctatlo,

continued

8180   "Limitless Limits." Argues that each art in a multiperf provides boundaries for the others, allowing them to flourish safely. The press is silenced.

8181   Kvevely abolishes the Dept. of Whakani, the traditional playwrighting program, located on the Isle of Whaka (original scene of the rape), which lies vacant for years after.

8182   Groundbreaking ceremony for Ctatlo's design for Myrna B. Netalo Multiperf Center.

8183   Dies in final construction phase during electro-textural mishap. Kvevely delivers eulogy at opening night of Multiperf Center.

How sad. Again Cachay took in the decrepit bathroom stall and felt sorry for herself. What was she doing in this life? What was happening to her? Who were these people she was sharing lives with? For example, Porcy drove her crazy with her meddling, so she could have played this trick. But how did she have access to Cachay's lifetime? No, Elvi must have done this.

Cachay remembered that morning, when she had heard a voice telling her bits of a story in her head. A story about Sheherazade and creating a collection of Arabic stories. Cachay had dismissed the voice, chalked it up to stress on the job. The qaraq had recalled many Arabic or Persian lives already, so she was either nostalgic for them or chanelling them in some weird way triggered by the catastrophe. No, that was crazy. Amazing, but crazy.

She got up from the toilet and headed back to her desk, finishing the chronology on the way.

A Chronology of Pr Winood Ctatlo, conclusion

8184 - "The Cycle of Romance." Unproduced multiperf concerning colleagues, each in love with the wrong person. Dedicated to Pr Daywa, later a neuromistressa at Draill U.

"The Climate of Narrative." Posthumous essay, the only one co-authored with Kvevely, an investigation of whether multiperf arts should echo, contrast, or complement each other. The 'climate' of the narrative determines the nature of interaction at any given moment.

Kvevely's contribution describes 'the complexity of unisons.' "A whakatan fugue can echo the airturns of a nerve dancer while the entire theater revolves around its audience." The essay sits on Kvevely's desk until his death.

ق

Finishing the biography, Cachay was reminded of last year's Draill U recalls, which centered on a production that proved the brilliance of Ctatlo's theories. My theories, Cachay mused. How strange that the

124

show was based on a tale from the 'Nichts Alhmbr'n,' a tale Sahara identified. Why do the Nights appear everywhere we go, especially in our
past lives?

Cachay felt an inner pride. The document did not trigger any memories, but she felt happy to receive a past life recall in some form. The
group thought her a curmudgeon doubting the work, but she was growing fond of this past life nonsense. In need of it.

Suddenly Cachay felt guilty at her pleasure. People were dying! She
stuffed the paper in her purse and reached her desk, ready for a new
onslaught of anxious phone calls.

16

———≈≈≈———

September 13. Day 3 (2nd day after Impact).

Because of Sahara's distress over the attacks, Dr. Lake suggested she rest at home during the final days of her pregnancy. She had chosen Dr. Lake because Dr. Hajjaj had insisted on six months of bed rest, but she needed to be active, now more than ever. Immobile, her distress could be worse for the twins. Ignoring all advice, she went back to work when the public libraries re-opened. The government had issued a list of banned books because of their incendiary nature. Terrorism was being equated with Islam, which meant Sahara's beloved texts would be banned. She needed to be at the front lines of this outrageous action.

It was worse than she feared. Librarians were asked to track borrowers of targeted books, such as weapons manuals, anarchic political tracts, or the *Qu'ran*. Next they'll be arresting children reading Ali Baba! Refusing to support policy against the First Amendment, during the first hour of her ill-advised day at work Sahara shot off angry emails to the state and federal library systems.

At lunch she should have calmed herself for the twins' sake, but instead she called Prof. Agib, her thesis advisor at the University of Chicago. With little greeting, she began:

"What's happening at the Oriental Institute? It's already a fascist state at my suburban public library. If this is a new world order, I hate it. I can't imagine what the Feds will do with the largest holding of Middle Eastern materials. Or what they'll do to the faculty."

"I am fine, Sahara, but thank you for the call. We're holding our breath for a backlash, but so far so good. It's U of C, you know, a tolerant community. There've been a few calls for translators, for whatever's about to happen. No one's banning any books."

Sahara was relieved, but said goodbye when he asked for her latest chapter. She called other friends and colleagues in the field, worried especially for her Muslim friends. Everyone was shaken and nervous, but except for some unpleasant looks on the train, no one was hurt. One young scholar who wore a veil had been scared to leave her three-year-old daughter at daycare. But the child had been safe, and her neighbors had offered their homes as safe havens in case of retaliation.

Later when Sahara signed an online petition against the book banning, a squirrely librarian warned she would end up on a government checklist. Sahara answered defiantly, "I'm an Arabic scholar; if they don't have my name already, they do now."

Toward closing, Sahara received an unexpected visitor. She had not seen Bax since the attacks, so he was glad to see him. But he was hesitant to speak. Last time he came to the library, they had processed the revelation that in his previous life Bax had been Sahara's sister, who died when they were children. It was a difficult, transformative talk, leading to Bax's commitment to Ooma. Sahara smiled: Bax feels safe coming here when things are difficult. She liked this change in their relationship, so much better than the changes in the world.

They spoke quietly at a table near the periodicals, tenderly asking each other how they were holding up. Then Bax asked if Sahara had received the series of recalls about the origin of the Nights as an Arabic text. Sahara had sensed them floating in her mind, but was too preoccupied with Amar and Naji to focus on them. Plus, the Arab lives were confused with others, like Draill U.

127

"I think we all had access to them," Bax said. "Bizarre. Thought I was crazy."

Sahara touched his hand. "You must've gone through a lot going to the Towers." Now Sahara felt like a big sister. "Why don't you see Dr. Machiyoko? To help with the shock."

"But I'm great! My past lives made me such a freakin' scaredy cat. My world has changed!"

"The whole world has changed. Even our falsely elected President has come into his own."

"The war on terror," Bax said. "I've had my own personal war on terror these past years, in my soul. But as I walked to the Twin Towers, as I saw them crumble, I wasn't scared."

"You've overcome your fears? That's amazing." Sahara was dubious, but did not wish to threaten Bax's positive mood. "Now tell me about the recalls. Everything." Bax astonished Sahara with the Seven Kisses tales. The qaraq had changed the Scheherazade story!

The uptight librarian crept up. "You're talking about the *Arabian Nights*? How could you?"

Sahara's eyes were daggers. Grabbing Bax, she packed up her things, and left the closing to her colleague. They sat on a bench near the library as Bax continued. When he got to the fifth kiss, his memory of Sheikh Ba'Tr's early life, Sahara insisted on the details and Bax complied.

The Tale of the Basran Spy

What was I, Ba'Tr, to do? I wanted so much more. I wanted to see a wider world. A new world order. A vision of life beyond this world. So I studied.

Newest translations of oldest Greeks. Pythagorean tenets of reincarnation. Surprised by early Christian writings on subject. More recent

Manichaeism spread past life credo to Sasan Persia. What about Islam? Reincarnation in some Shi'a sects. Began collecting texts.

Scholarly life not enough for me. Looked to Basra's burgeoning port. Easy to gain fortune in Abbasid Empire. Access to many cultures. Many beliefs. On docks I learned from great Arab navigators. Julius Caesar recorded Druids' reincarnation as core creed. Buddhism spread from India to China. The more I heard the more I saw truth. Metempsychosis dominant belief in the world. North South West and East.

During reign of Harun al-Rashid I sought every work on reincarnation. Visited Baghdad for information. Wahid blocked my access to books. Sought revenge at Barmaki majlis. Turned court against Sahra. Embarrassed Wahid. Sweet. Barmaki clan took me under wing. Introduced me to powerful people, beautiful women. Then Vizier Ja'far lay with Harun's sister. Clan exiled. Ja'far hanged by neck. I reverted to court failure.

Retreated to Basra. Baghdad a past life. Read deeper into Buddhist thought. Soul conceived as number of vortices or whorls. At death vortices spin off. Parts of soul pass to other beings. We contain elements of each other. Upset by this idea. Preserve my soul as I want it? Avoid death to avoid afterlife? I had lived over a century! Maybe destined for eternal life. Hu Ma's arrival fortuitous. Magic sex worked! Terrible about her coma. Returned to my youthful self.

Now I wanted more from life than ever! Bored with Basra. Wandered docks. Sex with foreign travelers. Even secretive Umayyads from Spain. The 'other' Islamic court in Cordova. Met Hasan, Umayyad page boy. Confided my true feelings. Abbasid court fell apart after Harun's death. Empire divvied up to losers. Hasan loved my anti-Baghdadism. Invited me to speak to his masters. Cordovan spies. Wanted goods on Caliphate.

Could not blur the borders anymore. Had to make a choice. Voice deep inside my head. "Be done with it and become celibate." No logical sense. But felt right on a cellular level. Went to work for Umayyad court. Traded secrets about my trade secrets. Felt good to be subversive.

What did a career as a spy have to do with my fascination with rein-carnation? My wanting to taste a new world? My escape into past lives became escape into world of intrigue. I was invited to Spanish court. al-Andalus. Umayyads there a century in exile. Court of al-Rahman II. Met at gate of Cordova with great respect. Eight decades feeling inferior in Basra washed away in eight seconds.

Budding culture. Bursting with youthful energy. Fiction taking hold. Arabic versions of story collections making rounds. Islamicized adapta-tions. *The Thousand Nights.* Old familiar night tales from my first youth. Scheherazade framed splendid compendium. With changes.

One character bothered me. Originally sex slave to demented Queen. Now slave to adulterous wife of King. First to die. Ignoble. Gratuitous plot detail. I determined to help poor slave. Gave him name. Sa'eed. If sex slave, make it good. Favorite lover of Queen.

How sell it to Umayyad scribes? Islamic spin on tale made King sym-bol of Pre-Islamic authority. Immoral behavior takes him down. Sa'eed takes aim at old Empire. Breaches palace wall. Rebel with a cause. Violates Queen to protest King. Contemporized idea of old Abbasid order crumbling. Umayyads as righteous rebels. Fuck Baghdad behind its back.

Court went wild for my variant. Symbol of a new world order. I had found what I sought. Lived out days in al-Andalus. Looked back on eternity of events. Looking forward to Eternity.

ق

Sahara marveled at the gamut of information from the New Year's recalls. She could write a dozen dissertations. It was too much to absorb. She focused on Ba'Tr's variant of Scheherazade. "Bax, your Persian incar-nation was a sex slave, Ba'ash. Ba'Tr cleaned up your image."

"Yes, I was fearless as the Sheikh, and gained power as a revolution-ary slave."

"Ushering in a new world order. I've wondered about Sa'eed. His Arabic nickname means Lucky. When the harem gets decapitated, does he go free out on the street?"

Bax shrugged. "It totally resonates with right now. I'm fearless again. There's a new world order coming. And I felt like a free man out on the street."

Sahara noticed the pink-orange rays of sunset. Talk of a new world gave her mixed feelings. "I've got to go, Bax. The qaraq needs to discuss all the tales. We'll get together soon."

Bax gave Sahara a farewell hug. She felt good in his arms. The conversation had been wonderful. He ached to see her go, but enjoyed a renewed sense of well-being. How could he feel so good at such a horrible time? Is such chaos, 9/11 or Ba'Tr's complex life, always necessary to find new order in the world?

17

—⌇∾∾∾⌇—

September 13. Day 3.

Verle saw Elvira Young sitting quietly as he walked by the sanctuary. Even for volunteers like Elvi, there had been no time to chat during the Unitarian Church's emergency work. Verle was on his way to supervise unloading of donated goods, but he ducked into the sanctuary.

"Ready for your break, young man?" Elvi said, before Verle could speak.

"A pleasant fantasy, Miss Elvi," Verle said. "I can spare eleven seconds."

"You're exhausted," she scolded. "Sit. Besides, there are things to discuss."

Verle was in his nineties, a remarkable age for the church's handyman. "I am feeling a bit poorly. Give me a minute with the boss. I'll get a break if the King gives his permission."

Forty-five minutes later Verle and Elvi sat down in To A Tea, a cafe on Abbey Street, the hip Glenclaire shopping district near the church. Though it was the first time Elvi had met Verle privately, her ritualistic chai tea service felt very familiar. Elvi was concerned with everyone's welfare. Verle filled her in, but itched to ask the facilitator what to make of his World Types recall.

"Remember the qaraq's collective lifetime as parts of a single dragonfly?" Elvi asked. "You were the brain, Verlin. You'll know what to do with the World Types."

Verle never pushed Elvi for more. "Fine. But there's something else. About Miss Cachay's Draill U bio. Appearing out of the blue. Know anything?"

Elvi smiled wickedly, but answered indirectly. "Remember being Dean of Draill U?

"As Do'en I produced a work by an old friend, a composer named Xlami. Highly provocative, but artistically successful as proof of Ctatlovian theory, the stuff of Cachay's lifetime."

"But you canceled the production, and estranged your beloved granddaughter, Siyam."

"Sahara. I also remember Ooma's self, a perky virtuoso xalatangist."

"Who you were so taken with," Elvi said, "because of your sad love life at Draill U."

"Really?" Verle trailed off, caught in Elvi's entrancing spell.

"Like to hear more? It would almost complete the set of lifetimes in that Sci-Fi World."

"So you *are* an expert on World Types!" The woman could be downright exasperating. But Verle could not resist the offer. Elvi poured more tea and told the tale.

The Little Known Tale of Do'en Waco Kvevely

There were other Do'ens of Draill U, perhaps an entire lineage, but no one thinks of that institution's history without thinking of Kvevely, to the point that, although he was once a student himself at the venerable arts conservatory, no one remembers his discipline. He studied on the Isle of Whakatan, but what was his talent: whakatangi (he accompanied Ctatlo at her historic recital), whakatang (his friendship with ecoscorist Xlami suggests this), or whakatani (his eagerness as Do'en to revive old scores implies acquaintance with the conductor's craft)?

He is remembered as the powerfully influential leader of Draill U, an adventurous supporter of wild talent and inter-disciplinary collaboration, and yet a conservative administrator of student discipline, faculty rigor, and budgetary limits. Added into this contradictory mix is his less publicized fixation on Pr Ctatlo: although his alleged violation of her was brushed off as sensationalist media, most of his unorthodox decisions as Do'en can be traced to Ctatlovian favoritism: hiring Ctatlo, encouraging her cross-training ideas, building aquatunnels to indulge her outdoor phobia, protecting her tenure during abusive teaching experiments, and commissioning theaters to house multiperfs.

The truth behind this anomaly to his otherwise sage judgment is that Kvevely chased after Ctatlo like a mythical hero chases after an elusive bird with a treasure in its beak: Kvevely promoted Ctatlo's career to such ends that she must have felt he was indebted to her from a past life. If Kvevely was Draill U's greatest leader, then Ctatlo was behind everything he accomplished.

There is one little known aspect of their relationship: around the time Kvevely proposed to her, something crushing happened between them. Ctatlo had a torrid affair with the whakatang Xlami, Kvevely's oldest friend; in intimate moments she observed his composing process, deriving her theory of inspiration coming from otherworldly sources. The affair was short-lived, Ctatlo returned to comfort Kvevely, but she had clearly drawn a romantic line in the sand. Never wishing to hurt Ctatlo, Kvevely took his ire out on Xlami, and ended his patronage; out of guilt, the Do'en revived his friend's brilliant ecoscore posthumously for the controversial production of *Asd and Ajd*.

After painful rejection by Ctatlo, Kvevely became aware that the academic community discouraged his bachelorhood as undignified. So the Do'en chose a wife among recent alumna, and had three children with her. It was a loveless marriage, and worse, a loveless fatherhood: his wife divorced him, noisily, after thirteen years; following a respectable period of time, Kvevely re-proposed to Ctatlo, unsuccessfully. His eldest son chose a field as far from Draill U as possible, Thermal Cybernautics; his second son moved to another planet, spitefully choosing Pnorienti, a world with no sexual taboos, and lit bonfires of scandal for the Do'en; his youngest, the beautiful tarakani, Ail-d'Roc, tolerated her father's coldness with uncomplaining resolve, graduated Draill U with top honors, famously danced with the Tarakan Royau, but eschewed a teaching job at Draill U to marry Schnaour Lochitrae VII, the Octowheel magnate.

Ail-d'Roc never gave up on the Do'en, so she encouraged her adorable child Siyam to follow in her toesteps and attend Draill U; before an untimely death from Szugmma Disease, Ail-d'Roc made Siyam promise to extract every ounce of love from her hard-hearted grandfather. This task was easier done than said, for, with a heart full of remorse from family estrangement, Kvevely gave Siyam everything he had refused his wife and children. Shamelessly favoring her at Draill U, the Do'en ran into trouble by blocking her performance with the telepactor Amat, her radiant partner onstage and true love. In doing so he lost Siyam, a karmic dagger to his heart.

At the base of his grief was his unrequited passion for Ctatlo, who had passed away years previously. He saw that, despite all the intellectual prowess he had developed, all the academic excellence he had nurtured, and all the creative energy he had fostered, his life came down to his love for Ctatlo, which had both sustained and destroyed him; it was as if she had set an emotional trap for him during their undergraduate years, which finally had sprung. But no, he had set the trap.

After his fatal cancelation of the *Asd and Asj* production at Draill U, he retired to the Kowya Heights, his home filled with books and objects that spanned his career; the Do'en's study served as a miniature universe of his life at Draill U. He reconciled with Siyam, but only after she was convinced he had had nothing to do with her true love's disappearance. In the end, he realized that no success of the mind could assuage a failure of the heart.

ق

Elvi finished the tale. "Forgive me for fillng your restful break with such sadness."

"Indeed," Verle replied. "Miss Elvi, does my organizational soul prevent me from a real emotional experience in the qaraq?"

"Waeo Kvevely had a real emotional experience, Verle," she began. "And despite the organizational features of the World Types structure, your work with it will have a real emotional impact on the group. Trust in yourself."

Verle smiled. "One more thing: if I am the brain of our dragonfly, who's the heart?"

Elvi returned the smile. "All of you. You're all the heart."

136

18

—∞∞∞—

September 11. 10:35 A.M. Hour 2.

Amar risked looking over his shoulder to see the Tower coming down. He had been right in feeling everything contained a potential danger. Ooma was sentient enough to run alongside him. As visibility was blocked by ash and dust, and the sound of the building's collapse was deafening, Ooma found Amar's hand. They kept moving blindly, several blocks away when the roar ceased.

They wandered the streets, blocked by crowds in one direction, doubling back toward the Twin Towers in another direction. Clasping hands, they also saw glimpses of memories and visions from each other and other qaraqis. They were students at Draill U, rehearsing a scene. They saw Naji lying in his crib, staring straight up into an unknown universe. They saw the den during the New Year's party. Embarassed that Amar saw her kissing Bax, Ooma focused on the street reality.

She was able to recognize the outline of Trinity Church, and led them toward the graveyard. A perfect place to rest our weary bones, Ooma thought, and Amar heard her in his mind. Is it safe here, Amar wondered: safe enough to stop. They sat at the edge of the sidewalk, their backs against the graveyard's iron fence. Neither of them could talk. They had been through too much, and minutes ago had faced feelings for each other that invested too much emotion. They needed to rest.

Ooma nestled into Amar's shoulder and the physical contact sent them back to the New Year's party. Ooma drifted off into Bax's fifth kiss. A new story unfolded in Ooma and Amar's minds together. It was Naji's lifetime, the innocent child soul of the qaraq. A gift to help them unwind, their souls received a breath of fresh air from the vision.

The Tale of the Two Albino Elephants

Once there was a poor mahout from northwestern India, who lost his wife to an incurable disease. He was left with his young daughter, Jali, and two of the strangest elephants ever seen. Being nearly white with pinkish eyes made them sacred to some, demonic to others. As a mahout, Narob trained and took care of the elephants, Zara and Zala, well-behaved and responsive creatures.

Narob, the mahout, struggled to be sole parent to his daughter, but who can resist a father who dotes on elephants? Zara adored Jali, Jali worshipped Zala, Zala followed Narob everywhere, and Narob was extremely fond of Zara. It was a happy family circle. Narob loved watching Jali grow, play, and help with the elephants. He did not know how to talk with her, other than about care of the animals, so he made up stories to share with her at night. Jali loved the tales, which Narob had heard from various sources. As she grew older, Jali wanted newer and longer stories, so Narob took to the market to hear fresh tales. When Jali was old enough he brought her along.

Narob was not a political man, preferring the company of elephants to men. But when Abbasid forces from Baghdad invaded his district, the safest thing for Jali, Zara, and Zala would be Narob's conversion to Islam. He was not a devout Hindu, though he never missed the festivals, where he decorated Zara and Zala for the town parade. Now he had to wake up from his religious sleepiness, and follow strict rituals to fit the new order. He did so with uncomplaining devotion, knowing it protected his odd family. He felt guilty he had betrayed his kind, but he had a sensation deep in his soul that he was the one betrayed, and he should run away from his homeland.

When Jali was ten years of age, they brought Zara and Zala to the market to perform tricks for the crowd. On Jali's insistence, Narob gave her the task of recruiting an audience by leading Zala to the central square and announcing the show. That evening, a crowd had already formed, and Jali saw that a representative of the Caliph was recruiting for an army. Behind him was an imperial officer, who frightened Jali with his stern appearance. After the show, the officer approached Narob with an offer. He wished that the two elephants travel with his battalion back west. He promised they would not engage in military operations. He hoped instead to present the unusual specimens to the Caliph.

Narob could not refuse the officer. He would only lose his precious animals by force. By accompanying them on the arduous voyage, he could insure their well-being and perhaps receive a handsome reward. He explained to Jali what was to happen, and that the safest thing would be for her to remain in India with her aunts and uncles. She refused, throwing a tantrum the likes of which Narob had never witnessed. The relatives saw the wisdom in leaving Jali with them, but many thought Narob and the elephants would be grateful for the child's presence.

Narob made it known to the platoon that the elephants had a special empathy for the child, could sense a threat to her from any distance, and would crush any heinous perpetrator. After this pronouncement, the family received great kindnesses from the soldiers, officers, cooks, and handlers on the long voyage to Baghdad. It was an arduous task to procure enough nourishment for Zara and Zala, who were not used to long hours of walking, especially with heavy goods on their backs. Narob was often in direct competition with the growing army for food, whose sullen men grumbled about the two huge feeders.

For months the army traveled, crossing through Mansura and out of India, passing many colorful towns in the Samanid Emirate, and finally entering Iraq and the City of Light. Narob enjoyed each new town, for he heard new tales to entertain his daughter. Jali loved the story of Sharazad, in many different versions from India to Persia to Iraq. In old Persian versions, an evil Queen murdered Sharazad's children. This version gave Jali nightmares, so Narob discounted it immediately. In a splendid version from the Affarid territories, one child survived to become Bahram Gur, the legendary Sassanian Shah. Narob understood that Jali's preoccupation with the children was her way of overcoming her grief for her missing mother.

When they reached Baghdad, Narob learned that a story glorifying Persian royalty would get him thrown in a dungeon. So Narob learned the latest version of the tale, where the brilliant Sharazad reforms the King. Jali adored this powerful woman. Most storytellers in the Baghdadi market were content to end the tale with the birth of a single child. Knowing that the story was a frame for a vast collection called *The Thousand Marvelous Tales*, Narob and Jali enjoyed a secret joke that during a thousand nights the King and Sharazad could have produced three children.

They transported the elephants to Ar Raqqah, where Caliph Harun al-Rashid had moved his administrative headquarters. The Caliph greeted Narob and his retinue with open arms, for he loved all that was new and fascinating from his territories. The albino elephants were a symbol of his ownership of the world, and a visual reminder of the greatness of Allah. Narob and Jali were given high honors, Zara and Zala fed extremely well, and all were offered small gifts, to them a fortune.

Their pleasures were short-lived. To establish relations with the Holy Roman Emperor, Charlemagne, Harun sent a water clock parading automated knights on the hour. To reciprocate, Charlemagne sent Harun Spanish horses and colorful Frisian cloaks. With the appearance of Zara and Zala, the Caliph's ambassadors saw the ultimate gift for their European rival. Before long Narob and Jali were on their next voyage with the elephants. Byzantine border wars raged, but the elephant caravan had diplomatic immunity to travel toward Francia.

Narob enjoyed the bright blue skies over the new lands. Jali delighted in the blue fabrics in the markets. The elephants gazed at the blue eyes of the pale settlers. At the Frankish court, Arab envoys introduced the animals as Abul and Abbas, portraying the giant beasts as the might of Islam. When Narob heard the new names, his heart sank, for it suggested his detachment from the elephants, and the end of his time with them.

But it was not to be: bewildered by the white gargantuans, the court begged Narob and lovely Jali to continue to be the elephants' caretakers. Their *mahouts*, Narob corrected, proudly. But as their good will promoted Harun's tolerant attitude toward the infidel, the Caliph's allowance of freedoms spawned dangerous attitudes. As Jali flirted with young Frankish men, conspiracy brewed among the new Umayyads in Spain. As the elephants bowed to delighted Europeans, the Idrisid clan in the Maghreb, the Aghlabid clan in Tunis, and the Kharijites all gained independence from Baghdad. As anti-Abbasid revolts exploded everywhere, Narob celebrated his good fortune.

ق

Amar and Ooma identified with the happiness felt by the elephants, Jali, and Narob in the midst of a crumbling, endangered Empire. They too sat in the midst of chaos and catastrophe, but felt safe and happy in each other's arms. Ooma had recalled her lifetime as the elephant Homma once, also set in Baghdad. It was not a restful delight like this recall, and she had panicked over it during a business trip with Amar. To escape her fears she had curled up in a hotel bed with him. Again, safe and happy despite horrors of the universe.

Naji's light-hearted memory was enough to allow them to relax and face each other again. In touch with their attraction, but still in trance, their minds returned to the New Year's party, but after all the kisses and past life visions, after Amar caught Ooma and Bax in his den, and after

141

Bax rushed out of the room. Amar and Ooma had stood there in the den, shame and desire loitering in the air, and something had passed between them, something unspoken, something wildly captured in their eyes. After a moment, Ooma assumed it was her boss' angry criticism of her.

In the present moment at the Trinity Church graveyard, their eyes met again, and they knew something more had passed between them that night. It had been a moment of pure honesty that communicated their deepest feelings for each other. They recognized the same feelings now, the same physical yearnings, and the same confusions. Amar was married, to a powerful woman, and Ooma was romatically entangled with Bax. They needed to take care of each other, not to pleasure each other, but tend to their wounds and traumatized souls.

Amar saw the confusing cluster of feelings show on Ooma's face as a stricken, wild creature. It was too much for her handle! How could he entertain such desires in this moment? They had revealed too much. He pulled away from her and sank back onto the graveyard wall. Unlike the childlike Narob, he had to face the current crisis and find help for Ooma.

19

—⟨ϱ⟩ϱ⟩ϱ⟩—

September 19. Day 9.

Sahara and Cachay were admitted to Glenclaire Hospital within hours of each other. Sahara had been anticipating a hospital emergency for eight months. Once they had begun seeing each other again, Amar had been concerned about her health. He did not want to repeat the scare during her pregnancy with Naji. After he returned from the Twin Tower attacks, Amar was even more vigilant. He insisted Sahara go to the hospital at the first sign of spotting and abdominal discomfort. After she had almost lost him, how could she deny his request for her safety? At Glenclaire Hospital, Dr. Lake wanted her under observation, perhaps until her due date, two weeks away.

Cachay's admittance was different. It had been a difficult week since the attacks. Cachay was ready to throw the phone out a window. Her boss, feeling pressure from superiors far up the governmental chain, made Cachay's life even worse. Cachay's strength was admirable, pushing sixty, fighting the fight on the state and federal level after a national emergency. But it was too much: mid-afternoon she fainted at her desk. At the hospital doctors diagnosed a mini-stroke.

"Are the drugs good at least?" Zack teased, sitting next to his mother's hospital bed.

"Zachary Goodkin, will you ever outgrow the Sixties?" When her son shook his head 'No,' Cachay sighed. "The medication is quite relaxing, if you wish to know." Maybe too relaxing?

"It's good for you," Zack said. "No joke, it's been a hell of a week."

"That worries me, Zachary. If I can't handle the pressure this week, how will I keep doing this work? I thought doing pro bono legal work was the right thing for me. But beside the hardship, I'm not cut out for helping others." Under the medication, Cachay's negative thinking wandered through her life. "I've failed everyone. My first husband. And your father."

"You're weirding me out, but you haven't failed me, Ma," Zack said. "At least you're not alone here. Sahara's checked in, on the floor above you. Making the twins safe for democracy."

Cachay's head spun. What was wrong? "My goodness, is everything all right?" The IV port in her arm felt tight and uncomfortable. Sounds in the hall of nurses and machine were menacing.

Zack saw his mother's unease and regretted burdening her. "You both just need your beauty rest." He would not tell her anymore, but he saw her concern for Sahara.

Porcy walked in holding Naji's hand. "I've brought some entertainment." Recognizing Cachay, Naji ran over to the bed and took hold of her arm. As Cachay delighted in the boy's presence, Porcy spoke quietly to Zack. "Everything's stable. Dr. Lake's going to do a full exam."

As Zack and Porcy consulted, Cachay's disorientation from the medication increased. She clutched Naji's little hands and closed her eyes. She felt a deep stillness for a blessed moment touching the child. But she sensed something else. What was wrong with his mother? What was wrong with Naji? Panic erased the deep stillness.

Cachay opened her eyes. In her hallucinating vision Naji now wore a white lab coat, at least a foot too long for him. Porcy and Zack were gone. Had they given up on her? The hospital room shimmered in a dreamlike light. The intercom and beeping machines provided an eerie soundtrack.

The Encounter with the Bobed Woman

Naji the dwarf doctor picked up her chart. An administrative voice boomed, as if reading:

"SYMPTOMS: Mild to severe depression. Rash behind the ears. Sleep-exploring."

"Sleep-exploring," Cachay said. "What in Heaven's name is that?"

In response, Naji tucked the chart into the billowing folds of his coat and beckoned.

Cachay threw off the hospital bed covers to discover that she was dressed in furs and jewels. Without thinking twice about it, she got down and followed Naji out of the room. The halls of the hospital seemed endless. At times she and Naji retraced their steps, at other times they reached a dead end, and once Naji opened a door with a golden key, directing them out of the hospital.

Naji pulled out the chart and she heard the voice again:

"VITALS: stable. STABLE: away in a manger. MANGER: protect the babies."

Cachay felt uncomfortable when she followed Naji outdoors. There were lovely gardens with hidden bowers, but Cachay knew there were no such places at Glenclaire Hospital. Shouldn't she be back in her room? She tried to keep up with the little doctor, but he disappeared frequently. She glimpsed many different scenes: Naji all alone in tears; the little doctor in consultation with an invisible figure; Naji chatting with twin, imperceptible forms. They seemed to be fading away.

Cachay awoke briefly from the dream state, the little boy still holding her hand, a plaintive expression on his face. He needed her to see more, understand more, so she drifted off.

145

"DIAGNOSIS: Transient Ischemic Attack, brought on by high brood pleasure."

Cachay emerged from the endless gardens to discover Naji in a public space full of beings dashing to and fro; the openness of the space made Cachay feel even more vulnerable and anxious. Naji chatted with a robed woman advising everyone around her. Cachay took in the scene, so uncannily familiar that she was jittery. She did not notice Naji leave.

"Where did he go, the little doctor?" Cachay did not remember approaching the robed woman. "What is this place? Who are you people?"

"If you do not know, Cta, then it goes well for you." Cachay found the name Cta strange but familiar. The woman had a calming demeanor. "You do Nozh a great service."

"What service? How could I possibly help him?"

"You became lost in this adventure, yet hung onto a thread of Nozh's image to guide you. You maintained your Self, and the world in which you belong. Otherwise you would recognize this place. Nozh learned he can pursue something, become lost, and still maintain his Self. From you."

Cachay did not know what the robed woman was talking about in the least. But she remembered a distant, old land where she too had observed someone, perhaps this Nozh. He had enabled her to learn something: how to breathe in air as well as underwater. How extraordinary!

She asked the robed woman, "Is Nozh lost? What is wrong with his mother? With him?"

"Lost in Time, pursuing a phantom. He will not find what he longs for, but he will find what he needs. His mother, and you, and the others also need it very badly."

Cachay thought hard about what she might need. "I am lost back in my world, aren't I?"

"You doubt yourself there, yes. But doubting is good. It will lead you to your correct path."

"So I am on the wrong path," Cachay pressed. "What should I be doing?"

"Make fair your inner Self, Cta, and you shall make fair your outer Self."

The second time Cachay opened her eyes in the hospital, Naji was gone, but Elvi sat next to her bed, with a warm smile, like the robed woman. Elvi whispered something significant, but Cachay could not hear. Instead, ideas popped into her drug-filled head: 1) she was not ready to return to her world; 2a) she had to find Naji and guide him back from the 17th Century; 3b - 1) this mission had risky consequences, but if the dangers threw into question her ability to help others, all the better; 11) it is not about selfish greed versus selfless service; 13²) one can help without being sheltering or meddling; 77 – x) it is worthy enough to consider the next worthy act.

"TREATMENT: Scheherazade notices dawn approaching."

ق

September 21. Day 11.

The third time Cachay awoke from her vision, confused and thirsty, it was a day and a half after she had been admitted to Glenclaire Hospital. Her chart showed an argument raging between her doctors about whether or not she had been in a coma. Although she sensed her son had spent many hours by her side, he was not there now. Elvi sat gazing at the sunrise.

Cachay gladly accepted a cup of water. The sights and sounds of the hospital were normal now, neither menacing nor bizarre. Cachay sipped her water and thought back to her unconscious state. Had Elvi been there? Was Elvi really here now? What had Naji seen in the interlife? She vaguely remembered that the twins were in danger. But she had been too pre-occupied with her own personal matters. The robed woman said

147

she had helped Naji. Had she cared? In horror, Cachay realized she was again focused on herself. She asked Elvi, "Did you check on Sahara?"

"Yes." Elvi frowned. "And you. And also on Naji."

Cachay was afraid to ask about the twins. "You heard Naji's reacted strangely recently?"

Elvi hesitated. "I knew he had not always been with us."

Cachay brightened. "But he's fine now. He's been a brave boy these days."

"If *you're* back with us, I know he's safe. For now."

Cachay did not know what this meant. But she understood she had been through something difficult with Naji. *The twins were in danger.* She put down the water on the bed tray. "I need to rest."

"You rest. But you're fine," Elvi said. "They're talking about discharging you soon. I need to see Sahara. The eleven days are almost up."

20

—◦◦◦—

September 20. Day 10.

The day after his mother slipped into unconsciousness, Zack passed the time at the hospital playing with designs for his website logo. He had brought a small pile of books into Cachay's room: 16ᵗʰ Century Chinese designs, ancient Bengali alphabets, and Maya calendar iconography. The geometric shapes of the old Mayan world captivated Zack. Deftly sketching copies on a steno pad, his eye and hand took control of his mind. He was drawn into a memory of his childhood in a Maya community (in the early Classical Era, according to the art book).

Or so Zack surmised on his way to Dr. Machiyoko's office later that day. Despite the therapist's ambivalence about having a patient whose past lives were entangled with hers, Zack argued he had work to do separate from past lives. Considering Cachay's mini-stroke, it would have been cruel for the therapist to refuse him.

After checking on Cachay's condition and Zack's feelings about it, the therapist moved on to the new relationship. "What's bothering you about Jobim? Are you still grieving for François?"

"I loved François, and couldn't commit to anyone after he died. But that's not it. I met Jobim during a terrorist attack, for God's sake! It's a relationship founded on a catastrophe."

"And you're sure the catastrophic feeling isn't related to François' death?"

"I'm not sure of anything." Zack paused. "Doc, there's been no sex. Well, little."

The therapist let silence fill the space. "Zack, do you feel guilty getting pleasure?"

"Why, because so many died, and I got lucky that day?"

"Yes. Survivor's guilt. I think this is a real relationship, but there's accompanying guilt. It will take time. But you deserve this happiness, Zack." Zack did not respond. "Zack, I understand the complexity of your feelings, but honestly I have so many patients suffering serious trauma."

"This is triage, isn't it? I found love, so take a number."

"I promised I'd work with you on the archives, explore our past life relationship there."

Zack felt ridiculous trying to convince his therapist to work with him! She'll bail on the archives, too. He had an idea. "Here's a deal. Something else bothers me about your rejection, but I want to think about it. But I'll tell you a new tale if you swear in blood to work on the archives."

Diana could not resist a new story. And Zack knew it. "Stinker. What's the lifetime?"

"It's a new place for the qaraq, a new World, as Verle says. I was a child in a Maya city, but far back in their history, before the 4th Century Sassanians."

"Why relate it to the Persians? They're on the other side of the world."

"How about that," Zack said. "Unbelievably, the two are related. Check it out."

The Tale of the Child Sacrifice from Uaxactun

No fair! You were only playing with the ball. They can't do this to you, can they? Mother and Father can't help; they were killed in the war with Tikal. They'll kill all of us from Uaxactun. Their *ahau*, Great-Jaguar-Paw, wants to make Tikal the most powerful of the Maya, and won't stop at anything, even hurting a child. Or a ballplayer. The ballgame is everything to us, Father said.

Great-Jaguar-Paw was not satisfied with capturing us. He had to defeat us in the ballgame. But he underestimated Uaxactun: we have great players and we humiliated Tikal. So Great-Jaguar-Paw banned us from the ballgame. You didn't know that included you, a child playing in the street, a rotten squash for a ball. Like when the twin hero Xbalanque tricked the Lords of the Underworld.

It wasn't fair! You didn't mean to go against any new rules. You weren't even playing the ballgame, just pretending the squash was your twin brother's head, after the Lords of Xibalba tested him in Fire House. The next thing the Tikal soldiers will say is you were making too much noise playing the ballgame, like when the Lords of Xibalba dragged the twins to the Underworld.

But they didn't say that. They grabbed you and put you in the pen and yelled at you though you're just a child. The Tikal woman explained the bad thing they were going to do to you. To please the Gods, Tikal needed human blood. Blood sacrifice. Like when the Lords of Xibalba sacrificed the twins in the ballgame, you asked? That is an old story, she answered, but yes.

Now you wait on the line to the temple. No one going in comes out again, not with a head. You are not scared, you are brave. You will show them. You will show them what happens when they don't fight fair. The

151

twins tricked the Lords of Xibalba by sacrificing themselves and coming back to life. The Lords were so impressed they wanted such powers, so they had the twins sacrifice them. Of course the twins never resurrected the Lords and conquered them for good.

The only way to be reborn is through the blood sacrifice, especially when they chop off your head. All of Tikal will want this secret of resurrection. You will let them play on the ballcourt, the playing arena for fighting, death, and rebirth. They will kill each other, lop off each other's heads, and use them for the ball. Then you will punish them for playing the ballgame, for kicking their squash-ball-heads, and you will scold Great-Jaguar-Paw himself for making too much noise and send him down to Xibalba. You won't resurrect any of them! The Lords of the Underworld will thank you for sending their souls, and resurrect Mother and Father so we can be reunited.

You enter the temple bravely. You welcome your blood sacrifice, for then Uaxactun will conquer Tikal. You will be a hero, without a twin, all reward for yourself. You are so lucky this day!

It is your turn. Take me! Mother and Father will be so proud. Take my blood! Tikal cannot see the tricks in store for it. Take my head! Uaxactun forever!

ق

When Zack finished, Dr. Machiyoko said, "In your story, the Maya had hero myths about reincarnation, played out the on the ballcourt. An important story for the qaraq. We need to heal ourselves by hearing about the universality of past life beliefs. See, my objectivity's down the drain."

"I see your problem," Zack said. "That's food for thought for a qaraq meeting, but it does me no good sorting out Jobim."

Diana ignored Zack. "I also felt a connection between this sacrifice and Ugrit's suicide. Ooma's incarnation stabbed himself with a sacrificial

152

knife from the Red Isle. But how can the knife magically travel from Africa to Meso-America over twenty-five centuries."

"Think that's odd? After my recall in the hospital room, I continued drawing the Maya designs in trance. I saw a bizarre image of a micro-organism drawing graphs to convince a carnivore to stop reducing the population. Then I drew a chart outlining karmic influence between the Maya ballplayer, the Maya child, Sharzad, and Purzai, the Persian woman who Queen Uzmeth sacrificed. When I told Elvi later, she explained that karmic pairings can have such cross-World connections."

"Elvi has been super active with us, compared to her usual coolness," Dr. Machiyoko said.

"And all roads lead to Scheherazade," Zack said. "We can't escape our roles in her story."

Dr. Machiyoko agreed. "When Shah Zaman asks to marry Dunyazade, she insists they live with her sister. Your archetype, Zaman, just imitates his brother. My character has balls."

"Thanks for the castration complex, Doc. Dunya was a slave in Persia. How'd she get to be Scher's royal sis?"

"We'll find out one of these days." Diana grinned. "Time's up."

Zack nodded. He may not have resolved a single personal problem, but he had completely engaged the therapist. It had been a fabulous session.

21

——⌇⌇⌇——

October 18. Week 6.

A month after Sahara and Cachay's release from the hospital, and two weeks after Naji's birthday party, Sahara called a qaraq meeting. Dr. Machiyoko was surprised by Sahara's request after all that had happened with her family, but no one denied how good it would feel to get together.

Diana and Zack helped Verle clean up, but as the other members entered the attic space, they commented bluntly on the clutter from the archives. Cachay tripped over a pile of Edgar Cayce books. Diana resented the group's criticism and realized she was feeling anxious about the meeting. Since Porcy claimed she had found the attic for meetings, she offered her real estate acumen to find a property to house the archives. Or maybe she could find somewhere else in the church. Porcy's pushiness made Verle nervous; he asked her to hold off until he talked with his colleagues.

It was the first time the qaraqis processed the stories where they changed the Scheherazade myth, during the transition from the Persian *Thousand Tales* to the Arabic *Thousand and One Nights*.

"Elvi, how did we share so many lifetimes in each other's minds?" Diana asked.

Elvi intoned her favorite catchphrase. "Everything is possible. The mind-boggling events of 9/11 literally unhinged your minds. Ooma was the catalyst, given what she experienced."

"You guys should have invited her," Bax said. "She's contributed so much."

"Amar says she's made herself scarce since then," Sahara said. "But I am grateful to her. Exploring the origins of the Nights could push me to deliver a chapter to Prof. Agib."

"I'm also happy we shared those recalls, however the devil we did it," Verle said. "The Arab World provides a precedent for a *Multiple* World Type, where we each had thirty to ninety lifetimes."

Diana was tired of hearing about Sahara's research or Verle's theories. What bugged her? "The recalls had emotional depth because they arose out of Bax and Ooma's intense bond."

"Bax, since not everyone received every story, do you feel up to reviewing the material?" Elvi startled Bax with her request. Porcy encouraged him. "You said you overcame your fears. Telling the tales should be a piece of cake." Cornered, Bax agreed, but as he recounted the Seven Kisses tales, his eyes twitched. Diana wondered about his new fearlessness.

When Bax got to Naji's lifetime as the mahout, Elvi inquired after the child. Sahara had thought it best to leave him home, though he had attended other meetings and even participated. "He's talking more baby gibberish, less coherent than most children his age, but more intense."

"At least he's coming out of his fog," Porcy said.

"Only half the time," Sahara said. "At other times I have no idea where he is."

Bax got to the sixth kiss, the last Nights recall he received at the disaster site. Diana recognized her lifetime as a scholar during the disintegration of the Abbasid Caliphate. "Maybe we'll get more wisdom about accessing each other's memories." She was uneasy exposing her memory.

"Or more wisdom about why Bax and Ooma accessed the Arab World at the New Year's party," Verle said. "Let's have it, son." Bax began the story.

The Tale of the House of Wisdom

You would have taken cover in the House of Wisdom, too, if you had lived in Baghdad then. Despite the growing strength of the rival Umayyads in Cordova and the civil wars everywhere, Caliph Ma'mun created the House of Wisdom, an attempt at the world's largest library and scholarly center. The Abbasid House of Wisdom was a refuge from civil strife, a sanctuary for your soul. Entering those splendid walls was like taking a breath of fresh air, even with the stale dust of scrolls, an odd sensation of being replenished and poisoned at the same time.

So many books, manuscripts, papyri, stela, histories, annals, tracts, oratories, suras, hadith, verses. And fictions. It would take seven lifetimes to comb through it all. Here is "The Prisoners of Love" in Latin, Pahlavi, and Arabic. Over there is a new Arabic version of the *Hezir Afsaneh*. You Islamic scholars enjoy slipping in Arabic stories to expand the small core of Indian and Persian tales. And no one can leave the frame tale alone! Including me.

I feel as anxious about one character in the Sharazad tale as I do about the chaos outside the walls of the House of Wisdom. Why am I fascinated with Dunyazad? Sharazad has an accomplice in most versions of the tale, usually a subordinate figure, a slave woman or housekeeper. One of the first Arabic translators made her Sharazad's wet-nurse, a gesture of intimacy I love. If I had my way, I'd make Dunyazad the younger sister, put her at the foot of Sharazad's conjugal bed. What better way to influence the King than by encouraging his happy mood, and begging for a story?

The other scholars mock me at the House of Wisdom for these thoughts. Why would the King allow Sharazad's sister into his marriage bed? The idea is to clean up the story for good Muslim ears, not desecrate it with further sinfulness. Soon you'll have Dunyazad join in the sex, they laugh. I don't dare defend that delicious notion. Sharazad's power disturbs them, so a second female force is too much. Let the Shah's brother advise him, they insist.

It is my turn to laugh: Shah Zaman, the King's brother, is such a weak character that the story needs Dunyazad to add spice. She marries him only to become a Queen. The staunchest opponent to these ideas is Zabbah ibn Sayyar al-Sakkak, an ancient scribe who acquired a little power during Harun's reign, lost it all at a majlis, and now hides in the House of Wisdom. He claims to have created the character, and defends Shah Zaman as if his soul depended on it.

Besides my nemesis Zabbah, there were other colorful characters in the House of Wisdom. Wahid, a kindly old papermaker, collected books and rare objects for the House. He loved showing off his finds: a precious manuscript that purports to be a list of incarnations for a group of souls; an eerie metallic oval piece from the Umayyad palace in Syria, which came to Abbasid coffers after a desert raid; an archaic map that fit around the oval piece, encasing it perfectly.

Yes, you would have enjoyed refuge in the House of Wisdom.

ق

Diana marveled at how she had transformed her Nights archetype. As in the qaraq's other stories, the Persian historical source, Dinzadeh, had improved. "It makes perfect sense she's Scheherazade's sister. A wet-nurse could not have protected her sister, or asked for a story."

"Allah knows what else she accomplished at the foot of the bed," Zack remarked slyly. "Do we really believe that during a thousand nights the King didn't dally with the convivial younger sib?"

Diana bristled at Zack's jocular comments. She felt incensed at Zack's incarnation Zabbah, who opposed her in the House of Wisdom, another sample of their karmic struggle. "Zabbah and Wahid shafted the Persian Uzmeth and her slave Dinzadeh in order to beef up the King, Zaman, and the vizier in the tale. It led to male dominance. Thank God for Scheherazade and Dunyazade!"

Verle cut short Diana's triumph. "What about this list of past lives, from Ba'Tr?"

"It's far-fetched to find past life evidence in the Nights," Cachay said, "so why impose it?"

"I think it's crucial! We need to re-connect to what matters to us." Empassioned, Diana thought back to Zack's argument about not being able to find another therapist. His worry had haunted her, and now she knew why. And why she was feeling so sensitive. The qaraq might be challenged to find professional help that would understand this complex karmic history, but each qaraqi suffered some trauma related to the Twin Towers. The attacks provided an opportunity for a journey of self-discovery. The task of being the qaraq's healer fell to her.

"Looking for reincarnation evidence in human culture can help us recover," Diana said. "Finding the link between past lives and the Nights is crucial and a big piece of our experience."

"Hence it's a Multiple World Type," Verle said, "whether or not it relates to reincarnation."

Diana felt dismissed, like she had in The House of Wisdom. "We need to look deeper into our stories, not just file them away in the right place. As if you could file anything in this mess."

There was a palpable silence in the room as Diana aimed her heated emotions at Verle. Everyone looked to Elvi, more active lately. "Let's all think about the questions raised. It's a lot to absorb at your first meeting back. I suggest Bax finish the tales at another meeting." She looked from Diana to Verle, and then to Sahara. "Are we up for another meeting?" When everyone nodded agreement, Elvi adjourned for the night.

22

———◈◈◈———

September 14. Day 4.

Sahara did not trust her teenage baby-sitters to be with Naji after his bizarre reaction right after the attacks. She looked to the qaraq for help, since she guessed her son's behavior related to the group's shared trance states, the interlife, and all things strange and magical. She was relieved when Porcy offered to spend Friday with Naji while Sahara was at the library.

No matter what she did Porcy could not engage the toddler. She chanted from sacred texts. She read aloud: "However, she received the King's permission," a passage from a fairy tale. Naji stared into space or babbled. Porcy put Naji down for a nap, but he was more outwardly distressed. Comforting the baby, Porcy attempted to see inside his mind. The effort put her into trance state, where she discovered Naji in the interlife World he occupied. Understanding his need to escape there, away from the harsh state of reality, she followed him. But she failed to reach Naji, just as she had failed at baby-sitting. She sat on a bench in the interlife, her soul withered.

Then Porcy saw a luminescent figure beckoning to her. The hypnotic appeal eased her distressed mind. Following the figure into a chamber reserved for quiet discussion, she slipped into a memory of her soul between lifetimes.

The Tale of the Soul and the Spirit Guide

We sat across from each other. I gladly accepted a mug of shai. Returning to conversation with my guide, especially after a difficult death, always renewed me, like someone who had choked on a bone and was revived by clearing the passageway. Breathing a new kind of air.

The spirit guide waited patiently as I sipped my shai. Shai had a wonderfully restorative effect. The guide asked, "What do you remember, Po?"

The first talking point: previous life, as if we had lived it together. "I mustered the Vawr. Built them up with a ritual. So much we know of reincarnation there. So little we think we know."

The guide saw my lack of clarity. "Po, we must deepen our attention on the past lifetime, not its relation to this world. Stay in touch with your passion back there, your forcefulness."

I focused my mind. Distant in my memory were billions of years before the first cells appeared, billions more before simple organisms. During all that time my spirit guide and I had argued about the advent of humanity on Earth, and when I could join that highly anticipated species. Then I tired of waiting, let go of humans, and felt inadequate. My latest lives renewed my yearning.

Reviewing all, I reached a moment of clarity. "That was my first human lifetime on Earth!"

"Yes, focus on the Vawr," the guide said. "Inciting them against the Borzi. The violence."

On the edge of impatience, the spirit pushed for every detail, every battle, every teardrop. I had vindicated my parents, but it was overkill.

My soul's exhilaration at entering the human world had led to extreme behavior. I had been harmful to everyone around me.

"They trusted you," the spirit scolded, "but you are not ready to live as a human."

"But human civilizations will come soon," I said. "I want to be there."

"You cannot contribute to society by bludgeoning everyone in your way. You behaved like an animal, Po, and so that is what you must be in the next life."

I lowered my head in shame, accepting my fate. We rose and walked the streets to a barnlike structure. An unfamiliar spirit met us at the front gates and I said farewell to my guide. The new one had bright red hair, unlike the typical shades of silver of most guides. She led me to a circular sand pit, where I sat. She pulled out a tiny handheld device from under her robe.

"You have been deemed inferior to your potential. You must incarnate as a lower animal form. Something humbling. You shall be a long-toothed tiger."

I knew these beasts from the previous life. We hunted and revered them. "These are beautiful creatures, noble and fierce. I would be made arrogant, not humble."

The redhead smiled cruelly. "If you wish to be contentious, you'll be an armadillo."

She held up a picture of the animal on her device. I had also seen these beasts. "It is not pleasing to look at, but it is strong, and tender with its young. Not a diminutive existence."

Sighing, she showed me a host of unattractive or aggressive beings: echidna, pathosaur, Ebola virus, slime mold, strangler fig. With each, I argued against its inferior status, pointing out something important about the creature. When she revealed the classic incarnation for a failed human, the red ant, I asserted the ant's intelligence and cooperative ability. Exasperated, the spirit pulled me back to the gate, where my former guide waited.

"She failed. Take her," the redhead said, with disdain. I decided she was a corrupted spirit who had no regard for the universe's myriad life forms.

"What do I do with you?" my guide asked, a strange expression on her face. "SWITCH?"

The Serendipitous Wish Intelligence Tracking Center of Heaven, or SWITCH, created meaningfully accidental events on various planes of existence. On some occasions, SWITCH picked up karma cases and suggested next lives, random and provocative. We walked toward the offices.

"What if SWITCH places me as a human?" I asked. "Won't that defeat your purpose?"

The guide smiled, again with hidden meaning. We entered the SWITCH building, and headed upstairs to the Information Collection. I waited quietly while the spirit chatted with an attendant. I could not hear their words, but the conversation seemed too casual.

Back at the guide's office, I refused a fresh mug of shai with an air of impatience. The guide asked how I felt about going to the corpyrooms.

Even for the interlife this felt interminable! I answered as calmly as possible. "We have talked about my mistakes. The corpyroom would only reinforce them and delay the consequences. But if it's the proper course, let's begin."

Another eternity passed; my guide smiled that strange smile again. "Po, I apologize for our little trick. We were testing your attitudes from previous existences. You're as contentious as ever, but you exercise a good deal of control. At the Animal Incarnation Bureau you showed great respect for other species. A worthy trait for any human incarnation.

"What remains are your latent abilities, which you've wasted while pining for the advent of humanity. It is time to exploit your multi-talented nature, through a series of human incarnations. While at SWITCH, I inquired about suitable human Worlds for you. Understand that we are not giving you a choice of these Worlds. I will design a sequence that challenges you. There is a wild core nature of these beings, which you mishandled. You will perceive much cruelty among these people. And face much suffering. But you are prepared to cope with hardship. It is time to pull your soul together, and burst forth with new talents."

I trembled at the warning of suffering, but knew there was nothing to be gained by fearing the unknown. I could not wait to return to Earth. I was curious about my hidden talents. I wept for joy and relief. I didn't have to be an armadillo!

ق

When Porcy came out of her trance, she was no longer holding Naji. She was lying down on Sahara's couch in the living room. She sat up. Her vision of the spirit guide was replaced by Elvi, who sat across from her, holding out a cup of tea.

"Where's Naji?" Porcy asked, still unsure which world she perceived.

"He's sleeping," Elvi answered.

"How? It takes years of mastery to get the kid down. How did you know to come over?"

Elvi flashed Porcy a smile. A familiar smile. "I have my methods." Elvi put the cup in Porcy's hand. "How was the interlife?"

Porcy took a sip of tea. She didn't ask how Elvi knew about the recall. Porcy was afraid she might learn Elvi had foreseen the World Trade Center disaster. The woman was full of surprises, and it felt best to go with the flow here. "Didn't Cachay experience a custom-made interlife, like I did? She was exiled from Heaven, but I was rewarded."

Elvi picked up Porcy's competitive attitude. "It's not a race. Everything in its own time."

"But is that how Heaven works? Custom-made?"

Elvi raised her own cup of tea. "There are as many different in-between worlds as there are souls. 'Heaven' is a particular brand. The Tibetan afterlife has a hundred deities, forty-two peaceful and fifty-eight wrathful, all living in a palace. Modern folks think they represent a

164

human being's positive and negative traits. But I've actually slept over. Given the dreadful plumbing, I guarantee you it's a real place.

"Just because a culture believes in an afterlife, does that make it a real thing?"

"Very real," Elvi said. "The Tibetan *bardo* system, six phases of consciousness, includes a Darkness where demons rip your soul to shreds. Better have a good reason for that work order."

Porcy couldn't read Elvi's wry smile. "Would I go through the bardos if I didn't believe?"

"Excellent question. But you might have believed in your previous life. Sahara recalled the six levels of existence between the Earth and Moon. For animals evolving up the chain of being."

"You tricking me again? Positing lower life forms, after I defended every living thing?"

"Why say *I* tricked you? Wasn't that your spirit guide?"

Porcy wrinkled her brow. "*My* spirit guide? Every soul has one?"

"At least one. Usually a whole team."

Porcy had a realization. "Do spirit guides ever oversee things during an actual lifetime?"

"If it's an important one. Especially involving a group of souls."

"Like a qaraq?"

Elvi nodded quietly. "Very perceptive. See, you're not so inadequate."

"Except as a baby-sitter," Porcy said. "So *you're* my spirit guide."

"Pleased to make your acquaintance." Elvi smiled her smile. "Again."

23

September 11. Hours 3-7.

Amar let Ooma rest at the Trinity Church cemetery. The sense of sanctuary relaxed Ooma's mind, and she drifted back into trance. This time her brain flickered from one recall to another, both influenced and influencing the other qaraq members receiving past life images in their minds. Ooma's mind jumped to her sixth kiss vision, an image of Hu Ma awakening from her coma.

The Seven Incarnations of Queen Uzmeth

Hu Ma moved from lifetime to lifetime in her mind, jumping from past to future, influencing the fragments Ooma saw, a parade of incarnations unfolding a saga of their soul, Umh, climbing out of the karmic mire created by the depraved Queen Uzmeth:

Uzmeth, sucking on a fingernail, watching Ardryashir clean up after liquidating another virgin, her insatiable senses delighting in his every motion

Udir, cleaning yak gofta off the streets, saving a magical relic from the dung heap, a book that imbued stories with power. The first rung out of the depths of Uzmeth's actions

Humai, granddaughter of Sharzad and Ardryashir, Uzmeth's depravity still lingering in her soul, begging for her night terrors to go away, sucking on her veil, pleading for another tale from her grandmother, commanding her father Bahram Gur to compile the calming stories into a collection, to relieve souls everywhere. Another rung up the karmic ladder, and first step to *The Thousand Tales*

Hu Ma, in her coma, envisioning the the qaraq's many lives that delivered tales from India to Persia to Iraq, from Sanskrit to Pahlavi to Arabic, transforming the Scheherazade story, and censoring out Uzmeth's character, the next rung up the spiral.

Hearing of emergency services, Amar woke Ooma out of her dreams so they could find medical attention. She resisted walking among the ash-covered ghouls, but Amar coaxed her over to the triage tents. They waited their turn, shifting from line to line and volunteer to volunteer. Amar noticed that Ooma struggled distinguishing between the reality of the situation and her visions. His focus and concern prevented him from receiving more images, even when touching her.

The paramedics found nothing urgent about their cases, and bandaged the minor lacerations. When Amar asked if they should worry about all the smoke and fumes they had inhaled, the medics gave the best answer they could, but suggested they wait for transport to St. Vincent's Hospital for a more extensive look. When Amar grew impatient waiting in another line, he asked Ooma if she could handle the forty-five minute walk uptown. He thought getting away from the site for fresh air might help them. She managed the walk, often stopping to rest or wander down a side street.

Ooma's physical wanderings, which Amar indulged to not upset her, reflected the wanderings of her mind. When they finally collapsed onto plastic seats in St. Vincent's Emergency Room, facing another wait, Ooma let her mind go. This time the memories led to lifetimes neither Hu Ma nor Ooma had envisioned fully.

The Seven Incarnations of Queen Uzmeth, continued

Umh continued her incarnations to counteract Uzmeth's negative karma:

Hu Ma's child, born as post-coma Hu Ma dies in childbirth and instantly transmigrates into the screaming infant. A vulnerable being, sensing her harsh history, growing up, mourning the loss of her mother, her soul, and Uzmeth, and taking her life because of it

A logic puzzle, parsing out Sassanian Kings and spirals of karmic ascendance

Umnia, tipping the karmic scales back in Uzmeth's direction, restorer of the female element of desire in the Scheherazade tale, jumping off the karmic ladder to survey the landscape. Umh pleased with herself for the first lifetime in five hundred years, thus evolving to become

Oamra, seventh incarnation after Uzmeth, lover of Sanaa, story collector, reaping all the good karma since the demented Queen's downfall.

When Ooma saw Oamra in her vision, she recognized the young woman who had lived in Baghdad with Sanaa, Sahara's incarnation. Sahara had recalled a torrid love affair between the two, a passion in opposition to their current antagonistic relationship. Ooma leaned forward in the plastic hospital chair, captivated by Oamra. Studying the medieval Muslim woman, Ooma mouthed words she heard Oamra speak, imitated her gestures.

Amar grew concerned when Ooma did not stop this behavior. Assuming she was wrapped up in a recall, he touched her hand. But he could not access the vision. Was he too embroiled in the day's reality, the Maya Factor, to see another World? Or was Ooma so far gone that she was now trapped in her memories, a kind of madness? Amar had seen trauma experts giving treatment to some of the victims. He considered finding one for Ooma. But how would he begin to explain what was going on in Ooma's mind to a therapist? He wished Dr. Machiyoko were there.

Amar wanted an end to this craziness right now. They were physically fine, the waiting was endless to him, and now he worried the harsh hospital environment might stress Ooma's mind more. Delicately lifting her from the chair, he took her out into the fresh air of the street.

As Ooma began moving, her obsessed focus on Oamra disappeared. She vaguely heard voices near her. Then she was back with Hu Ma in the wandering recall. Umh surveyed her incarnations after Uzmeth, assessing the redemption of her burdensome karma.

The Seven Incarnations of Queen Uzmeth, conclusion

I see my lives unfold, and yet they are not my lives.

Hu Ma and Ooma heard the voice quietly near them and wondered who it could be. But the seven incarnations drowned out the voice. A single fact gave them clarity: the *Hazir Afsaneh*'s triumphal entrance into Baghdad, its rebirth in the new Arabic culture, an accomplishment in which each incarnation took part, from Humai crying for a story to Oamra pushing for a subversive manuscript, a cultivation analogous to the journey of the soul or the construction of Baghdad. Echoing that feat, an unexpected déjà vu flickered at them, the first great city on the planet, long before Ur: the City of Pebbles, the vast shoreline network of micro-organisms, matted together in the spirit of cooperation, the first organic beings to touch land.

I see my lives unfold, but they are not mine. Hu Ma and Ooma heard the voice clearly now: Umh, their soul, soothing Hu Ma in her last moments in the world, and Ooma in her first hours away from the Towers. *They are not mine, but Uzmeth's, who had such a corrupting effect that it took seven lifetimes to redeem her sins. Now I can embrace a life proudly again.*

ق

That life belonged to Oamra, a beacon of hope for Umh, for Islam, and for Ooma in the modern world. Ooma continued to see her, mimicked Oamra's gestures, and blurted out old Arabic words. Amar wandered the streets with Ooma, praying that motion, air, and time would bring her down from her hallucinogenic state.

170

24

October 20. Week 6.

When Sahara finally visited Ardra, she was apologetic about waiting so long since they had talked on September 11. She made excuses for Amar not being there, though she honestly did not understand why he kept his distance from his grandfather. Ardra brushed off her apologies.

She brought Naji with her, and the old man and the child made an instant connection. Given Naji's recent distance, Sahara was surprised. Instinctually, Naji knew Ardra was frail. He climbed on a chair to sit next to him. Ardra realized he could not understand Naji's baby talk, so he asked the baby to name objects in the living room, with little success. But when the old man requested that Naji look in the bedroom for a certain book, Naji understood and obeyed.

Ardra made a present of the book to his great-grandson: a child's compendium of Hindu Gods, a souvenir of Ardra's days in India. He explained that he had read it to Naji's father as a boy. Naji pointed insistently to a page in the book, a tale about Ganesha, the popular elephant God. Again, Sahara was confused Naji showed livelier interest in Ardra's book than her bedtime stories.

Sahara asked after Ardra's health, and when he deflected the question she insisted on the truth. Ardra confessed his breathing had been troubled, and his doctor had banned cigar smoking. When she asked how he felt after giving up cigars, Ardra said he felt no different, just unhappy.

Sahara remembered how much she enjoyed Ardra, and promised to return soon. Before leaving, Naji leaned close to his great-grandfather, and remained there, still, for a minute. At first, Ardra looked awkward, but then an expression of surprise filled his wrinkled face, and he listened intently. Was Naji communicating inside Ardra's mind, Sahara wondered?

November 1.   Week 8.

Sahara came to the second official qaraq meeting that Fall with Naji, intending to hand him off to her baby-sitter outside the church. Naji seemed to enjoy the sitter's company, so Sahara was shocked when he put up a great fuss. Crying inconsolably when touched, he ran into the church. Sahara found him standing on the stairs that led to Verle's attic space, calm and full of expectation. One final attempt by the sitter to snag him led to screams.

"Some young gentleman wants to attend the meeting." Having witnessed Naji's tantrum, Verle neared the child, and Naji pulled on his wrinkled hand to lead him up the stairs. Anxious, Sahara threw the sitter some money and hurried after them. To her relief, the qaraq was delighted to see Naji. He was silent throughout the meeting, but Sahara had not seen him so engaged in weeks.

Because Bax had spent all last meeting recounting the Seven Kisses tales, Verle insisted they get down to work on World Types. Now that they could classify particular Worlds, they should ascertain which Worlds were missing recalls by which qaraq members, and wrap up those Worlds.

Dr. Machiyoko sized up Verle's intense energy. "You getting OCD on us? We have so much new material, including our deep archetypes. Why waste time tidying up a dozen recalls?"

"Forgive me, Dr. Jung." The qaraq had never heard Verle react sarcastically. What was going on between these two? "I talked to the church about a new space for us and they got on my case about the mess up here being a fire hazard. If we want extra space we have to act in good faith and show some organization. I have to close out some files and I need your cooperation."

"But isn't finding reincarnation beliefs more important than inputting data?" Diana asked.

"The archive project is a noble effort," Zack said, in mock outrage. "We're working our asses off. But what if I had a new recall, an episode of a familiar story that will help complete a World, unearth reincarnation beliefs, and probe deep into our souls? Would everyone be happy?"

After many vigorous nods from the group, Zack launched into his story.

The Tale of the Staredown Between the Two Cliff Faces

You can do this, Zinc[ite]. You don't have to assert your strength, crush anything to dust, or move mountains. Just stay here, focus straight ahead, and beat him at his game. Copycat his stony outcropping. Be as passive as you want. The perfect job for you.

Forget about those birds, Zinc[ite]. All manner flying about, eagles, doves, feathered creatures that out of the corner of your rocky eye seem to transform into lovely human figures, like the ones diving into rain pools down in the valley. Don't let anything distract you, or you'll be tempted to blink. The game will be lost. There are changes all around, especially down below. Tap into some ancient attitude about evolutionary change, ignore what's new. Be the Rock you are!

This game could last thousands of years, Zinc[ite]. You might be distracted by the people below, but they comfort you. Without them, this life is lonely, with only an archrival to face. At first they came and went, decades in between each generation. You learned how to keep them around, allowing your minerals to enrich the soil for their use. You set an example for them: be still, do not move to other ground, and you will be rewarded in this valley. It worked: they looked up to you as an icon of stability, the power of fixity in your frozen glance. It helped your game, too.

Thousands of years. You felt activity around the valley. The rule of the Matriarchs and the Elders. Stone worship. Principices vying for power. Discovery of Licghurian crystal in your opponent's caves. Erosion from crystal mining. The reign of destruction as rock fell on the village.

Thousands of years. You eroded over time, sometimes sending waterfalls of rock down on the valley. It was a terrible distraction and many times you almost lost the game. Your landslides were not nearly as severe as those of your adversary. You wanted him to save the village and pack in the game. But he would never do that. You despised him for centuries because of the horrible dangers he caused. His stare became colder than ever. But you felt for the victims. Unmoving, you could be moved. You discovered compassion.

Perhaps as a reward, you won the staring contest. A bitter reward: by that time your enemy had razed the community. You smirked in triumph as your challenger blinked stone from his eyes. But your judgment of his lack of compassion was unfounded. As soon as he flinched, more rock wept from his eyes, a show of compassion that outdid your quiet discovery. You felt shamed, as if you were the real loser. The smirk froze on your face.

Thousands more years. Your two spirits departed the two cliff faces, the opposing cliff having borne several different souls. But the story remained permanently displayed in stone. Your rival's cliff continued to bleed dirt and rock, erosion carving out a wise and deeply felt facade.

Your cliff remained frozen, a slight upturn in its expression, with no sign of victory.

"I was your rival, sweets," Porcy said. "I recalled a cliff that shed rock tears. Amazing."

"Thank you, sir." Verle felt emboldened revisiting a World. "Another five-character World, like the Borzi versus Vawr. The two camps are the opposing cliffs, or the cliffs versus the tribes."

"I don't know what this culture has to do with reincarnation beliefs," Diana said. "At least there's a depth, Zack, getting to the roots of your passivity."

"Does every recall have to pass a test for depth?" Verle challenged.

Porcy intervened. "I want to know who the Principices are. Same as the Matriarchs?"

"Search me," Zack said. "But thank God this tale isn't about Scheherazade. But as Our Lady of Storytelling said: 'Oh King, this story is no more wondrous than the story of how I heard it.' The qaraq looked at Zack dumbfounded. "There's more to tell, and it ain't pretty."

The Epilogue of the Tale of the Staredown Between the Two Cliff Faces

Jobim is a Bennington alum, so we drove up to Vermont last weekend. After seeing the campus and dropping in on a few old professors, we drove around, lost on back roads. After the eleventh quaint town, we realized we had crossed the border into New Hampshire. Jobim was sick of covered bridges by now, but I got an insane sense I had been in that place before.

Jobim's a fast learner: just a month after I outed you all at the FunStop, he recognized I was going into past life trance. He made

175

me pull over and let him drive. I navigated, leading us northeast. We entered a beautiful valley, mountains all around, and at the north end there was a large group of people holding signs. After Jobim asked the locals what was happening, he drove us to an inn and insisted I lie down. That's when I received the full story about the two cliff faces.

Over dinner, I told him my tale and he said the people were protesting the abandonment of an old anti-erosion project. The north cliff face had been eroding for centuries, a stony face locally known as The Old Man in the Mountain. Legend had it that in anger at the people's sins, the Old Man hurled down rocks and debris. Wooden supports had shored up the Old Man's chin and eyes.

"It's a tragedy," Jobim said. "In a matter of years, the Old Man is doomed to collapse no matter what, so he's being abandoned. The locals believe more can be done."

"I unconsciously recognized the site of the Stone Cliff. And showed up for a milestone."

"You're uncanny," Jobim said. "I wonder if the present day Old Man is ensouled."

"Forget a soul, he can't even keep his chin. But it's a good question. You've got a knack for this stuff. You be recalling soon." Jobim gave me an uncomfortable look, which I ignored.

The next morning we returned to pay our respects. After the fog lifted, I got a good look at the rival cliff across the road, my stony incarnation. I saw a distinctive sneer on its face. I asked the locals if my cliff had a name, but they didn't even see a face in the stone.

I joined in the protest, to rectify my karma for humiliating the Old Man in the staring contest. At least Jobim absolved me. "That should do your karma nicely. Can we go now?"

Jobim's underlying tension from the day before surfaced. "What's wrong?" I asked. "You were the one who wanted to come up here. But if you want to go, let's go."

There was stony silence on the ride home, pun fully intended. Halfway down the Thruway I couldn't stand it any longer. I had never seen Jobim in a foul mood. I pushed him to explain.

"You could have driven off the road yesterday, going into trance," he said. "You've described flooding your kitchen while in a recall. I met you standing in the middle of a New York City street, lost in a fog."

"That was different," I said. "That was 9/11. That shit was real!"

"Don't quibble," Jobim said. "I'm worried about these past lives. I'm worried about you."

I was touched. I did my best to explain how safe regressions can be, especially when we have them together at meetings. Jobim asked me a lot of questions. I could tell we had crossed a line together, and that if I wanted to continue the relationship, I could keep nothing from him.

ق

Zack paused, as if done with the narrative, but then concluded. "I just wanted you to know that Jobim is part of my past life discovery process now. I may or may not be able to find a therapist outside the group who accepts us, but I've found a partner who does. I hope that's okay."

"Hallelujah," Verle said, and the group seconded him heartily. Elvi was silent.

"I appreciate it," Zack said. "I'm grateful for this group. It's important for us to stick together these days. I see us fighting. The Doc and the old man, God knows why. Sahara and the little guy have their moments. When Jobim and I went south, I knew it had to stop."

As if in answer, Naji jumped down from his chair and toddled over to Zack. The boy climbed up on Zack's lap and, as with Ardra, leaned in close to him. After an awkward moment, Zack's face widened into a huge smile. "Thanks, little man." As Naji got down from Zack's chair, Diana gave Sahara a look that questioned whether the child was back to telepathy. Returning to his chair, Naji knocked over a pile of books.

"Gotta clean this place up," Porcy said. "And we still don't know who the Principices are."

"The Principices," Verle repeated, his eyes staring out in space. "Principices."

"I think we've lost *our* Old Man," Elvi said. "Or I think he's found the Stone World."

In trance, Verle reported his lifetime there.

25

———⟨✦⟩———

The Tale of the Next Life Tales

Vlaler-rawk made sure everything was ready for the Spring Festival, half according to her own designs, and half according to the Principice's wishes. The Principice was the third ruler since the tribes had chosen to stay permanently in the valley and lead an agrarian life. Vlaler-rawk was tired of moving around, haggling with greedy souls, and worrying about attacks from all sides. The valley had a good natural defense: the narrow pass leading into it was easily guarded.

Most visitors were welcome regardless of their motives. The village wished to leave hostile ways behind, and create lasting peace. The greater the bounty, the stronger the harmony, so the Principice enticed people to work in the valley and remain there. The best lure was the Spring Festival. Despite Vlaler-rawk's ambivalence about newcomers, she worked harder than anyone to make sure each element blessed the crops, and satisfied the Principice.

Some wished the Spring Festival honor the Stone Cliffs looking down on the valley. Believing the Cliffs had a major influence on their lives, they thought the minerals in the stone had a sticking power that kept people there. Vlaler-rawk had heard this argument too many times, as well as endless debates about staying or migrating, a fight as old as the scum in the ponds. But the Principice was as generous as she was wise; she instructed Vlaler-rawk to make room at the Festival for those wishing to honor the Cliff Face. It was Vlaler-rawk's charge to give the Stone worshippers whatever they needed, to listen and nod as they talked of appeasing the 'Anger of the Stone' at human encroachment on the Cliff's territory, and to join in their rituals, face the proper direction at the offering pyre, and mouth their incantations. Captivated by the Stone rites, The Principice played the bright ambassador, promising acceptance of the most outlying beliefs in the valley. This tolerance went against Vlaler-rawk's nature; she did not want any new people, beliefs, or rites.

In the midst of the Festival, a small band of Stone worshippers arrived, forced off their lands and seeking the valley's welcome generosity. They vowed they would be grateful to the first thing they encountered, which of course was the towering Cliff Faces. Obligated to assist their offering of praise, Vlaler-rawk observed the tribe's adapted ritual.

Vlaler-rawk had seen the tomb carvings of the Wallinapopek peoples, but she had never heard of an ancestral ritual that told stories, not of the events of the deceased's life, but of an upcoming lifetime, to ensure the dead would return as that person or place or rock or animal. Her own people buried and honored their dead, believing one lived on in the natural surroundings, but not as a recognizable entity like an oak tree; she had never experienced a rite for the return of the dead. The newcomers needed only a fire circle and a few entrails, but Vlaler-rawk made a show of being at their beck and call; she wanted to see what this was all about.

The ritualistic elements were nothing new: hand-waving, burning of animal parts, mysterious holy words, a moment of silence, more smoke and entrails, and an edible substance, which Vlaler-rawk declined.

As darkness fell on the fire circle, the dozen visitors were deep in conversation: the dialect was not easy to follow, especially with hushed voices; eventually Vlaler-rawk understood they were deciding whose story to summon. They chose an elder woman in the circle whose mate had recently died; the tribe wondered in what form he would return. The stars appeared, more substance was consumed, and the old woman spoke in trance. Vlaler-rawk sat inside the fire circle and listened to the tale.

Three or four lifetimes ago, the old woman began, she and her mate had lived as wolves on the high plateaus of the lands to the south; after the aggressive hunt of that lifetime, they strove to become human and less victimized by the world. She remembered lifetimes where they died as small children, or existed as slaves. It was not until this current life that she realized the folly of viewing human existence as superior: she prayed for her mate's safe return as a non-human.

She imagined brave adventures of him once more as a wolf, running free and hunting fiercely, never killing without hunger, never wounding another creature to cause pain. She saw the two of them as wolf rivals in a mating contest, one overpowering the other, the other offering its neck for the finishing blow. This vision was so strong that she faltered, until her friends stopped her and announced she had found her mate's next reincarnation as the wolf.

The next morning Vlaler-rawk awoke at the fire circle, having stayed up listening to other next life tales. Pulling herself together, she fetched the visitors food, and prepared for the last day of the Festival, the most important day to the Principice, the time to persuade outsiders to stay and help with the coming harvest. Vlaler-rawk joined in, but asked the Principice's permission to concentrate on the fire circle visitors; she believed they would add to the valley's way of life. She spent half the day exercising her excellent organizational skills, and the other half at the fire circle entertaining her guests, sharing stories of valley life, and quoting crop fertility figures; she asked how the visitors liked the majesty of the Stone edifices, but they only nodded politely.

As night fell on the Festival, Vlaler-rawk listened to the next life stories with fascination and envy, for she wished for the imagination of these people. Two of her new friends explained that they were searching for a connection between their tribe's next lives and the Stone Cliffs. So far the Stone had no influence on their stories, which showed reincarnations in places outside the valley.

The group asked if Vlaler-rawk would like to see her next lifetime. When Vlaler-rawk resisted, the old woman who had spoken the first story revealed their custom to initiate a new tribe member by recounting his or her next life tale; they would perform this honor for Vlaler-rawk. Touched, Vlaler-rawk was eager to hear her story: the narrative went long into the night, with many episodes, leaving no time for other tales.

Vlaler-rawk awoke the next morning at the fire circle, where the visiting tribe packed their belongings. Vlaler-rawk was not heartsick at their departure; instead, she calmly went to the Principice, delivered her message, and bowed low when she received the ruler's solemn reply.

Like the other visitors, Vlaler-rawk's story from the night before had made no mention of the Cliff Faces, no reference to the valley and its people, and no allusion to stone. Turning her back on her quiet, peaceful life, she hoisted her belongings on her back and followed her new friends out of the mountain pass. She had seen her future, and it was beyond.

ق

When Verle came out of his trance, Diana addressed him. "I appreciate your Cliff tale affirming prehistoric origins of reincarnation beliefs. These people seem like an evolution from the gravestone painters of my recall."

"Which places them closer to 10,000 BC, my friend," Verle said, rubbing his eyes. "The other tales, when the Cliff Face was crumbling, was thousands of years later."

"I'm glad you two are being cordial," Cachay said, "but we still can't link reincarnation beliefs with our many Nights recalls."

"Remember that your souls have CHITS, traits that recur through lifetimes," Elvi said, "including an archetype based on the Scheherazade characters that effects your personality. That's a connection between the Nights and the transmigration of souls."

"Good enough for you, honey?" Porcy needled Cachay. "Though some of us never act like an archetype. Guess we don't have one, sugar." Cachay agreed. "Some of us wonder if the whole thing is a load of poppycock."

"The only clue I have is that I am 'The Pyypyl,' whatever that means," Porcy said. "A clue from a logic puzzle in the future, bless me."

Bax touched Porcy on the arm. "Remember our talk after we shared recalls of the Nights during 9/11? We didn't think I was Hammad the Bedouin, but maybe you were. Hammad starts with the initial of your last name, Honeywell. And he gave the court nicknames, like you do."

"Hammad beefed up the People's suffering in the Scheherazade tale," Verle said.

"Is 'The Pyypyl' the People? That's my archetype?" Porcy seemed dubious. "How can I be a whole population? And what about Cachay – she's got nada."

"If I may be so bold, my lady," Verle said to Cachay. "Over the last year or two, you and I have felt a deeper connection. Maybe not soul mates like Scheherazade and the King."

"Not remotely, old man," Cachay said, blushing in front of the group.

"But you admit the connection, I hope. Perhaps your archetype is related to the Vizier. One of his closest relationships is with the Court, the emirs and grandees in the palace."

"So I'm a Court? That's as ridiculous as the People!" Cachay said. "The type that kisses the ground before the King? Do I act that way to Amar?"

"Your relationship with him goes back to his childhood," Sahara pointed out. "Amar and Zack are archetypal brothers; you're close to both of them, as any court would be close to its rulers."

"Be that as it may, what does this far-fetched conceit mean to me?" Cachay said.

"For once, I side with my mother," Zack said. "I'm painfully aware of my archetype. But if our souls are controlled by the Scheherazade characters, what's the ultimate point?"

"And how can the archetypes affect us in lives before the Nights existed?" Verle asked.

183

Elvi was silent. Bax spoke up. "I'm the one brought in tales of us rewriting Scheherazade. We created variants that enhanced our arche-type. Like we were reborn to make the story right. We did more work on the Nights later. In Ooma's elephant recall, there's a storytelling collective."

Sahara rubbed Naji's head. "This guy told me, *in utero*, that the qaraq created a special version of the Nights. In my recall of Sanaa and Oamra, it's called a subversive anthology."

Enthusiastically, the group agreed it needed to recall the collec-tive that worked on the special Nights. Verle winked at Cachay. "Still don't know how my 'Next Life Tales' leads to the Arabian Nights. But we have somewhere to look for a connection between past lives and Scheherazade's court." Cachay smirked, and Elvi adjourned the meeting.

26

September 11. Hours 7-11.

Amar and Ooma wandered the streets for hours, occasionally stopping to rest or get a bite to eat. The exercise and food brought Ooma back to normal consciousness, but she was still fixated on the Arab World tales. Seated at a coffee shop, they discussed the visions.

"I know it's crazy," Ooma said, acknowledging her erratic behavior, "but I'm sure others in the qaraq are seeing these lifetimes, too." She pointed to the news on a television in the diner. "The government points its finger at Muslim terrorists, and the qaraq gets a history lesson in Islamic Lit."

"I agree, but I don't see an actual connection," Amar said. "Why fiction and Scheherazade?"

"Don't you see? It's not overtly political. I don't think we're being summoned to take sides or anything. But we've always been wrapped up in Arabic literature. You married a Nights scholar! As the world is on the brink of a new order related to the Mideast, the qaraq is on the brink of s breakthrough related to Middle Eastern culture. It's the right time for it."

"And you think Umh's incarnations are a key?" Amar worried about Ooma's answer, since it might make her break from reality again, and get lost in one of the incarnations.

Ooma chewed on her straw. "I don't understand about Hu Ma's child killing herself, or how a logic puzzle is an incarnation," she said. "But Umnia is the next step to understanding, and Oamra worked on a Nights version that involved the qaraq. I have to recall these lifetimes."

Amar reached for Ooma's hands. "But not now. It's too much for you." But it was too late. For the first time since escaping the Tower, Amar received a vision by touching Ooma. She had already willed herself back in time to receive her seventh kiss tale.

"It's all right," she reassured Amar, "I'm in control. I've tapped into the qaraq's memories. I see myself as Umnia, but this is her husband's voice. It's Porcy's lifetime."

The Tale of Hanbal and Umnia

We gathered that day in Cairo for the strangest of reasons. One of us had been in Ethiopia and brought back dark beans used to make a strong beverage with beneficial health effects. We tried adding the beans to a cup of hot water, unsuccessfully swallowing the horrid stuff. We boiled the beans in water: the taste was still too bitter. Baking the beans in the fire improved the flavor somewhat, but we abandoned the black, sticky stuff for mint tea. At least we enjoyed many an anecdote while suffering through our experiments.

Umnia was extremely jealous of the group of men. Then again, my wife complained about all my activities. Her barbed tongue curbed my few freedoms. If I enjoyed a few good yarns at Kashi the bookseller's shop every morning, Umnia bit my head off if I was gone more than two hours. As dependable as the rising sun, I walked through the door for luncheon, and she's anxiously chewing on a date nut, ready to criticize every word spoken and every coin spent. When I justified our meetings because we pass ideas onto the local council, she said we masked our storytelling and carousing with griping.

There was one way to her heart, and acceptance of the fellows: I shared a bit of the Second Lover's Tale, or a witty anecdote about Harun al-Rashid. If I didn't want her chasing me around the kitchen with a knife, then nothing but the Tale of Shahrazad soothed her fiery nerves. Sometimes it took four or five stories to cool her oven. If I offered her the latest tale, Umnia lowered her voice, showed me a bit of her face, and approached seductively. Great relief from nagging.

Umnia loved the Shahrazad story the most because of the strong female character. She would take over my telling of the tale, freely embellish it, and whip herself into a frenzy of passion. One of our group knew an old Persian version, with an evil, demented Queen. Umnia complained the Queen had been demoted to an adulterous wife, and should have a stronger voice.

"If Shahrazad is so strong, her nemesis should be too," she argued. "We should bring back the ancient Queen's sensual nature."

"That would be blasphemy, praise the purity of Allah," I pleaded.

"If we are to believe the King is a good enough soul to be reformed by Shahrazad, then a huge force, not a bit of adultery, must provoke his murderous streak. Let his Queen have orgies again. Let the whole harem join in!"

"You give too much power to this character, Umnia. She is but a woman."

"She is a Queen! She has power! King Shahryar is the old order, the rulers before Islam. He is reformed by the sweetness of Islam, the new order. The Queen and her streetwise lovers are the revolutionary transition, the subversive agents of change, the usurping thrust!" Worked up by her defense, we finished the discussion in the bedchamber. This story did wonders for our marriage.

The court of Baghdad had Arabicized *The Thousand Wondrous Tales*, but recently the collection hit the streets, became less courtly and refined, and emerged popular and vulgar. The men at the bookshop loved it, but given Umnia's erotic bent for the Queen, she felt a righteous responsibility for the rest of the collection. When an Arabic history was added, such as the epic of Umar, she bit down on a palm nut and declared that the manipulation of history could be as vulgar as fiction. "Does adding a surface layer of Islam onto a heathen core make it legitimate? Is it not the same as the edict against telling lies, against stories that change the truth?"

I did my best to calm her. "Honey lamb, there's an old copy of *The Thousand Tales* at the bookshop. It starts with an invocation to The Prophet, thanking Allah for vanquishing those cultures that supplied us with stories. It imbues the Arabic collection with a symbolic power of the Islamic Empire, of our conquests in Allah's name."

Umnia was not convinced. "I worry about this subjugation of other people's myths. We must purify this work, to make the collection popular in the street *and* in the pious Islamic *umma*. We must bring spiritual power to the stories."

I scratched my head. "This from a woman who wants the Queen to have orgies?"

"Precisely why." I had touched a raw part of her soul. "Talk to the bookseller. Find out if there are storytellers who share my desire for purity!"

Most bookshops, libraries, and market book stalls were meeting places for literary and philosophical discussions. The dealer suggested a few emporiums, but our local storytellers laughed at the idea of purifying a street frivol. Venturing into Cairo's grand marketplace, the collectors found Umnia's request amusing, but said we would only find sympathy for our cause in Iraq.

There was no satisfying Umnia. She insisted we save the money to travel across the sea and find the source. After five years we made it to Basra, where public libraries teemed with learned minds who instantly understood Umnia's problem. But among such literate men, who had consumed a great deal of fiction, no one treated stories with the same respect as the Qu'ran, *hadith*, or philosophy. Each edition of *The Thousand Tales* contained a new hodge-podge of stories. Who cared if they were truly moral?

Umnia was crestfallen. We returned to Cairo. The eve of the 4th Century after Our Prophet began ominously. Protective of Umnia, I minimized my visits to the group. Yet she thought about the problem constantly, assessing new tales for their Islamic potential. In her last years, she again begged for a voyage to Iraq, this time to the heart of the world: Baghdad. No destination was as important to Umnia as the Suq al-Warraqin, the bookseller's marketplace. Here dozens of vendors traded precious wares. Here new versions of *The Thousand Tales* flourished. Here they respected Umnia's question.

There were secret groups working on special editions, courtiers bridging the gap between popular and scholarly versions, imams banning the compendium and imams using it for moral education. I was locked out of these groups because of their elite status. After years of Umnia depending on me to infiltrate exclusively male groups, my lack of access was the final straw for her. The fact that in Baghdad there must be a group with her vision was no consolation; the fact that she could have no part in it broke my wife's heart.

ق

The story ended, but Ooma stayed in trance.

Amar squeezed her hands. "What's going on? Where are you?"

A single tear rolled down Ooma's soft, caramel-colored cheek. Still she said nothing.

Amar paid their bill and resumed walking Ooma through the streets. They had not yet been able to phone Ooma's parents, but Amar knew he must bring her home. He heard about the ferry shuttles and led them toward Chelsea Piers. He kept questioning Ooma until he got a response.

189

"It is I, Oamra," she said, in a distant voice. "Only I can resolve Umnia's tragedy. Only I can create a truly moral Nights, with the qaraq's help. Only I can protect the collective's work."

"You are not Oamra," Amar said. "You are Ooma. Are you seeing Oamra's lifetime?" But as at the hospital, despite holding her hand, Amar did not receive any visions from Ooma. "Ooma, come back to me. You are losing yourself."

Ooma came to semi-consciousness. "The qaraq is on an incredible path. I've been in the forefront, for bad and good. They need me. They need Oamra. They need to find the collective."

Amar embraced Ooma to his chest. "Thank God you're back with me. You scared me."

"I'm sorry." She looked deeply into Amar's eyes, the most lucid gaze he had seen from her all day. The intimate bond between them re-surfaced. "Amar, you must help me. The qaraq must let us in. I have so much to give them. After today, they know I do. But you must back me up."

"Of course, of course," he said. "But I'm worried about you, about you channeling these incarnations. You're going beyond regression, you're becoming these people."

"That's why we must go to meetings, where I can get help. If you love me, you'll help me."

"I'll do whatever I can, though there's little love between me and the qaraq." Amar knew he would protect her as much as anything. He had seen her slip into another reality, a fragile vulnerability. They started walking again. "I'll help you. But first let's get you home."

27

—ᴄᴏᴏ—

November 22.   Month 3.

On the Saturday before Thanksgiving, Sahara went on an outing to the Metropolitan Museum of Art with Ardra, Naji, and Porcy. She was so glad they had finally set up a date, since Amar kept dropping the ball; she felt she owed it to the aging man. He was frail getting out of his cab, but his plea for Porcy to help him up the many steps of the museum was full of spice.

"Don't blush, Miss Honeywell, but we're turning heads up and down Fifth Avenue." Porcy had only met Amar's grandfather once, but she remembered she had instantly liked him.

Inside the museum, Sahara and Porcy checked everyone's coats. Naji waited with his great-grandfather, pursuing a game of peek-a-boo, each laughing like little babies. "This is the second time Naji's perked up seeing Ardra," Sahara confided to Porcy. "Like there's nothing wrong. It drives me nuts." Rejoining them, Sahara told Naji not to tire his great-grandfather, but they continued the game. Naji covered his face going through the ticket entrance; Ardra peeked out from behind his hand as they entered the Egyptian wing.

"Time to get serious, Ardra," Porcy mock-scolded. "We got high culture here, sweets."

"On the contrary, my good woman," Ardra said, never ceasing the game. "Do you know why they built these tombs? To preserve souls after death, to aid in coming back to life. Peek-a-boo symbolizes the same thing: disappearance, reappearance, death, rebirth: the Hindus knew it, the Egyptians did, and every tiny child knows, before we ruin them."

Sahara and Porcy shared a look. Did Ardra know about the qaraq?

Before anything else was said, Naji laid eyes on the small tunnels and halls of the stone tombs in the Egyptian wing. He dashed off, summoning Ardra for a new game, hide and seek, a variation on the reappearance ritual. Naji was too fast for the old man, so Sahara ran ahead, caught up to her son, and led him back by the hand. They walked through the exhibit, and then on to the Temple of Dendur. The colossal edifice intimidated Naji: he snuck back to the child-friendly tomb replicas. He loved the maze-like structure, and flitted in between museum visitors. The magic of the space overtook him.

He peeked around the corner of a niche. To his surprise, the twins were waiting just around the next bend in the Egyptian maze. The twins had sought him out only in the interlife. It must be very important if they found their way to the physical world. The twins led Naji through a series of archways where there were no museumgoers. He had played this game with them before, but never inside an Egyptian tomb! When they reached a torch-lit vestibule, the twins spoke simultaneously.

"We have led you away from great-grandfather, so that he will not hear us."

"He'll be looking," Naji said, his voice trembling. "Why don't you want him to hear?"

The twins whispered in an eerie unison. "We are the comforters of the Near Dead, the Just Dead, and the Recently Dead. Ardra will be meeting us soon. He is very sick."

Naji's throat tightened. "Does he know?"

"He knows, but does not wish to believe it."

"Will you comfort him when the time comes?"

"No, we cannot be there. But we can teach you how to comfort him, how to ease his fear."

Naji knew the twins meant preparing Ardra for the interlife. "Will I do what the Egyptians did for their people? Is that why you came to the tomb?"

"Souls have done these things everywhere, for all time. We will tell you a story, your father's life in Egypt. At the time of the first Pyramids."

"But am I allowed to share the story with him?" Naji was confused.

"No, you know better. Just pay attention, and you'll know how to be there for him."

The Tale of the Animal Mummifier

How I despise this work! The odor of the oil mixtures is noxious. The slimy touch of the animal entrails is vile. Only with deft movements, quick slashes for disembowelment, continuous swipes for draining the fluids, and choppy stabs for stuffing the carcasses can I get through a day's work. The process is bad enough for human remains – but I embalm pets!

People have not forgotten the first reactions to The Great Pyramid. Ministers, priests, even slaves, thought the royals over-indulgent. It's one thing to decorate a tomb with images and texts; that practice goes back to grave paintings or next life soul tales, before Time began. But to cram your tomb with everyday objects, precious treasure, and statuary of your family – what a waste of resources. If Pharaoh is blessed with a divine afterlife, why take everything with him? Even food! Can't Osiris host a proper banquet?

Now they want pets by their sides, their bodies preserved the same way as humans. My great-grandfather was the first animal mummifier on record, my grandfather the first to mummify animals exclusively, and my father the most reputable at the trade. As for me, I go beyond what King Menkaure needs, by mummifying the cats, dogs, birds, and monkeys of his court. Disgusting!

It is two hours past sundown, if you can trust this new business of chopping the day into twenty-four sections. Can't tell if it makes things go faster or slower, but I'll try anything to ease my day. For example, there is a new wing of Menkaure's pyramid, unfinished and unguarded. Piles of gold and jewels lie about. I laugh at the glittering excess sitting in a darkened vault, where none of it will shine. I shouldn't mock the space, for it's been my comfort. I sneak inside after a long day of canine guts and monkey blood. All I need is an hour, a twenty-fourth of my daily existence, sitting quietly with a flagon of beer, focusing on nothing, and I'm a new man.

There is a belief that after the soul, the Ba, is released, it can return to the living world and travel from place to place. The priests use sacred objects that the Ba-soul can inhabit, project forth, and see its surroundings or move to new places. Royal demi-Gods use a small figurine to inhabit, a *shabti*. On one particularly bad day, I notice an odd oval-shaped metal object lying in a pile of treasure. Although it is not human-shaped, I assume the oval is a shabti for some bigwig's Ba. Hoping it's not keyed to any particular soul yet, I have the delicious idea to inject my troubled mind into it and go for a ride. At least pretending would give me respite from feline offal.

I hold the oval in my hands, close my eyes, and send my thoughts beyond the darkened chamber. My beleaguered soul clings to a sacred space, wherein lies the entire world, all the living and the dead, bonded together by a special magic.

I am totally unprepared for the next sensation. An unrecognizable force seizes my soul, my Ba. The torch-lit darkness becomes pitch black. My Ba spins about, and I lose consciousness.

The next thing I know I am in a similar room with Sha, my soul mate. It is the interlife.

"Where have you been?" Sha screams. "Did you do it?"

I am not sure what she means, but I know I am angry with her. "Why were you so difficult as a dog, refusing to be tamed, forcing me to come after you in the woods?"

"They took my pups!" she howls. "I hated the life in the caves."

"You were loyal to dogs," I say, "yet you took in a cat in your next life in Egypt. Now cats are Gods! You defaced the name of dog!"

"What do you care what I do? You've taken so long to find me! I despise you!"

"The qaraq will never stop feuding if we can't control these flare-ups. Be quiet!"

Our words become shouts, our howls become fiery blasts, and then one blast sends my Ba flying back. I awake in the tomb, convinced it was all a bad dream.

When Sahara realized that Naji was missing, she suspected where he had gone. Leaving Ardra in the gift shop, she and Porcy split up to search the Egyptian section. Porcy looked through the endless displays of Egyptian artifacts in the rooms beyond the Temple of Dendur. Sahara searched for Naji in the smaller tomb displays where they had started.

Sahara felt ridiculous, crawling on her hands and knees through the tomb display. As people walked by she squeezed against a wall or ducked under a ledge. Doing so, she had a déjà vu of tucking under the Earth's core during early geological time. Who had she been hiding from?

At last Sahara located Naji, in a side area, roped off to visitors. Naji's mind was somewhere else, so she held him for a few minutes, enjoying a quiet reunion with her child. Through their touch, she received glimpses of his recall. Sahara saw only a man in a chamber full of ancient objects, and surmised it was an Egyptian tomb. The man performed a ritual with an oval object that looked very familiar.

Sahara lifted up Naji, still lost to her, and went in search of Porcy, who was looking under a display case containing a replica of an Egyptian sailing vessel. They found Ardra at the gift shop, tired out from the day.

While Porcy fetched the coats, Ardra expressed his gratitude. "I cherish any time I can spend with family," he said. Sahara sensed more to his statement.

The Tale of the Animal Mummifier, conclusion

I do not wish to repeat my nightmare, but am intrigued by my success with the little oval. The next time I have a rough day, I grab the magical object. This time the oval works even better: I do not lose consciousness, and when I head toward Sha in the interlife, I will my Ba to go somewhere else. I land in a civilization more advanced than Egypt, with writing more practical than pictorial glyphs, and with the first magnificent cities. This time I am with Umh, in a passionate relationship that takes my breath away. As we make love, swirls of energy spiral around and through our pulsing bodies. I am aware that loving Umh means escaping the venomous relations with Sha.

I return to the tomb that night with visions of ziggurats and seal rings. I believe that I have not witnessed a dream, but envisioned a life in another world.

For months I experiment with soul traveling. One extraordinary trip I face off again with Sha, inside a cave that feels exactly like the tomb chamber, but exists four thousand years into the future. We are brothers, but I have died and return to haunt her/him. I reveal to my brother, and in consequence to myself, many lives we have shared. I understand now that the places I project my Ba are not dreams, but lifetimes my Ba will experience.

I strive to project my Ba to specific times and places, and re-visit lifetimes I have seen. I am after the same thing as Pharaoh: dominion over life and death, but my quest goes beyond cuddling up with Osiris. I have a great secret!

I have more ability to visit the near future, and so I focus on the land of Sumer and the city of Ur. Here my fervid lover Umh waits: despite my guilt avoiding Sha during this time, I need this desperate release. Then, after the most intense lovemaking session I have ever encountered, the oval shatters and loses all power! I cannot bring myself to return to the tomb.

ق

After the twins finished the story, Naji saw a panicked look on their faces. "Mom's back!" they cried, and before Naji knew it, they fled down the corridors of the Egyptian tomb. Naji followed, but the path became a long stairway; he realized he was awake, in his mother's arms, heading down the museum stairs to Fifth Avenue.

Everyone was relieved Naji was back with them, no one more than Ardra, who assumed the child had had a long nap. As they waited for a taxi, Ardra pulled out a bag from the gift shop. "Look what I got you, child. It's called a *shabti*." He showed Naji a small, adorable doll. "It's Egyptian; it will protect your soul, and give you advice." Ardra made the tiny figure talk: "If you're good, I will provide you with lessons of admonition. How 'bout that, kiddo?"

Naji giggled at his great-grandfather and begged him to keep playing with the shabti. Naji remembered what the twins had said about comforting the near dead, and how his father's Egyptian incarnation, Ankhar, had projected his soul using an object. Naji decided he would use the shabti to send comfort to his great-grandfather's soul. Ardra made the little doll jump for joy when the taxi pulled up, and Naji laughed hysterically.

As the cab pulled away, Sahara looked east, across the street to the building facing the museum, and noticed the address carved into its stone façade: 1001.

28

———◦◦◦———

December 6. Month 3.

By its fourth meeting, after the museum visit, the qaraq had chosen sides.

"We have to make more headway in completing Worlds we already know," Verle said.

"I refuse to approach our lifetimes in a shallow manner, just to rack up a tally, Diana said.

"So go swim out over your head, Doc," Zack said. "I'm for archive expansion."

"Our recalls are strange enough," Cachay said, "why push the emotional limits?"

"I'm with Diana,'" Porcy said. "I prefer stories of people to classifications."

The newly fearless Bax agreed, "I'm up for Diana's emotional challenges."

To break the palpable tension in the room, Sahara described Naji's recall at the museum. "The Egyptian projected his soul using an oval object. It reminds me of Diana's future life as Dizalegh, who learned to project her soul."

"Dr. Machiyoko will want us to try it, no doubt," Verle said.

"Don't be snide, love," Porcy said. "I'm working as hard as you. I don't need attitude."

Dr. Machiyoko knew Porcy had been helping at the church, helping Sahara with Naji, and helping Bax find jobs in a dried-up market. Porcy was especially sensitive to the suffering of people; watching trauma victims come into the church, she drove herself into a frenzy of work. The therapist recognized compensation for a harsh depression.

"Then, Miss Porcelain," Verle said. "You know how much work there is to be done!"

Bax struck a pose on the floor. "While you all argue, I'll project my Ba into those folders."

"While you're at it, project the contents into the computer," Zack said. "That's more than some people do around here."

Zack's jibe upset Diana more than she wanted. Her head ached deep in the base her skull.

Elvi intervened. "What about another lifetime in Dizalegh's era? That would explore past life beliefs and supplement a familiar World. Zack was Dizalegh's colleague and true love, Zizagh. Sahara was her rival Liligh, and Amar Dizalegh's defender. How about you, Verle?""

As the qaraq argued the suggestion, Diana's head throbbed. Eyes closed, she flashed on Dizalegh's passion for the story collections that bridged the ancient past with the near future. Images turned to words, and soon she was telling a story to the surprised group.

The Tale of Dizalegh's Early Career

You all may wonder how Dizalegh got herself mixed up in Zizagh's work. It did not transpire until she was forty years old; what early lifetime within a lifetime preceded it? Dizalegh's parents died when she was two, in a self-driven taxicab accident. Raised by her grandmother, a prominent Americanologist who was constantly away on lecture tours, Dizalegh learned to enjoy solitude. She wanted for nothing, except a doting adult. She consumed hundreds of reading lenses of every child's anthology of myths and legends. She saw visions of herself in foreign lands.

When old enough, she attended Miss Oprah's Liveaway School for Promising Girls, a dreadful place, complete with cruel initiations and every exclusionary mode known to rich girls. The school confirmed Dizalegh's love of privacy, but, like any unhealthy adolescent, she yearned to belong where she didn't, and listened to conversations while hiding in closets.

In the summers, she enjoyed a sleepaway camp in the Italian Garfagnana, close to her grandmother, who hosted the International Americanology Conference on Hostile Economics (IACHE) in Lucca. At camp, Dizalegh spoke Haute Milanese, learned how to load a crossbow blindfolded, and discovered the *Decameron* and the art of frame tale narrative. Most significantly for her soul, she made a tight bond with a boy and girl at The Little Alps Camp. The three of them shared distaste for the cheerier activities, and stole away for delightful hours. Dizalegh realized she could like people of both genders, but preferred private activity.

At university she became more social; she needed to go beyond a pattern of behavior that felt deeply limiting. A The University of Washington at Gatestown, where grandmother was Professor Emeritus at the Microsoft Institute, Dizalegh frequented a mystical group run by guru Jrasi. He claimed to read past life histories into myths and fables. Dizalegh concentrated hard on the parsing of the story material at meetings, sitting in the back of the room, legs crossed tightly.

Upon graduation she broke with the cult, landing her first job as a governess in Washington DC, where grandmother now advised a think tank on American-Singolian relations. To be part of an intimate family structure felt like redemption of her longtime indulgence in solitude and eavesdropping. Next, Dizalegh worked at the Global Licensing Organization for Cultural Action and Legislation (GLOCAL), which put local artistic best practices into the international spotlight, protecting them with international laws. For the second time, Dizalegh encountered the idea that past lives could be embedded into art and literature. The coincidence was too strong for her; she became curious about the link between reincarnation and ancient story collections.

After her grandmother passed, Dizalegh dove into research, coining words and phrases that resonated with story collections. For example, she became enamored of the term *recollection*. A story collection of past lives is a re-collection of recollections.

In her late thirties, Dizalegh had her first past life recalls. She grew consumed with proving the existence of reincarnation, and recalled a lifetime as a psychologist who performed past life regressions. With theoretical Physics positing time travel, Dizalegh came to believe metempsychosis had more to do with the nature of Time than with God or the Spirit. She proposed time travel experiments that could affirm reincarnation beyond a doubt.

Neither breakthroughs in Physics nor resources at GLOCAL allowed her to fulfill her work. An Algherman that GLOCAL frequently lobbied became concerned with Dizalegh's performance; her powerful grandmother was no longer there to protect her. She was removed from her position at age forty. Struggling to find work, Dizalegh was open to any career move.

Diana paused at this point in the story; semi-conscious, she searched her memory for a connection. "Do you remember the recall I had a couple weeks after 9/11?"

"In the Himalayas," Verle said, "the prehistoric tribe that made grave paintings."

"There was a figure observing their actions," Diana said, "hiding in the bushes."

"The future You watching the prehistoric You," Zack remembered. "You think Dizalegh mastered physics and time traveled?"

"I don't even know how she found another job," Diana said.

"I do," Zack said, relishing the moment. "I rescued her."

29

September 11. 10:55 A.M. Hour 3.

For the first twenty minutes Bax was at the World Trade Center, he looked around frantically to make sense of the scene. He was not allowed through certain barriers; people pushed past him to get away. He searched for Ooma among the temporary emergency shelters. Was that her waiting on that line? Was that her limping through the smoke and chaos? Or sitting against the wall of Trinity Church, wrapped in Amar's arms? Confused and vulnerable, he moved on with each sighting, second-guessing himself and choosing another direction to look. The chaotic scene and his inner turmoil led him into trance state once more. He found a bench and sat, his mind jumping to his seventh kiss tale, his final vision from the New Year's party.

The Tale of the Quarry in the Garfagnana

Nothing to do on such a hot day. Rest under the shade of the pines. Cool roots. By the marble quarry. Cooler up in the Garfagnana.

The little Alps. Let 'em bake in Lucca, Pappa says. Let 'em try to con-quer Castiglione. Impregnantable, he says. You are safe with us here, Balthasar. He lets me and Ursulina go to the quarry. By ourselves. We wait for the storm. Nothing else to do.

I am bigger than Ursulina. She was born 1111, the year of our Lord. I am jealous of that special number. Only ones. At least I am born 1110. Still many ones. And it makes me older. I am eleven, she is ten. My age has more ones. And I'm big for my age. Ursa likes that.

We wait for a heavy rain. The quarry will fill up fast. Then we can swim. Waiting is easy with Ursulina. Our heads fill up fast with ideas. I wonder what it's like to have many wives. Like the enemy people. Imagine yourself with four women, Ursa says. She puts her head on my chest. Giggles. I would like it, I say. Even if one wife was a Jew? Even if.

I play with Ursa's hair.

"Do you think there is another world, just like ours," she asks.

"With everything exactly the same?" I ask.

"Maybe not everything," she says.

"Maybe," I say. "You and me would lie here. Just like now. You look the same."

"The trees are the same. And the quarry." She shifts her head on me. Looks into my eyes. "Would my hair be the same?"

"Still long and brown. But not exactly." I pull out a strand. "This one would be different. And this one." She giggles. She stops giggling. Very fast. Few drops of rain.

"Do animals ever do it," she asks.

"Do what?"

"Kill themselves."

"You mean, like those people in Barga? The group in front of the church?"

"Yes, like the group," Ursa says. "Unholiest of acts, Mamma said. She crossed herself. What do you think?"

"You mean, if it's wrong?"

"No, silly, if animals do it," Ursa says. "In groups. And not lemmings."

"You mean, like zebras?"

"Yes, or those beautiful gazelles in Africa. The oryx."

"Why would they want to do it?" Ursa gives me a dark look.

The rain gets harder. Our clothes get wet. Even under the pines. My shirt is wet. Ursa rubs my chest. It is big and strong. She likes it. She jumps up. Grabs my hand. Pulls me up. We run out from under the trees. The rain is very strong now. Our clothes sopping wet. We look in the quarry. Fills up fast. I take off my drenched shirt. She takes off her shirt. An invitation.

Within moments we are naked. The water is almost high enough. The rain feels wonderful on my skin. Ursa's hand wonderful on my chest. Her hand explores further. Then she dashes off! Always dashes off. Dares me to dive in. Always a longer dive. Into shallower water. Where is she? The big rock! Highest point in the quarry! She stands at the edge. Her naked hand beckons me.

November 29.   Month 3.

Back at the qaraq's fourth meeting, the group acknowledged that Zack, as Zizagh, had shown up in Dizalegh's lifetime at the right time. Elvi invited Diana to continue.

The Tale of Dizalegh's Early Career, conclusion

You can imagine Dizalegh's desperation, having lost her reputation, and the community she had strived for all her life. She answered an ad for a research assistant, a job you understand was well below her position at GLOCAL. The job attracted her for two reasons: the researcher was at American University, an irony given her grandmother's career, and it dealt with story collections.

At the interview, the researcher, Zizagh, treated Dizalegh like a young student; you would forgive her if she had walked out the door and taken a job as a barista. But Zizagh confided in her that the work was confidential. What possessed him to share so much with a stranger? You may think he sensed Dizalegh was a soul mate; you may think he was as desperate as her. In any case, he sent away all the other candidates.

The texts hooked her. As she squinted from the reading lenses in her eyes, Zizagh plied her with multiple editions of *The Thousand and One Arab'an Nights*, and articles on Embedded Theory. Zizagh explained: there are no pure collections. Any anthology contains embedded structures, imposed over time, *horizontal* variants, like differing Arab'an Nights story sequences, *vertical* variants, like conflated versions of particular stories, and hidden social meanings.

Zizagh was studying a unique collection, which combined a history of past life tales from a particular group of people, a unique sequence of the Nights, and embedded structures. This version was not the first of its kind. Zizagh's work sought ancient versions that influenced the one he was decoding. He was aware of a version created by similar minded collectors called *The 379 Group*, which existed during the evolution of the Nights in ancient Baghdad.

As Zizagh described evidence for the imposed structures and incarnation tales, Dizalegh realized her life had led her here: the serendipitous encounters with past lives, the love of story anthologies, and the yearning for a passionate commitment. This odd man's fascinating project contained them all. By the end of the interview, Dizalegh was suggesting possible meanings for the story sequence, and Zizagh was asking her opinion about certain hidden structures. Their work together started at that first meeting and continued for twenty good years.

ق

Sahara made the first response to Diana. "Dear sister, I apologize for any grief I gave you while living at your house. You are fabulous! You filled in a World for Verle, found a connection between the Nights and reincarnation, and picked up a clue about this group from 1001 AD."

"How do you get 1001 for The 379 Group, Sahara?" Porcy asked.

"A connection I've made before: 379 AH by the Islamic calendar equals 1001 AD."

"Is this group putting Islamic morality into the Nights," Porcy said, "like in my lifetime as Hanbal? That took place in the 10th Century, right before 1001."

"Marvelous," Sahara said. "Can't wait to meet The 379 Group in an Arab World recall."

Although the discussions at the qaraq meeting made Sahara feel relatively normal, it had only been eleven weeks since 9/11. Her resilience was extraordinary, given that only eleven days after the Twin Tower attacks, Sahara suffered something equally catastrophic.

September 21. Day 11.

It was when she checked herself into the hospital, when Cachay was there too. After she was admitted, Sahara noticed less kicking inside her. The twins had been relatively inactive, but she assumed they had less room to move. She had back pain, and the nurses were concerned about her blood pressure. On the fourth morning, she noticed a bit of bleeding. She waited for Dr. Lake to make his rounds, but by lunchtime, it was too late. She heard a loud pop in the bathroom. Blood poured out of her.

September 11. 11:25 A.M. Hour 3.

Near Ground Zero, Bax continued his recall.

The Tale of the Quarry in the Garfagnana, conclusion

I'm always the first one to dive. I like to dare Ursa. Once in the water, shout at her to jump. But today she chooses Big Rock. Highest one in the quarry. Mamma forbid us. Too dangerous!

Ursa scrambles up Big Rock. I stare at her naked body bending and gripping. I am excited! I run to catch up. I have to accept her dare. She arrives at the top. Raises her arms in victory. I arrive behind her. Grab her arms. Pretend to push her off. She screams. I laugh. She turns and hits my chest. Ow! She rubs it in apology. Then hits me again. Another dark look in her eyes.

We look over the edge. So high! We've been up here, but never to dive. Is the water deep enough? Depends on the storm. Rain splashes everywhere. Hard to see bottom. Must be deep.

I dare Ursa to go first. No fair, she scolds. It's my dare today. You always go first anyway, she teases. Let's hold hands, I say. Go together. A double dare. Her face tightens. She is so beautiful! Why have I never noticed? Maybe I've always noticed.

Ursa lets out a big breath. Builds up courage. Her face relaxes, but gets serious. Makes me scared. She looks down again. Fine, we'll go together. But you must jump. I command it. Say you will. Obey my command. No backing down. No tricks. No letting go of my hand. Take an oath.

She's so strange. Did she plan this? Why command me? I'm so scared but I must take the dare. Why not? I take the dare every time. Just summer fun. Forget your fears. Dive and be done.

Ursa takes my hand. We shiver from head to foot. Naked hips touch. So excited! She shouts: UNO! I squeeze her hand. DUE! She's so fearless! Screams: TRE! We leap into the air.

I remember three things. UNO: a rock ledge juts out. We have not leaped wide enough. We hit the lip of the ledge. Our hands fly from each other. I feel a terrible scrape on my leg.

DUE: we bounce off the ledge. I shoot a glance at Ursa. She is shocked. Then smiles. Sheer determination. So much in her mind. A last dark look. Why has she commanded this?

TRE: before we hit the water, I see bottom. The rainwater is crystal-line clear. But not full enough. Dangerously shallow. We will hit bottom the moment after we hit the water.

My last thought: I am about to die.

ق

Bax snapped out of his recall, his heart racing. Haunted by the look in Ursalina's eyes, Bax knew beyond a doubt that Ursulina had planned the quarry dive as a double suicide. Or rather a suicide and a murder. The girl seemed to love him. Why would she cause their deaths? A harder question: if Ursa was Ooma's incarnation, what evil karma fes-tered between them?

Bax regained his senses, got off the bench, and continued search-ing for Ooma. Was he just imagining seeing her? Would he ever find her again? He noticed that the victims from the Towers had to identi-fiy themselves when they sought treatment. Boldly for him, Bax asked emergency workers if Amar and Ooma appeared on any lists. But Amar had been too impatient to wait in the lines. As Bax failed to locate their names, Amar and Ooma were walking uptown to St. Vincent's.

September 21. Day 11.

At the hospital, Sahara was quickly sent for an ultrasound, the nurses and doctors barely hiding the grave looks on their faces. While she waited for other tests, Sahara called Amar. He had been called into Bruckner Associates' temporary office in Jersey City, the first time back

208

to work since the attacks. He was upset he had to leave work since he was worried about being laid off with the fragile economy. But he was more concerned about Sahara when he arrived at the hospital to find his wife going through a fetoscopy, non-stress test, and electronic fetal monitoring.

Unable to get a clear answer from anyone, Amar thought to call Dr. Hajjaj. An expert in fetal trauma, Sahara's other Ob/Gyn was able to consult with Dr. Lake about tests results and the course of action. When Amar briefly saw Sahara and explained about the consult, she cursed herself: she had chosen Lake over Hajjaj because Dr. Lake had given her more latitude in her daily activity. She had let her determination to work, free of Amar's grip, prevent her from listening to Dr. Hajjaj's cautions. Their cursed relationship might be destroying the twins! Amar kissed her forehead and insisted she remain calm and cease such overwhelming thoughts.

Dr Hajjaj advocated an immediate operation. The fetuses might be 'monoamniotic twins,' sharing the same placenta and sac, interfering with each other's umbilical cords. There was no apparent entangling of cords, but something constricted them. There was a remote possibility that one of the twins was gripping the cord and suppressing blood flow. Sahara's fists clenched at the horrifying thought. She was given a sedative as she went into surgery.

November 29.   Month 3.

At the qaraq meeting, Diana came out of trance, but remained inside her own thoughts. The recall had been triggered by the tension within the qaraq, which Diana had fomented with her attack on Verle. She did not like the negative influence she had on the group; it gave her too much social responsibility. She felt burdened with responsibility for the group's well-being.

And the therapist was acutely aware of the psychological wounds her friends were nursing from September 11. Amar was jumpy and saw potential catastrophes everywhere. Bax was taking crazy risks, untypical of him. And Ooma: where to begin? If Diana was the group's therapist, then she needed to commit to this special role. The challenge frightened her. In her future life she had trouble committing to people; how could she ever pass this test as a healer?

When Diana did not respond, Verle said, "Dr. Diana, are you feeling poorly? If it helps, I am very grateful you added to a World. A Multiple, Near Future World."

Diana had heard enough. The weight of her responsibility toward the group and her self-doubts pushed against her negative attitude toward Verle's scheme. The friction was like two tectonic plates rubbing against each other. She could no longer hold back, and her feelings erupted.

"Verlin Walker! Do you realize everyone in this group is suffering from Post-Traumatic Stress? And with different symptoms. Zack's been having trouble sleeping. Sahara complains about her distance from Naji. We've all lived through a disaster, talked to dozens like us, but we're the only ones dealing with it through past lives. And I'm the only therapist who understands this instantly. So I say that sorting recalls into neat little piles is not the way to go! It's insulting."

"Actually, Di, the piles ain't so neat." Zack tried to break the tension in the room. "So you're giving out free sessions for PTSD?"

Diana chortled at the pathetic joke, but tears streamed from her eyes. "Of course. Any of you, my door is open."

Porcy asked tentatively, "You really think we've got trauma stress, Doc? Like soldiers?"

Diana took a deep breath. "Look at yourself, Porcy. You're working constantly, sometimes without noticing you haven't eaten. Pardon me, Cachay, but have you been more irritable recently? Me? Most days I feel helpless to help anyone, like I've lost control. These are all classic Post-Traumatic Stress symptoms."

Diana took a sip of tea. She looked at Verle, saw his overwhelming exhaustion. He had not admitted his stress, but she read it in his grayish wrinkles. "I should apologize, Verle. Elvi asked me to watch my tongue after the last meeting, and I blew it."

"You blew nothing, young lady," Verle said. "But why do you hate the World Types so?"

"I don't hate them, but I feel responsible toward the group so I want our memories to illuminate what we're going through. Dizalegh's breakthrough to commit to Zizagh could be a beacon for me when I feel helpless. Just promise me you'll look for beacons in the dark. When the group assented, Diana added, "And Verle, will you forgive me?"

"Only if you promise to call this old fool out on anything. Anytime."

Porcy looked at Elvi, knowing she was her spirit guide. "So, fearless leader, you conspired to have the Doc and Verle kiss and make up, didn't you?"

With the resolution, Elvi smiled broadly. "Anyone else for tea?"

September 11. 4:30 P.M. Hour 8.

After hours of searching for Ooma at the disaster site, Bax doubted he had ever seen her. He was unafraid of the lingering smoke or the wounded bodies everywhere, but this did not relieve his agony over Ooma and her life as Ursalina. Ursa's lifetime occurred centuries after the other recalls from the New Year's party. How did a clearly Christian locale relate to the closely tied Islamic lifetimes? The tragic tale stuck out from the Arabic tales and stuck in Bax's mind. Why had Ooma wanted them to die in the quarry? Why had Bax seen this memory at the climax of kissing Ooma, but also during this day of devastation? Were Christians pitted against Muslims in his mind because of the tensions in the world right now? Did he recall Ursa's death because he imagined the worse happening to Ooma in this life?

He was not going to figure this out anytime soon. He had failed to rescue Ooma, but had made the attempt. He couldn't think about it any-more. He finally gave up and boarded one of the cruise liners ferrying people back to New Jersey. As Ooma and Amar wandered the evening streets to shake off the horrors and recalls of the day, Bax yearned to go home.

September 21. Day 11.

Because of fear of blood clotting, Dr. Hajjaj induced Sahara's labor immediately. A Caesarian section was ill advised and dangerous in the situation, and carrying one or more dead fetuses would be emotionally traumatizing. After twelve hours, Sahara delivered the twins, then lay there, spent. Across the room, she made out the infant bodies, lying still and quiet.

"Bring me my children." Sahara thought she was screaming out loud, but the sound barely left her lips. Why were they not crying? The nurses looked at each other tensely. The head nurse consulted with Dr. Hajjaj. Finally, she brought the twins to Sahara's bedside.

"You must thank Allah for them," Dr Hajjaj said gently, "and love them always."

The nurse encouraged Sahara to look at them and touch them, to help her let them go. Sahara did not understand what the nurse said, but once she saw her beautiful, peaceful twins, her tears flowed uncontrollably. She stroked them tenderly. How could she be so strong? Was she in shock? She placed her hands on the babies' heads one last time, and closed her eyes. Silently, the nurse took away the twins.

Amar comforted Sahara as best he could in her recovery room. But after the trauma of 9/11, he could barely accept the loss of the twins. He reassured his wife that she was blameless, but he could not provide much more emotional support than that. He could not bring himself to cry.

Sahara's visitors commented on the inexplicability of the tragedy; no one in the qaraq dared suggest that the twins would pass on to another life. Doctors weakly explained that with stillbirths at full term, often the cause of death is unknown.

All through the day and night Amar remained by Sahara's side. Grateful for his presence, she renewed her joy at his return from the Twin Towers disaster. She also felt his distance. Neither of them could take in all the emotion experienced in the last eleven days.

September 11. 8:10 P.M. Hour 11.

After several hours of waiting for the ferry, and then the train to Glenclaire, Bax finally arrived to an empty house. He called Porcy, got through, and found she was at Sahara's home. He collapsed on his sofabed. He thought back to the consummation of his relationship with Ooma on the sofabed just weeks ago. He considered going to the Qadir house, but if Ooma was not home he would not know how to talk to her family.

Amar and Ooma returned to New Jersey around ten o'clock that night. Amar escorted Ooma to the Qadir home, where he witnessed her joyous reunion with her parents and younger sister. Although the Qadirs were grateful for Amar's protection of Ooma, he felt a coolness from them. He felt hurt by this attitude, given all that he had endured to save her. But he could not say anything at that moment, perhaps ever. When he left the house, Ooma did not look at him.

After Porcy came home, she called Sahara often until she heard the news that Amar and Ooma had returned. Now Bax wished to visit Ooma, but Porcy prevented it. Sahara had said that every time a siren sounded or building cracked, Amar flinched like an animal. Ooma must be suffering, too, and needed rest and her family's care. Porcy went to bed and Bax let himself cry.

October 10. Week 5.

Two weeks after her release from the hospital, Sahara insisted her life return to normal, much to the complaints of her friends. If Scheherazade could sleep with the King every night knowing she might die the next morning, Sahara could go work at a library. She launched into her chapter for Prof. Agib, and tried to be attentive to Naji and Amar. Naji was still in his own world, but Sahara decided to let that be. Amar was home many days, while Bruckner Associates regrouped. He was restless, but Sahara assumed it was work related.

Sahara was not looking for coddling, but she felt a wall rising between her and Amar. They had been so intimate only a month ago! After the stillbirths, he seemed only adequately sympathetic. She understood his fragile state after surviving the Twin Towers, accepting his distance as shock. She rationalized that she was being over-sensitive to the nightmarish situation. But Sahara grasped that Amar was more concerned about Ooma. His assistant had not returned to work or communicated with anyone since September 11. Amar was worried in a heightened way, the same way he now overreacted to loud noises. What had happened between them that day?

It was too hard for Sahara to push Amar to disclose any of the deeper emotions he must be experiencing. With her determination to get back to her life, she could not dredge up their feelings toward the tragic loss of the children. She knew she should, or call on Dr. Machiyoko to help them through this horrible moment, but it was too painful. She threw herself into work and trusted that their souls and the relationship would heal over time. Time was her solace.

September 21. Day 11.

As his mother was in surgery, Naji stayed with his father at the hospital. Amar attempted to play games and tell stories, but was soon frustrated with his son's lack of response. On their visits, Porcy, Zack, and Cachay took turns holding Naji. Did the child know what was happening?

Naji continued his search for the twins, which had started eleven days earlier. He felt the two figures slowly letting him gain on them. At one point, they led him into a beautiful park with cottonwood trees. Sitting down on a bench, the twins finally let Naji approach them.

"Are you my twin brothers?" Naji asked. "Inside my Mommy's belly?"

The twin on the right side of the bench answered. "No. We are twin souls. But there are no souls inside her belly. We are sorry."

Naji gasped. "Why are there no souls there?"

The twin on the left answered. "Your Mommy's babies were not ensouled."

"Not ensouled? Who told you that?"

"The Infinite Intelligence. Not every living creature is ensouled."

The right twin concurred. "Creatures and objects are ensouled at different times, for different durations."

"Why does that happen?" Naji shook his head. "It's awful."

The left twin responded. "Yes, sometimes it is. But sometimes it is good. There are many different reasons it happens. The Infinite Intelligence always has its reasons."

"Why did it happen to my Mommy?"

Both twins said, "We do not know. They did not tell us."

Naji was crestfallen. "They said nothing else?"

The twins looked at each other. The left one nodded, and then the right one said to Naji: "They said that this time there would not be three, only one. You are the Child."

Naji did not know what that meant. "So you are not my brothers?"

"No," both twins said.

Naji felt like crying. He fought back tears because the twins watched him closely. He did not know what else to say or ask or do. After a long time, he finally spoke.

"Will you be my friends?"

END OF PART ONE

PART TWO

30

—⟨~~⟩—

Sept. 15. Day 5 (4 days after Impact).

Ooma Qadir slept two full days after returning home. The harrowing escape from the Twin Towers combined with her psychic time traveling burned out her core being. Her exhaustion worried and frightened her parents, convincing them to keep her far from the world. On the third day, Ooma resumed consciousness in fits and starts. Her mother cooked all kinds of soups and breads and pastes to aid Ooma's recovery, an overflow of kitchen love. During Ooma's short passages of clear-headedness, her parents ranted that she should never return to work. Given the state of the world, she might meet violent prejudice. It took every ounce of Ooma's weakened will to persuade her parents to contact Bruckner Associates for her. On the fourth day, Ooma's father did so, on condition that Ooma not call Bax or any so-called friends, especially Amar. He might have rescued her, but he was still linked to the treacherous World Trade Center.

Ooma regained consciousness with the help of nightmares. Her dreams replayed images of falling debris, screams and shouts, an endless stairway. Startled awake by these dangers, Ooma would slip into protective trance and escape into a past life fragment. In one, a solitary sentence from the Scheherazade tale jumped out at her. It was a hopeful reminder that the recalls about the evolution of the story could insure Ooma's acceptance at qaraq meetings.

More dramatically, she received glints from a mysterious period when a version of her soul from ancient Egypt merged with her wounded anima from the 1600s. The two souls, 'old' and 'new' Umh, moved fluidly between a half a dozen lives. These visions mixed with the nightmares.

The Timeline of the Merged Souls

The merging of the souls is a healing: old Umh summoned from 12th Century BC Egypt to rescue her future soul that had fallen into solipsistic crisis, unable to continue. Since old Umh is also in crisis festering in the reign of Ramses III, she has a spiritual mission to travel forward in time and heal herself, not with eternal life but with nine or eleven cat lives that will see her/us/me through this ordeal this devastation this attack this mass violence

so there is a terrible beautiful collision a crashing of two souls in the night of 1600 AD, but new Umh's shattered soul is a blessing in disguise because it is pliable and enables old Umh to get in between the parts weave the fragments together into the loom of her own anima

the reconstruction is not complete without the merged souls entering a corporeal form a metaphor for new Umh's need to quit an intensely anti-social period and rejoin the body of the world old and new Umh we/I need a test lifetime in some deeply incubating world for we are still two souls separate locked in a not so friendly dialogue about how to complete the spiritual mission, until we incarnate as an English lady-in-waiting into a small crammed study in London for a night of debauchery with the transcendental poet John Donne

Donne's room becomes our quarantine area the hot kisses from the enlightened poet ignite our two souls and old Umh delivers the breath of life to the hungry mouth of new Umh forcing her from solipsism and the sexual crucible of the Donne room forges together

our two souls and the morning after I am at last I and we are no longer We

and Donne is equally empowered for that same morning he sketches
the Idea of a room-as-a-universe an Idea that emanated from the chambers of the Pyramids full of rooms of everlasting Time even new Umh's
solipsistic vision of the universe contained only within her soul was a
precursor to the Idea that Donne poeticizes for the world

As Ooma gained more hours of waking consciousness, her parents'
sequestering of her from the world reinforced her anguish over Sahara's
blocking her from meetings. Deep feelings had erupted between her and
Amar, secretly making the possibility of the qaraq including them more
frsaught than ever. Ooma thought the warmth she felt for Amar might be
a comfort, but the emotions were too volatile. She pushed her yearning
back down into her churning unconscious.

One positive thing could come out of the horrors of the Trade
Center attacks. Sahara would cherish the flood of Nights evolution
tales Ooma received that day. Ooma made a deep vow to record every
detail of the stories in her journal. Writing would ground her unstable
mind, too.

The Timeline of the Merged Souls, continued

Made flesh on that first glorious night in John Donne's eternal safe-
house, old and new Umh we/I gracefully sashay from one body to another,
the first new life on planet Aklanon where I am Om-na virtuoso open-
hearted collaborator at Draill U weeping at the keyboard as I accompany
a heart-wrenching rehearsal and when I depart this life of aesthetic pleasure I cannot imagine this tragedy who could have predicted the sheer
audacity of the Tower attacks

we re-merge our souls into a new cat life and land by the edge of the
North Sea handmaiden to the forlorn cousin of Ophelia she too a lost soul

221

I use her to strengthen my powers I summon the magical Ba force that projected old Umh's soul from Egypt

I come into full power as the Lady in Red spy broker of multi-national coffers of the Thirty Years Whirlpool and seduce Colonel Walker who is my downfall

I am replenished in a Scottish witches' coven but old Umh gets trapped in a mirror never-space and new Umh comes out of full power to fall Fall FALL the way so many fell down from the Towers seeking relief from the flames

On the fourth night Ooma lay recovering in her bedroom, she jerked awake as the monstrous building fell in her mind. The visions still plagued her, crumbling Towers jumbling up with merging souls. She turned on the nightstand lamp and reached for her journal. Despite her determination to record the recalls, her mind played tricks. Was she Ooma living in modern New Jersey, or old Umh from ancient Egypt, or new Umh from the 17th Century?

As she transcribed, she wondered why she had not received any new Nights tales. She had moved on to another set of lifetimes in her soul's journey. Ooma observed that the memories were about the travails of a lost soul, exactly her current state. Her recall suggested a new understanding of the qaraq's history before and after 1600, a journey into and out of madness.

Verle had once concocted a timeline for the Umh twins' adventures, but Ooma now saw the origin of the merged souls. If she could make herself see beyond the severing of the two souls in the coven, she could gain more currency to buy her way into the meetings. Ooma embraced her nightmares, her soul's madness, and extended the vision.

The Timeline of the Merged Souls, conclusion

Old Umh's leap of folly into a shard of magic mirror in hopes of escaping back to Egypt also caused new Umh to be stuck in the body of the Witch in Red brain dead and helpless, nurtured for the rest of her days by the good Christian souls of the coven, and old Umh stuck in never-space

after years vegetating as the Witch in Red new Umh escaped that trap to fly into another one: a facsimile of John Donne's study in London, the 17ᵗʰ Century incarnation of the qaraq's very own room-as-a-universe dating back at least to the Egyptian tomb not the chamber where Amar as animal mummifier sought refuge in the Old Kingdom nor the Kharman family tomb of the Middle Kingdom nor even old Umh's launching pad in the New Kingdom but all of these

for there is an ethereal space that exists in timeless conditions and any soul at any time may enter it or seek refuge in it or get stuck in it co-inhabiting the space with souls entering from wildly different time periods but recognizing them and these souls might spend a lifetime in this Donne room of the cosmos or move in and out quickly within one life

new Umh entered the refuge trap and there met the qaraq each soul trapped inside an object due to events of various and sundry lifetimes, so she incorporated into the image of a mirror in a painting on the wall that by some magical property reflected the actual objects in the room

and new Umh remained there for decades after she split from old Umh even after the close of the Thirty Year War and entrapped inside the painted mirror she enabled old Umh to be released from the never-space inside the mirror shard in the coven's cave new Umh sacrificed herself in one glass so old Umh could free herself from another

a happy sacrifice since by releasing old Umh she ensured her evolution as a soul: if old Umh had not resumed her life in ancient Egypt she never would have evolved through Time. New Umh would have been lost, too.

ق

When Ooma recalled old Umh escaping the never-space (her suburban bedroom felt like a never-space, too), she remembered that, hours after escaping the South Tower, she had received a memory unlike all the others. The anomalous recall had baffled her until now. It was old Umh's journey from the 17th century back to ancient Egypt. If she couldn't recall any new Nights tales, the key to Sahara's approval, at least Ooma might find a connection between the Nights, the ancient Mideast, and old and new Umh's stories.

31

——⟨ ⟩——

Sept. 11, 2:22 P.M. Hour 6.

The Tale of the Priestess and Ramses III

As I fall backward in never-space, images of incarnations speed past me a reflection of my desperation to escape the mirror shard: a mythical roukh, teeth clenched in fury; a desperate sailor, surrounded by nothing but waves, clinging to a splinter of the mast; fruits, vines, and flowers, intertwined, blossoming in a garden of paradise

and as I approach my life in the 20th Dynasty in the time of Ramses III, I see Egypt on the cusp of a great Dark Age dividing the golden ages of Egyptian rule from the later advances of Greece and Rome I see the sack of territories forcing every people to look for new ground, the first known labor strike, and the arrested tree growth from befouled atmosphere that limited sunlight

and I see my own demise as I overshoot the local clouds of my home town and jump in Time to my play for glory centuries before as Queen Oumkratania how I was broken by my failure and how at my rebirth in

Egypt I was ready to do anything to regain the balance of my spirit just as I am ready to do anything to leave never-space and as I lose full consciousness of my soul's history I remember my life in Egypt in the time of Ramses III, as if reliving it.

I knew the priests were as scared as the rest of us that great Ramses could not stem the invasion of the Sea Peoples so I knew something was going on behind the Pyramid pylons about special life forms that could hide or protect you from danger I was frustrated I could not see through the walls the way a sky spirit is frustrated not to see what lurks beneath the oceans

I was a powerful priestess and the clergy needed me for my dominance over thousands of female souls who followed and adored and respected me I had always done the priests' bidding usually suppressing my female supplicants' questioning of male authority still despite my great value they hid from me this great secret experiment tomfoolery

it was a century since we started calling our King by the name of Pharaoh meaning Great House a great irony since our last Kings weren't worth it but Ramses III deserved the title and so deserved my advice so I went to him a daring move since I had only met him once but he looked kindly upon me and asked me what my heart desired

I laid it all out: the priests had devised some method of protecting themselves and Pharaoh was displeased and desired the execution of the priests but I gently suggested he not let the secret die with the priests but partake of the protection himself and Pharaoh heard me and I offered to discover the secret if Pharaoh would grant me access to the priests' inner sanctum and he inquired how I would gain the information and I explained that priestesses have a powerful charm that exposes anything and I showed him my charm and we exposed much to each other that night

I gained access to the priests through the highest Minister who did not trust me and set a condition that I test this arcane technique to ensure that it was safe for Pharaoh and I was reluctantly escorted to the deepest darkest corner of the Pyramid into a special chamber as old as the oldest

Pyramids and as fresh as a newly decorated royal tomb and here were the priests' stores for their life in eternity all the jewels and wheat and oils they could possibly use but their treasure was not what Pharaoh sought and they breathed a sigh of relief when I requested their secret method they agreed heartily with a few laughs which did not ease my soul

their secret: we all knew techniques for projecting your Ba into objects for sure footing after death but the priests claimed they could project their living Ba into places they targeted and thus escape the ills to befall the Kingdom and when they hesitated to teach me this practice I mentioned how easily Pharaoh could reverse his decision to spare their miserable lives

I practiced projecting my Ba day and night for weeks reporting to Pharaoh the plausibility and safety of the method and promising to add it to the charms we enjoyed in his chamber but he grew impatient and pressured me until I realized the devilish priests had left out a key component: eavesdropping on their practice I observed they focused on an actual object a shabti a figurine so I got my favorite object in the world a statuette of a cat carved in stone and since I had been working so intensely I overdid connecting to the little cat and my entire Ba left my body traveled through the cat became endowed with multiple cat lives and I saw the future spread out and I shot ahead to rescue new Umh and merge our souls

I never returned to Pharaoh who had my body dragged through the streets and thrown in the Nile and returning from never-space I saw to my horror there was no life to inhabit and I regretted learning the secret of the priests but I did not regret fulfilling my spiritual desires in secret for whenever I do so in the public eye I fail I fall I fell

so after eight or nine lives projected through the cat shabti I was still lost without a home without a body without an incarnation, my soul doomed for all Time.

ق

Ooma awoke drenched in sweat, having felt the terror of being stuck forever between life and death. Her breathing was difficult, her head spun, and, strangely, her mind rang with phrases from the Nights. But where was the connection between the Nights and ancient Egypt? Knowing Sahara had studied at the University of Chicago and the Oriental Institute, Ooma wanted to ask her about Ramses III and the glory of Egypt on the wane. She yearned to be part of qaraq discussions.

Grabbing her journal, Ooma added Umh's lifetimes, deep in thought about the journey of her twin souls. What was new Umh's solipsistic nightmare all about? What events in the qaraq's 16th Century history had driven her crazy? In her current fragile state, the idea that she, like Uzmeth or new Umh, was fated to live on the edge of sanity sent a chill up her spine.

But her vulnerable mind was also highly receptive to lifetime visions, especially those enticing to the qaraq. She was indispensable in fleshing out the qaraq's role in developing the Nights, and she was *necessary* to the qaraq understanding its complex history. But to fulfill her crucial importance, she had to go willingly to wherever her mind journeyed, regardless of its cost on her mental state.

32

———⦿⦿⦿———

September 29. Week 3 (2 weeks after Impact).

During the week Sahara returned home after the death of the twins, Amar fawned over her.

"They say you still need rest, love. I can organize your meds, bring you tea, read to you. You gave me a hero's welcome when I came back from the Towers. It's the least I can do."

"I hardly did anything," Sahara said. It was true. She had been overjoyed to have Amar safely home, but he was encased in a jittery shell. She was not sure how to deal with him.

"You were a rock for me," Amar said. "Everything made me nervous. A slippery toy on the stair. Bacteria on the leftovers. I was a mess."

You still are, Sahara thought. But she said, "Now we both are, thanks to me."

It was too hard to hear her talk this way. Amar took his wife's hand. "Remember how happy we were the night before the attacks? It took us so long to get to that loving place again. We mustn't lose it. How we can we regain that happiness?"

How can we possibly regain that happiness? Sahara heard as much doubt as tenderness in his voice. It was too hard for *her* to hear. She twirled a chunk of hair around her finger, searching for a positive way forward. "I have an idea. If you'd like to read to me, there's been a flurry of *Alf Layla* articles coming out of places like Wayne State University. Read them to me."

"Wayne State? As in Scheherazade in Detroit?" Amar shrugged. "If it would sooth you."

"I'd be grateful." Seeing his doubt again, Sahara said, "But nothing will eliminate the pain."

October 6. Week 4.

Sahara had given up therapy after living with Diana, but the therapist insisted Sahara not push down her feelings. Porcy had eased Sahara by throwing Naji's birthday party. Being among children at FunStop reminded her of the twins, but the qaraq's company did wonders. Hopeful, she convinced Amar to go to therapy. Amar knew it was detrimental to bottle up his emotions; Sahara had left him after his violent episodes of blowing off pent up anger. He had to unload the horrors.

In his first session with Dr. Machiyoko, Amar shared his constant fears. Ooma had not returned to work: in his shaky state he knew something was dreadfully wrong.

The therapist asked Amar to return to his 9/11 saga. "Tell me about Ooma's state then."

"I was fascinated by the stories that came out of her, which you've heard," Amar explained. "But we were in severe danger and she couldn't see it. I was worried she was losing her mind."

"Did you feel you were going crazy, too?"

"No! I felt saner than ever, everything I feared was happening. I even felt the buildings would collapse, and they did, for God's sake! I saw the world more truthfully than I ever had."

"Do you still feel like you have a prescient ability?"

"Look, Diana, I was in a heightened state. I know it wasn't normal, and I'm not a prophet."

Dr. Machiyoko crossed her legs tightly and leaned toward Amar. "This will sound like a leap, but tell me more about 'the whole funeral process,' as you called it. How was that for you?"

"How was it for *you*? You were there. A funeral for two unborn beings. What can I say?"

"Nothing, if you don't want to. I just want you to look at your feelings."

"Sorry," Amar said. "It's hard to know how to grieve. We never knew them." Amar reflected in silence, then said, "It feels like a symbol of all the pain Sahara and I have endured."

"Do you mean in your past lives together?"

Amar looked at her, dumbfounded. "No, Diana. Just this one."

October 9. Week 5.

During the week after starting therapy, Amar would do either all or nothing for Sahara. On Wednesday, he brought home ice cream and a romantic comedy video. On Friday, he sulked in the morning, worked late at the office, and fell asleep when he got home. That weekend Sahara had two painful reminders of the stillbirths: sporadic bleeding and the stubborn flow of breast milk. Returning from his Saturday therapy session, Amar found his wife sobbing. He rocked her in his arms. On Sunday, he spent the day watching football, a rarity. He was completely erratic.

October 20. Week 6.

For a couple sessions, Amar had asked Diana to regress him, but no past life memories emerged. That Saturday afternoon, Amar came home determined.

231

"Hypnotize me, Sahr. Even if you end up having the recall. You've started qaraq meetings again and I'm pissed. I'm supposed to express my feelings, right? I can't have my own recalls, and you lot are swimming in them. This is something we can do. It'll help us move on."

"Move on?" Sahara was wide eyed. "It's only been a few weeks."

"But you're already going to work, fighting the Feds, meeting the qaraq. Please. Try."

Sahara saw his needy look, and no ulterior motive. Ooma had emerged from home, and appeared at the Jersey City Bruckner office. Soon she'd insist on joining the meetings. If Ooma was accepted and not Amar, there'd be hell to pay.

For the first attempts, the couple had no success. Lying on the new couch in the Arabian niche, Amar had trouble relaxing. Sahara lay next to him. Amar had received recalls in the past through her touch. She hoped it also would bring Amar closer to her.

After a few days of failed attempts, Sahara asked, "How did you receive the Nights recalls on 9/11? Many in the qaraq saw them, which was truly amazing. Was it the insanity of the day?"

Amar hesitated, but did not wish to lie to Sahara. That always got them into trouble. "Ooma had the recalls. Or picked up on them from others in the qaraq."

When he said no more, Sahara asked, "But you had physical contact with her, didn't you?"

"Sahr, I did the damn Fireman's Carry down seventy flights. Yes we had physical contact!"

Amar's over-reaction was as upsetting to Sahara as this intimate knowledge of the rescue. But they were attempting a calm hypnotic state. "I'm not attacking you. Just trying to help."

"And heal. I'm sorry, it's the nerves," he said. "Let's try again."

Eventually Sahara was able to regress Amar. But she wondered why Ooma had such better luck with him. And what that meant for the future of the qaraq.

232

November 3. Week 8.

"Are you still experiencing that heightened feeling?" Dr. Machiyoko asked.

Amar was tiring of his sessions. "You ask this every time. What are you after, Diana?"

"You're not depressed. But you flinch at loud noise and have a heightened sense of danger."

"So I'm paranoid? Are you paranoid if bad things actually happen to you? Ooma's only be back to work a few weeks. She's so fragile. I worry about her. Is that bad?"

"It's admirable. Healthy. But do you want your fears to rule you?" Dr. Machiyoko waited for a response. She could explore being ruled, given his lifetimes as a King. "I have an idea! This is perfect!" She jumped up, got a sheaf of papers, and moved to the stool at the foot of the futon.

"Is it story time, Dunyazade? I'm not paying for a mini-qaraq meeting here."

"Indulge me, your mightiness. To cope with survival, you suffered a deep brain response, which I believe you're stuck in. By reading your lifetime as another deep brain survivor, maybe we can free up something. Zack gave me some archive tales to edit, including Mr. Borzu, right here."

"You're gonna read my story? Hasn't Borzu caused enough problems?"

The Borzi world had stirred up ugly tensions between Amar, Bax, and Sahara a couple years before. Diana reassured him there was little to worry about (was he feeling that heightened state of fear?). She read aloud: Borzu's stubborn, heroic exploits, his taking on unwanted leadership.

Verle pestering her at the second meeting: she was the only qaraqi who had not recalled a Borzi lifetime. With each phrase she read, Amar's response pulled her into the World. Her anger at Verle and her heightened attention colluded to send her back to the end of the Borzi-Vawr feud.

The Tale of the Hotly Pursued Cavewoman

You know exactly why I went there! Borzu is dead to us now. You don't believe in him anymore than I do, even though you are a Borzi warrior. You may have crushed the Vawr and left a few families to gnaw the bones of their dead, but what has that made you? A desperate animal!

You chase me day and night, and have your way with me by force. I get it, I'm no huge-skull: you want me as mate, to tend your fire. But you all disgust me, stuffing your faces with half-cooked deer meat, gristle dangling from your teeth. The image plagues me; I picture you slobs up in a tree, underneath a damp rock, on the ocean floor. That's how little I want to be Borzi.

Do you understand my anger? When I escape and sneak over to the last remaining Vawr village, you track me there! If I went to another land, outside the Three Valleys, for a nice quiet dinner, there you'd be, guest of honor in the cave! I cannot escape your infuriating pursuit of me.

You insist on knowing why I went to the Vawr village. How could I go near them, they are dead to us. True enough, ever since heartless K'Chung killed the Vawr one by one. Long ago we justified killing Vawr for denying Winter a place at the table. Then they had another maddened scheme, draining blood from a Borzi warrior, to ensures his soul comes back as a Vawr. There was no influx of newborn Vawr, but the ritual did not fail them.

They discovered a world in between lives. Their energies were weak to fight the Borzi, but perfectly focused for death. Not your brutal idea of death, where you make a meal of someone's brains, but a sublime, hopeful death. I witnessed the Vawr's serenity in facing death, and I wished to join them. My desire was fraught by you and your warlord pals. No matter how radiant my soul felt, I suspected I would not live long enough to learn their rites.

You've shunned your hero Borzu, and shunned us who would save you from sinking into the mire. I yearn to join any tribe but yours. Even without the Vawr rite, I'll reincarnate into a group that opposes whatever idiotic herd you run with in the next life. It'll be the next round of an age-old war played out in the forests of our planet.

ق

When Diana came out of trance, Amar had his coat on. "Your 2:15's here, Princess."

Diana gasped. "See what happens to a soul entrenched in survival tactics?"

"But superior souls like you evolve to spiritual wisdom?"

"Amazing, right?" Diana got up from the stool. "Survival obsession alienates the soul."

"Nice try," Amar said, "but you're doing qaraq business on my dime. Conflict of interest."

"No charge, okay? And think about those ideas. For next time."

November 6. Week 9.

A month after Amar's attentions began to wane, Sahara detected a pattern. Ever since they had married, Amar's life had gotten in the way of her doctoral work, or she had let it. They had moved away from the University of Chicago because of his work; he had needed her to play housewife for the sake of appearance at his Wall Street job; his threatening reaction to her getting pregnant had sabotaged her peace; their separation had allowed her to work independently, but Amar had spent the year wooing her back; the rejuvenated sex alone had driven her to distraction.

Now she fretted over his lack of affection. Enough! She would not let *his issues* stop her research. Figuring how to incorporate these fantastic ideas about the origin of the Nights into a scholarly work might take months. At least she had to finish a chapter for Prof. Agib.

Amar supported her renewed attack on her thesis, but Sahara felt his gesture came too easily. Was he championing her work so she'd give him more space?

November 10. Week 9.

"You're concerned about how little they call you into the office?" Dr. Machiyoko asked.

"The writing's on the wall," Amar answered. "My stock's been rising and falling at work for two years now. Since 9/11, downsizing is very enticing to the big shots. Bruckner no exception."

"They'll fire you? Are you upset? You seem confident about it."

"It makes me think beyond it. To consequences."

"For you and Sahara? About financial security?"

"Of course." He hesitated. "And Ooma. My assistant. They'll let her go because of me."

Amar felt cornered. His heightened concern for Ooma played into Diana's theory about his fears. But if he explored his true feelings for Ooma, he was opening a major can of worms. Could he trust Diana's discretion as a doctor? She was also his wife's best friend.

The safer choice was easy. "Things are getting worse. Sahara's thrown herself into recalls and Scheherazade. My life almost ended, my newborns died, and my job is on the line. Why shouldn't I be in post-traumatic survival mode?"

"Of course *you* should," the therapist said. "But why are you so afraid for Ooma?"

Amar's stomach churned with emotion. "She's already so fragile. She avoids everyone's glance, but checks everyone out. Under that new veil she wears. She trembles going down stairs, like she's going to fall. If – when -- she loses her job, she might crash."

"Do you see what you're doing, Amar? Focus on it."

Amar let silence envelop him. He could not look at his feelings for Ooma any closer. And he refused to reveal them to Diana. But Diana wanted him to look at something else. He let his sensation of fear surface. It was more than fear. The Maya Factor, the illusion of everyday reality, weighed upon him: every building could fall, every stair could trip you, every feeling could make you burst. He felt a horrible rushing feeling.

Dr. Machiyoko let Amar cry for several minutes. Then she said very quietly. "It's called hyper-vigilance. It's not paranoia. It's a very real experience."

Amar shook his head. Crying felt very good. As did avoiding Ooma. "What do I do?"

"Just notice what triggers your fears. Don't worry about what's real and what isn't. You're not crazy. You're wounded. You'll heal just fine. And don't stop being concerned about friends and loved ones. If you can support Ooma, support her."

Amar looked up from his tears. Dr. Machiyoko handed him a tissue.

"Thank you, Diana. Thank you."

November 13. Week 10.

Before the qaraq's third meeting that fall, Sahara asked if Amar wanted to continue hypnosis. They had finally uncovered a lifetime, but it was so disturbing they could not discuss it. Like so many other fears and horrors from those weeks, the couple felt inadequate to help each other work through them. "Let's forget the hypnosis," Amar said. "It's not as if we're devoid of stories."

Sahara sensed Amar's distance. Fighting her anxiety, she dared probe a sensitive subject.

"Love, how are we doing? Is the death of the twins going to destroy us?"

Amar tensed. "I honestly don't know. Were we karmically destined to have three children?"

In the European variant, Scheherazade had three sons. "That version was fabricated by happy ending fiends. But you know what's horrible? I think how pure the Arabic original is. There must only be one child, like Naji. I'm using the twins' deaths to understand my thesis."

"It's a rationalization," Amar said. "There's no right or wrong way to think about something so terrible. Are you also thinking there's no happy ending for us? Can't we try for another child?"

Sahara noted Amar's half-hearted tone. "I couldn't face another loss. It'd drive me mad."

They sat in silence. The full weight of the loss fell on Sahara, and she began to cry. "Why does everyone die in my life? My babies, my mother. My sister when I was only three years old!"

Amar swallowed hard. "Let's not talk about this. We're gonna be fine."

Neither of them believed his statement. Sahara saw distress in her husband's eyes. Amar saw the damage in his wife's face. Neither had the strength to deal with the other's torment.

33

September 15. Day Five.

Leaving a note on her pillow for Amar, Sahara hoped she would find Verle at the church after midnight. Sure enough, doors were open, lights blazing, volunteers working into the night for families of World Trade Center victims. She found Verle nodding off in a pew.

Sahara gently touched him on the arm. "You look pretty useless, old man."

Verle started awake. "Goodness, woman! The qaraq ruins my few chances at rest."

"Can't sleep myself," Sahara said. "And I haven't seen you since the Towers came down."

"I heard Amar made it. Not all did. But the Unitarians are helping, twenty-four to seven."

Sahara smiled at Verle's attempt at current idiom. "And I heard Elvi took you to tea Saturday. That's a first. You must rate. Any reason?"

"Solidarity between church volunteers." Verle yawned loudly. "She shared a Draill U tale."

"No kidding. We're out of control sharing recalls." They traded bits of information from the last few days, realizing that the qaraq had received each other's memories from a distance. The strange phenomenon was hard for Verle's sleep-deprived mind to process. "I want to share another story with you, from before the attacks," Sahara said. "I recalled your life as Veronique d'O. She was a French courtier who supported the first European translation of the Nights."

Verle's heavy-lidded eyes struggled to focus. He too had received parts of the 18th Century memory, as had other qaraqis. "So it wasn't just this traumatic event that opened our collective mind," Sahara said, "it was already happening." She noticed she was losing Verle with this thinking. "There's some force at work here. Something about the Nights we're all supposed to know."

Verle tried to ask Sahara how Veronique d'O's lifetime related to the ancient Nights evolution. The thought triggered a memory of Veronique's later life in his dreamy mind.

The Tale of Casual Karma

Not every karmic encounter over lifetimes is clear in its meaning: two arch-enemies from the War in the Pacific of 1945 might share an elevator ride in their next life, on a rainy Tuesday, and never meet again; a fifteen-year-old boy feeling a hormonal urge toward a cute blond across the subway tracks has no clue that five lifetimes before they were vines growing up opposite sides of a stone church in Kecskemet, Hungary, unable to reach each other before the church was razed by Ottoman forces; a chance jostling of shoulders between two strangers, annoyance without consequence in that lifetime, is followed by gradually increasing nuisances in a parade of lives, accumulating to a pitched clan war. Even in a qaraq, not every soul reunion is comprehensible at first glance.

Take Veronique d'O, secret love child of the translator of the exotic Nuits, Antoine Galland, and the Marquise d'O, his patroness. Having divined the secret of her birth, Veronique lured Galland to her mysterious family chateau, to share her vision of the Nights. With so many differing versions there could be no authentic text; she convinced him to add tales to his translation that did not come from a prized Arabic manuscript. Galland's scholarly sleight-of-hand spread to a chain of decisions that created a European Nights containing a thousand and one segments.

Veronique's vision of a book that simulates Eternity, 1001 standing in for the Infinite, was the same as the Idea of John Donne, the room-as-a-universe, the small, complex container existing as a World; the Idea is also manifest as a qaraq, a handful of souls representing the immortality of all creatures.

Galland died before his final Volumes appeared in print, not even topping three hundred Nights; at that time Veronique saw no successor to continue Galland's work: it was the end of a great age. She quit France, depressed; she could not bring herself to visit the Levant again; she went as far as Eastern Europe, froze in her tracks in the Carpathian Mountains, and lost her way.

The wandering woman saw a funnel of smoke, not unlike a vision of a Genie from the Nights; it instilled fear in her, simply from the rocks and branches the twister threw into the air. Hiding behind a tree, Veronique observed the funnel change direction and appearance every few moments: a prehistoric sea-worm burrowing into the ocean floor, a flying fish twisting into the atmosphere above the waves. These sights were as frightening to Veronique as the physical danger.

The crazy funnel kept its distance, but after a while Veronique swore that it paused, then moved off a bit, as if to beckon her to follow; Veronique dared take a few steps from the tree, and the twister lifted up in joy and moved a few yards further. After an hour following the dust column in this game of folly, the twister led Veronique to a handsome estate outside the village of Tluste.

Standing still outside the gate, the funnel of smoke lessened in intensity until it stood no higher than Veronique, who was no longer afraid, but considered it an ally. Simultaneously, she received a compelling thought: I must find a place that feels like home, a refuge at once contained and comfortable, yet vast and all-encompassing. Veronique recognized the room-as-a-universe Idea, but was also put in mind of a group of souls guiding each other in the world.

The twister had guided Veronique to an estate that was unoccupied and for sale; she had her business agent purchase it (she did not explain the decision came on the advice of a dust devil). She used the estate as a base to establish an enormous library, full of folktale anthologies, histories, and literature, the stuff of Scheherazade's own bibliographic universe, which Veronique sought in the great libraries of Vienna, Prague, and Budapest, specializing in local editions, such as the 1715 Yiddish translation of the Nights. Estranged from her family, court, and country, she replaced those special groups with her vast library in the remote estate, her own room-as-a-universe.

Veronique enjoyed life there for many years; during this time she experienced one casual, non-karmic encounter with a member of her qaraq: Shemuel, the hermit of Okopy, older brother of Noam (whose ghost haunted the Carpathian countryside as the whirlwind of smoke). Drawn to the estate by hunger, Shemuel climbed over Veronique's wall, collapsed in her backyard, and awoke in the enormous library, a steaming bowl of broth before him. Encouraged by his gentle treatment from the lady of the house, Shemuel invaded the library without permission, locating the Yiddish edition of the Nights. To improve her command of the local language, Veronique had been reading the tale, "Seif et Mulouk," so the book naturally opened to the first page of the story.

Several hours later, her servant reported that the vagabond was gone, the glass door onto the veranda had been shattered, and the Yiddish Nights lay amid the pile of shards; Veronique puzzled over whether it was a sign about the fate of the Nights in the world. Unable to see any significance, she surmised that the encounter bore greater consequence for the distraught man than for her.

ق

After Verle recovered from his vision, he introduced World structures to Sahara. He saw two Multiple Worlds at work in his recall, the recurring Nights tales, and a large sequence set in modern Eastern Europe. Since the evolution of the European Nights was intertwined in the latter stories, Sahara thrilled that the qaraq midwived the Nights from its origins to modern development.

Nonetheless, Sahara and Verle questioned the connections between the Donne Idea, Veronique and the Nights, and the Jews. Did the present qaraq need to locate Veronique's library? If both the qaraq and the Nights embody the Idea, how did that relate to the recent raft of Nights recalls? As The 379 Group, did the qaraq bridge the early Nights with the European versions?

Sahara saw such mysteries weigh on Verle's sleepy head, his dreads hanging low. She urged him to rest and bade him good night. She needed to sleep as much as he did.

34

—⟨∘∕∘⟩—

October 20. Week 6.

Ooma's family kept her in hiding for a month. She had made a few calls to Amar and Bax, then returned to work a week ago. But when Amar told her the qaraq had had its first meeting without her, it hit her as hard as any of her nightmares. Sahara had broken her promise to let her join. Amar made a half-convincing argument that Sahara could not stand complications since the twins had died. Then why have meetings at all, Ooma insisted. His hurt look told her the stillbirths were sensitive ground for him, too. It was not a good idea for him to plead her case to his wife.

To support her right to enter the qaraq meetings, Ooma had recorded every detail of her Medieval Arabic lifetimes in her journal. Reliving her Islamic past through writing shielded her from nightmares and anxiety. She felt safe inside the memory of Umnia or Oarma, so she adopted those personas as sanctuaries for her vulnerable soul.

Ooma showed up at Bruckner Associates wearing a *half-niqaab*, covering her head and shoulders, and exposing only her eyes and lower forehead. It was a choice beyond the simple headscarf she had worn previously. Her mother worried about hostility toward Ooma because of the terrorist attacks, but Ooma wanted to face the prejudice, secure inside the protective veil of her chosen identity. Amar's co-workers questioned his acceptance of her veil. Given the economic repercussions of the attacks, Ooma's controversial choice of attire might hurt him.

Knowing Bax was on friendlier terms with Sahara, Ooma thought about enlisting his aid to gain entry to the meetings. But Bax had treated Ooma with greater respect lately, and attempted to rescue her at the Twin Towers. Ooma would not force Bax to lobby for her, as he had in the past.

There was only one other thing Ooma could do.

"What a surprise," Verle said, as Ooma entered his attic. "Here for my next makeover?" The old man alluded to the outing to a beauty salon that Ooma had foisted on him, which had ended in humiliating disaster.

"Only if you want our friendship to end," Ooma joked. "The dreads look just fine."

Zack was there, too, at the computer. "The rumors are true. I like the burka. Very sexy."

"It's supposed to be chaste, not sexy," Ooma scolded. "And it's called a niqaab."

"A burka covers the body from head to toe," Verle said.

"Gold star," Ooma said. "America is learning this stuff for the first time right now."

"Hopefully for good," Verle said. "So, Miss Ooma, what brings you to my humble loft?"

Ooma looked around at the cluttered attic, but only saw it as a sacred space, with its cathedral ceiling and quiet niches. "I've never seen the inner sanctum." *The qaraq met here!* "I know you've been recording stories, and since I've recalled many of them, I'd like to help."

Zack feigned a bow. "At last! A reasonable member of the group."

"Like to see the transcriptions of your recalls?" Verle asked. "You could edit them."

Ooma stepped over a few piles to take some folders from Verle. Looking over the texts, Ooma marveled at the accuracy of stories she had never directly told the group. Had the qaraq always been as attuned at accessing each other's recalls as during 9/11?

When Zack left later, she made her next move. "I brought my journal, with new stories about the Nights. There's one I want you to look at, Verle." When Ooma showed him a particular assortment of sentences, he was fascinated.

"They came into my mind randomly," Ooma said, "not like a story. Are they connected?"

"They look like clues in a puzzle. May I borrow your journal to study them?"

On Sunday Ooma returned, along with Zack and Diana, who noted Ooma's calm demeanor.

"Ooma gifted us with an unusual style of recall," Verle explained. "I once received one of these from the future. It's a logic problem: you're given fragments of information, and you logically deduce sets of facts. Like: of five houses, what are their colors, owner's nationality, and style."

"I remember," Zack said. "It's how we learned about souls' recurring Character Identity Traits. CHITS. Things like our Nights archetype and soul story language style."

"Yes," Verle said. "I have the soul of an adventurous vizier speaking in a complex syntax.

Ooma frowned. "And I am the evil Queen who rambles in stream of thought. So you put it together?" Ooma was eager to hear, but did not forget her mission to be invited to meetings.

"That I did," Verle said. "Ooma's logic puzzle is a history of Sassanian kings named Bahram. It may seem like gibberish, but I'll talk you through it." He laid a series of charts on the floor. "Maybe Ooma can shed light at the end of the tunnel."

As Zack and Diana listened to Verle, Ooma thrilled at how well her plan was going.

The Tale of the Logic Puzzle Suicide

LOGIC PUZZLE #477   BAHRAM-IT!   (Anonymous)

The Sassanian Empire of Persia was ruled by many kings. Of the six kings named Bahram who began their reigns between 273 and 635 A.D., each had a work of art associated with his family. One relative older than each Bahram inspired the work of art; Bahram then had the work created for a relative younger than him. The family relations were different for each Bahram.

Determine the starting year of each reign, the older and younger relative, and the name of the work of art. Then answer the questions at the end of the puzzle. Here are the clues:

1. Bahram VI's father inspired oral narratives; Bahram IV gave a harp piece to his cousin-wife.

2. *The Battle between the Fire Cult of Zoroaster and the Christ Worship of the Romans* was created during the reign that began 115 years after the start of a reign that created a work for a niece.

3. We ignore Bahram II (almost wiped out by Roman conquerors), so our sixth Bahram is actually Bahram VII, a fictional king ruling on the cusp of the Islamic takeover of Persia.

4. A mother inspiring a frame tale of a written story collection, created for her granddaughter, lived during the reign which began in 420 AD, 147 years after a reign started, which saw the rock carving, *The Triumph of Ardashir*, inspired by an uncle.

5. The grandfather who inspired *Ahura Mazda and the Sacred Fire* monument had a grandson who was Bahram III, V, or VII.

6. Bahram VII had the silver plate entitled *Bahram Gur and Azadeh* made for his bastard son: it depicted Bahram V, after his lover Azadeh accused him of using magic in some uncanny hunting archery, trampling her to death under the hooves of his steed.

7. The *Hazar Afsaneh* or *1000 Tales*, the popular, oral version of the written collection, was created for the king's step-brother right before the reign whose work was inspired by a step-mother.

8. A great-uncle inspired a work after a reign where a work was made for a grandson.

9. The difference between the number of the Bahram whose uncle inspired a work, and the Bahram promoting the written *1000 Tales*, is four. (*Prisoners of Love* was added to that collection.)

10. Bahram I began his reign in 276 AD; Bahram VII supposedly began his reign in 635 AD. For the other Bahrams, you can always cheat by looking up their dates in the records books.

Now answer these questions:

1. Who was the real Scheherazade?

2. Who wrote *The Book of the Tale of the 1000 Nights*?

3. If it is possible that one of the Bahrams' mothers was the historical Scheherazade, isn't it just as possible that these people did not exist, that the historical truth is so false a fiction that it undermines all precepts of Truth that the Prophet delivered us from Almighty Allah?

Verle finished: "The questions are atypical of a logic problem, and unanswerable given the information. An ironic joke by the puzzlemaker, not me, but maybe you, Ooma."

"Not me! I saw these as incoherent fragments, and now that they're clues, they're still incoherent fragments to me. I'm clueless." In fact, Ooma knew the puzzle was Umh's life as she redeemed her Uzmeth karma. But she hoped Verle could explain important links to her.

"But can you actually solve the puzzle, oh wise Vizier?" Zack asked. "Does it make sense?"

"Indeed. I won't bore you with the logic of the solution, which puzzles usually provide." Verle displayed a chart with a summary of the Bahrams, the inspirers and recipients, and the works:

Bahram I   273   Uncle/niece   Rock carving, *The Triumph of Ardashir.*

Bahram II   N/A

Bahram III   293   Grandfather/grandson   Monument, *Ahura Mazda and the Sacred Fire.*

Bahram IV   388   Great-uncle/Cousin-wife   Harp composition, *The Battle between the Fire Cult of Zoroaster and the Christ Worship of the Romans.*

Bahram V (Gur) 420   Mother/daughter   Written story collection, *The Thousand Tales.*

Bahram VI   590   Father/step-brother Oral story collection, *Hazir Afsaneh.*

Bahram VII   635   Step-mother/bastard son   Silver plate, *Bahram Gur and Azadeh.*

"You recalled all this, Ooma?" Zack asked. "Were you one of the Bahrams?"

"I was Bahram Gur's daughter, Humai, who started *The Thousand Tales.*" Now they're playing into my plan, Ooma thought.

"Ooma, I still don't get why you received the puzzle." Diana looked at Ooma intensely. "We've heard your story as Humai. Are you sure you weren't a different incarnation here?"

"Maybe you were the creator of the puzzle," Verle said. "Try and remember."

Ooma did not expect their response to go in this direction. She took a breath and imagined what Umnia or Oamra would do in the situation, her pillars of calm. Instead, Ooma gained contact with another from her soul's journey of redemption, Khadija, daughter of the Sheikh and Hu Ma. She fell into trance, narrating Khadija's story softly.

I have hit bottom shamed from my life as Uzmeth haunted by night-mare tales as Humai put into a coma by a Sheikh's magic sex and reborn as the babe I delivered on my death bed beautiful Khadija whose name means premature, but my torture continues: The Thousand Tales *disrespected my Queen in the frame tale my shame laid bare all eyes on me as if monsters with five eyes hunted me as Khadija my soul hit bottom so I went into the marketplace found an oval object that held the smallest of scrolls and wrote a farewell note to my family and placed the note inside the oval after I took my life I looked down at those grieving my dead corpse not yet finding the note and an urge possessed me not to reveal my despair so the Masters imbued me with the power to transform the note: I reincarnated into the note and worried that the world would forget the source of* The Thousand Tales *Humai's wish its roots in Uzmeth's one hundred and fifty years of Sassanian rule and I willed the knowledge of the Bahrams to enter the note, my soul reduced to a logic puzzle.*

ق

Diana put her arm around Ooma, acknowledging the pain of seeing a lifetime as a suicide. "You existed both as Khadija and the puzzle. You were the puzzle to rectify your Queen character."

"It fits our recalls about rewriting Scheherazade," Zack said. "To better our archetypes."

Zack's comment brought Ooma out of trance. *Here was her chance!* "How did you hear those recalls?" When Zack explained the collective sharing of memories, Ooma interrupted him. "I *knew* I was projecting my visions on 9/11, but I thought it was to Amar. I went through hell while getting those recalls, so the qaraq could witness this important step in its history. It's not fair. I risk death to share my lifetimes, but I'm still locked out of the group. Even Naji goes to meetings."

Diana tried to calm Ooma. "I know it seems wrong, but right now Sahara is dealing with –"

250

"What gives Sahara the power to say, 'I exempt you from your right'?' She hates me!"

Zack's turn: "It's the slaughtered virgins talking. We'll fix it. Promise."

Ooma looked relieved, so Verle changed tracks. "Ooma, after I constructed the puzzle there were sentences left over in your journal. I think this text is a warm-up for bigger things."

"What bigger things?" Zack asked. "About what?"

"Those lifetimes where we rewrote our Scheherazade characters were the past lives right before we were a group of story collectors. The 379 Group. Our collective created a special, subversive Nights version." Verle winked. "In 1001 AD."

Ooma laughed out of delighted surprise. She had accomplished her plan and then some!

251

35

September 16. Day Six.

The day after Verle recalled the second story about Veronique d'O in Sahara's presence, he invited Zack to have dinner at the church. While they ate in the meeting hall, Verle could not get a word in edgewise. Zack unloaded his soul about Dr. Machiyoko, Jobim, and his struggling Internet business. It was hard for Verle to listen to the barrage; he looked away at the banners of doves and flames he had hung up last year. Zack kept talking as they walked up to the attic.

Finally Verle interrupted. "Begging your pardon, but may I ask a favor of your Highness?"

"Oh Jesus, am I spewing? I'm so sorry. What do you need?"

"The qaraq is flooded with recalls, maybe a counter-reaction to our Maya Factor drought last year." Verle gestured to the stacks of papers and files on the floor. "We need a faster system."

The two brainstormed, and Verle stressed World Types as a key in processing lifetimes. Then Zack wanted to transcribe a new tale right away, so Verle recounted Veronique meeting the twister as Zack typed the story. Feeling pressure to work fast, Zack's fingers got ahead of his brain. After Verle stopped, Zack continued to type furiously. Looking over Zack's shoulder at his automatic word processing, Verle recognized the voice of Shemuel, hermit of Okopy, and Veronique's intruder. It was Sahara's incarnation: Verle noted they were continuing to access each other's memories. Verle read Shemuel's Carpathian saga as Zack typed in trance.

The Tale of the Talking Twister

Four times I was entreated to end my days as a hermit and return to my community. The first appeal came from Rebbe Yisroel of my home-town, Okopy. The BeShT, great spiritual leader of the Jews, was also born there. I wandered a hundred kilometers to Brody, years before the Good Master of the Name moved there; the BeShT's path followed mine in a canon thirteen years apart.

The second appeal to end my hermitage came from my late brother Noam, on the road to Brody, at the end of my adolescence. My broth-er's ghost appeared as a dust devil, and lured me into a nearby pine grove. His head whipped about at the top of the little twister as he spoke.

"Our people are falling apart like a rotting log. Pogroms decimate the population. The rich scholars look down on the poor so the poor reject spiritual knowledge. The rebbes sink into a Talmudic fog; the vil-lagers cling to amulets. All of them are lost, lost to each other. But you have vision, otherwise you could not see me. You must reenter the world and guide Jews back together."

I was terrified of this whirling specter of a man, a bizarre version of my childhood playmate. But I recognized his voice, understood clearly his meaning, and despite my fears, reacted honestly.

"If you are my dear brother Noam, then you know our family fell victim to the massacres. Gd knows what horror you suffered to end up in this wretched state."

Noam's apparition burst into smoke, then flickered back to human-oid form. "You've no idea what I experienced in the afterlife. Have you passed through Recollection, Rest, Transition? Seen our soul family reunited? You have Unpaid Debts, brother, and must return to the villages."

"I won't return to where I was cruelly orphaned."

"But you have … overcome your grief," Noam said with difficulty, "in the quiet of these groves and streams. Bring that peace of mind to the people."

"Let them flee the anti-Semites and find Gd in the wilderness." The tormented soul before me was just a frightened boy. I remembered Noam on the bed we shared, clutching a favorite blue rag. "Go to the people and scare the matzah out of them," I teased. "Chase them into the woods."

The spirit took umbrage at my remarks and sparks shot from the funnel. Then a look of recognition flashed across Noam's face: the child got the joke. "Can you see me tearing up Reb Yisroel's kitchen? Smiting a chicken as he wets his prayer shawl?"

We both laughed, Noam's guffaws chucking small rocks from the dirt funnel. "I do help the people," I said, "but the less human contact I have, the greater my link to Gd."

I watched the seven-foot tall tornado shrink in dejection. "I failed," my brother lamented. "You're as stubborn as ever." I did not know how I had previously appeared stubborn to Noam, but an image of a feisty cat lurking near the Pyramids popped into my head. No stranger than a talking twister.

Noam was crumbling into dust. "Wait, brother," I cried. "Don't go."

Noam's confident voice contrasted with his fading body. "I am doomed to remain attached to the sufferings of my family. You alone could have freed me."

"I promise to fight for our people. Do not go!"

"Too late, Shemuel, you made your choice. I'm being pulled away." Barely a foot tall, what remained of Noam looked me in the eye. "There is a magical place, a place of power. It has been an ancient cave on a desert mountain, a subterranean cavern guarded by mer-people, a locked strongbox opened by seventy-seven keys, and a secluded room, hidden in wartime, full of wondrous blue objects. This place contains all things, and all souls meet there. There you will find me, your family, and the truth you seek. If you insist on the illusion of solitude, then at least find this hermitage that will connect you to the world."

As Noam spoke, a memory of a place of dark infiniteness terrified me. I described to my brother a flaming numeral 1001, a vast abyss below it. "Is this terrible place what you mean?"

Noam laughed, and the remaining bit of the twister spun off into wisps. "Gd of Abraham, no, Shemuel. I'm talking about a cave in the hills." With a snicker, he vanished into thin air.

ق

When Zack snapped out of his writing trance, he questioned why he had received Sahara's recall. Because of the Character Trait of initials recurring in names, Verle surmised that Noam was Naji's lifetime. An Internet search about the BeShT dated the tale years before Noam's twister appeared to Veronique.

"Where is my soul in all this?" Zack asked. "It's like my life. I've lost myself in the chaos."

"I hate to channel Dr. Machiyoko," Verle said, "but do you feel anything in the story?"

"I feel a strong connection," Zack admitted, "like I met one of them."

"Perhaps after Veronique settled into the estate," Verle suggested. The two men let the thought sink in. Between Zack's constsnt talking at dinner, his recall, and his confusion now, Verle had had enough. "That'd be enough slacking, son. We've got work to do."

36

—◦◦◦—

October 22. Week 7.

By the time meetings started again, Verle and Zack were sold on targeting lifetimes. Since Diana fought them on the superficial task of filling in lives in specific Worlds, Verle and Zack pioneered the technique on their own. It seemed an impossible task, but they hoped for success as a team. An obvious target was Zack's presumed lifetime connected to Veronique, Verle's incarnation.

When Cachay invited her son and Verle to dinner, they were surprised to find Jobim there. Like everyone else, Zack's mother had hit it off with the new partner; Zack was both relieved and anxious about Cachay's ease with the young Brazilian-American. Jobim was in the living room, hunched over Cachay's new laptop, a novelty in the budding digital world of 2001.

Zack watched in awe. "God, how'd you do that so fast? My desktop's way too slow."

"I spend way too much time on it," Cachay said. "Verle, is that why I can't recall?"

"You will, you will." Verle whispered. He too was smitten by the machine.

Jobim offered the laptop to Zack; on the sofa the two men exchanged a warm smile. Jobim had re-entered his apartment three weeks before, but its proximity to Ground Zero caused him great anxiety. Mostly, he went there to pick up clothes to bring to Zack's Glenclaire home, but only on days when he had business downtown. Invariably, on those nights he had nightmares.

Zack tried the laptop's Internet software. "Wow!" He explored other import-exporters on a search engine. "Look at that!" He cross-referenced the keyword, 'Arabian Nights.' "Lordy Lord! Someone's looking for artifacts related to the Nights. That's not in the Yellow Pages!" Zack placed his hands on the machine, felt its warmth, and closed his eyes. "I found you, chaste, pure, ingenuous, pious!" Joy overcame him: confidently slipping into trance, he willed himself to see his Eastern European lifetime with Veronique.

The Tale of the Carpathian Exile

With the first murky images, Zack understood he was witnessing the final chapter in *Veronique's* lifetime, three decades after she migrated to the region where the Ukraine, Poland, and Romania juggle their borders. Veronique had long ago given up returning to France, slowed down on collecting volumes for her library, and used her servant Zadek for business in the village. Zack recognized himself as Zadek.

Veronique's Carpathian home felt satisfying as a hideaway. She had looked at the Nights as an advancement of the Idea of the Contained representing the Limitless; with Galland's death and the discontinuation of the Nights translation, she replaced one variation of the Idea with another, her secluded existence on the estate with a massive library.

Veronique never forgot the disturbing incident of the vagabond, who picked up the Yiddish Nights and shattered her patio door. Twenty-five years later, she mentioned the incident to Zadek.

257

"The vagabond was Shemuel, long since dead," Zadek explained to his mistress. "The new righteous movement among the Jews was inspired by mystical behavior of men like him."

Veronique rewarded him for the information, with a higher position and the estate keys. At her age, she needed more help around the house.

A new position emboldened Zadek. "Mistress, I perceive a sadness in you. What ails you?"

"Curb your insolence, Zadek," Veronique scolded. "That is not for you to ask."

He did not give up. "You should be content with your peaceful domicile, so I'm guessing the problem is philosophical."

"Now you are incomprehensible as well as insolent," Veronique said.

"The new mystical teachings profess that God exists in all things, all things thus contain the Infinite and the Holy."

Marveling at the parallel between the young man's words and the Idea, Veronique disclosed her family history, her relationship with Antoine Galland, and the revelation of the European Nights. Her heart's desire was an edition containing a thousand and one Nights. With her library, she could concoct such a thing, but having severed her connections in France, the task was fruitless.

Zadek laughed. "But there is a simple solution to your dream."

Veronique returned her servant's laughter. "Now you are arrogant. You have no literary ability. What possible suggestion could you make?"

Stung by her scolding, Zadek gestured toward the estate library. "You hold a room full of inanimate objects in higher esteem than a humble servant's wish to satisfy your dream. Then I refuse to reveal my strategy."

Veronique remembered Shemuel, and felt like she was throwing Zadek through her glass doors into the cold: she hated the thought, so she showed him a few books needed to compile an ambitious story collection. Zadek understood some, could not read others. That afternoon she began his education.

The next day Zadek again refused to tell Veronique his solution to her dilemma, but inquired about a volume in Yiddish; the day after he again refused, but asked about the cultures represented in the library. On the third day she asked about his plan again; he beseeched her to teach him French; instruction in Greek, Latin, Arabic, Spanish, English, and German followed. During the years of Zadek's education, Veronique asked her pupil's plan, withheld instruction unless he confessed, tossed out questions fishing for a hint, and polled locals for information. Being put off by Zadek so many times, Veronique experienced it as a déjà vu. Finally she recognized Zadek would only confess when his education was complete.

Fifteen years passed, and Veronique came to love Zadek, his diligent study, sensitive soul, and loyal perseverance: was he not undergoing this course for her alone? Veronique stopped asking about Zadek's plan, for it became obvious. Approaching her eighth decade, Veronique knew her end was near, the time to endorse his strategy. Marshalling strength for one final trip, she accompanied her protégé to Vienna, where she selected a fashionable wardrobe for him; on their return she dictated letters of introduction, for her hands suffered from annoying tremors.

Veronique bequeathed generous funds to Zadek, and gave him final instructions, fully preparing him to realize her dream: Zadek would travel to Paris, inculcate himself in the appropriate circles, and rekindle the translation of a complete edition, armed with enough materials from Veronique's library to produce seven thousand and one Nights.

ق

Zack felt pulled back to his mother's living room. He resisted, wanting to see Zadek's life in Paris. But his targeting ability had its limits. Instead of 18th Century French architecture, Zack recognized he was in his mother's living room holding the warm laptop. Back from his vision.

"Damn, my life was just beginning!" He shared the tale with his friends.

"My Lord, you targeted a recall, lad," Verle said. "The goal we've been seeking! You stopped short because our lifetimes together ended. We were a team then as we are now."

259

Zack nodded agreement. Sensing Zack's lingering disappointment, Jobim rubbed his back gently. Their eyes met, and Zack noted Jobim's anxiety. It must have been strange for Jobim to see Zack in trance, out of control. Like when they had met, on 9/11. He needed to lighten the air.

Zack caught Cachay's eye, and smiled hungrily. "Mother, I'm stealing your computer."

37

November 2. Week 8. Washington, D.C.

Ellis looked away from the computer terminal and reached for his cup of coffee. The dreary basement office gave him the creeps; why wasn't he out in the field? Bad enough the government thought it could fight the War on Terror by surveying books checked out of public libraries; he had to wade through the surveillance. Emails from librarians! Humiliating!

He had stopped looking at each red-flagged book. Ellis searched libraries with the highest number of banned books checked out, and surveilled those branches. So far nothing popped out. With another gulp of coffee, he turned to the next branch, in Glenclaire, New Jersey.

There were many restaurants in Glenclaire, reflecting the urbane tastes of the commuter population. *Roy's* was closest to their house, but Sahara felt that was no reason to go there. The last time she and Amar had eaten there, they barely survived a heated fight. Amar wanted to give it another chance, and since it was Friday after an exhausting week, Sahara gave in.

Gaining strength from a chicken Caesar, Sahara unloaded political outrage on her husband, who attacked some mussels. President

Bush had ordered the first pre-emptive invasion of a foreign state in American history. After book bans, it was too much for her. "Have we learned nothing from history? Alexander the Great, three British armies, and a decade of Russians all met disaster in Afghanistan. Muslims were the only successful invaders. Now we think we can take them out?"

Amar tossed a shell aside. "We're going after bin Laden, not Muslims. We've got to do whatever it takes. The economy tanked because of him."

She grabbed his fork and downed a mussel. "That's so Republican. War at all cost, as long as it helps Wall Street. You should move to a red state."

"Since when is my liberal wife a slave of TV?" Amar drained his wine glass and poured them both more. "They invented that red state/blue state thing during the last election."

"The country's as divided as the Civil War, and war makes it worse. Who's next? Iraq?"

"Nonsense. There's a new spirit of camaraderie all over the city, and the nation."

"Maybe this Fall." Sahara put down her fork. "Even the qaraq's split. We barely started the last meeting with all the bickering. You're in good conservative company with Cachay and Porcy, even though they're women of color. Maybe Bax, our white cowboy. Zack and Diana share my misgivings about Bush. I'm sure your friend Ooma's nervous living in America right now. Thank God Verle and Elvi are neutral."

"Sahr, let's not fight over politics." Amar worried Sahara was still upset about the twins, throwing herself into work as a distraction. "You shouldn't get worked up."

"Don't shut me up. Would Scheherazade take this lying down? The government needs to hear our voices. I've stepped up my email campaign. Do you know we have more calls for outreach to help the community understand Islam? That's what we need, not censorship."

"If this is your inner Scheherazade, my Shahryar weeps when you talk so. Please be careful."

Sahara stopped arguing, but Amar's reproach to calm down insulted her. Lately he spouted advice because he did not know what else to say. Their grief from the twins' deaths had pushed him away, as if he stood on a shore as she drifted out to sea.

On the way home, Amar suggested they declare a truce and attempt a past life regression. This was an example of his inconsistent sensitivity to her: one day he made a connection, the next, nothing. When they got home, after paying the sitter, Sahara guided Amar to relax, then led his mind through a door into a realm beyond. She asked what he saw and waited patiently.

Out of the silence, Naji cried out. She left Amar lying on the couch, hurried to the nursery, and picked up Naji from his bed. Immediately quiet, the child pointed downstairs. Sahara carried him back to the living room, where he reached out to his father. If her big lunk wasn't going to recall anything, why not share a moment with his son? Naji stroked his father's hair, gave his nose a puckish squeeze, and then pressed lightly on his forehead.

With a sigh, Sahara again asked Amar what he saw. This time he answered.

The Medieval Crime World Regression

-- It is dark, outdoors. Houses with gardens, fountains. An old Arab world, like the Nights.

"What are you doing there?" Sahara asked. Amar paused to consider, then spoke.

-- Lighting a candle. Dripping wax on something. Planting the candle in the wax.

Naji still touched his father, listening intently. Sahara waited. "Now what?"

-- It's moving! The candle took off in the dark! Now I can see it better. The candle's stuck on the back of a turtle! The turtle creeps under a gate and into a courtyard. I watch it intensely.

"What are you looking for?" Despite herself, Sahara was interested.

-- I'm casing the joint. I'm a thief. Clever little bugger. In the candle-light I break the gate latch. My crew lights more candles; turtle-light guides us to a big haul. We go home and celebrate.

"Celebrate? Do you have any remorse?"

-- None. Trickery and guile are valued in our world. Not just in the storybooks.

"What is your world? What year is it?" Amar paused again.

-- My hero is Al-Uqab, 3rd Century master thief. A doctor wagered he could not rob his house. Appearing as Jesus -- using hypnosis! -- Al-Uqab stole the doctor from his own home!

"3rd Century?" Sahara wondered. "Are you in some Islamic land?"

-- Yes, Baghdad. Good potential for chicanery here."

If the dates are Islamic, then Al-Uqab lived in the 800s AD, Sahara surmised. *Amar's thief life would be later. But why another Arab recall?* "Do you have a gang? What are you up to?"

-- A powerful gang. Just now we get a tip about a group of storytell-ers who've made a collection, and they're worried about it getting into the wrong hands. A mere book, but with great power! If we nab this book, we make coin off those who want it or want it hidden.

Sahara held her breath. "What do you know about this book? The storytellers?"

-- Not much. Haven't seen it yet. But it's big. Got hundreds of sto-ries in it.

Sahara could only guess what it was. Amar suddenly looked afraid.

-- The book is in hiding. Kept safe by another ... criminal organization.

Naji whimpered. Sahara asked, "A rival gang? That sounds dangerous."

-- Worse than a gang. Madame Hunj. Doesn't know what she has, but it's at her house.

"Her house? Madame Hunj? You're afraid of a prostitute?"

-- She runs the best-known establishment in Baghdad. Everyone goes there. Criminals and caliphs. Go against her and she can have anyone in town destroy you.

"That is a problem. What are you going to do?"

Amar was quiet. Suddenly Naji jerked his hand away from his father's body.

ق

Startled out of trance, Amar looked from Naji to Sahara. "Was that Naji's lifetime?"

Sahara was not entirely sure. "You don't know?"

"Even when I have a memory, I can't tell if it's my own. Can't even recall my own recalls."

"If Naji triggered his own recall through you, that's incredible." Sahara hugged her baby tightly. "Did you, little one? You haven't given us a clue in months."

Amar winced. "Next you'll want to perform experiments on him. What's happening to us?"

"Relax. You've just seen a new World, like the Nights from a crime perspective. Something dangerous shut it down, and you feel anxious. I would, too."

"I don't know. But it's very weird. Getting recalls from my son. I'm losing faith in these sessions. I shouldn't have asked you. You're over-wrought about everything. Your research, Naji, even the library. Please stop the anti-government protests. You need rest."

The insult again! "You're saying what happened is my fault?" Irked, she picked up Naji. "I'm putting him back to bed." She left the room without waiting for Amar's response.

Ellis looked at the computer again, amazed at one public employee's background. Residence in a new country every three years, Arabic studies in graduate school, and a husband of East Indian descent, who worked at The World Trade Center! Ellis called his superior to report this unusual citizen. Time to start a file on Sahara Fleming.

265

38

November 7.   Week 9.

Bax and Ooma had had little physical contact since before 9/11. They finally had a rendez-vous in Ooma's bedroom when her parents were away from the house. They had enjoyed torrid moments here, so Bax was aroused just to see Ooma's bed and the little altar in her closet again.

Ooma needed to complain to Bax. "Sahara's locked me out of two meetings. I've lobbied Amar, Verle, and Zack, but she's got some ultimate veto power. *I've* recalled most of the Nights stories. I pointed the way to The 379 Group. Don't they want my help sorting it out?"

"Verle would rejoice at it," Bax said, "but it won't help you."

"Dammit! Bax, I didn't want to draw you into this, but I'm frustrated. I could be the champion of reincarnation for the group."

"You're becoming religious?" Bax swallowed. "Is that why you're wearing this thing?"

"It's called a niqaab. I've explained it before, don't be annoying. My people are under attack. The group's flooded with recalls about early Islam. I've never felt closer to my culture."

"Reincarnation, too? What's the niqaab got to do with that?"

"Does it bug you?" Ooma deftly removed the niqaab. "Better?" Removing her sweater, she unbuttoned her blouse. "Even better? Now you help me. What do we need to do?"

Ooma was always a bundle of contradictions. Unveiled seductress. Kindled by desire, Bax knew he had no choice but support her cause. "Verle wants to tie up Worlds. We need to interest the qaraq in wrapping up another saga."

Ooma considered while stroking Bax's leg. "How about my recalls about old and new Umh? Do you have any added info?"

"I received a memory during 9/11, but the details escaped me. A week later, when I tried to piece it together, my palms began to sweat from an odd sensation. A heightened clamminess on my fingertips, in the webbing by my thumb, and under the knuckles."

Ooma caressed Bax's hands. "Here? The sensation led you to a memory?"

"An alternate reality, I think. Related to the 1600s. A great mystery."

Emotions heated, Ooma continued her caresses. "Delve into that mystery. Tell me."

The Tale of the Magical Hairplay

The pox had good days and bad days for me. I was nine when it began. 1611. Gustavas crowned in Sweden. A bad day. Terrible itching on my arms. Scratched for hours. Mother slapped my hands. Bathed me in ice. Pox will spread if I don't stop! It spread. My hands. Under the knuckles. My head. Bugs living in my scalp. Don't scratch! Just lightly fingered strands of hair.

Gustavas was King! All was well. Itching subsided. My body grew. Very big for my age. Then just very big. A time of many battles. Gustavas was audacious. Wanted Sweden to control our seas. Pushed Danes out. Fought back Poles. Defeated Russians. Routed Ottomans.

The pox came and went in those years. Made no connection at first. During Polish clash Mother thought I was worried. Scratch out my fear. By Russian campaign I noticed coincidence. Bizarre rhythm between war casualties and rashes. A victory lessened itching. When Gustavas took on the Turks I girded my skin for battle. Sure enough. I scratched my head in misery. Hundreds died at sea. Gustavas declared North Sea a Swedish lake. The pox cleared up. Triumph.

The vicar spoke of Heaven's providence. Nothing chance. Under the surface everything has meaning. Heaven's design. The smallest coincidence. But many battles with many rashes? What is Heaven's design? What meaning under the surface of my skin? What power in the pox?

The Hapsburg Empire was everywhere on the continent. Its victims made bizarre alliances. Southerners with us Northerners. Western French with Turks: thorn in Eastern side of Europe. Hapsburg Empire was a bear in gaming pit. Stronger than any of us small dogs of nations. But many dogs can take down the most ferocious bear. So Gustavas entered the Thirty Years War.

1630. After victory at sea sought victory on land. Led an army onto German soil. My pox acted up. Save the Protestants from Catholic domination! Arms and head itched fiercely. Thirteen thousand men liberated Magdeburg. My arms and head itched fiercely. Beat Hapsburg general Tilly at his own game. But Tilly had already sacked the town. Scratched until hair fell out.

Though diminished by pox I was still a large man. Signed up to fight alongside Gustavas. Joined Swiss pikemen. Led arquebuses to the front. Next engagement Tilly killed. Felt heroic.

But could not defeat bedeviling rashes. And strange effect my scratching had on others. In ditch I scratch my head. Soldier across from me raises hand to head without thinking. I rub my forearm. Officer touches his elbow. Finger my hair, and young cadet twirls his locks.

This power even more pervasive. On the field I have a fit of scratching. A volley of shots downs many men. One night I lie awake fussing with a scab. Next day I learn a town was leveled. Or a platoon ambushed.

A general defeated. How could my pox be the cause? Fortunately misery inflicted on enemy. Germany free for Protestants! Gustavas was Warrior King. Not my vile pox.

I felt strange power along with mad itch. Images crept into my brain. Alien world where young performers trained. Keyboard score with challenging fingerings for a musician. Drama of lusty Queen sending love letter containing tresses. Queen's locks have same power as my hairplay. Delusional, I imagined all-encompassing power. My shadow gestures influencing lives throughout time and space. Could I vanquish enemies with touch of a finger?

1632. Our troops meet von Wallenstein at Lutzen. Bohemian general holding key position. Thick fog in morning. Safe in ditch I unleash my power. Nasty itch on shoulder. Horrid patch on torso. Project energy into the fog as I itch my face. In an hour I hear victory shouts. Not without tragedy. In the mist Gustavas catches three bullets. Shoulder, torso, face. The King is dead. What folly made me believe I controlled Fate? What destruction have I etched into the face of world?

Ooma interrupted Bax. "Did you really have this power? From scratching? Your hair? I need to know. As Ormgarde I had dominance through brushing my mistress Kristina's hair. Old Umh gained power from her hair. What's the connection? The qaraq will want to know."

"I don't know much more," Bax confessed.

"Then let's recall more, like we've done before," Ooma said. "Take off your clothes."

39

—⟨∞⟩—

Before Bax had his shirt and pants off, Ooma plied him with kisses and strokes. She pushed him down to the carpeted floor between the bed and her closet shrine. Ooma threw off the rest of her clothes, revealing her hungry body. When she had enflamed Bax with fingers, legs, and lips, Ooma climbed on top and gazed down into his eyes. She looked like a mad animal to Bax.

"Take me back," she whispered. "Make me understand. Show me your power."

Preparing to receive Bax inside her, Ooma massaged herself against him roughly. The act pained them; their bodies tensed. Ooma's crazed sexuality triggered new images in Bax's mind.

Ooma's eyes blazed. "Give me your strength," she hissed. "Do it to the enemy!" Her need to storm the qaraq meetings and prove her worth drove her to an aggressive lust. Forced back into his memory of the diseased soldier, Bax saw a vision equal to Ooma's vulnerable madness.

The Tale of the Magical Hairplay, conclusion

The army skirmished for two years after Gustavas' demise. Our King gone, the fight had just begun. But I determined not to curse another soul. Let the pox run its course. At Nordlingen our troops met utter defeat. My sores and pustules worsened. Did not scratch. Licked our wounds the following year. Itch drove me to wild need and rage. Fragile alliance of nations won victories. Screamed the night for mercy. Brain fevered. Demented, I was discharged.

Wandered through forests. Unable to take care of myself. Dying face down in lovely mountain stream. I saw the most frightening, bizarre hallucination. Like a lifetime inside my lifetime. Or series of lives appearing at moment of death.

ق

The Vision of the Swedish Soldier

Encounter with my Shadow Self. A Frozen Roukh. Mirror World. Collusion of Souls, Old and New. Coven of Witches. Local Spell-casters. Beat Power Wielders at their own shame. Not since Weird Sisters messed with Thane of Cawdor.

Magic Mirror was Coven's Secret Weapon. Tool to raise Spirits from the Living. See All Things. Coven observes me. Playing with my Enpoxed Follicles. Struggling against Horrid Power. Insane in German forest. Stare up at Forest Canopy. Imagine myself the Tallest Tree. Mightiest

271

Size. But Tiny Tetrapods scratch at my roots. My bark. All is scratching. Drive me mad.

Coven tries to save me. Search their special Book of Spells. Dormant for centuries. Reincarnated as Book of Magic. Appeared with Mirror Shard. Good for Healing Spells. Bad for me. No enchantment can save me. No escape from scratching. From Death.

My soul stays attached to Coven. Misery loves company. Now I observe them. Still fascinated with hairplay scratching power. A rent in fabric of the cosmos. Wild cross-influence across spacetime. A gesture on this continent wreaks havoc on that planet. Or in the next meadow.

Seeing all, Coven observes Umh's Twin-souled Nature. Ability to incarnate without Death. They experiment with hairplay. Link to her Soul through Ormgarde's hair brushing. Create ripples in Umh's life. Place Colonel Walker on her path. Thinks she seduces him with her power. But he undoes her with vision of past life suicide. Renders her vulnerable. Her seductive power backfires.

Ripe for intervention. Coven entreats her to Inchnadamp. As Witch in Red. Ensnared, Witch in Red very useful. Mentors young witch, Coven Leader. Helps summon roukh. And releases my Soul. I fly to the inter-life. Free from pox at last.

ق

Ooma pushed Bax off her, put on her clothes, and sat on the bed. Until that day, she thought Old Umh was a powerful being who controlled time, space, and other souls. Now she saw the Scottish coven had controlled her, trapping new Umh in a mirror in Donne's room, and throwing old Umh back to Egypt. "Allah be my witness," Ooma murmured, "I have no power in any lifetime."

Bax took the remark to include Ooma's helpless efforts to join qaraq meetings. As with Umh's failed seduction, Ooma's ploy to enlist his aid had backfired, and he felt used. He was reminded of them as children

272

in the Garfagnana, when Ursalina tricked him into a suicidal leap. Lying naked on the floor, Bax felt as distant from Ooma as he did from that past life. Like the Swedish soldier, he felt a great need to fly away from his entanglement.

40

October 11. Week 5.

"It's been a month. Naji still won't go down!" Sahara collapsed on the couch.

Amar brought his wife a cup of peppermint tea. Three weeks after the stillbirths, he was the doting husband, on his good days. "Forgive me, love, but God knows what's been happening with him for two years. Telling stories inside your brain. Leading a collective mindmeld with the qaraq."

Sahara felt his accusation. "He was stable during all that. Sweet. He's shut down."

"Maybe he feels all the sadness more than we realize. It's natural to shut down. A defense."

"But I should be able to get through and help him," Sahara said. "I'm his mother."

"But he's extraordinary, and you can't have super powers all the time."

Sahara nodded and sipped the warm comfort of her tea. "Can I ask you something?"

Amar gazed at his wife's radiant glow. "No, I wish you'd leave me alone."

Sahara laughed, despite the serious query she had prepared. "Ardra. Your grandfather. I told you he called on 9/11. Worried about you. He's sick. Why haven't you seen him?"

Amar knew he couldn't make excuses. He looked into Sahara's eyes. "I do love him. At times more than my mother and father together. I can't bear that he's leaving us. I can't face it."

"You'd let him die without a visit? He practically raised you. Deal with it. Visit him."

"All right!" Amar stared tensely into his mug. "So why can't Ooma join the meetings?"

"That's quite a leap!" Sahara said. "She's hounding you, now that she's back at work?"

Amar stared at Sahara. "You promised she could join."

"Yes, I did. Before I lost two babies. You can't deal with Ardra? I can't deal with Ooma."

"Don't pin this on me! Ooma *needs* the group. Like everyone else. God, you're stubborn!"

From his bedroom, Naji heard his parents' raised voices. He followed what they said, but did not want to. Their fights were becoming more frequent. Again. The twins in the interlife had explained the stillbirths, so he understood his parents' turmoil. They were stuck with only him now, and he was trapped between telepathy and speech. He wished the twins were there to advise him. He had asked them to be his friends, but did not hear from them. He should seek them out!

As quick as thought, Naji found himself on the Path of Heaven. There they were, a few paces ahead. He rushed to catch up, but they scooted up a flight of stone steps into an official looking building. Following them inside, Naji climbed a marble stair in an elaborate lobby. Above the staircase was a sign: INFORMATION COLLECTION: ROOM 40 A-X.

Upstairs, Naji glimpsed the twins turn down one of four grand hallways stretching away from the landing. As he followed them along side corridors, one twin checked over his shoulder to see if Naji was near. Finally, they all entered Room 40N.

Out of breath, Naji sat across from the twins at a long library table. "You'll be my friends?"

The twin on the left spoke. "We are here to warn you."

The twin on the right spoke. "Don't talk to anyone back home."

"Cause it's too scary right now?" Naji asked. "Not even in my mother's head?"

"Especially that. Don't speak in anyone's mind," the right twin insisted.

"What if I'm hungry? Or sick, or need something?"

"Of course, speak then," both twins said. "As much baby talk as you'd like."

Naji felt bossed, trapped. "My parents are sad. They need me. What about the qaraq?"

The left twin smiled at the right twin. "That is why we brought you here. This room contains your past life records. As a consolation for not sharing stories, you may see new ones."

The twins showed Naji a series of buttons under the tabletop, and told him how to use them while focusing on a specific time in his soul's journey. The qaraq was amassing tales about the making of *The Thousand and One Nights*, but Naji had not remembered one for himself. He thought back to that time, and was very surprised by what he heard in his mind.

The Tale of the Human Gastrointestinal Microbiome

There was once a soul in the middle of his lifetimes, who took human existences for granted. Entering his first non-human incarnation in centuries, $NO(z)^{14}$ could not understand this World. Technically, the World was still human, for NO(z)^{14} was reborn in the microbiome of a human gastrointestinal tract. But he saw nothing familiar for, as a bacterial cell, NO(z)^{14} had no eyesight.

NO(z)^{14} sought other ways to perceive his surroundings. Within his cellular walls, NO(z)^{14} noticed that he possessed clairsentience. Just as psychic humans receive mystic thoughts in their brains, ideas popped through his membrane like mitochondria. Packed in the human gut with nasty bacteriophages, clueless helminth parasites, and chatty yeasts, the microbiome felt like a dank prison. Soon he realized that all the organisms were busy conducting biological functions. An image flashed through his clairsentient soul: a dragonfly egg stuck in amber for millions of years. Not knowing his own role, NO(z)^{14} felt trapped in the bustling crowd of organisms.

How to figure his purpose? NO(z)^{14} picked up some of the local dialect and asked others like him. 'Check the esophagus,' 'Ask over at the pancreas,' and 'Get down to the colon' were typical responses. Swimming the many tubes and canals, NO(z)^{14} learned much about his new home. Although hosted by a relatively enormous human body, the microbiome boasted eleven times as many organisms as the human had cells. This news did not surprise NO(z)^{14}; from the dawn of Time nothing had evolved without microbes crawling all over it.

NO(z)^{14} met a plethora of his microbial cousins: noble members of the domain Archaea that traced their royal line back before multi-celled eukaryotes; viral thugs that had decimated ancient cities but presently succumbed to the weakest elixir; a luscious pear-shaped bacterium that NO(z)^{14} promised he'd visit later; and an iridescent blue organism, difficult to classify as bacterium, prokaryote, or remote control device.

An old germ told NO(z)^{14} that the blue creatures' function was a mystery. Delving into it brought great misfortune. Tempted to approach the blue sprite, NO(z)^{14} became entranced by its luminescence, and swore he saw a many-columned edifice under an infinite firmament of stars.

Turning from the hallucination, NO(z)^{14} vowed to find a mission. In the endless tangle of the intestine, he came across a forest of villi struggling to expel nasty looking vermin. The intruders forced their way past the villi's waving tendrils, hoping to invade the nutrient infrastructure. $NO(z)^{14}$ shook off his aimless state, recognized the toxic enemies of the human, and charged into the forest.

Drawing on powers he did not know he possessed, $NO(z)^{14}$ excreted a glutinous substance that hampered the enemies' movements. Smashing into the maleficent cells, he ground them into the intestinal wall. Stretching his fluid form *in extremis*, he swallowed the gang leader whole. $NO(z)^{14}$ decimated the entire colony of marauders, and the villi waved their branches in gratitude.

$NO(z)^{14}$ had found his purpose. As a benevolent phage, he was destined to rid the gut of poisonous foes. Although it was dangerous, violent work, $NO(z)^{14}$ established his reputation as the phage to call for a neighborhood purge. He felt no guilt in his exterminations; he was part of life's natural order. But eventually $NO(z)^{14}$ met a strain of plague cells that reduced him to enzymes.

ق

Naji flinched as his reincarnation crashed to a halt. Replacing the story, a list recited in Naji's head, the names of souls slain by $NO(z)^{14}$'s purges. Naji's lip quivered as he recognized one name: Po, Porcy's soul. He had murdered one of his own! Naji did not wish to listen anymore. He rose from the table. The twins stood behind him, silent and still. Naji gasped. No escape!

Breaking out of trance, Naji was in his bedroom, no longer in the interlife. Eerie and menacing, the twins had judged him for the microbe lifetime. How could he have killed Po, even as a virus? Porcy was so sweet to him in this life. Had she forgiven him?

Naji received the microbiome tale after wondering where he stood in the evolution of the Nights lifetimes. Assuming the phage's life had occurred during the same time period, Naji intuited that his soul ran away from the qaraq after murdering Po, in exile as the qaraq created

278

a special version of the Nights. That would explain Naji's absence from that history.

Naji cried quietly. *Did they miss me back then, or just hate me? The twins were right: I can't tell anyone about this. I'm too ashamed.*

An hour later, when his father looked in on the nursery, Naji was fast asleep.

41

—◦◦◦—

November 15.   Week 10.

When Zack brought Jobim to the third qaraq meeting that fall, he felt palpable tension in the room.   Zack was surprised: Verle had instantly appreciated Jobim's understanding of World Types structure.   Diana was supportive of Zack finding a good relationship.   Cachay not only approved of Jobim, but had invited him to dinner.

"I tell Jobim everything that's going on," Zack argued to the group. "Why not let him get the straight dope before I infect it with my attitude?"

"It's about boundaries," Dr. Machiyoko said.   "We've worked hard to feel safe exposing personal problems.   Any new member threatens that safety."

"I'm so sorry," Jobim said, "I never meant to intrude.   I hate to cause any drama."

"Can't he be a guest, like when Bax or I visited for the first time?" Cachay suggested.   "Is that protocol, Elvi?"

"Don't put in on Elvi, mother," Zack said.   "I thought you all approved of Jobim."

Everyone jumped to reassure Jobim the issue was not his character. Except Bax.

"Ooma's been knocking on the door for months. She deserves entry more than Jobim."

"My God," Sahara said. "We're just talking about a guest visit. Do you have to push this?"

"Please stop!" Jobim could not handle the tension in the attic. The nightmares triggered by his apartment being at Ground Zero had made him more sensitive to anxiety than he had ever been before. "I can't stand you fighting because of me." He rose and went to the door. "Zack, I'll wait downstairs. It's okay, enjoy your meeting." Zack stood as Jobim left, but his mother restrained him.

"I feel bad for Jobim," Cachay said, "but Bax's right. Ooma asked for a mini-qaraq lunch."

"What good would that do, Mother?" Zack said. "There'll be even more in-fighting."

"Ooma's popping out stories," Bax said. "She knows everything about old and new Umh."

"Even what nightmare devastated new Umh in the first place?" Verle asked.

"Can't handle that now," Bax said. "I'd recall it for her. I'm not scared of any of it."

Dr. Machiyoko's heart raced. Bax's delusion of invulnerability was an over-compensation for watching the Towers fall. "If Ooma's not ready to see her soul break down, don't push it, Bax. And don't encourage him, Verle, just to wrap up the 1600s World."

"Finish one World, and its neighbor pops up," Sahara said. "I recalled a new World close to the 1600s, but kept it at bay, given Verle's clean-up campaign. Prof. Agib approved my first pages, so I live at the computer now, tackling a chapter a month. I brought you archivists a gift."

Sahara handed Verle a typed manuscript of her recall. As he perused it, the conversation bounced between the Ooma problem, the Jobim problem, and the qaraq's Medieval work on the Nights. Cringing at the qaraq's patter, Verle strained at the first paragraphs of the tale. His effort intensified as he recognized something on the page. He dropped the manuscript. Sahara hushed the group and looked toward Verle. The old greylocks recited his own lifetime narrative.

The Tale of the Tin Beads of Malacca

He never should have let her near his penis. Why did he do it? It wasn't just that it was the latest thing in Malacca, the foreskin incision, nor simply his uncharacteristic giddiness about the launching of the great Chinese Treasure Ships; nor could he chalk it up to the closing of the Silk Road, separation from his family back in Mocha, and the double-edge yearning to reunite with them and to pursue life's offerings freely. But why this offering? To lie on a table, head numb with rice wine, penis kept thick but soft by her perfect touch, while the tiny-eyed surgeon, with his piercing focus, delicately slid the tin beads into the inch-long cut in the foreskin, slowly eased them around the ring of flesh, and then closed up with minute needle stitches – why did he suffer such madness to acquire an orbital system of the tiny spheres in the pleasure center of his universe? And why did she linger? Did she have to keep applying the fragrant anesthetic leaves, massage the shaft, moisten the tip of the head? For an hour after? And her eyes: did she gaze at every man having the surgery? That was the only explanation he needed: Si's eyes captured him, teased him, instructed him.

Days before, while waiting at the harbor for his Treasure Ship to sail, Vas ibn Bad'r Ens had heard that Malaccan women had a special way. Get ready to abandon the strictures of Islam, they told him: even if married, a woman will pleasure any man, offer their husband any woman, all for greatest happiness. And the tricks and techniques they have! When Vas first heard of tiny metal balls inserted in male genitals for giving and receiving greater pleasure, he felt a shiver of painful disgust; at her parents' inn, Si had laughed at his squeamish attitude.

"It's a prized custom," Si explained, "for status as well as pleasure. The average man uses tin balls but the wealthy man uses gold."

"How does anyone know the difference," Vas asked.

Si laughed. "Try it and find out. I know just the man to do the procedure, and I'm the ablest of assistants." She looked into his eyes for the first time. "I take special care with a man's pride so there is no pain. Sometimes a taste of pleasure," she teased.

And so Vas let himself go, but how much farther would he go? He came from Anatolia, the area near Mocha, and had a prosperous trading business, spending half the year in China and the other half with his sons, his wives, and their parents. On this last trip to China the Emperor shut down trade routes to protect the borders, threatened by the powers of Islam on the eastern end. Vas thought himself clever to wait out the dispute, but unlike his cleverness at landing a good trade, he had miscalculated. Had he wished to be trapped, to abandon his family?

Vas thought about this question during the week he recovered at Si's parents' inn, receiving her gentle ministrations and teasings (ah, how you'll please your lovers); the answer came in the form of the question he asked Si: will you come on the sea voyage with me? When she did not take him seriously, he imparted the scope of the journey: was she enticed or frightened? Was it enough to see eight hundred gargantuan box vessels from Emperor Zhu Di's Chinese fleet enter her harbor? Did she understand the plan to send ships out past India, around Africa, and into the western sea, to discover what lands lay beyond?

If only Vas could answer Si's resistance to going with a list of all the women who'd feel the thrilling orbit of the tin spheres in their inner galaxies, to show how generous he would be giving of himself during the course the great eunuch-admiral Zhou Ma charted in the newfound West. There would be Urhu, the copper beauty on the northern coast of the long southern continent; Milok, the captivating Maya sorceress he would meet on the voyage up the other coast of the new continent; Nipor Por, dark red-haired woman of the earth tribe on the continent back near

China, with strange hopping animals with pouches; Kwiatl, long-legged carver on the northwest shore of the new northern continent they visited on a return trip; Snow Blossom, the beauty living by the huge bay with fragrant eucalyptus a bit south.

But Vas could neither foresee the future nor eradicate Si's dismissal of his invitation. He beseeched her parents, insisting he would be her protector, promising she would return home with fame and riches; they only wished their daughter stay with them. Si saw no benefit in abandoning her life: by assisting the tiny-eyed surgeon she met people from many lands, so why travel to them?

Still, she continued to gaze at him, until he finally saw it, when she declared his full recovery, his boarding pass to heights of pleasure: he did not wish to return to Mocha and his family. Now Vas understood he had made all his choices to be with her, to do anything she wanted – to sew metal balls into his cock, for Allah's sake. Now he knew what would convince her: he would share the gift she had made him, invite her into his bed the final night, and inaugurate his new apparatus.

She took the gift into her with such voracious delight that he realized she had been waiting for it all along; she cast off all inhibition and fear of this strange Arab, and when he invited her to travel for the last time, they stole away at dawn and cast off for places unknown. His own sweet concubine instructed Vas in her Malaccan ways of sexual generosity: Si offered him countless women on board the vessel and in every port; he offered her to those he felt were qualified, not the roughest sailors but the ambassadors, dignitaries, and hospitable natives they encountered.

But Vas loved her more and more and became jealous as they approached the Cape of Good Hope. Since it went against her beliefs, he hid his jealousy from her, complaining about the lovers as distractions from his work trading beans from Mocha. He rejected her Malaccan generosity.

At that point the great fleets went their separate ways in the journey; Si jumped ship to join Admiral Wen, who headed for the northern continent. Vas never saw her again, but roamed the seas with Zhou Ma to find Urhu, Milok, Nipor Por, Kwiatl, and Snow Blossom, all who felt his celestial tin pulses. Ships were lost, sailors drowned, and pregnant concubines left ashore at false paradises; Vas became protector of the last concubine, returned to Milok in Palenque, settled into a Maya hammock, and sired a dozen children that led to his great-great-great grandchildren.

Lying on the table back in Malacca, gazing into Si's eyes, Vas ibn Bad'r Ens had thought he had seized the life offered him, the glory of eight hundred Treasure Ships, and new sexual power. Later, Vas learned to let go of treasure and embrace rootlessness. In between, he became obsessed with his desire for Si, and so lost her, years later understanding she had escaped the trap of his love.

Should he never have let her near his penis? Better ask: should the Chinese never have sailed the tin globe of the planet in 1421, as Europeans name the year, only to be forgotten a century later by those usurpers who 'discovered' the New World?

ق

"Better ask: forget Jobim and Ooma – should we allow this lusty old soul in the group?" Cachay asked, a bit jealous that Sahara's soul had had her way with him.

"Nice try at lightening our problems, Mother," Zack said. "But I'd say the real question is: what are these Chinese explorations of the New World? Before Columbus?"

With his eyes still closed, Verle smiled. "Eight hundred vessels let loose on the world."

"Are you awake, old man?" Cachay poked him. "What are you saying?"

Verle opened his eyes, groggy, but perfectly conscious. "Actually, I saw something on the Net. Emperor Zhu Di, the same ruler who built The Forbidden City, built ships much larger than any European or Arabian boats. These Treasure Ships conducted extensive sea trade with India, Arabia, and East Africa well before Columbus. Zheng He, great

285

eunuch-warrior for Zhu Di, led many expeditions. He was Muslim, from an Islamic province in southern China."

Sahara commended Verle. "Thanks for turning my gift into a story. Glad you overcame your stricture against new Worlds. Though technically, you're adding to other Chinese lifetimes."

"When I was Lord Xa of the Seven Palaces," Bax said. "Was that also 15th Century?"

"Perhaps," Diana said. "My incarnation, Deng She, escaped your notorious court with the help of another eunuch, Zhou Dong. Maybe we sailed away on a Treasure Ship."

"The 15th Century will lead to the 1600s, and why Umh had a breakdown," Bax said.

Verle handed back Sahara's manuscript. "Honor us with your tale, Miss Si, love of my life."

Zack asked, "Aren't you two father-vizier and daughter-Scheherazade? Is this incest?"

"Maybe our souls created some kind of original sin, played out in this new, Multiple World," Verle mused. "Maybe it all became too much for Ooma."

Something struck Bax. "As Oolon, the sister of Lord Xa, Ooma lost it big time. Drove her brother away. Exposed every non-eunuch and fucked their brains out. Pardon." Bax thought of Ooma's recent erratic behavior. He felt a chill. "Can we hear Sahara's story?"

The idea that her story now threw Ooma into the spotlight upset Sahara. And with innocent Jobim becoming an issue, the tangle of conflicts overwhelmed her. But her tale was one of daring and adventure, like Verle's memory. Her soul had bravely fled to parts unknown. She gripped her manuscript tightly and read to the qaraq.

42

---∽---

The Tale of the Chinese Discovery of the New World

Perhaps it was for the best. I never would have left Malacca without Vas pushing me. I always did want more than to work in mother and father's inn. I liked working on the men, not for the sex, but for meeting all the different types: rich men wanting gold balls that rang out announcing their value, dashing loners with fiery stories, and most of all the foreignors.

Vas was one of them, having fled to parts unknown. An easy mark, just a little gazing into his eyes. But he returned my gaze (most men don't), stroked my arms after the treatment (few men even thank me), and asked me to sail on the Chinese monster boats (no sober man invites me anywhere). His love-making enchanted me. He made the dearest, oddest sounds of pleasure. Our pleasures transported me to a new world. I was ready to sail to the ends of the earth with him.

The ends of the earth – journey of a lifetime – soul mate – phrases echoing in my head as we sailed for Lakka and India. It was mostly soul mate that resonated, as if I had searched for one all my life. He sold me on the idea, consummate trader in love. I made him trade in love, too, with other women, but ultimately he was weak. Malaccan sexual generosity made him grab on, lose faith and pride in me, and admonish me like a royal adviser scolding a debauched Prince. In bed, his sounds were no longer novel. Would he force me to return with him to his beloved Mocha?

Mocha. The name, the place, and the substance still make me laugh. His grand plan. The silly little pots he had around his cabin, sprouting the plants he thought would make his fortune. The first time he revealed his secret boon I laughed for a day. These funny beans will make you rich? He explained that an herbalist had discovered the great value of the Mocha bean: to soothe every kind of itch. I had to bite my lip.

At each port his failure worsened. I teased him as the first traders jeered; I kept my tongue the next time when he lost his temper; I felt sorry for him, but grew tired of his obsession. I harbored a silent rage as he prattled on about new ways to demonstrate the remedy.

At the Cape of Good Hope it all fell apart. He chose to leave his family and sail on with me. That night he made violent love to me, clinging in desperation. The sound of his grunts was disgusting. I couldn't breathe. My image of a soul mate shattered.

I heard that Vas' fleet would bear south for a passage back to China, the other fleet north, where the weather resembled Malacca. At first light I boarded a ship of the other fleet. One of the concubines Vas had bedded took me in. The only drawback was the gift he had bestowed on her: Mocha plants, surrounding her bunk.

In the weeks ahead I felt adrift. What was I searching for? The ship made swift time in the ocean currents, but a crisis emerged in the new lands. The Chinese expected to conquer the world and bring back treasure and obeisance from civilizations. Where were these great peoples? Here a tribe lived in crude huts, there an island displayed nothing but

288

birds and monkeys. China, able to circle the globe, discovered its loneliness. My hopes had become illusions, too. I lost faith in love.

Then my monthly time stopped. Since Vas had eventually prevented me from sleeping with others, I knew it was his child. The concubines are experts at preventing pregnancy, but Vas had taken me by surprise. At a large island in the tropics several ships ran aground. Unable to support a child, the crew put me ashore with other women, children, and a few males to protect us. Food and water were plentiful, the beaches beautiful, and the natives peaceful. My journey was over.

Vas may have not been my soul mate, but he had altered my life radically. Still, after years on the island, I stopped thinking of him and searching for more. The days were balmy; the sun flowed in and out of the clouds like waves. Our Asian community made many children, and the children made children with each other, and occasionally with a native of such beauty and kindness that no one could resist. I lost track of which generation was which, of which mix of Turkish, Arab, Chinese, Malaccan, and Taino blood belonged to which gorgeous child.

The grandson of my granddaughter was the first child in many years to resemble Vas. Appropriately, he reveled in tending the Mocha plants that had survived. One day he came to tell me of white men landing on the shore. Long ago we gave up hope a Chinese vessel would retrieve us. It seems the Europeans had at last learned how to circle the Earth (perhaps they stole a map). I could have been a hundred years old, who knows; I was on my deathbed when the boy asked if he could travel with the white men to a new land. He hoped to trade the Mocha plant. I was too old to laugh, so I gave him my blessing. Perhaps it was for the best.

ق

"The Chinese discovered the Americas, *and* transplanted coffee there?" Zack challenged.

"The memory felt as true as anything else we recall." Still sensitive about Jobim and Ooma, Sahara was stung by Zack's doubt. "The recall

289

came a week after the Towers fell, and my body had its first weird pains. I got a massage, and the bodywork was sometimes unbearable, sometimes incredibly soothing. I felt something terribly wrong inside me."

Sahara stopped. Zack said, "I didn't mean to push you. You don't have to explain."

"No, it's good." Sahara had avoided the subject for weeks with Amar, sent him off to therapy, and stuck her nose in the books. Empowered by Si's brave exploration of a new world, she made the effort to explore her trauma. "I was splitting apart between the pain and the pleasure. No one will ever put me together again, all the Kings of Chosroes, in the Nights. I didn't know my babies were dying, but I needed to stop the pain, so my mind went to Malacca. It was real!"

The group sat in humbled silence. At that moment, no one cared about a revisionist history of the New World, or where the tale fit into qaraq history.

"It's a good time to wrap up," Elvi offered. "That was very brave, Sahara, but we won't push." The group slowly got up, and gave Sahara reassuring hugs. She felt she had just turned a corner, and could start healing. As long as another tragedy didn't strike any time soon.

As Zack headed out the attic door, he glanced back to see Elvi talking quietly with Diana. Was she scolding her for being on Verle's case lately? He hoped that was it, and not a tête-à-tête about him and Jobim. He felt awful seeing Jobim waiting on a hard bench in the church lobby.

"I felt like an intruder," Jobim said, "spying on something I wasn't meant to hear."

"Don't be silly," Zack said. "There's these other dramas in the group, that's all. You can be part of us. You're with me."

"I don't want to be part of the other dramas. And I don't like being ambushed. Not now."

"So you don't care about a group I've devoted my life to?"

Jobim exhaled sharply. "I didn't say that. I just don't need any more nightmares in my life."

Zack understood. He put his hands on Jobim's shoulders. "I'm sorry."

Jobim held still. "Forget about it. Just cool it on the qaraq parties and meetings."

"And dinners with my mother?" Zack removed his hands.

"Fine. Whatever." Jobim stood up to leave the church. "Can we go now?"

43

—⟊⟊⟊—

November 22. Thanksgiving.   Week 11.

The meal over, Sahara and Amar sat in the living room with their coffee, while Naji lay on his back on the floor, and Ardra sipped tea on the
sofa. As Ardra expressed his gratitude once again for the Thanksgiving
invitation, the doorbell rang. Sahara wondered if Amar's father Solomon
had decided to join them after all. She was surprised to greet Bax with a
young woman in a veil, each carrying a hefty cardboard box.

"Sorry to intrude, ma'am," Bax said. "Your husband might want these
right away."

"I snuck them out of Bruckner's Jersey City office yesterday," the
woman explained. "There aren't many new documents since September,
but it'll help him retain some clients."

As soon as she heard her voice, Sahara recognized Ooma. She had
not seen Ooma's new garb, and she noticed a new look in the young
woman's eyes, like a stranger gazing from within the veil. A wave of
dread shoved aside the awkward moment. Amar had not gone to work
yesterday, normal enough since the office was in flux. He had been
silent and ashen all day. Today he was cheerful during the holiday meal,
but she now feared the worst.

She called to Amar to help with the boxes. He took them and darted off to the den, avoiding Sahara's glare. "Forgive me, come in. Are you missing Thanksgiving for this?"

"My parents won't celebrate an American holiday after what's happened," Ooma said. "It kind of sucks; my mom makes the best turkey with apricots, dates, and almonds."

"Porcy dragged me to help at the church," Bax said. "Much rather be here."

Ardra poked his head in from the living room. "At least have a piece of pie. I remember this young beauty from your house closing. Not letting her out of my sight. You the lucky guy?"

Blushing, Bax bent down to shake Ardra's hand. He was surprised by the old man's strong grip. They settled in the living room. Ooma was glad Bax was there; it would have been doubly awkward on her own, though Ardra was sweet enough. Naji continued to stare at the ceiling.

Ready to face Sahara, Amar went into the kitchen as she cut up the pie. "I waited to tell you so I wouldn't spoil today. They canned me yesterday. Over the phone. The day before a holiday! Merciless Wall Street bastards."

Sahara did not respond. She thought she had gained some emotional ground since the last qaraq meeting, but she simply could not cope with another disaster. She handed the plates to Amar and sent him to the living room. Bax and Ooma happily accepted the pie, sweet shields from their discomfort. Sahara entered the room with tea. Ooma saw the tension between her and Amar.

"Sorry if I've ruined your Thanksgiving," Ooma said. "I figured you saw it coming, with the chaos of the election, the dotcom bust, and the economic mess after the attacks."

Sahara couldn't remain quiet. "The office used 9/11 as an excuse to finally get rid of Amar."

"You're next, Ooma," Amar said. "I may jump at the least thing, according to my therapist, but it doesn't mean I'm wrong. It saved us from the Towers." With a dismissive swipe at the air, he raised his voice.

"Good riddance! They can't handle someone making strong, quick decisions."

"*That* got you fired," Sahara said, "like when you threw your colleagues out our door." Sahara plunged them into a painful impasse with a reminder of the horrible New Year's party.

Seeing Naji close his eyes tightly, Ardra walked over to the child and extended his hand. "Time for young and old to retire upstairs." As they climbed the stairs, Naji knew Ardra was kind to take care of him right now. But the twins had told him to keep to himself. To comfort his dying great-grandfather by being with him, but nothing more. It was confusing. Where were they now when he felt so bad? It wasn't fair: he wished he could talk to great-grandfather.

A few weeks ago Naji had recalled his closest lifetime to when the qaraq's collective worked on the Nights. Since he had avoided them out of guilt for his microbial murder of Po, it made perfect sense that afterward he was a criminal stealing The 379 Group's special manuscript. He was sad he had been alone, separate from the qaraq. Like he was now. He wished he could speak to Ardra about it. Maybe the twins were wrong about keeping silent.

Ooma sat in the quiet tension of the living room. Perhaps it was an opportunity. "I can't imagine what you're going through. I know you've suffered greater misfortunes before now, but that doesn't make what's happened to Amar any easier."

"Thank you, Ooma," Sahara said, not insincerely. "I appreciate it."

"And here I've been hounding everyone about the meetings. I promise I'll back off."

Sahara looked in her teacup. "You have the right. I hope Bax keeps you informed."

"Absolutely," Ooma said, smiling at Bax. Sahara noticed Bax's shoulders stiffen.

"Have you had any new memories lately?" Sahara asked.

"All the time. The Arabian memories won't stop." Ooma saw Sahara's eyes widen, catching the bait. "I keep thinking about one big meeting

294

together. We could get all the lifetimes out." Ooma laughed. "Hey, we could do it on New Year's and purge the past."

Amar scoffed. "Lovely idea. I thought you were backing off."

"Sorry." Disliking her ex-boss' attitude, Ooma chose to mess with him. "There is a new lifetime from your husband. Did he tell you?"

Amar slammed his mug on the coffee table. "What are you talking about?"

Sahara saw his apprehension. "What's wrong?"

Amar looked down in shame. "It's the hyper-vigilance. Everyone in this damned group, even you Bax, has recalls day and night. There's something wrong with me. I'm from Delhi, for God's sake, my people are the original reincarnation mavens. I struggle to get one with my wife's help." Amar glared at Ooma. "So when you say I've recalled a lifetime, I jump."

"Sorry," Ooma said, "did I say *you* had the recall? It was my memory. Of your lifetime."

Sahara saw something was going on between her husband and Ooma, but could not deal with it at that moment. Fortunately, Bax said something.

"Haven't heard this one." He looked at Ooma, beseechingly. "It could pass the time." Ooma looked at Sahara and Amar for the go-ahead. Perturbed, trapped, and curious, they nodded.

The Tale of the Mountain that Looked Within

I am not the first who has stood here. The Fiery Mountain From The Sky crashed into the hills. Ice Rivers descended from the north. Many monuments to the earth have risen in this spot. I know I am a young mountain, but I also know you were here, among the giants of the past.

Where have you gone? Were you ground to dust, scattered through the Three Valleys? Or are bits of you inside my stone walls? Is that why I sense you near, whispering to me, teasing me? Or is this feeling a kinship with my neighbors in the mountain range? Not that titan across the valley, staring at me. Nothing loving about that one: a permanent scowl etched on his Cliff Face.

When I implore the other peaks for information about your disappearance, they humor me. One compliments me on my quick reaction to the loss, given the geological pace of mountain growth. Another giant suggests that the whispers I hear are the echoes of the people who once lived in the valley. This thought inspires stories from my neighbors, sordid tales about cutting open animals, and stuffing a human into the belly of a mule. Tawdry! Disgusting!

I shut out my neighbors and look within. Where is the spark of truth inside me, the faint trace of your remnants? I look past the shale, past the bedrock. There are glints of knowledge, encased in darkness. I see pockets of clear, shiny, luminescent crystal. There is a solid comfort in the substance. This must be what you left behind, gems of love, a gift for thousands of years!

Over time, new tribes drift into the valley, setting up primitive shelters protected by guarded mountain passes and a belief that we giants watch over them. You may be long gone, but you have left riches beyond compare for these future generations. I am saddened by your absence, but these clues of your existence shine with the warmth of an intimate caress.

I look deep into the crystal deposit of your cave. I open my heart to listen to your voice from beyond. A message comes loud and clear, the ancient voice of the Crystal: "I am the one who was here for millennia, even before your soul mate stood on this ground, before the first people traveled across the Great Land Bridge, before people lived in forests of magical creatures and buried their dead in sacred mounds. You mistake me for your long lost, still lost, soul mate. You buried me under a mountain of false memory. Bear witness to who I am: the Lighurian Crystal, the Corundum of Vision, the Solitaire who points the way forward in the darkness of Time."

The ringing voice of the Crystal falls silent. I turn my crushing disappointment toward you, but you are innocent of my folly. You had existed in this mountainous domain; my recognition is not entirely false. The Lighurian Crystal is familiar, but I am blind to my history with it.

Tired of my soul's exertions, I sink into the weight of my stone hulk. The valley inhabitants have not yet discovered the Lighurian Crystal, nor do they look up to me in rapture. These events are for future generations, and for future souls incarnating the mountain after me. If not for the settlements in the valley, I would be done with one swipe, send down an avalanche, and erode myself from the cliff face. I would leave no clues of being here, no false hopes, and no love lost.

ق

When Ooma finished, Bax asked, "How do you know this is Amar's lifetime?"

"A little help from my new colleagues at the archive," she replied. "Verle explained that the mountain epic of the Three Valleys is a "Five Character Conflict World." The qaraq is split into two factions within the World. Two of us are left to be mountains, the soul mates in this story. Most likely Amar and Sahara, or maybe Sahara and Naji."

"Or you and Amar," Sahara said, looking for a response from her husband. "Given the Nights archetypes, you two are King and Queen, after all."

"Point taken," Ooma said to Sahara, "but most ways Amar is Mr. Mountain."

"The impulsiveness feels like him," Sahara said, "ending it all with an avalanche."

Wary of Amar's silence, Bax said, "Have we run into these Ligoorian crystals before?"

"Sounds like they'll show up in new Worlds: land bridges and magi-cal forests," Sahara said.

Feeling she and Sahara were on a roll, Ooma pressed onward. "Amar's life is an important story. When we have this meeting all together, don't you think he should be there, too?"

Sahara smirked: she had not agreed to Ooma's New Year's meeting idea. "Even if the group bought in, I gave up hope Amar would come to meetings a long time ago. Ask him."

Ooma looked to Amar for a response, a knowing gaze that disturbed Sahara. What was going on between them? Could she rely on Amar for anything? On top of feeling Naji's distance, losing her babies, and fight-ing a spiral of depression, Sahara now had lost her partner's financial support, the one thing he had promised her when she moved back in.

Amar's response jolted Sahara out of her thoughts. "I'm a free man now. I once had better things to do than swap tales with a bunch of lunatics. Now I don't. I'm game."

Sahara felt the depth of her anger. With one look from Ooma, Amar had broken his principle of staying out of meetings, a principle based on wanting to hear stories only from his beloved wife.

She was on the verge of losing control. It was Thanksgiving. Ardra was upstairs with Naji. She had to keep it together. But all eyes were on her, waiting for an answer about New Year's.

"I'm not making any promises," she said. "I'll think about it. On one condition. No one pushes it at meetings, no one conspires to make it happen with the others. It's between us."

"No one?" Bax looked worried. "I have to keep this from Porcy?"

"Especially Porcy!" Sahara said. "She's the Gossip Queen. She'll tell everyone and they'll be all over me." Sahara was near tears. "I can't take any more pressure. I've got my work to do. And right now, I'm check-ing on my child." She fled the room, leaving Amar to deal with Ooma and Bax.

44

—⟨∂∂⟩—

December 13.   Month 4.

The qaraq meeting following Thanksgiving was when Verle fought Diana over World Types, Diana faced her life in the future as Dizalegh, which led to her story collecting work with Zack as Zizagh, and the therapist exposed the group's post-traumatic stress. All during the meeting, Bax exchanged charged looks with Sahara, but kept his promise not to bring up Ooma's New Year's idea. The qaraq could not have taken in the suggestion.

Ooma was not happy with Bax's report after that fourth meeting of the Fall, and took aggressive action in preparation for the meeting the following week. Struggling not to expose the New Year's idea to Verle and Zack, she spent every free hour inputting her recalls into the archive computer. When the qaraq climbed the stairs for the fifth meeting, there was Ooma working furiously in one corner of the attic.

Sahara and Naji were the last to arrive. As soon as they did, Ooma let out a cry, silencing the surprised crowd. "Before you all kick me out, please let me share something. I come to you as Oamra, whom you met in Sahara's recall of Sanaa. We were lovers in 10th Century Baghdad, but ended in Cordova, Spain, where we worked on a subversive version of the Nights."

"10th Century Cordova?" Sahara remarked. "al-Andalus?"

Verle nodded. "We've been hoping for recalls about The 379 Group. Is this it?"

"Who's Al Andaloose?" Bax was upset Ooma had not already told him about this.

"What do you mean: I come to you as Oamra?" With growing concern, Dr. Machiyoko observed Ooma's eyes twitching. She wondered who was actually peering out from her veil.

"If we wish to profit from all she has to say," Verle said, "let's listen." The group looked to Ooma, then Elvi. Ooma licked her lip in satisfaction. Elvi nodded. Ooma gestured for the qaraq to sit. Announcing the story with great bravado, Ooma strode around the attic as she spoke.

The Tale of the Flight to Spain

It was a very bad time to live in Baghdad: Sanaa and I did not notice because we were in each other's arms every chance we could; we had met only two years after the Buyid dynasty took power; many thought the shift a change for the better, the Abbasid Caliphate bullied out of their power by the ghulams, their Turkish mercenary soldiers, but soon the Buyids were in bed with the ghulams as Sanaa and I were in bed rapturous illicit against all social odds wooing each other with endless tales from the marketplace storytellers

so we were oblivious to the divisive forces inside the Buyid court until it was too late for me, oblivious as Sanaa fearlessly searched the seediest corners of the market gathering stories while I hid in the back of great-grandfather al-Malaq's shop who loved Sanaa's hunger for narrative

so al-Malaq gave her the magical oval object and said that in the last century the oval had been smuggled out of the House of Wisdom seven days after he was born and as a child he had stolen it from a blind sausage maker because of the oval's glittery surface and that he saw what the object could do after the lotus leaves he purchased from the sidr seller took over his brain but when I scolded him for such talk he warned me that one day I too would look upon the oval's magic

with Sanaa's first experience with the oval she implored me help and I crawled in her bedroom window to watch her sleep and saw images from the oval surround her beautiful body shining in the moonlight images from her dreams congealed into a storyline with fantastical settings

and I understood why al-Malaq chose Sanaa to be my comfort after he died, to be my public face in the market set the oval aflame with tales hunt for new myths, and Sanaa wished more than anything to join a storyteller group for she dreamed of a mighty anthology

she devoured all gossip about poetry and song and story at court but winced as the Buyids took a step backward in fiction's advancement in Islamic society attempted a prestigious literary circle around vizier al-Muhallabi by limiting stories to historical narratives or moral parables and kicked both common tales and ambitious fictions back into the market, where Sanaa celebrated the liberation of *The Thousand Tales* from the Buyids and gathered new frame tales such as "The Malice of Women" whose inclusion would no longer be met with scorn but with loving smiles.

I received so many vicarious delights from Sanaa's discoveries that I could never have foreseen what was waiting for me: with the Turkish guard as our street police breathing down the neck of the market I took pleasure in al-Malaq's practice of selling inferior goods to the mercenaries at triple the price but the Buyids had many spies and detected my pesky business methods and the heavy set ghulams visited my shop ripped up bolts of fabric overturned fragile vases bruised my arm spat in the entryway infuriating my proud soul to the point that Sanaa's reasonable pleas to protect our shop and bestow gifts on the soldiers only maddened me further

and two of them returned when I was alone and demanded free merchandise as payment for my cheating ways and I spat in their faces and one of them held me down while the other ripped my garments mounted entered rammed and my eyes watered in searing pain

and though Sanaa's comforts were a gift from Allah I knew it was the end and though she took over the shop kowtowing to the authorities I never wanted to sell another trinket and though Sanaa buoyed up my spirits I could not laugh at the great irony of my condition: as far back as I can remember I never wanted children and felt giving birth was a danger to any woman and here I was impregnated by a brutish savage.

Early in the pregnancy Sanaa concocted the name Muhammad ibn ʿUmar though I implored her to wait until the seventh day and before he could even kick I felt sharp pains like he was trying to punch his way out like he had no patience for waiting in there but Sanaa found toys and clothes in the market like the elephant statuette she thought would bring him luck

but it was another elephant that undid me when I was about to give birth so uncomfortable in the Baghdad heat hiding in my cool back room sanctuary: one day I needed some light and air I staggered outside through the market and heard shouting and excitement coming from the square and dragged myself there saw a restless crowd waiting for an execution and I would have turned away but near the shackled prisoner was a wondrous sight an enormous beast with massive wrinkled gray skin huge white curved tusks and an extraordinary nose that hung all the way to the earth or swung trumpeted curled like a marvelous serpent a real version of the statuette I had only heard of them though it was said Caliph Harun kept them as pets and they fought in warfare from Hind to al-Andalus yet I felt this dignified docile animal shying from the noisome crowd would not hurt a flea

I was sorely mistaken for as the prisoner was brought forward the crowd screamed for blood the beast's handlers jabbed pulled provoked the poor thing until it became as enraged as the people so the executioner pushed the prisoner at the beast the crowd surged closer and I was shoved toward the awful scene squeezed into the barbarian throng and though I had no sympathy for the criminal I would never wish him trampled by the mad beast as the crowd ogled and cheered his broken bones and torn flesh as the violence erupted from beast to people I was jostled and fell down in danger of being trampled but random arms pulled me up pushed me aside dumped me into the sand at the edge of the square only then I understood the pain was not the usual jab from the unwanted one but true peril my water broke and there was no unhindered path so I crawled in the sand to find a way out

and my distress was unbearable I needed to stop and rest every minute though there was no time to do so I willed myself through the market to any drug seller physician midwife then drew close to my shop and screamed for Sanaa but by the time I arrived there was monstrous shooting back pain blood everywhere and then it was too late and the baby was lost.

Months passed. The dark back room engulfed me. Vizier al-Muhallabi initiated friendly envoys to the rival court of al-Rahman III in Spain. I could not face the loss of the child. Torn between relief of being unburdened and guilt at deriving gladness from an infant's death I saw only the noble elephant put to demonic purpose; even when my grief and numbness lifted after a year or two the elephant haunted my dreams and though Sanaa saw it as a symbol of the lost babe and wished me to release it I swore the elephant was a deeper symbol

in the third year after the child's death al-Hakam son of al-Rahman III and Prince of al-Andalus invited the writer Ali al-Qali to Spain; the invitation was a deeper symbol for the Andalusian court at Cordova was the remnant of the Umayyad dynasty ousted from power two hundred years ago who fled through North Africa gained assistance from the Moors drove the Vandals out of southern Spain (the land 'of the Vandals' or al-Andalus) and claimed true legitimacy against the reigning Baghdadi Caliphate

but each eastern visitor to Cordova described an elegant aristocracy conscious of its dependence on Baghdadi innovation, a lush and fertile land, Muslim harmony with Christian Jew and Berber so news of Al-Qali's grateful acceptance of al-Hakam's offer turned all eyes toward Cordova including Sanaa who saw a journey to Spain as a healing force for my emotional demise and begged me flee our troubles take only what we could carry stowaway in al-Qali's caravan follow a herd of imported war elephants westward to the idyllic setting of al-Andalus

arriving on Spanish soil I experienced a familiar sensation of being unhappy in one world and deciding to leave it and my soul transformed breathing the coastal air smelling the varieties of exotic flowers and when the Umayyad welcome party discovered us stowaways they were so flattered by Sanaa's entreaties for asylum that to save face al-Qali consented for us to join

and traveling north over the mountains the serene blue sky washed away my sorrows the dry climate cooler than Arab lands soothed my skin and Sanaa asked our guides many questions and was surprised to learn that the founder of the Cordovan Umayyad line had not only been a successful military invader but also the first significant al-Andalus poet thus this culture was steeped not only in blood but the flower of language so perhaps it was more welcoming for fiction than Baghdad

and arriving at the Cordovan patios fountains gardens wall decorations palm frond motifs that equalled the finest Baghdadi neighborhood our guides challenged our loyalties by asserting that thirteen years ago al-Rahman III declared himself rightful Caliph of the Islamic empire in brazen defiance of Baghdad and there was a great moment of tension until I claimed that al-Rahman III was capable of the declaration because the Buyids had ruined Baghdad a legitimate culture no longer resided there so what better place for the center of Islam than this garden of paradise

then wine flowed and our new friends spoke warmly of the acceptance of every culture in al-Andalus despite occasional tensions and alluded to the first Muslims mixing with Christian women of northern Spain their descendants with pale skin blue eyes, and Christian and Jewish communities being Arabicized accepting the desert tongue joining the invaders' customs while adhering to their own rituals without persecution and I marveled at this harmony contrasting Baghdad's intolerance and drunk with our welcome Sanaa and I gaped at the smiling people of many skin tones

no ancient city rivaled its picturesque detail, no modern city rivaled its open-armed embrace; our flight to Spain happened at both the perfect time in our lives and the pinnacle in the history of this jewel of the future: we were in the right special place at the right special time, a time to do great work, Sanaa whispered to me, and a time to heal wounds, I whispered back.

ق

Ooma whispered these last words directly in Sahara's ear, but loud enough for the group to hear. Tensing, Sahara took in the implicit actions in Ooma's histrionic gesture: pointing out the strangeness of them as lovers in a past life, offering an olive branch, charming her way into the qaraq, and praying Sahara could heal her own wounds. Since Amar lost his job, Sahara had soldiered on numbly, using her chapter on a revisionist Scheherazade as motivation to live, Scheherazade as a patron saint to give her strength. How deal with Ooma?

Ooma broke the spell over Sahara and sat down next to her. To everyone's surprise, she removed her niqaab, as if to look more directly at Sahara. "I apologize for my story. From it, I felt the sheer agony of losing a child at birth. I'm sorry to remind you of the anguish."

Sahara acknowledged the apology with the smallest of nods. The statement released some tension, but Sahara was uncomfortable in the spotlight. She worked so hard to keep her torments at bay. Facing them in public was excruciating. She was grateful Ooma did not want a response.

"I must also thank you for something, Sahara. Though I did not recall this tale at the 1999 New Year's party, it continues those memories. That night radically changed my life: linking minds with Bax, revealing a part of myself to Amar, even gaining a nasty reputation in your eyes. It was all meant to be, started us all on a path together, and I thank you for that."

Sahara was speechless. Ooma rose ceremoniously and re-fastened her niqaab. "You may wonder when I recalled our escape from Baghdad. It was on September 11, after escaping the falling Tower, at a first aid station. I was out of my mind for hours, but when I regained reality, and saw how distressed Amar was, it triggered this horrid memory of losing him."

Dr. Machiyoko had followed Ooma's shifts in mood from possessed storyteller to calm dispenser of compassion. "Are you saying the baby you lost in Baghdad was Amar?"

"It was his lifetime I recalled," Ooma replied, backing away from the circle of chairs.

Bax spoke up. "I received bits of the recall on 9/11, too. We all heard stories that day."

"Ooma's mindset opened a chamber of memory that anyone could enter," Elvi explained. "Such a chamber is free of linear time constraint. Like a multiplex of films playing simultaneously, where you can watch any scene from any film, the qaraq could experience any of Ooma's recalls."

"Organizing recent recalls for the archives," Verle said, "I felt Time playing tricks with us."

"A major symptom of post-traumatic stress is a feeling of floating in Time," Dr. Machiyoko said. "You disassociate from a harsh reality or memory and lose your time linearity."

"This was very specific," Verle said. "A set of recalls on 9/11, another set in the days after, and another weeks later. The sets seem related."

"Whatever are you talking about, old man" Cachay questioned.

"Something special is going on these days. Can we take advantage of it, Miss Elvi?" Verle asked. "Take revenge on the Maya Factor?"

"With a marathon session?" Ooma addressed Elvi, but looked to Sahara for acceptance. "Exploring The 379 Group?" Sahara nodded wearily. Ooma beamed. "On New Year's?"

"Fun idea!" Porcy said, relieved Ooma was herself again. "Time's playing with us, and New Year is Time's holiday."

"And a recurring one for the qaraq," Zack said. "I'm sick of spoiling my New Year's."

"New Year is a rebirth ritual the world over," Porcy said. "No wonder it recurs for us."

"Thanks a lot. Jobim and I have plans. Careful or I'll bring him."

"If we explore The 379 Group, both Ooma," Bax hesitated, "and *Amar* should be there."

"Hold on," Diana said, "we're all working through traumas. Are we really ready for an intense psychic *marathon*?"

Silence fell on the group. Ooma adjusted her niqaab, then spoke. "I've seen many other fragments. I want to collect the bits into the next chapters of the tale, but I need your help."

Sahara faced Ooma. "Honestly, I love the idea. And I agree you and Amar should be there. But I'm too fragile right now."

"Girl, you been saying that for weeks," Porcy blurted. "Not that you haven't seen trouble. But you look beautiful, and you work your butt off. We strong women burn through the pain."

"Burn through and burn out," Diana added.

Bax looked up. "Porcy's right, we got to make it happen. I don't beg, but please, please, please have the New Year's meeting. I'm sick of playing errand boy between Ooma and the group."

Shocked by this rare outburst, the group stared at Bax, then Ooma, who now stood by the gable niche, her back turned to the circle. Cachay weighed in. "I'm skeptical about this marathon. We'll all dream back to 1001 AD? Like last Halloween, when baby Naji led us to Draill U?"

"Yes, a group hypnosis session," Elvi confirmed, "but under my guidance, not Naji's."

"It'll work, I promise!" Suddenly Ooma thrust herself back into the circle, shooting a finger at Cachay, and sweeping her arm around the group. "I'll show you."

Standing in front of a chair between Verle and Cachay, Ooma raised her arms to the ceiling. Cachay looked extremely nervous as Ooma took a full minute to descend into the chair next to her. "With the power of the qaraq around me, I can do anything. Pieces of my life in Cordova float before me. A swirl of recollection, to get us beyond our recent terrors." On Ooma's other side, Verle felt a jolt of energy, bewilderingly erotic for his many years. "Shards of memory! Bind together into a tale worth telling." Seated now, Ooma grabbed Cachay and Verle's hands, calling on the group to join. *Is this spooky or what*, Bax thought?

Then, by ancient Islamic storytelling craft, Ooma shepherded the qaraq toward al-Andalus.

45

—⟨∿⟩—

The Tale of the Cordovan Marketplace

Khurafa, contemporary of Muhammad, carried off by djinn, returning to tell the tale, too fantastical to be truthful, lent his name to a word that means Tall Tale or Fish Story or Night Tale. There are not a thousand and one Arabic names for such stories, maybe only eighty-nine, including names for storytellers: Khatib, the preacher who delivers the sermon Friday noon, might stir in a story about The Prophet; Qussa, who told religious stories in the mosque, scholarly apocryphal, or dubious, banished to the street in the first centuries of Islam; Nadim, the courtly cup-bearer, pleasing his patron in physical appearance witty conversation astute political views; Hikaya, the artist who could mimic anyone and tell the odd story, who evolved into the coffeehouse raconteur; Rawi, transmitter of recitation, spreading a poem or prophesy, possessing great power in pre-Islamic times, when Arabs gathered in Mecca for an annual poetry contest at the Kaaba, the Black Rock in the House of God, where Muhammad revealed the Qu'ran, the prophetic words of Allah only spoken for decades, a rawi re-citing text from memory.

Understand this: despite all we have learned about Islamic injunctions against fiction, leading into the 10ᵗʰ Century the truth is that fiction, storytelling, and recitation have had more complex status than simply being Banned in Baghdad; on the one hand the medieval storyteller had as low a reputation as a juggler in the souk, on the other there are many stories in the Qu'ran, truths not fictions, but stories nonetheless, with all their power.

They try so hard here in Cordova so hard to outdo every facet of life in Baghdad so hard to have the best assortment of delicacies almond date concoctions shady fountains of cool bliss so hard to keep up with the latest fashions the best literary practices and in the street the most novel tales

everywhere I go there is more juggling sword swallowing or storytelling than in any Baghdad alleyway; Oamra, it is your sensitivity to every new thing, Sanaa tells me; the breathlessness of being in the throng of Moors Arabs Jews Christians Berbers Franks each with their own niche stall meeting place a market so full of separate spaces how can a place contain such a density of life

but I shy from connecting with anyone retreat into my secretive self but replenish my wounded soul; there is power here opportunities riches abundance but how acquire them I wonder as I hide behind my veil; how will Sanaa fit into this new world and I let the breeze blow the veil's fabric into my mouth; Sanaa is in full thrall with our new home I muse as I suck and chew on the delicious veil giving me a simple peace

Sanaa! My only love! My salvation! who collected a hundred stories from the marketplace by her first moontime who inherited the magical talisman Sanaa with her good will and confidence Sanaa will be my mouth and ears in the bazaar with her power to kindle marvelous narratives: Sanaa will make our fortune, Sanaa will guide the ovoid, so I must guide her into the world.

In the complex Islamic world of the 10ᵗʰ Century AD/4ᵗʰ Century AH the demand for stories and the ethical criticism of performers was seen from a myriad of angles in the cracked mirror of public reflection:

309

in Abu al-Hasan ibn al-Husayn al-Masudi's many-volumed history
The Meadows of Gold, *the famous chronicler identified the hikaya as*
street performers, like Medieval street actors in Europe

another writer-historian al-Nadim observed that while fables night
tales and other asmar were in great demand during early 10ᵗʰ Century
in Muqtadir's Caliphate some scribes were serious in their classification
of the tales but others lied about origins and variants

Muqtadir's son who became Caliph al-Radi in the 930s had a princely
education but among his books could always be found lowbrow fictions
and legends such as Sindbad

although tales from collections like the Nights came from the oral tra-
dition many storytellers from court or street used written texts as prompt-
books during their recitations

another blurring of distinction: the literati deemed two kinds of reci-
tations the acceptable kind at court and the unrefined kind in the street
but some orators mixed the two to the point that jurists ruled what was
acceptable

Understand this: all this clouding of oral/written, court/street, accept-
able/popular texts shook up both the literari and public taste: works like
the Nights threatened the establishment

despite the charms of Cordova and acceptance by the people it was
rough establishing a shop: with so much diverse merchandise Moroccan
leathers Spanish wines Frankish cheeses we had nothing of value to offer
without capital to bring goods from Baghdad so at first we minded others' shops took in sewing and grew produce for market in a tiny patch
of earth behind our hovel

I knew what we needed to do but Sanaa hoarded her stories: dreams
of beings with limbs like straw bundles with tendrils of light flowing out
the tips Jewish merchants in cities of monstrous buildings scholars of
ancient lore with texts held in shiny discs images so vivid and unexplain-
able that Sanaa felt unsafe sharing them with anyone but me

still I encouraged her to try one out on the blind raconteur she had
met or the poet-tanner who told her new verses from the Levant and I

even made alterations to the wild dreamscapes I had a talent for transforming the merest crumb of sleepy invention into an irresistible tale, so I drove Sanaa to tell a few tales to friendly storytellers and I celebrated every positive response pushed every narrative on scribe or rawi and I enjoyed this new role as Sanaa's sidelines scripter

but both of us knew the dangers of this business because inevitably word would get to more traditional reciters who scoff or spit at a woman telling tales in a man's arena despite wonderful female poets or harem girls who enact stories: on the street it was punishable by the sword

I refused to foster Sanaa's dreams only to have her hawk a story to a discrete hikaya for a few coins; I insisted my lover appear before crowds emanate the joy she had felt since a child deliver the people her most delectable tales; I wandered the market puzzling this conundrum chewing on my veil watching other veils float by holding my head high to counteract the misery

then I spotted them: two marvelous veils two sand-strewn veils of the desert and in the narrowest space a pair of dark eyes peering out, I looked below at their robes I examined their gait as they marched through the souk – *these were men* -- I learned that these men with fully covered heads were the Tuareg of West Africa whose women do *not* wear the veil, men who don the veil to ward off evil spirits who cover all but their eyes speeding across the desert blasted by wind and sand

Our saviors! When I came home with two Tuareg outfits I lifted from the baths on al-Rahman Boulevard Sanaa shrieked we would be caught and killed by such men; when I altered them to fit so she could appear in public as a storyteller she gave me all kinds of problems lowering her voice as a man or chatted up by Tuaregs in a strange tongue or exposed as a woman and executed; I understood it was pure fear talking so when I offered to accompany her in disguise despite my own terrors Sanaa saw how serious I was

we took to the streets learning to walk as men at first how to feel strong and comfortable in the thick outfits thicker veils than my own more gratifying to suck tougher to chew if that helped me to appear more masculine then what motivated Sanaa was promise of displaying her stories: she dared speak to shopkeepers rub elbows in the tavern try a West African accent eventually respond to a question with a short tale a travel account of the desert a bedtime tale from a Tuareg mother

it took a year but Sanaa finally ventured out without me thank Allah and one evening stood up to narrate a sheaf of stories I had arranged into a charming frame tale and as I listened hidden in the back of the crowd I stood in awe and ecstasy as not one soul questioned Sanaa's true identity because each was enraptured by her performance by my composition of stories and in tears hearing the tale of the roukh defending its nest egg I realized I had hatched something wonderful for our time in al-Andalus for our livelihood for the people be they Umayyad Jew Egyptian Frank or Tuareg and loving my underground role, from somewhere inside me, from a past redemption of perversion, from a deep hope for spiritual growth, I envisioned a grand project destined for immortality

Given the intensity with which the literati denounced the street story-tellers and the growing number of written collections, it was obvious that fiction was exceedingly popular that audiences demanded written copies and that vulgate and erudite were intersecting in a rich mixture, the Nights being one such crazy stew to please any class or creed

given its wonderful open-mindedness this burgeoning movement challenged the old order stormed the scriptural gates of the palace, the compilers of the Nights plentiful aware of their rebel public: their re-cloth-ing of tales in Islamic robes deferred to one faction, the popularizing of histories catered to another, and the blatant theft of the court's beloved anthologies incited the whole mob to break the possessive grip of the lite-rati and take the verbal wildfire to the streets

Sanaa may have been the one to face the crowd in her Tuareg veil and spout stories from her dream-addled mind but I was the one nag-ging: Since when did Sharzad become the professoress of Islamic vir-tue? Did you remember to ask al-Qasim for that copy of *The Thousand Nights*? Is there or is there not a collection being compiled in Cordova?

I may have dreaded walking through the marketplace but if I came upon Sanaa deep in argument with the haughtiest of scribes doubting whether an Islamic coloring of a night story made it more acceptable as fiction I did not hesitate to lambast the pontificating buffoon with a panoply of paradoxical but sure-fire retorts: Are stories in the Qu'ran unclean? Does adding a layer of Islam to the Nights worsen the lies by rendering an older tale's cultural origins false? Is your mind bloated with goose fat?

Yes! Sanaa and I became fanatics about the Nights and the intersection of Nights and Islam fascinated us: in a two hundred year old version Sanaa found through her favorite bookseller the dedication on the first page thanks Allah for vanquishing all the cultures that created the stories what a haunting statement for it assumed that the book was a literary meeting place for every culture to gather together and speak as One even in the veiled disguise of Muslim ethics a true collection of multiple heritages like the streets of Cordova

and Sanaa and I wondered if there were any scribes storytellers courtiers booksellers itinerant scholars or plain old book lovers who shared this burning question: was the cultural conglomeration of the Nights a prideful appropriation of Islam's victims or could it be re-fashioned into a hallmark of harmonious co-existence respecting all life courtly or common Faithful or heathen male or female

it was the search for the answer to this question that would ease my fear of exploring Cordova and inspire Sanaa to gather her own multicolored group of storytelling misfits.

ق

The qaraq sat in silence as Ooma looked around the room with a proud gaze. Everyone recognized the import of the story: Sanaa and Oamra had lived as story collectors in Cordova, and would instigate The 379 Group and a special version of the Nights.

Zack broke the tension: "I'm dying to know who we were back then, especially if the Nights offended the court and challenged the Caliph. It's

313

like the Beat poets bucking the system with vulgar language and obscenity trials. Maybe I was El Lenny ibn Bruce al-Cordova."

"So are you ready for a group recall experience?" Elvi asked. "A New Year's meeting?"

"I vote for it," Porcy said, "but how about in the sanctuary? Verle, we have growing pains."

Verle frowned. "I've been inquiring about another space, but I can check."

Diana said, "I'm still worried about our fragile state."

"Me, too." Sahara looked at Ooma, who met her gaze. "Convince me we'll be all right."

Ooma nodded, accepting the challenge as if she had been waiting weeks for it. She spoke in a quiet voice beyond her years. "All I want is to take my rightful place among this gathering of souls. I have been excluded and it has been hurtful, especially after years of exclusion as a Muslim in this nation. If you are punishing me for my actions as Queen Uzmeth, I had lifetimes of shame after that. I learned we must transcend the past and move forward. You must also forgive me. Accept me into the group. My soul is at stake. Help me, and we all benefit. The whole world benefits."

Sahara was moved by the speech. Despite Diana's misgivings, it was time to let Ooma's needs have sway. "New Year's it is," Sahara said. Ooma looked up with the faintest of smiles.

"With Amar, too, correct?" Cachay made it sound like a statement.

"I'll put up with him," Porcy said to Cachay, "if you be wild about group hypnosis."

Elvi cast her gaze on Diana, who glanced at Sahara for a second, feeling betrayed by her. But Diana confirmed with a nod. Consensus was a healing factor, too.

"Ooma, the New Year's meeting will be a trial," Elvi said. "Only after will the qaraq decide if you should join. And everyone: this is a New Year's meeting, in *place* of celebrating. If we meet after you party, you won't have the psychic energy required. Understood?"

Everyone nodded, but Zack sighed. "Everyone I love can come to this meeting except Jobim, and now I'm not allowed to party with him. What's next – flagellation?"

46

—⟨∞∞∞⟩—

December 17.   Month 4.

Due to the New Year's plan, the group did not meet again in December. Elvi used the time to pay a visit to Diana. "I love your home," Elvi said of Diana's Asian-inspired décor. Diana gave Elvi a tour, served her tea, and tried to make awkward small talk. Finally, she confronted Elvi.

"You visited to admire my shoji screens?" Diana asked. "You never visit our houses."

"And I never force votes on important qaraq issues," Elvi responded. "Like New Year's."

"Yes, you've been more pro-active. Like telling me to back off Verle and his World Types."

"The qaraq is near a turning point. You need to be united, and my hand a bit firmer."

"What turning point? About all the trauma?"

"I know you're the group caretaker right now. But there are other issues. The qaraq is about to experience something that will galvanize or shred the group dynamic."

So Elvi recognized the pressure Diana felt. "Something worse than living a nightmare?"

"I'm happy Zack's found love, but he's too wrapped up," Elvi said. "He brought Jobim to a meeting. If Zack deludes himself into a false expectation, he'll get sorely hurt."

Diana pushed back. "Why are you interfering in his personal life?"

"Actually, I need you to interfere with Zack. The situation is serious. Jobim is the card that sends the house crashing down. Not Ooma. Not Amar."

"So along with healing the group, I have to save the house from burning," Diana said.

"I apologize," Elvi said. "I think I can help you understand better. Can we step outside? I need a cigarette." Outdoors, they walked around the neighborhood. Though it was almost Winter, Diana felt warm in Elvi's presence.

They came to a public park and Elvi gestured for them to sit on a bench. "You know you have a karmic relationship with Zack. I'd like to underline the complexity of that bond, to impress on you the importance of your role in his life."

"Great, you're guilting me into this." Diana heard an ethereal, mesmerizing music in her head. "What is that music, Elvi?"

"The music of Draill U." Elvi put her arm around Diana and gently placed her hand on the therapist's neck. "I want you to hear a story about your dance student days as Daywa, a tarakani. Zack was I-zaea, an indaki, accompanist for your dance class. He will be speaking."

Diana wondered how Elvi controlled her. The lushness of I-zaea's music put her into trance. Elvi's touch pulled her into a music-driven memory of her time with Zack at Draill U.

The Tale of the Indaki and the Neuromistressa

You said it to yourself a thrillion times, I-zaea old chawmp: you're nothing like them. These Draill U students were immature, neurotic, competitive, aggressive, unresponsive, and very, very talented. So what if you weren't as technically gifted? In your specialized skill you had more talent than a sophmorist class. The art of the indaki. No virtuoso could accompany tarakani like you, watching dance movement and creating sound that's supportive, rhythmically alive, and perfectly appropriate in quality. If a tarakani let the sound release her she flew through the air. It was called Nerve Dancing, but, cheena chaw, without a good indaki it was all nerve and no dancing.

Take beautiful, graceful, serene Daywa. Sure, she had plenty of neurotic territory. Her specialty: punishing self-criticism. Daywa started over and over, stopping at the slightest error, anger subsuming her. But the movements got better and better, until your scorn at her false starts melted away when she performed the phrase immaculately, with more artistry than anyone in the school. She took your breath away each class.

Like Daywa, you were drawn to Draill U because of Pr Ctatlo's mythic status for cross-training vocalists in movement, acting, and politics; the rumors that the Do'en was wrapped around her finger; her outrageous remarks infuriating the Neo-Authouritariunist Party. With her *Whakatica*, a poetics of the inter-disciplinary multiperf, Ctatlo influenced artists like Daywa and you to bust things up. Rebuked in traditional circles, Ctatlo was hell-bent on proving herself at Draill U.

Given the high turnover for the lowest paying job in the arts, you offered your services as an indaki to the Tarakan Dept., and they grabbed you up. With your lack of experience, they stuck you in a freshling technique class where you could do the least harm. There was Daywa, in the back corner, hiding from the world. But she replicated every move and neuro-motor pathway as if right in front of the instructor, the venerated neuromistressa Pr Fughini.

In the next class Fughini invited Ctatlo to observe, since the radical planned an experiment with tarakani. She had worked more with singers, her vocal techniques now standard practice, so whatever she had up her sleeve was untried and daring. You noticed Daywa's nerves charging her muscles more than ever. Were you the only ones excited by Ctatlo's presence?

It got better: Ctatlo was interested in your music! She was the Supreme Cross-Pollinator, so the marriage of tarakan with whakatan held a fascination. After class Ctatlo asked about your experience. Something told you to answer honestly: I'm as fresh as a freshling. Ctatlo was delighted; she did not want an indaki set in his ways. Likewise the tarakani: she asked for volunteers, anyone willing to be open, work hard, and take risks.

The Nerve Dancing Workshop is now famous in the history of Draill U, both for its invention of extended neuro-movement and the controversial ethical debate it provoked. Ctatlo's hypothesis: if tarakani motivated movements with pure nerve impulses, then the audience should be stimulated on a direct emotional level. Before the Workshop nerve dancing was known for tricks, like moving from lying down to leaping in a fraction of a second. To replace exhibitionism with emotional transcendence, Ctatlo needed a total commitment from performers.

Using her exegesis of the myth "Heyatt uy Budoyr" as fodder for the Workshop, she believed the content of the myth was radical political action: the female Budoyr, disguised as a Prince, must bed a Princess; after facing the truth, the two women preserve the deception and live together. To convey controversial content, Ctatlo required a radical form. She wanted tarakani nerve impulses to imprint edgy meaning on the audience; she wanted the audience to feel a thought.

Ctatlo assigned scenes from the story to small groups of participants. You and Daywa had the scene in which King Apatrus offers the Princess' hand in marriage. Daywa was to dance Budoyr's fearful inner monologue, considering how to respond. Your accompaniment was the voice of the King in Budoyr's mind, reacting to each possible response.

For example, Budoyr imagines lying that 'he' already has a wife: Daywa moved as the supposed wife, a dance of deception. You moved your fingers casually in and out of the sounding holes: the King dismisses

319

the problem by pointing out his multiple wives. Budoyr imagines revealing her true identity: Daywa nervously exposed her sexual identity.
Barely able to contain your desire, you revealed the King's own flirting
with thrusting, percussive strokes on the plectra-plane.

Ctatlo was coolly supportive of your initial efforts, but demanded
much more. You were crestfallen after the first day. You wanted to process your work with Daywa over dinner, but she retreated into her reclu-
sive world to lick her wounds. The second day of the Workshop was a
week later due to Ctatlo's busy schedule. She scolded the participants
for playing it safe and using old tricks. Daywa galvanized her will in a
fierce tightening of her body.

Ctatlo pushed the two of you to focus deeply on only one of Budoyr's
thoughts. Daywa expressed Budoyr's imagined refusal of the Princess'
hand with gracious but jittery movements; you reacted with ominous
bass tremolos: the King's rage and threats. Ctatlo ordered you to force
Budoyr to cower. On her knees, Daywa submitted with a wicked gleam
in her eye, seeing your molten fury for what it was, frustrated lust for
her exquisite body. By the end of the day you were both pouring sweat,
spent and speechless.

The final session of the Nerve Dancing Workshop came a month later.
During the wait, you approached Daywa many times, but her reticence
stopped you. Was she remaining 'professional' because the Workshop
was not over? Nonsense, there were teams driven into each other's arms
by Ctatlo's emotional demands. Some participants were unhinged by the
work. Was Daywa holding onto her sanity by avoiding you? Should you
check on her? Console her?

When the final session arrived, Daywa was eager to work on Budoyr's
final inner thought: what if she accepted the marriage offer and let events
play out with the Princess? Daywa contracted tight poses for Budoyr's
hiding of her female parts, gestured intimately to test the Princess' trust,
and exposed nerve endings for revealing her womanliness. Then: neu-
ronic thrashings for the Princess' shock, quiet glissades for Budoyr's
explanation, and a dance of carnal bliss.

320

Stirred by Daywa's erotic display, sustained chords hanging in the charged space betrayed your fixation on her. Where had such sensuality come from this obedient student? How had she overcome her controlled personality to exhibit this abandonment and wild pleasure?

Ctatlo eyed you from her bench. Get with the program King Apatrus! How would Budoyr imagine the King's reaction to accepting his daughter's hand? Delight: a fugue on a love theme, young royals intertwined in a marriage knot; vicarious pleasure: lush harmonies, the King's fantasy of Budoyr mounting the girl; pomp: martial rhythms with too much syncopation, the King's lust for his daughter sublimated by epicurean wedding feasts, just as you sublimated your urges for Daywa.

At the climax of the work, Daywa made eye contact, acknowledging that a power united you two, and boundaries disappeared between tarakan and whatakan, gesture and sound, Budoyr and the Princess, Daywa and I-Zaea, thoughts and feelings.

Daywa disappeared for days afterward. After a week, you went to her dorm room.

"It's me, I-zaea," you called through the unanswered door. "Everyone's worried. Show me you're okay. Or holler if you're dead." You talked through the door for a long time, using every trick of good will. "Open up. It's King Apatrus. I've got your stay of execution."

That did it. Perhaps she was inside the emotional world of the myth, perhaps she was sick of you going on and on. The door opened a crack. You waited. You pushed it open. On the bed, Daywa was still in her dance clothes from the Workshop, shivering, in a strange reverie.

"What's happened to you?" Thinking better of sitting on the bed, you pulled up the desk chair. "Have you eaten in days? What can I do?"

Without looking up, she spoke. "Everyone's worried? Even you?"

"Of course me! Ctatlo especially. Even the Do'en's been asking for you."

"So why didn't you come before now? It's been days."

Your stomach gripped. "I'm so sorry. I didn't think you wanted to see me."

"I didn't want to see anyone." She looked at you for the first time. "Except you."

You returned her look. "I don't get it. You were incredible in the Workshop. Fierce. Beautiful. So connected to me. But outside the Workshop, nothing. I thought you hated me."

Surprisingly, wondrously, she gave you the most radiant smile. "I did hate you at times. You pushed me so hard, forced me to go to dangerous, frightening places."

"Cheenus, that was Ctatlo! She pushed us both."

She barely heard you. "After the last session, I couldn't shake the work. I became Budoyr."

You reached out and touched her hand. "You poor thing. All this time?"

She gripped your hand, tears forming. "Yes. Until you came. Your voice freed me."

You fixed eyes on each other. Since you had known Daywa, you had fantasized about holding her in your arms, smothering her with kisses, sinking down on the floor with her. But at that moment all you felt was compassion and concern for her; physical love was out of the question. Daywa pounced. It was a shock. A tangle of embraces. Awkward, blissful coupling. Each kiss brought you back to your desire for her.

The passion restored Daywa's spirit. She returned to class and visited Ctatlo on the Isle of Whakatan, where the theorist hid out, writing furiously. On the first visit, Daywa brought you along for moral support, but soon developed a tight relationship with Ctatlo. Encouraged, Daywa suggested further experiments with tarakani (see the short article "Out of the Loins of Babes").

You and Daywa toiled tirelessly in classes and rehearsals; each night you ransacked each other for every bit of love. In the beginning it was joyous, but as Daywa became overpowering, you balked. You missed trysts, made excuses, left her waiting under a chilly moon in the Forest of Karlerosin. Ironically, as your fears grew, Ctatlo became fascinated with you and Daywa as a couple. Perhaps she enjoyed your affair as a substitute for her unsatisfied relation with Do'en Kvevely.

Sensing your withdrawal, Daywa clung to you like her tarakard clung to her skin. She moved from the back of class to next to your instrument. Your brow furrowed in deep lines from the closeness; she claimed your favorite pastime was worry. One night in a dream a voice complained of the cowardice of drifting continents who would not settle down. You awoke in a sweat.

In an attempt to give you space, bless her tarakani soul, she assisted Ctatlo in the famous Whatakan Lectures, the first step in the cross-training of artists. Throwing herself into transcription of the Lectures, Daywa struggled to keep up with her own training. Creeping in late to class, she resumed her position in the back of the studio, far from you. By midyear the relationship ended.

In Daywa's jugeniur year, Pr Ctatlo eschewed you and Daywa and started the invention of the Space Drama. Faced with separation from both mentor and lover, Daywa went berserk with sexual experimentation. She copulated with tarakani, friends, roommates, friends of roommates, roommates of tarakani, and most of the varsity whockaball team. You were in extreme pain.

You doubled down on your indaki improvisations. That year was the scandalous triangle between Ctatlo, Do'en Kvevely, and the ecoscorist Xlami. Picking up gossip from fellow whakatani, you divulged juicy bits to Daywa. By spring break, you were back on friendly terms. In her senieur year Daywa had a new attitude toward you. Flirty looks during slower exercises, gracious thank yous after class. She cleaned up her slutty reputation. She resumed taking class near the accompanist, not due to infatuation with you: she was training to teach and collaborate with indaki. In her last term she taught freshling technique. The two of you entered a new partnership.

Daywa's graduation party was a sprawling, drunken masquerade ball. She came as the sexiest of dragonflies. Her costume was all wings:

if not covering her bare torso with the top pair, or her perfectly shaped bottom with the lower pair, she would envelop a partygoer in all four. You were smitten all over again, as if you had never seen her, never been her lover, never left her. She made it clear that she was there, in that moment, in that get-up, for you. Wrapping you inside her voluptuous costume she told you, quietly, firmly, breathlessly: this was your last chance to have her.

You swooned, full of drink. You wanted her so badly, but the memory of her driving love frightened you. You excused yourself, sat in a restroom stall, took deep breaths. When you returned, an army of hungry bugs surrounded the lovely dragonfly. Thinking Daywa was back open for business, the male population swarmed her. You froze, gulped down one more drink, and left.

Having sweet-talked Kvevely into a facility for her experiments, Ctatlo came through for Daywa and got her hired as a dance instructor. As your neuromistressa, she told you she could never be lovers again, given the professional relationship. Once again she fended off the pain of your ambivalence by rejecting you. She embraced her by-the-book personality, controlling her life by controlling her students. In class, you and Daywa worked together brilliantly.

Then came the years when accusations of Kvevely's rape of Ctatlo in their ancient past pushed Ctatlo to hide in the construction site of her multiperf center. Seeing Daywa's sadness over Ctatlo's hibernation, you pursued Ctatlo to visit. Traveling to the construction area, you engaged Ctatlo in discussions about the interaction between artists. She surprised you and Daywa with a new tome, *Limitless Limits*: "The nerve dancer without the time structure of the indaki is formless; she might as well be flying through outer space, burning up, invisible to the world."

Grateful for this nod to Daywa, you offered acoustical assistance with the construction. While supervising an electrical installation related to acoustical tiling, you crossed two wires with no business being together. Sparks flew, lives were lost. Was it not the same between you and Daywa? Looking back from the interlife, your only regret about the electrical mishap was that it killed Ctatlo, too. But from the corpyroom, you admired the richly creative World of Draill U.

ق

On the park bench, Elvi released her sway over Diana. "That story was the culmination of the qaraq's Draill U memories."

"Ironic that I should complete a World," Diana said. "Verle will get a kick out of it."

"And Zack," Elvi said. "Your intimate contact at Draill U mirrors the complications still existing between you. You encourage a deeper under-standing of past life emotions."

"So I should deal with our complex relationship and confront Zack about Jobim? How do you know Jobim is a threat to the qaraq?"

"Jobim is no threat, just his situation with Zack. How do I know?" Elvi paused. "Because I am your spirit guide. I have counseled you in countless interlives. And stuck my nose in plenty."

Diana was dumbstruck. Was Elvi joking? Manipulating her? "I'm sorry. What?"

"I usually sit back, but if I see danger, I may reveal my true nature." Elvi sent a serene warmth through Diana's body. "Especially if I need help."

Do spirit guides have power to regress people, or warm their inner being? Diana felt a quiet thrill to possess the key to Elvi's mysterious character. "Of course I'll help." She stared at Elvi's smoldering cigarette and wondered what business an angel had with nicotine.

47

———∽∽∽———

December 21. Month 4.

Somewhere deep inside her psyche, Diana accepted Elvi's revelation as familiar knowledge. But with ten days before the New Year's meeting, the therapist felt an urgency to her spirit guide's request. She called Zack to her office. He sat on the futon couch. Diana pulled up a stool close.

"I've wanted a session for months," he said. "Out of nowhere you summon the lord of the land to your throne room. Do you fuck with all your patients or just me?"

"Just you," Dr. Machiyoko said. After a beat of silence, therapist and patient burst into forgiving laughter. "I want to talk about Jobim. How is it going with him?"

"Better," Zack replied, "even with 9/11 for an anniversary. I see it now: a French bistro, candlelight, the memory of smoke and screams. But it's made our bond fierce."

"Was there tension after you brought him to the qaraq meeting?" Dr. Machiyoko asked.

"I couldn't suggest anything for weeks without Jobim mistrusting it. Served me right."

"So you blame yourself? What's that been like?"

Zack shrugged. "I'm no Christian martyr. And Jobim's no picnic. He still has nightmares. He went to a therapist, but it didn't take. So he won't talk about it. Or have sex. Much."

"Is that okay with you? The not talking about it? Is he facing his place downtown?"

"He can take as much time as he needs to go back. I love having him at home," Zack said.

"So you're both flawed, working through it. You don't feel mothered or fathered by him?"

Dr. Machiyoko had probed the tight grip with his mother. After his father had died when Zack was a teen, he had clung to his mother in grief. He had tried to release the hold they had on each other: moving to Europe, copping a bad attitude, flaunting his boyfriends, which she enjoyed.

"No, it feels very equal between us." Zack considered. "But kind of a stalemate, also."

Diana leaned forward, seeing her first way in to something bigger. "What do you mean?"

"I'm waiting for Jobim to work out his trauma, and Jo's waiting for me to decide how the qaraq figures in our relationship. But neither of us want to push things."

Dr. Machiyoko grabbed an opportunity. "Sounds complicated. But what about the qaraq?"

"I tell Jo everything. I'm the only qaraqi who does that. So what does that make him?"

"Indeed. Hold that thought. I'd like to hypnotize you and see what comes up."

Zack laughed loudly. "Where'd you get your license? Shrinks R Us? I thought past life work threatens our boundaries in session."

Caught in her ploy, Diana froze. Should she express Elvi's concerns about Jobim directly? They gazed at each other, unsure how to proceed. Diana let the silent impasse fill the space. The feeling was extremely familiar to Zack. He recognized he was transforming into an altered state. Was he seeing a past life already? Zack squinted at something with the intensity of a wild animal.

The Gomphotheri's Stalemate Regression

"Zack, are you all right?" A light went on behind Zack's glare.

-- Doc! How'd you do that? I've gone somewhere.

Still caught in Zack's gaze, the therapist asked, "Where are you? What do you see?"

-- A pair of eyes, staring at me. Fierce eyes.

Dr. Machiyoko wondered if she was the object of Zack's attention. "Who's looking at you?"

-- You mean, *what's* looking at me. Short, fat, four cropped legs. A huge snout, maybe it's a trunk, and nasty sharp tusks. A pigmy punk elephant with an attitude.

"What attitude? Are you one of these creatures, too? What do you feel?

-- I'm pissed. There's a standoff. A turf battle. Jungle all around, prehistoric. We're the same animal. I see my tusks if I squint. We could be enemies, hunting each other. Or mates.

"Mates? Really? You look ready to move in for the kill."

-- Or maybe angry mother and cub. With me the lucky kid. She has something that belongs to me! That I found and she took away. That's why she feels like my enemy.

"Is there something there?

-- Yes, on the ground. She has her foot on it. Shiny, metallic, not prehistoric. But a few million years old, that's the message: a gift from aliens?

Zack tilted his head as if searching for an answer. He nodded off for a moment. But words kept coming in his mind, which Diana heard in hers. *The object is a magical relic. An ovoid! It travels through the stars. Forty star systems in this universe. Containing ... stories? prophecy? Version 1?*

"What is Version 1?" Diana asked.

-- Don't know. I'm pulled back by gravity. I was only been gone for a moment, but I saw other worlds and times. Now I see the glint off the metal ovoid on the jungle floor again. I'm back, trapped in the jungle standoff. Her power over me is greater than any force in the cosmos.

ق

"That was intense!" Zack said. "Who was I looking at? It wasn't you."

Diana felt sad at this statement. "Who has that kind of power over you. Cachay?"

Zack looked distressed. "Really? Whatever universe I hide in, she's there?"

"This is a powerful moment for you, Zack." Diana saw a way to help Zack and deal with Jobim. "Sure, there's a huge entanglement between you and Cachay. You and I have one, too, Buddha help us. But when you joined the qaraq you established independence from your mother."

"But that was spoiled when she joined," Zack said. "Remember how hard I blocked her?"

"Yes," Diana said. "But now that you've found Jobim, you can diffuse Cachay's presence in the group. I totally support your relationship with him, it's so healthy. Especially if it thrives independently from the qaraq. And from Cachay."

"Are you saying I shouldn't tell Jo qaraq business?"

"Not at all." Was she pushing too hard? "I'm saying the relationship is strong, and that's all you need right now. If you blur it with 9/11 trauma, or your mother, or Jo's relation to the qaraq, it's too complicated. You'll only add to that stalemate you described."

Zack mulled over the therapists's words. Even for their unorthodox relationship, he felt something strange about her active suggestions. What *was* she suggesting? That he keep Jobim and the qaraq on separate

329

turf. To avoid a stalemate. Wasn't that what the recall was about? A turf battle? The basic standoff echoed how he had described his relationship with Jo.

"Oh, my God!" Zack jumped up from the therapist's futon. "You're a genius, Doc. That other animal wasn't my mother. Or an enemy. It *was* a mate. It was Jobim! This is the first time he's appeared in a recall. The turf battle is all about how he fits in with the qaraq."

Diana was horror-stricken. "What are you saying?"

"You're so right. Jo can diffuse Cachay's presence in the group. But not by being independent, but by being part of it. Jo's a member of the qaraq!"

The dam had burst. "But Zack, what if he isn't? That could be so awkward. So hurtful."

"Don't worry, Doc." Zack paced the room. "I'll be cool. I'll wait for the right moment. More proof. We've got the big meeting coming up. I won't get in the way of that. I won't even tell Jo yet. I'll just let it all happen organically. But this is incredible." Zack grabbed his coat. At the door he turned back. "I know you called me here, but I'll pay for the session. Thanks, Doc!"

As Zack closed the door, Diana wondered if spirit guides were allowed to murder humans.

48

—⟨ɷ⟩—

December 31. Month 4.

A number of hours before midnight, Verle and Zack worked hard in the church sanctuary to prepare for the New Year's qaraq meeting. Normally a modestly adorned space, with some cloth banners hanging on the sides, the sanctuary now held the potential for a more festive appearance.

"How did you talk me into this, old man?" Zack grumbled as he hung up a string of wooden Javanese frogs acquired from his import-export business.

"If I have to decorate the church sanctuary, then you do, too." Verle placed a small statue of the elephant God Ganesha on a side table. "Porcy forced me, I force you."

"I'm punishing you for good reason." Porcy entered the church sanctuary, Bax trailing behind with a box of Christmas lights. "You lied to us, didn't ask for a space. We need new digs."

"I hate asking for things for myself," Verle said. "I couldn't bring myself to ask the boss."

"So I made you ask! They promised to look into it, and gave us the sanctuary. That's that."

Verle helped Bax find an extension cord, then sat down, tired and helpless. It was true that climbing to the attic was getting harder. So he supervised: Zack and Bax cleared the front of the congregational area and brought in several platforms used for theatrical events. As Zack and Bax configured the platform seating area on one side of the congregation, Porcy created an overflowing table of food and drink on the other side. Verle marveled at the little group's speed and accord; they created something unique, but awfully familiar, too.

"Now the pièce de resistance from my collection, for medieval Andalusian ambience." Zack hung some olden Spanish festoons, moaning loudly to tease Verle. "You're lucky I don't hold grudges. Much. Otherwise I'd repeat your Tale of Ugliness."

Verle's grey-brown skin went ashen. He left Bax holding a string of lights. "Don't you dare mention that terrible time. I don't want … certain people to know about my past deformity."

Zack saw how much his teasing affected Verle. Was it sensitivity to his past? Deciding not to probe, Zack said, "I wouldn't dream of singling out my vizier; I treat him with utmost kindness." Zack mock bowed on the ladder, almost falling off. Verle laughed, handing up more festoons.

At that moment Diana and Sahara, carrying a sleepy Naji, entered the sanctuary. In spite of the family's misfortunes, Naji had been sleeping better. Sahara settled on a platform, hoping to put the child down. With the alleys and niches Zack and Bax created between the platforms, and the Moorish feel from the lights and ornaments, Sahara felt an odd familiarity to the space.

Diana was grateful that Zack had not brought Jobim. After his delighted hope that Jobim was part of the qaraq, she half-expected he might. She was relieved to put aside the issue for the night and focus on what would be a challenging meeting.

"One touch and we're ready, boys." Porcy placed a plastic statue resembling a stack of three mushrooms in the center of her food cornucopia. "Batteries included!" She flipped a switch, the statue lit up, and water splashed from the top mushroom down the other two. Touched

332

by her love of fountains, Sahara's vision went out of focus: the disorientation, the space, and the burbling fountain put her into trance. Holding
onto Naji, Sahara had a vision of Sanaa as she wandered the streets of
Medieval Cordova, disguised as a Tuareg man hiding behind a thick veil.

*Sanaa searched for something. Oamra was foremost in the young
woman's thoughts. Today Oamra had sent Sanaa on a hunt to find "treasure hidden in plain sight." Sanaa tried to concentrate on the clues from
Oamra's handmade treasure map, but the street distracted her.*

*To Sanaa, the mix of humanity was magical. Jews and Christians
became Arabicized: the dhimmi, the protected "Peoples of the Book," and
the muwalladin, those of mixed Arab and non-Arab blood. Christian
practice was public in their cathedrals, compared with Jewish private
devotions. The current Vizier, the most powerful man in Sepharad, as
the Jews called al-Andalus, was Hasdai ibn Shaprut, Arabic scholar,
European emissary, trusted advisor to the Caliph, and Jewish leader.*

*As Sanaa pondered the different skin colors and colorful costumes
throughout the city, she forgot Oamra's mission. The stories she collected contained the same assortment of cultures as Cordova. If Jews,
Christians, or Franks showed up in those tales, it was often in a place far
from their origin, a diversified city like Cairo or Damascus. They were
dislocated populations, sharing troubled separation from a homeland,
struggle for opportunity, nostalgic loss of a past place, and a communal
space of exile such as a marketplace – or a storytellers guild meeting.*

*Sanaa searched with desperation. Was there a secret meeting place
for storytellers? Would she be safer there, enough to abandon her male
disguise? Tolerant diversity in Cordova brought good fortune to Jews and
Berbers, but for women it was business as usual. Which was no business
as usual. Was someone following her? Was she chasing someone? She
sweated beneath the veil.*

"Whoa, girl, don't make the twos any more terrible." Zack scooped
Naji out of Sahara's arms. In her disturbed trance, she had almost

dropped the child on the sanctuary floor. Zack sat on a bench to comfort Naji. Porcy asked after Sahara, and the disoriented woman described her vision.

"We moderns didn't corner the market on multiculturalism," Sahara said. "In al-Andalus, the more everyone's differences were accepted, the more everyone's fortunes rose."

Porcy looked over at Naji. The child's eyes were closed, he looked content on Zack's lap, but now Zack was in another world. Physical contact with Naji had triggered Sahara's memory, and now Zack's. Was it about how they set up the space? Sitting down with Zack, Porcy spoke gently.

Infanta Bishi's Address to the Assembly: Introduction

"Zack, what's going on?"

-- Not sure. It's blurry. I think I'm seeing a life of Naji's. But it feels close to me.

"Maybe you're both in the story, sweetheart."

-- Maybe. But I can't sort through Naji's mind. There are images of the interlife, classical buildings, endless hallways. And two white elephants.

Verle joined them. "Naji lived as a mahout. Gave two albino elephants to Caliph Harun."

-- That's right. There he is, sitting with them in a barn, daydreaming.

"Or remembering a past life," Verle offered.

-- You think I'm seeing Naji seeing himself as a mahout remembering a past life?

Porcy hmmphed. "Where are you?"

-- Not with the elephants. Different story. Another planet. Folks have tangerinish skin. Definitely humanoid. It's another school. Graduating Draill U must've summoned a new one. I'm the Science teacher, God help us! I'm cowering in my lab.

"Cowering?" Verle, Porcy, and now Bax spoke all at once. Sahara listened, still groggy.

-- I've been asked to host a guest speaking on Career Day. Give her a tour, chat her up, take her to lunch. All terrifying to me. Tried to get out of it, but there was no one else available.

"Are you afraid of people?" Verle wondered, knowingly. "Is it the tangerine skin?"

-- Mine is purplish. Seriously, I'm hosting our most illustrious alumna. Her books are known everywhere; they're part of the curriculum. There's a club devoted to her: the Unfanta Club.

"Her name is Unfanta?" Porcy asked.

-- Uor Unfanta Rishi. Uor is an honorific, like Ms., and surnames are first, like the Chinese.

"So she's called Rishi." Sahara finally joined in. "Like Rash. Must be Naji."

-- Kids call her Rashi as a nickname. I was pathetic showing her the school. Said nothing, just "English Building," "Gym," "Law School." Rishi was so tense she got a kink in her neck.

"Is Naji telling you all this?" Sahara felt hopeful and frightened simultaneously.

-- Not like talking in my head. But knowledge came to me as soon as I held him.

"Okay, I'm pulling the plug on this right now." Sahara jumped off her platform. "I'm glad he's finally communicating, but I'm worried for him. My visions from him were murky and dark."

Zack gasped as Sahara pulled Naji away. "Wait! My visions were clear. Wee bit jealous?"

"It's strange," Verle said. "Why did this school recall happen with the Cordova vision? Is there a connection, or is Naji confused? He hasn't spoke in our minds for months."

"Troubled, I think." Sahara sat back down with her child, and combed her fingers through his hair. As soon as she held him she was back on the streets of Cordova.

Oamra had hidden, in plain sight around town, sixteen gifts for Sanaa's thirty-second birthday, and sent Sanaa off with the map. Before Sanaa became distracted, she had uncovered half the gifts: a small basket of jasmine and myrrh body oils; a lavender silk bag to contain the oval artifact; a book of Persian legends, translated into Arabic; a metal stencil, to be used with a candle to shape smoke into a camel; three beeswax candles tied with a jute ribbon; a book of Chinese legends with preface by al-Nashi ibn Sfut. Sahara's final discovery was a star lamp, sold in Cordova by Sheikh Ba'Tr, after he moved from Basra. The antique had passed through the ancient Parthian palace at Ctesiphon, the Sassanian harem where it inspired Queen Uzmeth's orgies, and the House of Wisdom near Baghdad. And Oamra had located it!

Sanaa's search took her into narrower and narrower lanes. She felt she was walking in circles, until she curved around a blind alley and came upon a quiet courtyard. At the end, a doorway stood open. Feeling urgency in the pit of her stomach, she walked through the entrance.

Sanaa returned home hours later. Oamra knew the quest would take a while, but when Sanaa appeared late at night with only seven of the sixteen offerings, and a crazy tale of what she had discovered instead, something more important than the thoughtful gifts, Oamra was furious. She bit her lip during Sanaa's diatribe about a magical building with tiny enclosures that opened up onto spacious meeting halls, pleasure rooms, and living quarters.

In one of the spaces, a lovely fountain flowed near one end, a group of scholars sat on platforms at the other. To great delight, Sanaa eavesdropped on story collectors planning a new anthology. Oamra bristled when Sanaa mentioned this book without acknowledging her birthday books. Sanaa raved on about being brought before the group's leader, a Cairene twice her age named Hanbal. Fortunately, Hanbal recognized Sanaa as the Tuareg storyteller from the souk. Himself locked out of scholar groups for years, Hanbal welcomed the newcomer.

Sanaa described the hours sharing stories, listening to the fountain trickle, and munching delicious treats. The group's benefactor was a wealthy Frank with much real estate in Cordova; sympathetic to Hanbal's estrangement from the erudite community, he donated the building. The group sought a worthy idea for an anthology using Cordova's massive library. Sanaa suggested The Thousand Tales, *and Hanbal explained his late wife's desire to make it an Islamic morality tale.*

The mention of Hanbal's wife Umnia sent a shiver up Oamra's spine. The end of Sanaa's tale, when she was ushered out of the building, not through the alley but a grand gate on a crowded avenue, gave Oamra the impression of the building as a sinister, unpredictable place. Worst, Oamra saw Sanaa more captivated by the group's camaraderie than by her companionship.

Oamra felt inner dread rather than conscious understanding, so all she could do was scold Sanaa for ignoring her gifts, which probably were stolen by now. They ended in tears, with days of silence following. After years of support, Oamra felt malice toward Sanaa's storytelling enterprise.

As Sahara reached this part of the memory, tears began to flow. Porcy instinctively reached for Naji, but Verle stopped her for fear of a new trance. The little group sat helpless for a minute. Then Zack shrugged his shoulders, approached Sahara, and gently lifted Naji. Instantly he was back on the planet with the arts school, he told the others. The inhibited teacher brought Rishi to the assembly hall, and listened in awe as the illustrious alumna spoke with great ease to the students.

Unfanta Bishi's Address to the Assembly: Text of the Speech

Thank you for that sensationally loud welcome *(laughter and hoots)*, and sweet hush as I speak to you. Today I share the significance of my career choices, not in the arrogant manner I am known for *(single hoot)*, but hopefully in a modest tone. I won't be listing my accomplishments, with which you are already painfully familiar *(scattered chuckles)*. No, you all want to know the same thing *(long pause)*. How did I start out in a pit like this and end up a world famous writer and personality *(surge of shouting and rhythmic applause)*?

Once upon a time there was an ordinary girl in the country of Asu. Let's call her Rashi *(laughter)*. Like the other girls, her parents had high hopes she'd become a great nation-dancer. Little Rashi went to school to learn good technique: physical skills, musicality, spatial awareness, social interaction, intra-personal searching, and the poli-rhetorical for-mulae she'd need on this path.

Rashi was tempted by many prestigious callings, sonoral-physic, econo-art-visualizer, and legal-dramatist. She loved psychowriting, but at that time lit-therapy was a lesser art. "If you're not careful you'll end up in medicine!" her parents scolded. So Rashi tried out for the Dance Team, dreaming of life as a professional Sport Dancer, performing proudly in a sky blue costume, thrilling millions at the Balletta Bowl, and earning a huge salary.

With effort, Rashi got into a small and … somewhat respectable uni-versity *(laughter and hooting)*. Her parents pushed her toward a higher degree from the University of Frankovic, to deal with political heavy-weights in the Dance Diplomacy that runs our world. But Rashi despised the backstabbing and clutched under academic pressure. On a good day, it felt like the salt-woman pouring salt on her wounds; the worst felt like the cellar-woman dumping her corpse on a pile. She hated the elitist dictums of the arts: go to High Dance School, marry your dance partner, buy a big house. It was all so predictable.

Rashi finished school with bad marks and a worse attitude *(cheers)*. She said goodbye to her horrified parents and crossed the ocean for some "travel time" on the other continent. At first, she felt terribly foreign in strange lands, but then anonymity empowered her. She could be anything. Reinventing herself as an explorer, she embraced her love of writing.

In Afthanland she followed a family caught in the tragic civil war; tears wet the pages she wrote about a father betraying his sons to their death. Her words ripped like electricity through the journalistic network, and she received her first awards *(applause from faculty who lived through those times)*. She met Silvuno Smoth, the neglected Experimentalist who discovered a cure for Ranther Disease; she befriended Aon, the impoverished scientist who sold old books to support his experiments, which proved the vital Theory of Genomactivity. Rashi took socially downtrodden figures of science, medicine, and mathematics and carved impassioned stories.

In short, Rashi reinvented our value system. She upended our glorification of the arts at the expense of highly useful but endangered fields. Just as the swimming Wavebug transforms into the soaring Bellfly, she, I, all of us can find our true path in a new or 'inferior' field of study.

I was lucky: as a writer I had a little edge. Literature's only a bastard cousin of music and dance. But please respect math, science, or the medical 'art' (that's what it's called in Afthanland). Excel in any career path, and be praised for it! Good luck to you! *(wild applause, standing ovation)*

ق

A voice came from the back of the sanctuary. "What was that? Are we conjuring up any new World? Aren't we focusing on the creation of the special Nights?"

339

Amar appeared out of the shadows with Ooma trailing behind him. With multiple New Year's events in downtown Glenclaire, it had taken forever to park the car. Amar had run into Ooma on the street. They had slipped in during Zack's recall.

Ooma took in the space. "Shooting for magical Medieval Cordova? Cute."

Nervous her husband and Ooma arrived together, Sahara tried to be calm. "It's a bit much, but I like the fountain." She shot a glance at Amar. "It's why we bought our house."

Ooma sat on a bench. "So how *does* a school assembly relate to 10th Century Spain?"

"There may be a connection with the college recall." Bax did not like Ooma's tone; his answer had an edge. "If you'd been here, there were bits about Cordova, Sanaa, and you."

Zack managed to lay Naji on the bench, sound asleep. "I saw some after-images. Including the room Sanaa saw. With the fountain. There's definitely a connection."

49

—⟨❧⟩—

"An alien arts school and our meeting in Cordova in the same vision?" Amar questioned.

"We got World types, karmic history, CHITS," Zack said. "We're equipped to deal with anything. Don't wimp out."

"We should stick to The 379 Group," Amar said firmly.

Zack smirked. "If you play the noble King, why don't you recall the next life?"

Knowing Amar's sensitivity about his recalls, the group hushed, but only momentarily: Elvi and Cachay walked in. "Forgive us," Elvi said. "I took Cachay out to dinner and time flew."

Everyone was surprised by Elvi's social gesture. As the group recapped the new tales, Porcy and Diana wondered if Elvi had shocked Cachay with the spirit guide truth.

As far as Zack and Amar's tiff, Elvi offered advice. "You surmised that the soul of Oamra's lost baby was Amar. A tormented soul often returns to the same location for another chance. Amar, I could regress you: you may be reborn in the center of the action in Cordova."

Surprised by Elvi's directness, Sahara suspected that Elvi's offer was a test for Amar's entry into the group. She still shivered at the last time

Amar had come to a meeting, two years ago, when he lost it and ordered her to leave the group. It made sense he should work to gain entrance.

"In fact," Elvi said, "since Ooma's given us so much lately, I have no objection to her hypnotizing Amar." With a shrug from Sahara, Amar played the noble gamesman and agreed.

Standing in the shadows behind a bench, Ooma had not even taken off her coat. She felt guilty: no one knew how much she had hypnotized Amar, or how pleasurable it was to her. She made a show of reluctance to the group, but inside she was ecstatic. She stepped inside the grouping of platforms and benches and took off her coat.

Only then did the qaraq see that she was wearing a dark red robe under her niqaab. It appeared as if she wore a full-body veil. Ooma approached Amar. Sahara tensed as Ooma massaged his temples and whispered things in his ear. She gestured above him, as if bestowing a splendid robe of honor. His face took on a haughty, sly, and weathered countenance. He introduced himself, from the 10th Century, to the qaraq.

The Tale of the European in al-Andalus

I am 'Umar ibn Anbari al-Raqa'maq. I may not be as astute as our Grand Vizier Hasdai, the wise Jew who stands at the Caliph's ear, but I have an erudition few possess. I am that European, a born Nestorian Christian and a self-taught atheist, who by his escapades through Western, Near Eastern, and African climes, has the ability to fathom the philosophy of any culture rearing its head in al-Andalus. I may be a refugee from enemies, but I can benefit any cultural endeavor in town.

What escapades? What enemies? I look over my shoulder remembering my early years in Europe, which benefit me in acquisition of Frankish, Saxon, Latin, and Greek, but later threaten my existence as I enjoy the company of lusty wives and run down the street too often holding onto my clothes, escaping past broken windmills and offspring of albino elephants.

I run clear out of Europe, east toward holy lands, and latch onto the revolutionary Bedouin brigands of Banu Adi, not always escaping arrest. I flee to Antioch, rest under the patronage of Sayf al Dawi, and pause to pen the *Culture of Strangers*, under my new name of 'Umar ibn Anbari al-Raqa'maq, my first expression as a white face in a sea of beautiful, courageous color. Gaining a literary reputation, and adding Arabic to my repertoire, I brave the critical landscape of Baghdad.

There is much competition in the Buyid court, so I re-invent myself as an Aristotelian translator with a wide outlook. My confidence gets me into trouble when I expose the *Sirr al-asrar*, or "Secret of Secrets," as falsely attributed to Aristotle. I am correct, and it nearly costs me my life.

I flee Baghdad for Cairo, where my polyglottal handle on philosophy is not tolerated by the new Fatimid regime. Rogues attack my caravan, pound my flesh, and destroy my manuscripts. I crawl across the Sahara desert, roll senseless onto a Moorish ferry, and cling to a horse that transports me to the city limits of Cordova. I hope for sanctuary and an end to violent intolerance I've met everywhere. What I find is astounding: running water from Roman aqueducts, paved, well-lit streets, an encyclopedia of faces I have seen on my travels. An oasis of culture and acceptance, Cordova influences Frankish lands in everything from animal fables to ceramics.

At a majlis offered by Grand Vizier Hasdai, I announce the arrival of al-Raqa'maq. I present a translation of a letter from Aristotle to his pupil Ishkander, known in my childhood as Alexander the Great. Like the kingly advice in the *Kalila al Dimna*, the letter is chock full, including bits of magic, demonstrating that Aristotle was no pedant. Enticed, Vizier Hasdai requests my opinions.

Hasdai plays host at the Caliph's dazzling new palatial city, the Madinat al-Zahra. The Caliph dispatches the Christian Bishop Racenundo to parlay with the Bavarian nun Hroswitha, mystic and composer-librettist. With this surefire triad of Islamic Caliph, Jewish Vizier, and Christian ambassadors, al-Andalus connects to the world. I do not offer direct advice about this parlay, for any failed suggestion means a flogging; instead I send witty, relevant quotes to Hasdai.

Thus I enter the political and literary life of Cordova. I wander the streets, and follow personages who arouse my curiosity. I spy a man in the most ambitious veil, to fend off sandstorms. He ducks into a bookshop I know, run by a marvelous Jewess, Masiama ibn Ishaq ibn al-Di'nam. Upon his death, Masiama's husband bequeathed her the establishment, my favorite of dozens in Cordova. I felt an instant liking for Masiama: her goggle-eyed face, her literary knowledge. Although a native, fully Arabicized Jew, her religion and gender mark her, just as my European appearance blots out my Islamic expertise.

Masiama and I spend hours talking literature. I pick up some Hebrew for Iberian-Jewish poetry; she practices her Greek to skim the classics. But Arabic is the cultural and business language of the day, so this failed Christian and Friday night Jew crave Arabic words. As with Latin centuries ago, Arabic has the forked tongue of elitist expression and vulgate street slang. We love both.

I tease Masiama. "You are so provocative, a woman running a book business."

"In Cordova we have seven hundred libraries and countless copyists, including one hundred and seventy females. Is there not room for one good woman who can find any book you imagine?"

The day I follow the thickly veiled fellow into her shop, Masiama greets me with a smile. "Here are the Seneca plays you ordered, and the latest sales numbers from the souk."

I smile and thank her, but my eyes gesture toward the man, now at the back of her store.

Her brow furrows, worried and protective. "This is a Tuareg garment, a tribe from deep desert country in Africa. They never remove the veil, even for family."

Curious about what the Tuareg reads, I discretely keep my distance but steal peeks at the mystery man. Unaware of me, the figure takes off the headpiece to reveal a cascade of light henna colored hair. This is not a man who never removes his veil. This is not a man! Seconds later, the headpiece is back on. I creep closer, hiding behind stacks of books until I reach an open bookcase the false Tuareg is inspecting. I raise my head so books veil my own eyes, gaze into the narrow slit in the headpiece, and dare to speak. "Your secret is safe with me," I whisper.

The figure starts. Then, in a low, oddly hoarse voice: "What did you say?"

"No man of the desert has locks as soft as yours. Why hide your beauty?"

The eyes inside the veil pierce mine, assessing the danger. I send back a peaceful look, and we make a connection through the bookcase, across a gulf of foreign identity.

She removes the headpiece. "Something tells me to trust you, though I have no reason."

"You have Reason," I say, "which is enough to know the right thing."

Masiama appears, without surprise at the beautiful woman's disguise or disclosure to me. After formal introductions, over tea I describe my literary adventures; Sanaa tells me of a quest to compile a new version of *The Thousand Nights*. She describes a strange building where collectors meet, whose location eludes her. Over the past decade she learned that Sheikh Ba'Tr, reputed to have found the secret of eternal youth, owned the building and imbued it with a magical power to appear and disappear. At his self-imposed death, the world-weary Sheikh donated the building.

"My partner Oamra pushed me to give Scheherazade tough wiles to transform Shahryar into a morally Islamic ruler." Sanaa's eyes twinkle. "Perhaps you'd like to alter the King's character." I've found a literary cause beyond Aristotle. She may be twenty years my senior, but I am infatuated with this creature, a mix of desert warrior and storytelling charmer.

"Oamra discourages Sanaa's work on the Nights, out of a lover's spite," Masiama tells me. My burning heart sinks as I realize Sanaa is unobtainable. Noting my reaction, Masiama takes my hand and reminds me of her widowhood. That night I comfort myself in her arms, seeing Sanaa in her eyes. I will woo Sanaa, I will captivate her as she has me. Pilfering a copy of *The Thousand Tales* from the shop, I am inspired to bring Shahryar up to date with Sanaa's reforms. I am surprised the murderous King starts as a just and fair ruler. This perception restores my soul.

I look for Sanaa, easily find the Tuareg delighting the marketplace crowd. She is fearful of my exposing her. I write her a discrete note, pledging my loyalty. We meet, but Sanaa is nervous about Oamra. When I insinuate that transgression contains secret pleasures, she runs away.

Allured by the Nights, I abandon my dry translations for *muwashshah*, a trendy Spanish poetic form. The goal of poetry is *ta'ib*, or amazement; the ta'ib in this form makes me a blissful addict. After receiving seventeen perfumed poems, Sanaa agrees to see me again.

"Kill off the Tuareg," I tell her. "Cordova will accept you. Display your natural beauty."

She shivers with emotion, sans male veil, and rejects my advice. But she allows my loving pressure to encase her, like an insect shell before a great metamorphosis. "Your muwashshah poetry is kin to my tales. If you love this rebel poetry, if you love al-Andalus' repudiation of Baghdad, and if you love me, embrace the outlaw Fiction, and join my quest to render a fully literary Nights!"

I am her slave: I soak up any new trends in fiction. All the rage in Baghdad, a rascal named Ahmad ibn al-Husayn Badi' al-Zaman al-Hamadhani, 'The Wonder of the Age,' composes ornate epistles backwards, dazzles Buyid viziers, and entices Cordovan courtiers to Baghdad to hear him. Having no problem going against courtly or Islamic tenets, he invents fiction sanctioned by the literati. He calls his pieces *maqammat*, roughly translated as 'a standing,' which thumbs its nose at courtly majlis, meaning 'a sitting.'

His maqammat take almost any form: sermons, riddles, parodies of a father's advice to a son, cursing matches. At literary salons, Hamadhani challenges anyone to toss him a topic, and then improvises a maqama satirizing the issue or the style of the person who foolishly suggested it. As protection, Hamadhani creates characters to 'do the talking' for him, legitimizing fictional technique, four centuries into its condemnation.

I lay this information at Sanaa's feet like a bouquet of fragrant flowers. The advances of al-Hamdhani make a path for her glorious anthology. Sanaa is pushing sixty, I am in my thirties, and we have now known each other for almost a decade. I finally pass the test, join the project, and am part of her fantasy of an esoteric group meeting in a magical space no one can find. I am hers.

ق

The words rolled off Amar's tongue with a confidence and clarity the group had not heard. Ooma's hands never left his shoulders, though she trembled when Sanaa betrayed Oamra and met with al-Raqa'maq. When the tale finished, she released her hands with a force that jolted Amar, glared at Sahara wickedly, and, reacting in Oamra's name, spat on the ground.

"Really, young lady," Cachay reprimanded, "this is a sanctuary, after all."

The qaraq burst into spontaneous reactions, some seconding Cachay's comment, some congratulating Amar, some marveling at the story. All agreed they had a full night ahead of them. And one thing remained unspoken from that moment forward: Ooma and Amar had indeed passed an initiation test and were clearly vital, necessary members of the group that night.

347

50

———◁∾∾∾▷———

Amar sat in thought. Who were the other members of The 379 Group? Would Oamra ever join? What about the mysterious space? Amar looked at the space the others had created in the sanctuary. The configuration of platforms on the left side of the altar area formed four different levels. They could sit on the edge of a platform, lean back against a higher platform, or even lounge on an upper level, thanks to an assortment of pillows. Porcy had found an old rug in the library and strewn it in front of the altar area. To the right of that stood the table with food and the little fountain. The burbling of the fountain reminded Amar of home. But also something else.

Elvi had not quieted the group, so with a slow, dignified gesture, Amar silenced the room. "I regret my resistance whenever Sahara encouraged me to join meetings. I've missed a lot." Seeing Ooma bristle at the mention of Sahara, Amar faced her. "Thanks for enabling me to enter a new world. You make it easy for me to be here." It was Sahara's turn to tense at Amar's praise of Ooma; he did not notice her reaction. "Like old King Shahryar, I can't get enough tales. Don't take this for granted. It's a miracle. I feel ecstatic not to be on Wall Street. Thank you all!"

The qaraq saw in Amar a nobility and leadership they had never witnessed. Verle noted the character traits al-Raqa'maq had reclaimed for King Shahryar: fairness, kindness, a sense of justice. He would be proud as this man's vizier; he understood why he stuck by Shahryar in his darkest days.

Elvi spoke. "I think we owe Amar something. We agreed to group hypnosis, and he was on the front line, not easy for him. So own up and let me send the group back to Cordova."

The group murmured assent, especially after Amar's magnanimous appreciation. Everyone got comfortable on the platforms and pillows. Sahara seemed ill at ease with the experiment; Ooma sat farthest from the group. Elvi led the group through breathing exercises, then invoked the atmospheric sanctuary as a gateway to enter the magical space.

"Amar blessed us with an unusual recall. The most crucial portion of al-Raqa'maq's life is about to come, and all of you, except our sleep-ing child, will be part of it. So imagine a door in front of you, a door behind which lies the rest of our story, and a magical work of architec-ture we'll inhabit for the next few hours. When I tell you, walk through the door."

Before Elvi uttered the command, Ooma spoke up. "May Allah pro-tect you, as you enter this place. I have seen it, and it is not what it seems. You will each experience something different, for if anything it is changeable. Allow me to conjure another magical place for you, the jewel of my Muslim ancestors, the Versailles of the Middle Ages."

As Ooma spoke, she wandered among the qaraq, gesturing with her flowing robes. Dr. Machiyoko observed that Ooma seemed tongue-in-cheek at moments, strangely focused at others.

"Imagine a palace of fantastical design, right out of *Alf Layla*. Built into a mountain, the palace's reception hall has a ceiling of gold and sil-ver with an enormous pearl hanging from it. Pools and fountains inter-rupt the outdoor paths. A moat surrounds a zoo with exotic animals.

"This is the Madinat al-Zahra, fifty years in the making, surviving only thirty-five. The vision of al-Rahman III, last great Caliph of Cordova, completed by his son. Located eight miles west of Cordova in the foot-hills of the Sierra Morena. Descending from the highest ridge, a series of terraces housed the buildings of Caliph, viziers, and town. Gardens bejeweled a maze of paths."

Ooma nodded to Elvi, who brought the qaraq through the door into Cordova. She guided them to see milestones in their lifetime, interactions with the others, and the second of their deaths. Then she gave them time to come out of trance and gather their thoughts.

Ooma took the reins again. "Bax should start." He glowered at her. He was uncomfortable in the spotlight, and his visions disturbed him, especially in his relationship to the others.

Ooma pressed him. "You know your recall was amazing, I saw it on your face. And I know you hold the key to the space."

Everyone looked at Bax. Influenced by his memory, he felt a tension from the qaraq, as if he did not belong there. But Ooma was right; he had also seen wonders in his vision. "I reckon I should start. Remember my magic Sheikh Ba'Tr, who ended up in Cordova and zapped some space with complicated magic? I returned to Cordova in my next life."

To appease the group's curiosity, and Bax's anxiety, Elvi invited Bax to share his vision.

The Tale of al-Turtushi and the Secret Space

Twenty years old when I found my rhythm. Summers in Spain. Where I'm from. Winters in Baghdad to avoid the Spanish chill.

Roots in Catalonia. Tortosa. Why I'm called al-Turtushi. Abu ibn Ahmad al-Turtushi. The Tortosan. Now I live in the great city of Cordova.

Visited Baghdad at an early age. Wanted more knowledge than in Tortosa. Fell in with Isma'ili group. Attracted to their belief in reincarnation. Heretical to some. Logical to me. Learned about The Brethren of Purity. Mysterious encyclopedists. Reincarnation secrecy danger. Sign me up. Strict rules for attendance and hierarchy. Fifteen years to achieve next rank. I had no patience. Ran back to Spain. So pleasant. First idea of summer/winter rhythm. Soaked up the sun in Cordova. What a host of foods! The booksellers! Met Masiama. Jewess with a thing for me.

Back to Baghdad. Why am I here? Wine and singing girls. Raucous humor. Lowdown literary forms. I discovered *sukhf*. Not for the refined. Then came *mujun*. Basic feature was obscenity. What's diff between sukhf and mujun? Mujuniyyat's about hedonism. Offensive to the prudish. But stops short at scatology. Not so sukhf. Gross imagery to upset the squeamish. Fart jokes. How could I have been a Brother of Purity? Good riddance.

Couldn't wait to return to Cordova. Freer and wilder. Checked out mujun scene. Asked Masiama for books with sukhf. She was not pleased. Met fellow at a majlis. Called himself Izjis. Not sure why. From Cairo. Too tight-laced there, too. Curious about my interest in sukhf. Took me to unorthodox storytellers. One in particular. Tuareg. Fantastic array of tales. Could use a little mujun. Too urban for a desert dweller.

Bounced from Baghdad to Cordova. Good life. Wine women and sukhf. But something missing. Wandered the Cordovan streets. Shadowy corners call to me. Closed doors tempted me to open them. Buildings invited me upstairs.

One day entered an alley with a dooryard in an alcove. On the stoop sat an older woman. Sixty. Sobbing. Seeing me, she got up to run. Grabbed her. A face of torment and great beauty.

"What is troubling you?" I asked. "Unburden yourself."

Her eyes focused. She recognized me? "You wouldn't understand. You understand only filth. I've seen you listen to the Tuareg. Only raunch and debauchery interests you. Sukhf."

I confessed. "I am interested in the profane. It is only appropriate."

She pulled her arm from my grasp. "It is never appropriate."

"Except in the street? Of Cordova? There's a place for everything here. I wager you are not from here. You escaped from somewhere else."

She frowned. "What business is it of yours?"

"I knew it!" I chuckled. "Cordova accepts anyone. And everything. Even filthy words."

"You play with words to make your case," she said. "But you are good at it."

"Tell me your tale of woe. Maybe I can play with words to make it better."

The woman looked me up and down. Peeked up the alley. Gestured to the stoop. Positioned herself for a prompt escape if need arose. I obeyed, calmly, to gain her trust.

She told me of the souk storytellers. Hesitated with the Tuareg. Protective. Tuareg sought a space for story collective. One he saw many years ago. She searched for it. Led to this door. Knocked many times. No answer. Locked. Frustrating and sad.

I questioned why group so important. She would not say. I questioned why space had been hard to find. She actually said: it moves. I laughed. She started to cry again. I wished to comfort her. Improper to touch her. She would run. On instinct I tried the door.

It opened! Her tears ceased. Magnanimous gesture for her to enter. She balked. I saw long hallway lit with torches. Took a few steps in. The woman followed. Gave her warm smile. One tight edge of her lip curled up. We walked down the hall. A rush of exuberance. Then a chill breeze. Torches snuffed out. Woman ran back to the dooryard. In blackness I ran after her. In the alley no sign of her. Walked back to the door. It was *gone.*

That winter in Baghdad I couldn't get the incident out of mind. How did I open that door? So elusive to others. Memories of the Tueareg's tales plagued me. No amount of sukhf consoled me. I ate and drank with agitation. Gained three stone.

Next summer in Spain saw Izjis again. Told him Tale of Woman and the Door. To my surprise he recognized the woman. Oamra. Knew all about story collection. Didn't everybody? Tuareg, man named al-Raqa'maq, and Masiama! New Version of the Nights. Izjis had been approached. For his knowledge of Cairene tales.

Spent a week at Masiama's shop. Asked her everything about the Nights. Scheherazade. Liked Sa'eed character. Masiama called him poor slave. I preferred latest versions. Big stud in a harem orgy. Very sukhf. If this dirty version was in I was in. Masiama had me read al-Tawhidi. Hot new Buyid historian. Nights referred to racy nocturnal narratives. Boil a vizier's blood. Was this what I yearned for? The door? The Nights? I asked Masiama for an introduction to Tuareg.

I went looking for Oamra. Instead found the door. Many times. Never in the same place. Never same door. Never same place on entry. But knew it by a rush of exuberance. First entries led somewhere. Open patio back to the street. A lone tower.

Meanwhile Tuareg wouldn't speak to me. But I saw Oamra. She saw I had penetrated the space. Still disturbed. Invited Izjis and Masiama. Hoped they'd tell the Tuareg.

Made more discoveries in the space. Lovely rectangular garden patio. Another day garden had a suite of rooms above it. Then a large chamber. Nothing but fountain in center. Another day banquettes on one side. Fountain moved to other corner. Then stone benches dotted the sides.

One time I entered suite of rooms. Rugs everywhere. Wood carvings adorned ceiling. Lions and birds. On a whim I spent the night. As night fell I heard sounds. Exuberance turned to fear. No way out. Lions and birds became monsters and dragons. At dawn found exit. Ran for it.

I received a visit from al-Raqa'maq. Proxy for the Tuareg. European. Not to be trusted. "What are your intentions?" he asked.

"To help with Nights revision. Street it up." I appealed to his foreignness. "Nights has gone more Islamic. King gets morals and all that. But it's an anthology of many cultures. Euro tales can be told inside its walls. Why not pieces of the street? Dirty fun."

Ruckamuck was outraged. "Your views are a corruption of Cordovan openness. Of the good faith of Islam. I'll have none of it."

But I had an edge. I told him the spaces I had seen. This shut him up. He said he would report to the Tuareg. Then fled like a scared lamb.

I returned from Baghdad next summer with a theory. The times I entered the space with someone had been pleasant. New room or décor. Times alone were unpredictable. Dead ends. Traps. The space encouraged me to bring visitors. I was destined to bring the group into the space.

Visited Masiama and Izjis. Got feeling they were happy I'd been gone. Winter/summer rhythm a relief to them. I was a lot to handle. Raggymock had swayed them against me. Still, I presented my theory. Reluctantly they accepted my invitation. We entered through a cellar door in the Jewish quarter. Masiama liked that. Found what I called the meeting room. With the fountain. New alcove off the side. Beautiful filigree ornaments.

Sat them down. Put forth my ideas for reform of Nigts. What's so vital about including filth, they ask? Not filth: the people's energy. Mustn't a house have a privy? My poetry must have obscenities. Isn't court wine poetry off-color? What about image of paradise? Virgins awaiting every man. So honor any pleasure! Izjis bought in. Masiama turned up her nose.

But they were enthralled by the secret space. Promised to speak with Ruckamuff and the Tuareg. Oamra had new courage to find space's wonders. Stairwells down to torchlit tunnels. Gates to magnificent gardens. No such sights in Cordova. Where were we?

My dreams were haunted. Forced to fly. Off parapet? By an over-soul? Consumed too much food and wine. Never been heavier. So-called colleagues happy when this elephant wintered in Baghdad. On return I demanded to see Tuareg. Oamra confided group argued about me. I played hard to get. Last chance for them to accept me. To enter space. Such deceit Turtushi!

It got Rickydick's ear. Took him right into meeting place. Fountain burbling like crazy. New cushions on banquettes. Very funny. Supportive.

"Let me repeat," he said, "there's no place for smut in the Nights."

Blah blah. Oamra had told me he wanted to make Nights legit fiction. Used Hamadhani's cutting edge work to snare him. "Look what passes for art in the *Maqammat*. Rogues, devils, cursers. The main character, Abu al-Fath, vagabond scholar, tricks for money. The highest mysticism and lowest obscenity in the same breath. This low tone is the newest trend. The new fiction. Accept it and you must accept sukhf. And me."

After my parse of *Maqammat* Rockymuck lost in thought. I had him explore the mysterious halls. As we wandered I went for the kill. "Don't let my sukhf peddling fool you. I got as much literary chops as you. You want fiction for the ages. I want same for human urges. Farting to fucking. Together we'd make a powerful team. Add the others and praise Allah!"

al-Raqa'maq looked convinced. Not ready to admit it. Must save face. Walked in silence. Then: a golden light at end of passage. Left shadowy interior for the outdoors. Most splendid garden. Sunken into flowing water. Palms. Fruit trees. Lounging maidens. Strolling courtiers.

Raqa'maq gasped. He'd been here before. Impossible but true. A place well outside of the walls of Cordova. Up in the hills.

"Where are we?" I asked.

"You don't know?" he responded. "You who controls our entry into this alchemical territory, which transforms large distances into short spans?" He gestured toward the beauty surrounding us. "We are at the palatial city of the Caliph. The Madinat al-Zahra."

ق

205

51

—⟨ΩΩ⟩—

Zack peered at Ooma. "How could you know Bax's tale would end at the Madinat?"

Porcy thought she understood. "Bax had her speech in his head while he was going under."

Bax was relieved the qaraq focused on Ooma's prescient mention of the Madinat, and not the disdain The 379 Group felt for Turtushi. In this life he was a welcome member of the tribe.

"Even with Ooma's travelogue," Zack said, "it's major serendipity. Did you know, Ooma?"

Ooma strode over to sit next to Bax. "Oamra knows many things. Turtushi's tale is just the start. As usual, Bax is just a frightened pawn in the midst of larger events." She stroked his hair, a cold, distant look in her eye. "We should continue."

Ooma had shattered any relief Bax felt about the group accepting him. Porcy saw the hurt look on his face. "Not until you apologize to him," she snapped. "That was pure mean, girl."

Before Ooma could answer, the group realized Sahara was muttering to herself, spouting a tale in trance. Bax's story had triggered another memory in her mind, and the tensions in the room caused her to replace present reality with an assured, haughty lifetime. The group listened carefully.

The Tale of the Licghurin Crystal

Once upon a time there was a young Princess, the Eversolid Fourth Principice Nongsch of the Three Valleys. Principice Nongsch came by the Stone Crown at a very early age, young enough to whine about the temperature of bark tea and the sweetness of morning buns. Keenly critical of the realm, disgruntled by former Principices, Principice Nongsch set out to change the rituals of the Village, and the myths of the land. These were the very foundations of her community, so to avoid resistance Nongsch played the innocent child, which she was. She used charm and playfulness to skirt her detractors and win the hearts of the people. A well-timed screaming fit didn't hurt either.

For centuries, the Principices of the land had argued with their Matriarchs and Elders. Growing up in the Court, Nongsch thought that the business of government was to offer the longest, loudest speech. The Court's sense of history was that the very faces of the Cliffs above stared each other down, towered in the sun victoriously, and crumbled in the throes of defeat. The people in the Village loved to recite and re-enact these legends, but Nongsch felt the mythology was static and stone-like. The tales wielded images of hills of shale burying the Village. This tone of sadness and terror kept the people out of touch with reality.

Burdened by Court feuds and outmoded beliefs, the Three Valleys had accomplished nothing for generations with their greatest resource. In the caves halfway up the central Cliff in Nongsch's valley, the Principices had mined exquisite Licghurin Crystal as long as anyone remembered. It was sacred practice, as if the soul of the Original Inhabitant was made of Crystal. Crystal extraction was treated with the dread of a human sacrifice. Originally, Crystal was used only to bejewel the scepter of the Principice. It was a profound secret that contact with Licghurin Crystal stimulated an altered state of mind, with the ability to see past and future.

In the lineage of Principices leading up to Nongsch, mining occurred in the lower caves, in easy reach of villagers. Crystal objects filled the treasury, and common uses overshadowed the sacred purpose. Principice Nongsch wanted to enter the entire network of caves. She envisioned extraordinary grottos as ceremonial spaces, to unify the people, smooth over conflicts at Court, and return to magical use of the Crystal. She wanted greater connection with the Cliff, a path to the top. The Elders laughed at her. She held in her fury and laughed with them. They would see.

Nongsch had loved Licghurin Crystal since she was little. Enthralled by the bluish haze radiating from the Principices' scepters, she insisted on garments of the same hue, her bedchamber in shades of sapphire, and champions at the Three Valley Mock Battle bearing banners of cyan. When she came of age, her Mooncharm wish was a trip to the mines, believed impolitic at Court, which made Nongsch want it more. She climbed the rocky path with an entourage, and marveled at ancient letters carved into the entry to the cave: "I am the Licghurian Crystal, the Corundum of Vision, the Solitaire who points the way forward in the darkness of Time." Few surmised the meaning of the words, and none their origin.

Four miners brought her inside. At first Nongsch could see nothing in the penumbrae. Slowly the girl got used to the reflected light of the Crystal shapes, and saw obscure mirror images of herself. At times things appeared upside-down, then strangely curved, then elongated. She felt she floated amid the thousand-fold refracted angles of the Crystal.

The Court fought her every proposal to expand mining and discover new properties of the substance, but Principice Nongsch won every time. These endeavors were a clever distraction from her true design. Nongsch already felt the power of the Crystal through her scepter, a power of prophecy that had allowed past Principices to steer their community. The Principice wished to see more than blurry images, so she commanded that Crystal icons line the Cliff path. Standing in their midst, Nongsch thrilled at the clarity of her visions.

Rather than prophecy, she saw the history of the Three Valleys, a collective memory of coronations and harvests. Nongsch saw nothing of the future. What was wrong with her? Seeking the truth, the Principice proposed an enormous project, a path to reach the heart of the cave network. When several enormous caves were discovered, Nongsch selected the grandest cave for a Temple. She would see the future clearly in such an edifice.

It took years to complete the Crystal Temple. An enormous slab of stone served as a foundation for the floor of the cave. Seventeen pillars of mixed rock and Crystal supported the cave ceiling. In the center, a large Crystal plinth functioned as altar, stage, and storage case. The weight of this enormous box strained the stone foundation that held the pillars in place.

Though the Court thought her indulgent and unhinged, Nongsch wanted the people to enjoy fruits of all the labor. She instigated a seasonal pilgrimage up the mountain, stopping at each Crystal icon for ritual meditation. At first, the Temple was only a destination since it was far from complete. Later, short services occurred at the lip of the cave, where the people could gawk at the progress on the Temple. During each pilgrimage, Principice Nongsch clung tight to her scepter, hoping her visions would turn prophetic. Finally, the Temple opened for ceremonies and the people marveled at the display of Licghurin Crystal. If she could not foresee the future, at least she had created a better one for her people.

No one foresaw the true bane of Principice Nongsch's good works for the community. Erosion and slippage had already threatened the infrastructure of the mountainside from generations of mining. Adding further excavation, weight from the Temple's stone slab and pillars, and micro-erosion from the footpath traffic of the Villagers, Nongsch caused greater stress on the Cliffside. During her lifetime, many landslides occurred along the path to the Temple. After her death, the path to the top was abandoned due to minor quakes and toppling from above. If Nongsch had received the power, she would have foreseen her ambitious project crack the mountain until the Cliff Face came crumbling down and destroyed the Village.

But Prinicipice Nongsch never envisioned the future of her community, only images deeper into the history of the Three Valleys, and the geology of the North American supercontinent. In the interlife, Nozh, the Principice's soul, would understand why her vision was so limited, so extensive in an unintended direction. Nozh would see where his time was headed, a series of troubled lifetimes, and actions against his qaraq. An epiphany would lead to admirable lifetimes.

Ultimately, Nozh would pay for the twisted path he carved into the mountainside and the damage it caused. His karma would inflict a gouge that whirled up his soul.

ق

As soon as Elvi brought Sahara safely out of trance, Ooma went on the offensive. "What are all these superfluous stories, Sanaa? Are you avoiding our life in Cordova?"

Ooma's odd rebuke irked Sahara. Hurt from Ooma's previous insult of him, Bax took the temperature of their relationship by throwing support to her. "Yeah, Sahara, how did Elvi's regression possibly lead you to that story?"

Sahara glared at Bax and Ooma. "I have no clue! It was Naji's lifetime."

"Yes, Nozh's life," Verle said. "Why is he sending recalls in his sleep now?"

Sahara threw up her hands. "He wasn't part of The 379 Group. Maybe he wants in now."

Verle frowned. "It was a five-character World, with feuds between Principices and Cliffs."

"Forget categories," Amar said. "*Are* you avoiding Sanaa's life, Sahara?"

"What is wrong with all of you?" Sahara had had enough. "10th Century versus Stone Age. Old Worlds versus New. Categories versus depth. The real conflict here is our astonishing ability to remember past

360

lives versus our infuriating ability to constipate that process. Aren't we trying to heal from recent horrors? Shouldn't we embrace new things? New hope, new Worlds, new whatever!"

The group was shocked by Sahara's tirade, but knew the many issues underneath it. The tension magnified when Ooma walked over to hug Sahara from behind, arms brushing her breasts.

"I'm so sorry, my sweet, sweet Sanaa. Oamra will make it up to you."

Sahara felt a shiver of pleasure. Mortified, she quickly raised her arms to dislodge Ooma, and continued heatedly. "I'm the first who wants info on the Nights, or how the King intended to marry Scheherazade, or a link to prehistoric reincarnation practices. And I felt a connection to the Madinat during Nozh's story. So here's a thought. Principice Nongsch used a crystal cave and objects to receive visions. We've encountered the Kharman tomb where objects accompanied the dead into the inter-life. In John Donne's room, we incarnated as the same objects in a condensed universe outside Time and Space. On the heels of Oamra planting objects around Cordova, Sanaa discovered a magical space, and al-Turtushi came to the Madinat, a journey that defied Space. There's a connection between these magic spaces, objects, and our work with the Nights."

Seeing Sahara had gained the group's interest, Elvi said, "I hope all your recalls from the regression clarify this connection. Now I challenge you to recount tales that flow one to another."

206

52

—◦◦◦—

Zack jumped up from his bench. "I'll start!" Realizing he had no reason to stand, he walked with dignity around the space, taking in the configuration they had mysteriously agreed upon, and looking for the perfect spot to perch. He chose a platform and sat ritualistically, as if that was the sacred spot to deliver past life stories. "My recall starts perfectly where Bax ended. The first meeting of The 379 Group, except it's 366 AH."

Verle did the math. "Or 988 A.D. Thirteen years before 1001. Excellent, son."

Zack bowed his head with false modesty. "They kissed the ground before him. It's an excellent, full recall. Though it starts with a random image: a pair of eyes staring at me."

The Tale of the First Meeting in The Maqaraqan

Why is she staring at you? You, Izjis, of all of us. So strange meeting like this. The Tuareg sits silently in the corner. Oamra nearby, with

Masiama on the platform. Grotesque al-Turtushi languishing on the rug, rolls of fat this way and that. And al-Raqa'maq acting like our leader.

But what a glorious place! Years of searching, years to get underneath the magic. Who cares if Turtushi holds the key to enter? To have access to the Madinat al-Zahra from some back alley in Cordova, without the endless ride across the plains -- it's a miracle! You never know where you'll turn up, the Madinat is so huge: receptions halls, residences, baths, gardens, the Mint, the Mosque. When al-Rahman III built it on Roman aqueducts for prestige and water, he was criticized for focusing more on the Madinat than government business or Friday prayers. But the glory's worth it.

When al-Turtushi led us here the first time, we had no idea where to meet. With the Tuareg whispering in one ear and Oamra the other, al-Raqa'maq ordered the group to scout for a space. Each of us had seen enchanting spaces on previous visits, but where were they? We scouted in pairs, women accompanied by men in case of trouble. You went with Masiama, climbing up an enticing Tower with open arches and gorgeous vistas. A lovely place for solitude or trysts, but you both agreed it was too drafty for a comfortable meeting.

When you rejoined the others, Turtushi and Oamra had found a suite of living quarters with a garden on the floor below, which Turtushi had seen before. It was handy for late nights, but not meetings. Like the Tower and other chambers, the area was empty, as if meant for us and unreachable by others. You joked that it was no wonder since we could barely find them.

The Tuareg and al-Raqa'maq were the most successful. They discovered a chamber separated from the rest of the Madinat al-Zahra, hidden in plain sight from the Court. We'd all seen it before, in dreams or visits with al-Turtushi, as if this space exists in our minds from another incarnation. A large room, grand, with monumentally high ceilings. At one end, several levels of stone platform banquettes, like a steam bath at the hammam, with benches nearby, perfect for a group meeting. Between the other end and center, an ornate marble fountain, gurgling continuously.

363

Side alcoves suggested private chats, with alabaster scrollwork, wood-carved lions and flying beasts, and calligraphed quotations on the walls.

The group searched for hours to find the space again. The Tuareg and Raqa'maq retraced their steps, but only received clues: if too far from the space, the Madinat appeared, merchants and courtiers crowding the halls; if nearing the goal, paths emptied and private spaces reappeared.

The group never found the chamber that day, but on returning there it was! The previous time Raqa'maq had entered from the platform banquette end; now the group came through a side room near the fountain. The Tuareg gasped: there were carpets and throw rugs, overlapping on the floor, lining the walls like tapestries, even hanging like banners. Before there had been none. You joked that they rolled out the carpets to welcome us. But no one was there, and no one in the group laughed. Everyone marveled at the beautiful designs, subtle colors, and soft weaves of the rugs.

What good fortune had brought you, Izjis, to this magical, malleable, surprising place? The same fortune that brought you to al-Andalus. Here you can present any idea without recrimination, love any kind of person without chastisement, and find any book in the Warraqa, the great bookseller's market. There you met Masiama, with the latest volumes from Cairo and a flirtatious smile. Would you have bed a widowed Jewess in Egypt? Here it was the thing to do.

Except al-Turtushi showed up first. No perfume could cover up his musty obesity. What Masiama saw in him you did not fathom. He pushed his extroverted sexual rawness on her, and you backed off, shunning an adolescent competition over a woman. Masiama loathed al-Turtushi's hedonistic eating sprees, but the wild lout entertained her with his flattery. Before long, she called him on his advances and took him to bed.

The affair did not last. Masiama graciously hid the truth about what happened, though it was hard to imagine sparks flying. al-Turtushi bragged he had made the conquest of the century and flouted his filth more than ever. The thought of following him into Masiama's arms disgusted you. You kept your distance and let go of feelings for her.

Soon Maisama invited you to the secret group and al-Turtushi's tours of the elusive space. Turtushi was furious, and alleged that Masiama bore no love for you. One look from Masiama hushed the lout: she had something on him. You felt Masiama looked at you in a new light, but only due to your civility, so you did not read this attitude as an invitation. The triangle settled into a partial truce. One gaze at the magical meeting space convinced you that working together harmoniously was more valuable than petty entanglements.

And yet her eyes pierce you. No wonder: no one knows how to start the first meeting. What are we working on? Why? Nothing to do but stare at each other.

"We must name this space," al-Turtushi says. He takes credit for the space, obnoxiously, but the others are happy to have a task. Masiama says, "The Arabic word for space is *makan*."

Raqa'maq blurts out, "What about *maqaraqan*?" Again you suspect glory-seeking, since the made-up word contains the sound of his name. But we instantly take to it, formalize it. The Maqaraqan. It has a familiar ring to it. Satisfied, the group is silent. The fountain seems louder.

You suggest introductions, a personal story, an era of our lifetime that feels like a past life. You volunteer to start. The group concurs and you bow your head in false modesty. "They kissed the ground before al-Izjis," you jest. None laugh. As you begin, does the fountain quiet down?

You grew up in Egypt when the Fatimids conquered. Shi'ites proliferated, tracing power back to a member of Muhammad's family, may Allah praise them. The Buyids in Baghdad trace their line to son-in-law Ali, but the Fatimids gain their legitimacy from Fatima, Ali's wife. A new elite culture began to grow with the founding al-Qahira in the delta of the Nile.

You had been the pupil of Abu Ya'qub al-Sijzi Ishaq ibn Ahmad, an influential thinker not in line with Fatimid orthodoxy, but supportive of Caliph al-Mu'izz. al-Sijzi was an itinerant poet and scribe, who wrote that his wanderings had been tormented by The Qird, or the Ape of Evil Fortune. As a student, you were a contrarian, disagreeing with al-Sijzi for the sake of argument. Loving your critical spirit, he said, "Our young protégé defines the nature of reflection by turning my teachings inside out, the way a mirror reflects images." He named you al-Izjis, the mirror image of al-Sijzi.

The one idea you seldom countermanded was al-Sijzi's belief in metempsychosis. He claimed jinns and demons from the afterlife inspired him to write about mystical worlds. As a Moslem, expounding on reincarnation could get you into great trouble. You were less discrete than your master; before al-Sijzi could intervene, you were escaping a hostile posse across the Sahara.

Taking a moment to breathe, you look around the space at your audience. You check to see if your literary credentials impress Masiama. She is attentive, but not enthralled. The fountain gurgles more intensely. You launch into the next part of your tale with renewed gusto.

On your flight across the desert you never missed performances by local musicians. Unlike the effete Buyid court music, out in the desert you heard the haunting shrill of a snake charmer's pipe, the delicate tones of a one-stringed tortoise shell lute, or the enflamed keening of a female mourning choir. Most of all, you loved the interlocking rhythms of the drum circles, including sub-Saharan ensembles that played wooden slat drums with mallets. The melodic fragments and elaborate rhythmic sequences sounded like coded signals. You bought an instrument at an oasis.

Entering the Maghreb further west, you relished the local legends. The Arab Musa ibn Nasyr, who had conquered the Maghreb for the Umayyads, found a hidden city with an unassailable entrance. When Musa's lieutenant penetrated the daunting walls, he restrained his temptation for the plunder within, a moral exemplar for every good Muslim. At every new dune rise, you searched the horizon for the City of Brass, knowing full well it was fantasy. But the spell was cast: the magic of the desert softened your heart, the promise of an Islamic nation across the Mediterranean tingled your bones. One more outsider yearning for al-Andalus' embrace.

So you discovered the group, the Nights, but not the approach to the new anthology. Despite your tangle with al-Turtushi, who juxtaposes smut with courtly elegance, you defend his position. To reflect the beneficence of al-Andalus, include everything! With a nod to al-Raqa'maq, you support this openenss by praising modern fiction. You think back on samples you heard at desert campfires. Here was *hija*, invective or satire, where tribal rivals roast each other over the verbal pit. Here was *hazl*, the attitude of joking, which derives from legends that when Muhammad laughed his molars showed. Here was *mudhika*, which makes a man laugh out loud, to the point of 'falling on his back.' Arab culture has the greatest body of humorous narrative of any people around the Mediterranean. But our collection should contain any form, from hadith to asmar.

For al-Raqa'maq, too much conflicting style jumbles the collection. It is like a flying creature whose right eye seeks out mates and left eye seeks food. In the end, it crashes into the earth. So the group argues at our first meetings between a selective, elite collection, and a sprawling romp. We continue to bring in stories, and you prove an excellent writer, able to merge different languages and cultures into a whole. The work is off to a roaring start.

We return to the same magnificent space, The Maqaraqan, sometimes entering through new corridors in the Madinat al-Zahra, sometimes finding a new configuration of banquettes and alcoves, sometimes with a deafening noise from the fountain, sometimes a reverent silence. At each meeting the same pair of eyes examines you, pierces through you, or throws you kind looks as you argue for the most diverse Nights possible. Her gaze warms your heart, and gives you hope that there's still a magical space for you in Masiama's heart.

ق

Ignoring the final tender moment between Izjis and Masiama, a deep link between Zack and Diana, Bax jumped in. "This is why we set up these platforms? A memory of the Maqarayna?"

367

"Yes, this is how we found the Maqaraqan," Diana corrected, grateful for the distraction from her 10th Century love life. "We also found the Donne room and the Kharman tomb. We have a knack for rooms outside Time and Space."

"Don't forget my challenge to let the tales flow into each other," Elvi said.

"Since she was ogling me in the tale, I hope the Doc is up next," Zack said.

Diana was miffed by Zack's frankness. "He's right, my recall picks up the first years of meetings for the group." There were a lot of intimate details she didn't want to divulge. "I'm not sure where to start. The first image I saw was an open book or journal, a symbol of reading a past life, but also of Masiama in her bookstore, perusing a volume."

"Take your time," Elvi said. "You know best where to begin."

Diana blushed at the thought of where the tale actually started. But there was nothing to do but begin at the beginning.

53

—◦◦◦—

The Prepared Statement of Masiama ibn Ishaq ibn al-Dínam

Masiama had been only thirteen years old, just coming into her womanhood. In her Cordovan neighborhood was a Sheikh some of the old folk claimed had been alive for years beyond his youthful appearance. Traveling back and forth from Iraq, Sheikh Ba'Tr held some secret to eternal youth. To innocent Masiama, he was the most handsome man in the world. She devoured books, and every time the Sheikh saw her reading, he asked her sweetly how she liked the book. She and her friend Ynez spied on Sheikh Ba'Tr, enflamed to watch him flirt with many women in the quarter. Soon Ba'Tr seduced the vulnerable girl. She threw herself into the affair with a desire beyond her years, surprising even the world-weary Sheikh.

But things were not as blissful as Masiama expected. In a final act of lust, an explosion shuddered through Ba'Tr's body, his skin cracked and crumbled, and he perished in her arms. A deadly nightmare for Masiama, she fell into a private haze, fascinated by whatever dark power had cursed the Sheikh. Masiama retained her love for the Sheikh and saw no other suitors, until a matchmaker took over her fate. Masiama's family shed relief when an older, wealthy man accepted her hand in marriage, overlooking her lack of virginity and paltry dowry. Respectful of Jewish tradition, Masiama had to consent. There was no love in the marriage, but the old man cherished his fresh-faced bride, and Masiama loved working in his extensive bookshop. The sad union paid off when her husband died and left her the business.

Diana knew that Masiama's later attraction to Turtushi was because he was the incarnation of the Sheikh. Zack, as al-Izjis, was different: Diana felt Izjis' bowing out after her Turtushi affair was an act of self-sacrifice to respect her space. In contrast to her adolescent crush on the Sheikh, Masiama fathomed the depth of Izjis' love. Diana saw her unusual bond with Zack outlast the centuries.

In her lifetime before Masiama, she had been in seclusion at the House of Wisdom, the storehouse of the Abbasid Caliphs. In her inherited warehouse of books, Masiama retained her predilection for isolation. When her affair with Turtushi fizzled, she dove happily into the group's work, sublimating romance with a zealous hunger for literary knowledge. Defending herself, Diana kept these thoughts private, picking up the narrative after a brief pause.

Masiama defended a diversified Nights, and scoffed at a trend in the Western Empire. Despite a rage for anthologies in Baghdad, some editions of the Nights stopped well short of one thousand stories, or even a breakdown of tales into a thousand parts. This stance took the *Thousand* of *The Thousand Tales* as a slang expression for an endless supply of tales, even if the amount supplied was modest. It was a decadent fad typical of the weakling Buyids, Masiama argued. She considered not stocking the slim volumes in her shop, but they were bestsellers. Easy reads for lazy minds!

It became Masiama's mission to create a full *Thousand Nights*. Only this would satisfy her repressed cravings; only this would establish her as a real player, not just an object of desire. To convince her colleagues, she worked on a speech to deliver at a special meeting, nearly two years after the first time in The Maqaraqan. She asked Turtushi to bring her to the space ahead of time. When they arrived, the banquettes rose like an amphitheater, and the fountain gurgled in a steady tempo, like a crowd rhythmically chanting in support of the Jewess. When the group arrived and took their seats facing Masiama, the spray formed a halo behind her. She delivered her discourse.

"You all know my position. Let me first justify myself as an authority you should heed. I have worked in my late husband's bookshop for twenty-five years. Though I am a woman, I have haggled with hardened book dealers, balanced my own accounts, and kept up with the trends in the market. Bookshops and libraries are the literary centers of sophisticated cities like Baghdad and Cordova. I am at the center of these centers. If our endeavors, bless the Lord Almighty, end in a worthy manuscript, I am the one to know how and where to disseminate it.

"I have business relationships with people like al-Nadim, a Baghdadi bookseller who wrote the *Fihrist*, a many-volumed catalogue of Arabic writings throughout the empire. My friends are the marketplace professionals, phlebotomists, letter writers, and all who dupe the market inspector. I am in touch with the Cordovan world of scribes, lawyers, and bureaucrats who staff the royal chanceries. I have access to the Court resources for us, literary and financial.

"I know who runs the paper factory in Jativa, on the prosperous coast of Valencia. I possess a Romanian translation of the Nights, from a Ninth Century Persian source. I have a map from the House of Wisdom; I believe it relates to the object Oamra received from her great-grandfather."

The Tuareg produced the oval object from beneath his cloak, Masiama brought out the map, and the group marveled that the tattered map fit neatly around the ovoid like a wrapper. This sleight-of-hand impressed the group more than any credential Masiama had offered. She continued.

"I am not a scholar like some of you, but as a Jew I am aware that our writers use Hebrew for their highbrow styling, and Arabic for their expression of daily matters. Many Muslim authors avoid the *fusha* style set forth in the Qu'ran, and employ a healthy vernacular Arabic. I vote for this no-nonsense language for our Nights, for it will reach the people. I know this style well.

There is a mania for books in Cordova. Earlier in the century, Caliph Muktadir's court was crazy for fables and yarns, such as the *Hazar Afsana*, the Persian *Thousand Marvelous Tales*. I cannot tell you how many manuscripts are copied every day, with or without Scheherazade, which plunder the Nights. Or how many manuscripts the Nights plunder, for that matter.

"As a dealer in the Warraqan book market, lately I've noticed a new travel literature, of some interest to you seasoned wanderers. Unlike old travel manuals, the fashionable *aja'ib* is travel writing with a pinch of the wondrous, Persian sea captains logging about mermaids, dragons off the isles of Waqwaq, and strong women in every port. This genre's popularity proves the public craves a new Nights. I have my finger on the Warraqan pulse, and I tell you we stand only to profit."

Masiama requested a short break. Her strong pitch had aroused the males in the group. She sat quietly, her legs crossed tightly, a bundle of nerves. Dizzy, she felt she was flying in circles, veering toward an object of desire. She took a drink from the fountain and continued.

"I am not here to boast, but give weight to the following argument. As you know, Tuareg, the collection has had many names, recently either *The Thousand Tales* or *The Thousand Nights*, vastly different titles, as you shall see. I propose we construct a full version with all thousand offerings. If the market is hungry and an anthology boasts a thousand chapters, then the people will not be satisfied until all thousand appear, scribes, bibliophiles, book dealers, and storytellers alike.

"You may know, Turtushi, from your winters in Baghdad, that the Buyid Court attempted a complete version. The Vizier's scribe al-Jahshiyari essayed to compile a thousand separate tales, each no less than fifty pages! Death claimed him before he reached five hundred. Too daunting.

"From your skulking through the streets, Oamra, you know the public wants a literal product. So what of *The Thousand Nights?* Each night Scheherazade begins a story, but interrupts the tale at dawn; the King wants more and she saves her neck. Just so, our public wants more, so we give them a thousand *nights*, not complete stories, but parts of tales, as Scheherazade dishes them out. We can serve three hundred stories thus, fulfill the promise of our title, and save your necks.

"I see that look, Raqa'maq: you know the trend at Court now, the selective anthology. A few delicious morsels of poetry, a small set of linked stories, a miniature history. You think this fad threatens our comprehensive anthology, but I say it's lazy work of decadent snobs.

"One final note. My plea fits beautifully with Izjis' concept of a diverse, all-inclusive Nights. My plan enables as many kinds of tales as possible."

Unhappy being described as a skulker, Oamra shushed the Jewess. "I share your enthusiasm for Izjis' concept, but I'm terrified the group could get in hot water if word leaked out. Turtushi's bawdy material alone could aggravate the authorities. Though I like the orgies of the Queen, I insist on a moral Islamic compass to counterbalance the unsavory tales. But keep our work hushed."

There were jeers at Oamra. "It's just a cornucopia of literary pleasures," Turtushi said.

"Mind your lofty notions, Oamra, we'll all think you mad," Izjis said. "Let Masiama finish."

"I am finished," Masiama said. "But do we all concur with the goal of a full version?"

The group unanimously agreed to a work with one thousand portions. Oamra went along with the vote, but in her heart she wondered if she could prove her worthiness to the group.

ق

"I see none of us gave Oamra any hugs back then," Amar said to Ooma. "I'm sorry."

Ignoring Amar, Sahara said, "Diana, your expertise was impressive as Masiama."

Diana exhaled. Relieved she had finished her story, skirted the intimate details, and pressed Masiama's defense of herself and a full Nights, Diana was grateful for her friend's support.

Sahara continued her praise. "You recalled some amazing details. There really was a Romanian translation of a 9th Century Persian Nights. Always found it weird, but there you go."

"Know what else is weird?" Verle asked. "Hints of our dragonfly life in Miss Diana's story, like confused flying images. How can the dragonfly be in these tales, Elvi?"

"Don't forget the Cordovan group had your souls," Elvi said, "and your past lives."

"Ooo, they could recall the same things we do.," Zack said. "Weirdness."

"Please don't dwell on it," Elvi said. "Who's got the next tale?"

54

———⟨∾∾∾⟩———

Verle let out a huge sigh. "This is as good a time to share my recall."

"Is there something wrong?" Elvi asked.

"Been a rough night. Scolded for not asking for the space. Couldn't focus on my recall."

"Sorry about the scolding, sweetums," Porcy said. "So you didn't have one?"

"I did, woman, don't concern yourself. I was hoping I was a Vizier, my archetype, so I'd be at the Cordovan court. It'd be nice to be a Vizier, since they're respected. Instead, I got sweaty hands, tried to let clammy palms pull me into trance. But each time I re-focused I saw someone else's perspective in The 379 Group. I learned that, after a few years of meeting, tensions got hot."

The Tale of the New Members of The 379 Group

Just as my attic room was a higher ground for the qaraq, but now is an undesired place, so the people disliked the high ground the Madinat took away from their daily life. After his father died, Caliph al-Hakam II put finishing touches on the Madinat and shifted focus onto the Great Mosque. Heartened the new Caliph returned his energies to the city, the people hoped for an open, democratic space in the Mosque. But al-Hakam created his own higher space inside, reserved for the prayers of royalty. The people felt alienated by the spatial separation of the classes. The Madinat and Great Mosque were crowning accomplishments of the Cordovan Umayyads, but as al-Hakam's reign ended in 354 AH, these edifices were ticking bombs inside the Empire.

The Tuareg: in the Nights assemblage, the main arbiter of which stories to select, and what order to put them in. Although a master storyteller, it is not retelling of tales that matters to him, but rather the arrangement of the stories, the nesting into little frames, and the reflection of the moral lessons of the Scheherazade frame tale. From this primitive desert man comes a refined sense of order: *nazm*, they call it in the Madinat, the perfect sequence of pearls on the necklace, to show off each pearl while maintaining the beauty of the strand as a whole. He works in tandem with al-Raqa'maq, whose ability to adapt any tale complements the Tuareg's talents as a framer. When the Tuareg needs a new transition to fit one story next to another, Raqa'maq is the man for the job.

Raqa'maq: not an ideal collaborator with other members beside the Tuareg. Oamra is jealous of their close work. Worried about dangerous content, Oamra pushes the Tuareg to sequence tales to support Scheherazade's re-education of the King into a paragon of Islam. Diminishing of the King's power ignites Raqa'maq's anger toward Oamra. Izjis and Turtushi infuriate him, and Masiama riles him with her flirtatious eyes. But he must work in harmony with the group, so he channels his anger through stories loaded with violence and character assassination.

Izjis: uneasy about fitting into the group, he wants to make his mark. He chooses Raqa'maq as a target. The two men argue incessantly about the treatment of the King's murder of the virgins. Masiama suggests Raqa'maq edit the story to his liking. Inspired, he has Shahryar's brother, Shah Zaman, also a cuckold, make the deadly rounds of virgins in his own nation. Izjis complains this is overkill for the story, but agrees with the compromise. Tensions mount.

Oamra: when Raqa'maq and Izjis argue over the orgies that trigger the murders, she has a deep memory of an ancient Queen named Uzmeth. She becomes convinced it was her past life. She keeps the belief to herself, for fear of vitriolic response from the men. When Oamra confides in her lover, Sanaa understands hiding something, given that half the group knows about her Tuareg disguise and the other half does not. Their secrets press on Sanaa so much that at one meeting, as the Tuareg, she confides that Oamra has had a profound past life memory of the Queen, and claims a similar bond with the Scheherazade character. Oamra feels both furious and supported by Sanaa.

Masiama: the group goes mad in reaction to Oamra's outrageous belief, but the bookseller bravely confesses that she feels a strange connection to a character, Dunyazade. When she finds versions that call Dunyazade Scheherazade's slave, Masiama takes them off her shelves. Dunyazade should be near the lovemaking between King and concubine so she can request a story night after night. Masiama claims that in a past life she revised Dunyazade to be Scheherazade's sister.

The bookseller insists each member look into their soul for a true feeling toward the frame tale. Raqa'maq and Izjis concede they boil to protect Shahryar and Shah Zaman's roles. Turtushi just laughs; all he admits is a huge erection from Sa'eed infiltrating the Queen's orgies. This grotesque image persuades the others that he too is a reincarnation. Turtushi argues that attraction does not prove this blasphemous tenet, and displays proof of his phallic response to Oamra.

The fight tops all other group tensions due to its spectacular implications. The collective is silent about the topic for weeks. Meetings are unbearable. The Tuareg and Raqa'maq realize the group has hit an impasse. They force a consensus to find new members to buffer the conflict.

Li Yu: at the very next meeting, a beautiful middle-aged woman of Chinese descent waits for the group, seatly quietly in a niche. Masiama

377

notices that the usual figures woven into the rugs have changed to elaborate dragons and palanquins. Raqa'maq inquires how the woman arrived
at the space. In response, Li Yu simply asks if it is customary for a new
member to present a biographical sketch. Without waiting for an answer,
she has Izjis usher her to a banquette to present her life.

"I come from central Western China, whose population is a mix of
Muslim, Confucian, and indigenous religions. Given in marriage to an
itinerant diplomat, I moved east, where I admired the tenets of Buddhism,
in particular the mystique of reincarnation." At this statement the group
tenses, Oamra viewing a potential ally, Turtushi a suspicious intruder.

"When my husband passed away," Li Yu continues, "I returned to my
native land, and met a blind Sufi sage. The sage had a large following,
due to his charisma, unique thinking, and memory of anything he had
ever heard. I traveled with the sage, and opened up to Sufi mysticism
and its relation to Buddhism. In the territories that link Western China
with the Mideast, the sage's retinue encountered that of al-Mas'udi, the
great Muslim writer and historian, famed for his *Fields of Gold*."

Masiama winces at his name, and reconsiders her good opinion of
their visitor. But as Li Yu describes Mas'udi's universalist approach to
history and his respect for differing cultures, the group favors this connection to their diverse Nights. "Joining Mas'udi's caravan, I became
his constant companion, translator, and advisor on Asian thought and
spirituality.

"Upon al-Mas'udi's death, I spent some years in Baghdad, until I
tired of the stagnant court. I wandered through Mediterranean nations
and arrived in al-Andalus. Taken by the pluralism of Cordovan society, a
reflection of Mas'udi's philosophy and my personal experiences, I settled
down for the first time in my life. I heard rumors of your secretive group
and its work on the Nights, a work I always admired and felt Mas'udi did
not take seriously."

With this news, Masiama brightens and inquires what the Chinese
woman would contribute to the collection. Li Yu smiles, anticipating the
question, and rattles off a list: certain Chinese legends, well-known and

rare; an ability to read moral and karmic information encoded into tales (an idea that baffles and impresses the group); an interest in expanding historical sagas in the Nights.

Before her list is complete, Turtushi asks a burning question. "Have you ever suspected yourself an incarnation of a character from the Scheherazade tale?"

Without batting an eyelash, Li Yu rejects the notion for herself, which pleases the rotund man, but says she is aware of her past few lifetimes, which distresses him. Nonetheless, the group is so impressed with her that she is accepted spontaneously, a referendum Li Yu expected all along.

Ali ibn Abd Allah ibn Wasif al-Wa'wa: unlike Li Yu's mysterious appearance, al-Wa'wa had been a fixture in the marketplace for years, and a devotee of Nights legacy. A Persian Zoroastrian by birth, al-Wa'wa converted to Islam on relocating to Cordova, although he is rarely seen prostrate in prayer. A tall, robust, loud-voiced chap fond of arguing and jesting, his advanced years do little to diminish his energy, or his excellent set of teeth, which he displays proudly, along with an exotic knife with a crystal-encrusted handle he unsheaths regularly, gestures with to make points, and uses to peel, core, and slice apples with one hand. Despite his overbearing behavior, the group finds Wa'wa to be a caring and communicative individual.

al-Wa'wa has a single-minded passion: he will not let go of the Shu-ubiyyah Controversy. From the beginning of Islam, there was a tension between non-Arab, or Shu-ubiyyah, and Arab Moslems. Many Shu'bis maintained that all peoples were equal in Allah's eyes. Persians held the controversial position that Arabs were not a superior culture; many Persians excelled in Arabic, the holy language of the Qu'ran, over their Arab counterparts. Moving into the current century, Arabs punished Shu'bi partisans; the controversy died with assimilation of the Persian population.

al-Wa'wa is the exception: concerned that Persian contribution to Islamic culture will be forgotten, he is with the group to convince them of his point of view. He reminds them of the Barmaki clan, a Persian family of Viziers that frequently appears in Nights tales, and a long line of Persian scribes fluent in Arabic and other tongues, like his family. He views the Scheherazade tale as a moral threat to absolute power, because it is a Persian story, a call to arms to any outsider force.

The storytellers love al-Wa'wa as a friend, but have trouble taking his political rants seriously, and hesitate inviting him to meetings. But when the in-fighting motivates them to find new members, he is as spontaneous a choice as Li Yu. When Turtushi asks Wa'wa the inevitable question, the old Persian replies that Scheherazade's father tugs at his heartstrings. He loves the idea of incarnating as a prototypical Persian Vizier, and believes in a magical power of the Nights.

"I was always an eccentric old lout: in my fifties I burned all the books I'd written. Then I frequented the great libraries of Cordova, studying collections like *The Thousand Tales*. I marveled to find esoteric studies mentioning the Nights. An essay on prophecy contained a chapter on *zojy*, a phenomenon influencing historical and mythological events, which cited *The Thousand Tales* as a direct result of embedding zojy in human culture. A tattered sheaf of papers with a list of lifetimes, donated by Sheikh Ba'Tr, includes Persian historical figures resembling Scheherazade characters. These discoveries made me value the Nights mystique."

Wa'wa's shocking revelations cause ripples of emotion through the group. Oamra revels in a victory, and the Tuareg comments that the group owes Oamra credit for unveiling an extraordinary side to their work. Raqa'maq recognizes something familiar about zojy, but understands none of it. Masiama yearns to see the obscure documents. Li Yu nods knowingly. Izjis makes a few jokes about Wa'wa's sanity and laughs the loudest. Turtushi stews in his anger and farts more than once.

The good-natured Wa'wa takes the reactions in stride, and shares his latest thoughts on the subject. He believes the sequence of tales follows a mathematical pattern: so many demon tales (representing the King) followed by so many romances with a strong female character (representing

Scheherazade). Oamra and the Tuareg delight in Wa'wa's compatibility with a sequence they are discussing. Then Wa'wa pushes his credibility: the idea came to him in a dream about the unpredictable flapping of iridescent wings.

Welcoming Wa'wa into the fold, no one believes the tensions are about to dissipate. Li Yu, the coolest about such problems, suggests the group launch a period of intense, distracting toil. There is unanimous agreement.

ق

"You weren't kidding," Porcy said to Verle, supporting his perspective to make up for her harsh treatment of him earlier, "you can cut The 379 Group's conflicts with a knife."

"And they don't see the source of their beefs," Zack added. "Raqa'maq and Izjis, that's Amar and me, had past lives as Ardryashir and Zaman. Talk about tension."

"Yes," Amar agreed. "I talked you into murdering your wife."

"They're becoming aware of reincarnation, however," Cachay said, dismayed that a thousand years ago the group was more in touch with past lives than she was now.

"They've also heard about zojy," Zack said. "What's that have to do with the Nights?"

Ooma scoffed. "I don't trust this addled old man's recall." Sahara saw the hurt in Verle's eyes. After his appeal for respect from the group, and a generous contribution to the meeting, Verle deserved better. The group sat in disbelief at Ooma's behavior. Oamra had been victorious in transforming The 379 Group's approach to their work. What was wrong with Ooma, that she would contradict something so positive?

Zack looked at his watch. "Here's another wrinkle. It's midnight. Happy New Year."

381

55

January 1, 2002. Month 4.

"How 'bout a break?" Zack brandished a couple of champagne bottles from his pack. "The King lavished them with gifts. A little bubbly okay, Elve? Can we drink in the sanctuary, old man?"

"Hold on, Zachary," Cachay said. "Elvi, can you give us a hint about the Nights and past lives? What did the group know in the 10th Century?"

Elvi smiled, then paused. "A break's a good idea. Champagne's fine."

"Darling, at least confirm that you were Li Yu," Porcy said to the facilitator.

"No contest," Verle said. "Use your CHITS. Li Yu is a thin stretch for Elvira Young."

"But you rarely appear in our stories," Diana said, thinking of Elvi as her spirit guide.

"I told you last Halloween that it was the first time the whole qaraq had gathered together in a long, long time. When you do, like in Cordova, it's convenient for me to be on hand."

"And we are reborn for your convenience," Zack joked. "Can we get a drink now?"

The group swarmed the food table, diving into the hummus, olives, and sweets Porcy had laid out for Mediterranean atmosphere. Zack handed out plastic cups full of Moet and Chandon.

As the qaraqis toasted each other, Verle announced, "If The 379 Group culminated their work in 1001 AD, right now is exactly 1001 years later!" The group emitted a mock-mystical "Woooo!" and broke off into little chats.

Verle's numerological detail hit Ooma as a searing truth: the symmetrical dates signified a powerful link between the two groups. Her role within The 379 Group was a crystal clear reflection of her situation in the qaraq now: an outsider. Her past life beliefs in Cordova threatened the group, but she fit the 10th Century Islamic world; in New Jersey she accepted the qaraq's past life beliefs, but her Islamic lineage threatened the post-9/11 world. In both times she was desperate to feel accepted by the group, tremendously alone. Her only ally in this world was her boss, the man who had carried her to safety, who sought entry into the group like her. Ooma glided over to Amar, sat beside him, and put her head on his shoulder. He accepted without qualm.

Sahara watched the action from the bench where Naji slept. With her complicated feelings for these two people, Sahara could not accept the scene. She took another glass of champagne. She had worked so hard to trust Amar again, and now was she losing him? Was she still Wife? Mother? Scholar? Qaraqi? She was losing how she fit into the world. The champagne went to her head. She felt Naji's pull into the world of memory. Her head whirled with visions.

She saw trees: was she glancing at a pattern of leaf veins and reading memories, in a primeval jungle with dinosaurs, or a manmade arbor in a palace? With this thought she saw Sanaa, walking the Madinat at night, in an area meant for the Caliph's retinue. Sanaa turned into an underground maze of dirt paths lit by torches. Lost in the dark passages, Sanaa felt she was in a dank prison, and panicked that she was in a never-space, a dark vision of Eternity. Summoning every nerve to calm down, a story came to Sanaa. She was inside a womb.

The Tale of the Magickwald

As Gods, many of us were created at the beginning of the universe, through cosmic forces releasing vast amounts of energy, giving us our strength and ability. Thus Kronos, Zeus, Odin, or Ilmatar, the Creation Goddess of the Far North, all have nuclear origins. Also known as Lounnotar the Sky Mother, she connects to the sky above, the waters below, and Space itself, through a vein of energy linking her to the Instantaneous Creation, the source of her immense powers.

The downside of these powers is that controling a cosmic enterprise disables anyone, even a Goddess, from handling smaller bits of information. That is why the Virgin Daughter of the Air had no clue she was with child, how she conceived, or how long she had carried the fetus. It was not until a young Hero-God crawled out of her lap and bounded off that she asked around. Rauni, the Thunder Goddess who rules over childbirth, was embarrassed to ask a mere Spirit, lower on the totem. Voinenpeller, Spirit of the Forest, shared this news:

Ilmatar-Luonnatar remained pregnant for seven hundred years, forgetting her dalliance with a warrior, since her spawn was half-mortal. The result was a very bored fetus, full-grown for many centuries, doomed to squirm in a dank prison cell. This was no ordinary Hero-God, content to sip ambrosia in the clouds. No, this was one stubborn Hero, Faina. After seven hundred years, during which time he grew so much hair, stained by blood and placenta, that it glowed bright red-orange, he clawed his way up his neglectful mother's womb, squeezed into her vaginal cavity, tore a hole in her still intact hymen with his left big toe, and escaped.

The God-Hero Faina's actions impressed me to no end, so I, Voinenpeller, wished to adopt him, especially after his birth mother's heedlessness. But after he birthed himself he disappeared from sight.

384

Later I rescued him, and nourished him to health. In gratitude, he told his tale:

For centuries I lay still in the womb, dearest father-rescuer, Voinenpeller (who lets me call him Voinen). I must have suffered endlessly in a previous life, for I wanted to turn to stone, numb and cold. Seven centuries cured me of this denial of existence, realizing my mother would never release me. Seven centuries in the womb dumbfounds a man, so I was not prepared for the world.

My father is Anniddi, despite the rumors of mother's warrior dalliance. How else was the hymen intact? Anniddi is your God-father as well, Voinen, Spirit of the Forest. Anniddi is the primal God of the Wood, whose beard and clothes are made of bramble and branch and tree trunk. He lies over the Earth, covering it in forest. Mortals nestle in his beard and pockets for shelter. It's a happy arrangement, unless something disturbs him. Then he shakes and shivers, causing storms.

When Anniddi sensed I had come into the world he tossed and shook, from joy and fear of my time in the world. Thunder exploded right at my ear, a frightening phenomenon for which I was unprepared. I ran at full speed, which given my great strength caused me to travel many leagues out of your sight, oh true father, unlike my Earth father who scared the daylight out of me. Tired of running, I hid in a warm cave away from the pounding thunder, and fell into a deep sleep.

The next thing I knew there was a crowd of surly mortals over me, kicking and beating me, shouting that I had trespassed on their home. I had never experienced pain and out of shock and terror I lay there, unable to leave their cave. They beat me for seven days and seven nights, until my cries reached you, wonderful guardian Voinen, who vanquished the beasts.

I am grateful for your hospitality, and for answering my questions. When I wanted to understand this world, you sent me into the woods, lighting my path with your Spirit, and led me to a very friendly mortal,

Grlll Graundhrn, who described this special forest in the following manner:

Sorry about your mama, chappa, but you know what they say: sometimes Gods are denser about which end is up than us lowly mortals. We've been working on our smarts for a long time, as long as there's been a difference between folk and beasts, which in a pinch there isn't. What I'm telling you is that you've come into a world where for the first time there's a blurry edge between who's a God, who's a mortal, who's an animal, and who's a rosebush. There's also lots of different mortals, like the smart ones and the ones still have to light their fire with a neighbor's log. There are the human-animals, an interesting lot, good to keep clear of in a full moon. The wood's alive with all kinds of bodies. But you're a Hero-God or half-mortal, even if Anniddi topped your mama, for he added a spice of human to your blood. So you're gonna blend right in, have na fear.

It's a world of great power, too. My folk believe our dead ancestors are still around in some form, helping out or messing about our lives. We do our best to honor them, just as you do with Sir Voinen, a very powerful character in these parts. We also use whatever magick we can get our hands on, with the help of the Spirits, even the Gods, and believe it or na, sometimes there's magick in a beast or a little plant. The wife took ill last Leaftide and an old crone with bad breath and a hide bag gave me a few sprigs of some weed. Boil it up and have her drink it, she told me. The wife was up hounding me to take out the bones the next day. Never know where help lies in the wood.

Don't take my word for it, Mr. Faina, come into the wood. I'll take you to a very special place, the cave of one of our most noteworthy bears, worshipped, feared, and revered as a great Spirit, though he's a beast, especially when he wakes up in Spring. Ach, he's at home! O'ursha, how's berries? Let me introduce Mr. Faina, recently born out of Luonnatar herself. He'd benefit from your views on the woods. Go right ahead:

Love the wood like your self. Already there are places on this Earth where animals cannot talk to mortals. Where mortals have forgotten they can speak to any living creature, beast, flower, or stone. They pray to their Gods but no longer see them. Some say the Gods have left.

But we are blessed. We are still on speaking terms. Even I chat with your master Voinen about coming storms. A bear and a Spirit! To prove the magick of this place I will take you to someone who knows why the wood is the way it is. Not a God, or even a Spirit. Not a Hero like you or a mortal like my friend Grlll Graundhrn here. Not even a beast like me. Here we are. The Tree of Magickwald. Ask him anything. Ach, excellent question. Now be patient and listen:

I am the center of the Magickwald. Geographical and spiritual. For solace and certainty, find your way to me, young Hero. If you need a talisman, carve it from my bark. If you need to temper your club, do so on my trunk. You are in need of answers. Of origins other than your own. Know this: the Magickwald is an experiment of the Gods. Which Gods we do not know. Some say they came on ships from other worlds. Some say they are our most ancient ancestors.

The experiment is this: to let every creature live as long as they wish. To die when you choose, unless by violent means. To choose which life you'll be born into next. So tree may become Spirit, mortal become Hero, or animal remain animal.

The Tree of Magickwald was silent after its pronouncement. Faina was astonished by the answer to his question. The bear O'ursha spoke to him softly as they walked back to her cave:

The spell cast on the Magickwald takes many forms. Because we can be reborn in many forms. Some creatures can transform while alive. I can change to a Spirit at the height of summer. You may have the power to transform to animal, Spirit, or even God. Everything is possible.

Faina stayed deep in thought as he and Grlll Graundhrn bid farewell to O'ursha and walked through the wood to Voinen's dooryard. Arriving, the kindly mortal conveyed one last secret:

I must whisper a legend that's passed from one mortal tongue to another. It is said this experiment will ultimately fail, that our ability to choose death shall cause the downfall of the Gods. They will die out, or get back in their skyships, or transform into rock or animal or legend. This catastrophe will befall from the actions of a God-Hero and a mortal woman. Beware, Faina, for you may cause these woes. Walk carefully in the Magickwald. You will find boons and allies there, chappa, and also dangers and enemies. But you may be the hope of mortals everywhere. Fare well.

With that, Faina God-Hero entered Voinen's home. Once inside, he recounted every detail of his journey into the Magickwald, ignoring that this generous Spirit might be his future enemy. At the end Faina said:

I am left with a thousand and one questions. Since you are a Spirit, I must ask first who is responsible for this grand experiment? Are they Gods? Some kind of Oversoul? Are they as big as me? Vast like my father Anniddi? What power allows them to control Life and Death?

Voinen bid Faina take off his boots and sit by the fire. He made him a mug of waldbark tea and sat down facing him by the hearth. Only then did Voinen answer:

What a marvel, this world of transformation and endless existence. Only here could you hear of a legend told by a God, within which a Spirit tells the myth of a Hero telling a fable of a mortal telling a story of an animal telling a tale of a tree spinning a yarn, at the end of which tree, animal, mortal, Hero, Spirit, and God conclude the saga. Enjoy it, come what may.

Don't bother with these questions, my son. The answers would confuse you, not give you what you need to know. Rather ask who you are and how you fit into the world.

Thus Voinenpeller concluded his mythic account, and thus the Hero's adventures began. We Gods looked down in curiosity. It was time for us to back away, and let Hero, Mortal, and Animal shape the world and name it as their own. Some find these names and beings on Finnish soil, some in other Scandinavian cultures. Looking down, we saw these creatures in the landmass of Greenland, before it settled in its northern space to become covered with ice, back when it was still a Green Land, covered with the dense forest of the Magickwald.

ق

January 1, 2002. Month 4.

During the champagne break, the group noticed Sahara in trance state by Naji's side. After Elvi gently brought her back, Sahara recounted a tale far from the heat of Spain. Ooma seethed on the bench next to Amar. This was her chance to impress the group with her knowledge of al-Andalus, and Sahara was sabotaging her hard work. It felt like her struggle with the Cordovan group, and as the two groups merged in her mind, she could no longer tolerate Sahara's recall.

"Stop! This story is irrelevant! You're ruining everything!"

Cachay answered. "This tale started from Sanaa's vision in the Madinat. That's relevant."

Sahara agreed. "Maybe Sanaa was starting to recall past lives; the Forest tale might be hers." "It's a new World with pre-historic reincarnation beliefs," Diana said, "perhaps our oldest."

"Even if all that's true," Ooma said with a scowl, "what does it have to do with The 379 Group's work on the Nights? Sahara, isn't that what you're most interested in?"

Already on edge, Sahara hated being confronted with this girl's nonsense. "What is your problem? We share recalls. Get with the program. I don't know how we fit into this World yet."

"Why are you getting so angry?" Ooma demanded.

"I'm fed up," Sahara answered bitterly. "Anyone else lose a couple babies? Anyone's husband lose his job because of his fucking anger?"

"Bruckner laid off lots of people," Ooma defended Amar. "You weren't blameless."

Sahara's fury was beyond sense now. "He promised to support me after I worked hard to become independent. I trusted him. Maybe I should go it on my own again. Does that shock you? I'm not surprised. It's hard enough to try out new Worlds here. Christ!"

The group looked back and forth between Ooma and Sahara. Silence prevailed. Elvi collected the champagne cups as a sign to move on with more stories.

56

———

The tension in the sanctuary had reached such a pitch that it was no shock when Porcy and Cachay started fighting to go next. Cachay wanted to get it over with and relieve her anxiety. For Porcy, the smells of the food during the meeting triggered an olfactory memory of Cordova. She had been a street orphan named Paulina, drawn to a meeting by delicious smells coming from an open window. Inside was a table spread with roasted meats, and people hard at work, neglecting it. Paulina grabbed a handful of grub and got caught, her introduction to The 379 Group.

"I brought the street into the group." Porcy wrinkled her nose at Cachay, and told her story.

The Tale of the Christian Orphan from the Streets

When I got caught with my hand in the honey pot that day, the group had been gathering for almost seven years. They had their ups and downs, but they had knuckled down to work, adapting many stories and copying them into various chapbooks. Everyone had a special function, like al-Turtushi, one of my favorites, who spiced up dull stories with juicy slang. They accumulated piles of things to be read, bottles of ink, and paraphernalia. They could not store materials in the Madinat al-Zahra, so they did copy work in town, at residences, libraries, or Masiama's bookshop.

The Maqaraqan was weird, with that fountain drowning me out whenever I wanted to talk. The carvings on the walls kept changing, the lions looking at me hungrily, bird feathers waving to me. There were times when the group had so much to do that when we tried to leave, we kept re-entering the Maqaraqan, or ended up in the residence space with tables set up to work through the night. And beds, a garden, and food, so I had no complaints. I liked the bedroom with the rabbits and dogs in the tapestry; the bed was soft and the dogs chased the rabbits as I fell asleep.

When Caliph al-Hakam died, his son Hisham was only eleven. For the next twenty years the Vizier made him a prisoner in his own palace. Ignoring lessons from the greedy construction of the Madinat and Great Mosque, the evil Vizier built his own palace on the other side of Cordova. He was so aggressive that he earned the name al-Mansur, "The Victorious." He captured Christian towns that had been peaceful for centuries. I was a Christian child during the *fitna*, this time of troubles. My parents worried about having named me Paulina, after the disciple Paul; my very name made me a target. During one of al-Mansur's bloodthirsty conquests, my entire family perished. In the chaos I escaped to Cordova. I lived on the street, learning the language of the downtrodden.

I was a breath of fresh air to the quibbling group of highbrows. At my first meeting, which the odd Li Yu insisted I attend, my first action was to pull off the Tuareg's beard. I asked why a woman came to the meetings in disguise. When Oamra protested, Li Yu confessed she had seen through the disguise. Wa'wa had guessed too, and all the others confessed they were in on the secret. Not much of a secret. Only

Turtushi was clueless: no surprise there. Oamra insisted for safety sake Sanaa stay disguised, but we all laughed at her fears.

The success of my first trick inspired me to be as playful as I wished. I made up for a missing piece of the group, a childlike spirit. I constantly reminded them the book was an entertainment and not as high blown as they wished to believe. Children might even read it some day. My attitude ruffled them: I was chided every ten minutes. Once I shouted, "I can't sneeze without being scolded," and they all shushed me.

What a bunch of pomegranates! Turtushi had the habit of running his hands all over Oamra. After I exposed Sanaa, Oamra confessed she had no interest in men and he should stay away. This revelation upset Turtsuhi greatly, not because of any prejudice (any sexual practice was acceptable to him), but because he wanted her so badly. Frustrated, Turtushi turned to the rest of us girls. Masiama could give him one look and he backed off. Li Yu seemed too otherworldly for desire. One knee in the groin and he steered clear of me. That left Sanaa.

Raqa'maq hated Turtushi's advances on Sanaa; his tensions with Izjis lessened with the escalation of his ire toward the obese Tortosan. Oamra confided to me that she saw what was happening to Sanaa. The two of them lived together, but Sanaa was getting restless, perhaps because Oamra was becoming secretive and fearful. Oamra saw Sanaa winding up in the sack with one of the guys, maybe even Turtushi (yucch), so she forgave her in advance. A bit weird that.

And the past lives! That continued to be a sore spot. As far as I was concerned, we might have had past lives or not. I was used to accepting other beliefs, growing up Catholic, and tolerating Islam even when it killed my parents. I had forgiven al-Mansur; to apply Christian forgiveness was enough revenge for me. With the poor on the street, I understood it didn't matter if they were African or Frankish, Moslem or Jew, selfish or nice. So I accepted that each group member felt a connection to past lives, even if all I wanted was a good tale to help me sleep through my tears.

Turtushi kept after Sanaa, so Raqa'maq comforted and fought for her, until she was under his protection. Then wonders: Turtushi worked in greater harmony with everyone, admitted a fear of new territory, and embraced reincarnation. Others divulged a surprising amount of knowledge on the subject. Masiama shared things she had learned from some fool named Ba'Tr. Wa'wa had studied Ba'Tr's list of incarnations, some of which are story characters, and concluded it was a disguised outline of an ancient story collection. We all marveled that a set of stories could be encoded messages about a set of lifetimes.

Li Yu couldn't resist throwing in her two coins. Some Buddhists think the soul breaks apart after death, the pieces floating around in a cosmic soup. When a soul is reborn, some pieces come back together, some don't, and new bits from other souls get mixed in. Li Yu asked if the bad blood in the group might be leftover from past lives. Sanaa answered that we'd be less likely to harbor resentments from life to life if we let go of parts of ourselves. Our conflicts could be overcome in this lifetime. This attitude did wonders for the atmosphere at meetings.

When I walked the empty hallways of the Madinat at night, I gave myself the willies thinking about these things. One night I found a beautiful side room with Persian carpets of dark blue and red geometric design. In an area strewn with pillows Li Yu lounged in silk robes. "Paulina, lie down next to me," she beckoned. She stroked my hair in a most soothing manner. I asked if she really knew what happened when we died. She explained that in the mountains between Sind and China, the people prepare for a series of afterlife psychic states, or *bardos*.

"Each bardo tests us: if we succeed, transcendence; if we fail, we enter a new life. In the Initial Bardo our soul starts in pitch-black." The carpet changed to shades of black on black. I imagined a completely dark, silent state of being. "In the Bardo of the Absolute, with benevolent and wrathful deities, we must recognize the most horrifying demon as our internal fear." On the rug, faces jumped out at me. If I flinched at these figments, how could I survive an onslaught of demons? I'd be reborn as a frog in a heartbeat. The carpets became a lake of blood-red tears.

Despite her lovely touch, Li Yu was a bit much to handle. Although pleased the group resolved its attitudes about past lives, the spiritual aspects disturbed me. I focused on the collection, brought new tales from the street, and developed opinions about the work.

One day I overheard Izjis and Turtushi flapping their tongues: the Hindu Krishna could have been reborn as Buddha, the Buddha reborn as Jesus, and at every time there could exist a great spiritual leader, just as there is always a Golden Age occurring in some land. I interrupted to ask for a corrected draft al-Raqa'maq wanted, hinting there were important things to do than prattle.

"What could be more important than life, death, and thereafter, young one?" replied Izjis. "Of course nothing," I said, "except the fried dough from Ali's."

"You making a run?" Turtushi drooled on himself.

"I'm demonstrating that this ethereal work on the Version has left street values behind."

"Impossible!" Turtushi said. "It's my job to keep it raw and earthy."

"Which you do expertly," I said, "on aristocratic texts. The street tales I bring are rejected."

"Poor Paulina," Izjis said. "Little girl's feeling hurt and neglected?"

"If that bothered me, I'd have slit my throat at age eight. No, you idiots, we've lost our link to the people. Our work will stagnate and die if it's not pumping with their lifeblood."

From then on I had my agenda. We had to grow the Version outside of court. They called me Paulina the Populist. As my skills evolved, I fought for direct prose over flowery style. I reminded Sanaa, Oamra, and Masiama that women were the strongest voice in our audience. In the streets I found writers who were fruit-sellers and herb vendors, social commentators parading as wise fools. I uncovered the obscure "Prisoners of Love," a satirical frame tale with a cult following. I pushed the group to re-conceive their mountains of written pages as a street event to end all street events. "Forget the damn book! Shout the tales to the rooftops!"

ق

Porcy turned to Cachay and said defiantly, "Okay, toots, your turn. Beat that."

Wincing at Porcy's attitude, Cachay looked around at the expectant group. It was time to confess the truth. "I didn't have a recall. I've got nothing."

57

—◦◦◦—

Elvi spoke up in Cachay's behalf. "You were all in the same boat last year, when your miraculous ability to recall dried up. Imagine being alone in that state, like Cachay."

Porcy felt terrible: she always kept the group spirit alive, so she hated making anyone feel uncomfortable. "I apologize, dear. Not to make excuses, but when I thought back to our time in Spain, I feel a competitive edge toward Cachay."

"Let's get to the bottom of it, then. The whole 379 Group is accounted for except Cachay." Ooma strode over to Cachay, all bright confidence, yet another tact for Ooma's soul. If she could help Cachay, she might gain points back. But her hope was another way she was out of touch with reality. The group felt Ooma's chipper demeanor as strange as any other change she had made.

With a flourish, Ooma placed her hands on Cachay's shoulders. "Come, just open your mind to me." Cachay had difficulty relaxing under the pressure of Ooma's touch, but she forced herself into stillness. Peering into a pale red aura around Cachay's head, Ooma felt a connection to her soul. She saw a male courtier wandering the halls of the Madinat at night. Concentrating on the vision, Ooma narrated to the group, starting as Oamra and alternating with the courtier's account.

The Tale of the Courtier who Crashed the Madinat al-Zahra

I see pages, from a manuscript a collection of notes a pile of drafts. They are strewn everywhere: in the tavern Turtushi frequents, in Masiama's bookstore, in Izjis' house in Raqa'maq's office under Wa'wa's bench in the Maqaraqan in the garden below the room where Sanaa and I sleep in the Madinat residence. And in a darkened hallway where Paulina carelessly dropped a page of a past life memory Masiama used as a source for a Nights tale.

It was this page that Muhammad ibn Darraq abd al-Qastali al-Khwarazmi came upon one midnight when he could not sleep. It was a tale of two ancient beasts, a mother and a daughter, who fought incessantly over the hazards of the adolescent's fads. The tale dumbfounded al-Khwarazmi: clearly a work of fantastical fiction, yet it had a ring of truth. The two beasts behaved as if they had human souls. al-Khwarazmi felt a kinship with the mother, which was preposterous since he was not a mother, yet uncanny because of its familiarity to him. He tucked the page in his robe.

The group hit its stride. Izjis and Wa'wa teamed up to organize the chaotic paperwork another friendship cemented but young Paulina beseeched them not to depend on bound books the true goal being oral presentation in the street yet since there was no agreement on this principle the group formed itself into sub-committees:

One to cull all the collected tales into a coherent list (Sanaa, Raqa'maq);

another to order the strongest choices (Sanaa, Masiama);

another to improve stories for interest and flavor (Turtushi, Wa'wa);
another to edit tales for consistent style and clarity (Raqa'maq, Izjis);
another to make fresh copies (Oamra, Masiama);
another to proofread and rehearse oral renditions (Sanaa, Paulina);
another to organize everything (Izjis, Wa'wa);
another to keep records secure (Oamra, Paulina),
each group with a differing notion of what to write down what to throw away which led to stray papers afloat everywhere such a foolish dangerous outcome.

On another midnight roam al-Khwarazmi found a second page, a real shocker. It was from a story cycle banned by Umayyad, Abbasid, and Buyid alike, each calling it treasonous propaganda. Khwarazmi recognized the ending, when prisoners are liberated and tyranny brought down, and two lovers sit in their opened cells, momentarily suspended in a dream of shocking Freedom. The language celebrated anarchy. The courtier scolded himself for feeling a shiver of excitement.

What real love did he have for the system that sustained him? The question kept him up for many weeks. The son of a noble's cousin and a Greek concubine, Khwarazmi never felt he had royal blood, so he mistrusted the Cordovan Court. He was one of the most distinguished poets in Cordova, including those locked up by al-Mansur, and the first considered half decent by Baghdad. But his Court spiraled down faster than a wounded sparrow. Cordova had once vied for the Empire. Now all that glory poured into the military, harassed the Christian north, and indulged in spectacles like the Madinat. Khwarazmi despised its outdoor gardens and vistas, which made him dizzy and nauseous. He searched for underground passages, with little known chambers and halls.

The worst example of a missing page was a draft of a frontispiece espousing the group's mission pinched by Paulina to defeat the idea of a written document or misplaced by Izjis since he authored the draft over a hasty lunch.

399

al-Khwarazmi found more pages, until he came upon a very unusual piece of paper, a description of an edition of *The Thousand Tales*. This was no ordinary version but the work of renegades, with female authors. Khwarazmi considered taking the dangerous evidence to al-Mansur's henchmen, to gain favor at Court, but people who try such things land in a dungeon.

Exploring deeper into the underground Madinat, Khwarazmi hunted for the perpetrators of the scandalous pages. He found right turns where there had been left turns, saw fleeting shadows just ahead, and fought off fear and yearning. Finally, he ran into an adolescent girl in a dark hall, unconcerned for her safety. When Khwarazmi questioned her, she was cold toward him because he was a courtier. He grabbed her arm, waved the page in her face, and demanded if she recognized it.

Paulina ripped the page from the obnoxious courtier's hand and demanded where he had found it. She pulled a large knife from her robes (in fact, Wa'wa's knife with crystal handle that she had pinched that morning), and aimed the knifepoint at Khwarazmi's throat. After a tense moment, Khwarazmi laughed from his belly and congratulated Paulina on her prowess. He explained that he was fascinated by the work and wished to meet her cohorts.

Paulina sized up the courtier and decided he was weak and merely curious. She lowered the knife but did not sheath it, and gruffly ordered him to follow. Khwarazmi's first heated encounter with the group required initiations on both sides to gain trust. Raqa'maq recognized the poet and revealed that Khwarazmi wrote panegyrics to al-Mansur championing Islam against Christianity. On hearing he was a collaborator with her parents' murderer, Paulina brandished the knife again. Retrieving his weapon, Wa'wa stopped her but pressed Khwarazmi to defend his actions.

Survival depends on favor at Court, the courtier claimed. Outside the establishment they might be poorer, but infinitely freer, for which he felt the deepest envy. When Khwarazmi warned them to be wary of eyes on them, the group asked his opinion of their mission.

"I do not know how your little cabal became installed in such a mysterious place. I have loved *The Thousand Tales* since I was a boy and admire your ambition. We live in a vast Empire, so I understand the instinct to speak to all peoples, even with Islamic morality in mind. But this is a dangerous concept now. al-Mansur is violent and unstable. He reaches out to Moors, Berbers, and extremist groups to strengthen his campaign, but could be taken down by these allies. There is no longer an atmosphere of tolerance, where Jewish mathematicians rub elbows with desert poets.

"If you claim your version contains hidden prophecy from an ancient time, it is heretical. If you have sequenced the stories in a mystical pattern grounded in politics, you will be burned at the stake. Twice. If your work crosses all borders, you'll be exiled to the other side of those borders.

"I only warn. I do not raise my hand against you. I find your work unsettling, outrageous. But years at Court made me accept open-arm policies with a comfortable conservatism. Many at Court remember the pleasant days of al-Rahman's reign, before this fiasco. They'd be overjoyed you're standing against the dark forces. I believe your work must be known at Court. I can help make the collection the finest written anthology of popular narrative. When may I start?"

Taken aback, the group told Khwarazmi they needed to discuss his plea. A week later Wa'wa met him: after days of stormy arguments, Paulina only accepted Khwarazmi for the sake of consensus, but refused to congratulate the courtier. Paulina's push for oral performance rubbed against Khwarazmi's revival of the group's interest in an outstanding manuscript for the ages. Paulina took back Wa'wa's knife. The courtier maintained calm and rose above the threats.

"al-Raqa'maq speaks wisely about the popularity of Hamadhani's *Maqammat*, combining the satisfactions of written fiction with your need for a bit of spice, Paulina. A new writer of maqammat in the Court's eye, al-Hariri, uses puns and palindromes, without the bad grammar of the street."

"The street don't care about grammar, stuffed shirt." Paulina cleared her throat and spat on the ground. "It makes folk tale, spicy or not, ring false."

"Spelling's hard enough." Wa'wa often tried to cool the flames. "Our heroine in Persian is *Scheherazade*, but in Arabic *Sharzad* or *Sharazade*." Seeing through his ploy, Paulina stabbed the table.

At another meeting, Khwarazmi raised the issue of including more poetry. "In the desert, it was the vernacular of the Arabs. A poem should express peak emotion at the climax of a story."

"The Court ruined poetry," Paulina said. "It's perfumed and fed on sugared dates. It no longer expresses the emotions of ordinary people."

And so it went, meeting after meeting. Worried they neglected the work, Sanaa gathered all finished versions of tales and suggested storing them in a locked container. Raqa'maq supplied a larger casket, and Sanaa offered the oval talisman to be fashioned into a clasp. Wounded by this use of her great-grandfather's lucky charm, Oamra called the plan preposterous. Paulina backed her up with a flick of the knife. Khwarazmi grabbed the weapon and asked Wa'wa's permission to melt down the knife as a key for the lock. Wa'wa's mind fogged with the pressure of the moment. Did the knife have ordinary quartz or rarer crystal? Did the blade's shape originate from a noble tribe?

The casket idea did not abate tensions. Paulina said, "You keep adding one frame tale embedded in another. Imposing these orders on folk tales is like the imperialistic Court imposing values on other cultures."

"But spreading motifs from a frame tale to stories inside it is like spreading culture from tribe to nation to everyone," Khwarazmi said. "We need a legitimate, moral, Islamic version."

Paulina stood up, knocking over her chair. "Is the current Islamic tyrant legitimate and moral? How can we kowtow to that insane al-Mansur? He murdered my family."

The comment silenced al-Khwarazmi. He was unaware of Paulina's family history. He had avoided learning anything about the ruffian. Truly shocked, he bowed his head deeply.

Raq'maq filled the silence. "We have stories about merchants that appeal to the middle class. We have ingenious adaptations of Persian classics that make the literati proud. And we have magic, adultery, and body odor for street folk. This is our desire, a collection for the whole world."

"Raqa'maq speaks true." Sanaa smiled at him. "Can't we make the most magnificent book, worthy of any Court, if not the current one, while the Tuareg and Paulina advertise it in the souk?"

"Quite right! It took us years to stop arguing about mysticism," Wa'wa said. "Do we really want to carry on a class war? When we hope to resolve such differences? A truce!"

ق

Ooma yanked her hands from Cachay's shoulders. "That's enough. Paulina and Khwarazmi get along fine now. Anyone want more to eat or drink?" The qaraq looked at her, bewildered.

Despite Ooma's bizarre behavior, Porcy was still on her side. Lord knows what the poor babe was going through, escaping that building to become a public enemy in America. Porcy chose to ignore Ooma's quirks and comment on Cachay's recall.

"Not so fast, Quicksdraw, give me and Paulina our moment of absolution. This is why I was cranky with Cachay. She and I were rivals in Cordova, class warriors."

"Don't you mean classy?" Cachay half-smiled at Porcy. "In the Scheherazade archetypes, I am simply 'The Court.' So reductive it's embarrassing. At least give me some class."

"I was also generalized as The People," Porcy said, "representing lost virgins and their mourning mothers. In Cordova we represented Court and People. Our archetypes. Cool."

"Cool for you," Cachay scoffed. I hate it."

"Why deny it, sweetie?" Porcy said. "You love this role. You bitch about lowlifes at Social Services. Even on 9/11 you sat on your high horse judging them. I should burn you in effigy."

403

"Shouldn't we just be grateful?" Verle said. "Ladies, as people of color we should be proud we collaborated on this multi-cultural book. A thousand years ago. A subversive manuscript."

"It's about to get better," Zack said. "I think Bax's gone back into trance."

At the mention of archetypes, Bax mused on his, Sa'eed, the Queen's lover, like Bax in size and sexuality, and fearless. Bax was proud to have braved the World Trade Center; it was a huge breakthrough. The thought sent Bax to a memory of one week after the attacks.

58

—◦◦◦—

September 18, 2001. Week 2.

That week Bax had tried to return to Ground Zero to test his new-found bravery. But he was frustrated by new security measures keeping him out. Riled, he tried tall buildings where he could climb onto the roof, and ended up in Soho, at a twelve-story apartment house with no door-man, dangling his legs over the side of the tarred roof.

Bax sat there, looking over the downtown skyline, marred by smoke and the two missing jewels in its crown. He wondered what it had been like for the poor souls who jumped from the fire, or for Ooma as she rushed to safety. Bax wondered if he could have withstood it. His dizziness from the height, rush of fear thinking back to the attacks, and pumping adrenalin from this experiment in fearlessness, all converged in his brain. He felt like he was floating, dreamlike and intense at the same time. As he drifted back to a past life memory, Bax kept a life-line of awareness. After his show of bravery he would hate to fall off a building.

At the meeting, Elvi gently questioned Bax in his trance, who was remembering Bax on the Soho rooftop, recalling al-Turtushi's lifetime. He explained all.

The Child's Dream of the Encoded Zujj

I am dreaming of a man dreaming of a child dreaming. Bax on the roof dreaming of al-Turtushi. Turtushi dreaming of his three-year-old self. All of this from The 379 Group pressuring Turtushi. Too little work for too little results. But Turtushi had magic to enter Madinat. Insurance.

All that changed. For years Masiama kept a special map. From House of Wisdom. Dating well before Islam. Unknown provenance. Every time Masiama perused it, it changed. Stars and constellations. Then continents. Matching coastlines. Then Spanish Empire. More changeable than Maqaraqan fountain. Latest: floorplans of the Madinat.

Little coincidences sprang up. The Jewish neighborhood appeared one week. That week portal to Madinat in that neighborhood. One week hallway under sunken gardens. Then group entered through that hallway. Masiama tracked it faithfully. The map predicted where and when to enter the Madinat. Didn't need Turtushi to find Maqaraqan anymore.

Masiama felt sorry for the blubbery lout. Already knew all bravado and no delivery in bed. Then blamed for group's lack of progress. Useless member. But Masiama could not withhold truth forever. Revealed map to group. If don't need Turtushi for entrance, don't need him at all. Treated us despicably, Oamra ranted. Izjis, Wa'wa, Sanaa added damning criticism.

It hit Turtushi hard. Didn't see it coming. His head swam. Felt like a man forced over edge of a cliff. Floating in thin air. His spirit dislodged from his body. Saw himself looking over edge of a tall building. Then floating above bed watching himself dream. Three years old.

The dream of the child unfurled to both Bax and al-Turtushi. It was a sophisticated dream for a three-year-old, but consider: young children are closer to the interlife from their birth, so the child accessed a wealth of information. His previous lifetime as Sheikh Ba'Tr, which spanned more than a century, was full of arcane knowledge and images the child found in his dream.

What unfolded in the child's mind were steppingstones of a cosmic journey, from a distant planet in another universe, to a distant planet in this universe, to the dawn of distant civilizations on this planet, to the evolution of *The Thousand Tales* in this civilization, to a distant future version of the collection. On the journey, the child encountered this grand saga:

the excavation of zojy, raw material of prophecy, from the mines of Veryx;

the ur-collection of events from the eleven universes, narrated by a great Seeress;

the smuggling of the ur-Version out of Veryx, to and from eleven planets;

the mathematical encoding of the zojy collection, the ur-Version, on Adad, Moon of Namboor, in the Yaaziyaat system;

the encapsulation of the Code into a metallic ovaloid vessel, bound for Terra;

the decoding of the vessel's contents into imagery of great influence on Earth;

the interpretation of the imagery as human culture, reincarnation ritual, and mythology;

the particular re-encoding of the Earthbound zojy into *The Thousand Tales*, embedded with the Seeress' Veryxian prophecies and past life correspondences;

the corruption of this second compendium of zojy-incarnation tales into *The Arabian Nights*;

and finally, future attempts to purify the collection through integrative encoding of corresponding collections of stories, past lives, prophecies, and mathematical data.

After the saga rippled through the child's mind, the dream circled back to locate his soul in this sprawling history. The child saw shamans read narratives into dried bones of ancestors, but also stacks of versions of *The Thousand Marvelous Tales*. Some versions contained correspondences between stories and past life narratives, which were encoded versions of the original zojy. Were the past life events prophesied in the zojy? If the truest version of the encoded collection had already been created, did every culture have the task of re-purifying their story collection?

The dream honed in on a conversation between Ba'Tr and al-Majriti, the Spanish Jew who served as al-Rahman III's astronomer. A mathematician by training, Majriti postulated that 1) since the original zojy traveled through eleven worlds, 2) with seven key objects accompanying the zojy's vessel, and 3) thirteen phases of the zojy's journey, then eleven, seven, and thirteen are numbers that can decipher encoded stories, or encode stories with past life information for any new collection.

al-Majriti invoked the notion of *Correspondences*, underneath all mystical meaning, for Jew, Christian, and Moslem. To comprehend something invisible and ethereal we depend on comparing it to something visible and known; to envision the unbelievably vast we liken it to the small and contained. Ba'Tr responded that if a man's head corresponds to the dome of Heaven, then an anthology corresponds to the history of many universes, its stories to past lives and prophecies.

When the child awoke, the dream left a deep impression on his unconscious, later guiding the adult Turtushi to return seasonally to Baghdad as if recovering the lost dream, and to support a group creating a gritty, mystical, human compendium.

The recall-dream affected 379 Group radically. Group was grateful for Turtushi's visison. Had been out on his ear. Now group all ears. Breakthrough in approach. Group inspired to encode the work. Make 'second compendium of zojy-incarnation tales.' Version 2. Ur-text influenced early progress of humanity. Version 1. Human archetypes.

Myths. What lies under everything we feel. Believe. *The Thousand Tales* are coded variants of this ur-Text. Same power to tap human depth. The group wanted to share this power with world. A version for all cultures.

Group started encoding process. Wa'wa listed prophecies from Madinat library research. Izjis listed past lives from Ba'Tr manuscript. Group needed to amplify their own recalling. Then organize its past lives. Categorize them. Look for correspondences. Between story and prophecy. Prophecy and lifetime. Lifetime and group recall. Raqa'maq organized the correspondences. Sanaa sequenced them according to her story order. How integrate correspondences into stories?

Back to the Madinat library. Techniques of correspondence. Mixing magic spells with narrative. History with fiction. Numerical schemes. Seven, eleven, thirteen as microcosm of the macrocosm. Oamra wanted math schemes kept secret. Group agreed with her fears!

al-Mansur raided Santiago de Compostela. Attacked cult of St. James. Irate Christians pushed back. Cult of Matamoros. The Moor slayer. Cordovan military in trouble. Internal strife among rival Islamic cities. With great social unrest comes great artistic development. Reflection of social tensions. Blossoming of fiction. Fascination with crime. Maqammat appeared victorious. Anthologies and obscenity. Turtushi in his element. Group committed to him in new way.

New harmony permeated group. Previous tensions fell. Izjis made peace offering to Raqa'maq. Expanded end of frame tale. After double wedding. New detail: two brothers share rule of kingdom. Take turns every other day. Raqa'maq: how will that work? Izjis: does it matter? Symbol of harmony. Raqa'maq smiled. Quite right, brother.

Spreading the love, Raqa'maq presented gift to Sanaa. Newly fashioned strongbox. Magical oval embedded as lock. Manuscript safekeeping. Wa'wa and Paulina worked together to remake knife into key. Sword into plowshare. Sanaa presented shiny casket to group. Paulina presented key. Oamra joked: now our book is safely subversive. It's inside the box.

Masiama kept locked trunk at bookshop. Khwarazmi proposed liaison with Court. Any interested courtier vetted by Masiama. Began to launch book. Li Yu teased: shall we finish it first? Good laugh from everyone. Returned to work. Never worked as smoothly.

ق

Still in trance, Bax felt like he was in an airplane descending through layers of cloud. The layers were the different versions of his self. He was Bax, perched on the roof edge in a precarious haze. He was Turtushi poring over past life correspondences with fantastical tales. And a three-year-old dreaming of a three-universe-old prophecy.

As his mind cleared, Bax felt an inner joy. He had seen Turtushi transform from pariah to a vital source of inspiration for The 379 Group. Inspiration that lifted their work to a new level, and brought harmony to the 10th Century qaraq. He felt vindicated in his past, and strengthened in the present, ready for any new visions. Or what Ooma might say to him.

Bax became aware of the group's discussion again. They were parsing the dense ideas in the recall. Verle said, "Are those three numbers the code?"

"The code sounds more complicated," Sahara said. "But remember: 7 X 11 X 13 = 1001."

Amar had been quiet, listening intently but also keeping his eye on Ooma's condition. Now he had to speak. "I remember when Sahara had a dark night of the soul over those numbers. 1001 was a horrible vision of Eternity. And 379 was the Islamic equivalent of 1001 AD."

"But The 379 Group calls their collection the *thousand* tales," Verle said.

Sahara nodded. "The first existing record of a title using 1001 hails from late 11th Century. A Spaniard named Ibn Said quoted al-Qurtubi, or the *Cordovan*."

"This Cordovan could have mentioned it at the time of our group," Verle said.

410

"We don't know that yet," Cachay said. "In fact, what do we really know? Bax's story is as fantastical as Sinbad. And Turtushi was duped by magic, alchemy, and sorcery."

"Before you debase my research world," Sahara said, "understand that a Medieval sorcerer didn't look at magic as tricks. It was a philosophical endeavor; Alchemy was Medieval Science. Demons, jinn, and charms in the Nights could have symbolized hidden scientific wisdom."

"And the stories laced with past life information?" Cachay asked. "How is that scientific?"

"It's mythic. There's death and rebirth in the stories of Gods and Heroes," Sahara said.

"You're swimming in an ocean of ideas," Elvi said. "Much pertains to this ur-Text and the zojy, but there is much to understand. I recommend you continue with tonight's focus. Lost in the arcane detail, you missed that our Cordova group finally hit their stride."

"Yeah!" Bax shouted. "A new era of love and harmony. Mixing in the zojy."

"About that," Verle said. "The 379 Group created what the last story called Version 2?" "Yes," Elvi said. "They layered in their past lives in imitation of the creators of Version 1."

"But what's the point?" Cachay sounded like she wanted her money back.

"Believe me, there's a point." Elvi was a bit annoyed due to the lateness of the hour. "For now, know there are correspondences between the stories and past lives. Prophecies will come later. Just be more aware. For example, Cachay, are you aware of what's going on with your son?"

Zack stared ahead into space. How had she missed it? Maybe she needed to be less critical and more sensitive to the group.

"The power of correspondences," Elvi said, "took Zack to another world."

59

——◦◦◦◦——

Zack's head slumped, inside a recall. But it was Izjis whose head slumped, sitting with The 379 Group on a banquette, the fountain a trickle, not to disturb their concentration as they encoded the stories with past lives.

As the year approached 378, the group became of one mind (had it been eleven years since the first meeting?), the better to resolve the unexpected complications to the original goal of an entertaining set of night tales. Immersion in the particular set of stories of Version 2 had unleashed a flood of past life memories. By some group-spun logic, any past life they remembered must be implanted in the collection for future generations.

At meetings, the group surrounded itself with objects believed to inspire their new literary alchemy, and boost morale for the arduous work. al-Mansur, struggling with his war, had set up Berber troops in Cordova as police. Centuries of tolerance in al-Andalus crumbled. Berbers rebels had the lofty Madinat in their sights; the unimaginable cache of books there was the bull's-eye of the target. For the group, a book was as important a talisman as a metal oval embedded in a casket. The dwindling of books threatened their work just as the Berbers threatened their lives.

Izjis and Paulina conducted experiments to access information from sources other than books. They tried Christian incense ablutions, Buddhist meditation, and Kabalistic numerology, but little helped. One day, Izjis casually played upon an instrument he had brought with him from Africa, a wooden percussion instrument hit with mallets. Striking the instrument gently, his resistance softened and he went into deep trance. On the other side of the room, Paulina felt the same sensation. They repeated this treatment many times, summoning ideas, stories, and recalls. So Izjis sat, head slumped, summoning a memory.

The Tale of the Chronically Shy Teacher

Imagine a great weight upon you, which prevents you from looking up into the eyes of anyone. It's a subtle weight at the base of the skull that slumps your head toward the ground, but also weighs on your speech center, your quick logic function, your wit—all disabled in the presence of another person. Undoubtedly, nasty events in your childhood deeply embedded this crippling shyness. You cannot battle this affliction because you are simply paralyzed.

This was how I felt in my life as a science teacher at the University of Frankovic, one of the foremost educational institutions on planet UrduniA, but in a society where the arts were not just entertainment but medial communication for diplomacy, trade, and philosophical inquiry. The sciences were a luxury, enriching but not necessary. No wonder I held my head low, as if wasting away at the edge of a swamp, forsaking all company.

But I knew science. My love for it got me through the day. Too shy to impart this love to my students, I gave instructions and answered their

413

questions, my sole contact with them. Students made me nervous. I had no idea what to say to them outside of class.

My colleagues had wonderful relationships with their students. They joked, shared personal data, and cared about each other. My students only talked about what kind of grader I was, or how weird I was. I was terrified of any duty involving social contact with students or faculty. Yet if I was assigned to chaperone students on a trip, I fantasized about them gathered around me at night as I told stories of my life. When tensions arose in faculty meetings, I imagined resolving debates with grace and brilliance, gaining deep respect from my fellows.

McDuff, Chair of the Math, Medicine, and Sciences Department (MAMESS), was a doddering academic who could not complete a sentence without fifteen pauses. McDuff tortured me with the chore of hosting the famous Unfanta Rishi, which included barely saying five words to her at lunch after her lecture. Graciously, she took matters into her own hands and drew me out.

"Have you taught Science here long, Zamen Shi?"

"About ten years."

"Fabulous! Do you get support for it?"

"There's always cutbacks. Everything goes to the arts."

"I'm sorry," Rishi said. "You should encourage your interested students to try their luck overseas. There's much more opportunity over there since Smoth and Aeron."

I gasped. "It's amazing you wrote about them."

"They're ordinary people, needing support. Anyone can work there."

I nodded, then wished my head would fall off to avoid Rishi's next question. "Do you have any experiments?"

"Yes.... something I dabble in. An INERT vaccine. Little hope of getting support."

"Nonsense. Just do it. Please contact me if I can help."

Rishi understood my pain. You cannot imagine my excitement meeting her. Joy! Terror! After school I went to the storage closet in my classroom and brought out a small vial of liquid from the refrigerator. I placed the vial carefully in a test tube rack and perused a sheaf of papers.

Rishi had given me the inspiration to continue a project I had let flounder. UrduniA has struggled against INERT—Internal Neuro-Energetic Reductive Tendency. At times thought a psychological disorder, at times a bio-chemical imbalance, the active center changes with each case. INERT suppresses energy, will, and simple desires like hunger. I had isolated a chemical that had positive effects on the action of the disease. Quite a feat, but I needed tissue samples and modern equipment, which required contacts and marketing. With Rishi's support across the sea, I might have the courage to contact foreign laboratories, where I was unknown.

I looked over my file of work and saw where I had left off. The material I had isolated was extremely delicate; it's a wonder a student hadn't destroyed it by accident. I performed a couple of simple tests to see if the chemical was still active. It was! I transferred the liquid to a new tube, carefully placed it in the rack in front of me, and considered my next moves.

First, I contact Rishi and ask her advice about how to proceed. She writes a letter of recommendation and helps me win a grant. I buy the tissue and equipment for the next phase of the experiment. I prove that my chemical suppresses the disease. With Rishi's help, I report my findings in a journal. I receive acclaim and more funding and set up my own lab. With my students, I conduct further tests and reproduce compounds to be used as a drug. Wanting in on the action, the university procures a large contract from a pharmaceutical company for my patent.

The drug gets tested and saves lives immediately. Rishi writes articles about my struggle. Students line up to take my class. The university triples my salary and expands the MAMESS Department. Royalties from the vaccine pour in. I move to a major city, buy a large house, and receive lab space at a university, without teaching duties. I marry the most beautiful of my lab assistants. Sweep her off her feet with intelligence and passion. We patent many other vaccines. Rishi writes a hard science romance novel about us. I am awarded the ASA Peace Prize, usually given to dancers or artists. Rishi writes my speech, praising the beauty and use of science. It is so inspiring I overcome stage fright, deliver it passionately as my wife looks on adoringly, and finish with a grand gesture of triumph, a salute to peace and welfare on the planet.

At the height of my reverie, I made a grand sweeping gesture with my arms, smashed into the tube rack, and sent the precious tube hurling across the room, where it broke into a thousand pieces. I leaped up to retrieve the contents, but the substance evaporated out of UrduniA.

With it went all my hope. I returned to my negative and fearful life.

ق

Zack came out of his trance, shared his tale, and Ooma went back to her rant about derailing the 10th Century recalls with extraneous lifetimes. Entering into trance state herself, she repeated key phrases like "You cannot do this," and "Go no further." Dr. Machiyoko sat next to her. Surprisingly, Ooma allowed the therapist to hold her hand in comfort.

Verle had an opposite reaction to the tangential recalls. "The 379 Group recalled past lives, incorporated them into their story collection, and even *categorized* them."

"Stop plugging your World scheme, old man," Cachay said. "What's your point?"

"The point, dear lady," Verle said, "is that *we* did all that. The 379 Group was a *qaraq*. Our qaraq. The extra stories tonight are their memories. We're recalling our recalls back in Cordova."

"So Zack's story was Izjis' recall in the 10th Century," Porcy clarified.

"And Sahara's Forest World tale was Sanaa's memory," Verle said.

"How did this 1001 qaraq seed the Nights with their past lives?" Sahara asked. "There's direct, verbal ways, like a Nights character having a déjà vu with a past life detail. But I think there are non-verbal methods to embed stories with past life details."

416

"That new research you were telling me about," Amar said. "Non-verbal layers in text."

Sahara was palpably excited. "It's the perfect way to encode a story. Objects like talismans or charms. A meal could symbolize a lifetime as a cook. Common behaviors like punishment or drunkenness could represent a life in the law."

"If I keep listening, I'll end up with a Ph.D.," Cachay said. "But I'm not convinced." Cachay was still sensitive about her lack of recalls. "Can we *prove* we're seeing their recalls?"

"You need a memory of a Cordovan going into regression for a story," Elvi said, perturbed as the group harped on an area she advised them to avoid. "Anyone not share a story yet?"

The sanctuary was silent. Even Ooma was still. Finally, Diana spoke. "If any of us could land an arrow in such a bull's-eye, it would be Sahara."

The group murmured their assent. Verle spoke for everyone. "We should apologize to Sahara, for suspecting her of random visions." Amar glanced at Ooma, who was coiled in tension.

Sahara brushed off the apology and asked for help. Porcy said, "How about the circle of hands thing, like a group recall." Forming a circle, the group prepared a path right to the Madinat. From outside the circle, Ooma listened attentively to Sahara, who spoke as Sanaa.

417

60

—◦◦◦—

Such a beautiful library. When we first came here, al-Hakam's agents procured books from every province, scribes copying volumes day and night. Four hundred thousand books! al-Mansur burned much of the collection, sold off the rest to generate money for his wars. What a tragedy. We need some missing treatises to finish our work. Masiama recovered a few on the black market. Is this our future, foisting copies of our work on crooked dealers?

Contrary to these woes, we've mastered past lives. We even target a specific time and place for an incarnation. This technique is necessary to fill in details of new Worlds for encoding stories. The group relies on me for the initial vision of many Worlds. Recently I recalled a Forest World complete with Spirits and talking animals. Raqa'maq asks me to explore a World he only glimpsed, a prehistoric people on a long migration. The manuscript casket before me, I find that the oval clasp still engenders deep sight. I close my eyes and see a barren, bleak steppe.

The Tale of the Great Bridge of Ice

I If it wasn't for the shaman's wife, we'd have been stoned to death. Naxi can't help himself but I, Xani, his mother, am the only one who knows this. Perhaps the shaman's wife too, but that no longer matters. Yes he is loud, unaware how noisily he speaks and sings and shouts. Yes he grabs what he wants and is unruly when the tribe works in quiet, and yes he has no understanding that his way is not the way of all others around him. He is an outrage – I know this in my bones, for they ache every time Naxi offends an elder or strikes another child. My bones ache for him.

The tribe no longer heard my pleas. They made me their enemy so they wouldn't care about mother Xani's tears for her child. They pointed at my sunshine red hair, so different from anyone in the tribe. She is not from here, she is not our kind, she birthed a demon from another world. The more I begged and fought, the more troubled Naxi became and the more the tribe despised him. Things rose to such a fever with Naxi's screams that the tribe lost all control. So bless you shaman's wife, for leading us safely to the edge of the land. Run out of Tuva. The fortunate banished.

II We walked for days on hard, mud-cracked earth, adrift on the steppes, my body and soul as numb as the stone and sand under my feet. Naxi shouted and screamed his way across the plains, but he was my saving grace. If not for him, I would have fallen to my knees. We heard of a bridge to another world, a very long way ahead, but it sounded like a salvation. A new world. The bridge is made of thick ice, which would enable us to cross the sea. So the story went, but who can trust a story? They are good for keeping warm around the fire, but do they hold the truth?

Naxi complained every five minutes about the endless trudge. He would drive me insane if I didn't kill him first, but I'd only kill him if I were insane. We followed the morning sun, but at night or in fog I was unsure. It was too much for me, so I made my own story, a story to shine a light on our path, and promise me a destiny on the other side of the bridge.

III   We arrived at a village, asked for directions, and sought shelter from the winds. No one answered us, but they talked about us, pointed to my sunshine hair, and winced whenever Naxi uttered a sharp sound. I asked about the bridge and they turned away. When I pleaded for a scrap of food for my child, and let Naxi release his hunger in a series of moans, they covered their ears. Incensed by this cruel treatment, I threatened a woman with a stick. The villagers would have let me strike the poor woman, to safeguard the tribe from their superstitious fear of us.

Naxi saved the woman. Grabbing my hand tightly, he took the stick with his other hand. Then he clasped his hand in mine. Understanding, I walked with Naxi to the village outskirts. As humiliating as being treated like Invisibles was, I marveled at Naxi's calm during the ordeal.

The Ice Bridge tale has so many parts, Sanaa explained, that it takes weeks in the Madinat to see the entire narrative. Though he is not with us in Cordova, I have met the child-soul, here as Naxi, in many lifetime tales.

As we near completion of the book, frustrated by missing documents, we hear rumors of copies in Baghdad libraries. Tensions flare in our harmonious collective as we flirt with re-locating to the Buyid capitol. We argue about abandoning the Umayyads to a corrupt state, versus the universality of our work transcending politics. Some of us may leave and others remain. Oamra and I can barely share our feelings; hadn't we fled Baghdad?

I seek counsel with Raqa'maq, devoted friend over the years. The more vulnerable I feel, the more our feelings go beyond friendship. We work together at night often. He confesses his true feelings for me, harbored for years. My guard shattered, I embrace him and weep tears of joy. It is too late in my life for a sexual bond, but I have never been so happy. This is no flirtation: I have deeply loved him in secret for years. I reveal all to Raqa'maq in the hushed night of the Madinat. I do not see Oamra in the shadows, witnessing the ultimate betrayal of her life.

The Tale of the Great Bridge of Ice, continued

IV   Naxi and I passed through more villages as we left the steppe, some generous, some not, none sheltering us as long as Naxi shrieked. We entered a territory rivalry between two tribes, their war raging in full force. There was no going around this enflamed land, so Naxi and I hid behind rocks and waited until dark to travel further along the treacherous path. As we watched the violent interactions of the clans, what had seemed righteous in our own tribe now felt senseless. I felt Naxi understood, too, for he was eager to leave.

Following our escape, we gained a new attitude. It was more important to be self-sufficient than interact with every tribe, even if it meant a little thievery. I had lost any inclination to explain my child, or barter for a handful of maize. Naxi joined me in this attitude toward survival. Still, I kept my hope of a great destiny beyond the bridge of ice.

V   Despite our new aloofness, we were fascinated with some locales, customs, or dress. In one such place we encountered a kind and generous people, who welcomed us into their rituals. We spent a week there, encountering no harm in worshipping with them. My interest in these people of the northeast, besides the warm fur skins they lent us to ward off cold, was their belief in an afterlife. Convinced the soul leaves us forty-nine days after death, the tribe believed our spiritual essence traveled to a place called Gasho. We could not re-enter a human form for seven lifetimes. Our host for the week claimed he had lived as a seal, a boulder, fire-ant, the wart on his grandmother's nose, a caribou, birch tree, and a salmon that had never been speared. Naxi sat quietly, enthralled by the villagers' stories of their past lives.

It is now a matter of life and death to set foot in the Madinat. Despite Khwarazmi's clandestine efforts to canvas courtiers sympathetic to the collection, spies spread word of a seditious fiction. So it is also a matter of life and death to disseminate our work. Sadly, the group agrees to flee to Baghdad. Oamra makes no preparations; she barely speaks to me. She culls her contacts in the underground to see who is loyal and who is tainted by the corrupt state.

The Tale of the Great Bridge of Ice, continued

VI As we neared the coast, peoples of every tribe directed us to the Northeast Passage across the ice bridge. The closer we got, the more information we received. Glaciers crept forth, the bridge gained huge ice sheets, and beaches grew with receding of the sea.

VII We reached a mountain pass that looked down on the coast. The air was crisp and cold, and afforded a magnificent view of the sea. Jutting into the infinite waters, the ice bridge emerged as a grassy extension of the land. Relieved by its solidity, Naxi spent the week exploring the coastal hills.

Every action that week felt like a farewell ritual to our native continent. Daisy chains of mountain flowers became a funeral wreath. Campfires were a goodbye signal to every place we had visited. In one cave Naxi found a beautiful chamber full of long, sharp crystalline formations. The mineral was strong and gave off a crystal clear vibration to the touch. We broke off bits to take as souvenirs. On our final night we giddily made gestures with the crystals, laughing at our mock rites. Our mirth masked a deep sadness.

422

VIII On the bridge Naxi and I walked on pure ice! The frost seeped up my legs and chilled every bone in my body. The discomfort was matched by the hordes of people pressuring us to move over, in dangerous proximity to slipping and falling. We fought to stay in the middle of the march, but Naxi was closely packed in clusters of people. Being touched normally discomfited the child. Straining, he controlled his outbursts, protecting us from the tense crowd. His efforts moved me.

I realized that the mass of refugees, like us, were escaping some foe or searching for a better life. How often have souls migrated to improve their lot, find safe haven? I felt I had witnessed this many times, perhaps in my lifetimes as a fire-ant, birch tree, or crystal.

Sanaa explained: through hints I knew Oamra had observed my tryst with Raqa'maq, but she contained her anger and deeply felt hurt. She neglected me, kept her distance from the group, and gave no indication whether she was leaving with us for Baghdad. I implored her to speak about it, but she hid from me.

By the time we realized she was seriously ill, it was too late. She completed her work in private, especially with interested parties in the underground. Only when I confronted her about a bloodstain did she haughtily confess she was suffering from a respiratory ailment. I screamed at her out of grief and anger; she responded with insults and accusations. We fought through the night, expelling our hopeless, passionate energies. By dawn I apologized for my betrayal. She apologized for any hurt she was to cause me (she cause me!), and collapsed in my arms.

The Tale of the Great Bridge of Ice, continued

IX The villages on the other side of the ice bridge were overflowing with recent nomads, so Naxi and I chose to press on. I noticed Naxi curb his behavior in each new community. He stood out no more than the fact that we were foreigners. The northwest people of the new continent were hospitable and generous, and warned us of hostile territories to avoid. There were marvels: Naxi loved seeing the variety of animals, horses, flying insects, and huge, majestic birds. Enjoying our journey, we continued east. The time to settle down would make itself apparent.

X   We were unprepared for the distances on our great migration across the new continent. We followed endless rivers, climbed insurmountable heights, and hiked many extras miles to avoid glaciers. At times seventy moons felt like two days, then two days felt like seventy moons.

XI   Halfway through our journey we met the horsemen of the central plains, with great herds of beautiful sleek creatures unlike any we had ever seen. Brilliant at training loyalty into the powerful creatures, the tribe taught us their ways. We learned to ride, and received a special boon: our own ponies. In a solemn ritual, the chieftain enjoined us never to cruelly hit or shout at our horses.

Sadly, we bid farewell to these incredible folk. Happily, astride his young colt, Naxi made a greater bond with the animals of this glorious land. My son overcame his instability by paying attention to the animal life and his mental classifications. He laughed at how he'd capture his favorite animals, take care of them, and allow visitors to watch the beautiful creatures at play. I believed he imagined this invention in his mind.

As painful as Oamra's death was, it was the signal for the group to abandon Cordova for Baghdad. As we traveled there, I realized that in creating a story collection for every group of people in the world, we must include folk who developed this work long before us, the Hindus, the Persians, even the Buyids. Despite my – and Oamra's -- distasteful history with them, I must accept the eastern Islamic world.

The Tale of the Great Bridge of Ice, conclusion

XII   As we galloped forward on our journey, we received indications that we were approaching the eastern coastline of the continent. Naxi talked often about his animal enclave, and in the evenings he made toy beasts and enclosures with local rocks, sticks, and mud.

We came upon a village with another fascinating belief in the afterlife: upon death our souls fly out of our mouths. Naxi laughed aloud when he heard this image, an embarrassing moment, but I realized he had not reacted in his old, rude manner since well before the horse peoples. Yes, he annoyed me when he neglected a chore, lost in his animal kingdom. But mostly he eased me with his steadiness. It was time to settle down, the oldest idea in the world.

XIII   We were told the ocean was less than a moon's walk away. Concentrating hard on locations, I spotted our new home when we entered a small mountain range that circumscribed three lovely valleys. In one valley there were breathtaking cliffs that seemed alive with human faces. Naxi cared nothing for this sight, but he was content to establish a home for his animals.

Taken by our beautiful mounts, the people of the Three Valleys welcomed us into their fold. Although a new land to me, I sensed I had been there before, as one of the Stone Cliffs. To honor the people, their rites, and the magnificent cliffs, I revealed to the incredulous villagers the crystals from near the ice bridge. I carried them up a path toward an opening in one of the cliffs, an enormous cave with special rock formations. Here I laid my crystals, a connection to the other continent, let go of my homeland, and released my emotion into the mountain rock.

In a thrilling moment, the cave rock absorbed the crystals like delicious nectar. Shiny substance disappeared into hard stone, but then the stone came to life, the cave vibrated, and a brilliant luster spread from wall to wall and floor to ceiling. By the new moon the entire cave had transformed into a crystalline palace worthy of the village's sacred rituals. The people called me Goddess Xani, sent over a magical bridge of ice, with many myths that included my magical sprite. Naxi and I were content to play with his toy animals and rest our weary feet.

Sanaa explained: on our arrival in Baghdad I thought through the ice bridge tale and understood that one journey reflected another; they even shared a strange aspect of return. Being back where I had fallen in love with Oamra, I reflected on her past lives. Uzmeth's early years had been filled with spiritual yearning, later corrupted. Now she had finally achieved spiritual redemption, not purification in the group's eyes, but a consciousness and fulfillment of immortality.

ق

With the group still holding hands, Elvi made a rare summation of the story. "What a beautiful tale of your mother-son bond, Sahara. So deeply felt. And what a culmination!"

"A prequel to the Stone Cliff stories," Zack said.

"Whopping evidence of prehistoric past life beliefs," Diana said.

Porcy added. "A sad culmination to The 379 Group's work in Cordova."

Cachay said: "But don't forget our initial goal: proof from Sanaa that the 1001 group recalled their own past lives."

"Our past lives." Stretching, Sahara commented, "It's ironic the Forest and Ice Bridge Worlds are brand new to us, since we recalled them a thousand years ago. New and old are completely relative."

Ooma let out a scream and rushed the circle. The group clutched hands even tighter. Ooma accused Sanaa of minimizing Oamra's death. She shot her arms out to Sahara.

61

———✦✦✦———

Ooma grabbed Sahara and Amar's shoulders, and a jolt of electricity raced through the circle, sparking the qaraq's collective mind. The group saw the trunk that held the precious manuscript and the oval clasp that ignited Sanaa's recall, and now their visions.

Ooma's mind split between the present and the 10th Century, where Oamra's spirit hovered after death, ready to incarnate into a being near the 1001 qaraq. The 2002 qaraq also splintered in Time. For a full ten minutes they perceived images of their arrival in Baghdad, their final work on the book, their struggles to disseminate copies, and the future of Version 2's journey into the world.

Here is what they saw:

a sign of good fortune in Baghdad, the group immediately finds a space near the Warraqan Bookseller's Market on the eastern side of the Tigris, in an alley off the Shammasiyah Road, a lovely, dark, carpeted chamber on the ground floor, not as magical as the Maqaraqan, but cozier and more intimate, with two portico windows looking onto the quiet alley, screened in for privacy if desired;

after final touches on the manuscript, each of six members, Sanaa, Raqa'maq, Masiama, Izjis, Wa'wa, and Khwarazmi, transcribes a copy of the book. Oamra has passed, Paulina lacks the skills, Turtushi, ecstatic to be back in Baghdad, is rarely at meetings, and Li Yu serves as proofreader;

during these carefree days basking in their accomplishment, the group laughs and feasts while transcribing; for example, Izjis, riffing off the suspicion they incarnate as archetypes in the Scheherazade tale, responds to Raqa'maq's flirtatious jests to Sanaa, "After hearing this, my brother, I'd be glad to have her younger sister as my wife;"

as they work, each member plans where to send a copy, writing letters so the reception will not endanger the group; grieving, Sanaa stares forlornly at her copy, sad at losing Oamra's trusted underground contact;

on the eve of the copies being shipped off, the group celebrates the New Year of 379 A.H.; Raqa'maq toasts the European New Year of 1001, Sanaa calls for a moment of silence for Oamra's death, and the group renames their glorious work The Thousand and One Nights, *in her honor;*

hearing news that Berber forces have razed the Madinat al-Zahra, the group mourns the loss, until Paulina brings Homma the elephant to one of the portico windows to cheer everyone; after arriving from Hind, elephant and mahout become frequent visitors; the qaraqis claim telepathic connection with Homma: in Paulina's mind she sees Homma caravaning by the Zagros Mountains in Persia, envisioning a prehistoric time when mountains fell and rose with new continents, and intuiting the infinite nature of her soul;

Wa'wa confirms that Homma, whom he calls Filaq, or "Little Elephant" in his Persian dialect, told him her kind is the oldest living creature in many universes, from before the ur-Version of the stories; Izjis accuses Wa'wa of a hilarious lie, so Homma humbles him by telepathically expounding on her lineage with Ganesha, Hindu God of Timelessness, asserting that his soul is as immortal as hers, and affirming she knows all this because elephants never forget;

Sanaa tearfully reports that Homma revealed herself as Oamra's incarnation;

honoring Oamra/Homma, Sanaa locks the original manuscript inside the casket, places it atop Homma, and fastens it with a blue elephant statuette adorning the creature; the group bids Homma and mahout farewell as the two depart for Portugal, a gift to the King, hoping this willy-nilly act is as wise as the other book shipments;

Paulina drifts away from the group, but meets Homma one last time on the road out of the city, and receives a final vision, of the criminal underground, the notorious Madame Hunj, owner of Baghdad's most prominent brothel, and a deadly contest with a rival criminal over a book.

As the qaraq recovered from the onslaught of visions, Elvi asked Ooma how she was doing. Releasing her hands from Sahara and Amar, Ooma said, "Thank you, Oamra's memory was honored. But her fears for the subversive Nights manuscript were accurate. She wanted the book underground, not in the underworld."

"At a price!" Porcy rubbed her temples in anguish. "I had a recall. Early November. Sahara had told me about troubles with Amar. I went home and did a Tarot. I dealt the Death card and the Ten of Swords, a horrid looking thing about violent separation. I freaked that it was all over between them." Amar glared at his least favorite qaraqi, but Porcy wagged a finger at him. "I kept quiet 'til now because I didn't want to shake your tree house. And a voice in my head said the cards were not about you, but something I got mixed up in a thousand years ago."

Porcy sat up, ready to share a vision. "This was the vision of the near future that Paulina received in 1001. Since I was Paulina, I received it as a memory of that crime World. I was Madame Hunj."

The Tale of Madame Hunj and the Book Thief

As celebrated in Arabic literature, the crime world thrived in Baghdadi society of the 10th and 11th Centuries. We all took part in it, and in other crime worlds in the West. It was how our incarnations after the 1001 qaraq launched the copies of Version 2 into the world. It was how Naji's soul, Nozh, rejoined his qaraq after hiding in shame from murdering me in our lives as microbes. The crime World befitted his debased self esteem.

Too inflammatory for legitimate channels, the first manuscript copies were destroyed by the Buyid and Cordovan Courts. The only route open to us was the Banu Sasan, the underworld, notorious pun on the opening lines of the Scheherazade tale, where King Shahryar is identified with the clan of Persian Sasan Kings, the Banu Sasan. We appreciated the joke, so our souls plummeted to the bottom of this World, walking alongside Nozh's soiled footsteps as the gang member Nadir. Reborn with no memory of our mission as The 379 Group, our souls did not know who wanted the manuscripts, who wanted them kept hidden, or who found value in these rare books, but we felt compelled to follow the money trail.

Madame Hunj was perfectly happy to collect anonymous payments for secreting a copy of some subversive book at her infamous brothel. Some of the girls got a peek at it, learned a few stories, and entertained clients with the night tales, hiding the collection in plain sight. No matter to Hunj: the girls' storytelling ability was good for business.

The good Madame would not have allowed any harm to come to the book; she was a woman of her word. Her irresistible swaying hips made her more seductive than any of her charges (only a Caliph could afford her ministrations). But her sexuality did not disguise her capacity for violence. If a client mistreated any employee, courtesan or cook, he should fear her flaring temper. If a girl swindled the establishment, Hunj blew into a rage and snuffed out the poor soul.

Madame Hunj's reputation in Baghdad was based neither on the pleasures of her house nor the extent of her rage. She was champion of the downtrodden, took in any unfortunate from the street, and saved them through training and employment. Compassion reigned over her house, protecting her singing girls, each of whom she nicknamed. Hunj's caring extended to street workers: the 'milk cows,' as men called them, the girls who had their own rooms and signaled to their clients with surreptitious little coughs or fingers in their mouths; the 'free cows' in red leather trousers who worked the Wax Candle Market; and the 'wild cows' who received guests in the great outdoors. If any of these women ran into trouble, they could graze at Madame's house.

By the mid-11th Century the only surviving member of The 379 Group was Izjis, at seventy-five. Unaware that a copy of the book was under the patronage of Madame Hunj, Izjis assumed he had the only manuscript copy left in Baghdad. Given his feebleness, he feared for the book's security and his own life. One day he brought the book to a younger friend for safeguarding. On the way, stopping many times to catch his breath, Izjis cursed the heftiness of the volume.

It so happened that a member of a notorious crime syndicate followed Izjis. Nadir was aware of a precious book in Madame Hunj's possession. Inquiring into its value, he learned of Izjis' copy. Taking advantage of the old man's condition, the shyster approached him at a resting place. Playing the kind soul, Nadir offered to carry the book, and Izjis happily agreed. In those days, cunning was of high value in the crime world: to simply run away with the book was bad form.

Feigning enormous curiosity about the heavy volume, Nadir got the elderly man to reveal his concern for the book's safety. Nadir played his con: as a respected client at Hunj's brothel, Nadir boasted he could put in a word to the good Madame, who protected precious objects from harm. Izjis would be free to visit the book (and the girls) at any time. Izjis found the offer unusual, but being tired and curious, he delivered the book into Nadir's clutches.

Nadir left the book with his gang and that night went to Madame Hunj's. He was a frequent visitor, but as a messenger from a rival gang, not a respected customer. In a private meeting with the Madame, Nadir warned of an old man named Izjis who insisted a precious object in Hunj's care belonged to him. Soon Izjis would visit demanding the object, and claim that Nadir presented it to him, utter nonsense since

Nadir had no idea what the object was. Nadir begged Hunj to be careful, since Izjis was of unstable mind and could become violent.

Madame Hunj was unsure why Nadir supplied this information. And, as far as she knew, the object was the book, perhaps the only copy in the world, which explained the price paid for its security. She had no idea of its history, though she knew a fifth of its stories were of Jewish origin, a fact she quietly cherished given her mother's heritage. She warily thanked Nadir, and sent him out the back door.

Nadir's exit was lucky, for poor Izjis sauntered into the establishment minutes later. He was almost tossed out on his ear, but then Hunj ushered him into her chambers. Izjis did exactly as Nadir warned, Hunj questioned how he could possibly know about the book, and he became obstinate and flustered. Hunj's henchmen roughed up the old man, pulling out teeth and cauterizing his temples to exact a confession, but he screamed, pleaded that the book was his, and threatened violence. Exasperated by his intransigence, Madame Hunj picked up a paring knife, slit the unfortunate man's throat, and ordered his body thrown in the Tigris.

Madame Hunj was never remorseful about doing violence to an oppressor of a victim, but by the same token, she recognized when unjust violence was perpetrated. When she felt remorse over Izjis' demise, as if part of her soul had been torn out, she suspected Nadir of duping the old man out of his true belonging. She had to act fast, before Nadir gained any more ground. Dressed in a gorgeous blue veil, she went with two guards to Nadir's home, and making a great seductive show of it, offered her luscious body in gratitude for the warning about the awful, old maniac.

They made love until dawn. Having gained Nadir's intimate trust, Hunj confessed she was in awe of him, since she guessed he had tricked another copy of the book out of the old man. With erotic flattery, she promised to put Nadir in contact with those paying mightily to protect the book. She needed to show Izjis' copy to them, a delicate matter only she could perform. As collateral she offered Nadir her book while she held his.

His lust satisfied, Nadir agreed to everything. That evening he returned to the brothel. Hunj made a show of retrieving a carefully wrapped volume, not the true book. Not knowing any better, Nadir handed over his copy. He was treated to the most wonderful evening, but by dawn he too was at the bottom of the Tigris. Near the end of this night, Hunj entered the room where three girls pleasured Nadir. Dismissing the girls, she spoke softly as she stroked his manhood.

"I do not like being used by anyone, especially my rivals. Your little trick with Izjis did just that, and worse: it forced me to murder an innocent man. For that you'll pay with your own life." She squeezed Nadir, just enough to match pain with pleasure.

Nadir had been tricked in equal measure. Hunj held his life in her hand. Surrendering to her touch, he imagined thousands of invisible organisms springing forth. The image brought him to another lifetime, though he did not understand it as such. He was one of those organisms, capable of endlessly generating precious copies of himself, and, as a germ, holding a gargantuan creature's life in the balance with a crippling disease. Nadir envisioned another microbe life, alongside Hunj's soul. Here he snuffed out her life, and she accepted it as the natural order.

Nadir looked into Hunj's eyes. *Here we are again, paying off debts. So be it, as it is in the natural order, it is in the criminal code. Kill and be killed, all part of a day's work.* "You have me by the short hairs, Madame. Well played. Tell me, since I take it to my grave, why are these books so important?"

Hunj smiled and eased up on Nadir's precious parts. "I do not know. It's a collection of old stories. The Court destroyed a copy because it threatens the Empire. My code demands I protect Izjis' copy, too. Or sell it to my patron, who wants the book protected."

Nadir laughed. "Our code is a marriage of greed and honor." With that, Madame Hunj brought her rival to the most outstanding bliss of his short life. At its climax, she motioned and her bodyguard gently ran his dagger across Nadir's neck. At that instant Nadir's ecstasy was mixed not with fear, but respect. Hunj served the mysterious books better than he had.

Thus we spent our next lifetimes, passing the books through the underworld, betraying each other, quickly forgiving our betrayals. The ideal harmony we reached as a qaraq vanished in 1001, but we held on to it for dear life.

ق

Looking at Naji sleeping, Porcy spoke of Nadir. "Sorry for offing your baby, Sahara."

Stroking Naji's head, Sahara said, "Sounds like he got his karma's worth. Poor soul."

The comment irked Ooma. "What about me? While I was alive you mocked my warnings about the book's security. Then you happily murder each other in the crime World to protect it."

"Shut it, girl!" Porcy had always championed Ooma, and had supported Oamra in Cordova as Paulina. But after this miraculous night, Ooma's nasty comment was the last straw. Ooma had denigrated Bax and screamed at Sahara. Porcy was done.

Dr. Machiyoko expressed genuine concern for Ooma. "Do you know who you are?"

Ooma stared intensely at the therapist. "You do not recognize me? You insult me this way? I am Oamra, she who has been abused by her qaraq."

Dr. Machiyoko took Ooma's hands. "We are not Cordovans. You're in the 21st Century. It's the church. There's Bax. There's Verle and Elvi. I know we've hurt you, but you are Ooma."

Ooma took in the last words, shamefully, her delusion slowly dawning on her face. She buried her head on Diana's shoulder. "Naji's not the only ravaged soul here," she mumbled. Amar approached and gently led Ooma to a bench.

434

62

—◦◦◦—

Stifling yawns and growing tired of the group's dramas, Elvi entreated the group to finish up the food and prepare for one final story. Making sure Ooma was stable, Elvi promised her the next tale would honor Oamra's memory further. Ooma smiled at Elvi, gathering inner strength.

Amid empty champagne cups and soiled napkins, Elvi reconvened the meeting. "First I want to acknowledge a crucial breakthrough. Your 10th Century incarnations saw past life tales, so now you can access recalls from the 1001 qaraq. I'd like to give you an example of such a story."

Before Oamra died, al-Turtushi took the old star lamp (one of Sanaa's birthday gifts), and re-fashioned it into a magnificent fixture that shot rays of light. He claimed it spread light on recalls and reflected Oamra's beauty.

At the 1001 qaraq's last meeting, Turtushi hung the brilliant lamp so all would remember Oamra. Its illumination cast a spell on Turtushi. Through ordained images, he foresaw that Europe, primitive in relation to Islam's accomplishments in science, mathematics, and arts, would catch up over the next five centuries, mixing many cultural identities. The qaraq's work to make Version 2 an amalgam of multiple cultures was way ahead of its time. Perhaps it would have a share of influence on the synthetic developments in Europe and the world.

Turtushi's soul, Bal, flew ahead to the 18ᵗʰ Century. During that time in his soul's journey, Bal had withstood bizarre challenges: time traveling as the roukh and being stuck in the Donne room as an iconic book. His immersion as a literary object led him to incarnate into a scriptorial life as a Christian monk in Syria.

The Tale of Dom Denis Chavis

Diyunisus Shawish was more drawn to the fables of the common people than the parables of the Good Book. The young priest took advantage of a travel opportunity by attending the Greek School of Athanasius in Constantinople. It was his first experience of foreigners interested in stories from the Levant, stories he had brought in manuscript and memory.

One such devotee was a Carpathian Jew named Zadek, come from Paris to find manuscripts of *Alf Layla wa Layla*. The rage for fairy tales had died down, and Zadek had the sad hope that discovering a complete version of *Alf Layla* might revive interest. When the priest asked, Zadek explained the European craze for the *Nuits*, demanding all one thousand and one portions of the meal. Antoine Galland had used a manuscript with a third as much. When Galland ran out of authenticated tales, Veronique d"O, Zadek's mentor, encouraged him to pad the edition. The Nuits was one version of a millennia-old entity, so there was no such thing as an authentic compilation.

Heartened by Zadek's confidences, the priest revealed a Syrian manuscript from Aleppo that contained marvelous tales akin to the Nuits. Perusing the fourteen delightful stories, Zadek told the priest that, with the revival of the fairy tale, he could set himself up nicely in Paris.

Zadek's words stayed with the priest, outliving Zadek, who never accomplished the mission for Veronique d'O. But the meeting between the two men set in motion the next chapter in the history of the Nights in Europe. In the 1780s, Minister Breteuil called the priest to Paris to do some Arabic research in the Bibliothèque du Roi. Jumping at the opportunity, Diyunisus Shawish became Dom Denis Chavis, and took a tiny flat near the neglected Jardin du Luxembourg.

As if Zadek exerted his will from Heaven, Chavis' arrival in the French capitol coincided with a new interest in exotic tales. In the great imperial library Chavis found Galland's Arabic manuscript and studied the French edition. Marveling, he saw where Galland had implanted stories from other sources, like the Tale of Sindbad, and how Galland had suppressed the Nights numbers that divide Scheherazade's narrations into small portions and tick off a countdown to a thousand and one. Chavis determined to continue where Galland had left off.

To cash in on the new hunger from the Parisian audience, publisher Paul Barde hired Chavis to translate new tales for a *Continuation* of Galland's Nuits. Chavis had the material, but his translations were awkward mixes of French and Italian, so Barde enlisted the elder raconteur Cazotte to clean things up. Happy for the comeback, Cazotte went to work. Barde falsely announced to the public that a full manuscript existed in the Bibliothèque, enabling a *Continuation*.

Elvi explained to the 2002 qaraq: Turtushi's vision was a feather in the 1001 qaraq's cap: their work would last centuries! But as Li Yu, Elvi explained to the 1001 qaraq that their subversive work would face great persecution. Nights manuscripts would be desecrated and destroyed. But Turtushi's image of the Nights achieving wonderful popularity stuck with the qaraq, not Li Yu's caveat. Their dream of a full, thriving Nights was false.

Bax lost track of how much champagne he had drunk, and the bubbles went to his head. When Elvi claimed the hopeful Nights' future was false, Bax knew in his heart that Turtushi's view of Chavis was in error as well. Bax had been Chavis: his family named him Diyunisus, but often called him Bacchus. Bax and Bacchus. He had a truer memory of Chavis, which he shared.

The Tale of Dom Denis Chavis, conclusion

Paris is expensive. A loaf of bread! Same as food for a week in Aleppo. A little translating, a little tutoring? The Minister's stipend helps. I need more. Need more tales. Add to Galland. My own manuscript's not Nights. Can I make a thousand and one? That would make my fortune.

Must create an Arabic Nights manuscript. Galland an inspiration. Start copying Arabic sources from Galland. Then insert his added tales. Translate them from French back into Arabic. Next add new tales from my Aleppo manuscript. Need more. Can pad a story with poems. Characters yearn: love poem. Add a whole Night with a poem. Push the collection to six hundred Nights numbers. Still need more.

Cazotte slows me down. So demanding. Barde breathes down his neck. Cazotte blames me. Slowpoke Syrian. Because I copy in Arabic. Plus translate to French! Cannot reveal this secret. Deceive them all. Sinful courtiers. Greedy publishers. Promise Barde there's a complete Nights. Will God forgive my lie?

I am not the only deceiver. Cazotte complains of my sloppy translation though he knows no Arabic. But he does more than tidy my French. 'Improves upon it', he says. Alters original language. Adds plot details. Whole characters. *Et maintenaut!* His own story! So why should I repent? Galland deceived public. Cazotte does him one worse.

Barde loses patience. Does away with Nights numbers. Just like Galland. No faith in reaching thousand and one. After first edition of *Continuation* Barde abandons project.

At first reviews are good. Call the work entertaining. Full of instruction about customs of the Arabs. Translated into many languages. But by close of 18th Century it's lambasted as false and unliterary. British hate it. Damn them! Dr. Patrick Russell. Brags of his manuscript from Aleppo. All is lost. I quit work on Nights. Sin of forgery. Voices chant in my head. Right wrong right wrong. Zadek encouraged me. Lead public toward Infinite! After Galland forgery easier. Write wrong write wrong. Thought I could pay the royal rent. Wrong rite. Unheroic. Abandon new Nights manuscript. At six hundred thirty-one nights. Let another sinner discover it.

ق

"That's Chavis' claim to fame," Sahara said, "not the *Continuation*, pretty useless as Nights material, but the unfinished manuscript he left in the Bibliothèque du Roi. It was the next crumb on the path to a full European Nights. Others found it, saw his methods, and 'topped it off'."

"So our 1001 qaraq had a vision of a glorious future," Porcy said, "but their Version was suppressed, and Chavis' work a sham. A sad way to end tonight's saga."

"There's another point of view," Sahara said. "There are many Nights versions, none truly authentic. Storytellers in the souk changed tales freely. Given this practice, European adaptations join an acceptable tradition. So we shouldn't lament or criticize the 1001 qaraq's misinterpretation."

"But I deceived the world," Bax said. "Chavis didn't do it in the open market."

"All right, enough 1001 qaraq for one night, if not a lifetime." Elvi was tired and losing patience. "You all have another purpose tonight. To accept Amar and Ooma or not."

The group tensed at Elvi's reminder of their problem. Mindful of his new risk-taking, Bax spoke. "I'm in the hot seat anyway. Never thought I'd say it, but I'm okay with Amar." The group nodded in assent. "But Ooma, you drove us crazy all night."

439

"You're blending yourself and Oamra," Diana said. "I'm concerned."

"I'm in no state to decide about you, Ooma baby." The group agreed with Porcy. "Too many sour notes. 1001 qaraq was clueless. Bax botched Version 3. Ooma's nuts. Hey, wanna hear something positive?"

"Spit it out," Zack said, "before I stick my head in the church oven."

"This space was awesome, brothers and sisters!" Porcy said. "Don't ya think? Verle?"

Feeling pressured, Verle chose his words carefully. "The Maqaraqan was like the Donne room, a universe unto itself. Not sure we can achieve that here."

"We'll help you look into it, if that worries you," Zack said. "Our own magical space."

"All right," Verle said, looking tired and old. "We'll look into our own Maqaraqan."

"Fabulous. I'm tabling your other decision about Ooma. Can I adjourn this meeting?" Elvi pleaded. "Before dawn interrupts?"

Humiliated, and disappointed her invitation to join was once more delayed, Ooma slipped out before Bax could say anything to her. Not everyone was ready to leave, so Elvi excused herself before she was grilled for more advice. Despite his continued concern for Ooma, Amar enjoyed his new status in the group. Verle supervised the restoration of order in the sanctuary.

Finally, it was time to go. Stepping into the cold morning air, Sahara and Amar saw a beautiful reddish glow on the horizon, illuminating the New York City skyline. Sahara thought of the moment at the end of each of the thousand and one nights, when the coming of dawn saved Scheherazade from the King. She looked at her husband and felt a chill run through her bones.

63

———❧———

January 1, 2002. Month 4.

Sahara sat in Naji's darkened room watching him sleep, a light drizzle pattering on the window. Naji slept through New Year's Day, and she was glad of it: if he reversed his sleep pattern in the New Year, perhaps other problems would resolve. She was most worried about his speech difficulties. He leaked stories at the meeting, but Sahara would forego this telepathic ability if it meant he could play naturally with other children. How wrong to be upset when his normal speech developed and storytelling powers diminished. She should have rejoiced!

Naji struggled out of sleep, wondering where he was. He imagined himself at a meeting in the Maqaraqan, a fountain warmly gurgling nearby. Then he remembered he was the only one not involved in those monumental events, and he was sad. The qaraq had not involved him in the meeting, though he heard bits of their tales. The twins had given him an injunction not to share recalls with the group, which made him sadder still. He yearned to interact with the group again.

Thinking of the twins in his half-awake state, Naji drifted back to his mother and Cachay in the hospital months before, when in his mind the twins approached him in the interlife.

September 20. 9 Days after Impact.

The Tale of the Eleven Gugglets of Water

The twins led him to a darkened library, a light drizzle pattering on the window. They procured one of the many volumes of the Akashic Record, the catalogue of souls and their lifetimes. Displaying a list of the qaraq's lives from the 1600s, the twins offered Nozh a ride down a rabbit hole of knowledge. But the child was incredibly thirsty. Ignoring his request for water, the twins urged him to travel back in time. When Nozh begged, the twins consented to give him a drink if he went on eleven visits to see eleven visions of eleven lifetimes. Nozh wept that he was only a baby.

Finally, one of the twins gave Nozh a gugglet of water and promised he'd get another after the first visit. The gugglet was so refreshing that Nozh felt fortified to go on an adventure. The other twin pulled out a key he had shown Nozh previously. He waved it over a page in the Akashic Record. With a deep gurgle, the three of them swooped into the World on that page. Nozh saw a pubescent boy, Baachetelle, on his baby-sitter's lap, fondling her. Nozh did not understand, but Baachetelle seemed very confident for someone his age and Nozh liked that. Even more, Nozh liked Baachetelle's toy, a set of cages with tiny people inside.

Nozh gasped in delight at the miniature Xoo, but the twin waved the key and they were back in the library. They gave Nozh another gigglet of water, waved the key over another page, and traveled to a different World. There Nozh saw a population following lighted paths on a city sidewalk. Each person muttered a unique non-verbal sound. A fish-like man rode into town on a bumper car. Arguing about a more accurate destination, the twins pulled back to the library.

After another gushlet, Nozh finally appeared in the 1600s, in John Donne's room. Satisfied they had located the correct century, the twins gave Nozh large gurglets as he watched scenes from Draill U, the Lady in Red's travels, and the Inchnadamp coven. Another substantial jiggeret and Nozh saw his 17th century lives: a waif traveling on the heels of an army during the Thirty Years War; a spirit flying over Europe, spreading a soulful Idea during the senseless War; the boy Nils, avoiding enemy soldiers while scavenging food.

Before each World there was pure darkness. The twins whispered in the child's ear to comfort him, though Nozh did not understand a word. But with the penultimate garglet, Nozh saw and heard nothing in the dark World; it was a never-space that trapped the Red Witch and the roukh. When Nozh saw the frightful creatures he panicked, but in the never-space he got terribly mixed up running in circles. The twins pulled him out, but Nozh thought it was a mean trick and refused to go on the eleventh excursion. They promised him an extra gulpert. He could not resist. Did each drink made him thirstier?

Nozh wandered in a vast storehouse containing all the plunder of the Thirty Years War. He walked miles searching for a way out, with no help from the twins. He didn't like how they played! Nozh tried to enjoy the booty, but everything was burned or scarred by the ravages of war. This was no place for a child! Nozh sat on a broken trunk and cried.

Between sobs, Nozh remembered Cta in the interlife, as lost as he was now but able to overcome. With her inspiration, he knew he would retain his soul. He embraced this hope, and reality shifted. He was out of the storehouse, out of the 1600s, out of the library, the twins' clutches, and the interlife, and back at the hospital, at Cachay's bedside, holding her hand. Soon they walked together, her health fully restored, on the way to his mother's hospital room.

When Sahara heard about Cachay rescuing Naji from the twins in the interlife, the full impact of losing her babies stormed down upon her.

Knocked from her numb state, the blow triggered an intolerable grief. She ordered Cachay to leave the room and take the child with her. Her reaction hurt Naji worse than any of the twins' devilry.

ق

January 1, 2002. Month 4.

Naji pretended to continue sleeping because his mother was at his side. If she had been that upset in the hospital, did the sight of him remind her of losing the twins? Is that why she worked so hard, and stayed away from father? The twins had no souls in her belly, and they were mean: why be sad? Naji did not want anything to do with them anymore.

Was it another mean trick when the twins told him to keep silent? If it would make his mother happy, why not tell her stories? Why not tell everyone stories? He thought of a lifetime to share; should he say it out loud, or inside her mind?

As he pondered, his mother touched his head. "My sweet little Prince, please come back to me. If you let me in, Your Majesty, we shall consent that you set up residence here." She touched her heart with her other hand. Then she caressed his soft locks as she curled a finger in her own sunshine hair. His mother's touch was wonderful, but deterred Naji from communicating. So much easier to let the delicate strokes soothe his soul.

In another minute, he was sound asleep.

444

64

—⟨∅∅∅⟩—

January 2. Month 4.

Two days after the New Years meeting, Sahara had a string of visitors, the ladies of the qaraq. Cachay brought an apple pie, Diana checked on Sahara's fragile balance with Amar, and Porcy just wanted company. Cachay grimaced as Porcy appropriated her pie and cut into it.

"I can't bear to be parted from my sister for more than hour," Porcy said. They revisited many moments, including Sahara's confession about losing Amar's financial support. They all supported her independence.

Amar entered the house, with a visitor. "Someone wants to apologize," he said, ushering in Ooma. Sincerely, Ooma acknowledged her odd behavior and asked for understanding from the women. She even let Sahara off the hook, promising to stay away from the group until she got her act together. The women brushed off her apology with kind words. But Sahara was quiet, and went to show the women out, leaving Ooma and Amar alone.

"I'll be loyal to you in the qaraq as you were to me at work," Amar said. "How is it there?"

Ooma deflected the question. "I was thinking back on the Fall, and remembered I had a recall at the office. The week I came back to work."

She patted the couch next to her. "Wanna hear?" Amar thought of his wife saying goodbye to her friends at the front door, still talking a blue streak. He walked over, sat, and gestured for Ooma to begin.

October 10, 2001. Week 5.

I was very loyal to you at Bruckner, and I wondered if your wife had such a pure loyalty, she who walked away from you two years ago who claims you as soul mate in stories but struggle with you: where do I figure in that?

I was very anxious coming back to work. I hadn't been near a corporate building since the attacks, I knew everyone would have an attitude toward me; I may have assimilated into American society but the terrorists had ruined it for all of us and I feared my co-workers weren't going to help.

But most everyone was kind in a forced not knowing what to say manner they said very little directly which drove me crazy so I adopted a direct approach, especially strangers I saw in the elevator: Don't worry I was in Building 2 during 9/11: I have no love for terrorism but they looked at me funny didn't see an Islamic woman but an assimilated person of indeterminate color so I had to make a statement and be clear to myself

I took up the veil no big deal I wore a headscarf all childhood abandoning it as a geeky teen but it was a big deal at work and I could explain that it's important that Islam is not punished but understood but people would rather gossip than understand a Persian-American girl's cultural dilemma so my attitude hardened toward everyone at Bruckner and I felt compelled to stand up for you at the end of that first week back I was at my desk feeling bad for myself and angry at the world and I thought back to old Umh during the 1600s exiled from ancient Egypt who had to take over new Umh's soul and take advantage of the geo-political situation and probably was a victim of it like I was currently and my heart opened to her heightened by my discomfort being back at work

446

I looked at my hands and saw patterns in my skin like henna treatment the shapes like letters and I saw a box a casket the symbols were filigree carvings on the outside; at the time I didn't know about the chest Raq'amaq gave Sanaa in Cordova hateful present that made Oamra jealous and snoop and discover the love between them breaking her heart this was that loathsome box but now it was laid to rest on a trash heap of war and I saw it in the 1600s but knew I witnessed another's life.

The Tale of the Ensouled Casket

The wars could not go on. The Hapsburgs had ravaged every nation, even some Islamic states, and now their own duchies suffered the same fate. The New World had been plundered of resources to fund the war. We were in desperate shape, the people responding with bitter revolts. Noble houses were sacked or forfeited their goods. Each enemy storehoused these goods. With the chaos of war, the storehouses fell into disarray, one treasure pile mistaken for another, a Spanish tiara thrown on a heap with a French necklace. Forgotten, luxuries lost all worth.

Many of our souls were lost in the Thirty Years War, but not destroyed. That would have been a kinder fate. We wandered the skies of Europe, looking down on a shredded continent and hoping for a belief to unite our spirits. We found comfort in the Idea, a philosophy contained in a poem, a universe in a room. Meandering through the ether, we sought that mystical space. Some of us found a refuge, some of us reincarnated, and some of us were trapped in a false hideaway.

I fell to Earth, into darkness, into one of the forgotten storehouses. I smelled metal: swords, chainmail, halberds, pikes, and daggers. A dragon's lair of weaponry, all left for dead by the human dragons of war. Was this the sacred place I had prayed for? Now I prayed to be rescued from it.

As my panic subsided, I noted that my soul inhabited a casket of medium size, too small for a dowry, too large for jewels. I knew this casket: it had been in my soul's history for centuries. Its important key had been lost, but worse, warriors had forced the lock, itself an important keepsake.

An ensouled object has its own unspoken history. When I embodied the casket, I perceived all its misfortunes, the love triangle it caused, the theft of its original treasure, the deceit of Oolon's brother Xa making off with it. Its metal was weary of the dessicating War. I took all into my being.

For lifetimes my soul had yearned to join the venture of humanity, and when it did my joy was so boundless that I accepted any pain befitting the human cause. But I grew tired of the fights and violence. What worth was this human folly, and why had I desired it so? This was the reason I claimed the miserable casket, to reflect on my overinflated expectations of a barbaric species.

With this revelation the casket transported to a magical never-space, the Donne room where my qaraq lay trapped in the particular objects of our fate. I sat across from a cudgel-shaped key with a nasty attitude, the key that could open the trunk. Disenchanted, we had no desire to accomplish such things. In that room-as-a-netherworld, we ensouled many objects. But our souls were lost.

ق

I pondered this recall for a long time, Ooma recounted, *ignoring work duties at Bruckner. At first I could not see why I had received this story, only recognizing details: my lifetime as the Chinese femme fatale Oolon whom I had not realized was betrayed for gold by her brother Xa (Bax!); or the loss of the casket's original treasure which I now understand was the Original of Version 2 but why had I envisioned this pathetic soul passively entombed as a casket and with that clarifying question the answer was clear: I was meant to see a cautionary tale of a soul in torment because I should not feel sorry for myself even if I too was a soul in torment hounded by people so the first choice I made back at Bruckner was to defend you, Amar, I could not stand by as a friend was treated badly and as I learned about our time in Baghdad I was proud to retain Islamic roots in the modern world and later when you were fired I felt guilty a lowly intern stayed on at the downsized offices downsized in Jersey City and I felt I owed you something to make amends so I became outspoken and defiant, verging on the mildly insane.*

January 2. Month 4.

Amar was touched by Ooma's loyalty and suffering. He felt an urge to comfort her, to do more than that. He placed his hand on hers and looked in her eyes. But as he leaned forward, Sahara entered the den. Amar removed his hand quickly.

"Sorry, I was waiting by the front door. Didn't want to interrupt a recall in progress."

"From the Fall." Ooma was surprisingly calm at Sahara's intrusion. "A foreshadowing of the Cordovan casket." She stood up. "I hope the ladies accepted my apology."

"You didn't have to apologize," Sahara said.

Ooma steeled herself. "No, I didn't. Seeing everyone here, it felt like the thing to say. I actually came to tell you something else. It seems my support of Amar has cost me my job."

"Oh my God!" Amar said. "I knew this would happen."

"I'm very sorry," Sahara said.

Amar leaned forward, shaking his head. Hyper-vigilance, Dr. Machiyoko called it, but when everything is falling apart, am I really imagining the worst? The attacks, then the twins, then the job, Ooma's fragility, and now *her* job. He was sick of it, especially everyone's anguish.

"I'll never work for Wall Street cretins again," he said. "It's the wrong response to the attacks, it's what the terrorists want, but I can't help it. Ooma, I'll do whatever I can to help."

Sahara listened to her husband in shock. She had not heard such sympathy when she lost the twins. He expressed more feeling to Ooma in a few minutes than she had received in months. A pillar of stone,

Sahara saw the truth of what had bothered her for weeks. Her friends were right: it wasn't about money. She was furious about Amar's lack of support for her loss of the twins. The depth of that grief had been too intense for her to see clearly. She was devastated by Amar's failure. Was it possible for them to live together in a semblance of a relationship?

65

———⟞ʘ⟝———

January 7. Month 4.

Cachay cursed the stairs leading to Verle's attic. She hoped the Maqaraqan would excite the group to find Verle a new space. When she finally made it, breathless, she was upset to find Porcy.

"Whatever you came to tell Verle you can tell me," Porcy insisted. "Come on, babe, we just went through an ordeal together. Surely New Year's means something."

"That ordeal," Cachay said, "included you accusing me of callousness during 9/11. Next you'll dismiss me as an evil aristocrat in the 10th Century."

Verle puttered in a corner, but decided to referee. "Did you bring some news, my friend?"

Cachay threw herself down on a chair. "Yes! The *ordeal* flipped a power switch for me. I'm having my own recalls again!"

"That is wonderful news," Verle said.

"Congratulations, sweetie, and I mean it," Porcy said. "What's the recall?"

"First, I'm going to gloat and tell you exactly how I got the vision. I was watching an old Jacques Cousteau documentary on television, with an underwater camera moving through bizarre plant life and odd-shaped creatures. I laughed to myself that I must have lived in a World like that. I let my mind enter the liquid jungle. I didn't end up in the ocean, but it was the first recall I'd willed in months! Complete with a scientific preface, which I wrote down." Cachay pulled out a small journal and read aloud.

The Tale of the Nasal Microbiome

Metagenomics provides the genetic description of a single microbial community, as well as on any individual aspect of that microbiome, such as the prevalence of a particular bacterial species.

Corpa Coustae! What a vile jolt, what violent expulsion! Hurtling with my compatriots, blown out of our world, through the opening of the cosmos. Thrust into a vast, light space, a terrible infinity of openness. Airborne thus, my flight slows, I float for a small eternity, then begin a gravitational descent. Falling! Cruel medium, or non-medium, not like our thick, moisture-filled substance, our life-water. Thin air is a death sentence: no resistance to stop me falling to my doom.

Gracia Gente! The air moves! We waft en masse in a horizontal direction, saving us. A strange breeze lifts us, sends us back down, then forward in a new direction. Is this worse than straight plunging? Should I have wished for a swift death? Now the air has a compulsive nature, pulling us in a single direction toward a focal point. Where are we headed?

Ah, familiar world! We enter an environment with substance, unlike the thinning air outside. But we are not where we started; this is new territory. The life-water is not as rich as my home world. There are fewer of my fellows and more of that disgusting fungal family, with the strange looking cousins. All that hair! Always asking for a loan. Where can I curl up and hide?

My wish is granted too soon. Before I find a hideaway the violent wind blows us into the bright void again. Mixed with those filthy fungi. It is not freefall or thin air I mind as much as being outdoors, in open space. Some find it liberating. For me freedom is our jungle-like world, full of branching arbors and soft membranous tissue to shelter us. Here there is too much space, too much emptiness. I scream aloud, then another inhalation of the wind pulls us to another environment.

Inside this jungle, I latch onto my own kind, nestled into a soft bower of mucus. Perfect harmony, as in our home world, where other organisms respected us, and everyone knew their place. I am grateful to be in a perfectly balanced society, with few fungal outliers.

But the expulsions continue from one world to another. At least we enter consistent host populations: human nasal cavities, evident from the hair forests. Each individual host is different in the make-up of its microbiome, the community of microorganisms colonizing the nasal cavity. The metagenome, the millions of genes constructing the organisms, has roughly the same ingredients, but each individual has a combination specific to its microbial recipe. This nose has a preponderance of *Cladosporium*, those pesky fellows with the funny dialect; that beak has barely enough *Candida*, the bedrock of the nasal crust; a third cavity is crawling with *Saccharomycetales*, who flatter you in that sugary-sweet way; a fourth is half *Aureobasidium* (Lord help us, such indulgence).

As the humans blow us from one nose to another, it is clear an epidemic plagues them. This is not a normal disease to cause such frequent expulsions, nor is there normal inflammation in the passageways we traverse. There is a toxic virus among us.

All this is deeply disturbing. My initial distress over obnoxious populations now seems petty. I can accept a few scrappy yeasts in my turf, in the face of this dread. What if one of my hosts is at death's door, and before expelling me, expires, abandoning me in a decaying body, my own death not far behind? The thought plagues me, as if I've undergone it over and over again.

I will not give up my standards. I scrutinize every bug and weed in every neighborhood. Maybe my quest for a highborn microbiome will lead us to a healthy host, safe from harm.

I make a startling discovery. The more streamlined a community, say with a preponderance of *Aspergillus*, with no *Fusarium* and *Cryptococcus* thrown in, the less healthy the human. The 'purer' the genetic population, the greater its vulnerability. A community with diverse gen-ethnicities is stronger. How ironic! To survive I have to mingle with the masses.

I had yearned for a replica of my original microbiome, the purest of human nasal societies. But a nasal nation with several shades of *Candida* might flourish compared to a community purged of *Cryptococcus*. Could a pure core even exist? I now value a messier polyglot of a society.

Because of the prevalence of disease, I did not last long in this lifetime. But I survived longer than my old, purist friends, and lived in harmony with many diverse groups. No longer am I grateful for an esteemed incarnation, but rather for my esteem of life's diversity.

ق

"That explains a great deal," Porcy said, in response to Cachay's tale, "a great deal."

Cachay did not like being appraised by Porcy. Diplomatically, Verle congratulated Cachay on receiving a story, then asked for Porcy's explanation.

"Naji's microbiome lifetime preceded his time as the thief of Version 2," Porcy said. "He exterminated me as a germ, then, ashamed, avoided the qaraq during The 379 Group. As Madame Hunj I killed the thief in karmic response. Maybe your life preceded *your* 1001 qaraq time."

"That explains a great deal?" Cachay spat out. "So what?"

Porcy exhaled. "I'm not done. You showed up at the Madinat as a haughty courtier. This microbiome World prepared you to work with aristocrats and commoners alike in the 1001 qaraq."

"On a book about diversity, to bring the world together," Verle added.

454

"Not a total soul correction," Porcy jabbed, "but you loosened up, honey."

"You know what? Honey?" Cachay's tone was pure venom. "I came here to share a recall with Verle and feel good about myself. Not to be rated on soul corrections. Or to enter a race, Verlin, about how our present racial diversity makes us open to diversity in our past lives. At least I didn't depend on crazy Ooma to have my recall like you did." Cachay stomped out of Verle's attic.

66

January 26. Month 5.

All month Sahara and Amar avoided what had happened between them at the New Year's meeting. Amar had been pre-occupied with Ooma, Sahara with the tangential visions that turned out to be The 379 Group's own recalls. But she had gone off on Amar, revealing her anger and sense of futility. The day after she had realized the depth of her despair over Amar's lack of support about the twins. It was too much to communicate, especially in light of Ooma's loss of her job. Again Sahara retreated behind the cover of her work. Three chapters and counting! Prof. Agib convinced her the end was in sight.

Amar did not impede her progress. The severance package from Bruckner was not enough to ease Sahara financially as she completed her thesis. The least he could do was get out of her way. It felt hypocritical to Amar that he confessed to Sahara's best friend, his therapist, and not his wife.

It was killing Diana, too, but she gave Amar a thumbs-up to help Ooma get back on her feet. Ooma was secure at home, finishing her business degree. She needed Amar's support, and it made him feel better. Amar did not admit his attraction to Ooma, which disturbed the therapist.

As for Amar's hyper-vigilance, Dr. Machiyoko had coached him to be relaxed and present. She listened to his job ideas; once he spread the word in the business community that he was leaving Wall Street, Amar felt better about himself. Convinced that problems with his marriage were real, he strategized talking heart-to-heart with Sahara, not losing his temper. But he feared the outcome.

Since Sahara remained at a distance, it was up to Amar to initiate conversation. He invited her to Roy's for a tête-à-tête. The talk was long overdue, and she too feared the worst, especially since the restaurant had been the scene of a bad fight. It was a local hangout for the town, and Sahara recognized several people there. They ordered, willing themselves to stay calm.

To allay her fears, Sahara took control of the conversation. "I'm heartened about Naji. He's talking more, clearer baby talk. Trying to connect again. He's come to terms with something."

"What do you think it is?" Amar asked. "I've noticed the change, too."

"I think he protected himself from our angst after 9/11. He's a super sensitive soul."

"And a baby. So he's healing from the shock, like the rest of us," Amar said.

"I think he retreated into a fantasy world. That prevented him from connecting somehow. But he sparked recalls on New Year's. I had glints before. Bax got one, too."

"You know Naji communicated with Bax?" Amar felt a flush of anger.

"Settle down, Godzilla." Their food arrived amid a tense silence. "I told you Bax checked on me after the attacks, and came over to the house."

"You did?" Amar dug a mussel out of its shell. "Remind me."

September 18, 2001.   Day 8.

Bax insisted on helping Sahara in some way. Was there anything needed in the house or yard? Although Bax worked as a groundskeeper,

Amar refused to hire him. Bax found lots to fault in the lawn, but seeing debris clogging the gutters, he was appalled. Naji was down for his nap, so Sahara showed Bax the ladder, watched him climb up safely to the gutters, and went back inside.

An hour later, Naji woke. Sahara carried him outside to check on Bax. The young man sat on the edge of the roof, staring into space. Frightened for his life, Sahara snapped Bax out of reverie and insisted he come into the house. Over lemonade, she asked what had happened.

"I was finishing up when I heard a voice calling. I must have gone into trance."

No wonder Sahara had stopped hearing work on the roof. She looked down at her sleepy child. Had Naji sent Bax into another world? "Where did you go, Bax?"

"The Jewish place you remembered last Spring, where you were one of three brothers."

"Okopy," Sahara said, "in old Poland. The shtetl. I was Shemuel, Amar was my older brother Alter, and Naji the youngest, Noam. They both died in pogroms. Is that right?"

"Yes. The story was told by Shemuel. Noam had just died."

Sahara held Naji tighter. "Tell me what happened to Shemuel."

The Tale of the Elusive Cave

What a nightmare to see little Noam deteriorate as a column of air! It was like that old tale, when a shipwrecked sailor sees a silver column turn into a ghoul. Noam was an afterlife apparition, but I got him to speak as my baby brother, and reveal a secret place where I could see him and Alter.

Now I had a mission, into which I could channel my grief. Find this magical place! I searched all the hills looking for caves, climbing down into their treacherous depths, wandering by torchlight through hidden trails. I broke my hermetic seal and craved unusual gossip in the taverns, like an Idea circulating Western Europe: a room containing the universe. As a hermit, this idea appealed to me as a safe haven. Poor Jews with little in their house fancied the notion. But all I got were analogies: this room is like a sacred book containing all the world's stories, like the Pentateuch.

For years I continued searching. I lived in various caves, hoping one would metamorphose. To aid this vain hope I steeped myself in magical lore, again intersecting with others to obtain kabbalistic texts, learn powerful incantations, or decipher sacred names. I used such thaumaturgy successfully in daily life: I could conjure a fish out of a stream for dinner, produce flame to illuminate a cave with the flick of my wrist, or put a spell on a ferocious animal to pass by safely.

In the towns I rendered myself physically invisible and took whatever goods I needed. I always returned the favor with a miracle or two. I put food on a table or patched up an argument; I might heal a child from fever, coax a deer into turning a mill wheel to aid a beleaguered worker, or even change the course of a river to save a village from flooding.

Life was good, but my success brought me no closer to my dearest goal of reuniting with my family. I had seen Noam for only minutes; he had influenced my life for years. I ceased to care about my appearance, and gained a reputation as an eccentric. My raiment resembled vines stuck together after a rain shower. Invisible at times and not others, I appeared unpredictably. Lost in thought, I pulled my fingers through my hair compulsively, earning the nickname "Matted One."

When villagers understood I performed miracles they begged me to contact dead relatives or change their fortunes. I obliged when I could, but in my preoccupation with the magical place, I often performed the wrong task. Once while resurrecting a young man struck down by influenza, I conjured up a hundred frogs in the town well. While exorcising a demon from a magistrate's daughter, I released the devil but also invoked the Kefitzah ha-Derekh, or "Shortening of the Way, and sent the poor girl to Lubin for the day. I was not showered with gold for this mitzvah.

My unease at losing my hermit status, the people's extremely mixed feelings about me, and the stubborn obscurity of the magical place led me to despair. In my youthful wisdom (I was barely in my twenties) I realized I was not looking for a specific cave, but rather a state of mind in which to perceive the charmed spot. But no amount of meditation or Magical Names brought me any closer.

One day, I fled into the Carpathian Mountains outside of Kassowa, determined to enter the first mystical cave I found. I hiked and climbed for days, dizzy from altitude and hunger, for I fasted and deprived myself of comfort on this journey. I trusted my instincts, letting my path go where it wanted, running down hillsides and disappearing into vales as my mood changed. I felt I was closing in on something, though what or where it was I did not know.

On the eleventh night of my travels I was caught in a terrible thunderstorm. I embraced the calamitous winds and biting rains and let myself be blown about. "Here it is," I cried, and hurled myself against a rock face. "There it is," I screamed above the deluge, and flattened myself against a tree. I collapsed in one spot on the mountain, retching violently. If I remained there I knew I would die, so I hurled myself to another area. I passed out, having no idea where I was.

By morning the storm abated. I awoke at the mouth of a hidden cave, mostly covered by fallen branches and debris. I cleared the mess to look inside; a light glowed at the back of the grotto. Still weak, I crawled forward until I discerned a figure seated next to a warm fire.

It was my older brother, Alter, who had died before I was born.

ق

January 26, 2002.   Month 5.

At Roy's restaurant, Sahara finished her narrative. "Weeks later, Zack and Verle received new Okopy recalls. Zack saw Noam as the ghostly twister convincing Shemuel to rejoin the shtetl community. But like Naji, Noam was lost between worlds."

Amar asked: "Was Naji sending a message through Zack? Rejoin the family, Mommy dearest. Get your head out of the books. Noam also led Veronique d'O to the house in Poland."

"Where she collected her library related to the Nights, which eventually led to Chavis adding to Galland's fake manuscript, which Veronique had justified in the first place."

Amar stopped following Sahara's history and remembered Bax on the roof picking up signals from his son. It infuriated him. "Did you finish telling me about Bax?"

Sahara dropped her fork. "You're changing the subject from the state of Naji's soul. You're as suspicious of Bax as I am of Ooma. I saw you two at New Year's."

Amar stopped eating. "I have a confession." Was the whole town eavesdropping on their conversation? "I feel as responsible for Ooma right now as anyone in my family." He called for the check. "Let's continue this at home."

461

67

—◈◈◈—

They drove home in silence. His frank concern for Ooma was understandable, but Sahara knew there was more to it. Amar shrugged off Sahara's connection with Bax. If they were to resolve things, they would have to leave everyone else out of the equation, including the qaraq.

After the baby-sitter left, Sahara and Amar sat down on the couch in the den. Sahara knew it was time to come forth. "My love, the simple fact is that you weren't there for me after the twins died. Sometimes out of duty, but not true caring. I saw the way you reacted to Ooma when she was fired; you were devastated, and let her feel that. We've been here before: you fought me on my pregnancy with Naji, almost killed me when I defied you, and struggled to accept fatherhood."

"Hold on, " Amar said. He did not want past conflicts to cloud his judgment. "The situation with the twins was different. The stillbirth was a thousand times harder for you than me escaping a burning monolith. But I had no reserves left to deal with it. My grief at the passing of the twins was as deep as yours, but I could not touch it right away. You pulled away immediately. Wasn't that your way of dealing with the trauma, just like my shutting down? I'm so sorry, love. But don't point your finger. You made choices, too."

"I know, I know. It's us, baby, it's not just you. That troubles me most of all. I simply don't know what we're supposed to do. Has Diana shed any brilliance? It's okay, tell me."

"She hasn't, actually. Just encouraged us to talk." He hesitated. Should he say the therapist encouraged him to help Ooma? Maybe not, that's Diana's choice. "There's no magic bullet."

"*Not good.* We've recalled some blissful lifetimes, but usually we're fighting, miserable."

Amar winced. "Are you thinking of that recall, the last time you hypnotized me?"

"In ancient Sumer? It soured us off regression. Didn't it start with a sequence of our lives?" "And went downhill from there." They let the memory fill a morose silence between them.

The Tale of Atu and Ur-zamma

It was a reincarnation thread looking for an eye of a needle. They saw their lives as primitive dogs, happily reunited souls, living in caves of early humans, but emotionally divided about their masters. Sha (Sahara's soul) rejected the humans and ran off to the woods. After, from the interlife, Amb (Amar's soul) witnessed Sha's life in Egypt at the time of the first Pyramids, shocked that she condoned the glorification of the Cat-Goddess Bast. He had wrung his soul dry with dog guilt and here she was living the ultimate insult to the name of dog! When Sha joined Amb in the world beyond, they fought like cat and dog, venting hostile feelings from a dozen lifetimes. Irreconcilable: Amb vowed to Sha's spirit-face that he would insult and humiliate her in their next incarnations.

Amb headed straight down to Egypt, to work as a mummifier of cats. You want to preserve the Cat as a sacred animal, fine, I'll gut and stuff them! His vindictiveness pained him immensely, for he was at heart a fair and generous soul. He immersed himself in powerful Egyptian magic: to escape his supposed soul mate, he practiced soul transformation and time travel. Creating a bridge to 17th Century Europe via the Donne room, he glimpsed old Umh trapped inside the mirror and determined to have her. He leaped into the never-space, freed her with his magics.

Amh flung his ravaged soul back to Egypt, but old Umh had not returned to her origin. He searched the Akashic records and learned she was in Sumer, in the city of Eridu in the third millennium BC. Pining to merge his new physical incarnation with Umh, his extreme reactions made him miss his aim. He was reborn as Atu, centuries after Umh's Sumerian life as Ur-zamma. She had long since died, her soul stuck in the Great Depths Below.

The ancient Sumerians believed that a soul descended into the Great Depths Below, disrobed to render itself vulnerable, and atoned for its transgressions in the dusty, dark kingdom ruled by Erishkigal. The soul ate dust and believed it was in the Land of No Return. Purified thus, the soul could ascend the link to the Great Above.

Every Sumerian assumed so firmly that this ascension was synonymous with rebirth that there was no record of this belief, despite the creation of written language at this time. In fact, superstition about mentioning reincarnation led to an interdiction against equating Ascent with rebirth. For all the myths where a Hero descends to the Great Below, few narratives elucidate the returning ascent.

As a priest, Atu oversaw the ritual for a soul's ascension from the Netherworld. But he was forbidden to mention the ritual's function, under pain of death. One benefit of his priestly office was Atu's access to a certain Egyptian ambassador and his sharing of that culture's innovations. Atu learned a practice that preserved the soul after death. Unfortunately, when the ambassador spoke of the spell, he transgressed the law against mentioning reincarnation, and Atu had him killed. He did so with a wave of his hand, insuring that his new knowledge was kept secret from envious priests.

To test the method, Atu attempted to contact the ambassador from beyond the tomb. The technique worked perfectly, allowing Atu to formally apologize to the poor soul before letting him descend to Erishkigal's domain. In his Ascension practice, Atu became adept at contacting souls.

This skill gave Atu a brilliant idea. Despite the priesthood's celibacy, Atu yearned for the most beautiful woman of the bygone dynasties. He searched archives and family histories for an enticing candidate. Reading of a lustful, proud, and fiery princess, Atu selected his mate, Ur-zamma. He invoked the Egyptian spell, using a portion of ghat powder acquired from the dead ambassador's belongings, and received a vision of the Netherworld. He spied the desirable soul, with which he felt an instant kinship. Searching for a way out of the dust, Ur-zamma cried out to Atu's apparition. He enticed her body up to Eridu, her flesh as supple as in life.

So ecstatic was Ur-zamma to be alive once more that she threw herself into the priest's arms. They made ravenous love for countless revolutions of the Moon. With the priest under her spell, Ur-zamma, now with Umh's knowledge, insisted he use magic to return her to her proper time in Egypt. Umh had been on a wild ride through the future, a never-space, a Sumerian incarnation, then down to the Netherworld dust. But the task was beyond Atu's knowledge.

Ur-zamma reviled Atu's impotence to help her. He was so insulted by her accusation against his manhood that he was compelled to prove his virility. He mounted her as the God Enlil ravished the Goddess Ninlil, and she fought back as Ninlil matched Enlil. Their passionate bouts continued for another countless set of lunar revolutions.

Spent, Ur-zamma pleaded with the priest to return her to the dust of Erishkigal's realm, where she could mourn her soul's demise. Atu was horrified at the thought of losing her. Her pleading turned to tender demonstrations, the woman raised from the dead overcoming the engorged male. Again they went at it over countless revolutions of Earth's best friend. Atu satisfied his deepest lusts while Ur-zamma remained insatiable. On the last revolution Atu reached purest epiphany and saw all: his soul Amh, his feud with Sha, the whirlwind soul ride, the sighting of Umh. Still hatefully bound to Sha, he had only sought Ur-zamma's embrace to spite his soul mate.

With this knowledge he released Ur-zamma. Enough was enough. He sent her back to Erishkigal, with a promise to help her re-enter her proper place in Time. After his epiphany, he knew his life was also some quixotic ricochet of his soul. Why not do some good while he had access to arcana? He experimented with every magic spell until his incantations bore results. In the temple repository he came upon a cold metallic oval that quivered to his touch. In the Netherworld purification, the soul is burned down to that primeval bit of metal, the seed from the Great Mother Ninhursag. Perhaps the oval was made of this eternal substance.

The silver-white ovoid in his palms, Atu invoked soul ascendancy. A dusty column of air appeared. Inside the spiraling smoke Atu saw Ur-zamma, a smile of delight on her face. She cried that she was at last free, felt pure power in her soul, and could set off to her true place in Time. In eternal gratitude, Ur-zamma/Umh approached Atu and engulfed him in her pulsing gyrations. Priest went from holy man to lusting beast as the happy corkscrew pleasured him. This time the tryst lasted only one circle of the Moon, but Atu experienced a release equal to all the others with Ur-zamma combined.

In the morning, Atu awoke on the floor of the chamber, limbs spread every which way, his member as flaccid as a goose's wrung neck. A two-inch layer of dust blanketed the floor. Ur-zamma was gone to her soul's rest. Atu was thankful for her liberation, but just as Janshah mourned the loss of his wife to the river monster, Atu mourned Ur-zamma's loss to the River of Time.

The ovoid was also gone. At the time Atu/Amh would not have under-stood, but for the first time in its age-old existence, the metallic object had shattered into seven pieces. This fragmenting was a devastating event that would take uncountable epochs to repair. A confluence of forbidding

466

forces caused the undoing: the raising of the dead, Umb's stray soul re-engaging with its path, a Sumerian priest tampering with a reincarnation ritual, and some of the hottest sex this side of Babylon. The oval's component pieces shot off in various directions in the cosmos, some following in Umb's wake, others in the opposing direction, some back to the past, others into the future.

Atu/Amb left the priesthood, found an obedient wife, and sexed her every full Moon, in memory of Ur-zamma and in unconscious vengeance against Sha. After death, Amb rested for an aeon in the interlife, healing his tie with Sha barely enough to reincarnate as Ambanari, God of the Red Isle, brother to Sha's Goddess Sahnra. Their feuding saw the ruin of Madagascar, and the hot and cold blowing of North and South winds.

ق

When he had first recalled this memory, Amar had been embarrassed by its content, no less so than when the couple remembered it the night of their talk. It exposed in lurid detail the two worst traits of their relationship: the triangular tension with Ooma, and their constant spite.

Sahara asked: "Am I your soul mate, or is Ooma? She's your Queen in the Scheherazade tale. I wonder if a romantic notion of soul mates is even valid. There's one positive thing in this awful memory. It's true there's no record of Sumerian afterlife beliefs, like with *The Egyptian Book of the Dead*. But this story once again reveals past life belief in an ancient culture."

Amar was impatient to resolve things. "Can this story shed light on what we should do?"

"What light is there, Amar? This tale makes me tired of dealing with you at close quarters. Maybe what we had last year is best: a safe distance, extreme caution, and a little sex thrown in."

Amar grinned. "Absence did make something grow. Especially in furniture showrooms." He thought back to a particularly passionate moment in public.

467

They sat in silence, each searching for a solution. *If we can't live together,* Amar thought, *then I need to do the gentlemanly thing. Would that be best for Naji? Could we still raise him together? Can he stand more disruption?*

Sahara thought about Amar's hyper-vigilance. He imagined the worst all the time, and it made him an inconsistent and unreliable mate. She could accept that. But perhaps the best thing for her, and Naji, was for Amar to live separately but remain close. The idea excited her. A surprise, since they had worked so hard and carefully to reunite. *Hadn't they done that lifetime after lifetime, a wearisome cycle? If they tried a separation with full consciousness, would that be an evolution?*

They saw the exact same solution. For Amar, it was a noble act, and a brotherly gesture. For Sahara, she liked the parallel to her moving out, to Diana's house. And for Naji, it would be an easy, organic, and probably fun change.

They spoke simultaneously: Amar said, "Why don't I move in with Zack?" as Sahara said, "Naji can live in this house with me, and Zack's house with you."

468

68

——◁∿∿▷——

February 9, 2002. Month 5.

In the first two weeks of Sahara and Amar's trial separation, Ardra Rash's health plummeted. Struggling to accept his grandfather's demise, Amar did little to formally move out. He worked out sleeping arrangements with Zack, who was gracious to a fault, as was the ever-friendly Jobim.

Zack explained that he and Jobim used the New Year to start fresh, forgetting they had met under the shadow of 9/11, and moving on to work out the details of life together. Including Amar and Naji in their household would be a pleasant test of their new bond. Zack said it would be good for Jo to live among qaraqis, a statement Amar did not quite understand. As for Naji, the first afternoon and evening he stayed with his father and the two men was a great delight.

Acting as a strong, positive team, Sahara helped Amar face his dying grandfather. On a Saturday they brought Naji to see Ardra, probably for the last time. With a key to Ardra's apartment he had never used, Amar opened the door to discover the ancient man propped up in his easy chair with pillows and blankets. Piles of clothes, newspapers, and empty food containers lay everywhere, evidence of Ardra's weakened state.

Despite the stale smell of the apartment and his ghastly appearance, Ardra's eyes had their usual twinkle. "Please excuse the mess. Come in, come in. A joy to see you all!"

The couple feigned good cheer. "We're here to feed and nurse you," Sahara announced, putting down bags of groceries.

"And pamper me, too, I hope." Ardra's smile revealed the sublime spirit still radiating from the tired body. "Because I won't be able to eat a single thing you brought."

"Even samosas and green curry?"

Ardra shrugged. "Maybe a little samosa. But I'd rather eat up this little morsel." Weakly he held out his arms to Naji, who gently ran into them.

"Ah-Dah," the boy said quietly. Ardra bathed in the serene sense of peace he had felt holding Naji at the art museum a few months before. He couldn't get enough of it.

Sahara admired the lovely bond. "Ardra dear, can we leave Naji with you while we cook?"

"Cook away, if you can navigate the disastrous seas of my kitchen," Ardra said. "Naji and I will discuss politics."

Naji broke his embrace and took a few steps backward, knocking over a stack of New York Times sections. The child raised his hands to his eyes.

"Ah, a game of peek-a-boo, your favorite." Ardra raised his own hands, then opened a few fingers. "Peek a boo!" The boy giggled. "Why do you like it so much?" Ardra repeated the game. Naji giggled again. As Ardra raised his hands a third time, Naji waved to him. "Bye-bye? A new game?" Ardra raised his hands again, and Naji waved.

"I take your point," Ardra said. "I'm about to leave you, is that it? Like disappearing behind my hands?" Naji opened his hands up in front of his eyes and smiled. "But I'll reappear? Ardra translated. "Is that crazy Hindu talk, your Indian blood? We're Jewish, didn't your Dad tell ya?"

Naji climbed onto the arm of the chair and nuzzled against the old man. "Love you, Ah-Dah." Seeing Ardra's condition, Naji had made his choice. It was time to communicate regularly with the world again. Damn the twins! Who better to share things with than the dying man, who doted on his comfort? "Momma and Poppa and me," he said aloud, "we know our past lives. So does our qaraq. Our friends in past lives. We tell many, many stories."

When Naji saw that Ardra was confused and dubious about the qaraq, he switched to telepathic communication: *I'm sad you're not part of our qaraq, but you're part of another one, which you'll remember in the interlife. Recalling past lives is a magical thing, like speaking in your mind.* Ardra was speechless with surprise at the voice in his head, so Naji continued. Naji wanted so badly to ease Ardra's fears about death and assure him all was not over. To do so, he wanted to demonstrate his ability, to share a past life story.

First, in Ardra's mind, Naji proudly announced that this was the two hundred and twenty-second past life the qaraq had recounted so far. He did not explain how he knew this esoteric fact; by Ardra's furrowed brow Naji knew it was already a lot to fathom.

Second, Naji had a better way to tell the story than reciting it in Ardra's brain. He had spent the Fall living in a fantasy world, brought on by a vision of the twins. They might not have been real, but one positive side effect of this delusion was a new ability. Naji could project visual images of what lay in his imagination, including past life memories.

You're in for a treat, Ah-Dah. The story is about Heaven! My time as a soul there. I can give you a preview of the sweet place you're about to enter. And then you'll see my story.

As Ardra's mind filled with people in robes with beatific smiles, he wondered if it was due to his pain medication, or Naji's bizarre abilities.

The Tale of the Master's Hut

There was once a soul named Nozh who walked the path of Heaven with a big chip on his aura. His last lifetime had ended in an unfair death, and he had vague memories of other unsettling lives. He roamed the walkways looking for someone who could hear his complaints. He was told a million things to appease him: 1) It was not time for his Dreaming Back; 2) The Guides Office was this way, or SWITCH was that way; 3) For now he should just rest; 4) He had wonderful lives ahead, including one with reptiles under the influence of potent flowers. Nothing satisfied him.

At long last Nozh found a shady alley; at the end stood a wooden hut with a crooked, wooden sign: THE MASTER IS IN. Nozh knew of the Masters, higher entities than the spirit guides, perhaps their immediate superiors. Nozh felt fortunate, but despite the sign, the hut was closed. He waited for days, roamed the area, and made inquiries, but no one knew about the hut.

One morning Nozh saw a bent-over man with a long, black beard delicately take down the sign, pop a latch under the front counterpane of the hut, and lift up the front panel. Nozh thought it would fall back on him, so he ran up and grabbed the heavy, wooden board. As soon as he did, the bearded man let go and nodded, as if he had expected someone to finish the task. The bent man disappeared with the sign around the back of the hut. In past searches Nozh had not located a door anywhere. The man popped up inside the booth, as if he had walked up a flight of stairs.

Nozh spoke first. "I've been waiting for days to see you!"

The bearded man nodded, without expression.

"Why do you leave that sign up when you are not in, and take it down when you are?"

Again the man nodded, this time with a slight look of approval. He did not speak.

Nozh tried once more. "You are the Master, are you not?"

The Master nodded, then looked at Nozh in anticipation of a question.

"I've come from a terrible lifetime, and I need to discuss it," Nozh said.

The Master gave Nozh a puzzled look.

"You're right," Nozh said, surprised he was in agreement with the mute Master, "it was a wonderful life, an advanced one. I was a flying fish before the age of fish even began."

Nodding satisfaction at Nozh's correction, the Master gave a look of understanding.

Nozh gave words to the Master's look. "You know how terribly I was killed. Why was I?"

The Master smiled for the first time, acknowledgement that Nozh found the true question. He disappeared, then re-emerged holding a tiny card with a single word: RECOLLECTION.

"You want me to remember all the events of the lifetime? Like the Dreaming Back?"

The Master shrugged, as if to say 'that's one way to think of it,' and gave Nozh the card.

Nozh could think of nothing else to ask. With slight embarrassment, he left the Master's hut and returned to the Path of Heaven, where he strolled for many days, lounging in the beautiful parks to recall his previous life. Did the Master want him to remember what he could until he had a revelation? All Nozh could think was how unfair a short life is. Many times he returned to the hut, but it was closed, the sign absurdly hanging in place. Nozh grew testy.

Finally the bent-over man came back. Nozh helped set up the shack, then lit into him.

"I've been waiting weeks this time. I remembered everything I can, but see no purpose in it." With that, he fished out the tiny card and slammed it down on the hut's counter.

The Master nodded, acknowledging Nozh's frustration. Then he picked up the card and handed it back to Nozh. Nozh was dumbfounded.

"What? You want me to remember more? I haven't worked hard enough?"

The bearded Master extended the card.

Nozh snatched the card. "Fine! You're the Master," he said with barely disguised contempt.

Nozh spent weeks racking his memory for other details. Perhaps the life's brevity was a karmic comment. He had done bad deeds previously, but paid severe consequences. If the guides meant to punish him even more, then the whole process was worse than he thought.

Months later (a fact Nozh pointed out to the Master the next time he appeared at the hut), Nozh asked if there was another lifetime which made sense of his tragic demise. The Master grinned from ear to ear at the question, took the card from Nozh, and once more handed it back.

"You want me to recall that other lifetime? You can't just tell me?"

The Master squinted, as if to say 'do you really think that would be for the best?'

Nozh snatched back the card, but vowed this would be the last time. Whole seasons went by as he recollected past lifetimes. Was the lesson about patience? Was this a test of how long he could remain focused on one thing? Obsessing about Time, Nozh remembered one past life that had lasted an inordinate length. The opposite of the tragic, short lifetime! Was his untimely death a gift from the guides, a tonic for that endless life?

A year later, the next time the Master returned, Nozh explained his theory, praising the Master for forcing him to wait for a revelation. The Master seemed pleased, but barely smiled as he reached for the tiny card. Nozh was anxious he would hand it back, but the Master wanted to press on. He disappeared under the counter, re-emerging with a new card.

Immensely relieved, Nozh took the card and read: REST.

"After all this time, you want me to do nothing now? Forever and a day?"

The Master shrugged, as if to say 'why not, give yourself a break, live a little.'

Nozh left feeling happy with the progress but disappointed in the next step. He did his best to enjoy what Heaven had to offer, but soon after he started to play and revel in music and make new friends, he felt restless. Over the years, he visited the hut, but the bearded man only handed the card back to him, either with a bemused nod, or an expression of reproach. After decades Nozh complained, and the Master seemed to listen with greater thoughtfulness.

One day Nozh found the Master waiting for him. The bearded man had a fresh, invigorated attitude and held out his hand for the tiny card. When Nozh handed it over, the Master ripped it up, flung the pieces to the ground, and disappeared. He re-emerged with a list on a small piece of paper:

RECOLLECTION
REST
TRANSITION
CENTRAL ISSUES
LONG TERM ISSUES
UNPAID DEBTS

The Master produced a large quill and scratched off the first two items, looking at Nozh after each one to acknowledge their hard-won achievement. Then he circled TRANSITION several times, jabbed a bent finger at it, and shoved the list over to Nozh. Before Nozh could ask about the nature of TRANSITION, the Master had come around, closed up the hut, and vanished.

This next step was murky to Nozh, but by fretting over it he came out of static relaxation. As soon as he had this thought, Nozh happened by the hut to find the Master again waiting for him. The man clapped his hands for the list, crossed off TRANSITION, and jabbed the quill at CENTRAL ISSUES. Then he was gone.

Nozh had considered the central issues of his previous lifetime decades ago. Was the issue his untimely death? Or the extravagant length of other lives? Or his self-destructive responses?

Soon after, Nozh strolled by the alley, where the Master beckoned vociferously. He demanded the list, again crossed out, quilled, and pointed, urging Nozh to LONG TERM ISSUES.

Something bothered Nozh about the Master's new impatience, but he excused it. To consider long term issues he had to distinguish between immediate concerns and long-range goals. Halfway through this thought he saw the Master running toward him on the Path of Heaven, waving his arms wildly. The Master grabbed Nozh's sleeve and pulled him back to the hut, the whole time poking about his clothes for the list. By the time they reached the hut, the Master had pushed Nozh to the final item, UNPAID DEBTS.

That night as Nozh went to sleep, he realized the Master's speedy rhythm was meant to make a point. Nothing else comes before unpaid debts. His previous interlife plus the untimely death had not been enough karma to repay his destructive lifetime as a disease-carrying germ! Nozh tossed and turned with this disturbing thought, but was awakened by an annoying scratching sound. It was the Master! He was furiously crossing off places he had already crossed off the list. Finally, he tore the sheet into bits.

"What are you doing?" Nozh asked, squinting at the bearded figure. "Are you saying I'm done? I barely began the last steps! This is maddening."

The Master shrugged, as if to say 'does it really matter?'

"Yes, it matters," Nozh shouted, despite his sleepiness. "It's my soul you're playing with!"

The Master nodded in understanding. He picked up a scattered piece and gave it to Nozh.

"REST?" You want me to go back to that step? It took forever. Now you rush me."

The Master raised his eyebrows meaningfully.

"That's supposed to be significant? I didn't like my long and short lives, and I don't like the long and short of this process either. So?"

The Master tilted his head to the side, as if to say 'you tell me, dear soul.'

"I don't get it. Unless it's about crossing out extreme choices and looking for alternatives."

The Master leaned back on his elbows, inviting Nozh to continue.

Suddenly Nozh knew the answer, an answer he had heard many lifetimes ago. He said it aloud, but did not truly understand its meaning: "The Middle Way."

And to Nozh's great surprise and delight, the Master spoke.

"There was a Prince who was deliriously in love with a foreign Princess, but the girl and her royal family rejected the Prince's suit. The Prince's father wanted to go to war against the Princess' kingdom, but the Prince knew that such a forceful action would backfire and cause the Princess to kill herself. He contemplated taking his own life to end his hopeless misery. In such tales, there was a middle way: not an obviously prescribed course, but one the Prince had to invent, a creative act unseen by anyone except his inner spirit. He might travel to the Princess' land in disguise and suit her in a fresh form; he might meet her in a land foreign to both of them and rescue her from grave danger; he might wait for Providence to throw them together in unexpected circumstances. Each outcome would be a middle way. There is always a middle way, even without two extremes."

Nozh thought of his recent struggles and knew there were many alternatives. He thought of a past interlife dilemma between choosing a simpler life versus a complex, evolving species. He should be ready for anything. A childlike freedom overcame him, a feeling he had not experienced in millennia. "I just have to invent what I want, right?" Nozh asked. "And stop complaining."

The Master shrugged, stood up, and left Nozh to sleep peacefully.

That was not quite the end of Heaven for Nozh. One day he passed the alley and saw the hut, which he had not thought about for a long time. It was closed and the sign was up, but next to the sign was tacked a piece of paper. Nozh took down the paper, read it, and knew it was meant for him. It was the list, a new copy, with nothing crossed out:

RECOLLECTION
REST
TRANSITION
CENTRAL ISSUES
LONG TERM ISSUES
UNPAID DEBTS

ق

At the end of the story, Ardra's body and soul was greatly eased, by the resolution of the tale, by its heavenly milieu, and by Naji's touch. Weeping for joy, Ardra was dumbstruck by the two-year-old's uncanny precocity. There was so much to discuss with the child, but they were interrupted when Amar cleared the paper strewn table and Sahara laid out the food.

"To prepare this feast, we sprayed scents from censers and burned aloes, wood, and perfumes," Sahara said. "And that was just for the samosas." Carefully, Amar helped his grandfather to the table, and propped his chair with more pillows.

"My goodness," Ardra said, before eating, "I forgot I have something for the little one. Naji dear, go to my bedroom. On my dresser -- ignore all the socks -- you'll find an odd looking thing. It belonged to your father as a boy in India." As Naji ran off to fetch the object, Ardra said, "I have to let go of things as my time draws near." Sahara shushed him as Naji returned with a metal, oval object, surprisingly shiny for its age. Sahara and Amar looked at each other in shock.

"Amar brought it home one day in Delhi," Ardra told Naji. "It was a worthless piece of junk, he wouldn't tell us where he found it, but he played with it for hours. Maybe you will, too."

Was it remotely possible this was the oval given to Sanaa by Oamra's great-grandfather? Was this a bizarre reincarnated ritual, a non-qaraqi elder handing down the silver gadget to a young qaraqi? Sahara already imagined herself stealing it from her sleeping child, to test its powers.

Amar's mind went elsewhere. He knew exactly where he had found it in New Delhi, at a condemned building where a young girl he had met had seen its glint, gone after it, and vanished with a scream. It was a terrifying memory he had never confessed to anyone, out of childish guilt.

"I can't even remember where I got it," Amar said, with a false laugh.

The appearance of the oval set the couple on edge during dinner. Ardra noticed their absurd tension over a simple piece of metal. Were they worried about Naji's safety playing with it? Was it anxiety over him? No, it was something else, that awkward tension, a couple in trouble.

After dinner, as Sahara and Amar cleaned up, Ardra probed Naji about his parents. He learned of their conflicts, one of the reasons Naji had retreated to a fantasy world. They had agreed peacefully to separate, probably for good. Naji explained the arrangement with Zack's house.

After maintaining good spirits despite his illness, Ardra now looked solemn. *Well, it's not a bad plan*, he thought, with Naji listening in to his mind. *Zack's a good boy: used to baby-sit your Dad at my jewelry shop. And he lives next door. You'll hop back and forth like a jackrabbit. But if the plan is permanent, as you suspect, my wise great-grandson, we must plan for your future. We need to protect all three of you. What's the best approach?*

Ardra faded into his thoughts. A minute later, Naji roused him by speaking aloud.

"I know, Ah-Dah. I have an idea."

END OF PART TWO

PART THREE

69

—⁓—

February 24.   Month 6.

Ardra's funeral was held at Riverside Memorial Chapel on the Upper West Side of Manhattan. A crowd of jewelers and Indian immigrants gathered to bid farewell to the well-loved man. Besides Amar, his father and brother, and Sahara and Naji, the guests included Cachay and Zack (with Jobim), who had known the family for years. Sahara also invited Diana and Porcy, for she needed much moral support. She thought she had experienced the worst of her troubles, but Ardra's death unearthed her buried grief.

Amar was equally disturbed, and wanted the funeral over and done. He helped his father with the details, and Solomon informed him that Ardra had changed his will at the eleventh hour, and that the changes would affect Amar enormously.

Unlike his parents, Naji was as content as a teddy bear. Though still receiving Wonderland-like visions, he managed to gain control of this image forest. No longer experiencing regression as a defense against trauma, he selected what he wanted to see. It was like a secret stash of candy.

Naji was happy so many qaraqis were at the funeral. His mind was full of their emotions and anxieties, about Ah-Dah, about death, and about what direction the group should take. His mother was particularly distressed. Naji loved being in the presence of so much feeling, in spite of the occasion. He had retreated for months, and wanted to be back.

In the mélange of thoughts he was absorbing, he heard a voice calling him. An unfamiliar voice, but calm and reassuring. It told him to contact the qaraq. *You did well with Ah-Dah, and you have an important message for the qaraq.* It felt like a voice from on high, like the twins. Even though they had plagued him, Naji loved the idea of his brothers as spirit guides.

Naji wondered what the message could be. Since January he had been playing catch up with all the recalls he'd missed. Zack was always talking qaraq history, so being at his house aided Naji's efforts. When Naji showed Zack the oval Ah-Dah gave him, Zack brought out all kinds of things he'd collected, including a blue elephant with little mirrors. Naji would return the favor now.

Seated next to Zack in the sanctuary, Jobim was the first to notice something was wrong. Zack's eyes twitched, his hands started sweating, and he made a lot of breathy sounds. As the rabbi presided over the gathering, Zack knew he was disturbing those around him. Before stepping outside, Zack turned to Jobim and said, "The little bugger's in my head." As Zack exited the sanctuary, Naji left his surprised mother, ran over and took Zack's hand. Waiting in the newly fallen snow for the service to end, Naji shared the images he saw with Zack.

The Idea and the Reunion of the Qaraq

After the 1001 qaraq disbanded, the great Diasporas that swept across the planet washed the members away from each other. Religious wars pushed aside Islam and expelled Judaism. Sailing vessels great and small scattered peoples over seven continents. Huge nomadic tribes flooded over plains and mountains to engulf entire populations.

484

In one vision, Naji saw an ice mummy of a Pazyryk chieftain of a Scythian tribe, from the Altai Mountains of Siberia. Naji's inner eye lingered on the beautifully executed tattoos on the Pazyryk's arms. Pleased with the icy blue details, Naji counted many animal forms: Argali Wild Sheep, Sanga Antelope, Mongolian Gazelle, Prezealski Horse, Siberian Ibex, Whooper Swan, and Lammergeyer Vulture. Needed for the nomad's survival, the wildlife possessed supernatural qualities, strength, courage, and longevity, befitting the high social status of the warrior.

Zack realized Naji was stuck in the swirling tattoo designs and gave the boy's hand a squeeze. At the same time, the mourners emptied onto the snowy street and into cars for the procession to the cemetery in Queens. Zack, Cachay, Diana, and Porcy had been assigned one car, with Jobim driving. Naji would not let go of Zack's hand when Sahara came for him. With a shrug of Zack's shoulders, Sahara understood that if her son was to be a regular in Zack's home, this game was inevitable. But to break from her child added to the pain in her heart that day.

In the car, Cachay riddled her son about leaving the service. Zack smiled and looked at Naji. To everyone's shock, the child greeted them in their minds, except for Jobim, who was driving. Naji noted Zack's sadness that his friend was excluded and forced to deal with New York traffic. Before anyone could comment further, the qaraqis went on the journey in Naji's mind.

The Idea and the Reunion of the Qaraq, continued

By the 17th Century the Explorations and the first global wars were in full swing, and the world found spiritual nourishment in the Idea,

485

inspired by a John Donne poem, which encouraged non-action, an acceptance of the Universe in the here and now, contained in a microcosm.

Naji saw his soul, Nozh, attached to the suffering European continent
from the beyond. It was time to leave off silly things, but retain the creative spark of the Child. Nozh spread the Idea through the ether, like a
Prince tossing coins to the crowd.

Nozh remained an attached soul in his lifetime as Noam, unable to
let go of the horrible suffering of the Jews. His ghost, the column of air,
pleaded with his brother Shemuel to rejoin and help his people, and was
humored and rebuffed. This was not just Noam entreating Shemuel, but
Nozh entreating Sha, and child entreating mother to rejoin the qaraq.

The car arrived at the cemetery, and the riders joined Sahara and
Amar at the gravesite. In the freezing air during the burial, Naji continued to reach out to the minds of the qaraq. Cachay got Naji to stop
when the rabbi spoke to everyone at the grave. But then it was time for
the message.

The Idea and the Beunion of the Qaraq,
conclusion

The Donne Idea soothed the grief of a continent of souls. The qaraq
slowly healed and re-connected one by one, like Num finding Nimeh,
Moses his birth mother, or the blind Jacob his beloved son. But could
the Idea reunite the entire group of dislocated souls?

ق

Once the funeral was over, a bizarre event for those with Naji's
vision in their heads, Cachay asked Zack about details in the 17th Century

history, and Porcy commented to Diana how painful a fractured qaraq was to her, especially with the group together now. Everyone agreed the recall implied a complex set of stories, linking the 1001 qaraq, the Diaspora, the Explorations, the Donne Idea, Eastern European Jewry, and some theoretical reunion of the qaraq. All yet to be recalled.

And the miraculous child was back with them. Miraculous, mischievous child, interrupting a funeral!

Sahara broke away from the other mourners, and came over to the little group, huddled in the cold. When Diana delicately explained that Naji had entered all their minds, Sahara wept for the first time that sad afternoon.

70

February 28.   Month 6.

A few days after the funeral, Diana went to visit Sahara. She was a regular guest at the house now that Amar had moved out. Naji was speaking again, and 'Auntie Di' wanted to soak up every word. When she arrived, the front door was locked and Sahara did not answer the bell. Diana knew she was at home, so she went to Zack's house for a key.

Finding Zack and Jobim playing with Naji, the therapist wondered if the new arrangement distracted Zack from believing Jobim was a member of the qaraq, or convinced him more than ever that he belonged. She had been heartened when Jobim remained separate from Naji's telepathic antics at the funeral. In fact, she hoped her days doing triage for the group's traumas were waning. Now she was caught between questioning Zack's state and worrying about Sahara.

She got the key, called out to her friend inside the house, and found Sahara in bed with the covers pulled over her head. "What's going on?" Diana sat on the bed and touched Sahara gently. "What do you need? You took Ardra's death very hard."

Very slowly, Sahara unbound her head from the covers. "I was doing so well. Or so I thought." She squnted at the light. "Pissed at Amar, but splitting with him felt like liberation. My thesis pouring forth. Even found evidence to support our Nights recalls."

"And Naji's talking!" Diana stroked Sahara's arm. "You were strong for Ardra at the end."

"Yes, I thought I had my reserves back. But it was a sham." Sahara curled into a fetal position, hardly looking at Diana. "Ardra was so caring and wonderful, and had this delicious bond with Naji. When he went, it broke a seal over all the pain I'd been containing in order to survive. My whole year has been a spiral down. Now I can't stop it."

"What are you talking about? What can't you stop?"

"The lack of control. All I can do is finish my work. Can't even face the group. I'm done."

"We can take a break," Diana offered. "New Year's was worth six months of meetings. But don't give up. Through past life work you know Ardra's death is just a transition for him."

"For him. For me he's gone." Sahara turned away from Diana. "Anyway, we have no proof of reincarnation."

Things were bad if Sahara was reverting back to early doubt. Diana spoke softly. "My obsession with tracing past life belief in human history was a way of confirming the truth. All those diverse cultures believing the same thing couldn't be a case of global cryptoamnesia, each group influencing the next. It had to be based on a reality, the reality we tap into every week."

Diana saw Sahara was numb to her efforts, but she felt a great desire to reach her friend. She willed herself to envision the origin of past life belief on Earth. She went to the empty side of the bed, lay on her back next to Sahara, and shut her eyes. Feeling her mind shift, she whispered, "Sahara, I'm going somewhere. Stay with me. It's important. I'm going to prove to you once and for all that metempsychosis is an actual fact. I hit a lifetime once, well, the life is in the future, so I *will* hit a lifetime, where despair leads me to doubt everything I believe. Are you listening?"

The Tale of the Expedition for Proof of Reincarnation

In the interlife after the lifetime, my spirit guide comforts me. The solution she comes up with is to travel in time and witness continuity between lifetimes. I gravitate toward passive observation, so maybe I'll see something convincing. The spirit guide teaches me a physical technique that uses my knowledge of Bu-rei-dkagh (to project my soul into inanimate objects), a fetal position (like when I twist my legs together), and a silver amulet.

We spin through a network of spacetime wormholes, and I search for evidence that certain souls reappear in new forms. My guide says we'll make enough stops for me to make up my mind. But, she insists, there is one place we should not go, and if I'm tempted I'll suffer the consequences. I have no idea what she's talking about.

We start in a highly advanced World near my last lifetime in the future. In this World they have technology that tracks data deep in the past, and scientific projects bridging the divide between myth and historical fact. Flouting such terms as mythflow and timeload, a few researchers claim they can track a soul through lifetimes. There are plenty of skeptics.

Trying a different tact, the guide brings me to the past, where we find a soul who believes he was one of the last dinosaurs on the ancient planet of Earth, and suffered a humbling capture by the first mammals. Maybe we'll see his story unfold on another stop. We focus on Earth and the evolution of reincarnation beliefs.

There were the Mayans, who thought the afterlife a ball field of retri-bution for souls in conflict. An ancient race of India possessed a manual for imbuing stories with the power to help souls transmigrate. This text derived from prehistoric bone readings, where a shaman recorded a soul's next life in a grave painting. When I witness such a ritual, lurk-ing behind a bush, I have the eerie sensation the shaman is my previous incarnation. The spirit guide feigns ignorance.

It was still possible that each civilization influenced another. Wormholing back to the dawn of humanity, when tribes were more iso-lated, we observe the Vawr preserve a corpse, a Cro-Magnon disturb his circle of elders with the audacious notion of a rebirth, and a primitive herd of ape-men howl and hurl rocks at an early believer in metempsy-chosis. Again, where is the proof?

The guide prepares me to tuck in tight, and we travel to the demise of the dinosaurs. Miraculously, I recognize the dinosaur that the future soul remembered as a past life. An impressive feat on the guide's part, but how do I actually know this dinosaur shares the other soul? Maybe the future soul has the dinosaur on his brain for some other reason.

I doubt whatever my spirit guide hands me. Frustrated, she depos-its me in the astral ethers. I remember the one stop forbidden me; she had cruelly tempted me with coordinates. Spirit guides are less than subtle sometimes, so I wager she offers me forbidden fruit. I jump to the destination.

I travel to a period *between* the dinosaurs and the evolution of homi-nids. I also travel *toward* Earth now, from some distant planet. The ship that speeds me through the stars has made many stops, with Earth as its final destination. The oval vessel is an artifact destined for Terra.

Another jolt forward in Time, and the ovoid lies hidden in a cave on the Asian sub-continent. Creatures come in contact with the artifact's power, its contents, projected in images. Inspired, the natives strike ani-mal shells with beaters, recount stories, and smear berry dyes on their cave walls. They also devise reincarnation rituals.

Am I to believe that without this alien influence Earthlings never would have acquired culture, religion, or past life beliefs? This discredits reincarnation as a physical reality and humanity as a creative inventor of the belief. Is this why my guide did not want me near this truth, because it would taint my already jaded view?

But perhaps my devilish angel withholds the truth that reincarnation is real, and tricked me into this other view? Perhaps it is her duty to keep the truth an elusive mystery. I curl into a fetal position to free my assaulted brain from misery. But my posture triggers one final adventure. I travel to a time before hominids, but when another sentient species dominated the planet. They were proboscideans, a race with long trunks for noses. From the shadows of a firelit ceremony, I watch an invocation of immortal souls and endless lifetimes. After the rite, I overhear an argument between two creatures about the verity of metempsychosis, one pleading there is no other explanation for the mystery of life and death, the other claiming that there will always be doubt.

The next thing I know I am in the arms of my spirit guide, sobbing uncontrollably. She makes a final argument: if I am here in an interlife, isn't that proof of reincarnations? No, it's proof there's an afterlife, but not that I'll be reborn. Even when I line up for my next life, it could be a trick to send me off to oblivion. My feeling that I've gone through this process many times could be because everyone's convinced of it. If I do transmigrate, I will not remember once I've done so; if I think I'm remembering a previous life, I will doubt. That is what the forbidden detour taught me.

I did not mean to teach you that, my guide says, which is why I forbade it. I am sorry for your pain, but this is the way of the cosmos.

ق

"This was supposed to make me feel better?" Sahara had curled up in the crook of Diana's arm. "Then the eunuchs went forth and threw me in the dungeon of despair."

492

"I thought if I put the story together it would get to the bottom of things."

"It did, didn't it? Bottom's not too pretty."

Diana determined to salvage things. "You have to admit it's an awesome tale, jumping around in time like that. We saw the ovoid traveling through the stars! Its images, or zojy, not only inspired stories, but also reincarnation beliefs."

"Which means that ultimately, the Nights and the idea of rebirth came from the same place," Sahara said. "So if I kiss off reincarnation, I shouldn't put any stock in the Nights either."

"Or the memory of Ardra's good soul," Diana said.

Sahara mulled over the thought. She adjusted the covers to invite Diana to curl up under them. "But if I *don't* give up the Nights, I can't give up all the connections to it, the qaraq's history, the origins of human culture and reincarnation myths. Even with all the holes in your narrative."

"That's my girl." Diana wrapped her arm around Sahara's shoulder. "What holes?"

"How about: what planet did the zojy vessel come from?"

"That's a *worm* hole," Diana teased. "Like where did Version 2 go after the 11th Century?"

That's a *rabbit* hole." They giggled like girls at a sleepover. Suddenly Sahara sat up in bed. "You're right. I can't continue spiraling down. Naji's contacted everyone. I need him back. I need to free my finances from Amar. And I can't lose the qaraq. I'm the one to fill in these gaps!"

Relieved her friend was back in the race, Diana had an instinct Sahara might go overboard.

493

71

—◦◦◦—

March 5.   Month 6.

"What the hell are we doing?" Zack mouthed the words to Jobim so Naji wouldn't hear. It was better than thinking them, for who knew what the tyke heard in their brains. Jobim gave Zack a warm smile and handed him the plastic frog.

"Oh what the hell, I'm not keeping anything from you, kid," Zack said. Naji reached out his hand. "Not even my most exotic, favorite frog." Tossing the frog into the bath water, Zack squirted bubble bath liquid into the tub, and stirred up the water. "Don't get any ideas, you still have a Mommy and a Daddy, Satan bless them. Jo and I are just surrogate baby-sitters. Your Dad's just downstairs. Waiting for Ooma, may Allah keep her from the psych ward."

"Be nice," Jobim said. "They've both lost their jobs and are helping each other plan the next step. No need to get catty in front of Naji."

"It's okay, right Naj? Take me with a grain of bath salt." Zack scooped up foamy suds and flicked them at Naji's head. The two-year-old giggled, and flicked some suds back. It was the most delicious sound Zack had heard in a long time. He had not seen Naji smile in months.

Jobim saw the gleam in Zack's eyes. "You're the best, Naji. It's good to see you happy."

Naji stared at Jobim, that fixed look children get when they size up an adult. Naji turned to Zack and whispered, "Grain of bath salt." They flicked suds at Jobim.

"Kid got his sense of humor from his catty neighbor." Jobim splashed Zack. Naji roared.

"Okay, okay, too much fun," Zack said. "We don't want Sahara or Diana to think we like this. Or the brides next door will want us to perfume the hammam bath for *them*."

"Ha Mom?" Naji sat still in the bath.

"Do keep up," Zack said. "Hammam's a bathhouse. Like in the Nights."

Understanding, Naji lay back and spread his arms, like a fat man relaxing. "Hammam."

"Exactly," Zack said. "Mom's gonna be happy with how well you're using your words."

Downstairs, Amar made coffee for Ooma's arrival. So far the four male housemates had enjoyed nothing but good times, with no awkwardness. Ooma coming over would be a test. When she arrived, Amar discussed job prospects. Later Zack and Jobim came downstairs, and Amar went up to read Naji a story. Jobim had never met Ooma, but he put her at ease instantly.

"So," Ooma said, "you think Sahara and Amar ..."

Jobim answered. "They're both saying it's for good. As long as it works for Naji."

Ooma sipped her coffee. "What's that like? Naji has three Daddies?"

"Too politically correct for you? You the one to judge weird?"

"I can judge weird." Ooma knew Zack liked to joke, but it still hurt. Perhaps following his humorous lead would ease the pain. "Just 'cause the qaraq thinks I'm psycho. Any news?"

"They be targeting," Jobim said. "Do I have it right? Choosing a World."

Amar entered the living room. "Naji didn't sleep for months, and now he's out like a light."

"It's the bath salts," Zack said, with a wink at Jobim. "So yeah, targeting is us."

Ooma poured Amar a cup of coffee. "I feel less like targeting than a target right now."

Amar sat next to her on the couch. "The qaraq's tough. Jo, think twice about joining."

"Oh, I am. Zack thinks I'm one of you, but I couldn't recall to save my past life."

"Nonsense," Zack said. "If Ooma can recall Oamra recalling an elephant recalling a neutrino foreseeing the end of the world, you can remember our last lifetime together."

Amar said, "Seriously, Ooma, don't you want to move on from your visions of Oamra?"

"Yeah, a recall to clear the palate," Zack said. "And your reputation. Like my World as a terminally shy science teacher. Since I'm the thread there, I could help you recall it."

"You can do that?" Jobim was impressed. "So *that's* targeting."

Taking the challenge, Zack stood behind Ooma and placed his hands on her shoulders. There were a couple false starts, and Amar and Ooma tensed with the pressure.

"Weren't you called Hra Zamen?" Jobim said. "Maybe saying your name would help."

Dramatically, Zack whispered the name into Ooma's ear. "Champion of Science at the University of Frankovic." Ooma let out a hiss and her eyes became slits, trancelike, but also hostile. Zack let go of her shoulders as if receiving a shock. "Jeez, Jo, you got more moxie than I thought."

Before Jobim could temper Zack's esteem of him as a qaraqi, Ooma spoke.

The Tale of the Political Ballerina

I don't know why I am obsessed with Zamen, that mouse. He has no power in the school, being in the sciences, and he's the least popular instructor. He was always shy, but as of two years ago, when he destroyed some stupid closet experiment, he's barely spoken a word; he has less contact with his advisees, who no one remembers after they graduate, and he hides from all of us. I'll put an end to that, I'll expose him, I'll destroy the little worm.

I know why I loathe him. I was Uor Qxalm Taki, high-level ballerina in the Diplomat Corps, Principal Lead in Overseas Choreographed Negotiations, La Prima in Political Pas de Deux, the most starseeking diva in Political Performance. But the physical injuries began, and making a comeback proved difficult; resting on my laurels and needing to be the center of attention I let the University of Frankovic snatch me up with the admins wrapped around my fingers

I thought I would settle into the comforts of retirement but I felt severed from my life literally haunted by the image of all my friends and close colleagues drifting away on an island while I stayed fixed to shore suffocating and every time I saw that weasel Zamen he represented this narrow environment and made me feel the limits of my body and see that I was surrounded by lesser-thans but worst of all I could see how he disliked being here exactly my feelings I looked at his pathetic mug and saw we were alike and wanted to annihilate him my degradation

my one comfort was the faculty commons a room with a warm wood interior soft armchairs upholstered with Darkeibeest suede a deep-seated sofa eating table small kitchen area and fireplace for those chilly mornings a rather special accommodation for a small arts faculty though we had to share it with the professors of MAMESS. Uch.

I spent more time in my beloved faculty room than the dance studio I held court seated in a favorite chair from my Diplomatic office a
darkwood throne with lioness carvings at the end of the arms and plush
cushions in the seat big enough to hold two people if their bodies were
entwined

when I first met Zamen he was attempting to grade papers in the
commons room but couldn't keep his gaze off my chair so I strode in
regally sat down with perfect posture:

"And you are?"

"Hra Zamen. Science."

"Science," I groaned, settling down in the plush scarlets. I pulled a
Cinn Stick from my bag, sat back, and placed it in my mouth. "How is
science, Hra Zamen?"

"It's good," he muttered. "You're Uor Qxalm." Barely got the name
out.

I rose, strolled over to stand behind him. "You may call me Taki."
I riffled through his papers. "Do my dancers have to take science?" I
chewed on the Cinn Stick. "Poor dears."

"I wouldn't know. I don't follow my students' interests."

"Hra Zamen, you're one of those sci-types who ignores the allure of
the arts." I placed a foot on his chair, allowing my thin ballet skirt to rise
up my thigh. It was my surest test the use of my body enter the physical
space of the subject see their kine-sexual response gauge their appreciation of my grace.

Zamen failed the test miserably he did not know what to do responded
with some weak defense of science kept his eyes on his papers; I considered making a conquest of him in the lioness chair for his physique was
not abhorrent but after one minute he revolted me I've never disliked
anyone so much on first meeting.

"Just as I suspected, Hra Zamen, your only interest is in piddly
games." I sat in the lioness chair and stared at him. Within minutes he
excused himself.

I gave the school my best shot I lived for my students and appeased the fawning faculty but every time I saw Zamen I cringed inside from his lack of appreciation of me yet I showed nothing only looked for a plan to bring Zamen down

first I brought Zamen to faculty awareness since he was so inconspicuous then in private I made nice apologizing for our initial meeting respecting his work so I got a small mouthful from the weasel how math and science are overlooked in favor of music and dance and I encouraged him to raise the issue at meetings but he was too shy so I did it for him, mentioned he was against the arts pushed him into unpopular pro-science statements put words in his silent shocked mouth

best of all I heard about Zamen's secret projects in his classroom; ecstatic I took Chancellor Demus to lunch and inquired if he encouraged faculty to pursue pet projects on school property adding that though I'd love to perform highly classified negotiations at the university given its neutral ground I'd never dream of a conflict of interest to which the Chancellor replied that it was unethical subject to recrimination although he'd love to make an exception for me and probed why I had asked and I said Hra Zamen had these fabulous experiments going on in his storage closet

at this the Chancellor reinforced his position: such behavior was misuse of school equipment funds time space but he was curious what I had going on in my closet then with absolute seriousness assured me that he would investigate Zamen's activities I feigned horror that I had hurt Zamen and invited the Chancellor to search the dark corners of my studio shameless ballerina

I learned Zamen had gotten nowhere on his project but this inspired a marvelous idea: I had overheard a dancer's boyfriend complain about his science grade from Zamen bitching he could never approach the professor without him running away so with a little seductive assistance from the dancer/girlfriend I convinced the vengeful student to work on a little project in Zamen's storeroom for extra credit and soon after a device set off a chemical reaction that demolished the storeroom and set fire to the school's science texts and equipment

Uor Qxalm Taki, Supreme Negotiator for the Ballet Corps, triumphed again.

ق

Zack and Ooma turned away from each other. The tale had been an awful struggle between their souls. Zack could not break from the memory with his usual humor, so Jobim tried. "You messin' with my man?" The mock attack won a smile from Ooma.

Zack did not smile. "Ooma, we got a situation here. You were out for blood."

Ooma bowed her head. "What is wrong with me?" The answer was out of reach.

Amar came to her rescue. "There's got to be an explanation. Your immediate dislike of Zamen is like a karmic reaction driven more from past life events than current ones."

"We don't know this World's time," Ooma said, "so who knows what karma there was."

"Zack, you've mentioned a clan war," Jobim said. "This tale has feud written all over it."

"That makes more sense," Ooma said. "You guys are sweet. But let's face it. I'm evil."

"No, you're not. You're pretty." All heads turned. Naji was downstairs from bed. Had he heard the recall? "I want some water," Naji said. "That's all. No past lives."

72

—◦◦◦—

March 8. Month 6.

Returning from the reading of Ardra Rash's will, Amar, Sahara, and Naji sat silently in a three-person seat on a New Jersey Transit train. Sahara and Amar were too shocked to talk. It was not the inordinately generous amount of money Ardra had bequeathed. It was not that Ardra had left Sahara and Amar independent legacies, though they wondered how he had learned about their separation before passing. It was not even the terms, which were unorthodox.

The will specifically referred to: 1) supporting Sahara so she was financially independent from Amar, 2) funding Amar to envision a new business enterprise, and 3) setting up a trust fund for Naji, whose management Sahara and Amar had to share. These were unusual but fair terms, encouraging both financial independence and cooperation in the family.

It was the preface to the will that silenced the parents. Ardra stated he had consulted with Naji on the current needs of his family, grateful for the child's foresight. And the shocker, in language twinkling with Ardra's humor: Naji's fund was custodial only until his sixth birthday.

At the reading, Sahara and Amar had questioned their son, but Naji was close-lipped. How did a child just beginning to form sentences, Sahara asked herself, influence Ardra to completely revamp his will? Amar wondered if it was legal; was Ardra of sound mind?

Breaking the tense silence, Naji spoke aloud. "Staying at Uncle Zack's. Not a new thing."

The parents were so surprised by the statement, they asked him to repeat it.

"It's okay I stay at Zack's. I did it before."

"What are you talking about?" Amar asked. "Why bring this up now?"

"You mean the time I visited Ardra by myself after 9/11?" Sahara clarified for Amar. "I didn't know what shape Ardra was in, so I didn't want Naji to see him. Zack and Jobim baby-sat."

Amar remembered: at the time he could not face his grandfather ill. He got angry with Sahara for visiting. The memory humbled him; ending the marriage is the right choice.

Naji perceived his father's distress. "We took care of Ah-Dah. Now he's taking care of us. He's good *faqaf*."

The kid was full of surprises today. "Faqaf?" both parents asked.

"Not part of the qaraq," he answered, "but close friend to it. Even for lifetimes."

Was this a private language, Sahara wondered. "So you enjoyed being with Zack and Jobim. Didn't they give you a haircut that time?"

"Yes!" Naji was more animated than they had seen in months. "They clipped their hair first, so I wouldn't be scared. Then Jo cut my hair and Zack told me about Egypt." His parents probed. "How they prepared the bodies. Cut the hair. Cut the toenails. He played Little Piggie."

Sahara gasped. "He told you about preparing mummies? What is wrong with him?"

"It calmed me. Uncle Zack knows all about tombs. Sent me back to Egypt."

"Moses and Vishnu!" Amar exclaimed. "A haircut, mummies, and then a regression?"

Naji recognized his father's scolding voice. He needed to nip this in the bud. This was a good day. The best day. His mother and father should be happy. He and Ah-Dah had made sure of it. "I saved my Egypt life story for you. For both of you." *It's a special day. Wanna hear it?*

Naji spoke these last words inside their minds. Sahara looked at Amar, who nodded approval. They sat there on the Glenclaire train, approaching Watsessing Avenue. Amar held Sahara's hand as she closed her eyes, overwhelmed by the day's events. Naji told his tale.

The Tale of the Festival for the Welcoming of Aapep

I was mad at you, Momma Sha, so mad and hurt for what you did to me. I carried on for many lifetimes, no matter what they said in the interlife. It is time for you to let go of your unruly side, child, but I want one more go, I told them. This time I want to be the most expert thief, so I chose the richest, juiciest place to be one.

The Twelfth Dynasty had restored Egypt's wealth and power in the world. The heirs of the two Sensuret Pharaohs did more than consolidate their hold on immediate neighbors. Egypt was trading with China! The treasures in the royal coffers were amazing, but off limits to any thief, no matter his expertise. Thank Khnum that decades ago the Dynasty had allowed middle class Pyramid tombs. Security was not as elaborate. I had a way in.

The great Festival for the Banishing of Aapep was in full swing. Aapep was the Demon of darkness and chaos, opponent of Ma'at, who brings light and order. The priests constructed an effigy of Aapep, which was burned to protect us for another year. Of course, much more went on to honor Khnum, the local deity for the town of Elephantine: dancing, singing, imbibing of sacramental spirits, and general free license, men having their way with women, slaves with masters, and thieves with loot. My gang called it the Welcoming of Aapep.

I waited until the brilliant blue of the sky, the reflection of the mighty Nile, started toward pink and orange. The giant effigy was receiving final prayers and songs. Looking back one more time, the ghastly face of Aapep burned into my mind's eye. As I slipped out of town and neared the Pyramid, I passed workers heading the other way, toward the effigy. No one missed the final night; once the pyre started, any behavior was acceptable. Dozens of cleaners, guides, and, finally, guards left the Pyramids. I arrived at the south gate and snuck in the secret way my gang had discovered.

My stomach tightened. Getting inside a Pyramid was easy, getting into one of the tombs was the trick. The Kharman family burial suite was no exception: a maze of hallways to navigate and then three locked gates. The gang had paid off an acolyte for a map, but even with his life threatened, the pawn did not give up every tip. He promised that a clever man could figure out the rest. I volunteered for the job.

The acolyte did not lie. I whisked through the halls, only hesitating through fear. With all the stories and songs promoted by the new government, I imagined what Gods and Demons followed me down the halls. I rushed through the first gate, pushed a combination of stones in the wall and the second gate popped open. The third gate was another matter.

Outside the tomb stood a massive statue: an elephant with a mighty horse atop it, and a monstrous snake riding the horse. There were jewels enough right there, but I knew who the snake was: Aapep, the Demon itself, who froze its victims with a magical gaze. I avoided the snake's eyes, but after a terrifying eternity, surmised the gate switch must be on the snake's face. Who would want to look there? I yanked at the jewels in the eyes, the head, the fangs. A loud click!

I was in! The chamber resembled living space in the Kharman household, so the immortal souls could rest out eternity in comfort. That meant ghosts were all around me! Chilled, I saw insects swarming in every corner. Fool! They were only bejeweled scarab beetles, representing immortality, which adorn every tomb. Then I remembered the Festival priests performing symbolic actions to banish the Demon: spitting upon Aapep, defiling him with the left foot, or dismembering him. I imagined Aapep ripping me up in retaliation. I saw visions of strange machines that traveled to other times. What brought these images to my mind? Fear was powerful.

I sat down on a facsimile of a favorite Kharman bench. I had to pull myself together. I'd suffer equally frightening consequences from the gang if I failed. The burning ritual would be soon, and then the guards would return. I did a sober perusal of objects for the taking. There were jewels, gold versions of objects such as wheat and hammers, and expensive belts and necklaces. I got my tools and went to work dislodging gems. As I pried loose the beauties, I shook, and sliced my hand three times. The blood made me think of Aapep being dismembered. Renewing my resolve, I gathered loose items and made a pile. In one corner, I noticed an oval object, apparently hovering in mid-air. Nearing it, I felt a peace come over me, my fears abating. I stared at the ovoid and new visions came, this time not fearful ones.

I saw a soul traveling through Time, then settling into human form in Sumer many centuries ago. I saw the man-soul perform a ritual with the same ovoid, which exploded and shattered apart, hurling itself into never-space, retracing the soul's journey and ending in Egypt! I marveled to see it whole again, sequestered inside the magical powers of a Pyramid before my time. I saw the ovoid appear to several Egyptians: an acolyte tested by his master; a priest, ancestor to the Kharmans; and a drunken Kharman, celebrating the opening of the family tomb, thinking he had too much beer.

Enthralled, I touched the miraculous talisman. Doing so, I tore a sacred veil protecting it, which had forestalled its shattering. Tapping into the destructive energy, I completed the inevitable catastrophe started in Sumer. The object broke into seven pieces, pitching me across the chamber.

I felt the greatest shame. I knew I could not understand the devastation even if seven priests explained it, but my sadness was boundless. In my soul I knew I had undone something that had required uncountable amounts of time and energy, and benefited untold populations. I had to leave!

I threw as much treasure as I could into my bag. As I did, I found a fragment of the oval shell. I flinched, but out of some perverse instinct, I stuffed it into my pocket. Wildly searching for the other parts, I found a set of metal bars woven together by thin fibrous cording. What else had the shattering loosed? I bolted from the tomb.

Outside I froze before the giant elephant statue, lest the snake lunge at me. About to place the string of bars inside the bag, I tapped lightly on each metal slat and heard a pleasant ringing tone. The sound cleared my head and gave me courage. I could not remain a minute longer, but the paltry amount of loot would cost me my life. I had to escape to another land, away from the gang. I wished to project my soul to a safe place, the way priests claim the deceased soul can. With the tones ringing in my head, I reached into my pocket and clutched the oval shell.

I faced the statue. At that moment the priests set Aapep on fire, and smoke and flames from the pyre released magic into the libidinous festival grounds, the township of Elephantine, and the nearby Pyramids. I felt the magic as I gazed into the snake's eyes. I banished Aapep from my soul. I glanced down at the charging horse and willed it to whisk me away. Finally, I gazed lovingly at the elephant, placing my soul in its care. Gripping the oval tighter, I cast the bars at the elephant, and felt the chiming chord vibrate through me.

A flash of light and I was gone. Mimicking the shattering of the oval object, the musical bars dispersed to some isles below China, since in my mind China is the farthest place from the gang. The ovoid fragment scattered to the North, for across the great sea at the Nile Delta is the surest escape route. My Ba stayed right there, entered the great statue, and transformed into a smaller form that the guards found the next morning, at the foot of the elephant. I was no longer human, I could not move, but I had banished all fear.

ق

Momentarily forgetting the wonder of Naji speaking in their minds, Sahara and Amar sought connections to other past lives. "Remember later visitors to the Kharman tomb," Amar began, "the Minister from the Red Isle, and another thief, Nazir, who was Naji as well."

"Both of them found the tomb plundered, but noticed debris from objects," Sahara said.

"They found remains from the seven pieces," Amar said. "Nazir hid two of them in a desert cave. The top half of the oval and a map. He made a knife and a pocket mirror from two others."

"Leaving three," Sahara said. "The bars went to Indonesia, returned to Africa as the Instrument. And Oamra's great-grandfather got the base of the ovoid, millennia later."

"The Minister saw an elephant statuette lying near the big statue," Amar said. "That must be the small form the thief inhabited, that the guards found. The seventh fragment."

"We keep running into these object fragments. Elephants, knives, ovals," Sahara said.

"They're looking for each other," Naji said. "To be put back together. As the ovoid."

Amar startled. "But we keep messing things up, starting with me shattering the oval."

"And me helping." Naji mashed his head against Amar, cuddling. "At least Ah-Dah gave us one of the pieces. Though Uncle Zack and I haven't had any luck with it."

Amar squeezed Sahara's hand. "I know it's hard, Sahr. Just when Naji splits his time away from you, he starts to speak. But it's a blessed sign. Something's right with this change. Ardra's rewarding us, too." Sahara refused to respond, so Amar continued. "After a lot of trauma,

Naji figured how to sequence his development so he can speak aloud *and* in our minds. Right, buddy?"

Sahara stroked Naji's hair and let Amar's words sink in. If this was true, the child showed tremendous self-determination. "Naji, you said you saved this story for us. Made a big deal of receiving it with Zack and Jobim. You just wanted to let us know you're happy there?"

"It's good we're all near," Naji said. "Zack and Jo will need us."

"*They'll* need *us*?" Now Amar was confused. "Why?"

"Something bad may happen. Not sure what. Auntie Di tried to help. But can't."

Naji's father scolded. "You can't say this stuff and not be sure what you mean."

Naji made a sad face. "Sorry, Poppa. I'm not seeing things that clear. Not since talking."

"It's okay, sweetie," Sahara said. "If something bad happens between Zack and Jo we'll be there for them. You're not a bad boy for saying something." She gave Amar a warning look.

"But you were a real bad boy in Egypt," Amar said, saving face. "On the day we learn, with great difficulty, that you told your great-grandfather how to leave his money, why remind us you were a thief in many past lives? Does that help us trust you inheriting when you're six years old?"

"I only told Ah-Dah what you two wanted. He figured out the rest." Naji grappled with how to speak his next thought. "At end of the story the thief didn't steal anything. He found the ovoid. First thing you talked about. Important. Turned himself into elephant piece. Thief did my soul and qaraq good. Strange way to do it. Like a baby … cuting Ah-dah's will."

"Cuting?" Sahara worked out the word as she worked out Naji's amazing defense.

"*Executing* Ardra's will!" Amar delighted in his discovery. "Yes, we should trust you because you are a marvelous child handling the strangest of circumstances in the strangest ways."

508

"Yes, miraculous child," Sahara said, now that she understood. "I was my parents' world-traveling hippie waif, adjusting to the strangest of circumstances. Naji fits right into the family line."

"A World-traveling karmic waif," Amar agreed. He wiped tears from Sahara's face, and she gave him a small kiss. Then they looked down at the beaming boy, worrying the same thing.

The miraculous child spoke. "I know. You're not together anymore. And things are great with us now. But it's more than okay. It's the only way everything works out."

"The only way what works out?" Sahara asked. "What do you know, little swami?"

"I know it's for a really big reason. But I can't remember. I'm growing up. I'm not as close to the interlife."

Naji started to cry. "I'm losing my memories."

Sahara pulled him into her arms.

Amar looked out the window. "Damn! We're so wrapped up. Glenclaire was a half-hour ago. Quick, everyone off!"

They leaped up, and through hysterical tears and laughter, stumbled off the train.

73

March 11. Month 7.

The qaraq had not met since New Year's. By March, the qaraqis were restless. Taking the situation in hand, Cachay invited Verle, Zack, and Diana to her house for a 'mini-qaraq' meeting. She cleaned the house immaculately, and served an elegant high tea with sandwiches and cakes.

"Ooma's not making noises about joining," Zack reported. "Just hangs out with us lads."

"You mean with Amar," Cachay said. "I see that heading nowhere good."

"Let's not judge," Diana said. "Sahara seems content apart from Amar."

"And off in her own World." The small group startled as Porcy walked into the living room, Elvi close behind. "Hope it's okay to crash the party. I brought a facilitator. And brownies."

Cachay's hackles went up. She glared at Verle, who must have spoiled her careful plan. Oblivious, Porcy put down her platter and picked up a brownie. "Sahara's been trying crazy stuff to target stories. Donning raiments and ornaments. She wants me to regress her in that fountain."

"I'm coming over when she tries that," Cachay said. "Since crashing meetings is condoned."

Porcy ignored Cachay's high dudgeon. "Fine. You can baby-sit Naji."

Elvi called the meeting to order. Verle insisted the group become as good at targeting recalls as the 1001 qaraq. Eyeing Porcy, Cachay bragged that she had targeted a recall the other night. "Zack helped Ooma enter his shy teacher's World, so I asked him to do it for me."

"But I failed," Zack said. "So Jobim guided her through a visualization. Success! I'm telling you he's a natural born qaraqi. He should be at this meeting."

Diana caught Elvi's glance at her. She nodded, silently admitting there was no stopping Zack's fantasy. "There are others who should be at this meeting," Elvi said with a critical edge.

"May I continue?" Cachay said. "I visualized a devastating diary written by Hra Zamen."

The Tale of the Shy Teacher's Probation

Uiysdae, 4/113/00f6

After Uor Qxalm Taki disgraced me in the eyes of the university, I was put on probation. My fate would be determined end of next school year. A year to prove myself, not something I'm good at. Knowing Taki's spidery circles, the worst is yet to come.

Klvetsdae, 7/115/00g6

Start of the school year. I noted Eldon Kor's arrival with interest. A new teacher in the Math, Medicine, and Sciences Department always promises greater ease for me. Someone might feel shyer in the first year in MAMESS than I feel any time. Kor was a sweet man with pale complexion and thin black hair that hung down in his face. Extremely friendly. No outdoors type, but an attractive slender physique. Could be one of Taki's arrogant dancers, but he has a passion for math.

Frankovicsdae, 2/117/00g6

The students love Hra Eldon Kor. They flock to his classroom and love to hang out. Math is an elective students take to fill in their schedule. Eldon's draw was that Math is serious fun. And beautiful, surprising. If he saw elegance in your answer it wouldn't matter if it were correct.

Eldon was assigned to teach Astrobotany, bane of every new teacher's life. Begrudging arts students took it to graduate. Eldon did not prejudge. He avoided textbook classifications and started with the Uiywuit galaxy, our homeworld. He got everyone excited about what goes on in the stars, and from there, galactic plant life. His classroom was the secret pleasure palace of the school.

Wuitsdae, 5/118/00g6

All the teachers liked Eldon Kor. I extended a helping hand his first semester, answering any questions. For me to hit it off with anyone is implausible, but the two of us discovered common interests. We delighted in Unfanta Rishi's books, and shared a fascination with the Z-Endor Theorem. Within a few months I had found an ally in MAMESS. I shared my project ideas.

Hrursdae, 11/119/00g6

Taki also had luck with Kor. She was attracted to his ease with students. And his passion and delicate build. I was forced to watch Taki, from her lioness chair, flirt incessantly with Kor.

"A waste of a gorgeous body! I'd turn you into a scrumptious Dancer Diplomat in a year!" Kor blushed at Taki's taunts. "You can't believe Math is good for the students," she said. "They fall in love with you, then Math, then, Whoosha!, they're paupers without any way to make a living."

Taki had Kor wrapped around her finger, and soon his body was wrapped around hers, too.

"Take my dance class. Look at that rotation!" Taki sucked a Cinn Stick as she felt his inner thighs? "That's the secret. Oh, what's this? No little Cinn Stick for you!" She was shameless!

Dvonsdae, 1/121/00f7

Taki despised the alliance between Kor and me. But she used the friendship as new material against me. At the new semester, Chancellor Demus announced with regrets a series of cutbacks. Under review, I confided to Kor I'd be the sacrificial lamb for MAMESS. Kor knew Taki was behind this. One day Kor shared good news. He was on my review committee; I had one vote in my favor. I guessed how he had won his spot; Taki welcomed him with open arms. Begging me not to be jealous, he argued that his bond with Taki was going to save my ass.

Uiysdae, 4/122/00f7

As a new teacher Kor was vulnerable as well. It was horrible when he was sacked. That was not all. The chancellor excised the entire Math curriculum. Tenured Calculus professors were going, too. The money saved was going to Taki's creation of a new dance extravaganza.

Kor was furious. When Kor asked me what he could do to save his hide, the answer was obvious to me. "You need to use your bond with Taki."

Wuitsdae, 5/122/00f7

Kor went to confront Taki today. Would he beg her to save his job, or unleash his fury? I imagined the scene: Kor's tirade as dusk threw shadows on Taki lounging on her throne.

"I love that passion," she would say when Kor was finished. "Give it to me, baby."

Kor plants his hands on the lioness arms. "I'm dumped thanks to your greed."

513

Taki turns cold. "What more do you want? I got you on that worm's review committee." She sits up, and a fold of her robe exposes the curve of her breast. "Kor. I have the chancellor in my pocket. Say the word and you have your job back."

"What are you saying?" Taki's charms weaken Kor; he is not sure he can resist.

Taki puts her hands on Kor's face. "I don't want you fired. I want you here."

Kor pulls back. "I'm tired of your game. Your teases are like a rich man inviting a starving man home, and then pretending to eat food that is not there. Taki recognizes the story: the starving man pretends to get drunk, and slaps the rich man. The rich man forgives the jest.

"Are you going to slap me?" she taunts, and removes the sash from her robe. Taki relaxes back and Kor thrusts himself onto the lioness chair. At the height of their passion, Taki holds back and purrs into Kor's ear: "I go no further until you promise not to defend Zamen at his review."

Kor protests: "How can you do this? How can I betray a close colleague?"

"I am saving your life! Oppose Zamen or lose me." Taki undulates so Kor cannot resist, and during their horrible, gorgeous climax, tangerine skin turning lavender, Kor shouts his promise. Spent, Taki wraps her robe around her and exits. The last bit of twilight disappears.

Lethesdae, 9/124/00f7

Kor screwed Taki, but Taki screwed me. My review was a sullen execution. Kor bowed his head as others gloated. He glared at the triumphant Taki, which displeased her.

I can teach one more year, still under probation. What can I do in a year?

ق

"The journal ended there." Cachay poured some more tea. "I was concerned with what I, as Kor, had done to poor Zamen. What an untenable position I lived through! I was inhuman."

"Actually, a tangerine human," Zack said. "But I forgive you for shafting me, Mother."

"Cachay, I know you dislike your Nights archetype as the Court." Diana gestured to the tea service. "But the tale's tragedy is a perfect reflection of it. Kor was schooled in messy politics."

"Maybe the experience made you more human, after lives as a courtier," Verle said.

"You all see me as a conspiratorial bureaucrat? How come I hate Social Services?"

Porcy swallowed a brownie. "You hate all the needy people there. Courtly and cold."

"Your struggle may have been balancing politics with the needs of fellow creatures," Diana said. "Social Services is a painful replay, pitting your inner bureaucrat against your humanity."

"Mom, you went back to Law School so you could do *pro bono* work, helping others in the bureaucracy," Zack said. "And you've been an excellent mother. Even after Dad died."

The painful memory stunned Cachay. She blurted out, "Let's move on. Have some food."

Grabbing another brownie, Porcy jumped in. "All right, if you're the Court, I'm the People. If we're in contention, then let's tousle. You target a recall, so will I. Verle babe, pick a bull's-eye."

74

Verle stroked his chin. During the weeks after New Year's he had taken stock of his World types. The 379 Group lifetimes were only part of a much larger Multiple World. The mythic Forest and Land Bridge Worlds opened up a time period between the prehistoric Boreus and Stone Cliff Worlds. This period outlined human evolution up to the first civilizations, and a Five-Character type qaraq feud. Verle was also troubled by Diana's recall about the origin of reincarnation beliefs on Earth, which pointed to alien influence. Did Version 1 come from the stars? Verle had an idea.

"We've been so busy with the Nights that we stopped pursuing our oldest lifetimes. The seeds of the Versions are hidden there. Remember Zack's Starseeker tale? He was from the planet Ga-men, part of a lineage of planets with dominant proboscidean races."

"Like elephants, a qaraq's best friend," Zack said. "As a Starseeker, I had an ancient Aleph'iant mission to find alien, sentient species compatible with Ga-men's value of compassion."

"You sought a planet where the Xoo had moved after Suissam," Verle said. "From your clues, I calculated the planet was Earth before the dinosaur mass extinction. If the mission survived that catastrophe, was the species that Ga-men sought mammalian? Hominid?"

"We want a lifetime on Earth, after the dinosaurs, about what Ga-men found." Porcy produced a candle from her handbag and lit it on the coffee table. Seeing Cachay smirk at her gesture, she said, "I know you dears are sensitive about New Age stuff, so I'll keep it simple. *May this amber light trigger projections in my mind.* Boom!" Porcy took one more bite of brownie, focused on the flame, and soon recited a tale.

The Tale of the Projoscola

Everyone on Ga-men knows that famous image. We see it every New Round's Eve in the montages of great historical events. The Aleph'iant have always sought new life forms. This image celebrates those compassionate discoveries, passing our knowledge to new species.

Even before the discovery, Moeriterrium was a rare find. The Clairtemporant prophesied a world with a primitive form of our species, the Starseekers located it, and for two hundred and fifty years, nearly a million and a half Terrium years, the Machines sent back images of Mammalian species. But none resembled us. Funding came and went for the mission on Moeriterrium. I joined the Starseekers because our world gave up on it. Only seven Projoscola left on the Terrium surface.

The Projoscola Machines are a wonder. We plant them on a world in relative obscurity, and they observe life, send images, and record data for Ga-men or Starseekers. The Projoscola see into the soul of any sentient being, monitor its sensory perceptions (the sights it sees, sounds it hears), and project them back to the Starseekers. The Machine's ability is based on technology from our ancestors in previous universes, the silent sharing of thoughts between two minds. The projective ability is a more recent invention, which employs light to project information into space.

The Projoscola choose creatures they can relate to, either due to familiarity of behavioral patterns or assessment of potential wisdom. Since they use these beings as eyes and ears, sometimes the images lightcast to Ga-men do not include the creatures themselves. If one being looks at another one, we receive the information, but if they keep to themselves, we only see their habitat.

So it went on Moeriterrium. The host organism looked down at the ground because its pod community was more interested in rooting out food than engaging in social intercourse. As the creature evolved, so did a protuberance jutting into its field of vision, between the eyes. All of Ga-men were insanely curious at these images lightcast by the Projoscola. Pressure mounted.

I had personally named each Projoscola: Podling, Infanta, Ogle, Sweet-eye, Cootya, Babe, Dopey. When Ga-men lost patience and cut funding, they were recalled to Ga-men. I felt I had lost a family member or favorite pet Hmnd. I feared the Terrium expedition had seen its final rest, three Ga-men millennia for nothing. I suggested our crew move the Projoscola closer to the species.

The beauty of a Projoscolum is that it is non-invasive: we control it from space, it reads its target from afar, and the light projected blends with the atmosphere. For millions of Terrium years no organism ever detected our presence! Our crew was divided about breaching this strict protocol, especially Blo-mon, who quoted the Starseeker Guide chapter and verse about non-interaction. The moderates argued that by favoring this species we rendered natural selection unnatural. But to stick slavishly to the rules meant the end of our work. Stubbornly contentious, I knew what I wanted, to look at the face of this species and discover once and for all if they resembled us.

Blo-mon threatened to contact Starseeker Central, have me stripped of rank, and recall every last Projoscolum. Blo-mon and I came to blows, but thanks to the moderates we worked out a compromise. Blo-mon recalled Ogle, Sweet-eye, and Dopey (who was useless anyway). Cootya remained at a distance, but Podling, Infanta, and Babe moved closer.

The experiment turned to disaster. With the appearance of three Projoscola, many creatures fled in terror. The alpha males stood their ground, threatening and kicking up dust at the Machines. Re-programmed to approach, Babe was attacked and de-activated. The Mammalians fought each other over what to do. Seizing the moment, Podling flew to a distracted creature, bound it in plas-wire, and prevented its exit. Worked up, Podling forgot to project any image back to our ship.

Before further mishaps, I ordered the third Machine, Infanta or Unit No. 1664.125.211211-246.11520.2552121, to retreat, seek shelter, and harm no Mammalian. Infanta set its sights on a nearby oasis where the Machines hid from passing animal life. At the same time, a family of the frightened creatures escaped to the oasis. Detecting the presence, Infanta entered the eyes of a child as it shook in fear and gazed up at its caring mother. This image changed our world.

Back on Ga-men the media sent the image to every netscreen and holostage on the planet. Everyone saw the baby's fearful parents nuzzling each other, head to head, eye to eye, and best of all, nose to nose. There was the evidence to prove our kindred genotype, the feature linking us to universes of ancestors: a classic proboscis. It was the trunk seen round the world.

The fever from the home world was momentous. We were rewarded handsomely, and sent new Projoscola to probe inside the host minds. Intervention is tricky, but once Ga-men finds a compassionate species, they track its intelligence, ready to be allies. Why not tip the scales sooner?

Proboscidean life on Moeriterrium was extremely primitive compared to our ancient civilization. On Ga-men, citizens stared in awe at *Anthracobn*, its origins in the Reptilian era, evolved over millions of years, still snuffling the earth floor with its snout. There was *Barythierre*, remarkable for its eight sawed-off tusks, still foraging on four legs. And *Moeritherion*, which we named after the mysterious planet, tugging at our heartstrings with its piggish-doggish-hippoish muzzle and torso. It insulted our sleek grace but reminded us of our humble origins. We loved them all!

Content that life on Moeriterrum was evolving nicely, we were secure in the knowledge that a century on our world meant a million years of biological history for our future companions. All was well until, for some unknown reason, the Projoscola broke down and stopped their reports.

ق

Verle responded to Porcy. "The tale reminds me of a very short life of yours. You were murdered as an infant, perhaps over control of the zojy. On planet Veryx, which had zojy *mines*."

"Then I had a lifetime near it, with iconic images and the God Vishnu," Porcy said.

"We had a hint of a lifetime in between the infant and Vishnu tales involving a proboscidean species," Verle said. "Elephants with sacred devices. Your latest tale supports my theory that a device smuggled out of Veryx ended up on Ga-men, before humans evolved on Earth."

"This zojy device," Zack said. "Aren't we talking about the metal ovaloid thingie that keeps showing up in our lifetimes? The parts littered the Kharman tomb, the oval helped Sanaa envision stories. It probably powers my menorah that projects stars on the ceiling." No one laughed.

"The zojy have many forms," Porcy said. "They're raw ore on Veryx, projected images seeding Earth culture. They can be prophecies, or past lives embedded in Version 1 of the Nights."

Listening to the contradictory information, Cachay felt defeated. She had exposed her soul in her recall, then Porcy one-upped her with an all-encompassing vision. The confusion exacerbated Cachay's dark mood. "It's too much mush! Which are the true zojy?"

Hoping to bring some peace, Elvi said, "All of the above are true. All of the above."

75

—⚬⚬⚬—

April 2.   Month 7.

Naji and his unemployed father spent a lot of time in their new home, playing games, watching cartoons, and handling Zack's less fragile collectibles. Jobim joined in the fun when he could; Zack succumbed to distraction from his online business constantly. Everyone, including Naji, got sick of the playground, Yummy Yammies, and FunZone.

To give Amar and Zack a little credit, they had a lot of discussion before deciding to bring Naji to Woodie's, Glenclaire's only cigar bar. They assumed if it were the wrong choice, Woodie's would not allow a child through the door. But the hostesses gazed in delight, their eyes became sharper then unsheathed swords, and their lashes bewitched all hearts. Within minutes the two men enjoyed fine stogies, careful to blow smoke away from Naji, who savored a lollipop.

"No clue what sort of business I want to create," Amar bemoaned after a glass of Merlot, "especially in this economy. Ooma needs my help, but I hit nothing but obstacles."

"Didn't Doc Mach give this a name," Zack said, "seeing doom everywhere?"

"Hypa-viglitz," Naji said, with the authority of Sigmund Freud.

"Hyper-vigilance," Amar corrected, astonished that, with his new verbal skills, Naji had picked up the term. "I'm not making these things up. You two know I don't fret day and night."

"Every day," Naji corrected, "but not every night. Poppa, you need to relax."

"Did you get that from Momma?" Amar displayed his cigar. "What's Poppa doing now?"

"Fretting," Naji said, "and it's night. Ah-Dah gave us money. No worries. Need a tale."

Zack perked up. "You got a story? From a new World?"

"Momma started it New Year's," Naji said. "Forest Spirits and Mortals. Five-Character Feud. I got a recall when I saw the Forest in Poppa's mind."

Disturbed by his son's eerie knowledge, Amar felt enshrouded by the smoke of the cigar bar. He was uneasy re-visiting the Forest, a World on the edge of catastrophe, a feeling too close to home. Clearing a cloud of smoke with a wave, he asked, "When did you see my mind, young man?"

Naji took a slow tug on his lollipop. "Sit back, and I'll tell you all about it."

November 22. Thanksgiving.   Week 11.

Naji stayed lying on the floor after Bax and Ooma came to the house that day. In his brain he was searching for the twins. A futile task, Naji realized he was bounding back and forth inside the minds of the people in the living room. When he saw his father gazing at Ooma, he glimpsed a dense forest. In Poppa's head? What did it have to do with Ooma? Allured by the Magic Wood, Naji entered his own shadowy lifetime there.

The Tale of the Dark Lord's Summons

Lo, the Dark Mistress of the Magickwald, Nouhi Shadowbranch, summoned every God and Goddess, every Spirit and Nymph, both Dark and

Light, calling upon Trucement so neither side cast a tremulous glance, so each side would heed Nouhi's words clearly, and so a tone of collaboration might prevail. Nouhi was to put forth a Warning, that without action from the divine element of the Wood, their existence would soon be at an end, brought about by human, animal, and plant.

Sending dark Spirits forth, Nouhi spread this exhortation: if you love to gaze upon the vast blue beauty of the Sky as much as I do, (I, a deity of wrath and destruction who oft prefers the sight of mud and leaf decay, so you love Sky even more than I), if you wish to continue enjoyment of Ilmatar's Blue, then run fast to this gathering of Gods, and hear of the Doom weighing upon us all.

Nouhi's minions were nervous about the gathering, for there were so many details to solve. Refreshment alone presented a serious dilemma. The Dark forces preferred thick meads and brown ales, whereas the Light liked fruit drinks and crystal waters; the Dark gnawed tough meats and bones, the Light seeds, nuts, and flowers. The Dark would mock the Light fare, while the Light would not wish the coarse foodstuffs to touch their delicate morsels. It was enough to ignite a war.

Then there was the treacherous business of the seating chart. No matter how satisfying the wine and victuals, Tuoni, Lord of the Underworld, might smack Jumala, Thunder God, on the back of the neck, if seated near him. Kalma, his daughter, Goddess of Death, would trade insults with Roonikka, Jumala's wife, if they were within shouting distance. Yambe-Akka, the Old Woman of the Dead, could hurl a leg of mutton at Ukko the Rain God, who helps with the Impossible.

Yet Nouhi insisted everyone sit close enough to hear her speak! Which knoll sufficed to provide an intimate enough space? Which tree would provide enough shade for the company?

Nouhi was Goddess of Sorcery and Dark Magick, who ruled over witches, sorcerers, and necromancers, and who governed spells, invocations, chants, and sacred drums. Working her way up the Magickwald hierarchy, from mischievous imp to playful and vengeful Forest Spirit, Nouhi had earned a reputation as a sprite joking and teasing one minute, and bifurcating a corpse the next. Nouhi demonstrated an inventive, wizened maturity as well, a role model for Dark creatures of the Wood. She had cast aside her earlier pranks, and earned a spot in the ruling class of the Magickwald. No one could make a potion or cast a curse without authorization from the Goddess of Sorcery.

When the fateful night of the Gathering came, the highest degree of Sorcerer beat a drum to raise Gods and Spirits to approach. Hiisi, Dark Spirit and Nouhi's assistant, who had worked out all the troublesome concerns, paced nervously. Only three or four fights broke out as the deities took their seats. Nouhi climbed up a high branch of the designated Tree to calm any more outbursts. Despite a few snickers from the Light side, everyone fell silent as Nouhi began to speak.

"Gone are the days when we immortals delighted in every new creature come into this world, be it flying with rustling wings, bushy with long tail, or rooting with snoutish nose. Now we must trust no human, animal, or plant, old or new.

"Gone are the days when our forefathers left us to ward this planet, when the last dominant race receded from its power, and when the creatures of this Earth held equal sway over the land. Now we must keep a watchful eye, lest one group seizes control.

"Gone are the days when Yambe-Akka agreed to leave each soul alone, to allow it to choose its passing from this world into Tuoni's unliving realm. Now we must distinguish between us, immortal from birth, and them, immortal by our granting.

"Gone are the days when mortal spoke to immortal as friend, when animal conversed with human over the hedge, when Spirit communed with flower to receive a love nectar. Now these ties are breaking: some men think animals dumb, some plants cringe at approaching feet, and most have forgotten we Gods exist. We ceased listening to mortal cries.

"A fatal Hero has come into our midst, one Faina, with hair of bright flame. He will bring us all down, one by one, or all at once. He is both mortal and immortal, man and God, half of each and none of either. Faina is prophesied to take the power of Undying gifted to mortals, and turn it against us. Voinen, dear enemy, you have taken this nemesis into your home and given him warmth, counsel, and broth. Your good heart will betray all of us. Reconsider your generosity.

"Trouble is about to fall like leaves of the Wood in Autumn. We must put away differences and work together to save our existence on Earth. Some mortals may love us still, but these same will be content to do away with us eventually, for a good tale to tell their grandchildren.

"We must act fast. Inhibit growth wherever you tread, be it procreation, germination, or population. Withhold secret lore. Watch over each other, Light over Dark, Dark over Light. Kalma, Goddess of Death, I call you to revoke the Gift of Undying to any newborn. Do so silently and unobtrusively, so none will rise in protest.

"Most of all, Dark Ones, sow anger and spite among all mortals, for only violence can undo the Undying they enjoy. Cause war. I do not ask the Light to participate in such horror, only to accept its necessity. Help the innocents accept their mortality. We will work together in this.

"Lastly, I call for a small group of Dark Volunteers to hunt down Faina. We must trick Fate in this, for She comes not to this Gathering; Fate stands outside and receives no influence from what we fear. Those who would bring down Faina must be stealthy, quiet, and deadly. If ye desire the task, come to me. All others, think grimly on my words, and prepare. Strength be with us."

And Lo, the company dispersed, Dark plotting with Dark, Light strategizing with Light, with the occasional Light approaching a Dark. Hiisi cleaned up the mess, grousing bitterly. Finally, only the Tree of the Magickwald remained, who had shaded the Gathering. Being the only mortal privy to deadly information, and ally of Faina, the Tree thought long on its next action.

ق

At the cigar bar, when Naji finished, the effort of conveying the story, combined with the smoke, made him drowsy. Quickly, Zack asked, "Naji, why was the Forest in your Dad's mind? Was this his recall?"

525

Naji's eyes fluttered. "No. I was Nouhi."

Zack gave Amar a puzzled look. "Sahara introduced the Forest World at New Year's. How were you thinking about it before, at Thanksgiving?"

Amar had arrived at the real reason he dreaded re-visiting the Forest World. "I saw this World the week before Thanksgiving. When Ooma hypnotized me."

76

———〰〰〰———

Before Amar divulged the truth to his shocked friend, he waited until Naji was fast asleep. After a long drag on his cigar, Amar described events the week before Thanksgiving.

November 17. Week 10.

Amar and Sahara had had their final hypnosis session, when Amar recalled the disturbing tale of betrayal in Sumer. Amar was frustrated with his wife's attempts at regression, so Ooma offered her services in exchange for his support in helping them join qaraq meetings. Amar was resistant to her offer, since he could not tell Sahara about it. But he accepted.

Ooma had regressed Amar successfully in the past, but when she laid hands on his shoulders in the most sensual manner, the act felt illicit. Amar received mere flickers of the Forest World, so Ooma stood in front of him, placing his hands on her body. Amar could barely control his lust! The experience was marvelous, but as unsuccessful as any regression with Sahara.

In his therapy session that week, Amar confessed the incident, including fragments of the Forest World. The slightest detail sent Dr. Machiyoko into a full memory of her lifetime there.

"Dammit!" Zack interrupted. "That woman gets the best visions on everyone's dime."

"Don't be mad, big brother," Amar said. "I'll tell you what she recalled."

The Tale of the Sleeping Giant's Dream

Gielikkin, Great Tree of the Magickwald, foe of those at the Gathering (they realized it not as they enjoyed her shade), shook her leaves and canopy, sending out a warning to all mortal creatures, that deities of the Wood meant them harm. The animals and humans were smart enough to comprehend the awful message, but not confident enough to know what to do about it.

Nyyrikki and Tuulikki, children of the Goddess of Water, listened to Nouhi's dreadful speech, and spread the news to their mother, Mielikki. Before she could alert her husband Anniddi, harts and hares, men and women, strangler figs and crawling vines all descended upon the gentle God of the Wood. Anniddi expanded his many-branching body to gigantic proportions, so that all who wished to nest in his forestal arms did so. Those who lived in the photosynthetic system that was Anniddi, and those who rushed into his arms out of fear, made their own Gathering that night. By firefly-light they beseeched Anniddi to help them and give them a course of action. Accustomed to moving slowly, Anniddi listened to the plaints well into the next day, then addressed the throng.

"You all know I love and protect you," the great God said. "Now curl up and sleep in my branches and twigs and leaves, and I will send a dream to comfort you."

Anniddi transformed into the Sleeping Giant, which some saw as a long hillside resembling a man lying prone, while others heard as the rustling of the wind in the trees. Mortals yawned and lay down in Anniddi's beard of lichen; mothers fell asleep in his eyebrows of moss, suckling their babes; young lovers fell asleep on the banks of his eyes, which were bottomless lakes.

In the God's message, he dreamed he was a Spirit flying over green landscapes, alighting in the trees to catch a snooze. Once asleep, the Spirit dreamed he was a man hunting in the forest. After an exhausting day, the human collapsed and dreamed he was a stag. The wondrous animal, wounded by the hunter, fell down in a swoon on a pile of leaves, and dreamed it was a vast tree. The tree dreamed it was a rock outcropping, and the rock dreamed it was a God.

Anniddi sent the dream as a test. The dream represented the interconnections that came with the gift of immortality, the ability of a leaf to hear the cry of a wolf pup, or a young girl to hear a Satyr fawning over her, or the population to understand the symbols within Anniddi's dream. But only a select few understood, while another group perceived it as comfort, the silly stuff of dreams. A third group, the largest, did not receive the dream, just a sound sleep, which incensed Anniddi. Who were these souls, who did not hear the God's voice? They did not deserve the precious gift of Life! They were the souls Nouhi spoke of, the Doom, the failure of the grand experiment.

Anniddi quelled and quaked down to his roots; he rumbled and shook, and a great storm ranted through the land. Every sleeper awoke, even those resting deep inside Anniddi's dream, who understood all. Whatever calm the sleep had brought was broken by the God's rage.

Anniddi raised cold winds and called on his ally Baqbaqa, the Spirit of the Wind, to carry him through the air. And Anniddi flew with Baqbaqa to Nouhi's side, and told the Dark Lord of his test. Anniddi said he would stand aside, but not participate in Nouhi's cause, though he understood it. He loved the mortals, even the ignorant ones, and did not wish them direct harm.

Nouhi accused Anniddi of complacency, of observing all and reacting occasionally with a storm, but never truly aiding God or mortal. Anniddi disagreed, for by stretching his limbs he provided homes and protection. Nouhi felt Anniddi was weak, and said that harsh treatment of people, if well intentioned, is often more beneficial than soft, kind treatment, which ends in calamity without hope. Anniddi argued that constant war with dark forces perpetuates those forces.

The two divinities remembered other visitors on the planet who had argued about interceding with the natives or maintaining a safe distance. Nouhi mentioned caged prisoners and sandship fleets; Anniddi recalled ancients with long nasal protrusions. Knowing they were neither the first nor the last facing this struggle, they gave up their debate.

Anniddi announced that if Nouhi and the divine host brought down Faina and changed mortals forevermore, then Anniddi would leave the world. Nouhi accepted this promise, but was sad she might cause Anniddi's departure from the Magickwald, and end their alliance.

As Nouhi and Anniddi bid farewell to each other, the God-Hero Faina heard from Voinen about the Gathering. Voinen ignored Nouhi's warnings about abetting Faina, for he loved him as a son. He thought: *Sometimes it is not whether we act harshly or kindly that determines our love, but it is our love that determines how we act.* And Faina marveled that Gods and Spirits, Light and Dark, looked to him as a malevolent force. Confused about his role in the world, he sought the Tree of Magickwald, to hear the text of the Gathering, and whatever advice the wizened arbor offered. Even in passive listening, Faina launched the Fate that would change the world forever.

ق

April 2, 2002.   Month 7.

"From this tale," Zack responded, "you knew the Doc and Naji, Anniddi and Nouhi, faced off about Faina's fate. Why didn't you say anything when Sahara recalled Faina?"

"It would've led to the fact that Ooma and I had a rendez-vous," Amar said. "Still secret."

530

"But we chewed off Sahara's head for recalling new Worlds. It wasn't new!"

"I know, it was bad." Amar snubbed out his cigar. "And if Sahara knew Diana was keepng information from her, even for professional reasons, she would've been mighty pissed. Diana and I had one more session. We discussed the awkward situations cropping up. She terminated me."

"For the best." It was Zack's turn to demolish his stogie. "Little Miss Dunyazade is so weird. She's been hounding me about Jo for the longest time. Maybe she's jealous. Or feeling obsolete. Jo and I got our act together without her. Even the sex is great now."

"I'm glad he's not screaming from nightmares anymore," Amar said. "But he still screams."

"Sorry about that " Zack gestured to Naji. "Especially for this little guy's sake. Seems to sleep through everything these days, though. Anyway, maybe Di needs some lovin' of her own."

"Oh, please. Sahara and I are doing fine separated. Di's fine, too. Just let it go, bro."

"Yes, it seems like you're more entangled with good Queen Uzmeth." Amar dismissed Zack with a wave of the hand. "She's not evil. Just struggling."

"Struggling? The girl was a horny predator in Borzi World. Who knows what power she'll grab in the Land Bridge or Stone Cliff Worlds. She went glory-mad on the Red Isle, and Bang! "Uzmeth. Not a bad sequencing of Worlds. I wonder where the Forest fits. If the Gods were really aliens, it's well after Ga-men. The mortals seem like early humans developing Nature myths. More sophisticated than Borzi, but no cultivation like the Three Valleys."

"The Forest is smack-dab in the qaraq's feud," Zack said.

Amar said, "It feels like the end of the world, with immortality and reincarnation at stake." "We know how to pick our battles," Zack said. "We're still fighting them."

"Sahr and I tried to resolve the feud in our dog-cat fights, but I ended up in hotter waters."

"With Ooma. In Sumer." Zack stared at Amar. "Was she good in the ziggurat?"

Amar glared back. "How did you find out? That memory ruined Sahara and me."

"She told Diana. Diana took pity and told me. And I told Porcy."

"Shit! Now everyone knows. It *is* the end of the world."

"It's mythic." Zack gave Amar a fiendish smile. "Just let it go, bro. We all should know everything. The bigger question is what happens now. With Ooma. How *are* things with her?"

Amar wondered how much Zack understand of his feelings for Ooma. How much did he himself understand? Did he need Zack as a new therapist?

Before they went any further, Naji woke up. Time to air the cigar smoke from the baby.

77

—⊰∅∅∅⊱—

April 16. Month 8.

When the qaraq reinstated regular meetings, Ooma was invited; the group knew she would decline. But Amar was there. Since Porcy was still on Verle's case to secure a better space at the church, Amar and Zack took pressure off the old man by hosting the meeting at Zack's house.

Besides Ooma and a sleeping Naji, Sahara was the only member not present. After the risky regression in her patio fountain, she wanted to slow down and sort out her last vision. Diana insisted the group was the place to process those thoughts, but Sahara begged off. She was closing in on sending her last chapter to Dr. Aziz. She needed space.

Everyone expected a night of catch-up, but Elvi had made the rounds, sharing their recalls.

"You've gotten much more *familiar* with us," Zack said. "Are we doing something right?"

"As always." Elvi looked around the group. "It is the way it is." Diana, Cachay, Porcy, and Verle gave her knowing smiles. She was their spirit guide. Zack shrugged.

Naji staggered into the room and plopped himself down on the couch next to Verle. With the little one nuzzled against his shoulder, the elderly man looked downright uncomfortable.

Amar, next to Verle, whispered, "Someone misses their great-grandfather Ardra."

Verle tensed. "Pardon me, but I ain't no surrogate."

"Our archetypes make you father to Scheherazade or Sahara," Porcy said, "so you'd be the child's grandfather. If I have to represent the masses, you can pony up to a kid."

When Verle looked horror-struck by the little kiss Naji gave his shoulder, Cachay said, "You old coot, would you rather he call you Grand Vizier than Grandfather?"

Aware of Naji's new speaking abilities, the company encouraged him to say the honorific: Gran Va Ziwo, Ganva Zio, Gasii. With each attempt, Verle softened. By the time Naji settled on *Gravi*, the group, and Verle, cheered. Taking his cue, Naji said, "Can we start?" Everyone laughed.

"Actually, Naji's been keeping pace with recalls," Elvi said. "I have ways of keeping tabs on everyone, including what you've learned. Call it a professional secret."

"Familiarer and familiarer," Zack said.

As if New Year's was the night before, the group fell into arguments about which Worlds to explore. Bax's head moved back and forth like watching a tennis match. Finally, Naji silenced the qaraq by switching deftly between speaking inside their heads and out loud. He described his Heaven, microbiome, and crime World visions. Every target hit was amazing, but he had had no control over why it was hit. "So stop fighting," he finished, aloud. "We need a clear target, and Gravi should pick it." The group was overwhelmed with the child's sensible wisdom.

"I be honored, lad," Verle said. "Let's go with Ga-men. We're onto something there."

Complying, Elvi guided Verle back to his life on Earth between dinosaurs and humans.

534

The Tale of the Phiomian Harem

I fulfilled a mission, discovered a beautiful new home, and found all the love I could ever want. Why am I miserable? Why lament this glorious experiment; why not rejoice?

It started with a journeyman's errand, a repair call to fix the Projoscola, which had ceased projecting images of life on Moeriterrium. Ga-men had observed for millions of Terrium solar years, only a few centuries in our time dimension, so I thought I wouldn't be gone long. I had seen images of kindred life on the planet, albeit smaller-nosed, four-legged, and unintelligent. But when I arrived I was smitten: the planet was lush and beautiful, the atmosphere unbelievable hues of green and blue. Proboscideans or no, I was ready to move here! The Mammalians were more hunted than hunters. Alongside the proboscids, they seemed equally good candidates for future companions.

There was nothing wrong with the Projoscola: power sources activated, systems enabled. But rather than operating camouflaged, the Projoscola were out near watering holes and herding grounds. No longer just observing, their assemblies whined for touches from the scurrying animals, they clicked greetings to passers-by, and near a tribe of primates, one Projoscolum clanked away in a rhythmic display of an 11/4 meter against a high pinging polyrhythm in seven. The apes danced madly in the moonlight to the looping accompaniment.

After the initial shock of witnessing Projoscola mingling with natives, I appreciated the beautiful innocence of it. With this fragrant, peaceful environment, no wonder the Machines let their guard down. But why had they stopped projecting data to Ga-men?

Uprooting the rhythmic Projoscolum from its dance with the apes, I made a note of its serial number (2254.21211-25121.854) and installed it in my airpod. I flew off in search of Moeriterrium's proboscideans; equipped with a Starseeker's endless micro-supplies, I took my sweet time exploring the planet. As I did, I analyzed 2254's datatracks (millions of years of them!), and discovered that ages ago Starseekers repro-grammed the Projoscola to interact with the species.

The airpod sailed through gorgeous glens and over mountains recently sculpted by continental collisions. Drifting over an endless marsh, I spotted my first proboscis: a medium-sized *Numidatian*, whose tusks braided around its trunk. Not much farther was a herd of *Bifurcia*, each with a trunk for inhalation and another for exhalation. Still further roamed the *Tethyrions*, whose probosces retracted or extended in accor-dion-like segments. 2254's files suggested this inventive biodiversity was due to the Machine's aggressive encouragement of mating habits. During this frenzy of generating new sub-species, they must have lost the logic to contact Ga-men.

A new mystery reared its head: the Projoscola reported to someone else! I trained the airpod to navigate toward where 2254 was sending its rhythmic signal. Along the way I kept track of each new species, check-ing against 2254's endless data, like filling in a giant Numeroniat cross-hatch puzzle. Halfway to the signal source, I had counted over three hundred species, every imaginable size, shape, and design of mutated proboscis. The Machines had spawned a chaos of creation!

Finding 2254's contact point was my next jolt. When ancient Starseekers discovered that planet Suissam had moved its Xoo to Moeriterrium, they enabled Ga-men to locate this proboscidean world. But with the evolutionary acceleration of the species, the Xoo showed great concern that its caged political radicals might some day influence and harm the proboscideans. Taking action, the Xookeepers made the Projoscola report all genetic data to Suissamese authorities. Learning this, my troubles began, perhaps the source of my sleepless nights now.

I went to the Xoo, ambassador of the Eleph Osciant, made the proper intros, paid the proper respects. I received a tour of the Xoo, so forlorn with the many radical thinkers exiled in a wasteland near the planet's Pole, so valuable in their ideas (bio-shreddable materiel; polymath disemployment schemes; mood inoculation), and so wasted on the Xoo's tiny flow of visitors. I sat down with the Xoo officials, using 2254 as my translator, who was on casual terms with them. They wanted nothing to do with Terrium evolution, and wanted the planet desolate and backward. This planet is teeming with life, I argued, especially proboscidean. I apologized for the Machines' actions and assured them Ga-men would control the population. I left, saddened by what I had to do.

It was not a matter of extermination – I could never do that -- but the process would take a great deal of time. First, I had the Machines calculate how long I could remain on Moeriterrium and how often I had to return to space to slow down my aging in our parallel spacetime. Next, I left for Ga-men and reported my plan to reverse the Machines' catalytic effects, arrest evolution, and let Nature select the most successful proboscidean families. I journeyed back and forth between my two homes, mourned as mutation after mutation died out over thousands of years, mere months on Ga-men. I cheered on the survivors, delighted in *Patamonstria*, the short-tusked brute luxuriating in beautiful streams, and felt reassured as *Mastodians* developed thick fur for the freezing tundra.

But my favorite was adorable *Phiomia*, closest in form to mine, if Ga-men was inhabited by four-legged nymphets with modest probosces and tiny, delicate heads. The Phiomia loved me, too: on cold nights they wandered into my encampment to huddle by the fire. I taught them rudimentary language, helped them develop skills to work alongside me, and even enjoyed sport with them. On crisp nights under Terrium stars I fell in love with that world, not wishing another race to die. If Nature would not protect the Phiomia, I would myself.

Back on Ga-men they humored my rants. The Projoscola offered no support, since they still only reported to the hostile Xoo. The species count was down from its pinnacle at four hundred to less than eighty. Was this when my misery began? The Xoo fretted about the intelligence of specific families; Ga-men pushed me to nurture those species. Both paths were wrong. I cut off contact with my tormentors and sought physical comfort with the Phiomia. As I released my tensions with the sweet one with the turned up snoot whom I named Phi-li, a grand plan fell into my lap.

Since they recognized me as their Alpha, I mated with as many as possible, with no idea as to what we would produce. After a few dozen calves were born, by necessity I traveled to Ga-men, knowing that on return my advanced genetic material would have influenced many generations.

As my airpod returned from the mothership back into Terrium atmosphere, I saw the semi-circular formation of huts that comprised a community of evolving Phiomia, already agrarian. More beautiful than ever, the bipedal tribe members greeted me as a God. The Phiomians were more obliging than ever; they vied for me. I feared combats, so I chose a clever one, with the popular name of Phi-li, to organize a harem to share me equitably.

Others were waiting, too, Xoo officials with Projoscolan representatives. Ignorant of the source of the Phiomia's progress, the Xookeepers laughed at my defense of the tribe's wondrous nature. Insulted, I left the Machines to dicker with the Suissamese, rutted the entire harem in revenge, and escaped to Ga-men. Returning later, I saw small cities thriving throughout the Dominion of Phiomia, with fortifications, schools of higher learning, and rich cultural traditions.

Projoscolan spies informed the Xookeepers of my complicity in this evolution. I argued that my breeding with the Phiomia safeguarded the Xoo's future: by creating a civilization loyal to the planet, I had provided protectors from alien liberation of the Xoo, chaotic interplay between the prisoners, and get-rich-quick mercenaries. The Suissamese banished me from the Xoo.

To get over the affront, I visited the Popushkavalle Gardens, thermal pleasure baths designed for proboscideans' thick muscles and water-spouting trunks; wallowing in the fresh mud soup, I splashed with my kindred proboscids, amazed that I passed for a Terrium creature. There were obvious differences (fewer toenails, more fuzz on their backs), but no one stared.

I was no longer an alien from Ga-men; nobody recognized me from previous visits. I had loved them, given them my vital essence, and fostered their growth. Now they looked the other way when I passed in the street, and taught their children alternate histories to how they had really evolved. They had advanced past my influence.

Here was the true reason for my misery. I had lost their love. I was heartbroken.

I wandered the streets of Popushkavalle, frequented the fermenteries, and met a young beauty named Phi-li. Together, we raised a precocious family.

ق

The qaraq marveled at Verle's story, not only because of his deft targeting. "You found a missing link to evolution on this planet," Diana said. "A whole other history."

"Did these creatures influence early man?" Zack asked. "Amar, how about Ganesha?"

Amar had a troubled look and did not respond to the question about the elephant God.

"One thing's certain," Porcy said. "Verle the Starseeker had a caring side to him, loving little Phi-Li and the rest. That CHIT re-surfaced today, Verle, snuggling up to Naji."

The old man's grayish-brown skin reddened, but he did not contradict Porcy. Naji nuzzled him again on the couch. Amar squirmed next to them.

"We still haven't seen a missing link to Version 1 and the zojy," Porcy said.

"Cause they haven't happened," Naji said. "Not quite yet."

The group stared at the child, who looked at Elvi for confirmation. She nodded casually.

Amar could not contain his discomfort any longer. "Enough! Version 1 will reveal itself in time. But what about all those New Year's recalls tracking Version 2? We've let the trail run cold. We must target this history now!"

"Poppa, relax," Naji said. The group burst into laughter.

539

78

—◦◦◦—

"Since King Shahryar here wants to bring the elephant majlis to an end and move on to V2," Cachay said, "I shall obey. I tried automatic writing. Sent me back to medieval Baghdad."

"Who *are* you?" Zack said. "Mother, you usually pooh-pooh this stuff."

"Whatever works," Cachay said. "I got fragments, about the fate of our Version 2 copies."

"Excellent catch, woman," Verle said. "Sanaa sent the Original, in a trunk fastened with the silver oval atop Homma the elephant, to the King of Portugal. Six of us sent off a copy."

"Exactly right," Cachay said. "In my interlife after Khwarazmi, I perused the journey of the copies after The 379 Group."

"Instant karma for your flexibility in the 1001 qaraq," Elvi said. "I remember it well."

"You do?" Zack's eyes bugged out. "Who are *you?*"

"Zachary, please, it's my turn." Cachay opened her journal and read the fragments.

The List of the Surviving V2 Manuscripts

-- Raqa'maq's copy headed for Rome, where Vatican officials confiscated it; desired by some religious authorities and execrated by others, it will remain tucked away in the Papal Library;

-- Wa'wa sent his copy to a scholar friend in Persia, who in turn made an Urdu copy to be sent to India; there, a translation is made into a rare Sanskrit dialect, but the Urdu copy washes up on the banks of the Ganges, page by page, its owner's throat cut in a back alley of Jhabalawad; the Sanskrit copy will bounce from Ceylon to the Islamic court on Java by the 16^h Century;

-- Khwarazmi's copy (mine!) went to a trusted courtier in Cordova, who had a second copy made, but the scribe hands over his copy to the wife of a corrupt official, in exchange for erotic services; with the ink still wet, the wife delivers the copy to her husband, the corrupt official exposes the copy, Khwarazmi's ally is assassinated, and the Cordovan court orders a manhunt for Khwarazmi, his copy, and any others;

-- Izjis' copy, sent by Li Yu to one of al-Mas'udi's disciples, was duplicated, its copy sent to China, where it was committed to Mandarin; the Emperor gifts the Arabic copy to Marco Polo in the 13th Century, who trades it for spice on his return, to a caravan somewhere in the Syrian desert; the Mandarin translation perishes in the Forbidden City fire of the 15th Century;

-- Masiama's copy was secure in al-Nadim's library in Baghdad; al-Nadim males another copy, leaked to the Buyids, who burn it and outlaw all copies; the initial copy comes under intense scrutiny by the Caliph's spies, until al-Nadim's grandson bargains with Madame Hunj to safekeep it;

-- on her death, Sanaa bequeathed her copy to Izjis, who, in his seventies, loses it to Nadir the thief; Hunj murders Nadir to secure this copy, thus rescuing the two Baghdadi copies;

-- al-Mas'udi's disciple's copy will inspire a secret cult, rousing rabble from Corfu to Kiev;

-- with the assassination of the Cordovan courtier who received Khwarazmi's copy, this manuscript will wallow in a series of shady deals, making its way deeper into low life intrigue;

-- Wa'wa's copy, purloined from the Persian friend/scholar's home, fetches a handsome price on the black market, worth five Ethiopian slaves and a bridal dowry, then barters its way from Merv to Thessaloniki, where a Greek noble purchases it for a secret society with ties to Rome;

-- The Original languished in its trunk in Portugal; by the 13th Century Royal Librarians shelve it; Portuguese navigators, perusing maps in the Royal Library for the Explorations, find the Original and smuggle it aboard a ship bound for the New World.

From the interlife, I vowed to steer one copy on a safe path. I was tempted to support rabble-rousers to resolve bad karma I had accrued from crushing popular uprisings. The New World was also tempting, but I did not wish to wait long. That left diving into the World of Crime.

I got a whiff of Madame Hunj when I lived in Baghdad, but she repulsed me. And the Cordovan copy's location was shady, and it had been mine! I packed my soul suitcase for Spain.

I dreaded being exposed to the street, the sun, and pickpocketry, anathema to a former courtier. I would take pleasure in breaking and entering: it'll get me indoors. I was grateful to stay connected to Version 2, but wasn't looking forward to a seedy world. So what good is gratitude? The intrigue, murder, and betrayal propagated to move these copies will be topped by my heinous activities. The irony is that the book contains the seeds of world harmony.

Allah grant me the luck and skill of Delilah and Quicksilver Ali, master thieves of the Nights!

ق

The group wondered whether the intrigue was related to Version 2's multi-cultural agenda. They were most curious if the manuscript bound for the New World might still be close. Elvi adjourned the meeting with a knowing smile: Cachay's list determined that the qaraq's investigation into Version 2's history was far from over.

79

May 19. Month 9.

Spring was in full bloom in Glenclaire, the time between when azalea and rhododendron bushes bloom. Amar had not checked on Ooma for a while and felt guilty. Was their bond easing up? Not such a bad thing. But seeing Bax weed and mulch the flower beds next door at Sahara's house only reminded him of his entanglement with Ooma. The trauma they experienced on 9/11 was not limited to the catastrophe; the intense past life regressions had taken their own toll. Who was he kidding: the recalls unearthed illicit emotions and ancient attractions between them.

When Amar called, Ooma was elated. She had missed him, though Bax had been visiting and comforting her every few days. She felt guilty, happier to see Amar than Bax, but there it was. Just as images of the falling Towers still haunted her, so did her awakened feelings for Amar. Their bond grew, renewed by exiting Bruckner Associates and their vulnerable futures.

Always nervous coming to Zack's house (what if Sahara saw her from next door?), Ooma took the beautiful Sunday weather as inspiration to invite Amar to the Glenclaire Rose Garden. The many varietals were bursting in a seduction of color as Ooma walked through the gate. A wedding reception was in full swing in the lower part of the garden.

When Amar arrived, Ooma pulled him up the hill to the Red Velvet flowerbeds, away from the wedding group.

They sat on a bench, taking in the aromatic air. Each sensed they were at a crossroads. Chatting about job interviews or company ideas was not enough. Amar gazed at the Persian beauty before him, and Ooma got lost in his dark, penetrating eyes. Cheers erupted from the wedding party, which Ooma took as a sign to express her true feelings. Amar would not cross a line soon after separating from Sahara, so the ball was in her court. "I have an awful confession."

"That sounds bad," Amar said, "even if it's good." Was there hope in his voice?

"After 9/11, in bed with visions, I had a vivid dream. I woke sweaty, crazed, and horny."

"Ooma, please, if it's not appropriate, I don't think ..."

"It was a recall, a continuation of one with Bax. We were Umh and Bal, our two souls escaping rough times in the late 19th Century, hiding out in an unread book."

"That crazy tale! About the book whose copies all disappear without ever being read?"

"All four hundred forty-four," Ooma said. *The Wedded Couple*, by Eleanor Younglass. There may be one copy remaining in Little Uckington-in-the-Marsh in the Cotswolds. It's as if the book was not meant for public consumption."

"But as a hideout for you and Bal. Weren't there zojy in the book, too?"

"In the library of the Viennese estate where the book takes place," Ooma replied, "there were false books, like set decoration for a film, and one contained the mysterious Version 1."

Amar frowned. "You and Bal had other uses for the library."

"We were bored! It was a neglected book. It pushed my buttons being left out of the group, even back then. I'm sorry, but in *The Wedded Couple*, Bal and I are a Baron and Duchess in a tryst."

"I thought the Baron was scheming something," Amar said.

545

"Absolutely, and he got me involved," Ooma said. "That was what my dream was about."

"So that's your terrible confession?" Amar asked.

"Not exactly." Ooma took a huge breath. "Listen to the story first. With an open mind."

The Tale of The Wedded Couple

Umh felt constrained inside the book. In touch with more past lives than Bal, she thought of a wall constructed around the imprisoning Xoo. Bal promised they had free will to play with events in the book, since it was unread. To ease her mind, he suggested reviewing the story line, so they could conceive an alternate course of action.

The Wedded Couple is a sordid tale set in the Vienna of Masoch's perverse sexual romances and Breuer's budding influence on Freud. Encased in the antiseptic body of an 18th Century morality tale, it exposes abuse of the lower class by a sinful aristocracy. Two innocent newlyweds from an extremely poor neighborhood go to a seedy hotel for one night of passion on their honeymoon. Lying in wait is the Baron, to the couple a handsome and distinguished gentleman. Learning of their nuptials, he gallantly whisks them to his suburban manor for a proper honeymoon, paying all expenses, if they simply comfort some older colleagues with their youthful presence.

The Bride is so charmed by the Baron that she delights at their good fortune. The Groom is extremely reluctant, on the point of hauling away his bride, when the Baron winks at his valet, and offers the Groom a conciliatory drink and snack, which consists of an opium cocktail and a banana dipped in honey with enough henbane to fell an elephant, whereupon the Baron valet Bride and unconscious Groom ride in a tattered coach out to the manor.

Sleeping off the elephantine cocktail the Groom is spread out on a guest bed upstairs while the Baron escorts the Bride on a tour continuing his charms and flirtations and making light of the old social convention of a noble taking a commoner bride to bed the Baron claims to be too late for this act historically though he manages to free a breast from the Bride's knotted blouse strings

the Duchess arrives and immediately sends her husband the Thuringian to cavort with other guests and instead of berating the Baron welcomes the Bride with open arms admonishes her to restore her bosom to its proper place and brings her to the dining rooms for a meal during which time the Groom is revived with coffee and pastry and promised more riches if he joins the fun and the Bride wins him over and they spend a truly wonderful night alone plied with champagne

meanwhile the Baron and Duchess (Bal and Umh) discuss plans and next day more nobles arrive and Bride and Groom have a special arrangement to be photographed and a servant leads them to a dressing room filled with gowns and costumes and the servant lays out a set of clothes with a Viennese version of Arabia low-cut bodice and slits for the Groom's pantaloons but the couple in good humor after their conjugal glee don the costumery

and enter a chamber to be photographed set up like a small theater with props and set pieces on a stage for the photograph but also chairs and tables for guests to sit as audience and the newly arrived aristos fill up the seats to watch as the photographer asks for poses static and formal at first then playful and exotic then more sensual but in good humor the guests egg on the couple

again that night the couple is wined and dined and next day asked for more pictures the photographer is missing so the guests request more lascivious poses even move into a dramatic presentation script them in suggestive situations and after a few more days the couple is obliged to perform sexual acts in front of the audience

the reader may wonder why the couple agrees to this enslavement so *The Wedded Couple* carefully delineates a journey into depravity and corruption for the couple starting with pay-offs mere baubles for the wealthy but riches for Bride and Groom and part of the Baron's scheme is to broker the cash jewels deeds and pocket most of the proceeds.

547

At the Rose Garden, Ooma sipped from a bottle of water. Plucking a blade of grass from the ground, she chewed on it while taking in Amar's shocked silence. She considered a disclaimer, but knew it made no difference. The next part of the tale disturbed Ooma, but she had to tell it.

The Tale of The Wedded Couple, continued

If there had been any critics of *The Wedded Couple*, they would have picked apart the book from this point, for little happens except a catalogue of sins, from wax burns to chocolate fellatio; there is an attempt to give sympathy to the Bride and Groom in the tradition of the morality tale when the couple refuses further services and is starved in locked rooms beaten by one gender while ravaged by the other and forced to fornicate with threesomes while begging for mercy

there is also a weak stab at the embryonic science of psychology with a hint that Baron and Duchess are parental figures with Bride and Groom desiring and hating them at different times, but despite this deeper level after a few weeks enjoying the depravities at the Baron's manor Bal and Umh grew tired and yearned for the other members of the qaraq and sent summons to the interlife and a few qaraqis came into the book and donned several of the characters' identities

when two qaraqis squeezed into the taut bodies of the Bride and Groom Bal and Umh knew it was time to take the story to another level and gladly relinquishing torture duty they pushed for a more democratic direction and since the aristocrats' sexual acts with Bride and Groom were forced and heinous the Baron and Duchess now approached the Bride and Groom romantically

the Baron began the fun with a serious conversation with the Bride assuring her it was a test of character and he was so happy the Bride had the moral fiber to set limits survive punishments that it made the Baron unable to resist her powers at the same time the Duchess approached the Groom with similar arguments telling him she controlled her husband the Thuringian by supplying the finances and that she had made it clear she must have the Groom and she caressed him and bathed his wounds

Ooma paused again, knowing what came next in her dream had awakened her and wracked her with guilt. She confessed the horrible truth: she had dreamed the tale the night Sahara was in the hospital fighting for the twins' lives. Ooma's heart had ached for Sahara, but more for Amar.

The Tale of The Wedded Couple, conclusion

at the climax of the dream Ooma as Umh as Duchess delighted in the most graphic prurient unabashed act with the Groom and as they clutched pushed released into oblivion they screamed each other's names My Duchess my wonderful one and she called out his given name my dearest Anselm and they also called out their soul names even while playing roles in the unread drama oh my Umh my one and only soul and Umh cried out my Amh my soul my desire my beloved

awakening from the dream Ooma pushed away her bared feelings because of Amar's marriage his true Bride her hospital tragedy and Ooma realized with great confusion that her lust in the unread book for Baron/Bal was a cover for her true desire for Groom/Amh and her feelings for Bax cooled from then on and Ooma fell into a deep depression knowing this truth.

ق

Amar and Ooma sat in silence, the sounds of the wedding party down the hill mocking them. Amar thought of a hundred things to say,

549

and said none. After a moment so prolonged it felt like a civilization's history could fit into it, Amar mumbled, "If Shah Zaman was astounded seeing his brother's Queen conducting orgies, then what would he -- what should I -- think of all this?"

"I know, I know," Ooma said. "I thought Umh was redeemed from Uzmeth's orgies in the Middle Ages. I'm a good girl. But a hundred years ago I was seducing the qaraq into debauchery again, and now I have the most inappropriate desires for you. What hope is there for me?"

Desperate to distance himself from the intensity of his feelings, Amar said, "What about *Bax*? Aren't you two working things out?"

"Don't know where it's heading," Ooma said. "He's been weird. Stunts, sitting on roofs."

"We've all been weird this year." Amar let out a huge sigh. "Especially Sahara."

"I'm sorry to burden you with my feelings, but I've kept them in long enough."

It was the moment for Amar to confess his true feelings. The wedding party grew raucous. Wasn't he free to move on from Sahara? He sat with his beautiful Umh, their minds and bodies full of hope and doubt, while the birds and bees suckled the Red Velvets. What held him back?

Ooma felt Amar's resistance to opening up to her. It was all right. She had confessed her sins. That was the hard part. She had waited this long for him, she could wait longer. Just as she could wait longer for the qaraq to accept her. Maybe that had to happen first. Maybe it *should*.

Ooma eased Amar's tension by changing subjects and asking about the group. Amar told her about new investigations into the zojy, the ovoid, and the Versions. Discussing the fate of the copies of Version 2, Ooma thought of the strange book she harbored in her closet. She had found it sitting outside the Glenclaire Library: how could it be one of the subversive manuscripts? If things didn't go her way with Amar or the qaraq, at least she had an ace up her sleeve, another mysterious, unread book that just might provide her some insurance in the future.

80

⟶⟿

June 4. Month 9.

Vexed by his rendez-vous with Ooma, Amar took a safe route and released his pent-up passion with Sahara. He flew to his wife, not to revive the marriage, but with the most amorous and physical advances since they had first met. There was no divorce yet, he argued to himself, so he wasn't using her to escape his feelings. But of course he was.

Nonplussed, Sahara happily obliged nonetheless, for she was coming out of a dark phase. She was near a breakthrough connecting the Nights, past lives, and the various Versions. Integrating as much past life data into her research as she could, she submitted a thesis draft to Dr. Aziz. She would survive this horrible year! Reinvigorated to return to meetings, she hosted the next one be at her house, on the patio by the fountain. As it gurgled calmly, she announced a new vision.

"I received fragments of this life when I lost the twins, including rough patches with Amar. I blocked it all out until last week, when he and I … got together."

"Got together?" Zack probed. Amar cleared his throat in warning. Nervous laughter.

"Do I have to spell it out?" Sahara knotted a strand of hair around a knuckle. "Embroider it with images of birds and beasts? Do you want to hear the recall or not?"

"We're glad to have you back, darling," Porcy said. "Lay it on us."

The Tale of the Mythogorad

Karmically locked together, Amar and I had lived on another planet, where sex is not taboo, but laughter is. We told each other stories endlessly, some forbidden humorous ones. I got a feeling this place existed before our current universe; it was the first time Amar understood my power as a storyteller, the healing art of narrative. It felt huge.

This fragment framed another story, about karma from that nontaboo World lasting deep into the future. I watched a visceral image of this karma advancing over time, the flaming numerals 1-0-0-1, the gateway to Infinity that had terrified me before. I saw two paths into my future. On one path, by some miracle I transcended the path of desire. But it was short lived, for in one of my next lives I was horrid Liligh, stuck in a jealous triangle.

The other path put me on an evolution as a seeress. This persona reminded me of something Naji said inside the womb. I was a prophetess who could remember every lifetime and see every lifetime ahead. I was responsible for the zojy in the first place, for envisioning the thousand and one prophecies. I knew hidden truths about future Versions.

I felt pressed to choose one path. I knew that neither led to transcendence of the cycle of rebirth, so I chose the path with information about zojy and the Versions. My choice framed the next part of the story, set in a garden with marvelous birds, cushat, bulbul, merle, and ringdove, all feasting on rare fruitery, pomegranate, camphor-apricot, myrobalan, and shaddock. I recognized each species out of a story in the Nights, the tale of Gharib for instance.

I was in a future nation in what Westerners call the Mideast, a desert world transformed by high-tech irrigation into a garden paradise. Someone aware of the species from ancient tales, a Sheikh or Emir or Oilat, had gone to a lot of trouble to create this garden. Fortunate to enter it, I had been permitted an audience with this powerful man. I was equally respected, if notorious: Sohlabi Flavia.

These were the days of the Mythogorad, the secret police who controlled the import and export of stories from culture to culture. Centuries after 20th Century multi-culturalism, factions within populations hit a groundswell of reaction against the philosophy, citing unrest, confusion, and ethnic de-purification as an unholy consequence of mixing of cultures. Uniculturalism gained momentum: many divergent peoples bought into it, ironic for a movement seeking to homogenize society. As economies on the planet were fraught with meltdowns, every nation was loath to open its financial distribution to outsiders. *Pick up your chips and go home* lay behind Uniculturalism.

After decades of ignoring literary critics and philologists, the authorities finally accepted that the most lethal infiltrator of one culture into another was storytelling. Textlenses, fiction, film and TVid scripts, especially children's story anthologies, were ripped apart by Mythogorad, cleaned of extraneous cultural influence, and re-packaged in sanitized versions. From political speeches to bedtime tales, all written material was potentially dangerous subversion.

Ames Rondol was a crack agent for Mythogorad, on assignment in the Arabiin Octosphere. Rondol tracked underground transport and dissemination of multi-cultural story collections, old or new, including oral transmission of variants of myths. Currently he chased down an oral terrorist spreading ancient stories throughout Arabi lands, who claimed that since Eurocentric and Arabi tales had Hindian or Asiatic origins it was futile to attempt purification. On top of this sedition, the criminal described a multi-cultural story collection outweighing any Uniculturalistic mission.

I, Sohlabi Flavia, was this supposed oral terrorist. I was aware of illegal copies of a special Version of the Arabiin Nights, completed after the age of Multi-culturalism, rooted in work done in Medieval Baghdad, and mythologized to contain prophecies from other planets. The trail had led me to Dhunbai and the Oilat's garden. I waited with trembling anticipation, for I knew I would not leave empty-handed. I had little to offer, but the Oilat wanted for little. He was willing to entrust a copy to me, knowing I would do the dirty work of sharing it with the world.

To my shock, the Oilat appeared with Ames Rondol at his side. Someone had bought someone out, some multi-national deal had been struck. Whatever it was, I faced trial and prison, but worst, the Oilat would never reveal the story collection. Ten years on a trail utterly lost.

The Oilat stood on ceremony. Before any accusations or arrests were made, he called for tea. A servant brought gold-lined bowls, and we drank as the cushats cooed. The Oilat claimed he had no connection to the controversial Version, but shared what he knew. Every story in this collection had secreted within it a detail from a past life of one of its creators. An idyllic marriage of a couple in a mythical Suburb was disguised as a royal legend. A controversial production at an alien arts school buried in the tale of Q'mezmeron. A thousand and one lifetimes in all! The authors from a few centuries ago might be the same souls who made the original in Medieval Arabiin times.

The collection was thus a double boon, a collection of old myths from around the world, and past life stories from many times. With this discovery, Rondol's presence infuriated me all the more. But I saw in the Oilat's eye the need for me to trust him still.

The Oilat insisted Rondol and I spend the night, promising we would be kept safe. I entered a plush bedchamber with two armed guards outside. Did I have a choice when Ames Rondol came in the night, proving his reputation as a seductive partner? Did I have a choice when with my morning coffee I found a small key on the tray, promising a future liaison with the Oilat? Did I have a choice when Ames escorted me out of Arabiin territories, inviting me to stay with him?

554

The more time we spent together, the more liberal Ames became. To his credit, he had no moralistic stance against diverse storytellers; it was a job. I did not feel impure about our congress. We shared much forbidden information, trading tales and literary history. We were easy together, but that meant more to Ames than me. Cherishing my knowledge on all matters story-wise, he called me 'gorgeous and brilliant.' I could have turned him with a new shade of lip sparkle. But I felt nothing. I waited to give him the slip to see what the Oilat's key opened.

One night as he stroked my naked thigh, he told me of a set of past lives pre-dating human history, when proboscideans encountered many alien races and political entanglements. An influential philosopher cited an ancient petroglyph symbolizing a ritual to recall past lives. Feeding my new interest in metempsychosis, Ames boasted it was the earliest reincarnation belief on Earth.

I was impressed. Ames Rondol was a good man, no evil scion of Uniculturalism. We could work beautifully as double or triple agents. But there was something deeply dissatisfying about him. No, it was me. I was beyond love. I was searching for something he could not give.

I gave Ames a long, heartfelt kiss. Then I changed the subject from reincarnation to the Arabiin Nights. We shared unconventional interpretations of the Shaharemzod tale into the night. Toward dawn, after a passionate hour, I pointed out that the King said that after a year of her storytelling, in his mind he had spared Shaharemzod. A thousand and one nights is nearly three years. "Why did he prolong the charade, keeping her on edge? Why not grant her freedom?"

Ames did not hesistate. "He would have lost her stories! He was addicted to her."

"She would have continued her stories regardless, I'm sure of it," I said. "No, it's something deeper." I rose from the bed, slipped on my clothes, and checked that the key was still in my pocket. "Think about it," I said, and walked out of Ames Rondol's life.

ق

The fountain's waters came to a standstill. Amar looked at Sahara sadly. Not only did the tale reflect a growing apart in the future, but also their current separation. Had sex triggered a tale where Sahara coldly couples with Amar only to leave him? Is that what had just happened between them? Sahara did not return his gaze. Amar's stomach gripped. Did the group see any of this?

Zack's fascination with another aspect of the story eased Amar's self-consciousness. "The past life references are clearly our own memories. Why us? Why would a future collection on a level with the Nights be embedded with *our* lives?" The fountain sputtered to life, as if interested.

"Don't forget the 1001 qaraq embedded Version 2 with our mutual past lives," Verle said.

Zack asked, "But what about lifetimes *after* 1001 AD? Who embedded those lives?"

"Maybe the 1001 qaraq *foresaw* those lifetimes," Verle said.

Diana said, "Dizalegh and Zizagh could have added any lives after 1001 for Version 4."

"Version 4? What happened to V3?" Bax asked. "My head's spinning."

Amar nodded agreement. He still felt sick, like he had lost Sahara forever.

With a twinkling smile, Elvi said, "I challenge all of you. Can you sort out this mess?"

81

———✦✦✦———

"I can help," Cachay said. "One of my first recalls was way in the future. Dr. Machiyoko and I were office rivals at some research center. In our tales there was mention of a Version 4."

"Version 4-XYZ or something," Diana said, "a future Nights. The Rabyon Nits."

"I'd be happy to target a recall there," Cachay said, "to clarify the Versions."

Her competitive edge rising, Porcy resented Cachay playing the hero. "Weren't you a spiteful loser in that lifetime? Diana should target the story. She was much cleverer."

The qaraq stared at Porcy. The fountain spluttered, as if clogged. Everyone noticed the fountain's reactions, but took it in stride, given their memory of the Maqaraqan fountain. Cachay smiled with cool dignity. "Next you'll say Diana is the radiant full moon in a blue brocade dress."

"Enough," Elvi said. "Dr. Machiyoko, will you regress Cachay to see what we can find?" Within minutes the group heard new information. Elvi's idea of teaming Diana and Cachay to revisit their lives as rival researchers paid off in cryptic, futuristic language, challenging to decipher.

The Authentication of Version 2-x1

Pdr. Chimnoggia believed the map was a fabrication. No one could decipher it and find a location for "Version 1." The idea of an Ur-collection was a myth that should have been outlawed in the last universe by the Mythogorad. Even if an antique reading lens existed in some ruin of a library, the collection would be a copy of an edition of a variant of an anthology. Nothing original.

Chimnoggia was taking no chances, however. If interest in the map existed, then interest in Version 1 existed. That meant less bother about Version 2. Her baby. She launched a campaign to discredit an Original Version. She stamped every report with the Porticon Emblage, affirming that Version 2-x1 came through, not Version 1.

Aleksjandra Bibliathek Authentication Document 1805-1302-11a

In Receivership at Bibliathek Level 5, under the Stewardship of Pdr. Chimnoggia, held for investigation the past twelve annia, one hybrid story collection (henceforth called Version 2-x1), the first copy of unknown derivation. Version 2-x1 combines a sequence of the Raabiin Nhts with The Ynkahnatynn Tales, an admixture of past life stories. This document authenticates the collection, which traces back to the previous universe.

It is known that at the end of the previous universe, techniques existed to preserve material into the new cosmos. The forensic discipline called Urchaeologic began, the tracking of artifacts that pass through Time. We have evidence that by the end of the previous universe the following artifacts existed regarding Version 2-x1:

1. *Eleven paper fragments of the Raabiin Nhts, dating from 2nd and 3rd Centuries, AH.*
2. *An incomplete manuscript of the Nhts, from between 3rd and 4th Century, AH.*

3. *Personal accounts, an entry in al-Nadim's ledgers, and the famous "Rukamuk Love Letter," stating that the original Version 2 was completed in 379 AH.*

4. *All copies lost, a reconstruction of Version 2 appears in sketch form over a thousand years later.*

5. *A translation of this reconstruction in Universalese, annotating hidden structures.*

6. *References to a Version 3, made from latter day Eurocnetic story collections.*

Only items 5 and 6 made it through the Porticon to our universe. We know of the other items from the New Foreword to the Universalese translation, a nostalgic look at culture during a dying cosmos. The Universalese Edition, not Version 1 nor 3, comes down to us as Version 2-x1.

To give teeth to her perspective, Chimnoggia mocked the outdoor digs, claiming true authentication is made through indoor cyber-exploration. She spread rumors of a secret cult of scientists with access to Version 1, who claimed it contained coded information pertinent to the salvation of the world; if V1 got in the wrong hands, the universe was doomed. Starting with this straw man to bash, Chimnoggia satirized other cults, one with flying bird-women, another with crosslog puzzles hiding prophetic messages. She made sure the Society of Urchaeologicians received her invectives, encouraging them to put down research into the Original Version.

Aleksjandra Bibliathek Authentication Document 1805-1302-11c

The strongest evidence verifying the integrity of Version 2-x1 is its structural features. Literary analysis suggests that any Version should contain at least seven hidden structures.

The characters in the tales of Version 2-x1 display the Character Identity Traits (CHITS).

Though inconclusive, most of the World Types actively categorize the past life stories.

Initial examination of the relation between Narrative Order and Chronological Order of the lifetimes shows the requisite algorhythmic relationships.

Pdr. Irsis Chimnoggia

Chimnoggia's campaign undid her in ways she had not intended. Without it, the idea of an Original Version was esoterica, with it, the V1 craze caught on like wildfire. Small organizations, serious and satirical, formed to investigate Version 1. One group took the form of the winged women Chimnoggia had invented to malign such cults. Scholars used crosslog puzzle structures to determine whether a story collection from an old universe could doom the current world.

The man mocked by Chimnoggia for digging in the woods challenged her to a debate. During the proceedings she had a terrible feeling, like one of the déjà vus from Version 2-x1, that she had fought in an arena before. The outcome was that Version 1 was a myth, wasting enormous energy, a victory for Chimnoggia. But interest remained, undermining her work on Version 2-x1.

Worse, her opponent called for the construction of a Version 4, a quasi-fictional account of the creators' work on the Versions, including their past life stories. Whereas Versions 2 and 3 presented the Raabiin Nhts with lifetimes embedded, Version 4 presented the past lives with Nhts embedded. Chimnoggia's criticisms again fanned flames of desire for the first V4 volunteers.

Chimnoggia went back to the windowless Bibliathek. She was done plotting, and maybe not just for this lifetime.

ق

"So that's what Version 4 is," Verle said. "It's the creators' story. Our story."

The qaraq sat speechless. Sahara and Amar wondered how their Mythogorad tensions related to these events. Were they no longer connected as a couple by that point? Porcy worried that she would fall by the wayside in the future and Cachay's soul would dominate. Zack mused: if The 379 Group created V2, and European translators V3, who would create Version 4?

Elvi noted the puzzled faces of the group. "I know it's a lot to take in, your role in these subversive manuscripts extending deep into Time. But you've uncovered a lot. And something more important than all this arcane knowledge happened today."

The qaraq implored Elvi to continue. "Remember after the Towers fell, and the everyday world, which you had written off as illusory, became horrific, more real than recalls? You doubted everything you had come to believe."

"Lost our sense of wonder," Verle said. "But here we are, renewed by this crazy history."

Murmurs of agreement passed around the circle of qaraqis. Whatever individual traumas lingered, the qaraq had healed. Elvi congratulated everyone as she adjourned the meeting. The fountain sprayed little jets of water, like quiet fireworks.

82

June 13. Month 10.

Seven months after a file on Sahara was created in Washington, an unnamed government agency called her in for questioning. The book bans had been lifted months before, but she was very nervous by the summons. Inside a gray block of a building up the hill from downtown Newark, a dumpy woman, exhausted by it all, ushered Sahara into a windowless office. No one-way mirror, cameras, or cold interrogation table, Sahara observed, just a metal desk, a few folding chairs, a couple of file cabinets, and a cheap rug. The drab office did not look like it was used everyday.

After a long wait, two men entered the room. The one who introduced himself as Ellis sat behind the desk, a small file before him. Ellis was a plain but attractive man in his thirties who could have passed for one of the fathers at the local school. The other man, who Ellis introduced as Ingles, wore thick black glasses, a grey suit, and carried a legal pad to take notes. A quintessential G-man, Sahara thought: what does he want with me?

"I'm sorry for the disturbance, Ms. Fleming," Ellis began, "but since 9/11 government agencies have monitored information around the country. Your name came up because of your work at Glenclaire Public

Library." Ellis was deadpan, but underneath Sahara detected a tone of apology, as if he never dreamed of bothering ordinary citizens. "Is it true you sent a number of emails complaining about repression of certain books in the library system?"

Sahara tightened. *So this was it.* "Yes. I'm an Arabic scholar trying to finish my thesis. I needed those books at the time. Some of my professors and friends were being hassled. We work with ancient texts, hundreds of years old, completely non-political. I understand the need for security now, but I was making a reasonable request."

Ellis made no expression. "Are you still working on your thesis?"

Sahara smiled involuntarily. "I just handed it in."

Ellis looked at his notes. "To a Professor Agib? At The University of Chicago?"

Were they after Agib? "Yes, that's correct."

Ingles rose from his chair to whisper something in Ellis' ear, then sat down again. Ellis looked at his notes. "What is your thesis about, Ms. Fleming?"

"The origin of *The Thousand and One Nights.* You know, Scheherazade? Genies?"

"I'm aware of the work, Ms. Fleming," Ellis said. "What languages do you know?"

The question startled Sahara. "Arabic, of course, a working knowledge of Farsi and Urdu. Some Hindi, Sanskrit, Turkish. And French and German, for treatises."

"Are you fluent in any of these languages?"

Sahara paused to think. "Arabic and French for sure. I could get around as a tourist with my Farsi and Urdu, maybe Hindi. The others just for reading texts."

"And Ms. Fleming, what is your interest in the subject matter?"

Why is he asking me these questions? "I've always loved the Nights. We have no original version, which fascinates me."

"You became familiar with the work during your years in Morocco and Egypt?"

How did he know that? Sahara felt on edge again. "Yes, as a child. Why do you ask?"

Ignoring Sahara, Ingles rose to speak to Ellis again. Ellis nodded impatiently. Ingles sat.

"You've been meeting with a group at the Glenclaire Universalist-Unitarian Church. Do you mind telling me about the nature of those meetings?"

For a second Sahara considered lying, making up something about Apocryphal studies. She knew that would never work. *The whole situation is preposterous. I'm innocent of anything they could be investigating.* She chose the truth. "It's a support group for past life regression."

"Come again?" Ellis asked.

"There's about ten of us. We have memories of past lives. We share our stories, and sometimes hypnotize each other to recall more past lives. That's called regression."

"Why are the meetings secretive? The church didn't know much."

Sahara felt her anger rising. "I'm sorry, but why all the questions? Have I done something?"

"This is not an interrogation, Ms. Fleming. Just answer the question. Please."

"All right. Everybody would think we're crazy if we talked much about it. We're discrete."

"I don't understand," Ellis said. "Aren't there all sorts of spiritual groups at the church?"

Something in Sahara let go at that moment. She had an idea. Her inner Scheherazade wanted out. *A story can save your life!* "Would like me to demonstrate a regression for you?"

Ellis looked over at Ingles, who nodded. "And how would you do that?" Ellis asked.

"I go into a trance, target a past life, and share. You don't believe me, do you?"

After a few more moments, Ellis said, "All right, Ms. Fleming, we'll humor you."

Sahara censored her response. She needed to relax. "In this World a shy science teacher is persecuted; the Arts are more important than Science. I haven't remembered my lifetime yet."

"You all have lifetimes in the same worlds?"

"We travel through Time together." Sahara couldn't resist. "You guys have a group, too."

Sahara closed her eyes and raised her hand to ward off interruption. When Ellis asked her how long it would take, Sahara said, "Normally, I would dress as Scheherazade in a gown lined with gold. But I'll let it go today. Hra Zamen? Speak through me." Amazingly, she heard a voice in her head. Receiving a story, she conveyed it to the two skeptical, but curious government agents.

The Tale of the Shy Teacher's Ruse

Zamen had one more year to remain at the school. The dance teacher Taki had plotted against him and tarnished the sciences, which made Zamen spiteful. He had to repair the damage.

With extreme shyness comes a great desire to be recognized. In desperation Zamen hatched a plot for his lonely soul. Through cryptic notes and dropped hints, Zamen spread rumors that his students achieved great success after graduation. He used names of recent graduates who, like him, were relatively unknown, and older graduates long forgotten. The successes included wonderful job opportunities in Bioneutic science, important experiments, and to honor Rashi, conquests abroad.

I remember the first hints of these success stories whispered between lockers. The hints pointed toward Math, but none of our favorite instructors claimed credit. Eventually only Hra Zamen had not weighed in on the matter. Was it possible? Since he was leaving, perhaps the shy Zamen was finally revealing something about himself. Whenever asked, he just shrugged meekly.

Within weeks, students and colleagues beset Zamen. He was not used to this kind of exposure. Befuddled by Zamen's notoriety, Taki joined the crowd. In the faculty room she wooed Zamen, but he left her lying in her chair-throne. How we girls giggled at the gossip!

Sahara looked at the agents. Any questions? No, I'm not making this up. Yes, my group has discussed that question, and no, there's no proof that the stories *aren't* from our imaginations. Yes, I can answer you because the trance is light. Should I continue? Yes, I'll keep it short.

The Tale of the Shy Teacher's Buse, continued

My best friend Povi was the first to reap a benefit from Zamen's success stories. She had him for Intro to Star Systems, the kind of course where dancers pick up an easy credit. But now there was a sense of pride to be in his class, and everyone worked hard so it might lead somewhere. Povi felt entitled to success, but then realized she was more interested in stars than stardom.

Many students switched concentration to MAMESS, working beyond their potential on astral traffic projects and seventh dimensional equations. Hra Zamen improved as a teacher, worked more closely with students, and supported extra-curricular activities.

I was one of Taki's prize dancers, and after Zamen shunned her, she enlisted me to blow a hole in his science bubble. I was more than miffed Taki used me that way. I liked having things my way, and working only as hard as I wished. Academics were a joke to me, and if a dance move messed up my gorgeous tangerine hair, forget it. To research some sci-brain's claim to fame was more than I could stand.

Taki threatened to kick me out of the company (she wouldn't dare, not with Mummy bankrolling the concerts), but promised me a juicy role if I busted Zamen.

Luckily I barely lifted a fingernail to prove his stories false. Either the alumni were non-existent, or the awards were. Taki thrilled at the list of damning information. I could care less.

But it was too late. Povi won first prize at the Bioneutics Sci-Fair; Groy Tersling was awarded a scholarship to the Universitat di Frieschutz in Electrogall Engineering; Tove Nuscholtz made the President's Council on the Intersection of Math and Art. Zamen got credit for each student, and this time deserved it. His lies had inspired a wave of success. He was reinstated and became head of MAMESS. Taki was livid. I didn't get my juicy role. Which was just fine.

Ellis interrupted the tale. "So you launch into these stories at the drop of a hat?"

"Sometimes it takes work, sometimes we can't control it," Sahara answered. "Two years ago we were quite blocked. This year we're learning to target specific lifetimes."

"We're out of time for any more stories." Ellis looked over his notes. "That will be all, Ms. Fleming. If we have any more questions, especially about the Arab community, we'll be in touch."

Sahara was disappointed by the abrupt halt. Her inner Scheherazade had failed. She rose from her chair. "You never told me. Are you guys FBI? CIA? This new Homeland Security?"

Ellis opened the door. "Thank you for your time, Ms. Fleming. The girl will see you out."

Shaken and dejected, Sahara walked heavily down the gray halls. As she neared the exit, a side door opened and to her surprise Ingles motioned her into a different room.

For the first time, Ingles spoke to Sahara. "Ms. Fleming, was there more to the story?"

Sahara's inner Scheherazade snapped to attention. *She had hooked the quiet one!* "Yes, Mr. Ingles. Like to hear?" Ingles unfolded a chair for her, stood against a wall, and invited her to finish.

The Tale of the Shy Teacher's Ruse, conclusion

With the accolades, Zamen had to lunch with the Chancellor and dine with the President. The media invaded campus. The bigger the spotlight, the more Hra Zamen retreated into anonymous silence. The recognition made him nervous and jumpy, and not because of the sham. Fame did not become him.

Robust debate about Art versus Science took hold of academia. MAMESS students got more attention than performers. I thought Povi's head would burst. When Taki pressured me to go public, I told her I was sick of it all. But I showed Povi the exposing data. She accused me of jealousy, called me a spoiled brat. I pulled up documents and alumni lists: it was all there in plain sight. Even after conceding Zamen had betrayed everyone, she claimed none of it mattered. My best friend drifted away, like an island floating from the mainland. The loss of Povi crushed me.

Povi desperately clung to pride in her work. She needed to vent against me, against Zamen, against her terrible, guilty position. So rumors started again, this time exposing Zamen's ploy. Within days it was all over campus. But few confronted him. The campus did not wish to tarnish its awardees, which Zamen had promoted. Taki called for justice, but what crime was there?

In the end, Zamen was untouched, but also unthanked and ignored. He was thrilled to be reinstated, victorious over Taki, and left alone.

ق

"You're done?" Ingles asked. "What happened next?"

"I don't know," Sahara said, pleased with her Scheherazade-like spell over the agent. "That's part of someone else's past life story. This is why we meet, to complete each other's tales."

"Can you get information about someone else's lifetime?" Ingles asked.

"If you have a connection to that lifetime. Recently we recalled many connected incarnations in 10th Century Baghdad."

Ingles leaned forward. "Could you receive information from present day Baghdad?"

"You mean intelligence?" Sahara smiled. "Afraid not. We're not mind readers."

Ingles looked disappointed, but thanked Sahara and furtively showed her the door.

83

———◦⁄⁄⁄◦———

June 18. Month 10.

At the next qaraq meeting, back at the church, the group was upset about the June heat rising to the attic. Sahara's news about her mysterious meeting made everyone even pricklier.

"That is serious," Amar said. "How dare they probe you or the group. What can we do?"

"Relax, *The X-Files* ended last month," Zack said. "The Feds aren't after us paranormals."

"Who knows?" Bax said. "I'm from Colorado. People get into weird conspiracy shit."

Porcy was sweating hard. "Good reason for a new space, hidden, like in Cordova."

"Go find us a space in a parallel universe, Porcelain," Cachay said. "Leave right now."

Zack raised his hand. "Ladies, can we shelve it?" The group assented, squirming in the heat. "To move on from Sahara selling us out to the KGB, I have a recall, courtesy of Jobim. The qaraq hit a delta with Version 2, copies seeping out into the world. The trail picks up with

Version 3, the European Nights started by Galland. Jobim and I want a link between the 11th Century and the 18th.

"I re-read the tales with Veronique d'O and yours truly as Zadek, the servant she groomed to make a complete Nights. Jobim suggested I target their connection to Version 2. Regressing myself as Zadek, I met up with a soul mate. I'm convinced this person was Jobim."

"You recalled Jobim's incarnation in 18th Century France?" Verle clarified.

"Directly tied in with the Nights," Zack said. "Proof that Jobim's in the qaraq."

"Evidence, not proof, Zachary." Cachay looked concerned. Her son had been obsessing about Jobim being part of the soul group. She feared her son might be disappointed. Devastated.

"Let's hear the story," Elvi said, perspiring like everyone else. "Then we'll talk."

The Tale of a Faqaf in Paris

Breteuil, the Minister of Culture, liked you, Zadek. He commented on your little shrug, the one you do when you don't know an answer, or it's not your place to speak, or you find a bit of humor but French wit escapes you. Breteuil did not realize that every Jew masters that shrug at five years old. The Yiddish signature for laughing at the world. He understood its inherent meaning, and asked his followers to enjoy it. In a month the palace was full of people shrugging like Jews.

Thanks to the Yiddish shrug, you gained admittance to the most important salons in Paris. You had to learn to be less aggressive, however. Telling everyone you know seven languages and wish to revive the *Nuits* didn't work. How ingratiate yourself in this game?

After many months you got a big break. Minister Breteuil invited you to gander at the exotic manuscripts in the Bibliothèque du Roi. *Eh bien!* The library was astonishing, ten times more magnificent than Veronique's holdings. The French fables were as exotic as the Arabic collections. Breteuil loved appreciation of this literature, but when you brought up a continuation of the Nuits, he mocked you. With the Yiddish shrug. You needed a scheme to make him embrace the project.

One day in the library, you had a marvelous idea. At a salon you will hold a debate: which is the more enticing fairy tale, the homegrown French variety, or the exotic Arabian brand? Breteuil loved the idea, and shared the hope that the discourse will bring about a fairy tale renaissance.

The Minister did everything to host the debate. No expense was spared, the banquet table was plentiful, and important luminaries were present. Fabulists and raconteurs from Europe and the Levant spoke and recited stories. The salon was alive with high spirits. Breteuil looked in your direction as you hobnobbed with critics and courtiers. You felt a special connection to him.

In the weeks that followed, you attended twice as many salons, bringing *contes de fée* into the spotlight. Well-wishers humored you, but it was an uphill battle. You invoked Breteuil's name, as he had prompted you, but you spent more time promoting his good name than the Nuits.

Veronique had prepared you brilliantly for scholarly issues, but not court wit or finesse. You badgered Duchesses and browbeat Vicomtes. Madame Rouchald was livid when you didn't greet her dogs. Yet when you suppressed your speech, the court thought you an idiot.

Minister Breteuil was your lifeline. The two of you plotted to construct an edition together. Soon you understood the one thing you needed for success was a complete manuscript of *The Thousand and One Nights*. Tired of the shallowness of the French court, you went to Constantinople, fully funded by the Minister. Corresponding, you poured out your heart and findings to him, and fortified your soulful link reading his ardent replies.

In Constantinople you met Diyunisus Shawish, a Syrian monk interested in story collections. You inquired about a full manuscript of *Alf Layla* in Anatolia or Syria. He had no leads, but revealed a small manuscript of fourteen stories, including a few found in Galland's volumes. You told him to wait for a revival of fairy tales in Paris, then go could set himself up nicely. You added the Yiddish shrug. You wrote to Breteuil about hiring the monk for some task, to get his tales close at hand.

You never found a manuscript, and gave up your quest. Shawish went to Paris as Dom Denis Chavis. Breteuil informed you the monk started a *Continuation* of the Nuits. After your failed years at court, you followed Fate's course. You translated peace treaties on the battlefront, witnessing borders change on a piece of paper.

After a few years of this life, you became bored and depressed. When a Byzantine battle took you to Vienna, you quit the camp. Viennese life was good for a few months, but you knew why you had come. You headed for the Carpathian countryside and the hamlet of Tluste. You found Veronique's estate abandoned, with only the stray dust devil kicking up stones in the courtyard. The library was ghostly, untouched during the decade of your absence. Weary and broken-hearted, you died on the carpet in that holiest of rooms, a copy of the Yiddish Nights clutched to your heart, a shrug fixed on your shoulders.

Elvi asked Zack to indulge her. Regressing him beyond his death as Zadek, she instructed him to follow his soul Za into the interlife, seek out the Masters, and see what lesson he learned from the lifetime. He saw that for him direct action was fraught with problems, as in Paris. But the passive approach had failed him, too, and led to nothing but gloom. The lesson was to find a balance between the two modes. Za felt hopeless to accomplish this task.

As comfort, his spirit guide had him look down on the world. He rejoiced to see his mistress' hopes take the next step. Veronique d'O had not helped Zadek sway a soul at court, but she enabled him to sway Chavis to go to Paris. Za insisted that Zadek's task was no different

than an ape being trained to serve a flagon of wine at table, and that it
was Zadek's relation with Breteuil that helped Chavis fabricate a longer
Arabic manuscript of the Nights.

But Za's guide pointed out that the connection with Chavis was more
significant than with Breteuil. The real lesson: you can't always spot a
soul mate by the amount of time and energy they give. Sometimes a rela-
tion lasts years, as with Zadek and Veronique, sometimes it lasts an hour,
as with Chavis. The spark Zadek felt with Breteuil, no matter how sup-
portive, was misleading. A soul like that might help you out for a lifetime
or two, but is not part of your qaraq. Breteuil was a beneficial but false
member of Za's soul group, a faqaf.

ق

"A fakaff?" Amar exhaled heavily in the heat. "What is that?"

Fighting off his trance, Zack cut short the answer. "More crucial: is Veronique's library still intact? Is there valuable information for us? Field trip to Carpathia?"

"If it helps link the European Nights with Version 2," Amar said, "which your tale didn't."

"Hold on, this faqaf concept feels close to home," Cachay said. "Where's it from, Elvi?"

"It's an ancient idea, like a qaraq. It means a false qaraqi, someone that feels significant at the time, but isn't part of one's ongoing soul group."

Cachay fanned herself in the heat, brow furrowed. "Are we talking about Jobim?"

The qaraqis avoided looking at Zack, sweating in the heat and the situation. Elvi gave Diana a look: *this is the moment I warned you about, when Zack needs your help.* Amar broke the silence. "Zack, has Jo ever seen a lifetime? In Paris you latched onto Breteuil. Maybe you're prone to these faqafs."

574

"Do you hear yourselves?" Zack said. "Prone to faqafs? It makes no sense. Why not say: Jobim should shop for the third and fourth dresses of the month. It's blather."

"Naji used this term," Sahara said, "about our close relation to Ardra."

Diana eased Zack's defensive stance. "Yes, we're not dismissing Jobim. Or disrespecting him. We all feel comfortable knowing him. Everything about your relationship is absolutely right."

"Except foisting him on the qaraq," Amar said.

Dr. Machiyoko held up a hand, then wiped her brow. She'd handle this, not a high-spirited King. "Zack, I get it. You love Jobim. Including him in our crazy secrets felt natural. He seems a perfect fit. But think of Amar and Ooma: it's obvious they belong, but they were outsiders. Think how uncomfortable you were when Cachay joined. Look at why you want Jobim in the qaraq."

Zack's face hardened. "So now I get my therapy rolled into a meeting. With an audience."

"I don't mean to put you on the spot," Diana said. "I'm just worried for you. You've picked the right guy, but the wrong approach. Don't sabotage it."

"I've been in the middle of Ooma wanting in on the group.," Bax offered. "It's not fun." Surprised to hear from Bax, the group looked at him with a new sympathy.

"Zack, after 9/11, I felt like the group's healer," Diana said. "But we're healing now. I'm backing off that role. But I'm there for you. If you need to work this out with me, I will."

"I don't need you," Zack said. The group looked at him, perturbed. "Any of you." The air in the attic felt tight and unbearable. Zack stood up and walked to the door. He turned back to the qaraq, but, unable to say more, he left.

84

—⟨∞⟩—

Outside the church Zack walked up and down the block before deciding he should go home. Then he realized his mother had given him a ride and he had no car. He started to walk home, but rejected a hot four-mile hike. He sat down at a bus stop. The bus had recently arrived. A long wait.

Underneath his anger he felt chastised by the group. Did he think any close friend was a candidate for Qaraqi? Did he take the group's powers for granted? The thought exhausted him.

Another passenger sat down next to Zack, a young woman in a Sixties peasant dress. Hippie garb, Zack thought. *Please don't talk to me*, he prayed.

"How ya doin?" Hippie Woman asked. Zack barely nodded. "When's the bus come?" Zack shrugged. The gesture thwarted the woman, who took out a book. Zack saw the cover: *Reincarnation and Karma*, by Edgar Cayce. *Holy shit. No escape. Fuck off, Miss Serendipity.*

"Was there no other way to handle that?" Cachay was furious Elvi had hurt her son. "That was cruel. Why not send in judges, witnesses, and the police? Who made you God?"

A palpable tension filled the blistering attic space. Porcy began tentatively. "Elvi's got a few connections in that department. In one of my recalls she was my spirit guide."

"Don't change the subject," Cachay snapped. "Could you be any more insensitive?"

"She's telling the truth," Diana said. "Elvi revealed herself to me as a spirit guide."

When Sahara nodded in agreement, Cachay said, "To some, but not all of us?"

"Elvi helped us all more since the attacks," Porcy said, "while you were avoiding humanity." Porcy saw the tears welling in Cachay's eyes. How could she have lashed out at her? Cachay was in anguish for her child. Triggered by emotional stress, Porcy's fleeting past life visions burst forth.

"Damn you all, I'm having a moment." Dizzy from the heat, Porcy took a deep breath and let the visions return. As a story formed, she shared it with the group.

The Tale of the Ganesian Holdout

It's the best for *us*, you're telling me? What did you call it, or us, a karock? My soul friends are flying around the cosmos with an important document, trying to find it a safe and proper home? I'm stuck here on Ganesa, unable to lift a hoof to help? You expect me to swallow that, because you're a spirit guide? Giving crazy advice for ages?

Do you know what I went through to secure this precious document? I went against my own Council to sanction an assassination, against the wishes of every world in our sector. True, he was a Zogrozi smuggler I had killed. Ganesian spies saw he had acquired the precious *Zojy Zeojyy*. I harbored hope the Zojy might help our cause on Gaia.

577

Beloved Gaia. I jeopardized my own planet's reputation to save things there. And why not? At one time there were hundreds of proboscidean species on the poor planet. All with potential for intelligence, in need of our protection. What does the Council say these days? Not worth the trouble? Isn't it Ganesian duty to help them evolve?

The problem stretched back over countless billennia, back to when Gaia was Terra. The Hculari, miserable set of beings if you ask me, announced a sacred mission to restore the natural course of evolution on the planet. So they set the planet ablaze in nuclear fire! After decades, radiation cleared, we returned, and renamed it Gaia. But the Hculari had installed their chosen species in underground caves, each served by a sentient proboscidean. The Hculari ordered us to leave. The nuclear disaster had been to wipe out all trace of alien culture on the planet.

The Ganesians dug in their hooves. Retaliating, the Hculari reached accords with every world in the galaxy to avoid Terra. For centuries we kept our distance and our eye on the forlorn planet. The newer strain of mammals outran our compatriots, leaving only a dozen proboscidean species on Gaia. Gaian interest became a cult minority, with no support from the Starseekers.

Tired of Council members curling up their trunks at me in disgust, I heard about the *Zojy Zeojyy* and recognized an ingenious way to reconnect with Gaia. On Veryx, a planet near the Zogrozi spacehubs, a great seeress had left a controversial book of predictions, destined to bring Gaia into its rightful age of wisdom and achievement. So I hunted down classified documents, terminated a Zogrozi smuggler, and brought the Zojy to Ganesa.

You say my conscience should ache, but how was I to know the smuggler was a fellow karocky? We confiscated his belongings, and one of our techs got a silver cube to project a series of images, each a prophecy I guessed. But it was a mock-up. There were supposed to be a thousand images, not just two hundred forty-seven. And there was galactic history, but no future data.

I brought the Council the most significant image. The First One: a proboscidean from a previous universe, capable of seeing any event in Time, an ancestor of the Veryxian prophetess. Wasn't this image proof of our connection with the Zojy? Justification to promote the Gaian probosciedeans? Such knowledge could reverse their devolution into base animals. The Council enabled a mission to Gaia, a paltry budget, reluctant Starseekers, one projoscolum, and allowed only original materials, no copies. If the plan didn't work, I had no further recourse.

According to you, El, the mission failed before it began, since the device was a phony. On a small Gaian landmass, on some rock at the side of a cave, the Starseekers scorched the Ganesian emblem, a proud figure with its telltale trunk. A passing proboscidean didn't notice the image, but the destined species saw a clue where to hunt mastodons into extinction.

Hominids. That's what you call the chosen ones on Gaia. The proboscideans were chosen, too, but the cosmos abandoned them. You say some day the hominids will worship the image on the cave rock. They will create a deity in our image, a Ganesian, and praise him as the Destroyer of Impedimenta. As a final insult, you say that I, Po-ha, yearned for lifetimes to be connected to the hominids. Misled, I clung to Ganesa's ancient mission. If I let go of it, I'll gain my deeper wish.

All I can say, El, is that you are one miserable spirit guide.

ق

"I hand it to you, Porcelain," Cachay said, "your vision raises more questions than answers."

"I thought the connections were impressive," Porcy said. "Ga-men, Veryx, smuggling zojy."

"The bickering has to stop, ladies." All eyes turned to Elvi as she made her pronouncement. "There's too much work to do, well beyond what the qaraq has already revealed."

"Like expanding this hint about how the proboscidean missing link made way for human evolution," Diana said. "With the help of a nuclear holocaust!"

"Like recalling all thousand and one past lives we keep hearing about?" Verle asked.

"Like revealing yourself?" Cachay picked up on the qaraq's hungry eyes on Elvi.

"Yes, I am more than a facilitator," Elvi began. "I am your qaraq's spirit guide, and have been for hundreds of your lifetimes. You're helped by other guides, other Masters, other forces in the interlife, but I am the one keeping track of your interactions, karma, and soul journeys."

"Do you always interact with us when we're alive," Porcy asked, "in disguise?"

Elvi laughed aloud. "Not often. If there's a special need I visit you individually. In your tale, the qaraq had moved on from proboscideans to Earth humans. Po needed to be helped along."

"I do apologize, Elvira," Cachay said. "Or is it just El? Porcy, I'm done fighting. Truce?"

Porcy felt humbled that a spirit guide had to help her along in the past. "Truce." Cachay handed her a handkerchief to mop up her sweat-filled face. "Thanks, lovie. I'm sorry, too."

Sahara addressed Elvi. "And you're with us now because the whole qaraq's together?"

"Like Li Yu in Cordova," Amar said. "Are those the only times you appear?"

"Sometimes it's better to get out of your way. Or guide with a light, magical touch."

"Great Master," Verle said, "are you here to guide us to recall all thousand lifetimes?"

"First of all, Verlin," Elvi answered, "I am no more a Master than you, just a few lifetimes ahead. Someday you'll be a qaraq's spirit guide, and you'll see there's a lot to learn. And the 1001 stories? Yes, it's time to make a plan. You target lifetimes now, so you can tackle bigger chunks.

Your archives are going to be brimming. You're going to need Zack back for that. Can someone give him my apologies and bring him back into the fold?"

Sahara, Amar, Diana, and Verle all answered: "Absolutely. You bet. Of course. Yes ma'am." And Cachay: "Why don't you apologize yourself?"

In answer, Elvi insisted they adjourn before anyone fainted in the sweltering attic. She slipped out first.

Zack sat nervously next to Hippie Woman at the bus stop. When she saw Zack eye her book, she launched into a litany of the amazing discoveries she'd made reading it, and wondered if Zack realized that Edgar Cayce had envisioned many of his past lives. Her Christian upbringing, which boasted of Heaven, had nothing on the idea of reincarnation. What's more, Hippie Woman continued, without Zack's permission, have you ever wondered how far back these beliefs go?

Yes, I have, Zack replied, as courteously as he could. How humdrum it all sounded on this innocent girl's tongue. He was so over it, especially the qaraq's attitude about Jobim, and his delusions. He needed a break from recalls and immortality and the whole truth and nothing but. If he couldn't take Hippie Woman, how could he deal with a thousand and one stories?

He stood, left the bus stop, and started walking home.

85

—⟨∾∾⟩—

July 15. Month 11.

It's okay, Momma. Everything's okay.

Sahara jumped at the voice in her head. Naji was speaking more aloud, but rarely in her head. They were eating lunch on the patio. The fountain stopped its calm flow.

Sahara sent her thoughts to Naji's mind. *What do you mean?*

You're sad. Is it hard that Poppa's next door? Or Ah-Dah dying? Or Uncle Zack and Jo's troubles?

Sahara smiled. *No, they'll be fine. You're right, everything's okay. Eat your lunch.*

Ignoring her, Naji spoke aloud. "Is it the men from the government?"

How did he know about Ellis and Ingles? "Yes, I'm a little worried about them."

"They're not bad men. You'll help them save the books. In the Round City."

In Baghdad? What books? Version 2? "What are you saying!" She tickled him.

Naji giggled in delight. "Momma! Stop!" Then in her head again. *Please.*

Sahara stopped cold. She was out of her depression. Naji was speaking. But it was weird.

"Know what you need, Momma? A good bedtime story."

"It's noon! Lunch, young man." Yes, weird. Why not? "You're the little man for the job?"

"I am. I help Uncle Zack. He said he'll sowget a zillion tales all by hisself. Show everyone."

"Sowget? Oh, he's saying *target* tales, baby." Poor Zack. Compensating for the Jobim thing.

"Remember our lifetimes crossing the Ice Bridge? I was Naxi? I'm gonna towget it. You can help me." Naji twisted his body to look at his mother's face. *Just look at me.* He stared deeply into her soul, accessing the prehistoric time they crossed the Bering Strait and North America.

Uh oh. Naji hesitated. *This is gonna make you sad, Momma. Don't be, it's just a past life.*

Why will I be sad, baby?

Because when my story starts, you die.

The Tale of the Grieving Child

In the land of the Three Valleys there once lived a young brave named Naxi. At the start of his journey with his mother Xani across the land, Naxi had a loud, mean streak, but by the end, when they found the Stone Cliff tribe, he learned to control himself. Naxi and Xani presented glittering crystals they had collected to their new tribe. When the crystals transformed a cave in the Cliffside into a glowing chamber, the tribe looked upon mother and son as divine beings.

Naxi enjoyed a peaceful life with the tribe, choosing a squaw who bore him several strong children. He took care of the tribe's livestock, and loved to make figurines of the animals for his children. Xani doted on her grandchildren.

But all things beautiful come to an end, and when Naxi's children were of marriageable age, Xani passed from this world. Naxi was beside himself, and his children had never seen him so angry and loud. He yelled at them day and night, would not let his wife touch him, neglected his duties with the animals, and vowed to take his family back across the land to the Ice Bridge. Naxi felt time running out. The Ice was melting, and he had to find a better life for his family.

The elders did not want Naxi to leave because it would bring bad fortune to give up a divine being. They called him to a full moon ceremony, normally secret to none but elders. The ceremony transpired in the crystalline cave his mother had created. Naxi felt the weight of grief there.

Seated in a circle, the elders commenced with burning of rare herbs and inhaling of smoke. Arcane melodies of power invoked the spirits. After some minor business about slaughtered rams, the presiding elder swore Naxi to secrecy. Performing a blood ritual to seal the oath, he cut into Naxi's forearm, and cast a few drops of blood on the fire. Naxi gave all his attention to the elders.

The elders explained that the soul returned after death to a new lifetime; on special occasions the elders could envision someone's past or future life. On their journey Naxi and his mother had visited several groups with similar beliefs. Anorher elder shared visions of inexorable workings of the Earth, huge changes in weather, underground shelves of land that caused quakes and formed mountains, and the imminent demise of the Ice Bridge from these forces. The next elder spoke the wisdom of the ages: if a mountain does not last forever, a human life lasts a moment. So Naxi must allow his mother to pass. This attempt to keep Naxi with them only caused him new tears.

When the smoke reached full effect, the next elder offered Naxi a vision of his mother. Though a final ploy, Naxi could not resist seeing his sweet mother again. Two other elders chanted a dreamlike tune. Their neighbor in the circle asked Naxi in a hushed voice to look into the smoke for Xani. Naxi saw blurry and mercurial fire phantasms form into his mother's lifetime as a seer, with visions of her own: escaping from a catastrophe on the planet, playing near a vast desert, amassing a body of prophecy into a subversive volume, and seeing Naxi see her.

It was too much for the son of Xani. Jumping into the middle of the circle, Naxi shouted at the elders and kicked furiously at the fire coals. He refused to believe the last visions, calling them tricks. He blamed them for keeping their knowledge from the tribe. He threatened to reveal all.

Thoughe disastrous if Naxi abandoned the tribe, there was no bad fortune in stopping him from breaking tribal law. Accusing Naxi of sacrilege, the elders pronounced a sentence of death upon his family. Naxi cursed the elders and ran from the cave. Waking his wife and children in the dead of night, he exhorted them to grab their lightest belongings and flee.

The family had a head start, but the elders organized warriors to hunt them. Naxi followed the boulders by the riverbank, for it was easy to navigate at night and hide their tracks well. By the third daybreak Naxi thought they had lost their pursuers, but pushed his family onward. They did not stop until the next full moon.

They had traveled from what would become modern day New Hampshire to northern New Jersey. There, ancestors of the Lenape tribal nation befriended them. The family was allowed to rest, but then put into harmony with tasks to serve the community. After a couple moons of this new life, Naxi and family took some time to wander the woodland hills. Gratified to recognize animals, birds, and insects from the Three Valleys, Naxi also delighted in many new creatures. Naxi spotted a new type of bull, a variety of redbird, and an odd antlered beast: spirits blessing their arrival in a new home.

The family found a cliff overlooking the valley where the tribe lived, and marveled at the expanse below them. Naxi thought back on his life: once again he was an exile. He would never grieve in such a calamitous way again, causing disruption to his family. He would grieve quietly.

ق

"See what dying does to people? Naxi got so mad!" *Did the story make you sadder, Momma?*

Sahara was comforted by the voice in her head. Their bond had healed! *No, baby. It was a beautiful story. More prehistoric past life beliefs. Naxi had a wonderful family. And overcame a lot of troubles.*

"Yes!" Naji said, a little too loudly. "So don't give up, Momma. There are 1001 people to meet." To humor her, he quoted Scheherazade. *King Shahryar will order robes of honor and gifts for each of them. And don't worry about those strange men. Everything will work out.*

Marvelous child! *How do you know all this, baby?*

The child looked into his mother's eyes. *I overcame a lot of troubles, too. I've grown.*

Sahara kissed her sweet, amazing boy. "Grow some more. Finish your lunch."

86

———《*》———

July 24. Month 11.

Ooma felt a weighted sadness as she sat on the Sandy Hook beach at the Jersey shore. She was there with Bax, and it was time to end the relationship.

That year, everything had gotten in the way of her finishing Glenclaire State: getting laid off at Bruckner Associates, which threatened her internship; deeper devotion to the qaraq's work, which threatened her interest in the degree; and nightmares, visions, and a fragile mental state, which threatened everything. Bax had tried to support her, but repeatedly failed with imploding bravura. She didn't know why he was still interested, since she had been so mean to him.

She loved the big hunk, beyond sexual attraction. Ooma's sadness was a repressed guilt: she could make it work if she wanted. But the thought exhausted her, especially given the year's recalls about them. Their karmic history spelt trouble, abuse, and vitriol.

But Ooma knew the true reason she wanted to break up, her true guilt. She loved another. She desperately wanted to be a good Queen to her King this time. To make that happen, she had to devote herself to Amar, finish her degree, and dump Bax. Without revealing her true feelings.

Nestled in behind a dune, they had relative privacy. Ooma looked at Bax lying peacefully in the sand, and her wish not to hurt him ached deep in her core. The ache turned to stimulation: if she had to hurt him, she could at least pleasure him first. Repositioning herself on the blanket, she slipped off his swimsuit and snuggled between his legs. Bax gave a lovely groan. Ooma applied herself to Bax until he reached maximum size. The thrill of gratifying him consumed her.

Ooma caught herself thinking of Amar. It was unfair to use Bax to fulfill her yearning for another, but the wonderful fantasy increased her passion, as Bax's moans affirmed. She forced herself to think only of Bax, and the 1999 New Year's party returned to her mind. Amar in the den! She intensified her rhythm and focused on the seven kisses. Stay on Bax!

Another unwanted image popped into her head, the final recall from their seventh kiss, which she had never revealed. Instinctively, she drew her mouth away, but he protested and grabbed her head. As he did, their soul connection opened, which had enabled them to see each other's past lives during the seven kisses, or blocks apart on September 11. Ooma's mind appeared to Bax, and he witnessed how she had remembered the story from the seventh kiss.

November 7, 2001. Week 9.

Weeks after the attacks, Ooma lay awake after upsetting dreams, and prayed her anguish would end. She had shoddy memories of the events inside the Tower, all jumbled up with visions. Reliving the cataclysm was too much for her, so Ooma's brain jumped to the recall of the Italian children from the seventh kiss. As a summer storm filled the quarry with rain, Ursa climbed to the highest rock to dare Balthasar. They jumped hand in hand, glanced off a jutting rock on their way down. Before crashing to their doom in shallow waters, Balthasar saw a set of expressions on Ursa's face. Had she planned a double suicide, or wished to murder him?

Bax's version had not answered this question, but that night Ooma saw the truth.

The Tale of Ursalina's Unconscious Revenge

Ursalina's face looked shocked: of course it did idiot after slamming against that ledge your face looked shocked too dear Balthasar love of my short life born 1110 died 1121 whereas I was born 1111 died 1121 I am shocked for the truth has just hit me I intended to die wanted you to die also and have a a dark evil inside me but that is not the entire truth

my face changes to a smile: I see I was an evil Queen but lived many lifetimes atoning for my behavior so why did I jump darling Balthasar born in 1110 me in 1111 what is the significance of those numbers and why does a similar number, 1001, come into my brain the difference being 111 the age of a very old man sweet Jesu a very old Sheikh hunched over me

a fearful tightening of my face: Lord God his ancient withering cock hardens and enters me an innocent Chinese daughter of a highly respected man am I subjected to this disgusting act as penance for my past evil no he fucks me for a perverse magical spell to restore his youth the magic rips through my groin belly breasts head and I lose consciousness hang onto life with a vengeance and I swear vengeance against this horrid action

and a look of sheer determination crosses my face: I do not act against the Sheikh in this life or the next for he is important to my qaraq but I keep my distance and then rejoice in a karmic turn for my soul when my group attains something vast and monumental at great risk

589

a final look into his eyes, a last dark look: but I don't forget the Sheikh who ended my life as the Chinese girl not for a monumental purpose but to sustain his life so on an unconscious level I know this is the time to seek revenge on his soul and I recognize Balthasar's soul as one and the same as the Sheikh's so at great risk I make us fall into this rainy pit and my soul is nourished with karmic vengeance against the Sheikh, and poor sweet Balthasar.

ق

November 7, 2001. Week 9.

After this shocking revelation that week, Ooma hoped Bax would intervene with the qaraq, perhaps as a test of his soul and their karma. When Bax failed and Ooma remained excluded from meetings, she went to Amar. Hypnotizing him, a deeper connection ignited between them.

July 24. Month 11.

As these memories radiated from Ooma's mind on the beach, Bax halted his pleasure. He witnessed the awful revenge on his soul, then the tryst with Amar, even more unbearable to see.

To seek his own revenge, Bax pulled out of Ooma's mouth, pinned her down in the sand, and entered her with maddened lust. As tears streamed down her face, Ooma understood Bax's fury. Anger surged through her, anger at herself, the Sheikh, Amar, the qaraq. She grabbed Bax's hair and pulled his lips onto hers. The hot image of the seventh kiss flashed through their heads. They plunged into the quarry. She gave him a dark look. He thrust deeper into her.

The vision of Amar in the den returned, he and Ooma gazing longingly at each other. To Bax, that moment was more charged than all seven kisses combined. "I fucked you over as the Sheikh," he grunted, "so you fucked me over as Ursa." He punctuated his words with faster

590

motions. "You still punish me by fucking with Amar." With Bax's wild force, Ooma neared her climax. "Are you fucking your King?" Their two bodies shuddered in release.

Bax rolled off Ooma and collapsed in the sand. The connection broke. Ooma looked at Bax, tears and sand staining her face. She did not dare breathe a word. Under the thin skin of his anger, she had hurt him tremendously. His recent fearlessness burst in a cartoon bubble.

"Go ahead, do it." Bax could not look at her. "Break up with me for something I did a thousand years ago. But I no longer desire eternal youth. I'm just doing the best I can."

Ooma could do nothing more here. "Way better than me." She had ruined everything between them. After a long time, she whispered, "I'm so sorry, Bax. I'm so, so sorry."

87

August 2. Month 11.

Sahara invited Amar over for a glass of wine on the patio. The two praised each other on how far they had come that year, given all the tragedy and sadness. When Amar raised his glass to Sahara's promotion at the library, Sahara asked how he was doing with employment.

"Still taking my time. Looking over Zack's online import-export business. In truth, I'm thinking of using his set-up to hunt for our mysterious Version 2." The fountain sizzled in delight.

Sahara ignored a flush of excitement about this plan. "How about Version 1 and 4 while you're at it? Leave Version 3 to me. Seriously, what about all your contacts?"

"My former business kingdom? May Allah bestow it on whomever he chooses." He made a grand gesture to the sky. "I use the Internet for recall research, too. I can't target anything myself."

Sahara toasted how well he accepted his limitation. "And now we need 1001 stories!"

"Verle calmed Zack into archiving again. Elvi anointed Diana as quality control, maintaining depth while Verle organizes everything to death. It'll help Zack if the Doc's around."

"If," Sahara said. "The group is healing in many ways. Porcy and Cachay are re-channeling their negativity to work together on the oldest memories."

"Wow." Amar tensed a little. "I heard Ooma broke up with Bax. Wants to finish her degree, get herself back on track. A healing of sorts." The fountain slowed to a trickle.

"Except for poor Bax," Sahara said. "The guy can't catch any luck, in any life."

"It's better he move on from her," Amar said. "It's a tricky relationship."

"Is it now?" Sahara smiled wickedly. "Have we moved on? Enough to work together on this huge endeavor with the qaraq?"

"Absolutely! Remember a year ago when you told me about Veronique d'O convincing Galland to translate as many Nights as he could find? I feel we're at that exact place."

"That was nice." Sahara remembered moving back in and staying up the night before 9/11.

Amar sipped his wine. "Sahr, I'm still sad about something. The tale of Uniculturalism?"

"Sohlabi Flavia brought you over to the dark side," Sahara said. "Then dumped you."

"You were completely over me. I can't take it." He reached out and kissed her hands. Sahara knew it was not seductive. It took her back to the hospital, with Amar holding her hand.

"Amar, when I was in the hospital, I glimpsed another part of that lifetime."

"In the future? Do you remember the story?" Amar asked. The fountain gushed again.

"You sure you want to hear it?"

"Maybe it'll help me understand."

"Knock yourself out. It's your point of view, Ames Rondol. Holding hands will help."

The Tale of the Version 4 Caper

I'm going to find this document! The trail stretches on for years. I search for Sohlabi Flavia, too, and that distracts me. Why did she abandon our sweet love? Of course I'm agent of Mythogorad and she's the enemy. But I procured stories for her. Why break my heart?

It takes a long time to expose a false trail, especially when it leads to something that actually exists. One trail of breadcrumbs leads to the work of Zizagh, who collected collections. Buried in the stack of fogged up reading lenses from the Zizagh File must be V2. I read a thousand lenses, once again tempted to be a convert of Uniculturalism, free from Sohlabi's influence, believing in the dangers of mixing cultures. In short, I'm sick of stories.

I see what looks like Version 2, but back at Mythogorad HQ I am set straight by the Digi-librarian, the cute one who's tossed with me a few times. We already have four copies of said document in the stacks, but thanks for the extra. I've been duped! The trail is cold.

I spend months in the agency library, combing for a new lead. I come across a letter, written on Hotel Franquinor stationery, complaining of the advent of Mythogorad. The letter-writer suggests that rather than locate the special Nights with past life bits, it would be easier to invent a new version. To assuage the reader, the writer invokes a lineage of souls who toiled tirelessly to collect their own past life tales, mixed with *The Thousand and One Nights*.

The question remains: did this Version ever exist, a Version 4, a follow-up to the European Version 3? Not being folkloric, does V4 fall under

Mythogorad's aegis? The past life tales are either innocuous or molded from rarer clay, a greater danger to Uniculturalism. It's all confounding!

I let the Digi-librarian lick my wounds, and put her on a hunt for V4 evidence. She unearths a number of allusions, documents, and events. Within a week I have an itinerary for my next mission. She begs to come along, but I decline. The trail is hot!

The path starts innocently in a privatized Los Angelos library that houses a burned fragment of a title page, a publishing imprint with a logo of an elephant, and the number 1001. The next stops are publishers and scholars, mostly ignorant. Given my agent status, one professor is not forthcoming. A candlelit dinner opens her up. V4 had an underground network!

The mission continues overseas, New Anatolia, St. Leninsburg, Dakar, Brighton. I meet with blows, knives, and shady characters whose dealings with illegal volumes match their trafficking of drugs and endangered species. The trail leads back to an expected place: the Arabiin Octosphere.

After bribes, bartering, and a threat from a syndicate, my spying uncovers a tip on the location of a manuscript. It's been under guard for years and will require a foolproof plan, special team, and hefty budget. I hole up in Dhunbai waiting for HQ approval.

Funds deposited, my contact wants the wad up front, and I pray I'm not stiffed. Weeks pass, I hear nothing further, and I book a flight home, but then one deep-in-dreams night, I awake to a cold laser against my cheek. I am hooded, thrown in a car, and driven everywhere and back to disorient me. Hours later, I am prodded into a building. We ascend a curving flight of stairs: why do they feel familiar? Seated, still hooded, I hear a safe being opened.

At last, mission accomplished. I imagine the document gently pulled from its home. Why was I brought here? They must want me to authenticate the goods before leaving, but I sense another perusing it before me. For the first time I feel nervous. The hood is ripped off my head.

I am in the palace of my old friend the Oilat of Dhunbai. How did we break in here?

"Is this what you're looking for?" She steps from the shadows and gestures. "Give it to him." Sohlabi Flavia! By the tension I know she is not part of the crew. What's going down?

One of the thieves shoves a manuscript into my hand. A manuscript, not a reading lens, so we're talking off grid, two hundred plus year old paper, and not before the 21st Century. I flip through it: the stories are not old myths. A frame tale has a group of people recalling past lives. Then paydirt: I spot a word here, a sentence there, directly from a translation of the Arabiin Nights. This is Version 4, a collection of past life tales encoded with fragments of the Nights!

I nod confirmation. The palooka in front of me grabs the book and another thrusts the hood on my head. I do not see them do the same to Sohlabi, but on the ride back I smell her near. We reach a destination, and land in a small, empty room, unhooded. Someone mockingly thanks us for our business, throws the manuscript on the floor, and slams the door. Locked. Sohlabi and I look at each other. Did she cough up as much loot as me, expecting to end the night with the book?

"Don't even think about fucking me." Lots of anger in her voice.

"Nice to see you, too. Think they'll let us go?"

Reluctantly, Sohlabi says, "I know this crew. They do good business. We're free to go." "Except for the locked door. And each of us killing the other for the book," I say.

"Right." Sohlabi picks up the manuscript (why prevent her?) and begins reading. I try to engage her in conversation (whaddya been up to for fifteen years?). On my third attempt she reads out loud. Annoyed, I pace the room like a caged animal, looking for escape. There is a high window, but after my many failures to reach it, Sohlabi sniggers. Incensed, I make a great noise banging on the door for help. I smash the door off its hinges.

Here is the situation: I command the door, but Sohlabi holds the manuscript. Seeing stalemate, she resumes reading aloud. I march up to her, plant my foot against her windpipe, and pin her head against the wall. Hearing her suffer will soften me, so she speaks, barely audible.

"I see a past life, thanks to the pain. We're in the interlife. I have three choices: transcend the world, escape to an easy life, or enter a treacherous life with you and accomplish great work." "And you choose the life with me, right?" I spit, smelling a trick.

"With you. I always suffer difficult fucking lifetimes with you, because of you. I'm tired of it, Ames. I just want to rescue a few tales this world. A thousand and one. Some say that number points to Infinity, immortality. You and I suffer infinite lifetimes."

My anger subsides, her words calculated for that effect. I can't have what I want, so I settle for what I can get. Swiftly I replace my foot with my open hand, and drag her by the neck upward against the wall. I force my mouth on hers, find the correct spot on her neck, and apply just enough pressure. Her mouth blossoms into a half-smile. As Sohlabi falls unconscious, I gently lay her on the floor and retrieve the book. She is so beautiful! I yearn to stay with her, but it is impossible.

I bend down and kiss her hands. Then I walk out the ruined doorway.

ق

By the fountain, Amar let go of Sahara's hands. "If you'd told me that story last Fall, I'd have been furious. Last Winter, I would've been depressed. Pretended it meant nothing in Spring."

Sahara listened intently. "It's summertime."

"I'm still sad, but look how we've struggled. It makes me proud."

Sahara rarely felt proud; she liked acknowledging it. "I'm ready to keep struggling with you. Parenting Superboy. Respecting our independence. And tackling the next few hundred recalls."

"Seven hundred and sixty-one to go, according to Zack," Amar said.

"Seven sixty, with your story." They clinked glasses, hearing the fountain's constant flow.

88

———⟨ɷ⟩———

September 11, 2001. Hour 11.

It was hours after the Towers fell before Amar felt Ooma was stable. They had gone to medical services, a coffee shop, and on a long walk around Manhattan before she stopped disassociating into Oamra's persona. At least long enough to bring her to the stability of her family. By 7:00 PM, Amar's phone finally got through to the frightened Qadir family. He told them Ooma was safe, and they were on a ferry heading across the Hudson River to Weehawken.

Once there, they walked to the Hoboken train station on a weed-bordered path skirting the waterway. At one point Ooma gazed at the plume of smoke across the river. The horrific events of the day pierced her fragile mind again. She burst into tears and ran into the bushes along the path.

Hidden from the other desolate travelers on the path, Amar found Ooma seated on a large, flat rock, left over from New Jersey's tortuous geological past. She cried quietly, head in hands. As soon as Amar sat down next to her, she wrapped her arms tightly around him. He returned the electrifying embrace, and the inevitable happened. They moved into a long, passionate kiss, a kiss delayed for hours since their silent confession of love escaping the Tower.

The kiss triggered a leap back in Time, to an even more charged kiss between their two souls. Amh, after vengeful fury at Sha, and Umh, after confronting Pharaoh's priests, became unstuck in Time; to fix this upheaval, their Sumerian incarnations Atu and Ur-zamma mated so powerfully they shattered the ovoid. Echoing Ooma, the final kiss between them also triggered a leap back in Time, a memory of Ur-zamma's youth in early Sumer, and a third kiss.

The Tale of the Three Kisses (That Grew to Seven)

With this kiss I seal the accord for the symbol of power that will bring everything to our people and great budding civilization. The Gods were good to us since their arrival from the skies when they insisted we find this oval object so precious to them so important for our advancement hiding within it such beautiful images of great domiciles called cities and symbols called writing

with this kiss my seductive wiles earned me a place in Mahakavid's bed where he projected the pictures on the ceiling great waterfalls and gargantuan mountains all emanating from the tiny oval that he will render unto me as if it had been mine for lifetimes

the royal house of Sumer set up careful relations with Mahakavid ruler of Hind for he had skirmished into our territory this champion on the elephant downing our horsemen I understand his lust for entwined bodies and his lust for blood are the same and as I coil myself around him I show Mahakavid that this lust is more beneficial in the bedchamber all he has to do is return the bauble and all lands will be his without a drop of blood instead with a drop of lust from our mouths so with this kiss I control this King and it reminds me of previous power kisses such as when I was a vestal virgin my maidenhead untouched but my lips and tongue not inexperienced I had been brought to the center of the Sumerian world to join the priestesses and was chosen to be sacrificed to the Gods and I stood before four priests two holding knives two holding vessels to catch my blood and in between the God Enerka stood several heads taller than the tallest priest his skin glowing in the heat his thin shape awakening a sensation between my legs

urged by my lust for this otherworldly creature and my hate for the priests and with nothing to lose I undid the gold cord and let my robe fall and announced that all souls stand naked in front of Enerka and I placed my mouth on his shining lips with gentle grace

suffice it to say that by sundown I was neither virgin nor vestal neither sacrifice nor priestess instead Enerka took me into his entourage my kiss gained me status and power in the court and from a distance I observed many events and learned about the secret object at that time possessed by the Gods how to activate its prophecies and gain wisdom from past lifetimes

then a cataclysm: the Gods climbed back into their airboats and left us saddened and endangered from the vacuum of power but I was fortunate a delegation from Hind arrived and Mahakavid took a fancy to me and Sumerian courtiers planned a great conspiracy I was to pass him information about the silver-white ovoid demonstrate its magic falsely as a great weapon of power allow Kavid to make off with the object (and me) and my kiss tells the rest of the story convincing Kavid to relinquish the object and peacefully gain huge tracts of territory

but when the ovoid returned so did I and we gave no lands to Kavid he marched on us we blustered to wield the object against him and he backed down and announced to all that Sumer had a mighty weapon so then we conquered built enriched civilized just as the Gods had promised

all of this happened because of the potent kiss I bestowed upon Mahakavid and the potent kiss I bestowed upon Enerka before that but both were only possible because of a sweet kiss that excited my innocent life as a young girl previously undisturbed except for one dream

a dream of terrible squabbling among a court of royals in a strange world where I yearned to end all feuding and on a table were eleven volumes containing great wisdom foreshadowing the oval and the day after the dream I met a handsome boy in the wood and we practiced the lore of our mouths until we tasted the sweetest kiss of all conjuring hundreds of images in our minds of other worlds and Gods but my mother caught us in the act and sent me away to be a vestal virgin

and that sweet kiss of youth led to the kiss of the God and that kiss led to the kiss of Mahakavid and now Uruk and Sumer grow to greater glory I sit in the palace miserable that feuding did not end so I think back to that sweet kiss of youth.

ق

Ur-zamma's thrilling memory intensified Amar and Ooma's physical contact behind the bushes. Since their passionate kiss generated the Sumerian past life memory, Ooma thought of her seventh kiss with Bax at the New Year's Eve party. Amar had caught them in that kiss, and Bax had fled. In the den she had fantasized the seventh kiss happening with Amar, a more desired kiss.

Now that imagined embrace was real, as Ooma clung to Amar on the rock. Now Ooma fantasized more of these sweet kisses, though even in her tenuous state of mind she knew this yearned-for future was a long way off. But the world had changed that day, and relationships would never be the same. Things might shift between Amar and Sahara.

As the kiss waned, Ooma pictured herself embracing Amar in a year or two. At that time she would think back to this kiss on September 11, just as she had imagined kissing Amar that night of seven recall-laden kisses, and just as Ur-zamma had recalled embracing Mahakavid, the God Enerka, and a youthful boy. Ooma saw all of these kisses at once: innocent youth, vestal virgin, shrewd conspirator, passionate Ur-zamma, New Year celebrant, terrorist victim, and future hopeful.

She felt such a sense of fullness from these connected moments of love that when Amar broke off the kiss, Ooma looked him in the eye and thought: *maybe not today, maybe not soon, but I will have you, Amar Rash, you will be mine.*

END OF PART THREE

APPENDICES

THE TALE OF SCHEHERAZADE AND SHAHRYAR

Once there was a mighty King of the Banu Sasan named Shahryar, who ruled with equity and fairness. Shahryar expressed a strong desire to see his younger brother Shah Zaman, who had ruled far away in Samarkhan for twenty years. Shahryar's Vizier advised against a trip, so the King sent the Vizier to arrange a visit from his brother. The Vizier stopped at many cities where Shahryar was beloved, exchanged rich gifts upon arrival at Shah Zaman's palace, and entertained the King's brother in his tents before departing home.

After Shah Zaman made the long journey, Shahryar invited his brother on a hunt, but Shah Zaman declined, preferring to sit by the palace windows that overlooked the garden. As he rested he saw Shahryar's wife enter the garden through a secret door with twenty slave girls. To his shock he watched as the Queen and the slaves stripped off their clothes by the fountain, revealing that they were ten women and ten men. Then Shahryar's wife called out and a huge man named Sa'eed jumped down from the trees. He tossed the Queen to the ground and mounted her, as the male slaves enjoyed the girls. They satisfied themselves until sunset and then left through the secret door, except for Sa'eed, who climbed the tree and leapt over the palace wall.

When Shahryar returned from the hunt his brother Shah Zaman told him all that had transpired. Furious, Shahryar demanded that his brother prove his damning statements. So in a few days the King and his brother pretended to go hunting, but instead hid themselves in view of the garden. Once again Shahryar's wife and the slaves were joined by Sa'eed and satisfied their lusts for hours in the garden.

Despondent, Shahryar and his brother renounced their kingdoms and went off in search of someone suffering the same misfortune. Soon they met a woman enslaved by a jinnee, who coerced them to lay with her while the jinnee slept. She claimed that in revenge for her treatment by the jinnee she had lain with five hundred and seventy men. Marveling that a powerful jinnee suffered an even greater misfortune than his own, Shahryar vowed to never stay married long enough to be betrayed again.

Saying farewell to his brother, Shahryar returned to his kingdom, ordered his Vizier to execute his wife, and slew all his concubines and their male slaves with his own sword. As he had vowed, during the next three years the King married a maiden every night and commanded his Vizier to kill her the next morning. The people raised a great outcry against the King and parents fled with their daughters until there was not a single virgin left in the city. Fearing for his life, the Vizier, in charge of the executions, searched all over, becoming more and more distressed.

The Vizier had two daughters, Scheherazade and Dunyazade. It was said that the older one, wise and witty Scheherazade, had collected a thousand books and had read all the stories, histories, poems, philosophy and science contained within them. When Scheherazade saw her father's distress and learned of his plight, she asked, "How long will this slaughter of women last? Give me in marriage to Shahryar, that I may rescue the virgin daughters."

The Vizier refused, interrupting Scheherazade's pleas twice with parables explaining his fear of her plan. But Scheherazade stubbornly insisted until her father approached the King. The King, who had held Scheherazade exempt from his bloody practice, warned that the minister would have to kill his daughter the next day. But Shahryar rejoiced to wed and bed the ravishing Scheherazade.

When Scheherazade heard that the King agreed to marry her she rejoiced. She planned with her sister Dunyazade to divert the King from his evil deed. That night, as the King prepared to penetrate Scheherazade, she began to cry. When the King asked her what was wrong, Scheherazade begged to see her sister for the last time. Dunyazade was allowed to sit at the foot of the couch while the King took his bride's maidenhead. Later, she asked Scheherazade to tell a marvelous story. Pleased with the idea, the King granted permission and Scheherazade began her tale. When dawn arrived, she broke off in the middle and asked the King to spare her life so that she could finish the next night. Eager to hear the end of the story, the King agreed. The following night Dunyazade again sat at the foot of the nuptial bed and after the love-making requested the end of the story. When dawn approached the King granted Scheherazade another night to continue her storytelling.

So every dawn the King spared Scheherazade's life so she would continue the story that night. During the day Shahryar performed his official duties, never calling upon the Vizier to carry out the execution. Instead he judged and deposed, forbidding this and permitting that, while the Vizier stood beside him, fearfully anticipating the worst.

In this way Scheherazade prolonged her life for a thousand and one nights. During that time Scheherazade gave the King three sons and told him many stories full of moral lessons of admonition. Finally, she pleaded for her life for the sake of the children. Weeping, the King told her that he had pardoned her even before their first child had been born. He had never stopped blaming himself for his past actions and praised Scheherazade for rescuing the women of his kingdom. He brought his viziers and emirs together to prepare for an elaborate wedding, and the people rejoiced at the celebrations.

Shahryar's brother Shah Zaman came from Samarkhan to celebrate his brother's betrothal. Zaman explained that after every tragedy that befallen them, he too lost hope and slaughtered a new wife every day. After hearing from Shahryar how Scheherazade had told him countless proverbs, parables, quips, anecdotes, histories, and verses, Shah Zaman asked to be wed to her sister Dunyazade. Shahryar rejoiced that the brothers would be married to the sisters, and asked Scheherazade's permission. Scheherazade agreed only on the condition that she and Dunyazade take up residence together, since they could not stand to be parted. The two brothers agreed heartily, since they too never wanted to be separated again. Shahryar ordered sumptuous feasts to celebrate the nuptials, for the court and the people alike.

In due time Shahryar summoned chroniclers to write down all that had happened. That is the origin of *The Stories of the Thousand and One Nights*.

NARRATIVE ORDER OF
RECALLED LIFETIMES

VOLUME ONE, BOOK ONE

PART ONE

607

611

PART THREE

VOLUME ONE, BOOK THREE

PART ONE

PART TWO

PART THREE

CHRONOLOGICAL BIRTH ORDER OF LIFETIMES

(as far as the qaraq understands it)

Pre-Cambrian Supereon

The Tale of the Super-Continent — Formation of Earth, billions of years ago

Phanerozoic Eon

Paleozoic Era

The Tale of the Unborn

The Tale of the Clumsy Pollen Catcher

The Tale of the Enamored Roots

The Tale of the Bituminous Coal Deposit

The Tale of the Settling of the South Pole

The Tale of the Ascension to the Fourth Level of Heaven

Carboniferous Period, 360 million years ago

The Tale of the Swimming Insect   Permian Period, 286 MYA

The Tale of the Chitin Armor

The Tale of the Servant's Revenge

The Tale of the Compound Eye

The Tale of the Battle Between the
Right and Left Eye

The Tale of the Winged Insect

The Tale of the Dragonfly's Four Wings

The Tale of the Budding Brain

The Tale of the Vanishing Fossil   (after founding of Xoo?)

Mesozoic Era

The Tale of Vaaiik Laignaar,   Triassic Period, 248 MYA
Father of the Xoo

The Tale of Baachetelle Foote   Jurassic Period, 213 MYA
and the Theory of Rotational   Dinosaur extinction
Partnering

Cretaceous Period, 145 MYA

Cenozoic Era
Paleogene Period

The Tale of the Licgh Nuo   Paleocene Epoch, 65 MYA
    Advent of Mammals,
    pre-primates

The Tale of the Clairtemporant   Eocene Epoch, 56 MYA
The Tale of the Alienated   (after end of
Starseeker   Gondwana?)
The Tale of the Projoscola
The Tale of the Phiomian Harem

    Oligocene Epoch, 34 MYA
    First Primates

Neogene Period
Gondwana breaks up, 150-25
MYA

The Tale of the Last Piece of   Miocene Epoch, 24 MYA
Gondwanaland
The Tale of the Bird's Eye View
A Brief History of the Suissamese   (before end of Gondwana?)
Xoo
The Tale of the Infant   (before end of the Xoo?)
Assassination
The Tale of the Ganesian Holdout
The Tale of Vishnu and the Youth

Pliocene Epoch, 5 MYA
The Gomphotheri's Stalemate   4 MYA
Regression

Homonids
Quarternary Period
Pleistocene Epoch, 2 MYA
The Tale of the True Borzu   Homo Sapiens, 100,000 BCE
The Tale of the Haughty Fern
The Tale of the Strangler Fig
The Tale of the Tau Lepton
The Tale of the Epiphany of the
Borzi Rival
The Tale of the Miserable Weather
in the Ice Age
The Tale of the Three-Season Year
The Tale of the Hapless
Mammoth
The Tale of the Rapacious
Warlord
The Tale of the Rival Tribe of the
Borzi
The Tale of the God-Urge

619

The Tale of the Reluctant Glacier
The Tale of the False Borzu
The Tale of the Seven Trysts   Brawr, Ourm,
The Tale of the Borzi-Vawr   their child
Half-breed
The Tale of the Hotly Pursued
Cavewoman

The Tale of the Spirit and the   Atlantis, 200,00 - 28,000 BCE
Mer-Couple
The Tale of the Soul and the   ?
Spirit Guide

50,000 BCE?

The Tale of the Sleeping Giant's   Anniddi
Dream
The Tale of the Dark Lord's   Nouhi
Summons
The Tale of the Magickwald   Faina

Unfanta Rishi's Address to the   44,000 BCE
Assembly
The Tale of the Chronically Shy   Hra Zamen
Teacher
The Tale of the Political Ballerina   Uor Taki
The Tale of the Shy Teacher'   Hra Elden Kor
Probation
The Tale of the Shy Teacher's Ruse   Dance student/Povi

The Tale of the Great Bridge of Ice   25-20,000 BCE
The Tale of the Grieving Child   Xani and Naxi

The Tale of Saaaar and Argmhm, the First Cavedogs	Domestication of dogs, 14,000
The Tale of the Cavedogs in Heat	(after Stone Cliff?)
	Old Man in the Mt., 28,000 BCE
The Tale of the Mountain that Looked Within	13,500
The Grave Paintings Regression	Shaman, 12,000
The Tale of the Expedition for Reincarnation Proof	
The Tale of the Staredown Between the Two Cliff Faces	11,000 AD
The Tale of thc Next Life Tales	Vlaler-rawk
The Tale of the Licghurin Crystal	after 10,000?
The Tale of the Three Kisses (That Grew to Seven)	pre-Ur Sumer
The Tale of the Path of Stone	
The Tale of the Eyes of the Stone Cliff	
The Tale of the Old Man of the Mountain	Self-sculpture, 4000
The Tale of The Neopheline Tombleur	Cats tamed in Egypt, 3500
The Tale of the Messenger of Imhotep, Architect of the Step Pyramid	2650
The Tale of the Conspiracy of the Myw	
The Tale of the Animal Mummifier	2600
The Tale of Atu and Ur-zamma	2500, post-Ur Sumer
The Tale of the Writing on the Wall	Old Kingdom, 2400

623

Yazdegerd I, reigned 399-420

The Tale of Sharzad's Third Child,   Narses, b. 399
Bahram Gur

Bahram V (Gur), reigned 420-438

The Tale of the Lucky   Udir, b. 400
Untouchable   Humai, b. 430
The Tale of Princess Humai and
the Thousand and One Stories

Rise of Islam, Sharzad rewritten

The Tale of the Muhaddith   Muhaddith, b. 650
The Tale of the Bedouin Poet   Hammad, b. 725

Harun al-Rashid, reigned 786-809)

The Tale of the Basran Scribe Zabbah, b. 735
The Tale of the Introduction of Wahid, b. 740
Paper to the West
The Tale of the Basran Spy   Sheikh Ba'Tr, b. 760
The Tale of the Majlis of Ja'far ibn Ally of Zabbah and Wahid,
Yahya al-Barmaki,   or, The Sleepless Reader
                     b., 775
The Tale of the Two Albino   Mahout
Elephants

Caliph al-Mahmoud, reigned 813-33

The Tale of the House of Wisdom Scholar, b. 800
The Tale of the South Chinese   Hu Ma, Basra, b. 850
Harem Girl
The Tale of the 111-Year-Old   Sheikh Ba'Tr, reborn, 871
Sheikh
The Tale of the Logic Puzzle   Khadija's Puzzle
Suicide
The Seven Incarnations of Queen Umnia, b. 890
Uzmeth

The Tale of Madame Hunj and the
Book Thief
The List of the Surviving V2   1030
Manuscripts

The Tale of the Quarry in the   Balthasar, b. 1110
Garfagnana
The Tale of Ursalina's   Ursalina, b. 1111
Unconscious Revenge

The Tale of the Tin Beads of   Vas, b. 1400
Malacca
The Tale of the Chinese Discovery Si, b. 1400
of the New World
The Tale of the Seven Chinese   after Chinese Treasure Ships, 1438
Palaces
The Tale of the Corruption of the (which Dynasty?)
Seven Palaces
The Tale of Oolon's Revenge in
the Seven Palaces

The Vision of the Swedish Soldier Gustavas, reigned 1594-1632
The Tale of the Magical Hairplay Pikeman's Pox, 1611

The Tale of the Marriage of Silvie Richelieu, 1585-1642
Saintonge
The Locksmith's Tale

The Little Known Tale of Do'en   Kvevely
Waeo Kvevely
The Tale of the Indaki and the   I-zaea
Neuromistressa

A Chronology of Pr Winood   Ctatlo
Ctatlo, 8101 - 8183
Pr Daywa's Campus Tour of
Draill U
The Tale of the Freshman Tarakani
Class
The Romance of Amat and Siyam
The Tale of the Midnight Visit
The Conclusion of *Asd and Ajd* and
Amat and Siyam
The Saga of the Alien School of
Performing Arts
The Tale of the Auditions for *Asd
and Ajd*

The Tale of The Zyp   Hapsburg/Dutch conflict, early
                                         1600s
The Tale of Anno and the Witches'   after dike breaks
Mirror
The Timeline of the Merged Souls   old Umh, 1611
The Tale of the Seduction of John
Donne Among the Topiary Donne
joins priesthood, 1615
The Tale of the Key-shaped Cudgel   (later in Donne's life?)
The Tale of Kristina, Gentlewoman   North Sea battles, pre-30 Years
of Denmark   War
The Tale of Umh and Ormgarde,
Handmaid of Denmark
The Tale of the British Spy and the   Thirty Years War, 1618-1648
Lady in Red
The Tale of the Nine Thoughts dur-
ing the Endless Orgasm

The Tale of Dom Denis Chavis	1745?-1790?
The Tale of Henry Whitelock Torrens	b. 1806, d. 1852
The Tale of the Merman Reborn as a Seedling	(exact dates?)
The Tale of the Goldsmith's Paraplegic Apprentice	19th C. Eastern Europe
The Tale of the Doomed Tree	Newark Railroad, 1856
The Tale of the Unread Book	*The Wedded Couple*, 1888
The Tale of *The Wedded Couple*	Baron, b. 1845, Countess, b. 1845
The Tale of the Ugly Curse	Madame Penelope, b. late 19th C.?
The Tale of the Ugliest Bride in New Orleans	Verlin Walker, b. 1906
The Mysteries of Cachay's Early Life	Cachay Goodkin, b. 1939
The Tale of the Spiritual Oaf	Porcelain Honeywell, b. 1956
The Tale of the Romance in the Japanese Tea Garden	Diana Machiyoko, b. 1960
The Tale of the Condemned Building in New Delhi	Blidget Fairchild, b. 1967, d. 1975
The Tale of the Three-Year Migration Pattern	Sahara Fairchild, b. 1970
The Tale of the Lost Soul	Interlife after Blidget
The Tale of the Wombat	Pre-Wombat Protection Laws, 1978
The Tale of the Journey to the East	Baxter Tenderheel, b. 1978
The Tale of the Faithful Young Moslem and her Secret Book	Ooma Qadir, b. 1981
The Message of Verlin Walker	Verle starts church job, 1990

The Tale of the Prodigal Son's Return from Paris	Porcy's reading of Zack, 1993
The Tale of Common Ground	Sahara meets Amar, 1996
The Tale of the Demon and the Pregnant Wife	Sahara/Amar move to NY, 1997
The Tale of Ardra and Solomon Rash	Amar proves himself on Wall Street
The Tale of the Glenclaire Realtor	Porcy focuses on being realtor
The Tale of the Vision in the Attic	Porcy forms group, 1998
The Tale of the Five Women in the Celtic Cross	Bax settles in New Jersey
The Memory of the Seven Rooms	Ooma, New Year's Eve
The Recollection of the Seven Kisses	Ooma with Bax, New Year's 1999
The Tale of the Mi'raj of One Thousand and One	Naji Rash, b. 1999
The Tale of the Locked Corpyroom	Naji with Twins, 2001
The Encounter with the Robed Woman	Cachay, Interlife Vision
The Tale of the Eleven Gugglets of Water	Naji, Interlife Vision
The Tale of the Two Paths	Future lifetimes
The Tale of Dizalegh's Early Career	
The Tale of Zizagh and Dizalegh	
The Tale of Algherwoman Azarogh	
The Tale of the Imprisoned Collectrix	
The Tale of the Star Lamp and the Hidden Text	

INCARNATIONS

[brackets indicate this individual's story has yet to be recalled]

Sahara (soul name: Sha)
 Ur, super-continent
 Interlife, third level of Heaven
 Dragonfly, nymph-body
 Borzi female
 Faina, God-Hero of the Forest
 Dance student, friend of Povi
 Xani, exile crossing Land Bridge
 Saaaar, female cavedog
 Saqqarah, messenger for Imhotep
 Sahnra, Goddess of the Red Isle
 The South Wind
 Sharzad, daughter of Sassanid Vizier
 Sahra, scholar, ally of Wahid and Zabbah
 Sanaa, storyteller, lover of Oarma (379 group)
 Si, Malaccan courtesan
 Silvie Saintonge, wife of French locksmith
 Siyam, neurodancer, faculty, Draill U

Sondre, refugee in 30 Years War
Shemuel, middle of three brothers of Okopy
[Bride, *The Wedded Couple*]
Sahara Fleming, childhood migrations
Sahara, Near Eastern Studies grad student, lover of Amar Rash
Sahara, housewife
Sahara, in a parallel lifetime
[Liligh, mutilated sculptress, lover of Zizagh]
Sohlabi Flavio, dealer in contraband myths
Shaell Offmore, housewife, The Suburb

Amar (Amh)
Gondwanan at settling of South Pole
Dragonfly, Chitin Armor
[Aamii Rocher, Xoo Gladiorator]
Borzu the Hunter
Argmhm, male cavedog
Old Man in the Mountain, mineral core
Animal Mummifier, Egypt
Atu, Sumerian priest
Ambanari, God of the Red Isle
The North Wind (Boreus)
Ardryashir, slave to Uzmeth
Oamra's stillborn baby, Baghdad
al-Raq'amaq, European Arabic scholar (379 group)
Anno, Dutch child, adopted by Scottish coven
Amat, telepactor, Draill U
Deserting soldier, 30 Years War
Alter, oldest of three brothers of Okopy
Seedling of Glenclaire tree
Goldsmith's paraplegic apprentice
[Groom, *The Wedded Couple*]

Amar Rash, son of Solomon, grandson of Ardra
Algherwoman Azarogh
Ames Rondol, agent of Mythogorad
Ardmin the Rash, World Types scholar
Arand Offmore, husband, The Suburb

Dr. Diana Machiyoko (Du)
Dragonfly, Right Eye
D'n-Gwn, Gondwanan chosen by Licgh Nuo
Da-men-da, Clairtemporant experimenter
Historian of Suissamese Xoo
Pre-historic Strangler Fig
Reluctant Borzi female
Anniddi, God of woods, Forest
Prehistoric shaman
Du, future time traveler to prehistoric times
Eyes of the Stone Cliff face
d'Aulai, Queen of the Red Isle
Dinzadeh, slave of Uzmeth
Frequenter of the House of Wisdom
Masiama, Cordovan bookseller (379 group)
Deng She, seventh Chinese wife
Pr Daywa, neuromistressa, Draill U
Army camp follower, 30 Years War
Diana Machiyoko, first generation Japanese-American
Dizalegh, early life
Dizalegh, the imprisoned story collectrix
Dizalegh, Bu-rei-dkagh visionary
Mmymch, Kr., future Versions researcher
Du, atomic particle
[Dolgh, ?]
]Dmnmd, ?]

Zack (Za)

Dragonfly, Front Wings

Alienated Starseeker of Ga-men

Riled-up gomphotheres

Member of rival tribe to Borzi (the Vawr)

Interlife, attached soul near Atlantis

Hra Zamen, the Shy Teacher

Zinc[ite], Cliff Face in staredown

Zenkket, Egyptian apprentice to Ka Lal

Zancq, son of priestess of the Red Isle

Mayan child from Uaxactun

Shah Zabar, Sassanid Prince

Shah Zabar, transformed by Dinzadeh obsession

Sharzad's first child, murdered by Uzmeth

Zabbah, Minister of Literature, Baghdad

Izjis, writer (379 group)

Dike, The Zyp, Low Countries

I-Zaea, indaki, Draill U

Key-shaped Cudgel, John Donne's study

Zadek, Veronique d'O's apprentice

Doomed Tree, 19th Century Glenclaire

Zachary Goodkin, artifact collector and trader

Zizagh, future story collector

[Za, atomic particle]

Verle (Vl)

Dragonfly, Brain

Vaaiik Laignaar, Father of the Xoo

Ga-men Projoscola repairman, mate of Phiomians

Sea Bird, end of Gondwanaland

Varw, multi-generational inventor of the Three-Season scheme

[Vollen, Forest Spirit]

Vlaler-rawk, organizer of Three Valleys Spring Festival
Vraawr, the neopheline Tombleur
Ka Lal, Egyptian Priest
Vaalat, xalafon, antique Instrument of the Red Isle
Wahid, book maker and collector
al-Wa'wa, Persian scholar (379 group)
Vas, Anatolian trader on Chinese treasure ship
Do-en Waeo Kvevely, Dean, Draill U
Colonel Walker, British Spy during Thirty Years War
Veronique d'O, confidant of Antoine Galland, French translator of the Nights
Veronique d'O, self-exile in Carpathia, teacher of Zadek
Mr. V., victim of Ugly Curse
Verlin Walker, caretaker, Glenclaire Unitarian Church
[Vlmeer Rwelka, World Types scholar]
Master Puzzlemaker-Logician

Cachay (Cta)
Dragonfly, Oversoul
[Aakiin Cacheille, Xookeeper]
[Riled-up gomphotheres mother]
Haughty Pre-historic Fern
Tau Lepton, during time of the Borzi
Weather System, during time of the Borzi
Young Mammoth, during time of the Borzi
K'Chungh, warlord of the eastern Borzi
Hra Eldon Kor, ally of Shy Teacher
Manager of the Universal Wash and Dry, laundromat in parallel universe to Egypt
Kha-nen-set, Pyramid Tomb Salesman
Oumkratania's Minister
Khajy, Queen of the Red Isle
Kibondo, griot and xalafon player

Sharzad's second child, murdered by Uzmeth
Nasal microbe
al-Khwarazmi, literary courtier (379 group)
Cordovan criminal looking for Version 2 manuscript
Guilaum, French locksmith
Pr Ctatlo, aesthetician, Draill U
Kristina, gentlewoman of Denmark, cousin of Ophelia
Eleven-year-old Witch, Scottish coven
The young witch, transformed into an old hag
Cta, interlife of Heavenly bureaucracy
Henry Whitelock Torrens, Anglo-Indian official and scholar
Cachay Goodkin, mysteriously connected to qaraq earlier in present
lifetime
Cachay, in interlife vision
Chimnoggia, Urchaeologician against Original Version theory
Ccycch, future Versions researcher
[Ket, ?]
[Kasshe, ?]
[Crassida, ?]
[Cast-eye, ?]
[cWyll, ?]

Naji (Nozh)
Interlife, visitor to the Master's Hut
Dragonfly, Egg
Later member of the Vawr tribe
Nouhi, Dark Lord of the Forest
Unfanta Rishi, illustrious Francovic alumna
Naxi, son of exile crossing Land Bridge
Nongsch, Eversolid Fourth Principice of the Three Valleys
Nyw, pet cat of Imhotep
Thief, Tomb raider of ovoid pieces during Aapep Festival
Zanaj, the thief on the beach

637

Zananzi, African trader
Nazir ibn Zaj, Pyramid raider of the Instrument
Narses, Sharzad's third child, later Shahanshah Bahram V (Gur)
Narob, mahout during Abbasid era
NO(z)^{14}, bacterial microbe in human gastrointestinal tract
Nadir, criminal in medieval Baghdad
Naqoeo, telepactor, Draill U
[Hanger-on, with camp follower, 30 Years war]
The Idea, Donne's room-as-the-universe
Nils, six-year-old boy in 30 Years War
Disseminator of The Idea
Noam, youngest of three brothers of Okopy
Noam, attached soul as twister-ghost
[Photographer in *The Wedded Couple*]
Naji Rash, enlightened fetus
Nozh/Naji, in interlife vision, with the Twins

Ooma (Umh)
Dragonfly, Left Eye
Ice Mountain, end of Gondwanaland
[Imaa Cordaire, Xoo liberator]
Ourm, Borzi female, initiator of the God-Urge
Uor Taki, political dancer at Franconia
Ur-Zamma, early Sumerian royal
Oumkratania, Queen of the Red Isle
Ugrit, Phoenician trader
Ugrit, transformed by Vaalat's playing
Priestess, during reign of Ramses III
Uzmeth, 140-year-old Sassanid Queen
Udir, lucky Untouchable, Hind
Princess Humai, grand-daughter of Sharzad
Hu Ma, Chinese captive of Sheikh Ba'Tr
[Daughter of Hu Ma, suicide]

Logic Puzzle of the Bahrams
[Umnia, wife of Hanbal, story collector]
Oarma, lover of Sanaa, story collector (379 group)
Homma, elephant in medieval Baghdad
Ursalina, child in the Garfagnana
Oolon, Chinese aristocrat
Old Umh, 9 lives time traveler in 1600s
Lady-in-waiting, seductress of John Donne
Om-na, xalantangist, Draill U
Ormgarde, handmaid of Kristina, Denmark
The Lady in Red, Thirty Years War
The Witch in Red, Scottish Coven
Painting of a mirror reflecting a room, John Donne's study
The Duchess, *The Wedded Couple*
Madame Penelope, New Orleans
Ooma Qadir, Iranian-American daughter
Ooma, during the 7 Kisses at the 1999 New Year's party

Bax (Bal)
Seed-bearing plant, Carboniferous Period
Animal Fossil, fused with Dragonfly fossil
Baachetelle Foote, Xoo radical
Reluctant glacier, at the time of the Borzi
Rival tribe member, disguised as Borzu
Stone Cliff valley warrior
Roukh, ally of the Queens of the Red Isle
Ba'ash, slave and favorite of Uzmeth
Sheikh Ba'Tr, Basran book collector
Ba'Tr, life extension (inc. 1999 party)
Ba'Tr, Umayyad spy at end of life
al-Turtushi, pornographer (379 group)
al-Turtushi, vision of zojy and code
Balthasar, child in the Garfagnana

Xa, Chinese Lord of the Seven Palaces
Ecoscore of *Asd and Ajd*, Draill U
Swedish pikeman, 30 Years War
Swedish pikeman, in vision of coven and interlife
The roukh, transported to the Scottish coven
Dom Denis Chavis, European Nights contributor
The Baron, *The Wedded Couple*
Blidget Fleming, Sahara's older sister, killed in India
Interlife, Bal in despair
A Tasmanian wombat
Baxter Tenderheel, Coloradan runaway
Bax, handyman in Glenclaire

Porcy (Po)

Clumsy seed-bearing plant, Carboniferous Period
Plant fossilized into a vein of coal
Dragonfly, Back Wings
Starseeker, Projosola interacter
Epy, infant victim of assassination
Pre-hominid youth, with Vishnu
Ganesian, searcher for *Zojy Zeojyy*
Half-breed child of Ourm and Brawr
Interlife, with El
[Povi, Frankovic Shy Teacher's student]
Stone Cliff face
Purzai, Sassanian sacrificial virgin
Muhaddith, early Islamic era
Hammad, Bedouin poet
Hanbal, story collector
Paulina, Christian orphan (379 group)
Madame Hunj, Baghdadi brothel owner
Poito, scenewright, Draill U
Ensouled casket, Donne room

Rebbe Yisroel of Okopy
Porcelain Honeywell, Jill of many trades
Porcy, Glenclaire realtor
Porcy, gatherer of people for past life work

THE CHITS
(Character Identity Traits)

Soul Name	NJ Name	Nights Name	Style	Personality	Gesture
Sha	Sahara	Scheherazade	1st person,	plays with hair	frame tale
Amh	Amar	Shahryar	1st Present Just Likes closure Killer instinct Overreactive	Generous	swipes the air
Du	Diana	Dunyazade	2nd outward Clinging Radiant	Overzealous	crosses legs

Za	Zack	Shah Zaman	2nd inward / Skittish	Agreeable	jokester
Vl	Verle	Vizier	3rd complex / Puzzleful / Caring / Conservative	Adventurous	hopeless planner
Cta	Cachay	The Court	Documents / Sheltering / Greedy / Anal Retentive? / Conspiratorial	Grateful	hates outdoors
Nozh	Naji	Children	3rd folk tale / Childlike	Dazed	loves blue

Umh	Ooma	Evil Queen	1st stream Secretive Capable	Insatiable	something in mouth
Bal	Bax	Sa'eed	1st sparse Lusty Devious	Shy	outsized
Po	Porcy	The People	1st plural Spiritual Multi-talented All-suffering	Clumsy	nicknames

ACKNOWLEDGEMENTS

My deepest gratitude goes to my wife Sarah St. Onge, for her affirming first read of the first draft, an act of true love. Thanks to my editor, Barry Jay Kaplan, and folks at CreateSpace.

My research sins are multifold, including sins of omission and gratuitous inclusion for my own fascination. I take sole responsibility, but would prefer to blame the following:

The Thousand and One Nights: The third book started with my devouring all information about Islamic fiction in *The Routledge Encyclopedia of Arabic Literature* (eds. Julie Scott Meisami and Paul Starkey); it took years to finish this book because of the amount of beloved research I had to integrate and eventually bid farewell to. For further immersion into this wonderful literature I am grateful for *Kalila and Dimna*, Washington Irving, *Tales of the Alhambra*, Robert Irwin's anthology *Night and Horses & the Desert*, the *Maqamat* of al-Hamadhani, the *Maqamat* of Hariri, G. Willow Wilson, *Alif the Unseen*, and those kind folk at The University of Chicago, Nicholas Rudall, Tahera Qutbuddin, for her generous time and information, and Helen McDonald of the Oriental Institute. For inspiration about the great era of al-Andalus I thank Tariq Ali, Maria Rosa Menocal, *Ornament of the World*, A.B. Yehoshua, *A Journey to the End of the Millennium*. And for Nights scholarship I owe deep debt to Robert

Irwin (his inestimable *The Arabian Nights Companion*), Muhsin Mahdi (his incomparable study, *The Thousand and One Nights*), Ulrich Marzolph, (his prolific collections of articles such as *The Arabian Nights Reader*, and with Richard van Leeuwen *The Arabian Nights Encyclopedia*), Eva Sallis, Muhsin J. al-Musawi, and the many fine translators and editors of the great story collection, Antoine Galland, Richard Burton, Edward Laine, John Payne, J.C. Mardrus, Powys Mathers, Joseph Campbell, Jack Zipes, and Husain Haddawy.

Reincarnation and the Interlife: Dr. Brian Weiss, Edgar Cayce, Michael Newton, *The Egyptian Book of the Dead*, *The Tibetan Book of the Dead*, Carol and Philip Zalecki, *The Book of Heaven*.

Inspiring Literature: The Nights and a few of its followers, Boccaccio, Calvino, Barth, Rushdie; for Structural Genius, Joyce, Woolf, Faulkner, Jan Potocki, *Saragossa Manuscript*, Charles Palliser, *The Quincunx*; for Invention of Worlds, J.R.R. Tolkien, Frank Herbert, David Wingrove, The *Chung Kuo* series; for pioneering Karma Lit (along with myself), Anya Seton, *Green Darkness*, Joan Grant, David Mitchell, *Cloud Atlas*, M.J. Rose, *The Reincarnationist*; for other Unique Visions, Audrey Niffenegger, *The Time Traveler's Wife*, Katherine Neville, *The Eight*, and the Oulipo, especially Italo Calvino, *Cosmicomics*, Georges Perec, *Life: A User's Manual*, and Daniel Levin Becker, *Many Subtle Channels*, which made me realize I was using constraints without knowing it and knowing full well.

Science: Stephen Hawking, James Gleick, Brian Greene, *The Fabric of the Cosmos*, John McPhee, Ted Nield, *Supercontinent*, and my brother George Weinstock for inspiring information about the Human Microbiome Project (you'll see I stole a quote, if you ever read the book).

History and Myth: James Frazer, *The Golden Bough*, The *Mabinogion*; for Maya research, Linda Schele and David Freidel, *A Forest of Kings*, and Dustin Thomason, *12-21*; for the Chinese Treasure ships, Gavin Menzies' extraordinary *1421*; for Magickwald inspiration, Sara Maitland, *From the Forest* and Kenneth Macleish, *Myth* (Finnish pantheon).

And of course my years of collaboration with the marvelous students and faculty at Juilliard and LaGuardia High School of the Performing Arts (The Fame School), for dirt on Draill U.

ENDNOTE

Dear Reader,

Thank you for spending some time with my *1001* series.

I am hard at work conceiving Book Five and editing Book Four, *The Qaraq and the Evolutionary Explorations*. If you like what you read, please let me know. Half of my readers prefer the present day narrative and speed through the past life tales, while the other half favor the cornucopia of stories. Where do you stand? Or are you my ideal fan and enjoy both?

I'd love to hear from you at qaraqbooks.com. Or add a review to my Amazon page, or be a fan on goodreads. And join the newsletter! Thanks again!

Write a review: http://amazon.com/dp/0692477926

Favorite my Author Page: http://goo.gl/BnXsJR

Be a Fan on Goodreads: http://goo.gl/5I0DhS

Join the Newsletter: http://www.qaraqbooks.com/subscribe

FOR NEWS, STORIES, GIVEAWAYS, AND

ANNOUNCEMENTS ABOUT

UPCOMING TITLES IN

1001, THE REINCARNATION CHRONICLES,

SUBSCRIBE TO:

1001/QARAQBOOKS NEWS

http://www.qaraqbooks.com/subscribe

IT"S FREE!

48303156R00402